THE AQUITAINE PROGRESSION

Aquitaine—in years gone by a mighty kingdom, symbol of power and domination. Aquitaine now—no longer a kingdom, but the fearful symbol of a new obliterating power wielded by six warlords of the past, right-wing relicts of the Second World War. Seemingly civilized men, they seek to mould history to their own will; to conquer the world whatever the cost. Pitted against them is lawyer Joel Converse, an unwilling adversary, a cool man converted to whitehot vengeance. Both hunter and hunted, he becomes the most wanted man in Europe, running alike from the forces of good and the forces of evil. An instrument of the violence that he loathes, Converse is a puppet manipulated by both sides—his only object is to stop the conspiracy before it is too late.

THE AQUITAINE PROGRESSION

ROBERT LUDLUM

CHIVERS PRESS
BATH

First published 1984
by Granada Publishing Limited

This Large Print edition published by
Chivers Press
by arrangement with
Granada Publishing Limited
1985

ISBN 0 86220 136 5

British Library Cataloguing in Publication Data

Ludlum, Robert
  The Aquitaine progression. — Large print ed. —
  (The Windsor selection)
  I. Title
  813'.54[F]   PS3562.U26

  ISBN 0-86220-136-5

For Jeffrey Michael Ludlum
Welcome, friend
Have a great life

THE
AQUITAINE
PROGRESSION

PART ONE

Geneva. City of sunlight and bright reflections. Of billowing white sails on the lake—sturdy, irregular buildings above, their rippling images on the water below. Of myriad flowers surrounding blue-green pools of fountains—duets of exploding colors. Of small quaint bridges arching over the glassy surfaces of man-made ponds to tiny man-made islands, sanctuaries for lovers and friends and quiet negotiators. Reflections.

Geneva, the old and the new. City of high medieval walls and glistening tinted glass, of sacred cathedrals and less holy institutions. Of sidewalk cafés and lakeside concerts, of miniature piers and gaily painted boats that chug around the vast shoreline, the guides extolling the virtues —and the estimated value—of the lakefront estates that surely belong to another time.

Geneva. City of purpose, dedicated to the necessity of dedication, frivolity tolerated only when intrinsic to the agenda or the deal. Laughter is measured, controlled—glances conveying approval of sufficiency or admonishing excess. The canton by the lake knows its soul. Its beauty coexists with industry, the balance not only accepted but jealously guarded.

Geneva. City also of the unexpected, of predictability in conflict with sudden unwanted revelation, the violence of the mind struck by bolts of personal lightning.

Cracks of thunder follow; the skies grow dark and the rains come. A deluge, pounding the angry waters taken by surprise, distorting vision, crashing down on the giant spray, Geneva's trademark on the lake, the *jet d'eau,* that geyser designed by man to dazzle man. When sudden revelations come, the gigantic fountain dies. All the fountains die and without the sunlight the flowers wither. The bright reflections are gone and the mind is frozen.

Geneva. City of inconstancy.

Joel Converse, attorney-at-law, walked out of the hotel Richemond into the blinding morning sunlight on the Jardin Brunswick. Squinting, he turned left, shifting his attaché case to his right hand, conscious of the value of its contents but thinking primarily about the man he was to meet for coffee and croissants at Le Chat Botté, a sidewalk café across from the waterfront. "Re-meet" was more accurate, thought Converse, if the man had not confused him with someone else.

A. Preston Halliday was Joel's American adversary in the current negotiations, the finalizing of last-minute details for a Swiss-American merger that had brought both men to Geneva. Although the remaining work was minimal—formalities, really, research having established that the agreements were in accord with the laws of both countries and acceptable to the International Court in The Hague—Halliday was an odd choice. He had not been part of the American legal team fielded by the Swiss to keep

4

tabs on Joel's firm. That in itself would not have excluded him—fresh observation was frequently an asset—but to elevate him to the position of point, or chief spokesman, was, to say the least, unorthodox. It was also unsettling.

Halliday's reputation—what little Converse knew of it—was as a troubleshooter, a legal mechanic from San Francisco who could spot a loose wire, rip it out and short an engine. Negotiations covering months and costing hundreds of thousands had been aborted by his presence, that much Converse recalled about A. Preston Halliday. But that was all he recalled. Yet Halliday said they knew each other.

"It's Press Halliday," the voice had announced over the hotel phone. "I'm pointing for Rosen in the Comm Tech-Bern merger."

"What happened?" Joel had asked, a muted electric razor in his left hand, his mind trying to locate the name; it had come to him by the time Halliday replied.

"The poor bastard had a stroke, so his partners called me in." The lawyer had paused. "You must have been mean, counselor."

"We rarely argued, counselor. Christ, I'm sorry, I like Aaron. How is he?"

"He'll make it. They've got him in bed and on a dozen versions of chicken soup. He told me to tell you he's going to check your finals for invisible ink."

"Which means *you're* going to check because I don't have any and neither did Aaron. This marriage is based on pure greed, and if you've studied the papers you know that as well as I do."

"The larceny of investment write-offs," agreed Halliday, "combined with a large chunk of a technological market. No invisible ink. But since I'm the new boy on the block, I've got a couple of questions. Let's have breakfast."

"I was about to order room service."

"It's a nice morning, why not get some air? I'm at the President, so let's split the distance. Do you know the Chat Botté?"

"American coffee and croissants. Quai du Mont Blanc."

"You know it. How about twenty minutes?"

"Make it a half hour, okay?"

"Sure." Halliday had paused again. "It'll be good to see you again, Joel."

"Oh? Again?"

"You may not remember. A lot's happened since those days . . . more to you than to me, I'm afraid."

"I'm not following you."

"Well, there was Vietnam and you were a prisoner for a pretty long time."

"That's not what I meant, and it was years ago. How do we know each other? What case?"

"No case, no business. We were classmates."

"Duke? It's a large law school."

"Further back. Maybe you'll remember when we see each other. If you don't, I'll remind you."

"You must like games. . . . Half an hour. Chat Botté."

As Converse walked toward the Quai du Mont Blanc, the vibrant boulevard fronting the lake, he tried to fit Halliday's name into a time frame, the years to a school, a forgotten face to match an

6

unremembered classmate. None came, and Halliday was not a common name, the short form "Press" even less so . . . unique, actually. If he had known someone named Press Halliday, he could not imagine forgetting it. Yet the tone of voice had implied familiarity, even closeness.

It'll be good to see you again, Joel. He had spoken the words warmly, as he had the gratuitous reference to Joel's POW status. But then, those words were always spoken softly to imply sympathy if not to express it overtly. Too, Converse understood why under the circumstances Halliday felt he had to bring up the subject of Vietnam, even fleetingly. The uninitiated assumed that all men imprisoned in the North Vietnamese camps for any length of time had been mentally damaged, per se, that a part of their minds had been altered by the experience, their recollections muddled. To a degree, some of these assumptions were undeniable, but not with respect to memory. Memories were sharpened because they were searched compulsively, often mercilessly. The accumulated years, the layers of experience . . . faces with eyes and voices, bodies of all sizes and shapes; scenes flashing across the inner screen, the sights and sounds, images and smells—touching and the desire to touch . . . nothing of the past was too inconsequential to peel away and explore. Frequently it was all they had, especially at night—*always* at night, with the cold, penetrating dampness stiffening the body and the infinitely colder fear paralyzing the mind—memories were everything. They helped mute the sharp reports of small-arms fire, which were gratuitously explained in the mornings as necessary executions of the uncooperative and unrepentant. Or they blocked out the distant screams in the dark, of even more unfortunate prisoners forced to play games, too obscene to describe, demanded by their captors in search of amusement.

Like most men kept isolated for the greater part of their imprisonment, Converse had examined and reexamined every stage of his life, trying to understand . . . to *like* . . . the cohesive whole. There was much that he did not understand—or like—but he could live with the product of those intensive investigations. Die with it, if he had to; that was the peace he had to reach for himself. Without it the fear was intolerable.

And because these self-examinations went on night after night and required the discipline of accuracy, Converse found it easier than most men to remember whole segments of his life. Like a spinning disk attached to a computer that suddenly stops, his mind, given only basic information, could isolate a place or a person or a name. Repetition had simplified and accelerated the process, and that was what bewildered him now. Unless Halliday was referring to a time so far back as to have been only a brief, forgotten childhood acquaintance, no one of that name belonged to his past.

It'll be good to see you again, Joel. Were the words a ruse, a lawyer's trick?

Converse rounded the corner, the brass railing of Le Chat Botté glistening, hurling back tiny explosions of sunlight. The boulevard was alive with gleaming small cars and spotless buses; the pavements were washed clean, the strollers in various stages of hurried but orderly progress. Morning was a time for benign energy in Geneva. Even the newspapers above the tables in the sidewalk cafés were snapped with precision, not crushed or mutilated into legible positions. And vehicles and pedestrians were not at war; combat was supplanted by looks and nods, stops and gestures of acknowledgment. As Joel walked through the open brass gate of Le Chat Botté he wondered briefly if Geneva could export its mornings to New York. But then the City Council would vote the import down, he concluded—the citizens of New York could not stand the civility.

A newspaper was snapped directly below him on his left, and when it was lowered Converse saw a face he knew. It was a coordinated face, not unlike his own, the features compatible and in place. The hair was straight and dark, neatly parted and brushed, the nose sharp, above well-defined lips. The face belonged to his past, thought Joel, but the name he remembered did not belong to the face.

The familiar-looking man raised his head; their eyes met and A. Preston Halliday rose, his short compact body obviously muscular under the expensive suit.

"Joel, how are you?" said the now familiar voice, a hand outstretched above the table.

"Hello . . . Avery," replied Converse, staring, awkwardly shifting his attaché case to grip the hand. "It *is* Avery, isn't it? Avery Fowler. Taft, early sixties. You never came back for the senior year, and no one knew why; we all talked about

9

it. You were a wrestler.''

"Twice All New England," said the attorney, laughing, gesturing at the chair across from his own. "Sit down and we'll catch up. I guess it's sort of a surprise for you. That's why I wanted us to meet before the conference this morning. I mean, it'd be a hell of a note for you to get up and scream 'Impostor!' when I walked in, wouldn't it?''

"I'm still not sure I won't." Converse sat down, attaché case at his feet, studying his legal opponent. "What's this Halliday routine? Why didn't you say something on the phone?''

"Oh, come on, what was I going to say? 'By the way, old sport, you used to know me as Tinkerbell Jones.' You never would have showed up.''

"Is Fowler in jail somewhere?''

"He would have been if he hadn't blown his head off," answered Halliday, not laughing.

"You're full of surprises. Are you a clone?''

"No, the son.''

Converse paused. "Maybe I should apologize.''

"No need to, you couldn't have known. It's why I never came back for the senior year . . . and, goddamn it, I wanted that trophy. I would have been the only mat jock to win it three years in a row.''

"I'm sorry. What happened . . . or is it privileged information, counselor? I'll accept that.''

"Not for you, counselor. Remember when you and I broke out to New Haven and picked up those pigs at the bus station?''

10

"We said we were Yalies—"

"And only got taken, never got laid."

"Our eyebrows were working overtime."

"Preppies," said Halliday. "They wrote a book about us. Are we really that emasculated?"

"Reduced in stature, but we'll come back. We're the last minority, so we'll end up getting sympathy. . . . What happened, Avery?"

A waiter approached; the moment was broken. Both men ordered American coffee and croissants, no deviation from the accepted norm. The waiter folded two red napkins into cones and placed one in front of each.

"What happened?" said Halliday quietly, rhetorically, after the waiter left. "The beautiful son of a bitch who was my father embezzled four hundred thousand from the Chase Manhattan while he was a trust officer, and when he was caught, went bang. Who was to know a respected, if transplanted, commuter from Greenwich, Connecticut, had two women in the city, one on the Upper East Side, the other on Bank Street? He was beautiful."

"He was busy. I still don't understand the Halliday."

"After it happened—the suicide was covered up—Mother raced back to San Francisco with a vengeance. We were from California, you know . . . but then, why would you? With even more vengeance she married my stepfather, John Halliday, and all traces of Fowler were assiduously removed during the next few months."

"Even to your first name?"

11

"No, I was always 'Press' back in San Francisco. We Californians come up with catchy names. Tab, Troy, Crotch—the 1950's Beverly Hills syndrome. At Taft, my student ID read 'Avery Preston Fowler,' so you all just started calling me Avery or that awful 'Ave.' Being a transfer student, I never bothered to say anything. When in Connecticut, follow the gospel according to Holden Caulfield."

"That's all well and good," said Converse, "but what happens when you run into someone like me? It's bound to happen."

"You'd be surprised how rarely. After all, it was a long time ago, and the people I grew up with in California understood. Kids out there have their names changed according to matrimonial whim, and I was in the East for only a couple of years, just long enough for the fourth and fifth forms at school. I didn't know anyone in Greenwich to speak of, and I was hardly part of the old Taft crowd."

"You had friends there. We were friends."

"I didn't have many. Let's face it, I was an outsider and you weren't particular. I kept a pretty low profile."

"Not on the mats, you didn't."

Halliday laughed. "Not very many wrestlers become lawyers, something about mat burns on the brain. Anyway, to answer your question, only maybe five or six times over the past ten years has anyone said to me, 'Hey, aren't you so-and-so and not whatever you said your name was?' When somebody did, I told them the truth. 'My mother remarried when I was sixteen.' "

The coffee and croissants arrived. Joel broke his pastry in half. "And you thought I'd ask the question at the wrong time, specifically when I saw you at the conference. Is that it?"

"Professional courtesy. I didn't want you dwelling on it—or me—when you should be thinking about your client. After all, we tried to lose our virginity together that night in New Haven."

"Speak for yourself." Joel smiled.

Halliday grinned. "We got pissed and both admitted it, don't you remember? Incidentally, we swore each other to secrecy while throwing up in the can."

"Just testing you, counselor. I remember. So you left the gray-flannel crowd for orange shirts and gold medallions?"

"All the way. Berkeley, then across the street to Stanford."

"Good school. . . . How come the international field?"

"I liked traveling and figured it was the best way of paying for it. That's how it started, really. How about you? I'd think you would have had all the traveling you ever wanted."

"I had delusions about the foreign service, diplomatic corps, legal section. That's how it started."

"After all that traveling you did?"

Converse leveled his pale blue eyes at Halliday, conscious of the coldness in his look. It was unavoidable, if misplaced—as it usually was. "Yes, after all that traveling. There were too many lies and no one told us about them until it

13

was too late. We were conned and it shouldn't have happened."

Halliday leaned forward, his elbows on the table, hands clasped, his gaze returning Joel's. "I couldn't figure it," he began softly. "When I read your name in the papers, then saw you paraded on television, I felt awful. I didn't really know you that well, but I liked you."

"It was a natural reaction. I'd have felt the same way if it had been you."

"I'm not sure you would. You see, I was one of the honchos of the protest movement."

"You burned your draft card while flaunting the Yippie label," said Converse gently, the ice gone from his eyes. "I wasn't that brave."

"Neither was I. It was an out-of-state library card."

"I'm disappointed."

"So was I—in myself. But I was visible." Halliday leaned back in his chair and reached for his coffee. "How did *you* get so visible, Joel? I didn't think you were the type."

"I wasn't. I was squeezed."

"I thought you said 'conned.' "

"That came later." Converse raised his cup and sipped his black coffee, uncomfortable with the direction the conversation had taken. He did not like discussing those years, and all too frequently he was called upon to do so. They had made him out to be someone he was not. "I was a sophomore at Amherst and not much of a student. . . . Not much, hell, I was borderline-negative, and whatever deferment I had was about to go down

14

the tube. But I'd been flying since I was fourteen.''

"I didn't know that," interrupted Halliday.

"My father wasn't beautiful and he didn't have the benefit of concubines, but he *was* an airline pilot, later an executive for Pan Am. It was standard in the Converse household to fly a plane before you got your driver's license."

"Brothers and sisters?"

"A younger sister. She soloed before I did and she's never let me forget it."

"I remember. She was interviewed on television."

"Only twice," Joel broke in, smiling. "She was on your turf and didn't give a damn who knew it. The White House bunker put the word out to stay away from her. 'Don't tarnish the cause, and check her mail while you're at it.' ''

"That's why I remember her," said Halliday. "So a lousy student left college and the Navy gained a hot pilot."

"Not very hot, none of us was. There wasn't that much to be hot against. Mostly we burned."

"Still, you must have hated people like me back in the States. Not your sister, of course."

"Her, too," corrected Converse. "Hated, loathed, despised—furious. But only when someone was killed, or went crazy in the camps. Not for what you were saying—we all knew Saigon—but because you said it without any real fear. You were safe, and you made us feel like assholes. Dumb, frightened assholes."

"I can understand that."

"So nice of you."

"I'm sorry, I didn't mean it the way it sounded."

"How did it sound, counselor?"

Halliday frowned. "Condescending, I guess."

"No guess," said Joel. "Right on."

"You're still angry."

"Not at you, only the dredging. I hate the subject and it keeps coming back up."

"Blame the Pentagon PR. For a while you were a bona fide hero on the nightly news. What was it, three escapes? On the first two you got caught and put on the racks, but on the last one you made it all by yourself, didn't you? You crawled through a couple of hundred miles of enemy jungle before you reached the lines."

"It was barely a hundred and I was goddamned lucky. With the first two tries I was responsible for killing eight men. I'm not very proud of that. Can we get to the Comm Tech-Bern business?"

"Give me a few minutes," said Halliday, shoving the croissant aside. "Please. I'm not trying to dredge. There's a point in the back of my mind, if you'll grant I've got a mind."

"Preston Halliday has one, his rep confirms it. You're a shark, if my colleagues are accurate. But I knew someone named Avery, not Press."

"Then it's Fowler talking, you're more comfortable with him."

"What's the point?"

"A couple of questions first. You see, *I* want to be accurate because you've got a reputation too. They say you're one of the best on the international scene, but the people I've talked to can't understand why Joel Converse stays with a

16

relatively small if entrenched firm when he's good enough to get flashier. Or even go out on his own.''

"Are you hiring?''

"Not me, I don't take partners. Courtesy of John Halliday, attorney-at-law, San Francisco.''

Converse looked at the second half of the croissant and decided against it. "What was the question, counselor?''

"Why are you where you're at?''

"I'm paid well and literally run the department; no one sits on my shoulder. Also I don't care to take chances. There's a little matter of alimony, amiable but demanding.''

"Child support, too?''

"None, thank heavens.''

"What happened when you got out of the Navy? How did you feel?'' Halliday again leaned forward, his elbow on the table, chin cupped in his hand—the inquisitive student. Or something else.

"Who are the people you've talked to?'' asked Converse.

"Privileged information, for the moment, counselor. Will you accept that?''

Joel smiled. "You *are* a shark. . . . Okay, the gospel according to Converse. I came back from that disruption of my life wanting it all. Angry, to be sure, but wanting everything. The nonstudent became a scholar of sorts, and I'd be a liar if I didn't admit to a fair amount of preferential treatment. I went back to Amherst and raced through two and a half years in three semesters and a summer. Then Duke offered me an accelerated program and I went there, followed by some specializations at Georgetown while I interned.''

"You interned in Washington?"

Converse nodded. "Yes."

"For whom?"

"Clifford's firm."

Halliday whistled softly, sitting back. "That's golden territory, a passport to Blackstone's heaven as well as the multinationals."

"I told you I had preferential treatment."

"Was that when you thought about the foreign service? While you were at Georgetown? In Washington?"

Again Joel nodded, squinting as a passing flash of sunlight bounced off a grille somewhere on the lakefront boulevard. "Yes," he replied quietly.

"You could have had it," said Halliday.

"They wanted me for the wrong reasons, *all* the wrong reasons. When they realized I had a different set of rules in mind, I couldn't get a twenty-cent tour of the State Department."

"What about the Clifford firm? You were a hell of an image, even for them." The Californian raised his hands above the table, palms forward. "I know, I know. The wrong reasons."

"Wrong numbers," insisted Converse. "There were forty-plus lawyers on the masthead and another two hundred on the payroll. I'd have spent ten years trying to find the men's room and another ten getting the key. That wasn't what I was looking for."

"What were you looking for?"

"Pretty much what I've got. I told you, the

money's good and I run the international division. The latter's just as important to me."

"You couldn't have known that when you joined," objected Halliday.

"But I did. At least I had a fair indication. When Talbot, Brooks and Simon—as you put it, that small but entrenched firm I'm with—came to me, we reached understanding. If after four or five years I proved out, I'd take over for Brooks. He was the overseas man and was getting tired of adjusting to all those time zones." Again Converse paused. "Apparently I proved out."

"And just as apparently somewhere along the line you got married."

Joel leaned back in the chair. "Is this necessary?"

"It's not even pertinent, but I'm intensely interested."

"Why?"

"It's a natural reaction," said Halliday, his eyes amused. "I think you'd feel the same way if you were me and I were you, and I'd gone through what you went through."

"Shark dead ahead," mumbled Converse.

"You don't have to respond, of course, counselor."

"I know, but oddly enough I don't mind. She's taken her share of abuse because of that what-I've-been-through business." Joel broke the croissant but made no effort to remove it from the plate. "Comfort, convenience, and a vague image of stability," he said.

"I beg your pardon?"

"Her words," continued Joel. "She said that I

got married so I'd have a place to go and someone to fix the meals and do the laundry, and eliminate the irritating, time-consuming foolishness that goes with finding someone to sleep with. Also by legitimizing her, I projected the proper image. . . . 'And, Christ, did I have to play the part'—also her words."

"Were they true?"

"I told you, when I came back I wanted it all and she was part of it. Yes, they were true. Cook, maid, laundress, bedmate, and an acceptable, attractive appendage. She told me she could never figure out the pecking order."

"She sounds like quite a girl."

"She was. She is."

"Do I discern a note of possible reconciliation?"

"No way." Converse shook his head, a partial smile on his lips but only a trace of humor in his eyes. "She was also conned and it shouldn't have happened. Anyway, I like my current status, I really do. Some of us just weren't meant for a hearth and roast turkey, even if we sometimes wish we were."

"It's not a bad life."

"Are you into it?" asked Joel quickly so as to shift the emphasis.

"Right up with orthodontists and SAT scores. Five kids and one wife. I wouldn't have it any other way."

"But you travel a lot, don't you?"

"We have great homecomings." Halliday again leaned forward, as if studying a witness. "So you have no real attachments now, no one to run back to."

"Talbot, Brooks and Simon might find that offensive. Also my father. Since Mother died we have dinner once a week when he's not flying all over the place, courtesy of a couple of lifetime passes."

"He still gets around a lot?"

"One week he's in Copenhagen, the next in Hong Kong. He enjoys himself; he keeps moving. He's sixty-eight and spoiled rotten."

"I think I'd like him."

Converse shrugged, again smiling. "You might not. He thinks all lawyers are piss ants, me included. He's the last of the white-scarved flyboys."

"I'm sure I'd like him. . . . But outside of your employers and your father, there are no—shall we say—priority entanglements in your life."

"If you mean women, there are several and we're good friends, and I think this conversation has gone about as far as it should go."

"I told you, I had a point," said Halliday.

"Then why not get to it, counselor? Interrogatories are over."

The Californian nodded. "All right, I will. The people I spoke with wanted to know how free you were to travel."

"The answer is that I'm not. I've got a job and a responsibility to the company I work for. Today's Wednesday; we'll have the merger tied up by Friday, I'll take the weekend off and be back on Monday—when I'm expected."

"Suppose arrangements could be made that Talbot, Brooks and Simon found acceptable?"

"That's presumptuous."

"And you found very difficult to reject."

"That's preposterous."

"Try me," said Halliday. "Five hundred thousand for accepting on a best-efforts basis, one million if you pull it off."

"Now you're insane." A second flash of light blinded Converse, this one remaining stationary longer than the first. He raised his left hand to block it from his eyes as he stared at the man he had once known as Avery Fowler. "Also, ethics notwithstanding because you haven't a damn thing to win this morning, your timing smells. I don't like getting offers—even crazy offers—from attorneys I'm about to meet across a table."

"Two separate entities, and you're right, I don't have a damn thing to win or lose. You and Aaron did it all, and I'm so ethical, I'm billing the Swiss only for my time—minimum basis—because no expertise was called for. My recommendation this morning will be to accept the package as it stands, not even a comma changed. Where's the conflict?"

"Where's the sanity?" asked Joel. "To say nothing of those arrangements Talbot, Brooks and Simon will find acceptable. You're talking roughly about two and a half top years of salary *and* bonuses for nodding my head."

"Nod it," said Halliday. "We need you."

"*We?* That's a new wrinkle, isn't it? I thought it was *they*. *They* being the people you spoke with. Spell it out, *Press.*"

A. Preston Halliday locked his eyes with Joel's. "I'm part of them, and something is happening

22

that shouldn't be happening. We want you to put a company out of business. It's bad news and it's dangerous. We'll give you all the tools we can.''

"What company?"

"The name wouldn't mean anything, it's not registered. Let's call it a government-in-exile."

"A *what?*"

"A group of like-minded men who are in the process of building a portfolio of resources so extensive it'll guarantee them influence where they shouldn't have it—authority where they shouldn't have it."

"Where is that?"

"In places this poor inept world can't afford. They can do it because no one expects them to."

"You're pretty cryptic."

"I'm frightened. I know them."

"But you have the tools to go after them," said Converse. "I presume that means they're vulnerable."

Halliday nodded. "We think they are. We have. some leads, but it'll take digging, piecing things together. There's every reason to believe they've broken laws, engaged in activities and transactions prohibited by their respective governments."

Joel was silent for a moment, studying the Californian. "Governments?" he asked "Plural?"

"Yes." Halliday's voice dropped. "They're different nationalities."

"But one company?" said Converse. "One corporation?"

"In a manner of speaking, yes."

"How about a simple yes?"

"It's not that simple."

"I'll tell you what is," interrupted Joel. "You've got leads, so you go after the big bad wolves. I'm currently and satisfactorily employed."

Halliday paused, then spoke. "No, you're not," he said softly.

Again there was silence, each man appraising the other. "What did you say?" asked Converse, his eyes blue ice.

"Your firm understands. You can have a leave of absence."

"You presumptuous son of a bitch! Who gave you the right even to *approach—*"

"General George Marcus Delavane," Halliday broke in. He delivered the name in a monotone.

It was as if a bolt of lightning had streaked down through the blinding sunlight burning Joel's eyes, turning the ice into fire. Cracks of thunder followed, exploding in his head.

The pilots sat around the long rectangular table in the wardroom, sipping coffee and staring down into the brown liquid or up at the gray walls, no one caring to break the silence. An hour ago they had been sweeping over Pak Song, firing the earth, interdicting the advancing North Vietnamese battalions, giving vital time to the regrouping ARVN and American troops who soon would be under brutal siege. They had completed the strike and returned to the carrier—all but one. They had lost their commanding officer. Lieutenant Senior Grade Gordon Ramsey had been hit by a fluke rocket that had winged out of its trajectory over the coastline and zeroed in on Ramsey's fuselage; the explosion had filled the jet streams, death at six hundred miles an hour in the air, life erased in the blinking of an eye. A severe weather front had followed hard upon the squadron; there would be no more strikes, perhaps for several days. There would be time to think and that was not a pleasant thought.

"Lieutenant Converse," said a sailor by the open wardroom door.

"Yes?"

"The captain requests your presence in his quarters, sir."

The invitation was so nicely phrased, mused Joel, as he got out of his chair, acknowledging the somber looks of those around the table. The request was expected, but unwelcome. The promotion was an honor he would willingly forgo. It was not that he held longevity or seniority or even age over his fellow pilots; it was simply that he had been in the air longer than anyone else and with that time came the experience necessary for the leader of a squadron.

As he climbed the narrow steps up toward the bridge he saw the outlines of an immense army Cobra helicopter in the distant sky stuttering its way toward the carrier. In five minutes or so it would be hovering over the threshold and lower itself to the pad; someone from land was paying the Navy a visit.

"It's a terrible loss, Converse," said the captain, standing over his charts table, shaking his head sadly. "And a letter I hate like hell to write. God knows they're never easy, but this one's more painful than most."

"We all feel the same way, sir."

"I'm sure you do." The captain nodded. "I'm also sure you know why you're here."

"Not specifically, sir."

"Ramsey said you were the best, and that means you're taking over one of the crack squadrons in the South China Sea." The telephone rang, interrupting the carrier's senior officer. He picked it up. "Yes?"

What followed was nothing Joel expected. The captain at first frowned, then tensed the muscles of his face, his eyes both alarmed and angry. "What?" he exclaimed, raising his voice. "Was there any advance notice—anything in the radio room?" There was a pause, after which the captain slammed down the phone, shouting, "Jesus Christ!" He looked at Converse. "It seems we have the dubious honor of an unannounced visitation by Command-Saigon, and I do mean visitation!"

"I'll return below, sir," said Joel, starting to salute.

"Not just yet, Lieutenant," shot back the captain quietly but firmly. "You are receiving your orders, and as they affect the air operations of this ship, you'll hear them through. At the least, we'll let Mad Marcus know he's interfering with Navy business."

The next thirty seconds were taken up with the ritual of command assignment, a senior officer investing a subordinate with new responsibilities. Suddenly there was a sharp two-rap knock as the captain's door opened and the tall, broad-

26

shouldered general of the Army George Marcus Delavane intruded, dominating the room with the sheer force of his presence.

"Captain?" said Delavane, saluting the ship's commander first despite the Navy man's lesser rank. The somewhat high-pitched voice was courteous, but not the eyes; they were intensely hostile.

"General," replied the captain, saluting back along with Converse. "Is this an unannounced inspection by Command-Saigon?"

"No, it's an urgently demanded conference between you and me— between Command-Saigon and one of its lesser forces."

"I see," said the four-striper, anger showing through his calm. "At the moment I'm delivering urgent orders to this man—"

"You saw fit to countermand mine!" Delavane broke in vehemently.

"General, this has been a sad and trying day," said the captain. "We lost one of our finest pilots barely an hour ago—"

"Running away?" Again Delavane interrupted, the tastelessness of his remark compounded by the nasal pitch of his voice. "Was his goddamned tail shot off?"

"For the record, I resent that!" said Converse, unable to control himself. "I'm replacing that man and I resent what you just said—General!"

"You? Who the hell are you?"

"Easy, Lieutenant. You're dismissed."

"I respectfully request to answer the general, sir!" shouted Joel, in his anger refusing to move.

"You what, prissy flyboy?"

27

"My name is—"

"Forget it, I'm not interested!" Delavane whipped his head back toward the captain. "What I want to know is why you think you can disobey my orders—the orders from Command-Saigon! I called a strike for fifteen hundred hours! You 'respectfully declined' to implement that order!"

"A weather front's moved in and you should know it as well as I do."

"My meteorologists say it's completely flyable!"

"I suspect if you asked for that finding during a Burma monsoon they'd deliver it."

"That's gross insubordination!"

"This is my ship and military regulations are quite clear as to who's in command here."

"Do you want to connect me to your radio room? I'll reach the Oval Office and we'll see just how long you've got this ship!"

"I'm sure you'll want to speak privately —probably over a scrambler. I'll have you escorted there."

"Goddamn you, I've got four thousand troops—maybe twenty percent seasoned—moving up into Sector Five! We need a low-altitude combined strike from land and sea and we'll have it if I have to get your ass out of here within the hour! And I can do it, Captain! . . . We're over here to win, win, and win it all! We don't need sugarcoated Nellies hedging their goddamned bets! Maybe you never heard it before, but all war is a risk! You don't win if you don't risk, Captain!"

"I've been there, General. Common sense cuts

28

losses, and if you cut enough losses you can win the next battle.''

''I'm going to win this one, with or without you, Blue Boy!''

''I respectfully advise you to temper your language, General.''

''You what?'' Delavane's face was contorted in fury, his eyes the eyes of a savage wild animal. ''You advise me? You advise Command-Saigon! Well, you do whatever you like—Blue Boy in your satin pants—but the incursion up into the Tho Valley is on.''

''The Tho,'' interrupted Converse. ''That's the first leg of the Pak Song route. We've hit it four times. I know the terrain.''

''You know it?'' shouted Delavane.

'I do, but I take my orders from the commander of this ship—General.''

''You prissy shit-kicker, you take orders from the President of the United States! He's your commander in chief! And I'll get those orders!''

Delavane's face was inches from Joel's, the maniacal expression challenging every nerve ending in Joel's body; hatred matched by loathing. Barely realizing the words were his, Converse spoke. ''I, too, would advise the General to be careful of his language.''

''Why, shit-kicker? Has Blue Boy got this place wired?''

''Easy, Lieutenant! I said you were dismissed!''

''You want me to watch my language, big fella with your little silver bar? No, sonny boy, you watch it, and you read it! If that squadron of yours isn't in the air at fifteen hundred hours, I'll label this carrier the biggest yellow streak in Southeast Asia! You got that, satin-pantsed Blue Boy, third class?"

Once more Joel replied, wondering as he spoke where he found the audacity. "I don't know where you come from, sir, but I sincerely hope we meet under different circumstances sometime. I think you're a pig."

"Insubordination! Also, I'd break your back."

"Dismissed, Lieutenant!"

"No, Captain, you're wrong!" shouted the general. "He may be the man to lead this strike, after all. Well, what'll it be, Blue Boys? Airborne, or the President of the United States—or the label?"

At 1520 hours Converse led the squadron off the carrier deck. At 1538, as they headed at low altitude into the weather, the first two casualties occurred over the coastline; the wing planes were shot down—fiery deaths at six hundred miles an hour in the air. At 1546 Joel's right engine exploded; his altitude made the direct hit easy. At 1546:30, unable to stabilize, Converse ejected into the downpour of the storm clouds, his parachute instantly swept into the vortex of the conflicting winds. As he swung violently down toward the earth, the straps digging into his flesh with each whipping buffet, one image kept repeating its presence within the darkness. The maniacal face of General George Marcus Delavane. He was about to begin an indeterminate stay in hell, courtesy of a madman. And as he later learned, the losses were infinitely greater on the ground.

30

Delavane! The Butcher of Danang and Pleiku. Waster of thousands, throwing battalion after battalion into the jungles and the hills with neither adequate training nor sufficient firepower. Wounded, frightened children had been marched into the camps, bewildered, trying not to weep and, finally understanding, weeping out of control. The stories they told were a thousand variations on the same sickening theme. Inexperienced, untried troops had been sent into battle within days after disembarkation; the weight of sheer numbers was expected to vanquish the often unseen enemy. And when the numbers did not work, more numbers were sent. For three years command headquarters listened to a maniac. *Delavane!* The warlord of Saigon, fabricator of body counts, with no acknowledgment of blown-apart faces and severed limbs, liar and extoller of death without a cause! A man who had proved, finally, to be too lethal even for the Pentagon zealots—a zealot who had outdistanced his own, in the end revolting his own. He had been recalled and retired only to write diatribes read by fanatics who fed their own personal furies.

Men like that can't be allowed anymore, don't you understand? He was the enemy, OUR enemy! Those had been Converse's own words, shouted in a fever of outrage before a panel of uniformed questioners who had looked at each other, avoiding him, not wanting to respond to those words. They had thanked him perfunctorily, told him that the nation owed him and thousands like him a great debt, and with regard to his final comments he should try to understand that there were often many sides to an issue, and that the complex execution of command frequently was not what it appeared to be. In any event, the President had called upon the nation to bind its wounds; what good was served by fueling old controversies? And then the final kicker, the threat.

"You yourself briefly assumed the terrible responsibility of leadership, Lieutenant," said a pale-faced Navy lawyer, barely glancing at Joel, his eyes scanning the pages of a file folder. "Before you made your final and successful escape—by yourself, from a pit in the ground away from the main camp—you led two previous attempts involving a total of seventeen prisoners of war. Fortunately you survived, but eight men did not. I'm sure that you, as their leader, their tactician, never anticipated a casualty risk of nearly fifty percent. It's been said often, but perhaps not often enough: command is awesome, Lieutenant."

Translation: *Don't join the freaks, soldier. You survived, but eight were killed. Were there circumstances the military is not aware of, tactics that protected some more than others, one more than others? One man who managed to break out —by himself—eluding guards that shot on sight prisoners on the loose at night? Merely to raise the question by reopening a specific file will produce a stigma that will follow you for the rest of your life. Back off, soldier. We've got you by simply raising a question we all know should not be raised, but we'll do it because we've taken enough flak. We'll cut it off wherever we can. Be happy you survived and got out. Now, get out.*

At that moment, Converse had been as close to consciously throwing away his life as he would ever have thought possible. Physically assaulting that panel of sanctimonious hypocrites had not been out of the question, until he studied the face of each man, his peripheral gaze taking in rows of tunic ribbons, battle stars on most. Then a strange thing had happened: disgust, revulsion—and compassion—swept over him. These were panicked men, a number having committed their lives to their country's practice of war . . . only to have been conned, as he had been conned. If to protect what was decent meant protecting the worst, who was to say they were wrong? Where were the saints? Or the sinners? Could there be any of either when all were victims?

Disgust, however, won out. Lieutenant Joel Converse, USNR, could not bring himself to give a final salute to that council of his superiors. In silence, he had turned, with no military bearing whatsoever, and walked out of the room as if he had pointedly spat on the floor.

A flash of light again from the boulevard, a blinding echo of the sun from the Quai du Mont Blanc. He was in Geneva, not in a North Vietnamese camp holding children who vomited while telling their stories, or in San Diego being separated from the United States Navy. He was in Geneva, and the man sitting across the table knew everything he was thinking and feeling.

"Why *me?*" whispered Joel.

"Because, as they say," said Halliday, "you could be motivated. That's the simple answer. A story was told. The captain of your aircraft carrier refused to put his planes in the air for the strike that Delavane demanded. Several storms had moved in; he called it suicidal. But Delavane forced him to, threatened to call the macho White House and have the captain stripped of his command. You led that strike. It's where you got it."

"I'm alive," said Converse flatly. "Twelve hundred kids never saw the next day and maybe a thousand more wished they never had."

"And you were in the captain's quarters when Mad Marcus Delavane made his threats and called the shots."

"I was there," agreed Converse, no comment in his voice. Then he shook his head in bewilderment. "Everything I told you—about myself—you've heard it before."

"Read it before," corrected the lawyer from California. "Like you—and I think we're the best in the business under fifty—I don't put a hell of a lot of stock in the written word. I have to hear a voice, or see a face."

"I didn't answer you."

"You didn't have to."

"But *you* have to answer *me—now*. You're not here for Comm Tech-Bern, are you?"

"Yes that part's true " said Halliday. "Only the Swiss didn't come to me, I went to them. I've been watching you, waiting for the moment. It had to be the right one, perfectly natural, geographically logical."

34

"Why? What do you mean?"

"Because I'm being watched. . . . Rosen did have a stroke. I heard about it, contacted Bern, and made a plausible case for myself."

"Your reputation was enough."

"It helped, but I needed more. I said we knew each other, that we went way back—which God knows was true—and as much as I respected you, I implied that you were extremely astute with finals, and that I was familiar with your methods. I also put my price high enough."

"An irresistible combination for the Swiss," said Converse.

"I'm glad you approve."

"But I don't," contradicted Joel. "I don't approve of you at all, least of all *your* methods. You haven't told me anything, just made cryptic remarks about an unidentified group of people you say are dangerous, and brought up the name of a man you knew would provoke a response. Maybe you're just a freak, after all, still pushing that safe Yippie label."

"Calling someone a 'freak' is subjectively prejudicial in the extreme, counselor, and would be stricken from the record."

"Still, the point's been made with the jury, lawyer-man," said Converse quietly but with anger. "And I'm making it now."

"Don't prejudge the safety," continued Halliday in a voice that was equally quiet. "I'm not safe, and outside of a proclivity for cowardice, there's a wife and five children back in San Francisco I care deeply about."

"So you come to me because I have no

35

such—what was it?—priority entanglements?"

"I came to you because you're invisible, you're not involved, and because you're the best, and I can't do it! I *legally* can't do it, and it's got to be done legally."

"Why don't you say what you mean?" demanded Converse. "Because if you don't I'm getting up and we'll see each other later across a table."

"I represented Delavane," said Halliday quickly. "God help me I didn't know what I was doing, and very few people approved, but I made a point we used to make all the time. Unpopular causes and people also deserve representation."

"I can't argue with that."

"You don't know the cause. I do. I found out."

"What cause?"

Halliday leaned forward. "The generals," he said, his voice barely audible. "They're coming back."

Joel looked closely at the Californian. "From where? I didn't know they'd been away."

"From the past," said Halliday. "From years ago."

Converse sat back in the chair, now amused. "Good Lord, I thought your kind were extinct. Are you talking about the Pentagon menace, *Press*—it is 'Press,' isn't it? The San Francisco short-form, or was it from Haight-Ashbury, or the Beverly Hills something or other? You're a little behind the times; you already stormed the Presidio."

"Please, don't make jokes. I'm not joking."

"Of course not. It's *Seven Days in May,* or is it *Five Days in August?* It's August now, so let's call it *The Old-Time Guns of August.* Nice ring, I think."

"Stop it! There's nothing remotely funny, and if there were, I'd find it before you did."

"That's a comment, I suppose," said Joel.

"You're goddamned right it is, because I *didn't* go through what you went through. I stayed out of it, I wasn't conned, and that means I can laugh at fanatics because they never hurt me, and I still think it's the best ammunition against them. But not now. There's nothing to laugh at now!"

"Permit me a small chuckle," said Converse without smiling. "Even in my most paranoid moments I never subscribed to the conspiracy theory that has the military running Washington. It couldn't happen."

"It might be less apparent than in other countries, but that's all I'll grant you."

"What does that mean?"

"It would undoubtedly be much more obvious in Israel, certainly in Johannesburg, quite possibly in France and Bonn, even the UK—none of them takes its pretenses that seriously. But I suppose you've got a point. Washington will drape the constitutional robes around itself until they become threadbare and fall away—revealing a uniform, incidentally."

Joel stared at the face in front of him. "You're *not* joking, are you? And you're too bright to try to snow me."

"Or con you," added Halliday. "Not after that label I wore while watching you in pajamas halfway across the world. I couldn't do it."

"I think I believe you. . . . You mentioned several countries, specific countries. Some aren't speaking, others barely; a few have bad blood and worse memories. On purpose?"

"Yes," nodded the Californian. "It doesn't make any difference because the group I'm talking about thinks it has a cause that will ultimately unite them all. And run them all—their way."

"The generals?"

"And admirals, and brigadiers, and field marshals—old soldiers who pitched their tents in the right camp. So far right there's been no label since the Reichstag."

"Come *on,* Avery!" Converse shook his head in exasperation. "A bunch of tired old warhorses—"

"Recruiting and indoctrinating young, hard, capable new commanders," interrupted Halliday.

"—coughing their last bellows." Joel stopped. "Have you proof of that?" he asked, each word spoken slowly.

"Not enough . . . but with some digging . . . maybe enough."

"Goddamn it, stop being elliptical."

"Among the possible recruits, twenty or so names at the State Department and the Pentagon," said Halliday. "Men who clear export licenses and who spend millions upon millions because they're allowed to spend it, all of which, naturally, widens any circle of friends."

"And influence," stated Converse. "What about London, Paris, and Bonn—Johannesburg and Tel Aviv?''

''Again names.''

''How firm?''

''They were there, I saw them myself. It was an accident. How many have taken an oath I don't know, but they were there, and their stripes fit the philosophical pattern.''

''The Reichstag?''

''More encompassing. A global Third Reich. All they need is a Hitler.''

''Where does Delavane fit in?''

''He may anoint one. He may designate the Führer.''

''That's ridiculous. Who'd take him seriously?''

''He was taken seriously before. You saw the results.''

''That was then, not now. You're not answering the question.''

''Men who thought he was right before, and don't fool yourself, they're out there by the thousands. What's mind-blowing is that there are a few dozen with enough seed money to finance his and their delusions—which, of course, they don't see as delusions at all, only as the proper evolution of current history, all other ideologies having failed miserably.''

Joel started to speak, then stopped, his thoughts suddenly altered. ''Why haven't you gone to someone who can stop them? Stop him.''

''Who?''

''I shouldn't have to tell you that. Any number of people in the government—elected and appointed—and more than a dozen departments. For starters, there's Justice.''

"I'd be laughed out of Washington," said Halliday. "Beyond the fact that we have no proof—as I told you, just names, suppositions —don't forget that Yippie label I once wore. They'd pin it on me again and tell me to get lost."

"But you *represented* Delavane."

"Which only compounds the problem by introducing the legal aspects. I shouldn't have to tell you that."

"The lawyer-client relationship." Converse nodded. "You're in a morass before you can make a charge. Unless you've got hard evidence against your client, proof that he's going to commit further crimes and that you're aiding the commission of those crimes by keeping silent."

"Which proof I don't have," interrupted the Californian.

"Then no one will touch you," added Joel. "Especially ambitious lawyers at Justice; they don't want their postgovernment avenues cut off. As you say, the Delavanes of this world have their constituencies."

"Exactly," agreed Halliday. "And when I began asking questions and tried to reach Delavane, he wouldn't see me or talk to me. Instead, I got a letter telling me I was fired, that if he had known what I was he never would have retained me. 'Smoking dope and screaming curses while brave young men answered their country's call.' "

Converse whistled softly. "And you think you weren't conned? You provide legal services for him, a structure he can use for all intents and purposes within the law, and if anything smells, you're the last person who can blow the whistle. He drapes the old soldier's flag around himself and calls you a vindictive freak."

Halliday nodded. "There was a lot more in that letter—nothing that could damage me except where *he* was concerned, but it was brutal."

"I'm certain of it." Converse took out a pack of cigarettes; he held it forward as Halliday shook his head. "How did you represent him?" asked Joel.

"I set up a corporation, a small consulting firm in Palo Alto specializing in imports and exports. What's allowed, what isn't, what the quotas are, and how to legitimately reach the people in D.C. who will listen to your case. Essentially it was a lobbying effort, trading in on a name, if anyone remembered. At the time, it struck me as kind of pathetic."

"I thought you said it wasn't registered," remarked Converse, lighting a cigarette.

"It's not the one we're after. It'd be a waste of time."

"But it's where you first got your information, isn't it? Your leads?"

"That was the accident, and it won't happen again. It's so legitimate it's legal Clorox."

"Still it's a front," insisted Joel. "It has to be if everything—or anything—you've said is true."

"It's true, and it is. But nothing's written down. It's an instrument for travel, an excuse for Delavane and the men around him to go from one place to another, carrying on legitimate business. But while they're in a given area, they do their real thing."

"The gathering of the generals and the field marshals?" said Converse.

"We think it's a spreading missionary operation. Very quiet and very intense."

"What's the name of Delavane's firm?"

"Palo Alto International."

Joel suddenly crushed out his cigarette. "Who's *we*, Avery? Who's putting up this kind of money when amounts like that mean they're people who can reach anyone they want to in Washington?"

"Are you interested?"

"Not in working for someone I don't know—or approve of. No, I'm not."

"Do you approve of the objectives as I've outlined them to you?"

"If what you've told me is true, and I can't think of any reason why you'd lie about it, of course I do. You knew I would. That still doesn't answer my question."

"Suppose," went on Halliday rapidly, "I were to give you a letter stating that the sum of five hundred thousand dollars to be allocated to you from a blind account on the island of Mykonos was provided by a client of mine whose character and reputation are of the highest order. That his—"

"Wait a minute, *Press,*" Converse broke in harshly.

"Please don't interrupt me, *Please!*" Halliday's eyes were riveted on Joel, a manic intensity in his stare. "There's no other way, not *now*. I'll put my name—my professional life on the line. You've been hired to do confidential work within your specialization by a man known to me to be

42

an outstanding citizen who insists on anonymity. I endorse both the man and the work he's asked you to do, and swear not only to the legality of the objectives but to the extraordinary benefits that would be derived by any success you might have. You're covered, you've got five hundred thousand dollars, and I expect just as important to you, perhaps more so, you have the chance to stop a maniac—maniacs—from carrying out an unthinkable plan. At the least, they'd create widespread unrest, political crises everywhere, enormous suffering. At the worst, they might change the course of history to the point where there wouldn't *be* any history.''

Converse sat rigid in his chair, his gaze unbroken. "That's quite a speech. Practice it long?''

"No, you son of a bitch! It wasn't necessary to practice. Any more than you rehearsed that little explosion of yours twelve years ago in San Diego. 'Men like that can't be allowed anymore, don't you understand? He was the enemy, *our* enemy?' . . . . Those were the words, weren't they?''

"You did your homework, counselor,'' said Joel, his anger controlled. "Why does your client insist on being anonymous? Why doesn't he take his money, make a political contribution, and talk to the director of the CIA, or the National Security Council, or the White House, any of which he could do easily? A half-million dollars isn't chopped chicken liver even today.''

"Because he can't be involved officially in any way whatsoever.'' Halliday frowned as he expelled his breath. "I *know* it sounds crazy, but that's the way it is. He *is* an outstanding man and I went to him because I was cornered. Frankly, I thought he'd pick up the phone and do what you just said. Call the White House, if it came to it, but he wanted to go this route."

"With me?"

"Sorry, he didn't know you. He said a strange thing to me. He told me to find someone to shoot down the bastards without giving them the dignity of the government's concern, even its recognition. At first I couldn't understand, but then I did. It fit in with my own theory that laughing at the Delavanes of this world renders them impotent more thoroughly than any other way."

"It also eliminates the specter of martyrdom," added Converse. "Why would this—outstanding citizen do what he's doing? Why is it worth the money to him?"

"If I told you, I'd be breaking the confidence."

"I didn't ask you his name. I want to know why."

"By telling you," said the Californian, "you'd know who he is. I can't do that. Take my word for it, you'd approve of him."

"Next question," said Joel, a sharp edge to his voice. "Just what the *hell* did you say to Talbot, Brooks that they found so acceptable?"

"*Resigned* to finding it acceptable," corrected Halliday. "I had help. Do you know Judge Lucas Anstett?"

"Second Circuit Court," said Converse, nodding. "He should have been tapped for the Supreme Court years ago."

"That seems to be the consensus. He's also a

44

friend of my client, and as I understand it, he met with John Talbot and Nathan Simon—Brooks was out of town—and without revealing my client's name, told them there was a problem that might well erupt into a national crisis if immediate legal action wasn't taken. Several U.S. firms were involved, he explained, but the problem basically lay in Europe and required the talents of an experienced international lawyer. If their junior partner, Joel Converse, was selected and he accepted, would they consent to a leave of absence so he could pursue the matter on a confidential basis? Naturally, the judge strongly endorsed the project."

"And naturally Talbot and Simon went along," said Joel. "You don't refuse Anstett. He's too damned reasonable, to say nothing of the power of his court."

"I don't think he'd use that lever."

"It's there."

Halliday reached into his jacket pocket and took out a long white business envelope. "Here's the letter. It spells out everything I said. There's also a separate page defining the schedule in Mykonos. Once you make arrangements at the bank—how you want the money paid or where you want it transferred—you'll be given the name of a man who lives on the island; he's retired. Phone him; he'll tell you when and where to meet. He has all the tools we can give you. The names, the connections as we think they are, and the activities they're most likely engaged in that violate the laws of their respective governments—sending arms, equipment, and technological information where it shouldn't be sent. Build just two or three cases that are tied to Delavane—even circumstantially—and it'll be enough. We'll turn it all into ridicule. It will be enough.''

"Where the *hell* do you get your nerve?" said Converse angrily. "I haven't agreed to anything! You don't make decisions for me, and neither does Talbot or Simon, nor the holy Judge Anstett, nor your goddamned client! What did you think you were doing? Appraising me like a piece of horseflesh, making arrangements about me behind my back! Who do you people think you are?"

"Concerned people who think we've found the right man for the right job at the right time," said Halliday, dropping the envelope in front of Joel. "Only there's not that much time left. You've been where they want to take us and you know what it's like." Suddenly the Californian got up. "Think about it. We'll talk later. By the way, the Swiss know we were meeting this morning. If anyone asks what we talked about, tell them I agreed to the final disposition of the Class A stock. It's in our favor even though you may think otherwise. Thanks for the coffee. I'll be across the table in an hour. It's good to see you again, Joel."

The Californian walked swiftly into the aisle and out through the brass gate of the Chat Botté into the sunlight of the Quai du Mont Blanc.

The telephone console was built into the far end of a long, dark conference table. Its muted hum was in keeping with the dignified surroundings. The Swiss *arbitre,* the legal representative of the canton of Geneva, picked it up and spoke softly, nodding his head twice, then replaced the phone in its cradle. He looked around the table; seven of the eight attorneys were in their chairs talking quietly with one another. The eighth, Joel Converse, stood in front of an enormous window flanked by drapes and overlooking the Quai Gustave Ador. The giant *jet d'eau* erupted beyond, its pulsating spray cascading to the left under the force of a north wind. The sky was growing dark; a summer storm was on its way from the Alps.

"Messieurs," said the *arbitre.* Conversations trailed off as faces were turned to the Swiss. "That was Monsieur Halliday. He has been detained, but urges you to proceed. His associate, Monsieur Rogeteau, has his recommendations, and it is understood that he met with Monsieur Converse earlier this morning to resolve one of the last details. Is that not so, Monsieur Converse?"

Heads turned again, now in the opposite direction toward the figure by the window. There was no response. Converse continued to stare down at the lake.

"Monsieur *Converse?"*

"I beg your pardon?" Joel turned, a frown creasing his brow, his thoughts far away, nowhere near Geneva.

"It is so, monsieur?"

"What was the question?"

"You met earlier with Monsieur Halliday?"

47

Converse paused. "It is so," he replied.

"And?"

"And—he agreed to the final disposition of the Class A stock."

There was an audible expression of relief on the part of the Americans and a silent acceptance from the Bern contingent, their eyes non-committal. Neither reaction was lost on Joel, and under different circumstances he might have tabled the item for additional consideration. Halliday's judgment of Bern's advantage notwithstanding, the acceptance was too easily achieved; he would have postponed it anyway, at least for an hour's worth of analysis. Somehow it did not matter. *Goddamn him!* thought Converse.

"Then let us proceed as Monsieur Halliday suggested," said the *arbitre,* glancing at his watch.

An hour stretched into two, then three, the hum of voices mingling in counterpoint as pages were passed back and forth, points clarified, paragraphs initialed. And still Halliday did not appear. Lamps were turned on as darkness filled the midday sky outside the huge windows; there was talk of the approaching storm.

Then, suddenly, screams came from beyond the thick oak door of the conference room, swelling in volume until images of horror filled the minds of all who heard the prolonged terrible sounds. Some around the enormous table lunged under it, others got out of their chairs and stood in shock, and a few rushed to the door, among them Converse. The *arbitre* twisted the knob and yanked it back with such force that the door crashed into the wall. What they saw was a sight none of them would ever forget. Joel lashed out, gripping, pulling, pushing away those in front of him as he raced into the anteroom.

He saw Avery Fowler, his white shirt covered with blood, his chest a mass of tiny, bleeding holes. As the wounded man fell, his upturned collar separated to reveal more blood on his throat. The expulsions of breath were too well known to Joel; he had held the heads of children in the camps as they had wept in anger and the ultimate fear. He held Avery Fowler's head now, lowering him to the floor.

"My God, what *happened?*" cried Converse, cradling the dying man in his arms.

"They're . . . back," coughed the classmate from long ago. "The elevator. They trapped me in the elevator! . . . They said it was for Aquitaine, that was the name they used . . . *Aquitaine*. Oh, Christ! Meg . . . the *kids!*" Avery Fowler's head twisted spastically into his right shoulder, then the final expulsion of air came from his bloodied throat.

Converse stood in the rain, his clothes drenched, staring at the unseen place on the water where only an hour ago the fountain had shot up to the sky proclaiming *this* was Geneva. The lake was angry, an infinity of whitecaps had replaced the graceful white sails. There were no reflections anywhere. But there was distant thunder from the north. From the Alps.

And Joel's mind was frozen.

49

2

He walked past the long marble counter of the hotel Richemond's front desk and headed for the winding staircase on the left. It was habit; his suite was on the second floor and the brass-grilled elevators with their wine-colored velvet interiors were things of beauty, but not of swiftness. Too, he enjoyed passing the casement displays of outrageously priced, brilliantly lit jewels that lined the walls of the elegant staircase—shimmering diamonds, blood-red rubies, webbed necklaces of spun gold. Somehow they reminded him of change, of extraordinary change. For him. For a life he had thought would end violently, thousands of miles away in a dozen different yet always the same rat-infested cells, with muted gunfire and the screams of children in the dark distance. Diamonds, rubies, and spun gold were symbols of the unattainable and unrealistic, but they were there, and he passed them, observed them, smiling at their existence . . . and they seemed to acknowledge him, large shining eyes of infinite depth staring back, telling him they were there, *he* was there. Change.

But he did not see them now, nor did they acknowledge him. He saw nothing, felt nothing; every tentacle of his mind and body was numbed, suspended in airless space. A man he had known as a boy under one name had died in his arms years later under another, and the words he had whispered at the brutal moment of death were as incomprehensible as they were paralyzing. *Aquitaine. They said it was for Aquitaine.* . . . Where was sanity, where was reason? What did the words mean and why had he been drawn into that elusive meaning? He *had* been drawn in, he knew, and there was reason in that terrible manipulation. The magnet was a name, a man. George Marcus Delavane, warlord of Saigon.

"Monsieur!" The suppressed shout came from below; he turned on the stairs and saw the formally attired concierge rushing across the lobby and up the steps. The man's name was Henri, and they had known each other for nearly five years. Their friendship went beyond that of hotel executive and hotel guest; they had gambled together frequently at Divonne-les-bains, across the French border.

"Hello, Henri."

"*Mon Dieu,* are you all right, Joel? Your office in New York has been calling you repeatedly. I heard it on the radio, it is all over Geneva! *La drogue!* Drugs, crime, guns . . . *murder!* It touches even us now!"

"Is that what they say?"

"They say small packages of cocaine were found under his shirt, a respected *avocat international* a suspected connection—"

"It's a lie," Converse broke in.

"It's what they say, what can I tell you? Your name was mentioned; it was reported that he died as you reached him. . . . You were not implicated, of course; you were merely there with the others. I

51

heard your name and I've been worried sick! Where have you *been?*"

"Answering a lot of unanswerable questions down at police headquarters." *Questions that were answerable, but not by him, not to the authorities in Geneva. Avery Fowler—Preston Halliday—deserved better than that. A trust had been given, and been accepted in death.*

"Christ, you're drenched!" cried Henri, intense concern in his eyes. "You've been walking in the rain, haven't you? There were no taxis?"

"I didn't look, I wanted to walk."

"Of course, the shock, I understand. I'll send up some brandy, some decent Armagnac. And dinner, perhaps I'll release your table at the Gentilshommes."

"Thanks. Give me thirty minutes and have your switchboard get New York for me, will you? I never seem to dial it right."

"Joel?"

"What?"

"Can I help? Is there something you should tell me? We have won and lost together over too many *grand cru* bottles for you to go alone when you don't have to. I know Geneva, my friend."

Converse looked into the wide brown eyes, at the lined face, rigid in its concern. "Why do you say that?"

"Because you so quickly denied the police reports of cocaine, what else? I watched you. There was more in what you said than what you said."

Joel blinked, and for a moment shut his eyelids tight, the strain in the middle of his forehead

52

acute. He took a deep breath and replied. "Do me a favor, Henri, and don't speculate. Just get me an overseas line in a half-hour, okay?"

"*Entendu, monsieur,*" said the Frenchman. "*Le concierge du Richemond* is here only to serve her guests, special guests accorded special service, of course. . . . I'm here if you need me, my friend."

"I know that. If I turn a wrong card, I'll let you know."

"If you have to turn *any* card in Switzerland, call me. The suits vary with the players."

"I'll remember that. Thirty minutes? A line?"

"*Certainement, monsieur.*"

The shower was as hot as his skin could tolerate, the steam filling his lungs, cutting short the breath in his throat. He then forced himself to endure an ice-cold spray until his head shivered. He reasoned that the shock of extremes might clear his mind, at least reduce the numbness. He had to think; he had to decide; he had to listen.

He came out of the bathroom, his white terry-cloth robe blotting the residue of the shower, and shoved his feet into a pair of slippers on the floor beside the bed. He removed his cigarettes and lighter from the bureau top, and walked into the sitting room. The concerned Henri had been true to his word; on the coffee table a floor steward had placed a bottle of expensive Armagnac and two glasses for appearance, not function. He sat down on the soft, pillowed couch, poured himself a drink, and lighted a cigarette. Outside, the heavy August rain pounded the casement windows, the tattoo harsh and unrelenting. He looked at his watch; it was a few minutes past six—shortly past noon in New York. Joel wondered if Henri had been able to get a clear transatlantic line. The lawyer in Converse wanted to hear the words spoken from New York, words that would either confirm or deny a dead man's revelation. It had been twenty-five minutes since Henri had stopped him on the staircase; he would wait another five and call the switchboard.

The telephone rang, the blaring, vibrating European bell unnerving him. He reached for the phone on the table next to the couch; his breath was short and his hand trembled. "Yes? Hello?"

"New York calling, monsieur," said the hotel operator. "It's your office. Should I cancel the call listed for six-fifteen?"

"Yes, please. And thank you."

"Mr. *Converse?*" The intense, high-pitched voice belonged to Lawrence Talbot's secretary.

"Hello, Jane."

"Good God, we've been trying to reach you since ten o'clock! Are you all *right?* We heard the news then, around ten. It's all so horrible!"

"I'm fine, Jane. Thanks for your concern."

"Mr. Talbot's beside himself. He can't *believe* it!"

"Don't believe what they're saying about Halliday. It's not true. May I speak with Larry, please?"

"If he knew you were on the phone talking to me, I'd be fired."

"No, you wouldn't. Who'd write his letters?"

The secretary paused briefly, her voice calmer

when she spoke. "Oh, God, Joel, you're the end. After what you've been through, you still find something funny to say."

"It's easier, Jane. Let me have Bubba, will you?"

"You *are* the limit!"

Lawrence Talbot, senior partner of Talbot, Brooks and Simon, was a perfectly competent attorney, but his rise in law was as much due to his having been one of the few all-American football players from Yale as from any prowess in the courtroom. He was also a very decent human being, more of a coordinating coach than the driving force of a conservative yet highly competitive law firm. He was also eminently fair and fair-minded; he kept his word. He was one of the reasons Joel had joined the firm; another was Nathan Simon, a giant both of a man and of an attorney. Converse had learned more about the law from Nate Simon than from any other lawyer or professor he had ever met. He felt closest to Nathan, yet Simon was the most difficult to get close to; one approached this uniquely private man with equal parts of fondness and reserve.

Lawrence Talbot burst over the phone. "Good *Lord,* I'm appalled! What can I *say?* What can I *do?*"

"To begin with, strike that horseshit about Halliday. He was no more a drug connection than Nate Simon."

"You haven't heard, then? They've backed off on that. The story now is violent robbery; he resisted and the packets were stuffed under his shirt after they shot him. I think Jack Halliday

55

must have burned the wires from San Francisco, threatened to beat the crap out of the whole Swiss government. . . . He played for Stanford, you know."

"You're too much, Bubba."

"I never thought I'd enjoy hearing that from you, young man. I do now."

"Young man and not so young, Larry. Clear something up for me, will you?"

"Whatever I can."

"Anstett. Lucas Anstett."

"We talked. Nathan and I listened, and he was most persuasive. We understand."

"Do you?"

"Not the particulars certainly; he wouldn't elaborate. But we think you're the best in the field, and granting his request wasn't difficult. T., B. and S. *has* the best, and when a judge like Anstett confirms it through such a conversation, we have to congratulate ourselves, don't we?"

"Are you doing it because of his bench?"

"Christ, *no.* He even told us he'd be harder on us in Appeals if we agreed. He's one rough cookie when he wants something. He tells you you'd be worse off if you give it to him."

"Did you believe him?"

"Well, Nathan said something about billy goats having certain identifiable markings that were not removed without a great deal of squealing, so we should go along. Nathan frequently obfuscates issues, but goddamnit, Joel, he's usually right."

"If you can take three hours to hear a five-minute summation," said Converse.

"He's always thinking, young man."

56

"Young and not so young. Everything's relative."

"Your wife called. . . . Sorry, your ex-wife."

"Oh?"

"Your name came up on the radio or television or something, and she wanted to know what happened."

"What did you tell her?"

"That we were trying to reach you. We didn't know any more than she did. She sounded very upset."

"Call her and tell her I'm fine, will you, please? Do you have the number?"

"Jane does."

"I'll be leaving, then."

"On full pay," said Talbot from New York.

"That's not necessary, Larry. I'm being given a great deal of money, so save the bookkeeping. I'll be back in three or four weeks."

"I could do that, but I won't," said the senior partner. "I know when I've got the best and I intend to hold him. We'll bank it for you." Talbot paused, then spoke quietly, urgently. "Joel, I have to ask you. Did this thing a few hours ago have anything to do with the Anstett business?'

Converse gripped the telephone with such force his wrist and fingers ached. "Nothing whatsoever, Larry," he said. "There's no connection."

Mykonos, the sun-drenched, whitewashed island of the Cyclades, neighboring worshiper of Delos. Since Barbarossa's conquest it had been host to successive brigands of the sea who sailed on the

57

Meltemi winds—Turks, Russians, Cypriots, finally Greeks—placed and displaced over the centuries, a small landmass alternately honored and forgotten until the arrival of sleek yachts and shining aircraft, symbols of a different age. Low-slung automobiles—Porsches, Maseratis, Jaguars —now sped over the narrow roads past starch-white windmills and alabaster churches; a new type of inhabitant had joined the laconic, tradition-bound residents who made their livings from the sea and the shops. Free-spirited youths of all ages, with their open shirts and tight pants, their sunburned skins serving as foil for adornments of heavy gold, had found a new playground. And ancient Mykonos, once a major port to the proud Phoenicians, had become the Saint-Tropez of the Aegean.

Converse had taken the first Swissair flight out of Geneva to Athens, and from there a smaller Olympic plane to the island. Although he had lost an hour in the time zones, it was barely four o'clock in the afternoon when the airport taxi crawled through the streets of the hot, blinding-white harbor and pulled up in front of the smooth white entrance of the bank. It was on the waterfront, and the crowds of flowered shirts and wild print dresses, and the sight of launches chopping over the gentle waves toward the slips on the main pier, were proof that the giant cruise ships far out in the harbor were managed by knowledgeable men. Mykonos was a dazzling snare for tourists; money would be left on the whitewashed island; the tavernas and the shops would be full from early sunrise to burning twilight. The ouzo would flow and Greek fishermen's caps would disappear from the shelves and appear on the swaying heads of suburbanites from Grosse Point and Short Hills. And when night came and the last *efharisto* and *paracalo* had been awkwardly uttered by the visitors, other games would begin—the courtiers and courtesans, the beautiful, ageless, self-indulgent children of the blue Aegean, would start to play. Peals of laughter would be heard as drachmas were counted and spent in amounts that would stagger even those who had opulent suites on the highest decks of the most luxurious ships. Where Geneva was contrary, Mykonos was accommodating—in ways the long-ago Turks might have envied.

Joel had called the bank from the airport, not knowing its business hours, but knowing the name of the banker he was to contact. Kostas Laskaris greeted him cautiously over the phone, making it clear that he expected not only a passport that would clear a spectrograph but the original letter from A. Preston Halliday with his signature, said signature to be subjected to a scanner, matching the signature the bank had been provided by the deceased Mr. A. Preston Halliday.

"We hear he was killed in Geneva. It is most unfortunate," Laskaris had said.

"I'll tell his wife and children how your grief overwhelms me."

Converse paid the taxi and climbed the short white steps of the entrance, carrying his suitcase and attaché case, grateful that the door was opened by a uniformed guard whose appearance brought to mind a long-forgotten photograph of a mad sultan who whipped his harem's women in a courtyard when they failed to arouse him.

Kostas Laskaris was not at all what Joel had expected from the brief, disconcerting conversation over the phone. He was a balding, pleasant-faced man in his late fifties, with warm dark eyes, and relatively fluent in English but certainly not comfortable with the language. His first words upon rising from his desk and indicating a chair in front of it for Converse contradicted Joel's previous impression.

"I apologize for what might have appeared as a *callous* statement on my part regarding Mr. Halliday. However, it *was* most unfortunate, and I don't know how else to phrase it. And it is difficult, sir, to grieve for a man one never knew."

"I was out of line. Forget it, please."

"You are most kind, but I am afraid I cannot forget the arrangements—mandated by Mr. Halliday and his associate here on Mykonos. I must have your passport and the letter, if you please?"

"Who is he?" asked Joel, reaching into his jacket pocket for his passport billfold; it contained the letter. "The associate, I mean."

"You are an attorney, sir, and surely you are aware that the information you desire cannot be given to you until the barriers—have been leaped, as it were. At least, I think that's right."

"It'll do. I just thought I'd try." He took out his passport and the letter, handing them to the banker.

Laskaris picked up his telephone and pressed a

button. He spoke in Greek and apparently asked for someone. Within seconds the door opened and a stunning bronzed, dark-haired woman entered and walked gracefully over to the desk. She raised her downcast eyes and glanced at Joel, who knew the banker was watching him closely. A sign from Converse, another glance—from him directed at Laskaris—and introductions would be forthcoming, accommodation tacitly promised, and a conceivably significant piece of information would be entered in a banker's file. Joel offered no such sign; he wanted no such entry. A man did not pick up half a million dollars for nodding his head, and then look for a bonus. It did not signify stability; it signified something else.

Inconsequential banter about flights, customs and the general deterioration of travel covered the next ten minutes, at which time his passport and the letter were returned—not by the striking, dark-haired woman but by a young, balletic blond Adonis. The pleasant-faced Laskaris was not missing a trick; he was perfectly willing to supply one, whichever route his wealthy visitor required.

Converse looked into the Greek's warm eyes, then smiled, the smile developing into quiet laughter. Laskaris smiled back and shrugged, dismissing the beachboy.

"I am chief manager of this branch, sir," he said as the door closed, "but I do not set the policies for the entire bank. This is, after all, Mykonos."

"And a great deal of money passes through here," added Joel. "Which one did you bet on?"

"Neither," replied Laskaris, shaking his head.

61

"Only on exactly what you did. You'd be a fool otherwise, and I do not think you are a fool. In addition to being chief manager on the waterfront, I am also an excellent judge of character."

"Is that why you were chosen as the intermediary?"

"No, that is not the reason. I am a friend of Mr. Halliday's associate here on the island. His name is Beale, incidentally. Dr. Edward Beale. . . . You see, everything is in order."

"A doctor?" asked Converse, leaning forward and accepting his passport and the letter. "He's a doctor?"

"Not a medical man, however," clarified Laskaris. "He's a scholar, a retired professor of history from the United States. He has an adequate pension and he moved here from Rhodes several months ago. A most interesting man, most knowledgeable. I handle his financial affairs—in which he is not very knowledgeable, but still interesting." The banker smiled again, shrugging.

"I hope so," said Joel. "We have a great deal to discuss."

"That is not my concern, sir. Shall we get to the disposition of the funds? How and where would you care to have them paid?"

"A great deal in cash. I bought one of those sensorized money belts in Geneva—the batteries are guaranteed for a year. If it's ripped off me, a tiny siren goes off that splits your eardrums. I'd like American currency for myself and the rest transferred."

"Those belts are effective, sir, but not if you

are unconscious, or if there is no one around to hear them. Might I suggest traveler's checks?''

"You could and you'd probably be right, but I don't think so. I may not care to write out a signature.''

"As you wish. The denominations for yourself, please?'' said Laskaris, pencil in hand, pad below. "And where would you like the remainder to be sent.''

"Is it possible,'' asked Converse slowly, "to have accounts set up not in my name but accessible to me?''

"Of course, sir. Frankly, it is often standard in Mykonos—as well as in Crete, Rhodes, Athens, Istanbul, and also much of Europe. A description is wired, accompanied by words written out in your handwriting—another name, or numbers. One man I knew used nursery rhymes. And then they are matched. One must use a sophisticated bank, of course.''

"Of course. Name a few.''

"Where?''

"In London, Paris, Bonn—maybe Tel Aviv,'' said Joel, trying to remember Halliday's words.

"Bonn is not easy; they are so inflexible. A wrong apostrophe and they summon whomever they consider their authorities. . . . Tel Aviv is simple; money is as freewheeling and as serpentine as the Knesset. London and Paris are standard and, of course, their greed is overwhelming. You will be heavily taxed for the transfers because they know you will not make an issue over covert funds. Very proper, very mercenary, and very much thievery.''

"You know your banks, don't you?"

"I've had experience, sir. Now, as to the disbursements?"

"I want a hundred thousand for myself—nothing larger than five-hundred-dollar bills. The rest you can split up and tell me how I can get it if I need it."

"It is not a difficult assignment, sir. Shall we start writing names, or numbers—or nursery rhymes?"

"Numbers," said Converse. "I'm a lawyer. Names and nursery rhymes are in dimensions I don't want to think about right now."

"As you wish," said the Greek, reaching for a pad. "And here is Dr. Beale's telephone number. When we have concluded our business, you may call him—or not, as you wish. It is not my concern."

Dr. Edward Beale, resident of Mykonos, spoke over the telephone in measured words and the slow, thoughtful cadence of a scholar. Nothing was rushed; everything was deliberate.

"There is a beach—more rocks than beach, and not frequented at night—about seven kilometers from the waterfront. Walk to it. Take the west road along the coast until you see the lights of several buoys riding the waves. Come down to the water's edge. I'll find you."

The night clouds sped by, propelled by high-altitude winds, letting the moonlight penetrate rapidly, sporadically, illuminating the desolate stretch of beach that was the meeting ground. Far

64

out on the water, the red lamps of four buoys bobbed up and down. Joel climbed over the rocks and into the soft sand, making his way to the water's edge; he could both see and hear the small waves lapping forward and receding. He lit a cigarette, assuming the flame would announce his presence. It did; in moments a voice came out of the darkness behind him, but the greeting was hardly what he expected from an elderly, retired scholar.

"Stay where you are and don't move" was the first command, spoken with quiet authority. "Put the cigarette in your mouth and inhale, then raise your arms and hold them straight out in front of you. . . . Good. Now smoke; I want to see the *smoke*."

"Christ, I'm choking!" shouted Joel, coughing, as the smoke, blown back by the ocean breeze, stung his eyes. Then suddenly he felt the sharp, quick movements of a hand stabbing about his clothes, reaching across his chest and up and down his legs. "What are you *doing?*" he cried, spitting the cigarette out of his mouth involuntarily.

"You don't have a weapon," said the voice.

"Of *course* not!"

"I do. You may lower your arms and turn around now."

Converse spun, still coughing, and rubbed his watery eyes. "You crazy son of a bitch!"

"It's a dreadful habit, those cigarettes. I'd give them up if I were you. Outside of the terrible things they do to your body, now you see how they can be used against you in other ways."

Joel blinked and stared in front of him. The pontificator was a slender, white-haired old man of medium height, standing very erect in what looked like a white canvas jacket and trousers. His face—what could be seen of it in the intermittent moonlight—was deeply lined, and there was a partial smile on his lips. There was also a gun in his hand, held in a firm grip, leveled at Converse's head. "You're *Beale?*" asked Joel. "Dr. *Edward* Beale?"

"Yes. Are you calmed down now?"

"Considering the shock of your warm welcome, I guess so."

"Good. I'll put this away, then." The scholar lowered the gun and knelt down on the sand next to a canvas satchel. He shoved the weapon inside and stood up again. "I'm sorry, but I had to be certain."

"Of what? Whether or not I was a commando?"

"Halliday's dead. Could a substitute have been sent in your place? Someone to deal with an old man in Mykonos? If so, that person would most certainly have had a gun."

"Why?"

"Because he would have had no idea that I *was* an old man. *I* might have been a commando."

"You know, it's possible—just *possible*—that I could have had a gun. Would you have blown my goddamned head off?"

"A respected attorney coming to the island for the first time, passing through Geneva's airport security? Where would you get it? Whom would you know on Mykonos?"

"Arrangements could have been made," protested Converse with little conviction.

"I've had you followed since you arrived. You went directly to the bank, then to the Kouneni hotel, where you sat in the garden and had a drink before going to your room. Outside of the taxi driver, my friend Kostas, the desk clerk, and the waiters in the garden, you spoke to no one. As long as you *were* Joel Converse I was safe."

"For a product of an ivory tower, you sound more like a hit man from Detroit."

"I wasn't always in the academic world, but yes, I've been cautious. I think we must all be very cautious. With a George Marcus Delavane it's the only sound strategy."

"Sound strategy?"

"Approach, if you like." Beale reached between the widely separated buttons of his jacket and withdrew a folded sheet of paper. "Here are the names," he said, handing it to Joel. "There are five key figures in Delavane's operation over here. One each from France, West Germany, Israel, South Africa, and England. We've identified four—the first four—but we can't find the Englishman."

"How did you get these?"

"Originally from notes found among Delavane's papers by Halliday when the general was his client."

"That was the accident he mentioned, then? He said it was an accident that wouldn't happen again."

"I don't know what he told you, of course, but it certainly was an accident. A faulty memory on

Delavane's part, an affliction I can personally assure you touches the aging. The general simply forgot he had a meeting with Halliday, and when Preston arrived, his secretary let him into the office so he could prepare papers for Delavane, who was expected in a half hour or so. Preston saw a file folder on the general's desk; he knew that folder, knew it contained material he could cross-check. Without thinking twice, he sat down and began working. He found the names, and knowing Delavane's recent itinerary in Europe and Africa, everything suddenly began to fall into place—very ominously. For anyone politically aware, those four names are frightening—they dredge up frightening memories."

"Did Delavane ever learn that he'd found them?"

"In my judgment, he could never be certain. Halliday wrote them down and left before the general returned. But then Geneva tells us something else, doesn't it?"

"That Delavane did find out," said Converse grimly.

"Or he wasn't going to take any further chances, especially if there was a schedule, and we're convinced there is one. We're in the countdown now."

"To what?"

"From the pattern of their operations—what we've pieced together—a prolonged series of massive, orchestrated conflagrations designed to spin governments out of control and destabilize them."

"That's a tall order. In what way?"

"Guesswork," said the scholar, frowning. "Probably widespread, coordinated eruptions of violence led by terrorists everywhere—terrorists fueled by Delavane and his people. When the chaos becomes intolerable, it would be their excuse to march in with military units and assume the controls, initially with martial law."

"It's been done before," said Joel. "Feed and arm a presumed enemy, then send out provocateurs—"

"With massive sums of money and material."

"And when they rise up," continued Converse, "pull out the rug, crush them, and take over. The citizens give thanks and call the heroes saviors, as they start marching to their drums. But how could they *do* it?"

"That's the all-consuming question. What are the targets? Where are they, *who* are they? We have no idea. If we had an inkling, we might approach from that end, but we don't, and we can't waste time hunting for unknowns. We must go after what we do know."

"Again, time," Joel broke in. "Why are you so sure we're in a countdown?"

"Increased activity everywhere—in many cases frantic. Shipments originating in the States are funneled out of warehouses in England, Ireland, France, and Germany to groups of insurgents in all the troubled areas. There are rumors out of Munich, the Mediterranean and the Arab states. The talk is in terms of final preparations, but no one seems to know what exactly for—except that all of them must be ready. It's as though such groups as Baader-Meinhof, the Brigate Rosse, the

69

PLO, and the red legions of Paris and Madrid were all in a race with none knowing the course, only the moment when it begins.''

''When is that?''

''Our reports vary, but they're all within the same time span. Within three to five weeks.''

''Oh, my *God.*'' Joel suddenly remembered. ''Avery—Halliday—whispered something to me just before he died. Words that were spoken by the men who shot him. Aquitaine . . . 'They said it was for Aquitaine.' Those were the words he whispered. What do they mean, Beale?''

The old scholar was silent, his eyes alive in the moonlight. He slowly turned his head and stared out at the water. ''It's *madness,*'' he whispered.

''That doesn't tell me anything.''

''No, of course not,'' said Beale apologetically, turning back to Converse. ''It's simply the magnitude of it all. It's so incredible.''

''I'm not reading you.''

''Aquitaine—Aquitania, as Julius Caesar called it—was the name given to a region in southwestern France that at one time in the first centuries after Christ was said to have extended from the Atlantic, across the Pyrenees to the Mediterranean, and as far north as the mouth of the Loire west of Paris on the coast—''

''I'm vaguely aware of that,'' Joel broke in, too impatient for an academic dissertation.

''If you are, you're to be commended. Most people are only aware of the later centuries—say, from the eighth on, when Charlemagne conquered the region, formed the kingdom of Aquitaine and bestowed it on his son Louis, and *his* sons Pepin

One and Two. Actually, these and the following three hundred years are the most pertinent."

"To what?"

"The *legend* of Aquitaine, Mr. Converse. Like many ambitious generals, Delavane sees himself as a student of history—in the tradition of Caesar, Napoleon, Clausewitz . . . even Patton. I was rightly or wrongly considered a scholar, but he remains a student, and that's as it should be. Scholars can't take liberties without substantive evidence—or they shouldn't—but students can and usually do."

"What's your point?"

"The legend of Aquitaine becomes convoluted, the what-if syndrome riding over the facts until theoretical assumptions are made that distort the evidence. You see, the story of Aquitaine is filled with sudden, massive expansions and abrupt contractions. To simplify, an imaginative student of history might say that had there not been political, marital and military miscalculations on the part of Charlemagne and his son, the two Pepins, and later Louis the Seventh of France and Henry the Second of England, *both* of whom were married to the extraordinary Eleanor, the kingdom of Aquitaine might have encompassed most if not all of Europe." Beale paused. "Do you begin to understand?" he asked.

"Yes," said Joel. "Christ, *yes.*"

"That's not all," continued the scholar. "Since Aquitaine was once considered a legitimate possession of England, it might in time have enveloped all of her foreign colonies, including the original thirteen across the Atlantic—later the

71

United States of America. . . . Of course, miscalculations or not, it could never have happened because of a fundamental law of Western civilization, valid since the deposition of Romulus Augustulus and the collapse of the Roman empire. You cannot crush, then unite by force and rule disparate peoples and their cultures—not for any length of time."

"Someone's trying to now," said Converse. "George Marcus Delavane."

"Yes. In his mind he's constructed the Aquitaine that never was, never could be. And it's profoundly terrifying."

"Why? You just said it couldn't happen."

"Not according to the old rules, not in any period since the fall of Rome. But you must remember, there's never *been* a time in recorded history like this one. Never such weapons, such anxiety. Delavane and his people know that, and they will play upon those weapons, those anxieties. They *are* playing upon them." The old man pointed to the sheet of paper in Joel's hand. "You have matches. Strike one and look at the names."

Converse unfolded the sheet, reached into his pocket and took out his lighter. He snapped it, and as the flame illuminated the paper he studied the names. *"Jesus!"* he said, frowning. "They fit in with Delavane. It's a gathering of warlords, if they're the men I think they are." Joel extinguished the flame.

"They are," replied Beale, "starting with General Jacques-Louis Bertholdier in Paris, a remarkable man, quite extraordinary. A

Resistance fighter in the war, given the rank of major before he was twenty, but later an unreconstructed member of Salan's OAS. He was behind an assassination attempt on De Gaulle in August of '62, seeing himself as the true leader of the republic. He nearly made it. He believed then as he believes now that the Algerian generals were the salvation of an enfeebled France. He has survived not only because he's a legend, but because his voice isn't alone—only, he's more persuasive than most. Especially with the elite crowd of promising commanders produced by Saint-Cyr. Quite simply, he's a fascist, a fanatic hiding behind a screen of eminent respectability.''

"And the one named Abrahms," said Converse. "He's the Israeli strong man who struts around in a safari jacket and boots, isn't he? The screecher who holds rallies in front of the Knesset and in the stadiums, telling everyone there'll be a bloodbath in Judea and Samaria if the children of Abraham are denied. Even the Israelis can't shut him up.''

"Many are afraid to; he's become electrifying, like lightning, a symbol. Chaim Abrahms and his followers make the Begin regime seem like reticent, self-effacing pacifists. He's a sabra tolerated by the European Jews because he's a brilliant soldier, proven in two wars, and has enjoyed the respect—if not the affection—of every Minister of Defense since the early years of Golda Meir. They never know when they might need him in the field.''

"And this one," said Joel, again using his lighter. "Van Headmer. South African, isn't he?

The 'hangman in uniform' or something like that.''

"Jan van Headmer, the 'slayer of Soweto,' as the blacks call him. He executes 'offenders' with alarming frequency and government tolerance. His family is old-line Afrikaner, all generals going back to the Boer War, and he sees no reason on earth to bring Pretoria into the twentieth century. Incidentally, he's a close friend of Abrahms and makes frequent trips to Tel Aviv. He's also one of the most erudite and charming general officers ever to attend a diplomatic conference. His presence denies his image and reputation.''

"And Leifhelm,'' said Converse, coming to the last of the foreign names. "A mixed bag, if I'm accurate. Supposedly a great soldier who followed too many orders, but still respected. I'm weakest on him.''

"Entirely understandable,'' said Beale, nodding. "In some ways his is the oddest story—the most monstrous, really, because the truth has been consistently covered up so as to use him and avoid embarrassment. Field Marshal Erich Leifhelm was the youngest general ever commissioned by Adolf Hitler. He foresaw Germany's collapse and made a sudden about-face. From brutal killer and a fanatic super-Aryan to a contrite professional who abhorred the Nazis' crimes as they were 'revealed' to him. He fooled everyone and was absolved of all guilt; he never saw a Nuremberg courtroom. During the cold war the Allies used his services extensively, granting him full security clearances, and later in the fifties when the new German divisions were mounted for the NATO forces, they made sure he was put in command.''

''Weren't there a couple of newspaper stories about him a few years ago? He had several run-ins with Helmut Schmidt, didn't he?''

''Exactly,'' agreed the scholar. ''But those stories were soft and carried only *half* the story. Leifhelm was quoted as saying merely that the German people could not be expected to carry the burden of past guilt into future generations. It had to stop. Pride should once more be established in the nation's heritage. There was some saber rattling aimed at the Soviets, but nothing substantively beyond that.''

''What was the other half?'' asked Converse.

''He wanted the Bundestag's restrictions on the armed forces lifted completely, and fought for the expansion of the intelligence services, patterned after the Abwehr, including rehabilitation sentences for political troublemakers. He also sought extensive deletions in German textbooks throughout the school systems. 'Pride has to be restored,' he kept saying, and everything he said was in the name of virulent anti-Communism.''

''The Third Reich's first strategy in everything when Hitler took over.''

''You're quite right. Schmidt saw through him and knew there'd be chaos if he had his way—and he *was* influential. Bonn could not afford the specter of painful memories. Schmidt forced Leifhelm to resign and literally removed his voice from all government affairs.''

''But he keeps speaking.''

''Not openly. However, he's rich and retains his

friends and contacts."

"Among them Delavane and his people."

"Foremost among them now."

Joel once more snapped his lighter and scanned the lower part of the page. There were two lists of names, the row on the left under the heading *State Department,* the right under *Pentagon.* There were perhaps twenty-five people in all. "Who are the Americans?" He released the lever; the flame died and he put the lighter back in his pocket. "The names don't mean anything to me."

"Some should, but it doesn't matter," said Beale elliptically. "The point is that among those men are disciples of George Delavane. They carry out his orders. How many of them is difficult to say, but at least several from each grouping. You see, these are the men who make the decisions—or conversely, do not oppose decisions—without which Delavane and his followers would be stopped in their tracks."

"Spell that out."

"Those on the left are key figures in the State Department's Office of Munitions Control. They determine what gets cleared for export, who under the blanket of 'national interest' can receive weapons and technology withheld from others. On the right are the senior officers at the Pentagon on whose word millions upon millions are spent for armament procurements. All are decision makers—and a number of those decisions have been questioned, a few openly, others quietly by diplomatic and military colleagues. We've learned that much—"

"Questioned? Why?" interrupted Converse.

"There were rumors—there always *are* rumors—of large shipments improperly licensed for export. Then there's surplus military equipment—excess supplies—lost in transfers from temporary warehouses and out-of-the-way storage depots. Surplus equipment is easily unaccounted for; it's an embarrassment in these days of enormous budgets and cost overruns. Get rid of it and don't be too particular. How fortunate in these instances—and coincidental—if a member of this Aquitaine shows up, willing to buy and with all his papers in order. Whole depots and warehouses are sent where they shouldn't be sent."

"A *Libya* connection?"

"There's no doubt of it. A great many connections."

"Halliday mentioned it and you said it a few moments ago. Laws broken—arms, equipment, technological information sent to people who shouldn't have them. They break loose on cue and there's disruption, terrorism—"

"Justifying military responses," old Beale broke in. "That's part of Delavane's concept. Justifiable escalation of armed might, the commanders in charge, the civilians helpless, forced to listen to them, obey them."

"But you just said questions were raised."

"And answered with such worn-out phrases as 'national security' and 'adversarial disinformation' to stop or throw off the curious."

"That's obstruction. Can't they be caught at it?"

"By whom? With what?"

"Damn it, the questions themselves!" replied Converse. "Those improper export licenses, the military transfers that got lost, merchandise that can't be traced."

"By people without the clearances to go around security classifications, or lacking the expertise to understand the complexities of export licensing."

"That's nonsense," insisted Joel. "You said some of those questions were asked by diplomatic personnel, military colleagues, men who certainly had the clearances *and* the expertise."

"And who suddenly, magically, didn't ask them any longer. Of course, many may have been persuaded that the questions were, indeed, beyond their legitimate purviews; others may have been too frightened to penetrate for fear of involvement; others still, forced to back off—frankly threatened. Regardless, behind it all there are those who do the convincing, and they're growing in numbers everywhere."

"Christ, it's a—a *network*," said Converse softly.

The scholar looked hard at Joel, the night light on the water reflecting across the old man's pale, lined face. "Yes, Mr. Converse, a 'network.' That word was whispered to me by a man who thought I was one of them. 'The network,' he said. 'The network will take care of you.' He meant Delavane and his people."

"Why did they think you were a part of them?"

The old man paused. He looked briefly away at the shimmering Aegean, then back at Converse. "Because *that* man thought it was logical. Thirty

78

years ago I took off a uniform, trading it for the Harris tweeds and unkempt hair of a university professor. Few of my colleagues could understand, for, you see, I was one of the elite, perhaps a later, American version of Erich Leifhelm—a brigadier general at thirty-eight, and the Joint Chiefs were conceivably my next assignment. But where the collapse of Berlin and the *Götterdämmerung* in the bunker had one effect on Leifhelm, the evacuation of Korea and the disembowelment of Panmunjom had another effect on me. I saw only the waste, not the cause I once saw—only the futility where once there'd been sound reasons. I saw death, Mr. Converse, not heroic death against animalistic hordes, or on a Spanish afternoon with the crowds shouting '*Olé*,' but just plain death. Ugly death, shattering death. And I knew I could no longer be a part of those strategies that called for it. . . . Had I been qualified in belief, I might have become a priest.''

''But your colleagues who couldn't understand,'' said Joel, mesmerized by Beale's words, words that brought back so much of his own past. ''They thought it was something else?''

''Of course they did. I'd been praised in evaluation reports by the holy MacArthur himself. I even had a label: the Red Fox of Inchon—my hair was red then. My commands were marked by decisive moves and counter-moves, all reasonably well thought out and swiftly executed. And then one day, south of Chunchon, I was given an order to take three adjacent hills that comprised dead high ground—vantage points that served no strategic purpose—and I radioed back that it was useless real estate, that whatever casualties we sustained were not worth it. I asked for clarification, a field officer's way of saying 'You're crazy, why should I?' The reply came in something less than fifteen minutes. 'Because it's there, General.' That was all. 'Because it's there.' A symbolic point was to be made for someone's benefit or someone else's macho news briefing in Seoul. . . . I took the hills, and I also wasted the lives of over three hundred men—and for my efforts I was awarded another cluster of the Distinguished Service Cross.''

"Is that when you quit?"

"Oh, Lord no, I was too confused, but inside, my head was boiling. The end came, and I watched Panmunjom, and was finally sent home, all manner of extraordinary expectations to be considered my just rewards. . . . However, a minor advancement was denied me for a very good reason: I didn't speak the language in a sensitive European post. By then my head had exploded; I used the rebuke and I took my cue. I resigned quietly and went my way."

It was Joel's turn to pause and study the old man in the night light. "I've never heard of you," he said finally. "Why haven't I ever heard of you?"

"You didn't recognize the names on the two lower lists, either, did you? 'Who are the Americans?' you said. 'The names don't mean anything to me.' Those were your words, Mr. Converse.''

"They weren't young decorated generals —heroes—in a war."

80

"Oh, but several *were*," interrupted Beale swiftly, "in several wars. They had their fleeting moments in the sun, and then they were forgotten, the moments only remembered by them, relived by them. Constantly."

"That sounds like an apology for them."

"Of course it is! You think I have no feelings for them? For men like Chaim Abrahms, Bertholdier, even Leifhelm? We call upon these men when the barricades are down, we extol them for acts beyond our abilities. . . ."

"*You* were capable. You performed those acts."

"You're right and that's why I *understand* them. When the barricades are rebuilt, we consign them to oblivion. Worse, we force them to watch inept civilians strip the gears of reason and, through oblique vocabularies, plant the explosives that will blow those barricades apart again. Then when they're down once more, we summon our commanders."

"Jesus, whose side are you on?"

Beale closed his eyes tightly, reminding Joel of the way he used to shut his own when certain memories came back to him. "Yours, you idiot," said the scholar quietly. "Because I know what they can do when we ask them to do it. I meant what I said before. There's never been a time in history like this one. Far better that inept, frightened civilians, still talking, still searching, than one of us—forgive me, one of them—"

A gust of wind blew off the sea; the sand spiraled about their feet. "That man," said Converse, "the one who told you the network

81

would take care of you. Why did he say it?''

"He thought they could use me. He was one of the field commanders I knew in Korea, a kindred spirit then. He came to my island—for what reason I don't know, perhaps a vacation, perhaps to find me, *who* knows—and found me on the waterfront. I was taking my boat out of the Plati Harbor when suddenly he appeared, tall, erect and very military in the morning sun. 'We have to talk,' he said, with that same insistence we always used in the field. I asked him aboard and we slowly made our way out of the bay. Several miles out of the Plati he presented his case, *their* case. *Delavane's* case.''

"What happened then?''

The scholar paused for precisely two seconds, then answered simply, "I killed him. With a scaling knife. Then I dropped his body over a cluster of sharks beyond the shoals of the Stephanos.''

Stunned, Joel stared at the old man—the iridescent light of the moon heightened the force of the macabre revelation. "Just like that?'' he said in a monotone.

"It's what I was trained to do, Mr. Converse. I was the Red Fox of Inchon. I never hesitated when the ground could be gained, or an adversarial advantage eliminated.''

"You *killed* him?''

"It was a necessary decision, not a wanton taking of life. He was a recruiter and my response was in my eyes, in my silent outrage. He saw it, and I understood. He could not permit me to live with what he'd told me. One of us had to die, and

82

I simply reacted more swiftly than he did."

"That's pretty cold reasoning."

"You're a lawyer, you deal every day with options. Where was the alternative?"

Joel shook his head, not in reply but in astonishment. "How did Halliday find you?"

"We found each other. We've never met, never talked, but we have a mutual friend."

"In San Francisco?"

"He's frequently there."

"Who is he?"

"It's a subject we won't discuss. I'm sorry."

"Why not? Why the secrecy?"

"It's the way he prefers it. Under the circumstances, I believe it's a logical request."

"Logic? Find me logic in any of this! Halliday reaches a man in San Francisco who just happens to know you, a former general thousands of miles away on a Greek island who just *happens* to have been approached by one of Delavane's people. Now, that's coincidence, but damned little logic!"

"Don't dwell on it. Accept it."

"Would you?"

"Under the circumstances, yes, I would. You see, there's no alternative."

"Sure there is. I could walk away five hundred thousand dollars richer, paid by an anonymous stranger who could only come after me by revealing himself."

"You could but you won't. You were chosen very carefully."

"Because I could be motivated? That's what Halliday said."

"Frankly, yes."

"You're off the wall, all of you!"

"One of us is dead. You were the last person he spoke with."

Joel felt the rush of anger again, the sight of a dying man's eyes burned into his memory. "Aquitaine," he said softly. *"Delavane. . . .* All right, I was chosen carefully. Where do I begin?"

"Where do you think you should begin? You're the attorney; everything must be done legally."

"That's just it. I'm an attorney, not the police, not a detective."

"No police in any of the countries where those four men live could do what you can do, even if they agreed to try, which, frankly, I doubt. More to the point, they would alert the Delavane network."

"All right, I'll try," said Converse, folding the sheet with the list of names and putting it in his inside jacket pocket. "I'll start at the top. In Paris. With this Bertholdier."

"Jacques-Louis Bertholdier," added the old man, reaching down into his canvas bag and taking out a thick manila envelope. "This is the last thing we can give you. It's everything we could learn about those four men; perhaps it can help you. Their addresses, the cars they drive, business associates, cafés and restaurants they frequent, sexual preferences where they constitute vulnerability . . . anything that could give you an edge. Use it, use everything you can. Just bring us back briefs against men who have compromised themselves, broken laws—above all, evidence that shows they are not the solid, respectable citizens their life-styles would indicate. Embarrassment,

Mr. Converse, *embarrassment*. It leads to ridicule, and Preston Halliday was profoundly right about that. Ridicule is the first step.''

Joel started to reply, to agree, then stopped, his eyes riveted on Beale. ''I never told you Halliday said anything about ridicule.''

''Oh?'' The scholar blinked several times in the dim light, momentarily unsure of himself, caught by surprise. ''But, naturally, we discussed—''

''You never met, you never *talked!*'' Converse broke in.

''—through our mutual friend the strategies we might employ,'' said the old man, his eyes now steady. ''The aspect of ridicule is a keystone. Of course we discussed it.''

''You just hesitated.''

''You startled me with a meaningless statement. My reactions are not what they once were.''

''They were pretty good in a boat beyond the Stephanos,'' corrected Joel.

''An entirely different situation, Mr. Converse. Only one of us could leave that boat. Both of us will leave this beach tonight.''

''All right, I may be reaching. You would be, too, if you were me.'' Converse withdrew a pack of cigarettes from his shirt pocket, shook one up nervously to his lips and took out his lighter. ''A man I knew as a kid under one name approaches me years later calling himself something else.'' Joel snapped his lighter and held the flame under the cigarette, inhaling. ''He tells a wild story that's just credible enough so I can't dismiss it. The believable aspect is a maniac named Delavane. He says I can help stop him—stop *them*—and there's a great deal of money for nodding my head—provided by a man in San Francisco who won't say who he is, expedited by a former general on a fashionably remote island in the Aegean. And for his efforts, this man I knew under two names is murdered in daylight, shot a dozen times in an elevator, dying in my arms whispering the name 'Aquitaine.' And then this other man, this ex-soldier, this doctor, this *scholar,* tells me another story that ends with a 'recruiter' from Delavane killed with a scaling knife, his body thrown overboard into a school of sharks beyond the Stephanos—whatever that is.''

''The Aghios Stephanos,'' said the old man. ''A lovely beach, far more popular than this one.''

''Goddamn it, I *am* reaching, Mr. Beale, or Professor Beale, or *General* Beale! It's too much to absorb in two lousy days! Suddenly I don't have much confidence. I feel way beyond my depth—let's face it, overwhelmed and under-qualified . . . and damned frightened.''

''Then don't overcomplicate things,'' said Beale. ''I used to say that to students of mine more often than I can remember. I would suggest they not look at the totality that faced them, but rather at each thread of progression, following each until it met and entwined with another thread, and then another, and if a pattern did not become clear, it was not their failure but mine. One step at a time, Mr. Converse.''

''You're one hell of a Mr. Chips. I would have dropped the course.''

''I'm not saying it well. I used to say it better.

When you teach history, threads are terribly important."

"When you practice law, they're everything."

"Go after the threads, then, one at a time. I'm certainly no lawyer, but can't you approach this as an attorney whose client is under attack by forces that would violate his rights, cripple his manner of living, deny his pursuit of peaceful existence—in essence, destroy him?"

"Not likely," replied Joel. "I've got a client who won't talk to me, won't see me, won't even tell me who he is."

"That's not the client I had in mind."

"Who else? It's his money."

"He's only a link to your real client."

"Who's that?"

"What's left of the civilized world, perhaps."

Joel studied the old scholar in the shimmering light. "Did you just say something about not looking at totalities but at threads? You scare the hell out of me."

Beale smiled. "I could accuse you of misplaced concretion, but I won't."

"That's an antiquated phrase. If you mean out-of-context, say it, and I'll deny it. You're securely in *well-placed* contradiction, Professor."

"Good heavens, you were chosen carefully. You won't even let an old man get away with an academic bromide."

Converse smiled back. "You're a likable fellow, General—or Doctor. I'd hate to have met you across a table if you'd taken up law."

"That could truly be misplaced confidence," said Edward Beale, his smile gone. "You're only about to begin.''

"But now I know what to look for. One thread at a time—until the threads meet and entwine, and the pattern's there for everyone to see. I'll concentrate on export licenses, and whoever's shuffling the controls, then connect three or four names with each other and trace them back to Delavane in Palo Alto. At which point we blow it apart *legally*. No martyrs, no causes, no military men of destiny crucified by traitors, just plain bloated, ugly profiteers who've professed to be super patriots, when all the while they were lining their unpatriotic pockets. Why *else* would they have done it? Is there another *reason?* That's ridicule, Dr. Beale. Because they *can't answer.''*

The old man shook his head, looking bewildered. "The professor becomes a student," he said hesitantly. "How can you do this?''

"The way I've done it dozens of times in corporate negotiations. Only, I'll take it a step further. In those sessions I'm like any other lawyer. I try to figure out what the fellow across the table is going to ask for and then why he wants it. Not just what *my* side wants, but what *he* wants. What's going through his mind? You see, Doctor, I'm trying to think like him; I'm putting myself in his place, never for a second letting him forget that I'm doing just that. It's very unnerving, like making notes on margins whenever your opponent says anything, whether he's saying anything or not. But this time it's going to be different. I'm not looking for opponents. I'm looking for allies. In a cause, *their* cause. I'll start in Paris, then on to Bonn, or Tel

88

Aviv, then probably Johannesburg. Only, when I reach these men I won't try to think like them, I'm going to *be* one of them."

"That's a very bold strategy. I compliment you."

"Talking of options, it's the only one open. Also, I've got a lot of money I can spread around, not lavishly but effectively, as befits my unnamed client. Very unnamed, very much in the background, but always there." Joel stopped, a thought striking him. "You know, Dr. Beale, I take it back. I don't want to know who my client is—the one in San Francisco, I mean. I'm going to create my own, and knowing him might distort the portrait I've got in mind. Incidentally, tell him he'll get a full accounting of my expenses: the rest will be returned to him the same way I got it. Through your friend Laskaris at the bank here on Mykonos."

"But you've accepted the money," objected Beale. "There's no reason—"

"I wanted to know if it was real. If *he* was real. He is, and he knows exactly what he's doing. I'll need a great deal of money because I'm going to have to become someone I'm not, and money is the most convincing way to do it. No, Doctor, I don't want your friend's money, I want Delavane. I want the warlord of Saigon. But I'll use his money, just as I'm using him—the way I want him to be. To get inside that network."

"If Paris is your first stop and Bertholdier is going to be your initial contact, there's a specific munitions transfer we think is directly related to him. It might be worth a try. If we're right, it's a microcosm of what they intend doing every-where."

"Is it in here?" asked Converse, tapping the manila envelope containing the dossiers.

"No, it came to light only this morning—early this morning. I don't imagine you listened to the news broadcasts."

"I don't speak any language but English. If I heard a news program I wouldn't know it. What happened?"

"All Northern Ireland is on fire, the worst riots, the most savage killing in fifteen years. In Belfast and Ballyclare, Dromore and in the Mourne Mountains, outraged vigilantes—on *both* sides—are roaming the streets and the hills, firing indiscriminately, slaughtering in their anger everything that moves. It's utter chaos. The Ulster government is in panic, the parliament tied down, emotionally disrupted, everyone trying to find a solution. That solution will be a massive infusion of troops and their commanders."

"What's it got to do with Bertholdier?"

"Listen to me carefully," said the scholar, taking a step forward. "Eight days ago a munitions shipment containing three hundred cases of cluster bombs and two thousand cartons of explosives was air-freighted out of Beloit, Wisconsin. Its destination was Tel Aviv by way of Montreal, Paris, and Marseilles. It never arrived, and an Israeli trace—employing the Mossad—showed that only the cargo's paperwork reached Marseilles, nothing else. The shipment dis-appeared in either Montreal or Paris, and we're convinced it was diverted to provisional extremists—again on both sides—in Northern Ireland.''

"Why do you think so?"

"The first casualties—over three hundred men, women, and children—were killed or severely wounded, ripped to shreds by cluster bombs. It's not a pleasant way to die, but perhaps worse to be hurt—the bombs tear away whole sections of the body. The reactions have been fierce and the hysteria's spreading. Ulster's out of control, the government paralyzed. All in the space of one day, *one single day,* Mr. Converse!''

"They're proving to themselves they can do it,'' said Joel quietly, the fear in his throat.

"Precisely,'' agreed Beale. "It's a test case, a microcosm of the full-scale horror they can bring about.''

Converse frowned. "Outside of the fact that Bertholdier lives in Paris, what ties him to the shipment?''

"Once the plane crossed into France, the French insurers were a firm in which Bertholdier is a director. Who would be less suspect than a company that had to pay for the loss—a company, incidentally, that has access to the merchandise it covers? The loss was upward of four million francs, not so immense as to create headlines, but entirely sufficient to throw off suspicion. And one more lethal delivery is made—mutilation, death, and chaos to follow.''

"What's the name of the insurance company?''

"Compagnie Solidaire. It would be one of the operative words, I'd think. Solidaire, and perhaps Beloit and Belfast.''

"Let's hope I get to confront Bertholdier with them. But if I do, I've got to say them at the right time. I'll catch the plane from Athens in the morning."

"Take the urgent good wishes of an old man with you, Mr. Converse. And urgent is the appropriate word. Three to five weeks, that's all you've got before everything blows apart. Whatever it is, wherever it is, it will be Northern Ireland ten thousand times more violent. It's real and it's coming."

Valerie Charpentier woke up suddenly, her eyes wide, her face rigid, listening intently for sounds that might break the dark silence around her and the slap of the waves in the distance. Any second she expected to hear the shattering bell of the alarm system that was wired into every window and door of the house.

It did not come, yet there had been other sounds, intrusions on her sleep, penetrating enough to wake her. She pulled the covers back and got out of bed, walking slowly, apprehensively, to the glass doors that opened onto her balcony, which overlooked the rocky beach, the jetty, and the Atlantic Ocean beyond.

There it was *again.* The bobbing, dim lights were unmistakably the same, washing over the boat that was moored exactly where it had been moored before. It was the sloop that for two days had cruised up and down the coastline, always in sight, with no apparent destination other than this particular stretch of the Massachusetts shore. At twilight on the second evening it had dropped anchor no more than a quarter of a mile out in the water in front of her house. It was back. After three days it had returned.

Three nights ago she had called the police, who in turn reached the Cape Ann Coast Guard patrols, who came back with an explanation that was no more lucid than it was satisfactory. The sloop was a Maryland registry, the owner an officer in the United States Army, and there were no provocative or suspicious movements that warranted any official action.

"I'd call it damned provocative *and* suspicious," Val had said firmly. "When a strange boat sails up and down the same stretch of beach for two days in a row, then parks in front of my house within shouting distance—shouting distance being swimming distance."

"The water rights of the property you leased don't extend beyond two hundred feet, ma'am" had been the official reply. "There's nothing we can do."

At the first light of the next morning, however, Valerie knew that *something* had to be done. She had focused her binoculars on the boat, only to gasp and move back away from the glass doors. Two men had been standing on the deck of the sloop, their own binoculars—far more powerful than hers—directed at the house, at the bedroom upstairs. At her.

A neighbor down the beachside cul-de-sac had recently installed an alarm system. She was a divorced woman too, but with a hostile ex-husband and three children; she needed the alarm. Two phone calls and Val was speaking to the owner of

Watchguard Security. A temporary system had been hooked up that day while a permanent installation was being designed.

A bell—not shatteringly loud but soft and gentle. It was the quiet clanging of a ship's bell out on the dark water, its clapper swinging with the waves. It was the sound that had awakened her, and she felt relieved yet strangely disturbed. Men out on the water at night who intended harm did not announce their presence. On the other hand, those same men had come back to her house, the boat being only several hundred yards off-shore. They had returned in the darkness, the moon blocked by a sky thick with clouds, no moonlight to guide them. It was as if they wanted her to know they were there and they were watching. They were waiting.

For what? What was happening to her? A week ago her phone had gone dead for seven hours, and when she had called the telephone company from her friend's house, a supervisor in the service department told her he could find no malfunctions. The line was operative.

"Maybe for you, but not for me, and you're not paying the bills."

She had returned home; the line was still dead. A second, far angrier phone call brought the same response. No malfunctions. Then two hours later the dial tone was inexplicably there, the phone working. She had put the episode down to the rural telephone complex having less than the best equipment. She did not know what explanation there could be for the sloop now eerily bobbing in the water in front of her house.

94

Suddenly, in the boat's dim light, she could see a figure crawl out of the cabin. For a moment or two it was hidden in the shadows, then there was a brief flare of intense light. A match. A cigarette. A man was standing motionless on the deck smoking a cigarette. He was facing her house, as if studying it. Waiting.

Val shivered as she dragged a heavy chair in front of the balcony door—but not too close, away from the glass. She pulled the light blanket off the bed and sat down, wrapping it around her, staring out at the water, at the boat, at the man. She knew that if that man or that boat made the slightest move toward shore she would press the buttons she had been instructed to press in the event of an emergency. When activated, the huge circular alarm bells—both inside and outside —would be ear-piercing, erupting in concert, drowning out the sound of the surf and the waves crashing on the jetty. They could be heard thousands of feet away—the only sound on the beach, frightening, overwhelming. She wondered if she would cause them to be heard tonight—this morning.

She would not panic. Joel had taught her not to panic, even when she thought a well-timed scream was called for on the dark streets of Manhattan. Every now and then the inevitable had happened. They had been confronted by drug addicts or punks and Joel would remain calm—icily calm —moving them both back against a wall and offering a cheap, spare wallet he kept in his hip pocket with a few bills in it. God, he was ice! Maybe that was why no one had ever actually assaulted them, not knowing what was behind that cold, brooding look.

"I should have screamed!" she once had cried.

"No," he had said. "Then you would have frightened him, panicked him. That's when those bastards can be lethal."

Was the man on the boat lethal—were the *men* on the boat deadly? Or were they simply novice sailors hugging the coastline, practicing tacks, anchoring near the shore for their own protection—curious, perhaps concerned, that the property owners might object? An Army officer was not likely to be able to afford a captain for his sloop, and there were marinas only miles away north and south—marinas without available berths but with men who could handle repairs.

Was the man out on the boat smoking a cigarette merely a landlocked young officer getting his sailing legs, comfortable with a familiar anchor away from deep water? It was possible, of course—anything was possible—and summer nights held a special kind of loneliness that gave rise to strange imaginings. One walked the beach alone and thought too much.

Joel would laugh at her and say it was all those demons racing around her artist's head in search of logic. And he would undoubtedly be right. The men out on the boat were probably more up-tight than she was. In a way they were trespassers who had found a haven in sight of hostile natives; one inquiry of the Coast Guard proved it. And that clearance, as it were, was another reason why they had returned to the place where, if not welcome, at least they were not harassed. If Joel were with her, she knew exactly what he would do. He would go down to the beach and shout across the water to their temporary neighbors and ask them to come in for a drink.

Dear Joel, foolish Joel, ice-cold Joel. There were times you were comforting—when you were comfortable. And amusing, so terribly amusing —even when you weren't comfortable. In some ways I miss you, darling. But not enough, thank you.

And yet why did the feeling—the instinct, perhaps—persist? The small boat out on the water was like a magnet, pulling her toward it, drawing her into its field, taking her where she knew she did not want to go.

Nonsense! Demons in search of logic! She was being foolish—*foolish Joel, ice-cold Joel*—stop it, for God's sake! Be *reasonable!*

Then the shiver passed through her again. Novice sailors did not navigate around strange coastlines at night.

The magnet held her until her eyes grew heavy and troubled sleep came.

She woke up again, startled by the intense sunlight streaming through the glass doors, its warmth enveloping her. She looked out at the water. The boat was gone—and she wondered for a moment whether it had really been there.

Yes, it had. But it was gone.

3

The 747 lifted off the runway at Athens' Helikon Airport, soaring to the left in its rapid ascent. Below in clear view, adjacent to the huge field, was the U.S. Naval Air Station, permitted by treaty although reduced in size and in the number of aircraft during the past several years. Nevertheless, far-reaching, jet-streamed American craft still roamed the Mediterranean, Ionian and Aegean seas, courtesy of a resentful yet nervous government all too aware of other eyes to the north. Staring out the window, Converse recognized the shapes of familiar equipment on the ground. There were two rows of Phantom F-4T's and A-6E's on opposite sides of the dual strip—updated versions of the F-4G's and A-6A's he had flown years ago.

It was so easy to slip back, thought Joel, as he watched three Phantoms break away from the ground formation; they would head for the top of the runway, and another patrol would be in the skies. Converse could feel his hands tense, in his mind he was manipulating the thick, perforated shaft, reaching for switches, his eyes roaming the dials, looking for right and wrong signals. Then the power would come, the surging force of pressurized tons beside him, behind him, himself encased in the center of a sleek, shining beast straining to break away and soar into its natural habitat. *Final check, all in order; cleared for takeoff. Release the power of the beast, let it free. Roll! Faster, faster; the ground is a blur, the carrier deck a mass of passing gray, blue sea beyond, blue sky above. Let it free! Let me free!*

He wondered if he could still do it, if the lessons and the training of boy and man still held. After the Navy, during the academic years in Massachusetts and North Carolina, he had frequently gone to small airfields and taken up single-engined aircraft just to get away from the pressures, to find a few minutes of blue freedom, but there were no challenges, no taming of all-powerful beasts. Later still, it had all stopped —for a long, long time. There were no airfields to visit on weekends, no playing around with trim company planes; he had given his promise. His wife had been terrified of his flying. Valerie could not reconcile the hours he had flown—civilian and in combat—with her own evaluation of the averages. And in one of the few gestures of understanding in his marriage, he had given his word not to climb into a cockpit. It had not bothered him until he knew—they knew—the marriage had gone sour, at which point he had begun driving out to a field called Teterboro in New Jersey every chance he could find and flown whatever was available, anytime, any hour. Still, even then—especially then—there had been no challenges, no beasts—other than himself.

The ground below disappeared as the 747 stabilized and began the climb to its assigned altitude. Converse turned away from the window and settled back in his seat. The lights were abruptly extinguished on the NO SMOKING sign, and Joel took out a pack of cigarettes from his shirt pocket. Extracting one, he snapped his lighter, and the smoke diffused instantly in the rush of air from the vents above. He looked at his watch; it was 12:20. They were due at Orly Airport at 3:35, French time. Allowing for the zones, it was a three-hour flight, and during those three hours he would commit to memory everything he could about General Jacques Louis Bertholdier—if Beale and the dead Halliday were right, the arm of Aquitaine in Paris.

At Helikon he had done something he had never done before, something that had never occurred to him, an indulgence that was generally attributed to romantic fiction or movie stars or rock idols. Fear and caution had joined with an excess of money, and he had paid for two adjoining seats in first class. He wanted no one's eyes straying to the pages he would be reading. Old Beale had made it frighteningly clear on the beach last night: if there was the remotest possibility that the materials he carried might fall into other hands—*any* other hands—he was to destroy them at all costs. For they were in-depth dossiers on men who could order multiple executions by placing a single phone call.

He reached down for his attaché case, the leather handle still dark from the sweat of his grip since Mykonos early that morning. For the first time he understood the value of a device he had learned about from films and novels. Had he been able to chain the handle of his attaché case to his wrist, he would have breathed far more comfortably.

Jacques-Louis Bertholdier, age fifty-nine, only child of Alphonse and Marie-Thérèse Bertholdier, was born at the military hospital in Dakar. Father a career officer in the French Army, reputedly autocratic and a harsh disciplinarian. Little is known about the mother; it is perhaps significant that Bertholdier never speaks of her, as if dismissing her existence. He retired from the Army four years ago at the age of fifty-five, and is now a director of Juneau et Cie., a conservative firm on the Bourse des Valeurs, Paris's stock exchange.

The early years appear to be typical of the life of a commanding officer's son, moving from post to post, accorded the privileges of the father's rank and influence. He was used to servants and fawning military personnel. If there was a difference from other officers' sons, it was in the boy himself. It is said that he could execute the full-dress manual-of-arms by the time he was five and at ten could recite by rote the entire book of regulations.

In 1938 the Bertholdiers were back in Paris, the father a member of the General Staff. This was a chaotic time, as the war with Germany was imminent. The elder Bertholdier was one of the few commanders aware that the Maginot could not hold; his outspokenness so infuriated his fellow officers that he was transferred to the field, commanding the Fourth Army, stationed along the northeastern border.

The war came and the father was killed in

the fifth week of combat. Young Bertholdier was then sixteen years old and going to school in Paris.

The fall of France in June of 1940 could be called the beginning of our subject's adulthood. Joining the Resistance first as a courier, he fought for four years, rising in the underground's ranks until he commanded the Calais-Paris sector. He made frequent undercover trips to England to coordinate espionage and sabotage operations with the Free French and British intelligence. In February of 1944, De Gaulle conferred on him the temporary rank of major. He was twenty years of age.

Several days prior to the Allied occupation of Paris, Bertholdier was severely wounded in a street skirmish between the Resistance fighters and the retreating German troops. Hospitalization relieved him of further activity for the remainder of the European war. Following the surrender he was appointed to the national military academy at Saint-Cyr, a compensation deemed proper by De Gaulle for the young hero of the underground. Upon graduation he was elevated to the permanent rank of captain. He was twenty-four and given successive commands in the Dra Hamada, French Morocco; Algiers; then across the world to the garrisons at Haiphong, and finally the Allied sectors in Vienna and West Berlin. (Note this last post with respect to the following information on Field Marshal Erich Leifhelm. It was where they first met and were friends, at first openly, but subsequently they denied the relationship after both had resigned from military service.)

Putting Erich Leifhelm aside for the moment, Converse thought about the young legend that was Jacques-Louis Bertholdier. Though Joel was as unmilitary as any civilian could be, in an odd way he could identify with the military phenomenon described in these pages. Although no hero, he had been accorded a hero's return from a war in which very few were so acclaimed, these generally coming from the ranks of those who had endured capture more than they had fought. Nevertheless, the attention—the sheer *attention*—that led to privileges was a dangerous indulgence. Although initially embarrassed, one came to accept it all, and then to expect it all. The recognition could be heady, the privileges soon taken for granted. And when the attention began to dwindle away, a certain anger came into play; one wanted it all back.

These were the feelings of someone with no hunger for authority—success, yes; power, no. But what of a man whose whole being was shaped by the fabric of authority *and* power, whose earliest memories were of privilege and rank, and whose meteoric rise came at an incredibly young age? How does such a man react to recognition and the ever-increasing spectrum of his own ascendancy? One did not lightly take away much from such a man; his anger could turn into fury. Yet Bertholdier had walked away from it all at fifty-five, a reasonably young age for one so prominent. It was not consistent. Something was missing from the portrait of this latter-day Alexander. At least so far.

Timing played a major part in Bertholdier's expanding reputation. After posts in the Dra Hamada and pre-crisis Algiers, he was transferred to French Indochina, where the situation was deteriorating rapidly for the colonial forces, then engaged in violent guerrilla warfare. His exploits in the field were instantly the talk of Saigon and Paris. The troops under his command provided several rare but much needed victories, which although incapable of altering the course of the war convinced the hard-line militarists that the inferior Asian forces could be defeated by superior Gallic courage and strategy; they needed only the materials withheld by Paris. The surrender at Dienbienphu was bitter medicine for those men who claimed that traitors in the Quai d'Orsay had brought about France's humiliation. Although Colonel Bertholdier emerged from the defeat as one of the few heroic figures, he was wise enough or cautious enough to keep his own counsel, and did not, at least in appearance, join the "hawks." Many say that he was waiting for a signal that never came. Again he was transferred, serving tours in Vienna and West Berlin.

Four years later, however, he broke the mold he had so carefully constructed. In his own words, he was "infuriated and disillusioned" by De Gaulle's accords with the independence-seeking Algerians; he fled to the land of his birth, North Africa, and joined General Raoul Salan's rebellious OAS, which violently opposed policies it termed betrayals. During this revolutionary interim of his life he was implicated in an assassination attempt on De Gaulle. With Salan's capture in April of 1962, and the insurrectionists' collapse, once again Bertholdier emerged from defeat stunningly intact. In what can only be described as an extraordinary move—and one that has never really been understood—De Gaulle had Bertholdier released from prison and brought to the Elysée. What was said between the two men has never been revealed, but Bertholdier was returned to his rank. De Gaulle's only comment of record was given during a press conference on May 4, 1962. In reply to a question regarding the reinstated rebel officer, he said (verbatim translation): "A great soldier-patriot must be permitted and forgiven a single misguided interlude. We have conferred. We are satisfied." He said no more on the subject.

For seven years Bertholdier was stationed at various influential posts, rising to the rank of general; more often than not he was the chief military chargé d'affaires at major embassies during the period of France's participation in the Military Committee of NATO. He was frequently recalled to the Quai d' Orsay, accompanying De Gaulle to international conferences, always visible in newspaper photographs, usually within several feet of the great man himself. Oddly enough, although his contributions appear to have been considerable, after these conferences—or summits—he was invariably sent back to his previous station while internal debates continued and decisions were reached without him. It was as though he was constantly being groomed but never summoned for the critical post. Was that ultimate summons the signal he had been waiting for seven years before at Dienbienphu? It is a question for which we have no answer here, but we believe it's vital to pursue it.

With De Gaulle's dramatic resignation after the rejection of his demands for constitutional reform in 1969, Bertholdier's career went into an eclipse. His assignments were far from the centers of power and remained so until his resignation. Research into bank and credit-card references as well as passenger manifests shows that during the past eighteen months our subject made trips to the following: London, 3; New York, 2; San Francisco, 2; Bonn, 3; Johannesburg, 1; Tel Aviv, 1 (combined with Johannesburg). The pattern is clear. It is compatible with the rising geographical pressure points of General Delavane's operation.

Converse rubbed his eyes and rang for a drink. While waiting for the Scotch he scanned the next few paragraphs, his memory of the man now jogged; the information was familiar history and not terribly relevant. Bertholdier's name had been put forward by several ultraconservative factions, hoping to pull him out of the military into the political wars, but nothing had come of the attempts. The ultimate summons had passed him by; it never came. Currently, as a director of a large firm on the Paris stock exchange, he is basically a figurehead capable of impressing the wealthy and keeping the socialistically inclined at bay by the sheer weight of his own legend.

He travels everywhere in a company limousine (read: staff car), and wherever he goes his arrival is expected, the proper welcome arranged. The vehicle is a dark-blue American Lincoln Continental, License Plate 100-1. The restaurants he frequents are: Taillevent, the Ritz, Julien, and Lucas-Carton. For lunches, however, he consistently goes to a private club called L'Etalon Blanc three to four times a week. It is a very-off-the-track establishment whose membership is restricted to the highest-ranking military, what's left of the rich nobility, and wealthy fawners who, if they can't be either, put their money on both so as to be in with the crowd.

Joel smiled; the editor of the report was not without humor. Still, something was missing. His lawyer's mind looked for the lapse that was not explained. What was the signal Bertholdier had not been given at Dienbienphu? What had the imperious De Gaulle said to the rebellious officer, and what had the rebel said to the great man? Why was he consistently accommodated—but only accommodated—never summoned to power?

107

An Alexander had been primed, forgiven, elevated, then dropped? There was a message buried in these pages, but Joel could not find it.

Converse reached what the writer of the report considered relevant only in that it completed the portrait, adding little, however, to previous information.

Bertholdier's private life appears barely pertinent to the activities that concern us. His marriage was one of convenience in the purest La Rochefoucauld sense: it was socially, professionally and financially beneficial for both parties. Moreover, it appears to have been solely a business arrangement. There have been no children, and although Mme. Bertholdier appears frequently at her husband's side for state and social occasions, they have rarely been observed in close conversation. Also, as with his mother, Bertholdier has never been known to discuss his wife. There might be a psychological connection here, but we find no evidence to support it. Especially since Bertholdier is a notorious womanizer, supporting at times as many as three separate mistresses as well as numerous peripheral assignations. Among his peers there is a sobriquet that has never found its way into print: Le Grand Machin, and if the reader here needs a translation, we recommend drinks in Montparnasse.

On that compelling note the report was finished. It was a dossier that raised more questions than it answered. In broad strokes it described the whats and the hows but few of the whys; these were buried, and only imaginative speculation could unearth even the probabilities. But there were enough concrete facts to operate on. Joel glanced at his watch; an hour had passed. He had two more to reread, think, and absorb as much as possible. He had already made up his mind about whom he would contact in Paris.

Not only was René Mattilon an astute lawyer frequently called upon by Talbot, Brooks and Simon when they needed representation in the French courts, but he was also a friend. Although he was older than Joel by a decade, their friendship was rooted in a common experience, common in the sense of global geography, futility and waste. Thirty years ago Mattilon was a young attorney in his twenties conscripted by his government and sent to French Indochina as a legal officer. He witnessed the inevitable and could never understand why it cost so much for his proud, intractable nation to perceive it. Too, he could be scathing in his comments about the subsequent American involvement.

"Mon Dieu! You thought you could do with arms what we could not do with arms *and* brains? *Déraisonnable!"*

It had become standard that whenever Mattilon flew to New York or Joel to Paris they found time for dinner and drinks. Also, the Frenchman was amazingly tolerant of Converse's linguistic limitations; Joel simply could not learn another language. Even Val's patient tutoring had fallen on deaf and dead ears and an unreceptive brain. For four years his ex-wife, whose father was French and whose mother was German, tried to teach him the simplest phrases but found him hopeless.

"How the hell can you call yourself an international lawyer when you can't be understood beyond Sandy Hook?" she had asked.

"Hire interpreters trained by Swiss banks and put them on a point system," he had replied. "They won't miss a trick."

Whenever he came to Paris, he stayed in a suite of two rooms at the opulent George V Hotel, an indulgence permitted by Talbot, Brooks and Simon, he had assumed, more to impress clients than to satisfy a balance sheet. The assumption was only half right, as Nathan Simon had made clear.

"You have a fancy sitting room," Nate had told him in his sepulchral voice. "Use it for conferences and you can avoid those ridiculously expensive French lunches and—God forbid—the dinners."

"Suppose they want to eat?"

"You have another appointment. Wink and say it's personal; no one in Paris will argue."

The impressive address could serve him now, mused Converse, as the taxi weaved maniacally through the midafternoon traffic on the Champs Elysées toward the Avenue George V. If he made any progress—and he intended to make progress—with men around Bertholdier or Bertholdier himself, the expensive hotel would fit

110

the image of an unknown client who had sent his personal attorney on a very confidential search. Of course, he had no reservation, an oversight to be blamed on a substituting secretary.

He was greeted warmly by the assistant manager, albeit with surprise and finally apologies. No telexed request for reservations had come from Talbot, Brooks and Simon in New York, but naturally, accommodations would be found for an old friend. They were; the standard two-room suite on the second floor, and before Joel could unpack, a steward brought a bottle of the Scotch whisky he preferred, substituting it for the existing brand on the dry bar. He had forgotten the accuracy of the copious notes such hotels kept on repeating guests. Second floor, the right whisky, and no doubt during the evening he would be reminded that he usually requested a wake-up call for seven o'clock in the morning. It would be the same.

But it was close to five o'clock in the afternoon now. If he was going to reach Mattilon before the lawyer left his office for the day, he had to do so quickly. If René could have drinks with him, it would be a start. Either Mattilon was his man or he was not, and the thought of losing even an hour of any kind of progress was disturbing. He reached for the Paris directory on a shelf beneath the phone on the bedside table; he looked up the firm's number and dialed.

"Good Christ, Joel!" exclaimed the Frenchman. "I read about that terrible business in Geneva! It was in the morning papers and I tried to call you—Le Richemond, of course—but they said you'd checked out. Are you all right?''

"I'm fine. I was just there, that's all."

"He was American. Did you know him?"

"Only across a table. By the way, that crap about his having something to do with narcotics was just that. Crap. He was cornered, robbed, shot and set up for postmortem confusion."

"And an overzealous official leaped at the obvious, trying to protect his city's image. I know; it was made clear. . . . It's all so horrible. Crime, killing, terrorism; it spreads everywhere. Less so here in Paris, thank God."

"You don't need muggers, the taxi drivers more than fill the bill. Except nastier, maybe."

"You are, as always, *impossible,* my friend! When can we get together?"

Converse paused. "I was hoping tonight. After you left the office."

"It's very short notice, *mon ami.* I wish you had called before."

"I just got in ten minutes ago."

"But you left Geneva—"

"I had business in Athens," interrupted Joel.

"Ah, yes, the money flees from the Greeks these days. Precipitously, I think. Just as it was here."

"How about drinks, René. It's important."

It was Mattilon's turn to pause; it was obvious he had caught the trace of urgency in Converse's brevity, in his voice. "Of course," said the Frenchman. "You're at the George Cinq, I assume?"

"Yes."

"I'll be there as soon as I can. Say, forty-five minutes."

"Thanks very much. I'll get a couple of chairs in the gallery."

"I'll find you."

That area of the immense marble-arched lobby outside the tinted glass doors of the George V bar is known informally as the "gallery" by habitués, its name derived from the fact that there is an art gallery narrowly enclosed within a corridor of clear glass on the left. However, just as reasonably, the name fits the luxurious room itself. The deeply cushioned cut-velvet chairs, settees, and polished low, dark tables that line the marble walls are beneath works of art—mammoth tapestries from long-forgotten châteaux and huge heroic canvases by artists, both old and new. And the smooth stone of the floor is covered with giant Oriental rugs, while affixed to the high ceiling are a series of intricate chandeliers, throwing soft light through filigrees of lacelike gold.

Quiet conversations take place between men and women of wealth and power at these upholstered enclaves, in calculated shadows under spotlit paintings and woven cloth from centuries ago. Frequently they are opening dialogues, testing questions that as often as not are resolved in boardrooms peopled by chairmen and presidents, treasurers, and prides of lawyers. The movers and the shakers feel comfortable with the initial informality—the uncommitted explorations —of first meetings in this very formal room. The ceremonial environs somehow lend an air of ritualized disbelief; denials are not hard to come by later. The gallery also lives up to the implications of its name: within the fraternity of those who have achieved success on the international scene, it is said that if any of its members spend a certain length of time there, sooner or later he will run into almost everyone he knows. Therefore, if one does not care to be seen, he should go somewhere else.

The room was filling up, and waiters moved away from the raucous bar to take orders at the tables, knowing where the real money was. Converse found two chairs at the far end, where the dim light was even more subdued. He looked at his watch and was barely able to read it. Forty minutes had passed since his call to René, a shower taking up the time as it washed away the sweat-stained dirt of his all-day journey from Mykonos. Placing his cigarettes and lighter on the table, he ordered a drink from an alert waiter, his eyes on the marble entrance to the room.

Twelve minutes later he saw him. Mattilon walked energetically out of the harsh glare of the street lobby into the soft light of the gallery. He stopped for a moment, squinting, then nodded. He started down the center of the carpeted floor, his eyes leveled at Joel from a distance, a broad, genuine smile on his face. René Mattilon was in his mid to late fifties, but his stride, like his outlook, was that of a younger man. There was about him that aura peculiar to successful trial lawyers; his confidence was apparent because it was the essence of his success, yet it was born of diligence, not merely ego and performance. He was the secure actor comfortable in his role, his graying hair and blunt, masculine features all part of a calculated effect. Beyond that appearance, however, there was also something else, thought Joel, as he rose from his chair. René was a thoroughly decent man; it was a disarming conclusion. God knew they both had their flaws, but they were both decent men; perhaps that was why they enjoyed each other's company.

A firm handshake preceded a brief embrace. The Frenchman sat down across from Converse as Joel signaled an attentive waiter. "Order in French," Joel said. "I'd end up getting you a hot fudge sundae."

"This man speaks better English than either of us. Campari and ice, please."

"Merci, monsieur." The waiter left.

"Thanks again for coming over," said Converse. "I mean it."

"I'm sure you do. . . . You look well, Joel, tired but well. That shocking business in Geneva must give you nightmares."

"Not really. I told you, I was simply there."

"Still, it might have been *you*. The newspapers said he died while you held his head."

"I was the first one to reach him."

"How horrible."

"I've seen it happen before, René," said Converse quietly, no comment in his voice.

"Yes, of course. You were better prepared than most, I imagine."

"I don't think anyone's ever prepared. . . . But it's over. How about you? How are things?"

Mattilon shook his head, pinching his rugged,

weather-beaten features into a sudden look of exasperation. "France is madness, of course, but we survive. For months and months now, there are more plans than are stored in an architect's library, but the planners keep colliding with each other in government hallways. The courts are full, business thrives."

"I'm glad to hear it." The waiter returned with the Campari; both men nodded to him, and then Mattilon fixed his eyes on Joel. "No, I really am," Converse continued as the waiter walked away. "You hear so many stories."

"Is that why you're in Paris?" The Frenchman studied Joel. "Because of the stories of our so-called upheavals? They're not so earthshaking, you know, not so different from before. Not *yet*. Most private industry here was publicly financed through the government. But, naturally, not managed by government incompetents, and for that we pay. Is that what's bothering you, or more to the point, your clients?"

Converse drank. "No, that's not why I'm here. It's something else."

"You're troubled, I can see that. Your customary glibness doesn't fool me. I know you too well. So tell me, what's so important? That was the word you used on the telephone."

"Yes, I guess it was. It may have been too strong." Joel drained his glass and reached for his cigarettes.

"Not from your eyes, my friend. I see them and I don't see them. They're filled with clouds."

"You've got it wrong. As you said, I'm tired. I've been on planes all day, with some ungodly

116

layovers." He picked up his lighter, snapping it twice until the flame appeared.

"We haggle over foolishness. What is it?"

Converse lit a cigarette, consciously trying to sound casual as he spoke. "Do you know a private club called L'Etalon Blanc?"

"I know it, but I couldn't get in the door," replied the Frenchman, laughing. "I was a young, inconsequential lieutenant—worse, attached to the judge advocate—essentially with our forces to lend an appearance of legality, but, mind you, only an appearance. Murder was a misdemeanor, and rape to be congratulated. L'Etalon Blanc is a refuge for *les grands militaires*—and those rich enough or foolish enough to listen to their trumpets."

"I want to meet someone who lunches there three or four times a week."

"You can't call him?"

"He doesn't know me, doesn't know I want to meet him. It's got to be spontaneous."

"Really? For Talbot, Brooks and Simon? That sounds most unusual."

"It is. We may be dealing with someone we don't want to deal with."

"Ahh, missionary work. Who is he?"

"Will you keep it confidential? I mean that, not a word to anyone?"

"Do I breathe? If the name is in conflict with something on our schedule, I will tell you and, frankly, be of no help to you."

"Fair enough. Jacques-Louis Bertholdier."

Mattilon arched his brows in mock astonishment, less in mockery than in astonishment.

"The emperor has all his clothes," said the Frenchman, laughing quietly. "Regardless of who claims otherwise. You start at the top of the line, as they say in New York. No conflict, *mon ami;* he's not in our league—as you also say."

"Why not?"

"He moves with saints and warriors. Warriors who would be saints, and saints who would be warriors. Who has time for such façades?"

"You mean he's not taken seriously?"

"Oh, no, he *is*. Very seriously, by those who have the time and the inclination to move abstract mountains. He is a pillar, Joel, grounded in heroic marble and himself immovable. He is the De Gaulle who never followed the original, and some say it is a pity."

"What do you say?"

Mattilon frowned, then cocked his head in a Gallic shrug. "I'm not sure. God knows the country needed someone, and perhaps Bertholdier could have stepped in and steered a far better course than the one we embarked upon, but the times were not right. The Elysée had become an imperial court, and the people were tired of royal edicts, imperial sermons. Well, we don't have *those* any longer; they've been supplanted by the dull, gray banalities of the workers' credo. Perhaps it *is* a pity, although he could still do it, I imagine. He began his climb up Olympus when he was very young."

"Wasn't he part of the OAS? Salan's rebels in Algeria? They were discredited, called a national disgrace."

"*That* is a judgment even the intellectuals must

reluctantly admit could be subject to revision. The way all of North Africa and the Middle East has gone, a French Algeria could be a trump card today." Mattilon paused and brought his hand to his chin, his frown returning. "Why on earth would Talbot, Brooks and Simon walk away from Bertholdier? He may be a monarchist at heart, but God knows he's honor personified. He's regal, perhaps even pompous, but a very acceptable client for all of that."

"We've heard things," said Converse quietly, shrugging now himself, as if to lessen the credibility of hearsay evidence.

"*Mon Dieu,* not his *women?*" exclaimed Mattilon, laughing. "Come now, when will you grow up?"

"Not women."

"What then?"

"Let's say some of his associates, his acquaintances."

"I hope you make the distinction, Joel. A man like Bertholdier can choose his associates certainly, but not his acquaintances. He walks into a room and everyone wants to be his friend—most claim he *is* a friend."

"That's what we want to find out. I want to bring up some names, see whether they *are* associates—or unremembered acquaintances."

"*Bien.* Now you're making sense. I can help; I *will* help. We shall have lunch at L'Etalon Blanc tomorrow and the next day. It is the middle of the week and Bertholdier will no doubt choose one or the other to dine there. If not, there's always the day after."

"I thought you couldn't get in the door?"

"Not by myself, no. But I know someone who can, and he will be most obliging, I can assure you."

"Why?"

"He wishes to talk with me whenever and wherever he can. He's a dreadful bore and, unfortunately, speaks very little English—numbers mainly, and words like 'In and out,' or 'Over and out,' and 'Dodger-Roger' or 'Roger-Dodger' and 'runway six' or 'Lift off five' and all manner of incomprehensible phrases."

"A *pilot?*"

"He flew the first Mirages, brilliantly, I might add, and never lets anyone forget it. I shall have to be the interpreter between you, which at least eliminates my having to initiate conversation. Do you know anything about the Mirage?"

"A jet's a jet," said Joel. "Pull and sweep out, what else is there?"

"Yes, he's used that one, too. Pull and sweep something. I thought he was cleaning a kitchen."

"Why does he always want to talk with you? I gather he's a member of the club."

"Very much so. We're representing him in a futile case against an aircraft manufacturer. He had his own private jet, and lost his left foot in one of your crash landings—"

"Not mine, pal."

"The door was jammed. He couldn't ground-eject where he wished to, when the plane's speed was sufficiently reduced for him to avoid a final collision."

"He didn't slap the right buttons."

"He says he did."

"There are at least two backups, including an instant manual, even on your equipment."

"We've been made aware of that. It's not the money, you understand; he's enormously wealthy. It's his pride. To lose brings into question his current—or if you will, latter-day—skills."

"They'll be a lot more in question under cross-examination. I assume you've told him that."

"Very gently. It's what we're leading up to."

"But in the meantime every conference is a hefty fee."

"We're also saving him from himself. If we did it swiftly or too crudely, he'd simply dismiss us and be driven to someone far less principled. Who else would take such a case? The government owns the plant now, and God knows it won't pay."

"Good point. What'll you tell him about me? About the club?"

Mattilon smiled. "That as a former pilot *and* an attorney you can bring an expertise to his suit that might be helpful. As to L'Etalon Blanc, I shall suggest it, tell him you'd be impressed. I shall describe you as something of an Attila the Hun of the skies. How does that appeal to you?"

"With very little impact."

"Can you carry it off?" asked the Frenchman. The question was sincere. "It would be one way to meet Bertholdier. My client and he are not simply acquaintances, they are friends."

"I'll carry it off."

"Your having been a prisoner of war will be most helpful. If you see Bertholdier enter, and express a desire to meet him, such requests are not lightly refused former POW's.''

"I wouldn't press that too hard," said Converse.

"Why not?"

"A little digging could turn up a rock that doesn't belong in the soil.''

"Oh?" Mattilon's brows arched again, neither in mockery nor in astonishment, simply surprise. " 'Digging,' as you use it, implies something more than a spontaneous meeting with odd names spontaneously thrown about.''

"Does it?" Joel revolved his glass, annoyed with himself, knowing that any argument would only enlarge the lapse. "Sorry, it was an instinctive reaction. You know how I feel about that topic.''

"Yes, I do, and I forgot. How careless of me. I apologize.''

"Actually, I'd just as soon not use my own name. Do you mind?''

"You're the missionary, not I. What shall we call you?" The Frenchman was now looking hard at Converse.

"It doesn't matter.''

Mattilon squinted. "How about the name of your employer, Simon? If you meet Bertholdier, it might appeal to him. Le duc de Saint-Simon was the purest chronicler of the monarchy. . . . Henry Simon. There must be ten thousand lawyers named Henry Simon in the States.''

"Simon it is.''

"You've told me everything, my friend?" asked René, his eyes noncommittal. "Every-

122

thing you care to."

"Yes, I have," said Joel, his own eyes a blue-white wall. "Let's have another drink."

"I think not. It's late and my current wife has *malaise* if her dinner is cold. She's an excellent cook, incidentally."

"You're a lucky man."

"Yes, I am." Mattilon finished his drink, placed the glass on the table and spoke casually. "So was Valerie. I shall never forget that fantastic *canard à l'orange* she fixed for us three or four years ago in New York. Do you ever hear from her?"

"Hear and see," answered Converse. "I had lunch with her in Boston last month. I gave her the alimony check and she picked up the tab. By the way, her paintings are beginning to sell."

"I never doubted that they would."

"She did."

"Unnecessarily. . . . I always liked Val. If you see her again, please give her my affectionate best."

"I will."

Mattilon rose from the upholstered chair, his eyes no longer noncommittal. "Forgive me, I thought so often you were such a—matched pair, I believe is the expression. The passions dwindle, of course, but not the *de suite,* if you know what I mean."

"I think I do, and speaking for both of us, I thank you—for the misplaced concretion."

"Je ne comprends pas."

"Forget it, it's antiquated—doesn't mean anything. I'll give her your affectionate best."

"Merci. I'll phone you in the morning."

L'Etalon Blanc was a pacifist's nightmare. The club's heavy dark wood walls were covered with photographs and prints, interspersed with framed citations and glistening medals—red ribbons and gold and silver disks cushioned on black velvet. The prints were a visual record of heroic carnage going back two centuries, while the evolution in warfare was shown in photographs as the horses and caissons and sabers became motorcycles, tanks, planes and guns, but the scenes were not all that different because the theme was constant. Victorious men in uniform were depicted in moments of glory; whatever suffering there might have been was strangely absent. These men did not lose—no missing limbs or shattered faces here; these were the privileged warriors. Joel felt a profound fear as he studied the martial array. These were not ordinary men; they were hard and strong and the word 'capability' was written across their faces. What had Beale said on Mykonos? What had been the judgment of the Red Fox of Inchon, a man who knew whereof he spoke?

. . . *I know what they can do when we ask them to do it.* Yet how much more could they do if they asked it of themselves? wondered Joel. Without the impediments of vacillating civilian authorities?

"Luboque has just arrived," said Mattilon quietly, coming up behind Converse. "I heard his voice in the lobby. Remember, you don't have to overdo it—I'll translate what I think is appropriate, anyway—but nod profoundly when

124

he makes one of his angry remarks. Also laugh when he tells jokes; they're dreadful, but he likes it."

"I'll do my best."

"I'll give you an incentive. Bertholdier has a reservation for lunch. At his usual place, table eleven, by the window."

"Where are *we?*" asked Joel, seeing the Frenchman's pressed lips expressing minor triumph.

"Table twelve. Now."

"If I ever need a lawyer, I'll call you."

"We're terribly expensive. Come now, as they say in all those wonderful films of yours, 'You're on, Monsieur Simon.' Play the role of Attila but don't overplay it."

"You know, Rene, for someone who speaks English as well as you do, you gravitate to the tritest phrases."

"The English language and American phrases have very little in common, Joel, trite or otherwise."

"Smart ass."

"Need I say more? . . . Ahh, Monsieur Luboque, Serge, *mon ami!*"

Mattilon's third eye had spotted the entrance of Serge Luboque; he turned around as the thumping became louder on the floor. Luboque was a short, slender man; his physique made one think of those jet pilots of the early period when compactness was a requirement. He was also very close to being a caricature of himself. His short, waxed moustache was affixed to a miniaturized face that was pinched in an expression of vaguely

125

hostile dismissal directed at both no one and everyone. Whatever he had been before, Luboque was now a poseur who knew only how to posture. With all that was brilliant and exciting buried in the past, he had only the memories, the rest was anger.

"Et voici l'expert judiciaire des compagnies aériennes," he said, looking at Converse and extending his hand.

"Serge is delighted to meet you and is sure you can help us," explained Mattilon.

"I'll do what I can," said Converse. "And apologize for my not speaking French."

The lawyer obviously did so, and Luboque shrugged, speaking rapidly, incomprehensibly; the word *anglais* repeated several times.

"He, too, apologizes for not speaking English," said Mattilon, glancing at Joel, mischievousness in his look, as he added, "If he's lying, Monsieur Simon, we may both be placed against these decorated walls and shot."

"No way," said Converse, smiling. "Our executioners might dent the medals and blow up the pictures. Everybody knows you're lousy shots."

"Qu'est-ce que vous dites?"

"Monsieur Simon tient à vous remercier pour le déjeuner," said Mattilon, turning to his client. *"Il en est très fier car il estime que l'officier français est l'un des meilleurs du monde."*

"What did you say?"

"I explained," said the lawyer, turning again, "that you were honored to be here, as you believe the French military—especially the officer corps

—to be the finest on earth.''

''Not only lousy shots but rotten pilots,'' said Joel, smiling and nodding.

''*Est-il vrai que vous avez participé à nombreuses missions en Asie du Sud?*'' asked Luboque, his eyes fixed on Joel.

''I beg your pardon?''

''He wants it confirmed that you are really an Attila of the skies, that you flew many missions.''

''Quite a few,'' answered Joel.

''*Beaucoup,*'' said Mattilon.

Luboque again spoke rapidly, even more incomprehensibly, as he snapped his fingers for a steward.

''What now?''

''He'd rather tell you about *his* exploits—in the interests of the case, of course.''

''Of course,'' said Converse, his smile now fixed. ''Lousy shots, rotten pilots and insufferable egos.''

''Ah, but our food, our women, our incomparable understanding of life.''

''There's a very explicit word in French—one of the few I learned from my ex-wife—but I don't think I should use it.'' Joel's smile was now cemented to his lips.

''That's right, I forgot,'' said Mattilon. ''She and I would converse in *notre belle langue;* it used to irritate you so—Don't use it. Remember your incentive.''

''*Qu'est-ce que vous dites encore? Notre belle langue?*'' Luboque spoke as a steward stood by his side.

''*Notre ami, Monsieur Simon, suit un cours à*

l'école Berlitz et pourra ainsi s'entretenir directement avec vous."

"*Bien!*"

"What?"

"I told him you would learn the Berlitz French so you could dine with him whenever you flew into Paris. You're to ring him up. Nod, smart ass."

Converse nodded.

And so it went. Point, noncounterpoint, non sequitur. Serge Luboque held forth during drinks in the warriors' playroom, Mattilon translating and advising Joel as to the expression to wear on his face as well as suggesting an appropriate reply.

Finally Luboque stridently described the crash that had cost him his left foot and the obvious equipment failures for which he should be compensated. Converse looked properly pained and indignant, and offered to write a legal opinion for the court based on his expertise as a pilot of jet aircraft. Mattilon translated; Luboque beamed and rattled off a barrage of gargled vowels that Joel took for thanks.

"He's forever in your debt," said René.

"Not if I write that opinion " replied Converse. "He locked himself in the cockpit and threw away the key."

"Write it," countered Mattilon, smiling. "You've just paid for my time. We'll use it as a wedge to open the door of retreat. Also, he'll never ask you to dinner when you're in Paris."

"When's lunch? I'm running out of expressions."

They marched in hesitant lockstep into the dining room, matching Luboque's gait as he thumped along on the hard, ornate parquet floor. The ridiculous three-sided conversation continued as wine was proffered—a bottle was sent back by Luboque—and Converse's eyes kept straying to the dining room's entrance.

The moment came: Bertholdier arrived. He stood in the open archway, his head turned slightly to his left as another man in a light-brown gabardine topcoat spoke without expression. The general nodded his head and the subordinate retreated. Then the great man walked into the room quietly but imperially. Heads turned and the man acknowledged the homage as a dauphin who will soon be king accepts the attentions of the ministers of a failing monarch. The effect was extraordinary, for there were no kingdoms, no monarchies, no lands to be divided through conquest to the knights of Crécy or anybody else, but this man of no royal lineage was tacitly being recognized—*goddamn it,* thought Joel—as an emperor in his own right.

Jacques-Louis Bertholdier was of medium height, between five nine and five eleven, certainly no more, but his bearing—the sheer straight shaft of his posture, the breadth of his shoulders and the length of his strong slender neck made him appear much taller, much more imposing than another might. He was among his own, and here, indeed, he was above the others, elevated by their own consensus.

"Say something reverential," said Mattilon, as Bertholdier approached, heading for the table next to theirs. "Glance up at him and look tastefully awed. I'll do the rest."

Converse did as he was told, uttering Bertholdier's full name under his breath, but loud enough to be heard. He followed this quiet exclamation by leaning toward Mattilon and saying, "He's a man I've always wanted to meet."

There followed a brief exchange in French between René and his client, whereupon Luboque nodded, his expression that of an arrogant man willing to dispense a favor to a new friend.

Bertholdier reached his chair, the maître d' and the dining room captain hovering on either side. The pavane took place less than four feet away.

"Mon général," said Luboque, rising.

"Serge," replied Bertholdier, stepping forward, hand extended—a superior officer aware of a worthy subordinate's disability. *"Comment ça va?"*

"Bien, Jacques. Et vous?"

"Les temps sont bien étranges, mon ami."

The greetings were brief, and the direction of the conversation was changed quickly by Luboque, who gestured at Converse as he continued speaking. Instinctively Joel got to his feet, posture straight, his eyes level, unblinking, staring at Bertholdier, his look as piercing as the general's, professional but without awe. He had been right—in an unexpected way. The shared Southeast Asian experience had validity for Jacques-Louis Bertholdier. And why not? He, too, had his memories. Mattilon was introduced almost as an afterthought, and the soldier gave a

130

brief nod as he crossed behind René to shake hands with Joel.

"A pleasure, Monsieur Simon," said Bertholdier, his English precise, his grip firm, a comrade acknowledging another comrade, the man's imperious charm instantly apparent.

"I'm sure you've heard it thousands of times, sir," said Joel, maintaining the steady, professional burn in his eyes, "but this is an occasion I never expected. If I may say so, General, it's an honor to meet you."

"It is an honor to meet *you*," rejoined Bertholdier. "You gentlemen of the air did all you could, and I know something about the circumstances. So many missions! I think it was easier on the ground!" The general laughed quietly.

"Gentlemen of the air"—the man was unreal, thought Converse. But the connection was firm; *it* was real, he felt it, he *knew* it. The combination of words and looks had brought it about. So simple: a lawyer's ruse, taming an adversary—in this case an enemy. The enemy.

"I couldn't agree with that, General; it was a lot cleaner in the air. But if there'd been more like you on the ground in Indochina, there never would have been a Dienbienphu."

"A flattering statement, but I'm not sure it could stand the test of reality."

"I'm sure," said Joel quietly, clearly. "I'm convinced of it."

Luboque, who had been engaged in conversation by Mattilon, interrupted. *"Mon général, voulez-vous vous joindre a nous?*

131

"Pardonnez-moi. Je suis occupé avec mes visiteurs," answered Bertholdier, turning back to Converse. "I must decline Rene's invitation, I'm expecting guests. He tells me you are an attorney, a specialist in aircraft litigation."

"It's part of the broader field, yes. Air, ground, oceangoing craft—we try to represent the spectrum. Actually, I'm fairly new at it—not the expertise, I hope—but the representation."

"I see," said the general, obviously bewildered. "Are you in Paris on business?"

This was it, thought Joel. Above all, he would have to be subtle. The words—but especially the eyes—must convey the unspoken. "No, I'm just here to catch my breath. I flew from San Francisco to New York and on to Paris. Tomorrow I'll be in Bonn for a day or so, then off to Tel Aviv."

"How tiring for you." Bertholdier was now returning his stare.

"Not the worst, I'm afraid," said Converse, a half-smile on his lips. "After Tel Aviv, there's a night flight to Johannesburg."

"Bonn, Tel Aviv, Johannesburg . . ." The soldier spoke softly. "A most unusual itinerary."

"Productive, we think. At least, we hope so."

"We?"

"My client, General. My new client."

"Déraisonnable!" cried Mattilon, laughing at something Luboque had said, and, just as obviously, telling Joel he could no longer keep his impatient litigant in conversation.

Bertholdier, however, did not take his eyes off Converse. "Where are you staying, my young fighter-pilot friend?"

"Young and not so young, General."

"Where?"

"The George Cinq. Suite two-three-five."

"A fine establishment."

"It's habit. My previous firm always posted me there."

"Posted? As in 'garrisoned?" asked Bertholdier, a half-smile now on his lips.

"An unconscious slip," said Joel. "But then again, it says it, doesn't it, sir?"

"It does, indeed. . . . Ah ha, my guests arrive!" The soldier extended his hand. "It's been a pleasure, Monsieur Simon."

Swift *au revoir*'s accompanied nods and rapid handshakes as Bertholdier returned to his table to greet his luncheon companions. Through Mattilon, Joel thanked Luboque for the introduction; the disabled pilot gestured with both hands, palms up, and Converse had the distinct feeling that he had been baptized. The insane three-sided dialogue then resumed at high speed, and it was all Joel could do to maintain even minimum concentration.

Progress had been made; it was in Bertholdier's eyes, and he could feel those eyes straying over to him even while the conversation at both tables became animated. The general was diagonally to Converse's left; with the slightest turning of either face, the line of sight between them was direct. Twice it happened. The first time, Joel felt the forceful gaze resting on him as if magnified sunlight were burning into his flesh. He shifted his head barely an inch; their eyes locked, the soldier's penetrating, severe, questioning. The second time was a half-hour later, when the eye contact was initiated by Converse himself. Luboque and Mattilon were discussing legal strategy, and as if drawn by a magnet, Joel slowly turned to his left and watched Bertholdier, who was quietly, emphatically making a point with one of his guests. Suddenly, as a voice replied across the adjacent table, the general snapped his head in Converse's direction, his eyes no longer questioning, only cold and ice-like. Then just as abruptly, there was warmth in them; the celebrated soldier nodded, a half-smile on his face.

Joel sat in the soft leather chair by the window in the dimly lit sitting room; what light there was came from a fringed lamp on the desk. Alternately he stared at the telephone in front of the lamp and looked out the window at the weaving night traffic of Paris and the lights on the wide boulevard below. Then he focused entirely on the phone as he so frequently did when waiting for a call from a legal adversary he expected would capitulate, knowing that man or woman would capitulate. It was simply a question of time.

What he expected now was communication, not capitulation—a connection, *the* connection. He had no idea what form it would take, but it would come. It had to come.

It was nearly seven-thirty, four hours since he had left L'Etalon Blanc after a final, firm handshake exchanged with Jacques-Louis Bertholdier. The look in the soldier's eyes was unmistakable: If nothing else, Converse reasoned, Bertholdier would have to satisfy his sheer curiosity.

Joel had covered himself with the hotel's front desk, distributing several well-placed 100-franc notes. The tactic was not at all unusual in these days of national and financial unrest—had not been for years, actually, even without the unrest. Visiting businessmen frequently chose to use pseudonyms for any number of reasons, ranging from negotiations best kept quiet to amorous engagements best left untraceable. In Converse's case, the use of the name Simon made it appear logical, if not eminently respectable. If Talbot, Brooks and Simon preferred that all communications be made in the surname of one of the senior partners, who could question the decision? Joel, however, carried the ploy one step further. After telephoning New York, he explained, he was told that his own name was not to be used at all; no one knew he was in Paris and that was the way his firm wanted it. Obviously, the delayed instructions accounted for the mix-up in the reservation, which was void at any rate. There was to be no billing; he would pay in cash, and since this was Paris, no one raised the slightest objection. Cash was infinitely preferable, delayed payment a national anathema.

Whether anyone believed this nonsense or not was irrelevant. The logic was sufficiently adequate and the franc notes persuasive; the original registration card was torn up and another placed in the hotel file. H. Simon replaced J. Converse. The permanent address of the former was a figment of Joel's imagination, a numbered house on a numbered street in Chicago, Illinois, said house and said street most likely nonexistent. Anyone asking or calling for Mr. Converse—which was highly unlikely—would be told no guest of that name was currently at the George V. Even René Mattilon was not a problem, for Joel had been specific. Since he had no further business in Paris, he was taking the six o'clock shuttle to London and staying with friends for several days before flying back to New York. He had thanked René profusely, telling the Frenchman that his firm's fears about Bertholdier had been groundless. During their quiet conversation he had brought up three key names with the general, and each had been greeted with a blank look from Bertholdier, who apologized for his faulty memory.

"He wasn't lying," Joel had said.

"I can't imagine why he would," Mattilon had replied.

I can, Converse had thought to himself. *They call it Aquitaine.*

A crack! There was a sudden sound, a harsh metallic snap, then another, and another—the tumblers of a lock falling out of place, a knob being turned. It came from beyond the open door to the bedroom. Joel bolted forward in his chair; then, looking at his watch, just as rapidly he let out his breath and relaxed. It was the hour when the floor maid turned down the bed; the tension of the expected call and what it represented had frayed his nerves. Again he leaned back, his gaze resting on the telephone. When would it ring?

136

Would it ring?

"Pardon, monsieur," said a feminine voice, accompanied by a light tapping on the open doorframe. Joel could not see the speaker.

"Yes?" Converse turned away from the silent phone, expecting to see the maid.

What he saw made him gasp. It was the figure of Bertholdier, his posture erect, his angled head rigid, his eyes a strange admixture of cold appraisal, condescension, and—if Joel was not mistaken—a trace of fear. He walked through the door and stood motionless; when he spoke his voice was a rippling sheet of ice.

"I was on my way to a dinner engagement on the fourth floor, Monsieur Simon. By chance, I remembered you were in this very hotel. You did give me the number of your suite. Do I intrude?"

"Of course not, General," said Converse, on his feet.

"Did you expect me?"

"Not this way."

"But you did expect me?"

Joel paused. "Yes."

"A signal sent and received?"

Again Joel paused. "Yes."

"You are either a provocatively subtle attorney or a strangely obsessed man. Which is it, Monsieur Simon?"

"If I provoked you into coming to see me and I was subtle about it, I'll accept that gladly. As to being obsessed, the word implies an exaggerated or unwarranted concern. Whatever concerns I have, I know damned well they're neither exaggerated nor unwarranted. No obsession,

General. I'm too good a lawyer for that.''

"A pilot cannot lie to himself. If he does so blindly, he crashes to his death.''

"I've been shot down. I've never crashed through pilot error.''

Bertholdier walked slowly to the brocaded couch against the wall. "Bonn, Tel Aviv, and Johannesburg,'' he said quietly as he sat down and crossed his legs. "The signal?''

"The signal.''

"My company has interests in those areas.''

"So does my client,'' said Converse.

"And what do *you* have, Monsieur Simon?''

Joel stared at the soldier. "A commitment, General.''

Bertholdier was silent, his body immobile, his eyes searching "May I have a brandy?'' he said finally. "My escort will remain in the corridor outside this door.''

4

Converse walked to the dry bar against the wall, conscious of the soldier's gaze, wondering which tack the conversation would take. He was oddly calm, as he frequently was before a merger conference or a pretrial examination, knowing he knew things his adversaries were not aware of—buried information that had surfaced through long hours of hard work. In the present circumstances there had been no work at all on his part, but the results were the same. He knew a great deal about the legend across the room named Jacques-Louis Bertholdier. In a word, Joel was prepared, and over the years he had learned to trust his on-the-feet instincts—as he had once trusted those that had guided him through the skies years ago.

Also, as it was part of his job, he was familiar with the legal intricacies of import-export manipulations. They were a maze of often disconnected authorizations, easily made incomprehensible for the uninitiated, and during the next few minutes he intended to baffle this disciple of George Marcus Delavane—warlord of Saigon—until the soldier's trace of fear became something far more pronounced.

Clearances for foreign shipments came in a wide variety of shapes and colors, from the basic export license with specific bills of lading to those with the less specific generic limitations. Then there were the more coveted licenses required for a wide variety of products subject to governmental reviews; these were usually shunted back and forth between vacillating departments until deadlines forced bureaucratic decisions often based on whose influence was the strongest or who among the bureaucrats were the weakest.

Finally, there was the most lethal authorization of all, a document too frequently conceived in corruption and delivered in blood. It was called the End-User's Certificate, an innocuously named permit that was a license to ship the most abusive merchandise in the nation's arsenals into air and sea lanes beyond the controls of those who should have them.

In theory, this deadly equipment was intended solely for allied governments with shared objectives, thus the "use" at the discretion of the parties at the receiving "end"—calculated death legitimized by a "certificate" that obfuscated everyone's intentions. But once the equipment was en route, diversion was the practice. Shipments destined for the Bay of Haifa or Alexandria would find their way to the Gulf of Sidra and a madman in Libya, or an assassin named Carlos training killer teams anywhere from Beirut to the Sahara. Fictional corporations with nonexistent yet strangely influential officers operated through obscure brokers and out of hastily constructed or out-of-the-way warehouses in the U.S. and abroad. Millions upon millions were to be made; death was an unimportant consequence and there was a phrase for it all. Boardroom terrorism. It fit, and it would be Aquitaine's method. There was no other.

These were the thoughts—the methods of operation—that flashed through Converse's mind as he poured the drinks. He was ready; he turned and walked across the room.

"What are you seeking, Monsieur Simon?" asked Bertholdier, taking the brandy from Converse.

"Information, General."

"About what?"

"World markets—expanding markets that my client might service." Joel crossed back to the chair by the window and sat down.

"And what sort of service does he render?"

"He's a broker."

140

"Of what?"

"A wide range of products." Converse brought his glass to his lips; he drank, then added, "I think I mentioned them in general terms at your club this afternoon. Planes, vehicles, oceangoing craft, munitions material. The spectrum."

"Yes, you did. I'm afraid I did not understand."

"My client has access to production and warehouse sources beyond anyone I've ever known or ever heard of."

"Very impressive. Who is he?"

"I'm not at liberty to say."

"Perhaps I know him."

"You might, but not in the way I've described him. His profile is so low in this area, it's nonexistent."

"And you won't tell me who he is," said Bertholdier.

"It's privileged information."

"Yet, in your own words, you sought me out, sent a signal to which I responded, and now say you want information concerning expanding markets for all manner of merchandise, including Bonn, Tel Aviv, and Johannesburg. But you won't divulge the name of your client who will benefit if I have this information—which I probably do not. Surely, you can't be serious."

"You *have* the information and, yes, I'm very serious. But I'm afraid you've jumped to the wrong conclusion."

"I have no fear of it at all. My English is fluent and I heard what you said. You came out of nowhere, I know nothing about you, you speak elusively of this unnamed influential man—"

"You *asked* me, General," interrupted Joel firmly without raising his voice. "What I was seeking."

"And you said information."

"Yes, I did, but I didn't say I was seeking it from you."

"I beg your pardon?"

"Under the circumstances—for the reasons you just mentioned—you wouldn't give it to me anyway, and I'm well aware of that."

"Then what is the point of this—shall I say, induced—conversation? I do not like my time trifled with, monsieur."

"That's the last thing on earth we'd do—*I'd* do."

"Please be specific."

"My client wants your trust. *I* want it. But we know it can't be given until you feel it's justified. In a few days—a week at the outside—I hope to prove that it is."

"By trips to Bonn, Tel Aviv—Johannesburg?"

"Frankly, yes."

"Why?"

"You said it a few minutes ago. The signal."

Bertholdier was suddenly wary. He shrugged too casually; he was pulling back. "I said it because my company has considerable investments in those areas. I thought it was entirely plausible you had a proposition, or propositions, to make relative to those interests."

"I intend to have."

"Please be specific," said the soldier, controlling his irritation.

"You know I can't," replied Joel. "Not yet."

"When?"

"When it's clear to you—all of you—that my client, and by extension myself, have as strong motives for being a part of you as the most dedicated among you."

"A part of my company? Juneau et Compagnie?"

"Forgive me, General, I won't bother to answer that."

Bertholdier glanced at the brandy in his hand, then back at Converse. "You say you flew from San Francisco."

"I'm not based there," Joel broke in.

"But you came from San Francisco. To Paris. Why *were* you there?"

"I'll answer that if for no other reason than to show you how thorough we are—and how much more thorough others are. We traced—*I* traced —overseas shipments back to export licenses originating in the northern California area. The licensees were companies with no histories and warehouses with no records—chains of four walls erected for brief, temporary periods of convenience. It was a mass of confusion leading nowhere and everywhere. Names on documents where no such people existed, documents themselves that came out of bureaucratic labyrinths virtually *un*traceable—rubber stamps, official seals, and signatures of authorization where no authority was granted. Unknowing middle-level personnel told to expedite departmental clearances — That's what I found in San Francisco. A morass of complex, highly questionable transactions that could not bear intense scrutiny."

Bertholdier's eyes were fixed, too controlled. "I would know nothing about such things, of course," he said.

"Of course," agreed Converse. "But the fact that my client does—through me—and the additional fact that neither he nor I have any desire whatsoever to call attention to them must tell you something."

"Frankly, not a thing."

"Please, General. One of the first principles of free enterprise is to cripple your competition, step in, and fill the void."

The soldier drank, gripping the glass firmly. He lowered it and spoke. "Why did you come to me?"

"Because you were there."

"What?"

"Your name was there—among the morass, way down deep, but there."

Bertholdier shot forward. "Impossible! *Preposterous!"*

"Then why am I here? Why are *you* here?" Joel placed his glass on the table by the chair, the movement that of a man not finished speaking. "Try to understand me. Depending upon which government department a person's dealing with, certain recommendations are bound to be helpful. You wouldn't do a damn thing for someone appealing to Housing and Urban Development, but over at the State Department's Munitions Controls or at Pentagon procurements, you're golden."

"I have never lent my name to any such appeals."

"Others did. Men whose recommendations carried a lot of weight, but who perhaps needed extra clout."

"What do you mean? This 'clout.' "

"A final push for an affirmative decision —without any apparent personal involvement. It's called support for an action through viable second and third parties. For instance, a memo might read: 'We'—the department, not a person—'don't know much about this, but if a man like General Bertholdier is favorably disposed, and we are informed that he is, why should we argue?' "

"*Never*. It could not happen."

"It did," said Converse softly, knowing it was the moment to bring in reality to support his abstractions. He would be able to tell instantly if Beale was right, if this legend of France was responsible for the slaughter and chaos in the cities and towns of a violently upended Northern Ireland. "You were there, not often but enough for me to find you. Just as you were there in a different way when a shipment was air-freighted out of Beloit, Wisconsin, on its way to Tel Aviv. Of course it never got there. Somehow it was diverted to maniacs on both sides in Belfast. I wonder where it happened? Montreal? Paris? Marseilles? The Separatists in Quebec would certainly follow your orders, as would men in Paris and Marseilles. It's a shame a company named Solidaire had to pay off the insurance claim. Oh, yes, you're a director of the firm, aren't you? And it's so convenient that insurance carriers have access to the merchandise they cover."

Bertholdier was frozen to the chair, the muscles of his face pulsating, his eyes wide, staring at Joel. His guilt was suppressed, but no less apparent for that control. "I cannot believe what you are implying. It's shocking and incredible!"

"I repeat, why am I here?"

"Only you can answer that, monsieur," said Bertholdier, abruptly getting to his feet, the brandy in his hand. Then slowly, with military precision, he leaned over and placed the glass on the coffee table; it was a gesture of finality—the conference was over. "Quite obviously I made a foolish error," he continued, shoulders square again and head rigid, but now with a strained yet oddly convincing smile on his lips. "I am a soldier, not a businessman; it is a late direction in my life. A soldier tries to seize an initiative and I attempted to do just that; only, there was—there *is*—no initiative. Forgive me, I misread your signal this afternoon."

"You didn't misread anything, General."

"Am I contradicted by a stranger—I might even say a devious stranger—who arranges a meeting under false pretenses and proceeds to make outrageous statements regarding my honor and my conduct? I think not." As Bertholdier strode across the room toward the hallway door Joel rose from his chair. "Don't bother, monsieur, I'll let myself out. You've gone to enough trouble, for what purpose I haven't the faintest idea."

"I'm on my way to Bonn," said Converse.

"Tell your friends I'm coming. Tell them to expect me. And please, General, tell them not to prejudge me. I mean that."

"Your elliptical references are most annoying—Lieutenant. It *was* 'lieutenant,' wasn't it? Unless you also deceived poor Luboque as well."

"Whatever deception I employed to meet you can only be for his benefit. I've offered to write a legal opinion for his case. He may not like it, but it'll save him a lot of pain and money. And I have not deceived you."

"A matter of judgment, I think." Bertholdier turned and reached for the outsized brass knob.

"Bonn, Germany," pressed Joel.

"I heard you. I haven't the vaguest notion what you—"

"Leifhelm," said Converse quietly. "Erich Leifhelm."

The soldier's head turned slowly; his eyes were banked fires, the coals glowing, about to erupt at the merest gust of wind. "A name known to me, but not the man."

"Tell him I'm coming."

"Good night, monsieur," said Bertholdier, opening the door, his face ashen.

Joel raced into the bedroom, grabbed his suitcase and threw it on the luggage rack. He had to get out of Paris. Within hours, perhaps minutes, Bertholdier would have him watched, and if he was followed to an airport, his passport would expose the name Simon as a lie. He could not let that happen, not yet.

It was strange, unsettling. He had never had any reason to leave a hotel surreptitiously, and he was not sure he knew how to do it—only that it had to be done. The altering of the registration card had been done instinctively; there were occasions when legal negotiations had to be kept quiet for everyone's benefit. But this was different—it was abnormal. He had said to Beale on Mykonos that he was going to become someone he was not. It was an easy thing to say, not at all easy to do.

His suitcase packed, he checked the battery charge on his electric razor and absently turned it on, moving it around his chin, as he walked to the bedside telephone. He shut the switch off as he dialed, unsure of what he would say to the night concierge but nevertheless instinctively orienting his mind to a business approach. After initial remarks, mutually flattering, the words came.

"There's an extremely sensitive situation, and my firm is anxious that I leave for London just as soon as possible—and as discreetly as possible. Frankly, I would prefer not to be seen checking out."

"Discretion, monsieur, is honored here, and haste is a normal request. I shall come up and present your bill myself. Say, ten minutes?"

"I've only one piece of luggage. I'll carry it, but I'll need a cab. Not in front."

"Not in front, of course. The freight elevator, monsieur. It connects below with our corridor for deliveries. Arrangements will be made."

"I've made arrangements!" said Bertholdier

harshly into the limousine's mobile phone, the glass partition between him and the chauffeur tightly shut. "One man remains in the gallery in sight of the elevators, another in the cellars where the hotel supplies are brought in. If he attempts to leave during the night, it is the only other exit available to him. I've used it myself on several occasions."

"This . . . is all *most* difficult to absorb." The voice on the line spoke with a clipped British accent, the speaker obviously astonished, his breathing audible, a man suddenly afraid. "Are you *sure?* Could there be some other linkage?"

"Imbecile! I repeat. He knew about the munitions shipment from Beloit! He knew the routing, even the method of theft. He went so far as to identify Solidaire and my position as a board member! He made a *direct* reference to our business associate in *Bonn!* Then to Tel Aviv . . . *Johannesburg!* What other linkage *could* there be?"

"Corporate entanglements, perhaps. One can't rule them out. Multinational subsidiaries, munitions investments, our associate in West Germany also sits on several boards. . . . And the locations—money *pours* into them."

"What in the name of God do you think I'm talking about? I can say no more now, but what I've told you, my English *flower,* take it to be the worst!"

There was a brief silence from London. "I understand," said the voice of a subordinate rebuked.

"I hope you do. Get in touch with New York.

His name is Simon, Henry Simon. He's an attorney from Chicago. I have the address; it's from the hotel's registration file." Bertholdier squinted under the glare of the reading lamp, haltingly deciphering the numbers and the numbered street written down by an assistant bell captain, well paid by one of the general's men to go into the office and obtain information on the occupant of suite two-three-five. "Do you have that?"

"Yes." The voice was now sharp, a subordinate about to redress a grievance. "Was it wise to get it that way? A friend or a greedy employee might tell him someone was inquiring about him."

"*Really,* my British daffodil? An innocuous bellboy checking the registry so as to post a lost garment to a recent guest?"

Again the brief silence. "Yes, I see. You know, Jacques, we work for a great cause—a *business* cause, of course—more important than either of us, as we did once years ago. I must constantly remind myself of that, or I don't think I could tolerate your insults."

"And what would be your recourse, *l'Anglais?*"

"To cut your arrogant Frog balls off in Trafalgar Square and stuff them in a lion's mouth. The repository wouldn't have to be large; an ancient crack would do. I'll ring you up in an hour or so." There was a click and the line went dead.

The soldier lowered the mobile phone in his hand, and a smile slowly emerged on his lips. They were the best, *all* of them! They were the hope, the only hope of a very sick world.

Then the smile faded, the blood again draining from his face, arrogance turning into fear. What did this Henry Simon want, really want? Who was the unknown man with access to extraordinary sources—planes, vehicles, *munitions?* What in God's name did they know?

The padded elevator descended slowly, its interior designed for moving furniture and luggage, its speed adjusted for room-service deliveries. The night concierge stood beside Joel, his face pleasantly impassive; in his right hand was the leather *bourse* containing a copy of Converse's bill and the franc notes covering it—as well as a substantial gratuity for the Frenchman's courtesy.

A slight whirring sound preceded the stop; the panel light shone behind the letters SOU-SOL, and the heavy doors parted. Beyond in the wide hallway was a platoon of white-jacketed waiters, maids, porters and a few maintenance personnel commandeering tables, racks of linens, luggage and assorted cleaning materials. Loud, rapid chatter, heightened by bursts of laughter and guttural expletives, accompanied the bustling activity. At the sight of the concierge there was a perceptible lessening of volume and an increase of concentrated movement, along with nods and fawning smiles directed at the man who, with the flick of a pen, could eliminate their jobs.

"If you'll just point me in the right direction, I'll be on my way," said Joel, not wishing to call further attention to himself in the company of the concierge. "I've taken up too much of your time."

"*Merci*. If you will follow that corridor, it will lead to the service exit," replied the Frenchman, pointing to a hallway on the left, beyond the bank of elevators. "The guard is at his desk and is aware of your departure. Outside in the alley, turn right and walk to the street; your taxi is waiting for you."

"I appreciate—my *firm* appreciates—your cooperation. As I mentioned upstairs, there's nothing really that secretive, or unusual—just sensitive."

The hotel man's impassive countenance did not change, except for a slightly sharper focus in his eyes. "It is of no matter, monsieur, an explanation is not required. I did not request it, and if you'll forgive me, you should not feel an obligation to offer one. *Au revoir,* Monsieur Simon."

"Yes, of course," said Converse, maintaining his composure though he felt like a schoolboy admonished for speaking out of turn, for offering an answer when he had not been called upon. "See you next time I'm in Paris."

"We await the day, monsieur. *Bonsoir.*"

Joel turned quickly, making his way through the uniformed crowd toward the hallway, apologizing whenever his suitcase made contact with a body. He had just been taught a lesson, one he should not have had to learn. He knew it in a courtroom and in conference: Never explain what you don't have to. Shut up. But this was not a court or a conference. It was, it suddenly dawned on him, an escape, and the realization was a little frightening, certainly very strange. Or was it? Escape was in his vocabulary, in his experience. He had tried it three times before in his life—years ago. And death had been everywhere. He put the thought out of his mind and walked down the corridor toward the large metal door in the distance.

He slowed down; something was wrong. Ahead, standing in front of the security desk talking to the guard was a man in a light-colored topcoat. Joel had seen him before but he did not know where; then the man moved and Converse began to remember—an image came back to him. Another man had moved the same way—taking several steps backward before turning—to disappear from an archway, and now he moved the same way to cross the corridor to lean against the wall. Was it the same man? Yes! It was the one who had accompanied Bertholdier to the dining-room entrance of L'Etalon Blanc. The subordinate who had taken leave of a superior then was here now under orders from that same superior.

The man looked up, the flash of recognition instantly in his eyes. Stretching, he raised himself to his full height and turned away, his hand slowly moving toward the fold in his coat. Converse was stunned. Was the man actually reaching for a *gun?* With an armed guard barely ten feet away? It was insane! Joel stopped; he considered racing back into the crowd by the elevators but knew it was pointless. If Bertholdier had posted a watchdog in the basement, others would be upstairs, in the corridors, in the lobby. He could not turn and run; there was no place to go, nowhere to hide. So he kept walking, now faster, directly toward the man in the light-brown topcoat, his mind confused, his throat tight.

"*There* you are!" he cried out loud, not sure the words were his. "The general told me where to find you!"

The man stood motionless, in shock, speechless. *"Le général?"* he said, barely above a whisper. "He . . . tell you?"

The man's English was not good, and that was very good. He could understand, but not well. Rapidly spoken words, persuasively delivered, might get them both out the door. Joel turned to the guard while angling his attaché case into his companion's back. "My name's Simon. I believe the concierge spoke to you about me."

The juxtaposition of the name and the title was sufficient for the bewildered guard. He glanced at his papers, nodding. *"Oui, monsieur. Le concierge . . ."*

"Come *on!*" Converse shoved the attaché case into the man in the topcoat, propelling him toward the door. "The general's waiting for us outside. Let's go! Hurry *up!*"

"Le général . . . ?" The man's hands instinctively shot out at the crash bar of the exit door; in less than five seconds he and Joel were alone in the alley. *"Que se passe-t-il? Où est le général? . . .* Where?"

"Here! He said to wait here. *You.* You're to wait here! *Ici!*"

"Arrêtez!" The man was recovering. He stood

154

his ground. Thrusting his left hand out, he pushed Converse back against the wall. With his right hand he reached into his overcoat.

"Don't!" Joel dropped his attaché case, gripping his suitcase and pulling it up in front of him, about to rush forward. He stopped. The man did not pull out a gun; instead, what he had was a thin rectangular object bound in black leather, from which a long metallic needle rose from the narrow flat top. An antenna . . . a radio!

All thought was blurred for Converse, but he knew he had to act instantly—only motion counted. He could not permit the man to use that radio, alerting those with other radios elsewhere in the hotel. With a sudden surge of strength he rammed his suitcase into the man's knees, tearing the radio away with his left hand, whipping his right arm out and over the man's shoulder. He crooked his elbow around the Frenchman's neck as he spun on the pavement. Then without thinking, he yanked Bertholdier's soldier forward, so that both of them hurtled toward the wall, and crashed the man's head into the stone. Blood spread throughout the Frenchman's skull, matting his hair and streaking down his face in deep-red rivulets. Joel could not think, he could not *allow* himself to think. If he did, he would be sick and he knew it. Motion, *motion!*

The man went limp. Converse angled the unconscious body by the shoulders, propelling it against the wall, shoving it away from the metal door and letting it drop in the farther shadows. He leaned down and picked up the radio; he

155

snapped off the antenna and shoved the case into his pocket. He stood up, confused, frightened, trying to orient himself. Then, grabbing his attaché case and suitcase, he raced breathlessly out of the alley, conscious of the blood that had somehow erupted over part of his face. The taxi was at the curb, the driver smoking a cigarette in the darkness, oblivious to the violence that had taken place only thirty yards away.

"De Gaulle Airport!" shouted Joel, opening the door and throwing his luggage inside. "Please, I'm in a hurry!" He lurched into the seat, gasping, his neck stretched above the cushioned rim, swallowing the air that would not fill his lungs.

The rushing lights and shadows that bombarded the interior of the cab served to keep his thoughts suspended, allowing his racing pulse to decelerate and the air to reach him, slowly drying the perspiration at his temples and his neck. He leaned forward, wanting a cigarette but afraid he would vomit from the smoke trapped in his throat. He shut his eyes so tightly a thousand specks of white light assaulted the dark screen of his mind. He felt ill, and he knew it was not simply fear alone that had brought on the nausea. It was something else, something that was in and of itself as paralyzing as fear. He had committed an act of utter brutality, and it both shocked and appalled him. He had actually *physically* attacked a man, wanting to cripple him, perhaps kill him—which he may very well have done. No matter why, he may have killed another human being! Did the presence of a hand-held radio

156

justify a shattered skull? Did it constitute self-defense? *Goddamn it,* he was a man of words, of logic, not blood! *Never* blood, that was in the past, so long ago and so painful.

Those memories belonged to another time, to an uncivilized time, when men became what they were not—in order to survive. Converse never wanted to go back. Above all things, he had promised himself he never would, a promise he made when the terror and the violence were all around him, at their shattering worst. He remembered so vividly, with such pain, the final hours before his last escape—and the quiet, generous man without whom he would have died twenty feet down in the earth, a shaft in the ground designed for troublemakers.

Colonel Sam Abbott, U.S. Air Force, would always be a part of his life no matter how many years might separate them. At the risk of torture and death, Sam had crawled out at night and had thrown a crudely fashioned metal wedge down the "punishment hole"; it was that primitive tool that allowed Joel to build a crude ladder out of earth and rock and finally to freedom. Abbott and he had spent the last twenty-seven months in the same camp, both officers trying to hold together what sanity there was. But Sam understood the burning inside Joel; the Colonel had stayed behind, and during those final hours before breakout, Joel was wracked by the thoughts of what might happen to his friend.

Don't worry about me, sailor. Just keep your minimum wits about you and get rid of that wedge.

Take care, Sam.

You take care. This is the last shot you've got.

I know.

Joel moved over toward the door and rolled down the window several inches more to increase the rush of wind from the highway. Christ, he needed Sam Abbott's quiet objectivity now! His lawyer's mind told him to get hold of himself; he had to think and his thoughts had to stimulate whatever imagination he had. First things first. Think! The radio—he had to get rid of the radio. But not at the airport—it might be found in the airport; it was evidence, and worse, a means of tracing him. He rolled the window further down and threw it out, his eyes on the rearview mirror above the windshield. The driver glanced up at him, saw the bloody face but showed no alarm; Joel took repeated deep breaths and then rolled the window back up. Think. He had to *think!* Bertholdier expected him to go from Paris to Bonn and when the general's soldier was found—and he had undoubtedly been found by now—all flights to Bonn would be watched, whether the man was alive or dead.

He would buy a ticket for somewhere else, someplace where connections to Cologne-Bonn were accessible on a regular basis. As the stream of air cooled his face it occurred to him to remove the handkerchief from his breast pocket and wipe away the moist blood that covered his right cheek and lower chin.

"Scandinavian Air Lines," he said, raising his voice to the driver. *"SAS.* Do you . . . *comprends?"*

"Very clearly, monsieur," said the bereted man behind the wheel in good English. "Do you have a reservation for Stockholm, Oslo, or Copenhagen? They are different gates."

"I'm . . . I'm not sure."

"We have time, monsieur. At least fifteen minutes."

The voice over the telephone from London was frigid, the words and the delivery an impersonal rebuke. "There is no attorney by that name in Chicago, and certainly not at the address you gave me. In fact, the address does not exist. Do you have something else to offer, or do we put this down as one of your more paranoid fantasies, *mon général?*"

"You are a fool, *l'Anglais,* with no more comprehension than a frightened rabbit. I *heard* what I *heard!*"

"From whom? A nonexistent man?"

"A nonexistent man who has put my aide in a hospital! A fractured skull with a great loss of blood and severe brain damage. He may not live, and if he does, he will no doubt be a vegetable. Speak to me not of fantasies, *daffodil.* The man is real."

"Are you serious?"

"Call the hospital! L'hôpital Saint-Jérôme. Let the doctors tell you."

"All right, all right, compose yourself. We must think."

"I am perfectly composed," said Bertholdier, getting up from the desk in his study and carrying the phone to the window, the extension cord

159

snaking across the floor. He looked out; it had begun to rain, the street lights diffused in the spattered glass. "He's on his way to Bonn," continued the general. "It was his next stop, he was very clear about it."

"Intercept him. Call Bonn, reach Cologne, give them his description. How many flights can there be from Paris with a lone American on board? Take him at the airport."

Bertholdier sighed audibly into the phone, his tone one of discouragement bordering on disgust. "It was never my intention to *take* him. It would serve no purpose and probably cut us off from what we have to learn. I want him followed. I want to know where he goes, whom he calls, whom he meets with; these are the things we must learn."

"You said he made a direct reference to our associate. That he was going to reach him."

"Not *our* people. *His* people."

"I'll say it again," insisted the voice from London. "Call Cologne, reach Bonn. Listen to me, Jacques, he can be found, and once he is, he can be followed."

"Yes, yes, I'll do as you say, but it may not be as easy as you think. Three hours ago I would have thought otherwise, but that was before I knew what he was capable of. Someone who can take another man and rush that man's head into a stone wall at full force is either an animal, a maniac, or a zealot who will stop at nothing. In my judgment, he is the last. He said he had a commitment—and it was in his eyes. And he'll be clever; he's already proven he can be clever."

"You say *three* hours?"

"Yes."

"Then he may already *be* in Bonn."

"I know."

"Have you called our associate?"

"Yes, he's not at home and the maid could not give me another number. She doesn't know where he is, or when he's expected."

"Probably in the morning."

"No doubt. . . . *Attendez!* There was another man at the club this afternoon. With Luboque and this Simon, whose name is not Simon. He *brought* him to Luboque! Good-bye, *l'Anglais.* I'll keep you informed."

René Mattilon opened his eyes. The streaks of light on the ceiling seemed to shimmer, myriad tiny clots bursting, breaking up the linear patterns. Then he heard the sound of the rain on the windows and understood. The shafts of light from the streetlamps had been intercepted by the glass, distorting the images he knew so well. It was the rain, he concluded; that was what had awakened him. That and perhaps the weight of his wife's hand between his legs. She stirred and he smiled, trying to make up his mind—or find the energy—to reach for her. She had filled a void for him he had thought would always be there after his first wife died. He was grateful, and along with his feeling of gratitude came excitement, two emotions satisfyingly compatible. He was becoming aroused; he rolled over on his side and pulled down the covers, revealing the swell of her breasts encased in laced silk,

161

the diffused light and the pounding on the windows heightening the sensuality. He reached for her.

Suddenly, there was another sound besides the rain, and though still wrapped in the mists of sleep he recognized it. Quickly he withdrew his hand and turned away from his wife. He had heard that noise only moments before; *it* was the sound that had awakened him, an insistent tone that had broken the steady rhythm of the downpour: the chimes of his apartment doorbell.

Mattilon climbed out of bed as carefully as he could, reaching for his bathrobe on a nearby chair and sliding his feet into his slippers. He walked out of the bedroom, closing the door quietly behind him, and found the wall switch that turned on the lamps in the living room. He glanced at the ornate clock on the fireplace mantel; it was nearly two-thirty in the morning. Who could possibly be calling on them at this hour? He tied the sash around his robe and walked to the door.

"Yes, who is it?"

"Sûreté, monsieur. Inspector Prudhomme. My state identification is zero-five-seven-two-zero." The man's accent was Gascon, not Parisian. It was often said that Gascons made the best police officials. "I shall wait while you call my station, monsieur. The telephone number is—"

"No need," said Mattilon, alarmed, unlatching the door. He knew the man was genuine not only from the information offered, but anyone from the Sûreté calling on him at this hour would know he was an attorney. The Sûreté was legally circumspect.

162

There were two men, both in raincoats spotted by the downpour, their hats drenched; one was older than the other and shorter. Each held out an open identification card for René's inspection. He waved the cards aside and gestured for the two men to come in, adding, "It's an odd time for visitors, gentlemen. You must have pressing business."

"Very pressing, monsieur," said the older man, entering first. He was the one who had spoken through the door, giving his name as Prudhomme, and was obviously the senior. "We apologize for the inconvenience, of course." Both men removed their hats.

"Of course. May I take your coats?"

"It won't be necessary, monsieur. With your cooperation we'll only be a few minutes."

"And I shall be most interested to know how I can cooperate with the Sûreté at this time of night."

"A matter of identification, sir. Monsieur Serge Antoine Luboque is a client of yours, we are informed. Is this so?"

"My God, has something happened to Serge? I was with him only this afternoon!"

"Monsieur Luboque appears to be in excellent health. We left his country house barely an hour ago. And to the point, it is your meeting with him this afternoon—*yesterday* afternoon—that concerns the Sûreté."

"In what way?"

"There was a third party at your table. Like yourself, an attorney, introduced to Monsieur Luboque—a man named Simon. Henry Simon, an American."

"And a pilot," said Mattilon warily. "With considerable expertise in aircraft litigation. I trust Luboque explained that; it was the reason he was there at my request. Monsieur Luboque is the plaintiff in just such a lawsuit. That, of course, is all I can say on the subject."

"It is not the subject that interests the Sûreté."

"What is, then?"

"There is no attorney by the name of Henry Simon in the city of Chicago, Illinois, in the United States."

"I find that hard to believe."

"The name is false. At least, it is not his. The address he gave the hotel does not exist."

"The address he *gave* the hotel?" asked René, astonished. Joel did not have to give an address to the George V—it knew him well, knew the firm of Talbot, Brooks and Simon very well, indeed.

"In his own handwriting, monsieur," added the younger man stiffly.

"Has the hotel management confirmed this?"

"Yes," said Prudhomme. "The night concierge was very cooperative. He told us he escorted Monsieur Simon down the freight elevator to the hotel cellars."

"The cellars?"

"Monsieur Simon wished to leave the hotel without being seen. He paid his bill in his room."

"A minute, please," said Mattilon, perplexed, his hands protesting, as he turned and walked aimlessly around an armchair. He stopped, his hands on the rim. "What *precisely* do you want from me?"

"We want you to help us," answered Prudhomme. "We think you know who he is. You brought him to Monsieur Luboque."

"On a confidential matter entailing a legal opinion. He agreed to listen and to evaluate on the condition that his identity be protected. It's not unusual when seeking expertise if one is involved with, shall we say, an individual as wealthy and as temperamental as Monsieur Luboque. You've spoken with him; need I say more?"

"Not on that subject," said the older man from the Sûreté, permitting himself a smile. "He thinks all government personnel work for Moscow. We were surrounded by dogs in his foyer, all salivating, I might add."

"Then you can understand why my American colleague prefers to remain unnamed. I know him well, he's a splendid man."

"Who is he? And do you know where we can find him?"

"Why do you want him?"

"We wish to question him about an incident that took place at the hotel."

"I'm sorry. As Luboque is a client, so by extension is Simon."

"That is not acceptable to us under the circumstances, monsieur."

"I'm afraid it will have to be, at least for a few hours. Tomorrow I shall try to reach him through his office in . . . in the United States, and I'm sure he'll get in touch with you immediately."

"We don't think he will."

"Why not?"

Prudhomme glanced at his starchly postured associate and shrugged. "He may have killed a man," he said matter-of-factly.

Mattilon stared at the Sûreté officer in disbelief. "He . . . *what?*"

"It was a particularly vicious assault, monsieur. A man's head was rammed into a wall; there are extensive cranial injuries and the prognosis is not good. His condition as of midnight was critical, the chances of recovery less than half. He may be dead by now, which one doctor said could be a blessing."

"No . . . *no!* You are mistaken! You're wrong!" The lawyer's hands gripped the back of the chair. "A terrible error has been made!"

"No error. The identification was positive —that is, Monsieur *Simon* was identified as the last person seen with the man who was beaten. He forced the man out into an alley; there were sounds of scuffling and minutes later that man was found, his skull fractured, bleeding, near death."

"Impossible! You don't *know* him! What you suggest is inconceivable. He *couldn't.*"

"Are you telling us he is disabled, physically incapable of assault?"

"No," said Mattilon, shaking his head. Then suddenly he stopped all movement. *"Yes,"* he continued thoughtfully, his eyes pensive, now nodding, rushing ahead. "He's incapable, yes, but not physically. *Mentally.* In that sense he is disabled. He could not do what you say he did."

"He's mentally deranged?"

"My *God,* no! He's one of the most lucid men I've ever met. You have to understand. He went through a prolonged period of extreme physical stress and mental anguish. He endured punishment, to both his body and his mind. There was no permanent damage but there are indelible memories. Like so many men who've been subjected to such treatment, he avoids all forms of physical confrontation or abuse. It is repugnant to him. He can't inflict punishment because too much was inflicted on him."

"You mean he would not defend himself, his own? He would turn the other cheek if he, or his wife, or his children were attacked?"

"Of course not, but that's not what you described. You said 'a particularly vicious assault,' implying something quite different. And if it were otherwise—if he were threatened or attacked and defended himself—he most certainly would not have left the scene. He's too fine a lawyer." Mattilon paused. *"Was* that the case? Is that what you're saying? Is the injured man known to you from the police files? Is he—"

"A limousine chauffeur," interrupted Prudhomme. "An unarmed man who was waiting for his assigned passenger of the evening."

"In the *cellars?*"

"Apparently it is a customary service and not an unfamiliar one. These firms are discreet. This one sent another driver to cover before inquiring as to their employee's condition. The client would not know."

"Very chic, I'm sure. What do they say happened?"

"According to a witness, a guard who's been with the hotel for eighteen years, this Simon approached in a loud voice, speaking English—the guard thinks angrily, although he does not understand the language—and forced the man outside."

"The guard is wrong! It had to be someone else."

"Simon identified himself. The concierge had cleared his departure. The description fits; it was the one who called himself Simon."

"But *why?* There has to be a reason!"

"We should like to hear it, monsieur."

René shook his head in bewilderment; nothing made sense. A man could register at any hotel under any name he wished, of course, but there were charges, credit cards, people calling; a false name served no purpose. Especially at a hotel where one was presumably known, and if one *was* known and chose to travel incognito, that status would not be protected if a front desk was questioned by the Sûreté. "I must ask you again, Inspector, have you checked thoroughly with the hotel?"

"Not personally, monsieur," replied Prudhomme, looking at his associate. "My time was taken up interrogating those in the vicinity of the assault."

"I checked with the concierge myself, monsieur," said the younger, taller man, speaking like a programmed robot. "Naturally, the hotel is not anxious for the incident to receive attention, but the management was cooperative. The night concierge is newly employed from the Hotel Meurice and wished to minimize the incident, but he himself showed me the registration form."

"I see." And Mattilon did see, at least insofar as Joel's identity was concerned. Hundreds of guests at a large hotel and a nervous concierge protecting his new employer's image. The obvious source was accepted as truth, another truth no doubt forthcoming in the morning from more knowledgeable men. But that was all René understood—nothing else. He needed a few moments to think, to try to understand. "I'm curious," he said, reaching for words. "At worst, this is an assault with severe results, but nevertheless an assault. Why isn't it a simple police matter? Why the Sûreté?"

"My first question, monsieur," said the plainspoken Prudhomme. "The reason given us was that the incident involved a foreigner, obviously a wealthy foreigner. One does not know these days where such things may lead. We have certain controls not available to the *arrondissement* police."

"I see."

"Do you?" asked the man from the Sûreté. "May I remind you that as an attorney you have an obligation to uphold the courts and the law? You have been offered our credentials and I have suggested you call my station for any further verification you might wish. Please, monsieur, who is Henry Simon?"

"I have other obligations, as well, Inspector. To my word, to a client, to an old friendship—"

"You put these above the law?"

"Only because I know you're *wrong.*"

"Then where is the harm? If we are wrong, we shall find this Simon undoubtedly at an airport and he will tell us himself. But if we are not, we may find a very sick man who needs help. Before he harms others. I am no psychiatrist, monsieur, but you have described a troubled man—a once troubled man, in any event."

Mattilon was uncomfortable with the blunt official's logic . . . and also something else he could not define. Was it Joel? Was it the clouds in his old friend's eyes, the unconscious verbal slip about a blemished rock in the dirt? René looked again at the clock on the mantel; a thought occurred to him. It was only eight-forty-two in New York.

"Inspector, I'm going to ask you to wait here while I go into my study and make a phone call on my private line. The line, incidentally, is not connected to the telephone on the table."

"That was unnecessary, monsieur."

"Then I apologize."

Mattilon walked rapidly to a door on the opposite side of the room, opened it and went inside. He crossed to his desk, where he sat down and opened a red-leather telephone index. He flipped the pages to the letter *T,* scanning the names until he reached *Talbot, Lawrence.* He had both the office and the house number; the latter was necessary because the courts in Paris were in operation before the East Coast of America was out of bed. If Talbot was not there, he would try Nathan Simon, then Brooks, if he had to. Neither alternative was necessary. Lawrence Talbot answered the phone.

"I'll be damned, how are you, René? You in New York?"

"No, Paris."

"Sounds like you're down the block."

"So do you. It's always startling."

"It's also late where you are, if I'm not mistaken."

"It's very late, Larry. We may have a problem, that's why I'm calling."

"A problem? I didn't even know we had any business going. What is it?"

"Your missionary work."

"Our what?"

"Bertholdier. His friends."

"Who?"

"Jacques-Louis Bertholdier."

"Who is he? I've heard the name but I can't place him."

"You can't . . . place him?"

"Sorry."

"I've been with Joel. I arranged the meeting."

"Joel? How is he? Is he in Paris now?"

"You weren't aware of it?"

"Last time I spoke with him was two days ago in Geneva—after that awful business with Halliday. He told me he was all right, but he wasn't. He was shaken up."

"Let me understand you, Larry. Joel is not in Paris on business for Talbot, Brooks and Simon, is that what you're saying?"

Lawrence Talbot paused before answering. "No, he's not," said the senior partner softly.

171

"Did he say he was?"

"Perhaps I just assumed it."

Again Talbot paused. "I don't think you'd do that. But I do think you should tell Joel to call me."

"That's part of the problem, Larry. I don't know where he is. He said he was taking the five o'clock plane for London, but he didn't. He checked out of the George Cinq quite a bit later under very odd circumstances."

"What do you mean?"

"His hotel registration was altered, changed to another name—a name I suggested, incidentally, as he didn't wish to use his own at lunch. Then he insisted on leaving by way of some basement delivery entrance."

"That's strange."

"I'm afraid it's the least of the oddities. They say he assaulted a man. He may have killed him."

"Jesus!"

"I don't believe it, of course," said Mattilon quickly. "He wouldn't, he couldn't—"

"I *hope* not."

"Certainly you don't think—"

"I don't know *what* to think," interrupted Talbot. "When he was in Geneva and we talked, I asked him if there was any connection between Halliday's death and what he was doing. He said there wasn't, but he was so remote, so distant; his voice sounded hollow."

"What he's *doing* . . . . ? What *is* he doing?"

"I don't know. I'm not even sure I can find out, but I'll do my damnedest. I tell you, I'm worried. Something's happened to him. His voice was like an echo chamber, do you know what I mean?"

"Yes, I do," said Mattilon quietly. "I heard him, I saw him. I'm worried too."

"Find him, René. Do whatever you can. Give me the word and I'll drop everything and fly over. He's hurting somewhere, somehow."

"I'll do what I can."

Mattilon walked out of his study and faced the two men from the police.

"His name is Converse, Joel Converse," he began.

"His name is Converse, first name Joel," said the younger, taller man from the Sûreté, speaking into the mouthpiece of a pay phone on the Boulevard Raspail, as the rain pounded the booth. "He's employed by a law firm in New York: Talbot, Brooks and Simon; the address is on Fifth Avenue. The assumed name, Simon, however, was apparently a convenience, and not related to the firm."

"I don't understand."

"Whatever this Converse is involved with has nothing to do with his employers. Mattilon reached one of the partners in New York and it was made clear to him. Also both men are concerned, worried; they wish to be kept informed. If Converse is found, Mattilon insists on immediate access to him as the attorney of record. He may be holding back, but in my judgment he's genuinely bewildered. In shock, might be more accurate. He knows nothing of consequence. I could tell if he did."

"Nevertheless, he *is* holding back. The name Simon was used for my benefit so I would not learn the identity of this Converse. Mattilon knows that; he was there and they are friends and he brought him to Luboque."

"Then he was manipulated, General. He did not mention you."

"He might if he's questioned further. I cannot be involved in any way."

"Of course not," agreed the man from the Sûreté with quiet emphasis.

"Your superior, what's his name? The one assigned to the incident."

"Prudhomme. Inspector First Grade Prudhomme."

"Is he frank with you?"

"Yes. He thinks I'm something of a mechanical ex-soldier whose instincts may outdistance his intellect, but he sees that I'm willing. He talks to me."

"You'll be kept with him for a while. Should he decide to go back and see Mattilon, let me know immediately. Paris may lose a respected attorney. My name must not surface."

"He would go back to Mattilon only if Converse was found. And if word came to the Sûreté as to his whereabouts, I'd reach you instantly."

"There could be another reason, Colonel. One that might provoke a persistent man into reexamining his progress—or lack of it—in spite of orders to the contrary."

"Orders to the contrary, sir?"

"They will be issued. This Converse is solely our concern now. All we needed was a name. We know where he's heading. We'll find him."

"I don't understand, General."

"News has come from the hospital. Our chauffeur has taken a turn for the better."

"Good news, indeed."

"I wish it were. The sacrifice of a single soldier is abhorrent to any field commander, but the broader tactics must be kept in view, they must be served. Do you agree?"

"Yes, of course."

"Our chauffeur must not recover. The larger strategy, Colonel."

"If he dies, the efforts to find Converse will be intensified. And you're right, Prudhomme will reexamine everything, including the lawyer, Mattilon."

"Orders to the contrary will be issued. But watch him."

"Yes, sir."

"And now we need your expertise, Colonel. The talents you developed so proficiently while in the service of the Legion before we brought you back to a more civilized life."

"My gratitude isn't shallow. Whatever I can do."

"Can you get inside the Hospital of Saint Jérôme with as little notice as possible?"

"With no notice. There are fire escapes on all sides of the building and it's a dark night, heavy with rain. Even the police stay in doorways. It's child's play."

"But man's work. It has to be done."

"I don't question such decisions."

"A blockage in the windpipe, a convulsion in the throat."

"Pressure applied through cloth, sir. Gradually and with no marks, a patient's self-induced trauma. . . . But I would be derelict if I didn't repeat what I said, General. There'll be a search of Paris, then a large-scale manhunt. The killer will be presumed to be a rich American, an inviting target for the Sûreté."

"There'll be no search, no manhunt. Not yet. If it is to be, it will come later, and if it does, a convicted corpse will be trapped in the net. . . . Go into the field, my young friend. The chauffeur, Colonel; the broader strategy must be served."

"He's dead," said the man in the telephone booth, and hung up.

5

Erich Leifhelm . . . born March 15, 1912, in Munich to Dr. Heinrich Leifhelm and his mistress, Marta Stoessel. Although the stigma of his illegitimacy precluded a normal childhood in the upper-middle-class, morality-conscious Germany of those years, it was the single most important factor in his later preeminence in the National Socialist movement. At birth he was denied the name of Leifhelm; until 1931 he was known as Erich Stoessel.

Joel sat at a table in the open café in Copenhagen's Kastrup Airport, trying to concentrate. It was his second attempt within the past twenty minutes, the first he abandoned when he realized he was absorbing nothing, seeing only black letters forming an unending string of vaguely recognizable words relating to a figure in the outer reaches of his mind. He could not focus on that man; there were too many interferences, real and imagined. Nor had he been able to read on the two-hour flight from Paris, having opted for economy class, hoping to melt in with the greater number of people in the larger section of the aircraft. The concept at least was valid; the seats were so narrow and the plane so fully occupied that elbows and forearms were virtually immobile. The conditions prohibited his taking out the report, both for reasons of space and for fear of the proximity to straying eyes.

Heinrich Leifhelm moved his mistress and their son to the town of Eichstätt, fifty odd miles north of Munich, visiting them now and then, and providing an adequate but not overly comfortable standard of living. The doctor was apparently torn between maintaining a successful practice—with no social blemishes—in Munich and a disinclination to abandon the stigmatized mother and child. According to close acquaintances of Erich Stoessel-Leifhelm, these early years had a profound effect on him. Although he was too young to grasp the full impact of World War I,

177

he was later haunted by the memory of the small household's subsistence level falling as the elder Leifhelm's ability to contribute lessened with the burden of wartime taxes. Too, his father's visits served to heighten the fact that he could not be acknowledged as a son and was not entitled to the privileges accorded two half brothers and a half sister, strangers he was never to know and whose home he could not enter. Through the absence of proper lineage, certified by hypocritical documents and more hypocritical church blessings, he felt he was denied what was rightfully his, and so there was instilled in him a furious sense of resentment, competitiveness, and a deep-seated anger at existing social conditions. By his own admission, his first conscious longings were to get as much as he could for himself—both materially and in the form of recognition—through the strength of his own abilities, and, by doing so, strike out at the status quo which had tried to emasculate him. By his mid-teens, Stoessel-Leifhelm was consumed with anger.

Converse stopped reading, suddenly aware of the woman across the half-deserted café; she was seated alone at a table, looking at him. Their eyes met and she turned away, placing her arm on the low white railing that enclosed the restaurant, studying the thinning, late-night crowds in the terminal, as if waiting for someone. Startled, Joel tried to analyze the look she had given him. Was it recognition? Did she know him? Know his face? Or was it appraisal? A well-dressed whore cruising the airport in search of a mark, seeking out a lonely businessman far away from home? She turned her head slowly and looked at him again, now obviously upset that his eyes were still on her. Then abruptly, in two swiftly defined motions, she glanced at her watch, tugged at her wide-brimmed hat, and opened her purse. She took out a Krone note, placed it on the table, got up, and walked rapidly toward the entrance of the café. Beyond the open gate she walked faster, her strides longer, heading for the arch that led to the baggage-claim area. Converse watched her in the dull white neon light of the terminal, shaking his head, annoyed at his alarm. With his attaché case and leather-bound report, the woman had probably thought he was some kind of airport official. Who was the mark, then?

He was seeing too many shadows, he thought, as he followed the graceful figure nearing the arch. Too many shadows that held no surprises, no alarms. There had been a man on the plane from Paris sitting several rows in front of him. Twice the man had gotten up and gone to the toilet, and each time he came back to his seat he had looked hard at Joel—studied him, actually. Those looks had been enough to prime his adrenaline. Had he been spotted at the De Gaulle Airport? Was the man an employee of Jacques-Louis Bertholdier? . . . As a man in an alley had been—*Don't think about that!* He had flicked off an oval of dried blood on his shirt as he had given himself the command.

"I can always tell a good ole Yank! Never miss!"

That had been the antiquated salutation in Copenhagen, as both Americans waited for their luggage.

"Well, I missed once. Some son of a bitch on a plane in Geneva. Sat right next to me. A real guinea in a three-piece suit, that's what he was! He spoke English to the stewardess, so I figured he was one of those rich Cuban spicks from Florida, you know what I mean?"

An emissary in salesman's clothes. One of the diplomats.

Geneva. It had started in Geneva.

Too many shadows. No surprises, no alarms. The woman went through the arch and Joel pulled his eyes away, forcing his attention back to the report on Erich Leifhelm. Then a slight, sudden movement caught the corner of his eye; he looked back at the woman. A man had stepped out of an unseen recess; his hand had touched her elbow. They exchanged words briefly, swiftly, and parted as abruptly as they had met, the man continuing into the terminal as the woman disappeared. Did the man glance over in his direction? Converse watched closely; *had* that man looked at him? It was impossible to tell; his head was turning in all directions, looking *at* or *for* something. Then, as if he had found it, the man hurried toward a bank of airline counters. He approached the Japan Air Lines desk, and taking out his wallet, he began speaking to an Oriental clerk.

No surprises, no alarms. A harried traveler had

asked directions; the interferences were more imagined than real. Yet even here his lawyer's mentality intervened. Interferences were real whether based in reality or not. *Oh, Christ!* Leave it alone! Concentrate!

At the age of seventeen, Erich Stoessel-Leifhelm had completed his studies at the Eichstätt II Gymnasium, excelling both academically and on the playing field, where he was known as an aggressive competitor. It was a time of universal financial chaos, the American stock market crash of '29 further aggravating the desperate economy of the Weimar Republic, and few but the most well-connected students went on to universities. In a move he later described to friends as one of youthful fury, Stoessel-Leifhelm traveled to Munich to confront his father and demand assistance. What he found was a shock, but it turned out to be a profound opportunity, strangely arrived at. The doctor's staid, placid life was in shambles. His marriage, from the beginning unpleasant and humiliating, had caused him to drink heavily with increasing frequency until the inevitable errors of judgment occurred. He was censured by the medical community (with a high proportion of Jews therein), charged with incompetence and barred from the Karlstor Hospital. His practice was in ruins; his wife had ordered him out of the house, an order expedited by an old but still powerful father-in-law, also a doctor and member of the hospital's board of directors.

When Stoessel-Leifhelm found his father, he was living in a cheap apartment house in the poorer section of the city picking up pfennigs by dispensing prescriptions (drugs) and deutsche marks by performing abortions.

In what apparently (again according to friends from the time) was a watershed of pent-up emotions, the elder Leifhelm embraced his illegitimate son and told him the story of his tortured life with a disagreeable wife and tyrannical in-laws. It was the classic syndrome of an ambitious man of minimal talents and maximum connections. But withal, the doctor claimed he had never abandoned his beloved mistress and their son. And during this prolonged and undoubtedly drunken confession, he revealed a fact Stoessel-Leifhelm had never known. His father's wife was Jewish. It was all the teenager had to hear.

The disfranchised boy became the father to the ruined man.

There was an announcement in Danish over the airport's loudspeakers and Joel looked at his watch. It came again, now in German. He listened intently for the words; he could barely distinguish them, but they were there. "Hamburg-Köln-Bonn." It was the first boarding call for the last flight of the night to the capital of West Germany by way of Hamburg. The flying time was less than two hours, the layover in Hamburg justified for those executives who wanted to be at their desks by the start of the business day. Converse had checked his suitcase through to Bonn, making a mental note as he did so to replace the heavy black leather bag with a carry-on. He was no expert in such matters, but common sense told him that the delays required by waiting for one's luggage—in the open for anyone to see—was no way to travel swiftly or to avoid eyes that might be searching for him. He put Erich Leifhelm's dossier in his attaché case, closed it and spun the brass combination disks. He then got up from the table, walked out of the cafe and across the terminal toward the Lufthansa gate.

Sweat matted his hairline; the tattoo inside his chest accelerated until it sounded like a hammering fugue for kettledrums. He *knew* the man sitting next to him, but from where or from what period in his life he had no idea. The craggy, lined face, the deep ridges that creased the suntanned flesh, the intense blue-gray eyes beneath the thick, wild brows and brown hair streaked with white—he *knew* him, but no name came, no clue to the man's identity.

Joel kept waiting for some sign of recognition directed at him. None came, and involuntarily he found himself looking at the man out of the corner of his eye. The man did not respond; instead his attention was on a bound sheaf of typewritten pages, the type larger than the print normally associated with legal briefs or even summonses. Perhaps, thought Converse, the man was half blind, wearing contact lenses to conceal his infirmity. But was there something else? Not an infirmity, but a connection being concealed. Had he seen this man in Paris—as he had seen

183

another wearing a light-brown topcoat in a hotel basement corridor? Had this man beside him also been at L'Etalon Blanc? Had he been part of a stationary group of ex-soldiers in the warriors' playroom . . . in a corner perhaps, and inconspicuous because of the numbers? Or at Bertholdier's table, his back to Joel, presumably unseen by the American he was now following? *Was* he following him at this moment? wondered Converse, gripping his attaché case. He turned his head barely inches and studied his seatmate.

Suddenly the man looked up from the bound typewritten pages and over at Joel. His eyes were noncommittal, expressing neither curiosity nor irritation.

"Sorry," said Converse awkwardly.

"Sure, it's okay . . . why not?" was the strange, laconic reply, the accent American, the dialect distinctly Texas-Western. The man returned to his pages.

"Do we know each other?" asked Joel, unable to back off from the question.

Again the man looked up. "Don't think so," he said tersely, once more going back to his report, or whatever it was.

Converse looked out the window, at the black sky beyond, flashes of red light illuminating the silver metal of the wing. Absently he tried to calculate the digital degree heading of the aircraft but his pilot's mind would not function. He *did* know the man, and the oddly phrased. "Why not?" served only to disturb him further. Was it a signal, a warning? As his words to Jacques-Louis Bertholdier had been a signal, a warning that the general had better contact him, recognize him.

The voice of a Lufthansa stewardess interrupted his thoughts. "Herr Dowling, it is a pleasure, indeed, to have you on board."

"Thank you, darlin'," said the man, his lined face creasing into a gentle grin. "You find me a little bourbon over ice and I'll return the compliment."

"Certainly, sir. I'm sure you've been told so often you must be tired of hearing it, but your television show is enormously popular in Germany."

"Thanks again, honey, but it's not *my* show. There are a lot of pretty little fillies runnin' around that screen."

An actor. A goddamned actor! thought Joel. No alarms, no surprises. Just intrusions, far more imagined than real.

"You're too modest, Herr Dowling. They're all so alike, so disagreeable. But you are so kind, so manly . . . so understanding."

"Understandin'? Tell you somethin'. I saw an episode in Cologne last week while on this picture and I didn't understand a word I was sayin'."

The stewardess laughed. "Bourbon over ice, is that correct, sir?"

"That's correct, darlin'."

The woman started down the first-class aisle toward the galley as Converse continued to look at the actor. Haltingly he spoke. "I *am* sorry. I should have recognized you, of course."

Dowling turned his suntanned head, his eyes roaming Joel's face, then dropping to the hand-tooled leather attaché case. He looked up with an amused smile. "I could probably embarrass you if

I asked you where you knew me from. You don't look like a *Santa Fe* groupie."

"A *Santa Fe* . . . ? Oh, sure, that's the name of the show." And it was, reflected Converse. One of those phenomena on television that by the sheer force of extraordinary ratings and network profits had been featured on the covers of *Time* and *Newsweek*. He had never seen it.

"And, naturally," continued the actor, "you follow the tribal rites—and wrongs—the dramatic vicissitudes of the imperious Ratchet family, owners of the biggest spread north of Santa Fe as well as the historic Chimaya Flats, which they stole from the impoverished Indians."

"The who? What?"

Dowling's leathery face again laminated itself into a grin. "Only Pa Ratchet, the Indians' friend, doesn't know about the last part, although he's being blamed by his red brothers. You see, Pa's no-good sons heard there was oil shale beneath the Chimayas and did their thing. Incidentally, I trust you catch the verbal associations in the name Ratchet; you can take your choice. There's just plain 'rats,' or Ratchet as in 'wretched,' or Ratchet as in the tool —screwing everything in front of it by merely pressing forward."

There was something different about the actor now, thought Joel, bewildered. Was it his words? No, not the words, his voice. The Western inflections were greatly diminished. "I don't know what you're talking about, but you sound different."

"Wal, Ah'll jes' be *hornswoggled!*" said

186

Dowling, laughing. Then he returned to the unaccented tones he had begun to display. "You're looking at a renegade teacher of English and college dramatics who said a dozen years ago to hell with old-age tenure, let's go after a very impractical dream. It led to a lot of funny and not very dignified jobs, but the spirit of Thespis moves in mysterious ways. An old student of mine, in one of those indefinable jobs like 'production-coordinator,' spotted me in a crowd scene; it embarrassed the hell out of him. Nevertheless, he put my name in for several small parts. A few panned out, and a couple of years later an accident called *Santa Fe* came along. That's when my perfectly respectable name of Calvin was changed to Caleb. 'Fits the image better,' said a pair of Gucci loafers who never got closer to a horse than a box at Santa Anita. . . . It's crazy, isn't it?"

"Crazy," agreed Converse, as the stewardess walked back up the aisle toward them.

"Crazy or not," added Dowling under his breath, "this good old rancher isn't going to offend *anyone*. They want Pa Ratchet, they've got him."

"Your bourbon, sir," said the woman, handing the actor a glass.

"Why, *thank* you, li'l darlin'! My oh my, you're purtier than any filly on the show!"

"You are too kind, sir."

"May I have a Scotch, please," said Joel.

"That's better, son," said Dowling, grinning again as the stewardess left. "And now that you know my crime, what do you do for a living?"

187

"I'm an attorney."

"At least you've got something legitimate to read. This screenplay sure as hell isn't."

Although considered by most of Munich's respectable citizens to be a collection of misfits and thugs, the National Socialist German Workers' Party, with its headquarters in Munich, was making itself felt throughout Germany. The radical-populist movement was taking hold by basing its inflammatory message on the evil un-German "them." It blamed the ills of the nation on a spectrum of targets ranging from the Bolsheviks to the ingrate Jewish bankers; from the foreign plunderers who had raped an Aryan land to, finally, all things not "Aryan," namely and especially the Jews and their ill-gotten wealth.

Cosmopolitan Munich and its Jewish community laughed at the absurdities; they were not listening. The rest of Germany was; it was hearing what it wanted to hear. And Erich Stoessel-Leifhelm heard it too. It was his passport to recognition and opportunity.

In a matter of weeks, the young man literally whipped his father into shape. In later years he would tell the story with heavy doses of cruel humor. Over the dissolute physician's hysterical objections, the son removed all alcohol and smoking materials from the premises, never letting his father out of his sight. A harsh regimen of exercise and diet was enforced. With the zeal of a puritanical athletic trainer, Stoessel-Leifhelm started taking his father out to the countryside for *Gewaltmarschen*—forced marches—gradually working up to all-day hikes on the exhausting trails of the Bavarian mountains, continually shouting at the older man to keep moving, to rest only at his son's commands, to drink water only with permission.

So successful was the rehabilitation that the doctor's clothes began to hang on him like seedy, old-fashioned garments purchased for a much fatter man. A new wardrobe was called for, but good clothing in Munich in those days was beyond the means of all but the wealthy, and Stoessel-Leifhelm had only the best in mind for his father—not out of filial devotion but, as we shall see, for a quite different purpose.

Money had to be found, which meant it had to be stolen. He interrogated his father at length about the house the doctor had been forced to leave, learning everything there was to learn. Several weeks later Stoessel-Leifhelm broke into the house on the Luisenstrasse at three o'clock one morning, stripping it of everything of value, including silver, crystal, oil paintings, gold place settings, and the entire contents of a wall safe. Sales to fences were not difficult in Munich of 1930, and when everything was disposed of, father and son had the equivalent of nearly eight thousand American dollars, virtually a fortune in those times.

The restoration continued; clothes were tailored in the Maximilianstrasse, the best footwear purchased at bootsmiths on the

Odeonsplatz, and, finally, cosmetic changes were effected. The doctor's unkempt hair was trimmed and heightened by coloring into a masculine Nordic blond, and his shabby inch-long beard shaved off, leaving only a small, unbroken, well-trimmed moustache above his upper lip. The transformation was complete; what remained was the introduction.

Every night during the long weeks of rehabilitation, Stoessel-Leifhelm had read aloud to his father whatever he could get his hands on from the National Socialists' headquarters, and there was no lack of material. There were the standard inflammatory pamphlets, pages of ersatz biological theory purportedly proving the genetic superiority of Aryan purity and, conversely, the racial decline resulting from indiscriminate breeding—all the usual Nazi diatribes—plus generous excerpts from Hitler's *Mein Kampf*. The son read incessantly until the doctor could recite by rote the salient outrages of the National Socialists' message. Throughout it all, the seventeen-year-old kept telling his father that following the party's program was the way to get back everything that had been stolen from him, to avenge the years of humiliation and ridicule. As Germany itself had been humiliated by the rest of the world, the Nazi party would be the avenger, the restorer of all things truly German. It was, indeed, the New Order for the Fatherland, and it was waiting for men of stature to recognize the fact.

The day came, a day when Stoessel-Leifhelm

had learned that two high-ranking party officials would be in Munich. They were the crippled propagandist Joseph Goebbels and the would-be aristocrat Rudolf Hess. The son accompanied the father to the National Socialists' headquarters where the well-tailored, imposing, obviously rich and Aryan *Doktor* requested an audience with the two Nazi leaders on an urgent and confidential matter. It was granted, and according to early party historical archives, his first words to Hess and Goebbels were the following.

"Gentlemen, I am a physician of impeccable credentials, formerly head surgeon at the Karlstor Hospital and for years I enjoyed one of the most successful practices in Munich. That was in the past. I was destroyed by Jews who stole everything from me. I am back, I am well, and I am at your service."

The Lufthansa plane began its descent into Hamburg, and Joel, feeling the drag, dog-eared the page of Leifhelm's dossier and reached down for his attaché case. Beside him, the actor Caleb Dowling stretched, script in hand, then jammed his screenplay into an open flight bag at his feet.

"The only thing sillier than this movie," he said, "is the amount of money they're paying me to be in it."

"Are you filming tomorrow?" asked Converse.

"Today," corrected Dowling, looking at his watch. "It's an early shoot, too. Have to be on location by five-thirty—dawn over the Rhine, or something equally inspiring. Now, if they'd just turn the damn thing into a travelogue, we'd all be better off. Nice scenery."

"But you were in Copenhagen."

"Yep."

"You're not going to get much sleep."

"Nope."

"Oh."

The actor looked at Joel, the crow's-feet around his generous eyes creasing deeper with his smile. "My wife's in Copenhagen and I had two days off. This was the last plane I could get."

"Oh? You're married?" Converse immediately regretted the remark; he was not sure why, but it sounded foolish.

"Twenty-six years, young fella. How do you think I was able to go after that impractical dream? She's a whiz of a secretary; when I was teaching, she'd always be this or that dean's gal Friday."

"Any children?"

"Can't have everything. Nope."

"Why is she in Copenhagen? I mean, why isn't she staying with you—on location?"

The grin faded from Dowling's suntanned face; the lines were less apparent, yet somehow deeper. "That's an obvious question, isn't it? That is, you being a lawyer would pick it up quickly."

"It's none of my business, of course. Forget I asked it."

"No, that's okay. I don't like to talk about it—rarely do—but friendly seatmates on airplanes are for telling things. You'll never see them again, so why not slice off a bit and feel better." The actor tried haltingly to smile; he failed. "My wife's name was Oppenfeld. She's Jewish. Her story's not much different from a few million others, but for her it's . . . well, it's hers. She was separated from her parents and her three younger brothers in Auschwitz. She watched them being taken away—away from her—while she screamed, not understanding. She was lucky; they put her in a barracks, a fourteen-year-old sewing uniforms until she showed other endowments that could lead to other work. A couple of days later, hearing the rumors, she got hysterical and broke out, racing all over the place trying to find her family. She ran into a section of the camp they called the *Abfall,* the garbage, corpses hauled out of the gas chambers. And there they were, the bodies of her mother and her father and her three brothers, the sight and the stench so sickening it's never left her. It never will. She won't set foot in Germany and I wouldn't ask her to."

No alarms, just surprises . . . and another Iron Cross for the Erich Leifhelms of the past, retroactively presented.

"Christ, I'm sorry," murmured Converse. "I didn't mean to—"

"You didn't. I did. . . . You see, she knows it doesn't make sense."

"Doesn't make *sense?* Maybe you didn't hear what you just described."

"I heard, I know, but I didn't finish. When she was sixteen, she was loaded into a truck with five other girls, all on their way to that different type of work, when they did it. Those kids took their last chance and beat the hell out of a Wehrmacht corporal who was guarding them in the van. Then

193

with his gun they got control of the truck from the driver and escaped." Dowling stopped, his eyes on Joel.

Converse, silent, returned the look, unsure of its meaning, but moved by what he had heard. "That's a marvelous story," he said quietly. "It really is."

"And," continued the actor, "for the next two years they were hidden by a succession of German families, who surely knew what they were doing and what would happen to them if they got caught. There was a pretty frantic search for those girls—a lot of threats made, more because of what they could tell than anything else. Still, those Germans kept moving them around, hiding them, until one by one they were taken across the border into occupied France, where things were easier. They were smuggled across by the underground, the *German* underground." Dowling paused, then added. "As Pa Ratchet would say, 'Do you get my drift, son?' "

"I'd have to say it's obvious."

"There's a lot of pain and a lot of hate in her and God knows I understand it. But there should be some gratitude, too. Couple of times clothing was found, and some of those people—those German people—were tortured, a few shot for what they did. I don't push it, but she could level off with a little gratitude. It might give her a bit more perspective." The actor snapped on his seat belt.

Joel pressed the locks on his attaché case, wondering if he should reply. Valerie's mother had been part of the German underground. His

194

ex-wife would tell him amusing stories her mother had told her about a stern, inhibited French intelligence officer forced to work with a high-spirited, opinionated German girl, a member of the *Untergrund.* How the more they disagreed, and the more they railed against each other's nationality, the more they noticed each other. The Frenchman was Val's father; she was proud of him, but in some ways prouder of her mother. There had been pain in that woman, too. And hate. But there had been a reason, and it was unequivocal. As there had been for one Joel Converse years later.

"I said it before and I mean it," began Joel slowly, not sure he should say anything at all. "It's none of my business, but I wouldn't ever push it, if I were you."

"Is this a lawyer talkin' to ole Pa?" asked Dowling in his television dialect, his smile false, his eyes far away. "Do I pay a fee?"

"Sorry, I'll shut up." Converse adjusted his seat belt and pushed the buckle in place.

"No, *I'm* sorry. I laid it on you. Say it. Please."

"All right. The horror came first, then the hate. In sidewinder language that's called prima facie—the obvious, the first sighting . . . the real, if you like. Without these, there'd be no reason for the gratitude, no call for it. So, in a way, the gratitude is just as painful because it never should have been necessary."

The actor once again studied Joel's face, as he had done before their first exchange of words. "You're a smart son of a bitch, aren't you?"

"Professionally adequate. But I've been there . . . that is, I *know* people who've been where your wife has been. It starts with the horror."

Dowling looked up at the ceiling light, and when he spoke his words floated in the air, his harsh voice quietly strained. "If we go to the movies, I have to check them out; if we're watching television together, I read the TV section . . . sometimes on the news—with some of those fucking nuts—I tense up, wondering what she's going to do. She can't see a swastika, or hear someone screaming in German, or watch soldiers marching in a goose step; she can't stand it. She runs and throws up and shakes all over . . . and I try to hold her . . . and sometimes she thinks I'm one of them and she screams. After all these years . . . *Christ!*"

"Have you tried professional help—not my kind—but the sort she might need?"

"Oh, hell, she recovers pretty quick," said the actor defensively, as if slipping into a role, his teacher's grammar displaced for effect. "Also, until a few years ago we didn't have the money for that kind of thing," he added somberly in his natural voice.

"What about now? That can't be a problem now."

Dowling dropped his eyes to the flight bag at his feet. "If I'd found her sooner . . . maybe. But we were both late bloomers; we got married in our forties—two oddballs looking for something. It's too late now."

"I'm sorry."

"I never should have made this goddamn

picture. *Never.*"

"Why did you?"

"She said I should. To show people I could play something more than a driveling, south-forty dispenser of fifth-rate bromides. I told her it didn't matter. . . . I was in the war, in the Marine Corps. I saw some crap in the South Pacific but nothing to compare with what she went through, not a spit in the proverbial bucket. *Jesus!* Can you imagine what it must have been like?"

"Yes, I can."

The actor looked up from the flight bag, a half-drawn smile on his lined, suntanned face. "You, good buddy? Not unless you were caught in Korea—"

"I wasn't in Korea."

"Then you'd be hard put to imagine it any more than I. You were too young and I was too lucky."

"Well, there was . . ." Converse fell silent; it was pointless. It had happened so often he did not bother to think about it anymore. 'Nam had been erased from the national conversational psyche. He knew that if he reminded a man like Dowling, a decent man, the air would be filled with apologies, but nothing was served by a jarring remembrance. Not as it pertained to Mrs. Dowling, born Oppenfeld. "There's the 'no smoking' sign," said Joel. "We'll be in Hamburg in a couple of minutes."

"I've taken this flight a half-dozen times over the past two months," said Caleb Dowling, "and let me tell you, Hamburg's a bitch. Not German customs, that's a snap, especially this late. Those rubber stamps fly and they push you through in ten minutes tops. But then you wait. Twice, maybe three times, it was over an hour before the plane to Bonn even got here. By the way, care to join me for a drink in the lounge?'' The actor suddenly switched to his Southern dialect. ''Between you and me, they make it mighty pleasant for ol' Pa Ratchet. They telex ahead and Ah got me my own gaggle of cowpokes, all ridin' hard to git me to the waterin' hole.''

''Well . . . ?'' Joel felt flattered. Not only did he like Dowling, but being the guest of a celebrity was a pleasant high. He had not had many pleasant things happen to him recently.

''I should also warn you,'' added the celebrity, ''that even at this hour the groupies crawl out of the walls, and the airline PR people manage to roust out the usual newspaper photographers, but none of it takes too long.''

Converse was grateful for the warning. ''I've got some phone calls to make,'' he said casually, ''but if I finish them on time, I'd like very much to join you.''

''Phone calls? At this hour?''

''Back to the States. It's not this hour back in . . . Chicago.''

''Make them from the lounge; they keep it open for me.''

''It may sound crazy,'' said Joel, reaching for words, ''but I think better alone. There are some complicated things I have to explain. After customs I'll find a phone booth.''

''Nothing sounds crazy to me, son. I work in *Holl*-eee-wood.'' Suddenly, the actor's amused

198

exuberance faded. "In the States," he said softly, his words floating again, eyes distant again. "You remember that crap in Skokie, Illinois? They did a television show on it. . . . I was in the study learning lines when I heard the screams and the sound of a door crashing open. I ran out and saw my wife racing down to the beach. I had to drag her out of the water. Sixty-seven years old, and she was a little girl again, back in that goddamn camp, seeing the lines of hollow-eyed prisoners, knowing which lines were which . . . seeing her mother and father, her three kid brothers. When you think about it, you can understand why those people say over and over, 'Never again.' It can't ever happen again. I wanted to sell that fucking house; I won't leave her alone in it."

"Is she alone now?"

"Nope," said Dowling, his smile returning. "That's the good part. After that night we faced it; we both knew she couldn't be. Got her a sister, that's what we did. Bubbly little thing with more funny stories about Cuckooburg than ever got into print. But she's tough as they come; she's been bouncing around the studios for forty years."

"An actress?"

"Not so's anyone could tell, but she's a great face in the crowd. She's a good lady, too, good for my wife."

"I'm glad to hear it," said Joel, as the aircraft's wheels made bouncing contact with the runway and the jet engines screeched into reverse thrust. The plane rolled forward, then started a left turn toward its dock.

Dowling turned to Converse. "If you finish your calls, ask someone for the VIP lounge. Tell them you're a friend of mine."

"I'll try to get there."

"If you don't," added the actor in his *Santa Fe* dialect, "see y'awl back in the steel corral. We got us another leg on this here cattle drive, pardner. Glad you're ridin' shotgun."

"On a cattle drive?"

"What the hell do I know? I hate horses."

The plane came to a stop, and the forward door opened in less than thirty seconds as a number of excited passengers rapidly jammed the aisle. It was obvious from the whispers and the stares and the few who stood up on their toes to get clearer views that the reason for the swift exodus of this initial crowd was the presence of Caleb Dowling. And the actor was playing his part, dispensing Pa Ratchet benedictions with warm smiles, broad infectious winks, and deep-throated laughter, all with good-old-wrangler humility. As Joel watched he felt a rush of compassion for this strange man, this actor, this risk-taker with a private hell he shared with the woman he loved.

Never again. It can't ever happen again. Words.

Converse looked down at the attaché case he held with both hands on his lap. Inside was another story, one that held a time bomb ready to detonate.

I am back, I am well, and I am at your service. Also words from another time—but full of menace for the present, for they were part of the story of a living man's silent return. A spoke in the wheel of Aquitaine.

The first rush of curious passengers filed through the exit door after the television star, and Joel slipped into the less harried line. He would go through customs as rapidly and as unobtrusively as possible, then find a dark corner of the airport and wait in the deepest shadows until the loudspeakers announced the plane for Cologne-Bonn.

Goebbels and Hess accepted Dr. Heinrich Leifhelm's offer with enthusiasm. One can easily imagine the propaganda expert visualizing the image of this blond Aryan physician of "impeccable credentials" spread across thousands of pamphlets confirming the specious theories of Nazi genetics, as well as his all too willing condemnation of the inferior, avaricious Jew; he was heaven-sent. Whereas for Rudolf Hess, who wanted more than his little boys to be accepted by the junkers and the monied class, the Herr Doktor was his answer; the physician was obviously a true aristocrat, and in time, quite possibly a lover.

The confluence of preparation, timing and appearance turned out to be more than young Stoessel-Leifhelm could have imagined. Adolf Hitler returned from Berlin for one of his Marienplatz rallies, and the imposing *Doktor*, along with his intense, well-mannered son, was invited to dinner with the Führer. Hitler heard everything he wanted to hear, and Heinrich Leifhelm from that day until his death in 1934 was Hitler's personal physician.

There was nothing that the son could not

have, and in short order he had everything he wanted. In June of 1931 a ceremony was held at the National Socialists' headquarters, where Heinrich Leifhelm's marriage to "a Jewess" was proclaimed invalid because of a "concealment of Jewish blood" on the part of an "opportunistic Hebrew family," and all rights, claims and inheritances of the children of that "insidious union" were deemed void. A civil marriage was performed between Leifhelm and Marta Stoessel, and the true inheritor, the only child who could claim the name of Leifhelm, was an eighteen-year-old called Erich.

Munich and the Jewish community still laughed, but not as loudly, at the absurd announcement the Nazis inserted in the legal columns of the newspapers. It was considered nonsense; the Leifhelm name was a discredited name, and certainly no paternal inheritance was involved; finally it was all outside the law. What they were only beginning to understand was that the laws were changing in changing Germany. In two short years there would be only one law: Nazi determination.

Erich Leifhelm had arrived and his ascendancy in the party was swift and assured. At eighteen he was Jungführer of the Hitler Youth movement, photographs of his strong, athletic face and body challenging the children of the New Order to join the national crusade. During his tenancy as a symbol, he was sent to the University of Munich, where he completed his courses of study in three years with high academic honors. By this time, Adolf Hitler had been swept into power; he controlled the Reichstag, which gave him dictatorial powers. The Thousand-Year Reich had begun and Erich Leifhelm was sent to the Officers Training Center in Magdeburg.

In 1935, a year after his father's death, Erich Leifhelm, now a youthful favorite of Hitler's inner circle, was promoted to the rank of *Oberstleutnant* in the Gruppenkommando 1 in Berlin under Rundstedt. He was deeply involved in the vast military expansion that was taking place in Germany, and as the war drew nearer he entered what we can term the third phase of his complicated life, one that ultimately brought him to the centers of Nazi power and at the same time provided him with an extraordinary means of separating himself from the leadership of which he was an intrinsic and influential part. This is briefly covered in the following final pages, a prelude to the fourth phase, which we know is his fanatic allegiance to the theories of George Marcus Delavane.

But before we leave the young Erich Leifhelm of Eichstätt, Munich, and Magdeburg, two events should be recorded here that provide insights into the man's psychotic mentality. Mentioned above was the robbery at the Luisenstrasse house and the resulting profits of the theft. Leifhelm to this day does not deny the incident, taking pleasure in the tale because of the despicable images he paints of his father's first wife and her "overbearing" parents. What he does not speak of, nor has anyone spoken of it in his presence, is the original police report in Munich, which, as near as can be determined, was destroyed sometime in August 1934, a date corresponding to Hindenburg's death and Hitler's rise to absolute power as both president and chancellor of Germany with the title of *der Führer* raised to official mandatory status.

All copies of the police report were removed from the files, but two elderly pensioners from the Munich department remember it clearly. They are both in their late seventies, have not seen each other in years, and were questioned separately.

Robbery was the lesser crime that early morning on the Luisenstrasse; the more serious one was never spoken of at the insistence of the family. The fifteen-year-old Leifhelm daughter was raped and severely beaten, her face and body battered so violently that upon admission to the Karlstor Hospital she was given little chance of recovery. She did recover physically, but remained emotionally disturbed for the rest of her short life. The man who committed the assault had to be familiar with the interior of the house, had to know there was a back staircase that led to the girl's room, which was separated from the rooms of her two brothers and her mother in the front. Erich Leifhelm had questioned his father in depth regarding the inside design of that house; he was there by his own admission, and was aware of the fierce pride and strict moral code held by the "tyrannical in-laws." There is no question; his compulsion was such that he had to inflict the most degrading insult he could imagine, and he did so, knowing the influential family would and could insist on official silence.

The second event took place during the months of January or February 1939. The specifics are sketchy insofar as there are few survivors of the time who knew the family well, and no official records, but from those who were found and interviewed, certain facts surfaced. Heinrich Leifhelm's legal wife, his children and her family tried without success for several years to leave Germany. The official party line was that the old patriarch's medical skills, having been acquired in German universities, were owed to the state. Too, there were unresolved legal questions arising from the dissolved union between the late Dr. Heinrich Leifhelm and a member of the family, questions specifically relating to commonly shared assets and the rights of inheritance as they affected an outstanding officer of the Wehrmacht.

Erich Leifhelm was taking no chances. His father's "former" wife and children were virtually held prisoners, their movements restricted; the house on the Luisenstrasse was watched, and for weeks following any renewed applications for visas, they were all kept under full "political surveillance" on the chance that they had plans of vanishing. This information was revealed by a retired banker who recalled that orders came from the Finanzministerium in

Berlin instructing the banks in Munich to immediately report any significant withdrawals by the former Frau Leifhelm and/or her family.

During what week or on what day it happened we did not learn, but sometime in January or February of 1936, Frau Leifhelm, her children and her father disappeared.

However, the Munich court records, impounded by the Allies on April 23, 1945, give a clear, if incomplete, picture of what took place. Obviously driven by his compulsion to validate his seizure of the estate in the eyes of the law, Oberstleutnant Erich Leifhelm had a brief filed on his own behalf, listing the articles of grievance suffered by his father, Dr. Heinrich Leifhelm, at the hands of a family cabal, said family of criminals having fled the Reich under indictment. The charges, as expected, were outrageous lies: from outright theft of huge nonexistent bank accounts to character assassination so as to destroy a great doctor's practice. There was the legal certificate of the "official" divorce, and a copy of the elder Leifhelm's last will and testament. There was only one true union and one true son, and all rights, privileges and inheritances passed on to him: Oberstleutnant Erich Stoessel-Leifhelm.

Because we possessed reasonably accurate dates, survivors were found. It was confirmed that Frau Leifhelm, her three children and her father perished at Dachau, ten miles outside of Munich.

The Jewish Leifhelms were gone; the Aryan

Leifhelm was now the sole inheritor of considerable wealth and property that under existing conditions would have been confiscated. Before the age of thirty, he had wiped his personal slate clean and avenged the wrongs he was convinced had been visited on his superior birth and talents. A killer had matured.

"You must have one hell of a case there," said Caleb Dowling, grinning and poking Joel with his elbow. "Your butt burned up in the ashtray a while ago. I reached over to close the goddamned lid, and all you did was raise your hand like I was out of order."

"I'm *sorry*. It's . . . it's a complicated brief. Christ, I wouldn't raise my hand to you, you're a celebrity." Converse laughed because he knew it was expected.

"Well, my second bit of news for you, good buddy, is that celebrity or no, the smoking lamp's been on for a couple of minutes now and you still got a reefer in your fingers. Now, I grant you, you didn't light it, but we're getting a lot of Nazi looks over here."

"Nazi . . . ?" Joel spoke the word involuntarily as he pressed the unlit cigarette into the receptacle; he was not aware that he had been holding it.

"A figure of speech and a bad line," said the actor. "We'll be in Cologne before you put all that legal stuff away. Come on, good buddy, he's going in for the approach."

"No," countered Joel without thinking. "He's

207

making a pitchout until he gets the tower's instructions. It's standard—we've got at least three minutes."

"You sound like you know what the hell you're talking about."

"Vaguely," said Converse, putting the Leifhelm dossier into his attaché case. "I used to be a pilot."

"No kidding? A *real* pilot?"

"Well, I got paid."

"For an airline? I mean, one of these *real* airlines?"

"Larger than this one, I think."

"Goddamn, I'm impressed. I wouldn't have thought so. Lawyers and pilots somehow don't seem compatible."

"It was a long time ago." Joel closed his case and snapped the locks.

The plane rolled down the runway, the landing having been so unobtrusive that a smattering of applause erupted from the rear of the aircraft. Dowling spoke as he unfastened his seat belt. "I used to hear some of that after a particularly good class."

"Now you hear a lot more," said Converse.

"For a hell of a lot less. By the way, where are you staying, counselor?"

Joel was not prepared for the question. "Actually, I'm not sure," he replied, again reaching for words, for an answer. "This trip was a last-minute decision."

"You may need help. Bonn's crowded. Tell you what, I'm at the Königshof and I suspect I've got a little influence. Let's see what we can do."

"Thanks very much, but that won't be necessary." Converse thought rapidly. The last thing he wanted was the attention focused on anyone in the actor's company. "My firm's sending someone to meet me and he'll have the accommodations. As a matter of fact, I'm supposed to be one of the last people off the plane, so he doesn't have to try to find me in the crowd."

"Well, if you've got any time and you want a couple of laughs with some actor types, call me at the hotel and leave a number."

"I probably will. I enjoyed riding shotgun."

"On a cattle drive, pardner?"

Joel waited. The last stragglers were leaving the plane, nodding at the flanking stewardesses, some yawning, others in awkward combat with shoulder bags, camera equipment and suit-carriers. The final passenger exited through the aircraft's concave door and Converse got up, gripping the handle of his attaché case and sliding into the aisle. Instinctively, without having a conscious reason to do so, he glanced to his right, into the rear section of the plane.

What he saw—and what saw him—made him freeze. His breath exploded silently in his chest. Seated in the last row of the long fuselage was a woman. The pale skin under the wide brim of the hat, and the frightened, astonished eyes that abruptly looked away—all formed an image he vividly remembered. She was the woman in the café at the Kastrup Airport in Copenhagen! When he last saw her she was walking rapidly into the baggage-claim area, *away* from the row of airlines' counters. She had been stopped by a man in a hurry; words had been exchanged—and now Joel knew they had concerned him.

The woman had doubled back, unnoticed in the last-minute rush for boarding. He felt it, he *knew* it. She had followed him from Denmark!

6

Converse rushed up the aisle and through the metal door into the carpeted tunnel. Fifty feet down the passageway the narrow walls opened into a waiting area, the plastic seats and the roped-off stanchions designating the gate. There was no one; the place was empty, the other gates shut down, the lights off. Beyond, suspended from the ceiling were signs in German, French and English directing passengers to the main terminal and the downstairs baggage claim. There was no time for his luggage; he had to run, to get away from the airport as fast as possible, get away without being seen. Then the obvious struck him, and he felt sick. He *had* been seen; they knew he was on the flight from Hamburg— whoever *they* were. The instant he walked into the terminal he would be spotted, and there was nothing he could do about it. They had found him in Copenhagen; the woman had found him and she had been ordered on board to make certain he did not stay in Hamburg, or switch planes to another destination.

How? How did they do it?

There was no time to think about it; he would think about it later—if there was a later. He passed the arches of the closed-down metal detectors and the black conveyor belts where hand luggage was X-rayed. Ahead, no more than seventy-five feet were the doors to the terminal. What was he going to do, what *should* he do?

NUR FÜR HIER BESCHÄFTIGTE
MÄNNER

Joel stopped at a door. The sign on it was emphatic, the German forbidding. Yet he had seen those words before. Where? What was it? . . . Zurich! He had been in a department store in Zurich when a stomach attack had descended to his bowels. He had pleaded with a sympathetic clerk who had taken him to a nearby employees' men's room. In one of those odd moments of gratitude and relief, he had focused on the strange words as they had drawn nearer. *Nur für hier Beschäftigte. Manner.*

No further memory was required. He pushed the door open and went inside, not sure what he would do other than collect his thoughts. A man in green overalls was at the far end of the line of sinks against the wall; he was combing his hair while inspecting a blemish on his face in the mirror. Converse walked to the row of urinals beyond the sinks, his demeanor that of an airlines executive. The affectation was accepted; the man mumbled something courteously and left. The door swung shut and he was alone.

Joel stepped back from the urinal and studied

the tiled enclosure, hearing for the first time the sound of several voices . . . outside, somewhere outside, beyond . . . the *windows*. Three-quarters up from the floor and recessed in the far wall were three frosted-glass windows, the painted white frames melting into the whiteness of the room. He was confused. In these security-conscious days of airline travel with the constant emphasis on guarding against smuggled arms and narcotics, a room inside a gate area that had a means of getting *outside* before entering customs did not make sense. Then the obvious fact occurred to him. It could be his way out! The flight from Hamburg was a domestic flight, this part of the Cologne-Bonn airport a domestic terminal; there were no customs! Of course there were exterior windows in an enclosure like this. What difference did it make? Passengers still had to pass through the electronic arches and, conversely, authorities wanting to pick up a passenger flying domestically would simply wait by a specific gate.

But no one waited for him. He had been the last—the second to last—passenger off the late night flight. The roped-off gate had been deserted; anyone sitting in one of the plastic chairs or standing beyond the counter would be obvious. Therefore, those who were keeping him in their sights did not want to be seen themselves. Whoever they were, they were waiting, watching for him from some remote spot inside the terminal. They could wait.

He approached the far-right window and lowered his attaché case to the floor. When he stood erect, the sill was only inches above his head. He reached for the two white handles and pushed; the window slid easily up several inches. He poked his fingers through the space; there was no screen. Once the window was raised to its full height, there would be enough room for him to crawl outside.

There was a clattering behind him, rapid slaps of metal against wood. He spun around as the door opened, revealing a hunched-over old man in a white maintenance uniform carrying a mop and a pail. Slowly, with deliberation, the old man took out a pocket watch, squinted at it, said something in German, and waited for an answer. Not only was Joel aware that he was expected to speak, but he assumed that he had been told the employees' men's room was being closed until morning. He had to think; he could not leave; the only way out of the airport was through the terminal. If there was another, he did not know where, and it was no time to be running around a section of an airport shut down for the remainder of the night. Patrolling guards might compound his problems.

His eyes dropped, centering on the metal pail, and in desperation he knew what he had to do, but not whether he could do it. With a sudden grimace of pain, he moaned and grabbed his chest, falling to his knees. His face contorted, he sank to the floor.

"Doctor, doctor . . . *doctor!*" he shouted over and over again.

The old man dropped the mop and the pail; a guttural stream of panicked phrases accompanied several cautious steps forward. Converse rolled to his right against the wall; he gasped for breath as he watched the German with wide, blank eyes.

"*Doctor . . . !*" he whispered.

The old man trembled and backed away toward the door; he turned, opened it and ran out, his frail voice raised for help.

There would be only seconds! The gate was no more than two hundred feet to the left, the entrance to the terminal perhaps a hundred to the right. Joel got up quickly, raced to the pail, turned it upside down, and brought it back to the window. He placed it on the floor and stepped up with one foot, his palms making contact with the base of the window; he shoved. The glass rose about four inches and stopped, the frame lodged against the sash. He pushed again with all the strength he could manage in his awkward position. The window would not budge; breathing hard he studied it, his intense gaze zeroing in on two small steel objects he wished to God were not in place, but they were. Two protective braces were screwed into the opposing sashes, preventing the window from being opened more than six inches. Cologne-Bonn might not be an international airport with a panoply of sophisticated security devices, but it was not without its own safeguards.

There were distant shouts from beyond the door; the old man had reached someone. The sweat rolled down Converse's face as he stepped off the pail and reached for his attaché case on the floor. Action and decision were simultaneous, only instinct unconsciously governing both. Joel picked up the leather case, stepped forward and crashed it repeatedly into the window, shattering the glass and finally breaking away the lower wooden frame. He stepped back up on the pail and looked out. Beyond—below—was a cement path bordered by a guardrail, floodlights in the distance, no one in sight. He threw the attache case out the window, and pulled himself up, his left knee kicking fragments of glass and what was left of the frame to the concrete below. Awkwardly, he hunched his whole body, pressing his head into his shoulder blades, and plunged through the opening. As he fell to the ground he heard the shouts from inside: they grew in volume, all in counterpoint, a mixture of bewilderment and anger. He ran.

Minutes later, at a sudden curve in the cement path, he saw the floodlit entrance of the terminal and the line of taxis waiting for the passengers of Flight 817 from Hamburg to pick up their luggage before the drivers collected their inflated night prices to Bonn and Cologne. There were entrance and exit roads leading to the platform, broken by pedestrian crosswalks, and beyond these an immense parking lot with several lighted booths still operating for those driving their own cars. Converse slipped over the guardrail and ran across an intersecting lawn until he reached the first road, racing into the shadows at the first blinding glare of a floodlight. He had to reach a taxi, a taxi with a driver who spoke English; he could not remain on foot. . . . He had been captured on foot once, years ago. On a jungle trail, where if he had only been able to commandeer a jeep—an enemy jeep—he might have . . . *Stop it!* This is not 'Nam, it's a goddamn airport with a million tons of concrete poured between flowers, grass and asphalt! He kept moving in and out of the shadows, until he had made a complete semicircle—one-eight zero. He was in darkness, the last of the taxis in the line ahead of him. He approached the first, which was the last.

"English? Do you speak English?"

"Englisch? Nein."

The second cabdriver was equally negative, but the third was not. "As you Americans say, only the asshole would drive a taxi here wizzout the English reasonable. Is so?"

"It's reasonable," said Joel, opening the door.

"Nein! You cannot do that!"

"Do what?"

"Come in the taxi."

"Why not?"

"The line. Allviss is the line."

Converse reached into his jacket pocket and withdrew a folded layer of deutsche marks. "I'm generous. Can you understand that?"

"Is also urgent sickness. Get in, *mein Herr."*

The cab pulled out of the line and sped toward the exit road. "Bonn or Köln?" asked the driver.

"Bonn," replied Converse, "but not yet. I want you to drive into the other lane and stop across the way in front of that parking lot."

"Was . . . ?"

"The other *lane.* I want to watch the entrance back there. I think there was someone on the Hamburg plane I know."

216

"Many have come out. Only those with luggage—"

"She's still inside," insisted Joel. *"Please,* just do as I say."

"She? . . . *Ach, ein Fräulein. Ist ja ihr Geld, mein Herr."*

The driver swung the cab into a cutoff that led to the incoming road and the parking lot. He stopped in the shadows beyond the second booth; the terminal doors were on the left, no more than a hundred yards away. Converse watched as weary passengers, carrying assorted suitcases, golf bags, and the ever-present camera equipment, began to file out of the terminal's entrance, most raising their hands for taxis, a few walking across the pedestrian lanes toward the parking lot.

Twelve minutes passed and still there was no sign of the woman from Copenhagen. She could not have been carrying luggage, so the delay was deliberate, or instructed. The driver of the cab had assumed the role of nonobserver; he had turned off the lights and, with a bowed head, appeared to be dozing. Silence. . . . Across the parallel roads, the travelers from Hamburg had dwindled. Several young men, undoubtedly students, two in cut-off jeans, their companions drinking from cans of beer, were laughing as they counted the deutsche marks between them. A yawning businessman in a three-piece suit struggled with a bulging suitcase and an enormous cardboard box wrapped in a floral print, while an elderly couple argued, their dispute emphasized by two shaking heads of gray hair. Five others, men and women, were by the curb at the far end of the

217

platform apparently waiting for prearranged transportation. But where . . .

Suddenly she was there, but she was not alone. Instead, she was flanked by two men, a third directly behind her. All four walked slowly, casually, out of the automatic glass doors, moving to the left, their pace quickening until they reached the dimmest area of the canopied entrance. Then the three men angled themselves in front of the woman, as if mounting a wall of protection, their heads turning, talking to her over their shoulders while studying the crowd. Their conversation became animated but controlled, anger joining confusion, tempers held in check. The man on the right broke away and crossed to the corner of the building, then walked beyond into the shadows. He pulled an object out of an inside pocket and Joel instantly knew what it was; the man raised it to his lips. He was talking by radio to someone in or around the airport.

Barely seconds passed when the beams of powerful headlights burst through the glass over Converse's right shoulder, filling the back of the taxi. He pressed himself into the seat, his head turned, neck arched, his face at the edge of the rear window. Beyond, by the exit booth of the parking lot, a dark-red limousine had stopped, the driver's arm extended, a bill clutched in his hand. The attendant took the money, turning to make change, when the large car lurched forward leaving the man in the booth bewildered. It careened around the taxi and headed for the curve in the road that led to the airport terminal's entrance. The timing was too precise; radio

contact had been made and Joel spoke to the
driver.

"I told you I was generous," he said, startled
by the words he was forming in his head. "I can
be *very* generous if you'll do as I ask you to."

"I am an honest man," replied the German,
uncertainty in his voice, his eyes looking at Joel in
the rearview mirror.

"So am I," said Converse. "But I'm also
honestly curious, and there's nothing wrong with
that. You see the dark-red car over there, the one
that's stopping at the corner of the building?"

"*Ja.*"

"Do you think you could follow it without
being seen? You'd have to stay pretty far behind,
but keep it in sight. Could you do it?"

"Is not a reasonable request. How generous is
the *Amerikaner?*"

"Two hundred deutsche marks over the fare."

"You are generous, and I am a superior
driver."

The German did not underestimate his talents
behind the wheel. Skillfully he weaved the cab
unobtrusively through a cutoff, swinging abruptly
left into the parallel exit road and *bypassing* the
entrance to the terminal.

"What are you doing?" asked Joel, confused.
"I want you to follow—"

"Is only way out," interrupted the driver,
glancing back at the airport platform while
maintaining moderate speed. "I shall let him pass
me. I am just one more insignificant taxi on the
autobahn."

Converse sank back into the corner of the seat,

his head away from the windows. "That's reasonably good thinking," he said.

"Superior, *mein Herr.*" Again the driver looked briefly back out the window, then concentrated on the road and the rearview mirror. Moments later he gradually accelerated his speed; it was not noticeable; there was no breaking away, instead merely a faster pace. He eased to the left, passing a Mercedes coupe, staying in the lane to overtake a Volkswagen, then returning to the right.

"I hope you know what you're doing," muttered Joel.

No reply was necessary as the dark-red vehicle streaked by on the left.

"Directly ahead the road separates," said the driver. "One way to Köln, the other to Bonn. You say you are going to Bonn, but what if your friend goes to Köln?"

"Stay with him."

The limousine entered the road for Bonn and Converse lighted a cigarette, his thoughts on the reality of having been found, which meant his name was known from the passenger manifest. So be it; he would have preferred otherwise, but once the initial contact had been made with Bertholdier it was not a vital point. He could operate as himself; his past might even be an asset. Also, there was a positive side to the immediate situation; he had learned something—several things. Those following him—who now had lost him—were no part of the authorities; they were not connected with either the German or the French police, or the coordinating Interpol. If

220

they were, they would have taken him at the gate or on the plane itself, and that told him something else. Joel Converse was not wanted for assault or—God forbid—murder back in Paris. And this assumption could only lead to a third probability: the violent, bloody struggle in the alley was being covered up. Jacques-Louis Bertholdier was taking no chances that because of his severely wounded aide his own name might surface in any connection whatsoever with a wealthy guest of the hotel who had made such alarming insinuations to the revered general. The protection of Aquitaine was paramount.

There was a fourth possibility, so realistically arrived at it could be considered fact. The men in the dark-red limousine who had met the Hamburg plane were also part of Aquitaine, underlings of Erich Leifhelm, the spoke of Aquitaine in West Germany. Sometime during the last five hours, Bertholdier had learned the identity of the ersatz Henry Simon—probably through the management of the George V—and contacted Leifhelm. Then, both alarmed that no passenger manifest listed an American named Converse flying from Paris to Bonn, they had checked the other airlines and found he had gone to Copenhagen. The alarms must have been strident. Why Copenhagen? He said he was going to Bonn. Why did this strange man with his extraordinary information go to Copenhagen? Who are his contacts, whom will he meet? Find him. Find *them!* Another phone call had been made, a description given, and a woman had stared at him in a café in the Kastrup Airport. It was all so through-the-looking glass.

He had flown to Denmark for one reason, but another purpose had been served. They had found him, but in the finding they had revealed their own panic. An agitated reception committee, the use of a radio at night to reach an unseen vehicle only a few hundred feet away, a racing limousine: these were the ingredients of anxiety. The enemy was off-balance and the lawyer in Converse was satisfied. At this moment that enemy was a quarter of a mile down the road, speeding into Bonn, unaware that a taxi behind them, skillfully maneuvered by a driver slipping around the intermittent traffic, was keeping them in sight.

Joel crushed out his cigarette as the driver slowed down to let a pickup truck pass. He could see the large dark-red car ahead on the long curve. The German was no amateur; he knew the moves to make, and Converse understood. Whoever was in that limousine might well be an influential owner, and even two hundred deutsche marks were not worth the probable enmity of a powerful man.

Probabilities . . . everything was probabilities. He had built his legal reputation on the study of probabilities, and it was a simpler process than most of his colleagues believed. The approach, that is, was simple, not the work; that was never easy. It demanded the dual discipline of concentrating on the minute and prodding the imagination to expand until the minutiae were arranged and rearranged into dozens of different equations. This exhaustive what-if process was the keystone of legal thinking; it was as simple as that. It was also a verbal trap, Joel reflected, as he thought back several years, smiling an uncomfortable smile alone in the darkness. In one of her moments of pique, Val had told him that if he would spend one iota of the time on the two of them that he spent on his "goddamned probabilities," he would "probably" come to realize that the "probability" of their surviving together was "very probably nil."

She had never lacked for being succinct, nor sacrificed her humor in the pursuit of candor. Her striking looks aside, Valerie Charpentier Converse was a very funny lady. Unable not to, he had smiled at her explosion that night years ago, then they both had laughed quietly until she turned away and left the room, too much sadness in the truth she had spoken.

Large picturesque buildings gradually replaced the quiet countryside, reminding Converse of huge Victorian houses with filigreed borders and overhanging eaves and grilled balconies beneath large rectangular windows—stark geometric shapes. These in turn gave way to a contradictory stretch of attractive but perfectly ordinary residential homes, the sort that could be found in any traditional wealthy suburb on the outskirts of a major American city. Scarsdale, Chevy Chase, Grosse Pointe or Evanston. Then came the center of Bonn where narrow, gaslit streets ran into wider avenues with modern lighting, quaint squares only blocks away from banks of contemporary stores and boutiques. It was an architectural anachronism—Old World ambience coexisting with up-to-the-minute structures, but with no sense of a city, no sense of electricity or

223

grandeur. Instead it appeared to be a large town, growing rapidly larger, the town fathers uncertain of its direction. The birthplace of Beethoven and the gateway to the Rhine Valley was the most unlikely capital imaginable of a major government. It was anything but the seat of a hard-nosed Bundestag and a series of astute, sophisticated prime ministers who faced the Russian bear across the borders.

"Mein Herr!" cried the driver. "They take the road to Bad Godesberg. *Das Diplomatenviertel."*

"What does that mean?"

"Embassies. They have *Polizeistreifen!* Patrols. We could be, how do you say, *known?"*

"Spotted," explained Joel. "Never mind. Do what you've been doing, you're great. Stop, if you have to; park if you have to. Then keep going. You now have three hundred deutsche marks over the far. I want to know where they stop."

It came six minutes later, and Converse was stunned. Whatever he had thought, wherever his imagination had led him, he was not prepared for the driver's words.

"That is the American embassy, *mein Herr."*

Joel tried to focus his thoughts. "Take me to the Hotel Königshof," he said, remembering, not knowing what else to say.

"Yes, I believe Herr Dowling left a note to that effect," said the desk clerk, reaching below the counter.

"He *did?"* Converse was astonished. He had used the actor's name in the outside hope of some possible preferential treatment. He expected nothing else, if indeed that.

"Here it is." The clerk extracted two small telephone memos from the thin stack in his hand. "You are John Converse, an American attorney."

"Close enough. That's me."

"Herr Dowling said you might have difficulty finding appropriate accommodations here in Bonn. Should you come to the Königshof tonight, he requested that we be as helpful as possible. It is possible, Herr Converse. Herr Dowling is a very popular man."

"He deserves to be," said Joel.

"I see he also left a message for you."

The clerk turned and retrieved a sealed envelope from one of the mailboxes behind him. He handed it to Converse, who opened it.

Hi, pardner.
   If you don't pick this up, I'll get it back in the morning. Forgive me, but you sounded like too many of my less fortunate colleagues who say no when they want to say yes. Now collectively in their case, it's some kind of warped pride because they think I'm suggesting a handout—it's either that or they don't want to meet someone who may be where I'm going. By the looks of you, I'd have to rule out the former and stick with the latter. There's someone you don't want to meet here in Bonn, and you don't have to. The room's taken care of and in my name—change that if you like—but don't argue about the bill. I owe you a fee, counselor, and I always pay my debts. At

225

least during the last four years I have.

Incidentally, you'd make a lousy actor.
Your pauses aren't at all convincing.

Pa Ratchet

Joel put the note back in the envelope, resisting the temptation to go to a house phone and call Dowling. The man would have little enough sleep before going to work; thanks could wait until morning. Or evening.

"Mr. Dowling's arrangements are generous and completely satisfactory," he said to the clerk behind the counter. "He's right. If my clients knew I'd come to Bonn a day early, I'd have no chance to enjoy your beautiful city."

"Your privacy will be respected, sir. Herr Dowling is a most thoughtful man, as well as generous, of course. Your luggage is outside with a taxi, perhaps?"

"No, that's why I'm so late. It was put on the wrong plane out of Hamburg and will be here in the morning. At least that's what I was told at the airport."

"*Ach,* so inconvenient, but all too familiar. Is there anything you might require?"

"No, thanks," replied Converse, raising his attaché case slightly. "The bare necessities travel with me. . . . Well, there is one thing. Would it be possible to order a drink?"

"Of course."

Joel sat up in bed, the dossier at his side, the drink in his hand. He needed a few minutes to think before going back into the world of Field

Marshal Erich Leifhelm. With the help of the switchboard, he had called the all-night number for Lufthansa and had been assured that his suitcase would be held for him at the airport. He gave no explanation other than the fact that he had been traveling for two days and nights and simply did not care to wait for his luggage. The attendant could read into his words whatever she liked; he did not care. His mind was on other things.

The American embassy! What appalled him was the stark reality of old Beale's words. . . . *Behind it all are those who do the convincing, and they're growing in numbers everywhere. . . . We're in the countdown . . . three to five weeks, that's all you've got. . . . It's real and it's coming.* Joel was not prepared for the reality. He could accept Delavane and Bertholdier, certainly Leifhelm, but the shock of knowing that ordinary embassy personnel—*American* personnel—were on the receiving end of orders from Delavane's network was paralyzing. How far *had* Aquitaine progressed? How widespread were its followers, its influence? Was tonight the frightening answer to both questions? He would think about it all in the morning. First, he had to be prepared for the man he had come to find in Bonn. As he reached for the dossier he remembered the sudden deep panic in Avery Fowler's eyes—Preston Halliday's eyes. How long had he known? How much had he known?

It is pointless to recount Erich Leifhelm's exploits in the early to middle years of the war other than to say his reputation grew, and—what is most important—he was one of the very few superior officers to come up through Nazi party ranks accepted by the old-line professional generals. Not only did they accept him but they sought him out for their commands. Men like Rundstedt and Von Falkenhausen, Rommel and von Treskow; at one time or another each asked Berlin for Leifhelm's services. He was unquestionably a brilliant strategist and a daring officer, but there was something else. These generals were aristocrats, part of the ruling class of prewar Germany, and by and large loathed the National Socialists, considering them thugs, exhibitionists and amateurs. It is not difficult to imagine Leifhelm, sitting among these men, modestly expounding on what was clearly noted in his military record. He was the son of the late prominent Munich surgeon Dr. Heinrich Leifhelm, who had left him considerable wealth and property. We need no conjecture, however, to understand how much further he went to ingratiate himself, for the following is extracted from an interview with General Rolf Winter, Standortkommandant of the Wehrbereichs-kommando in the Saar sectors:

We would sit around having coffee after dinner, the talk quite depressing. We knew the war was lost. The insane orders from Berlin —most we agreed would never be carried out —guaranteed wholesale slaughter of troops and civilians. It was madness, national suicide. And always, this young Leifhelm

would say things like "Perhaps the fools will listen to me. They think I'm one of them, they've thought so from the early days in Munich." . . . And we would wonder. Could he bring some sanity to the collapsing front: He was a fine officer, highly regarded, and the son of a well-known doctor, as he constantly reminded us. After all, young men's heads were turned in those early days—the cavernous soul-stirring roars of *Sieg heil,* the fanatic crowds; the banners and drums and marching beside ten thousand torches at night. It was all so melodramatic, so Wagnerian. But Leifhelm was different; he wasn't one of the gangsters; patriotic, of course, but not a hoodlum. . . . So we sent dispatches with him to our closest comrades in Berlin, dispatches that would have resulted in our executions had they fallen into the wrong hands. We were told he tried very hard, but he could not put sanity in the minds of men who lived in daily fear of death from rumor and gossip. But he maintained his own sanity—and loyalty—which were constant. We were informed by one of his adjutants —not him, mind you—that he was confronted by an S.S. colonel who had followed him in the street and demanded the contents of his briefcase. He refused, and when threatened with immediate arrest, he shot the man so as not to betray us. He was one of us. It was a noble risk and only a night bombing raid saved his own life.
It is clear what Leifhelm was doing and

equally clear that the dispatches were never shown to anyone, nor was there an S.S. colonel shot in the streets during a bombing raid. According to Winter, those dispatches from the Saar were so explosive in content that someone would have remembered them; no one does. Once again, Leifhelm had seen an opportunity. The war was lost, and the Nazis were about to become the ultimate twentieth-century villains. But not the elite German general corps—there was a distinction. He wiped another slate clean and joined the "Prussians." He was so successful that he was rumored to have been part of the plot to assassinate Adolf Hitler at Wolfsschanze, and called upon to be a member of Donitz's surrender team.

During the cold war, Allied Central Command asked him to join other key elements of the Wehrmacht officer corps in the Bundesgrenzschutz. He became a privileged military consultant with full security clearance. A mature killer had survived, and history, with the Kremlin's help, took care of the rest.

In May '49 the Federal Republic was established, and the following September the Allied occupation formally came to an end. As the cold war escalated and West Germany began its remarkable recovery, the NATO forces demanded material and personnel support from their former enemies. The new German divisions were formed under the command of ex-Field Marshal Erich Leifhelm.

No one had dredged up the questionable decisions of the Munich courts from nearly two decades past; there were no other survivors and his services were desired by the victors. During the postwar reconstruction when countless settlements and labyrinthine legal resolutions were being sought throughout Germany, he was quietly awarded all assets and property previously decreed, including some of the most valuable real estate in Munich. So ends the third phase of Erich Leifhelm's story. The fourth phase—which concerns us most—is the one we know least about. The only certainty is that he has become as deeply entrenched in General Delavane's operation as any other man on the primary list.

There was a rapping on the door. Joel lunged off the bed, the Leifhelm dossier cascading to the floor. He looked at his watch in fear and confusion. It was nearly four o'clock. Who wanted him at this hour? Had they found him? Oh, Christ! The *dossier!* The *briefcase!*

"Joe . . . ? *Joe*, you *up?*" The voice was both a whisper and a shout—an actor's sotto voce. "It's me, Cal Dowling."

Converse ran to the door and opened it, his breath coming in gasps. Dowling was fully dressed, holding up both his hands for silence as he glanced up and down the corridor. Satisfied, he walked rapidly inside, pushing Joel back and closing the door.

"I'm *sorry,* Cal," said Converse. "I was asleep. I guess the sound startled me."

"You always sleep in your trousers with the lights on?" asked the actor quietly. "Keep your voice down. I checked the hallways, but you can never be clear about what you didn't see.''

"Clear about what?''

"One of the first things we learned on Kwajalein in '44. A patrol doesn't mean shit unless you've got something to report. All it means is that they were better than you were.''

"I was going to call you, to thank you—''

"*Cut* it, good buddy,'' Dowling broke in, his expression serious. "I'm timing this down to the last couple of minutes, which is about all we've got. There's a limo downstairs waiting to take me out to the cameras over an hour away. I didn't want to come out of my room before in case anyone was hanging around, and I didn't want to call you because a switchboard can be watched or bribed—ask anyone in Cuckooburg. I don't worry about the desk; they're not too fond of our crowd over here.'' The actor sighed. "When I got to my room, all I wanted was sleep, and all I got was a visitor. I'm down the hall and I was hoping to Christ—*if* you came here—he wouldn't see you.''

"A visitor?''

"From the embassy. The *U.S.* embassy. Tell me, Joe—''

"Joel,'' interrupted Converse. "Not that it matters.''

"Sorry, I've an obstruction in my left ear and that doesn't matter, either. He spent damn near twenty-five minutes with me asking questions about you. He said we were seen talking together on the plane. Now, you *tell* me, counselor, are you okay, or are my instincts all fucked up?''

Joel returned Dowling's steady gaze. "Your

instincts are perfectly fine," he said without emphasis. "Did the man from the embassy say otherwise?"

"Not exactly. As a matter of fact, he didn't *say* a hell of a lot. Just that they wanted to talk to you, wanted to know why you'd come to Bonn, where you were."

"But they knew I was on the plane?"

"Yep, said you'd flown out of Paris."

"Then they *knew* I was on that plane."

"That's what I just said—what he said."

"Then why didn't they meet me at the gate and ask me themselves?"

Dowling's face creased further, his eyes narrowing within the wrinkles of bronzed flesh. "Yeah, why didn't they?" he asked himself.

"Did he say?"

"No, but then, Paris didn't come up until he was about to leave."

"What do you mean?"

"It was like he figured I was holding back something—which I certainly was—but he couldn't be sure. I'm pretty good at what I do, Joe—Joel."

"You also took a risk," said Converse, remembering that he was talking to a risk-taker.

"No, I covered myself. I specifically asked if there were charges against you or anything like that. He said there weren't."

"Still, he was—"

"Besides, I didn't like him. He was one of those pushy official types. He kept repeating things, and when he couldn't come up with anything, he said, 'We know he flew out of

Paris,' as if he was challenging me. I said *I* didn't.''

"There's not much time, but can you tell me what else he asked you?"

"I told you, he wanted to know everything we talked about. I said I didn't have a tape recorder in my head, but it was mainly small talk, the kind of chatter I get all the time from people I meet on planes. About the show, the business. But he didn't want to settle for that; he kept pushing, which gave me the opportunity to get a little pissed off myself.''

"How so?"

"I said, yes, we did talk about something else but it was very personal, and none of his damn business. He got pretty upset at that, and that let me get even angrier. We exchanged a few barbs but his weren't very sharp; he was too uptight. Then he asked me for about the tenth time if you'd said anything about Bonn, especially where you were staying. So I told him for the tenth time the truth—at least what you said. That you were a lawyer and here to see clients and I didn't know where the hell you were. I mean I didn't actually *know* you were here.''

"That's fine."

"Is it? Instincts are okay for first reactions, counselor, but then, you have to wonder. An aggravating Ivy League government man, waving an embassy ID and acting obnoxious, may be very annoying in the middle of the night, but he *is* from the Department of State. What the hell's this all about?''

Joel turned and walked to the foot of the bed;

he looked down at the Leifhelm dossier on the floor. He turned again and spoke clearly, hearing the exhaustion in his voice. "Something I wouldn't for the life of me involve you in. But for the record, those instincts of yours were right on, pardner."

"I'll be honest," said the actor, his clear eyes amused, peering out from behind the creases. "I thought as much. I said to that bastard if I remembered anything else, I'd phone Walter what's-his-name—except I called him Walt—and let him know."

"I don't understand."

"He's the ambassador here in Bonn. Can you imagine, with all the troubles they've got over here, that diplomatic yo-yo had a luncheon for *me,* a lousy television actor? Well, the suggestion that I might call the ambassador made our preppie more upset than anything else; he didn't expect it. He said—three times, as I recall—that the ambassador wasn't to be bothered with this problem. It wasn't that important and he had enough on his mind, and actually he wasn't even aware of it. And catch this, Mr. Lawyer. He said you were an in-house, State Department 'query,' as if a simpleminded actor couldn't possibly understand bureaucratic jingoism. I think that's when I said 'Bullshit.'"

"Thank you," said Converse, not knowing what else to say, but knowing what he wanted to find out.

"That's also when I figured my instincts weren't so bad." Dowling looked at his watch, then hard at Converse, his eyes now penetrating.

"I was a gyrene, but I'm no flag-waver, good buddy. However, I *like* the flag. I wouldn't live under any other."

"Neither would I."

"Then you make it plain. Are you working for it."

"Yes, the only way I know how, and that's all I can tell you."

"Are you looking into something here in Bonn? Is that why you didn't want to be seen with me? Why you stayed away from me in Hamburg —and even getting off the plane here?"

"Yes."

"And that son of a bitch didn't want me to call the ambassador."

"No, he didn't. He doesn't. He can't afford it. And, please, I ask you not to."

"Are you—Oh, *Christ!* Are you one of those undercover people I read about? I walk into a guy on a plane who can't be seen when he gets to an airport."

"It's not that melodramatic. I'm a lawyer and simply following up on some alleged irregularities. Please accept that. And I appreciate what you did for me. I'm kind of new at this myself."

"You're cool, good buddy. *Man,* are you cool." Dowling turned and walked to the door. He stopped and looked back at Converse. "Maybe I'm crazy," he said. "At my age it's allowed, but there's a streak in you, young fella. Part go-ahead, part stay-where-you-are. I saw it when I talked about my wife. Are you married?"

"I was."

"Who isn't? *Was* married, that is. Sorry."

"I'm not. We're not."

"Who is? Sorry, again. My instincts were right. You're okay." Dowling reached for the knob.

"Cal?"

"Yes?"

"I have to know. It's terribly important. Who was the man from the embassy? He must have identified himself."

"He did," said the actor. "He pushed an ID in front of my face when I opened the door, but I didn't have my glasses on. But when he was leaving I made it clear I wanted to know who the hell he was."

"Who was he?"

"He said his name was Fowler. Avery Fowler."

7

"*Wait!*"

"What?"

"*What* did you say?" Converse reeled under the impact of the name. He physically had to steady himself, grabbing the nearest solid object, a bedpost, to keep from buckling.

"What's the matter, Joe? What's wrong with you?"

"That name! Is this some kind of joke—a bad joke—a bad *line!* Were you *put* on that plane? Did I walk into you? Are you part of it, Mr. *Actor?* You're damned good at what you do!"

"You're either juiced or sick. What are you talking about?"

"This *room,* your note! *Everything!* That *name!* Is this whole goddamned night a setup?"

"It's morning, young man, and if you don't like this room you can stay wherever you like as far as I'm concerned."

"Wherever . . . ?" Joel tried to evade the blinding flashes of light from the Quai du Mont Blanc and clear the searing blockage in his throat. "No . . . I *came* here," he said hoarsely. "There's no way you could have known I'd do that. In Copenhagen, on the plane . . . I got the last ticket in first class; the seat next to me had been sold, an aisle seat."

"That's where I always sit. On the aisle."

"Oh, *Jesus!*"

"Now you're rambling." Dowling glanced at the empty glass on the bedside table, then over at the bureau top where there was a silver tray and a bottle of Scotch whisky provided by an accommodating desk clerk. "How much sauce have you had?"

Converse shook his head. "I'm not drunk. . . . I'm sorry. Christ, I'm sorry! You had nothing to do with it. They're using you—trying to use you to find me! You *saved my* . . . my job . . . and I went after you. Forgive me."

"And you don't look like someone who's that worried about a job," said the actor, his scowl more one of concern than anger.

"It's not the employment, it's . . . pulling it off." Joel silently took a deep breath to control himself, postponing the moment when he would have to confront the awesome implications of what he had just heard. *Avery Fowler!* "I want to

238

succeed in what I'm doing; I want to win,'' he added limply, hoping to conceal the slip he saw Dowling had spotted. ''All lawyers want to win.''

''Sure.''

''I *am* sorry, Cal.''

''Forget it,'' said the actor, his voice casual, his look not casual at all. ''Where I'm at these days screeching's an hourly occurrence—only, they don't say anything. I think you just did.''

''No, I overreacted, that's all. I told you I was new at this. Not the law, just this . . . not talking directly, I guess says it.''

''Does it?''

''Yes. Please believe that.''

''All right, if you want me to.'' Dowling again looked at his watch. ''I've got to go, but there's something else that might be helpful in saving that''—the actor paused convincingly—''job of yours.''

''What is it?'' asked Converse tightly, trying not to leap at the question.

''As this Fowler was leaving I had a couple of thoughts. One was that I'd been pretty hard on a fellow who was simply doing *his* job, and the other was just plain selfish. I hadn't cooperated, and that could come back and snap me in the ass. Of course if you never showed up here, I'd get my note back and it wouldn't matter. But if you did, and you wore a black hat, my tail could be in a bucket of boiling lead.''

''That should have been your first concern,'' said Joel truthfully.

''Maybe it was, I don't know. At any rate, I told him that in the course of our conversation I

239

asked you for drinks, to come out on location if you wanted to. He seemed puzzled at the last part, but he understood the first. I asked whether I should call him at the embassy if you took me up on either invitation, and he said no, I shouldn't do that."

"What?"

"In short words, he made it very plain that my calling him would only louse up this 'in-house query.' He told me to wait for *his* call. He'd phone me around noon."

"But you're filming. You're on location."

"That's the beauty part, but the hell with it. There are mobile telephone hookups; the studios insist on them these days. It's another kind of screeching called budgetary controls. We get our calls."

"You're losing me."

"Then find me. When he calls me, I'll call *you*. Should I tell him you reached me?"

Surprised, Converse stared at the aging actor, the risk-taker. "You're way ahead of me, aren't you?"

"You're pretty obvious. So was he, when I put it together—which I just did. This Fowler wants to reach you, but he wants to do it solo, away from those people you don't want to meet. You see, when he was at the door and we had our last words, I was bothered by something. He couldn't sustain the role—any more than you did on the plane—but I couldn't be certain. He kind of fell apart on his exit, and that you never do even if you've got to hold in a sudden attack of diarrhea. . . . What do I tell him, Joe?"

240

"Get his telephone number, I guess."

"Done. You get some sleep. You look like a coked-up starlet who's just been told she's going to play Medea."

"I'll try."

Dowling reached into his pocket and took out a scrap of paper. "Here," he said approaching Converse and handing it to him. "I wasn't sure I was going to give this to you, but I damn well want you to have it now. It's the mobile number where you can reach me. Call me after you've talked to this Fowler. I'm going to be a nervous wreck until I hear from you."

"I give you my word. . . . Cal, what did you mean when you mentioned 'the beauty part' and forgetting about it?"

The actor's head shifted back in perfect precision, at just the right angle for anyone in the audience. "The son of a bitch asked me what I did for a living. . . . As they say in the Polo Lounge, *Ciao,* baby."

Converse sat on the edge of the bed, his head pounding, his body tense. Avery Fowler! *Jesus!* Avery Preston Fowler *Halliday! Press* Fowler . . . *Press Halliday!* The names bombarded him, piercing his temples and bouncing off the walls of his mind, screaming echoes everywhere. He could not control the assault; he began to sway back and forth, his arms supporting him, a strange rhythm emerging, the beat accompanying the name—names—of the man who had died in his arms in Geneva. A man he had known as a boy, the adult a stranger who had manipulated him

241

into the world of George Marcus Delavane and a spreading disease called Aquitaine.

This Fowler wants to reach you, but he wants to do it solo, away from those people you don't want to meet. . . . The judgment of a risk-taker.

Converse stopped rocking, his eyes on the Leifhelm dossier on the floor. He had assumed the worst because it was beyond his comprehension, but there was an alternative, an outside possibility, perhaps under the circumstances even a probability. The geometrics were there; he could not trace them but they *were there!* The name Avery Fowler meant nothing to anyone but him—at least not in Bonn, not as it pertained to a murder in Geneva. Was Dowling right? Joel had asked the actor to get the man's telephone number, but without conviction. The image of a dark-red limousine driving through the embassy's gates would not leave him. *That* was the connection that had enveloped the shock of Avery Fowler's name. The man using it was from the embassy, and at least part of the embassy was part of Aquitaine, therefore the impostor was part of the trap. That was the logic; it was simple arithmetic . . . but it was not geometry. Suppose there was a break in the line, an insertion from another plane that voided the arithmetic progression? If there was, it was in the form of an explanation he could not possibly perceive unless it was given to him.

The shock was receding; he was finding his equilibrium again. As he had done so many times in courtrooms and boardrooms, he began to accept the totally unexpected, knowing he could do nothing about it until something else happened, something over which he had no control. The most difficult part of the process was forcing himself to function until it *did* happen, whatever it was. Conjecture was futile; all the probabilities were beyond his understanding.

He reached down for the Leifhelm dossier.

Erich Leifhelm's years with the Bundesgrenzschutz were unique and require a word about the organization itself. In the aftermath of all wars, a subjugated national police force is required in an occupied country for reasons ranging from the simple language problem to the occupying power's need to understand local customs and traditions. There must be a buffer between the occupation troops and a vanquished people so as to maintain order. There is also a side issue rarely elaborated upon or analyzed in the history books, but no less important for that lack. Defeated armies can still possess talent, and unless that talent is utilized the humiliation of defeat can ferment, at minimum distilling itself into hostilities that are counterproductive to a stabilized political climate, or, at maximum, turning into internal subversion that can lead to violence and bloodshed at the expense of the victors and whatever new government that is being formed. To put it bluntly, the Allied General Staff recognized that it had on its hands another brilliant and popular military man who would not suffer the anonymity of early retirement or a corporate boardroom. The

Bundesgrenzschutz—literally, federal border police—like all police organizations, was and is a paramilitary force, and as such the logical repository for men like Erich Leifhelm. They were the leaders; better to use them than be abused by them. And as always among leaders, there are those few who surge forward, leading the pack. During these years foremost among those few was Erich Leifhelm.

His early work with the Grenzschutz was that of a military consultant during the massive German demobilization, then afterward the chief liaison between the police garrisons and the Allied occupation forces. Following demobilization, his duties were mainly concentrated in the trouble spots of Vienna and Berlin where he was in constant touch with the commanders of the American, British and French sectors. His zealous anti-Soviet feelings were rapidly made known by Leifhelm throughout the command centers and duly noted by the senior officers. More and more he was taken into their confidence until—as it had happened before with the Prussians—he was literally considered one of them.

It was in Berlin where Leifhelm first came in contact with General Jacques-Louis Bertholdier. A strong friendship developed, but it was not an association either one cared to parade because of the age-old animosities between the German and French militaries. We were able to trace only three former officers from Bertholdier's command post who remembered—or would speak of—seeing the two men frequently at dinner together in out-of-the-way restaurants and cafés, deep in conversation, obviously comfortable with each other. Yet during those occasions when Leifhelm was summoned to French head-quarters in Berlin, the formalities were icily proper, with names rarely used and certainly never first names, only ranks and titles. In recent years, as noted above, both men have denied knowing each other personally, albeit admitting their paths may have crossed.

Where previously acknowledgment of their friendship was discouraged because of traditional prejudices, the current reasons are far more understandable. Both are spearheads in the Delavane organization. The names on the primary list are there with good reason. They are influential men who sit on the boards of multinational corporations that deal in products and technology ranging from the building of dams to the construction of nuclear plants; in between are a hundred likely subsidiaries throughout Europe and Africa which could easily expedite sales of armaments. As detailed in the following pages, it can be assumed that Leifhelm and Bertholdier communicate through a woman named Ilse Fishbein in Bonn. Fishbein is her married name, the marriage itself questionable in terms of motive insofar as it was dissolved years ago when Yakov Fishbein, a survivor of the camps, emigrated to Israel. Frau Fishbein, born in 1942, is the youngest illegitimate daughter of Hermann Göring.

Converse put down the dossier and reached for a memo pad next to the telephone on the bedside table. He then unclipped from his shirt pocket the gold Cartier ball-point pen Val had given him years ago and wrote down the name Ilse Fishbein. He studied both the pen and the name. The Cartier status symbol was a remembrance of better days—no, not really better, but at least more complete. Valerie, at his insistence, had finally quit the New York advertising agency, with its insane hours, and gone free-lance. On her last day of formal work, she had walked across town to Cartier and spent a considerable portion of her last paycheck for his gift. When he asked her what he had done outside of his meteoric rise in Talbot, Brooks and Simon to deserve a gift of such impractical opulence, she had replied: "For making me do what I should have done a long time ago. On the other hand, if free-lancing doesn't pay off, I'll steal it back and pawn it. . . . What the hell, you'll probably lose it."

Free-lancing had paid off very well, indeed, and he had never lost the pen.

Ilse Fishbein gave rise to another kind of thought. As much as he would like to confront her, it was out of the question. Whatever Erich Leifhelm knew had been provided by Bertholdier in Paris and relayed by Frau Fishbein here in Bonn. And the communication obviously contained a detailed description as well as a warning; the American was dangerous. Ilse Fishbein, as a trusted confidante in Aquitaine, could undoubtedly lead him to others in Germany who were part of Delavane's network, but to approach her was to ask for his own . . . whatever it was they intended for him at the moment, and he was not ready for that. Still, it was a name, a piece of information, a fact he was not expected to have, and experience had taught him to keep such details up front and reveal them, spring them quietly when the moment was right. Or use them himself when no one was looking. He was a lawyer, and the ways of adversary law were labyrinthine; whatever was withheld was no-man's-land. On either side; to the more patient, the spoils.

Yet the temptation was so damned inviting. The bloodline of Hermann Göring involved with the contemplated resurrection of the generals! In *Germany*. Ilse Fishbein could be an immediate means of unlocking a floodgate of unwanted memories. He held in his hand a spiked club; the moment would come when he would swing it.

Leifhelm's commanding duties in the field with the West German NATO divisions lasted seventeen years, whereupon he was elevated to SHAPE headquarters, near Brussels, as military spokesman for Bonn's interests.

Again his tenure was marked by extreme anti-Soviet postures, frequently at odds with his own government's pragmatic approach to coexistence with the Kremlin, and throughout his final months at SHAPE he was more often appreciated by the Anglo-American right-wing factions than by the political leadership in Bonn.

It was only when the chancellor of the Federal Republic concluded that American foreign policy in the early eighties had been taken out of the hands of professionals and usurped by bellicose ideologues that he ordered Leifhelm home and created an innocuous post for the soldier to keep him at bay.

Leifhelm, however, had never been a gullible fool, nor was he one now in his new, improvised status. He understood why the politicians had created it—it showed recognition of his own subtle strengths. People everywhere were looking to the past, to men who spoke clearly, with candor, and did not obfuscate the problems facing their countries and the world, especially the Western world.

So he began to speak. At first to veterans' groups and splinter organizations where military pasts and long-established partisan politics guaranteed him a favorable reception. Spurred by the enthusiastic responses he evoked, Leifhelm began to expand, seeking larger audiences, his positions becoming more strident, his statements more provocative.

One man listened and was furious. The chancellor learned that Leifhelm had carried his quasi-politicking into the Bundestag itself, implying a constituency far beyond what he really had, but by the sheer force of his personality swaying members who should not have been swayed. Leifhelm's message came back to the chancellor: an enlarged army in far greater numbers than the NATO commitments; an intelligence service patterned after the once extraordinary Abwehr; a general revamping of textbooks, deleting injurious and slanderous materials; rehabilitation camps for political troublemakers and subversives pretending to be "liberal thinkers." It was all there.

The chancellor had had enough. He summoned Leifhelm to his office, where he demanded his resignation in the presence of three witnesses. Further, he ordered Leifhelm to remove himself from all aspects of German politics, to accept no further speaking engagements, and to lend neither his name nor his presence to any cause whatsoever. He was to retire totally from public life. We have reached one of those witnesses whose name is not pertinent to this report. The following is his recollection:

The chancellor was furious. He said to Leifhelm: "Herr General, you have two choices, and, if you'll forgive me, a final solution. Number one, you may do as I say. Or you can be stripped of your rank and all pensions and financial accruals afforded therein, as well as the income from some rather valuable real estate in Munich, which in the opinion of any enlightened court would be taken from you instantly. That is your second choice."

I tell you, the field marshal was apoplectic! He demanded his rights, as he called them, and the chancellor shouted, "You've had your rights, and they were wrong! They're still wrong!" Then Leifhelm asked what the final solution was, and I swear to you, as crazy as it sounds, the chancellor opened a drawer of his desk, took out a pistol, and aimed it at Leifhelm. "I, myself, will kill you right now," he said. "You will not, I repeat, *not* take us back."

I thought for a moment that the old soldier was going to rush forward and accept the bullet, but he didn't. He stood there staring at the chancellor, such hatred in his eyes, matched by the statesman's cold appraisal. Then Leifhelm did a stupid thing. He shot his arm forward—not at the chancellor, but away from him—and cried *"Heil Hitler."* Then he turned in military fashion and walked out the door.

We were all silent for a moment or two, until the chancellor broke the silence. "I should have killed him," he said. "I may regret it. We may all regret it."

Five days after this confrontation, Jacques-Louis Bertholdier made the first of his two trips to Bonn following his retirement. On his initial visit he stayed at the Schlosspark Hotel, and as hotel records are kept for a period of three years, we were able to obtain copies of his billing charges. There were numerous calls to various firms doing business with Juneau et Cie, too numerous to examine individually, but one number kept being repeated, the name having no apparent business connections with Bertholdier or his company. It was Ilse Fishbein. However, upon checking Erich Leifhelm's telephone bills for the dates in question, it was found that he, too, had placed calls to Ilse Fishbein, identical in number with those placed by Bertholdier. Inquiries and brief surveillance further established that Frau Fishbein and Leifhelm have known each other for a number of years. The conclusion is apparent: she is the conduit between Paris and Bonn in Delavane's apparatus.

Converse lit a cigarette. There was the name again, the temptation again. Ilse Fishbein could be the shortcut. Threatened with exposure, this daughter of Hermann Göring could reveal a great deal. She could confirm that she was not only the liaison between Leifhelm and Bertholdier but conceivably much more, for the two ex-generals had to transmit information to each other. The names of companies, of buried subsidiaries, and of firms doing business related to Delavane in Palo Alto might surface, names he could pursue legally, looking for the illegalities that had to be there. If there only was a way to make his presence felt but not seen.

An intermediary. He had used intermediaries in the past, often enough to know the value of the procedure. It was relatively simple. He would approach a third party to make contact with an adversary carrying information that could be of value to him insofar as it might be deemed damaging to his interests, and if the facts presented were strong enough, an equitable solution was usually forthcoming. The ethics was questionable, but contrary to accepted belief, ethics was in three dimensions, if not four. The end did not justify the means, but justifiable means that brought about a fair and necessary conclusion were not to be dismissed.

And nothing could be fairer or more necessary than the dismantling of Aquitaine. Old Beale was right that night on the moonlit beach on Mykonos. His client was not an unknown man in San Francisco but instead a large part of this so-called civilized world. Aquitaine had to be stopped, aborted.

An intermediary? It was another question he would put off until the morning. He picked up the dossier, his eyes heavy.

Leifhelm has few intimate friends that appear to be constant, probably because of his awareness that he is under watch by the government. He sits on the boards of several prominent corporations, which have stated frankly that his name justifies his stipend. . . .

Joel's head fell forward. He snapped it back, widened his eyes, and scanned the final pages rapidly, absorbing only the general impressions; his concentration was waning. There was mention of several restaurants, the names meaningless; a marriage during the war that ended when Leifhelm's wife disappeared in November of '43, presumed killed in a Berlin bombing raid; no subsequent wife or wives. His private life was extraordinarily private, if not austere; the exception here was his proclivity for small dinner parties, the guest lists always varied, again names, again meaningless. The address of his residence on the outskirts of Bad Godesberg. . . . Suddenly

Converse's neck stiffened, his eyes fully alert.

The house is in the remote countryside, on the Rhine River and far from any shopping areas or suburban concentration. The grounds are fenced and guarded by attack dogs who bark viciously at all approaching vehicles except Leifhelm's dark-red Mercedes limousine.

A dark-red Mercedes! It was Leifhelm himself who had been at the airport! Leifhelm who had driven directly to the embassy! How could it happen? *How?*

It was too much to absorb, too far beyond his understanding. The darkness was closing in, Joel's brain telling him it could no longer accept further input; it simply could not function. The dossier fell to his side; he closed his eyes and slept.

He was plunging headlong down through a cavernous hole in the earth, jagged black rocks on all sides, infinite darkness below. The walls of irregular stone kept screaming in frenzy, screeching at him like descending layers of misshapen gargoyles with sharp beaks and raised claws lunging at his flesh. The hysterical clamor was unbearable. Where had the silence gone? Why was he falling into black nothingness?

He flashed his eyes open; his forehead was drenched with sweat, his breath coming in gasps. The telephone by his head was ringing, the erratic bell jarringly dissonant. He tried to shake the sleep and the fear from his semiconsciousness; he reached for the blaring instrument, glancing at his watch as he did so. It was twelve-fifteen, a quarter past noon, the sun streaking through the hotel window. Blinding.

"Yes? Hello . . . ?"

"Joe? *Joel?*"

"Yes."

"It's Cal Dowling. Our boy called."

"What? Who?"

"This Fowler. Avery Fowler."

"Oh, *Jesus!*" It was coming back, it was *all* coming back. He was seated at a table in the Chat Botté on the Quai du Mont Blanc, flashes of sunlight bouncing off the grillwork on the lakeside boulevard. No . . . he was not in Geneva. He was in a hotel room in Bonn, and only hours ago he had been plunged into madness by that name. "Yes," he choked, catching his breath. "Did you get a telephone number?"

"He said there wasn't time for games, and besides, he doesn't have one. You're to meet him at the east wall of the Alter Zoll as fast as you can get there. Just walk around; he'll find you."

"That's not *good* enough!" cried Converse. "Not after Paris! Not after the airport last night! I'm not stupid!"

"I didn't get the impression he thought you were," replied the actor. "He told me to tell you something; he thought it might convince you."

"What is it?"

"I hope I get this right; I don't even like saying it. . . . He said to tell you a judge named Anstett was killed last night in New York. He thinks you're being cut loose."

The Alter Zoll, the ancient tower that had once been part of Bonn's southern fortress on the Rhine—razed to the ground three centuries ago—was now a tollhouse standing on a green lawn dotted with antique cannons, relics of a might that had slipped away through the squabblings of emperors and kings, priests and princes. A winding mosaic wall of red and gray stone overlooked the massive river below where boats of various descriptions plowed furrows in the open water, caressing the shorelines on both sides, diligent and somber in their appointed rounds; no Lake Geneva here, far less the blue-green waters of the mischievous Como. Yet in the distance was a sight envied by people the world over: the Siebengebirge, the seven mountains of Wester-wald, magnificent in their intrusions on the skyline.

Joel stood by the low wall, trying to focus on the view, hoping it would calm him, but the exercise was futile. The beauty before him was lost, it would not distract him from his thoughts; nothing could. . . . Lucas Anstett, Second Circuit Court of Appeals, judge extraordinary and intermediary between one Joel Converse and his employers and an unknown man in San Francisco. Outside of that unknown man and a retired scholar on the island of Mykonos, the only other person who knew what he was doing and why. How in the space of eighteen hours or less could he have been *found?* Found and killed!

"Converse?"

Joel turned, whipping his head over his shoulder, his body rigid. Standing twenty feet away on the far edge of a graveled path was a sandy-haired man several years younger than Converse, in his early to mid thirties; his was a boyish face that would grow old slowly and remain young long after its time. He was also shorter than Joel, but not by much—perhaps five ten or eleven—and dressed in light-gray trousers and a cord jacket, his white shirt open at the neck.

"Who are you?" asked Converse hoarsely.

A couple strolled between them on the path as the younger man jerked his head to his left, gesturing for Joel to follow him onto the lawn beyond. Converse did so, joining him by the huge iron wheel of a bronze cannon.

"All right, who are you?" repeated Joel.

"My sister's name is Meagen," said the sandy-haired man. "And so neither one of us makes a mistake, you tell me who I am."

"How the *hell. . .?*" Converse stopped, the words coming back to him, words whispered by a dying man in Geneva. *Oh, Christ! Meg, the kids . . .* " 'Meg, the kids,' " he said out loud. "Fowler called his wife Meg."

"Short for Meagen, and she was Halliday's wife—only, you knew him as Fowler."

"You're Avery's brother-in-law."

"Press's brother-in-law," corrected the man,

256

extending his hand. "Connal Fitzpatrick," he added.

"Then we're on the same side."

"I hope so."

"I've got a lot of questions to ask you, Connal."

"No more than I've got for you, Converse."

"Are we going to start off belligerently?" asked Joel, noting the harsh use of his own last name and releasing Fitzpatrick's hand.

The younger man blinked, then reddened, embarrassed. "Sorry," he said. "I'm one angry brother—on both sides—and I haven't had much sleep. I'm still on San Diego time."

"San Diego? Not San Francisco?"

"Navy. I'm a lawyer stationed at the naval base there."

"Whew," whistled Converse softly. "It's a small world."

"I know all about the geography," agreed Fitzpatrick. "And also you, Lieutenant. How do you think Press got his information? Of course, I wasn't in San Diego then, but I had friends."

"Nothing's sacred, then."

"You're wrong; everything is. I had to pull some very thick strings to get that stuff. It was about five months ago when Press came to me and we made our . . . I guess you'd call it the contract between us."

"Clarification, please."

The naval officer placed a hand on the barrel of the cannon. "Press Halliday wasn't just my brother-in-law, he came to be my best friend, closer than any blood brother, I think."

"And you with the militaristic hordes?" asked Joel, only half joking, a point of information on the line.

Fitzpatrick smiled awkwardly, boyishly. "That's part of it, actually. He stood by me when I wanted to go for it. The services need lawyers too, but the law schools don't tell you much about that. It's not where they're going to get any endowments from. Me, I happen to like the Navy, and I like the life—and the challenges, I guess you'd call them."

"Who objected?"

"Who didn't? In both our families the pirates—who go back to skimming the earthquake victims—have always been attorneys. The two current old men knew Press and I got along and saw the writing they wrote on their own wall. Here's this sharp Wasp and this good Catholic boy; now, if they ring in a Jew and a light-skinned black and maybe even a not-too-offensive gay, they've got half the legal market in San Francisco in their back pockets."

"What about the Chinese and the Italians?"

"Certain country clubs still have remnants of the old school ties in their lockers. Why soil the fabric? Deals are made on the fairways, the accent on 'ways,' not 'fair.' "

"And you didn't want anything to do with that, counselor?"

"Neither did Press, that's why he went international. Old Jack Halliday pissed bright red when Press began corraling all those foreign clients; then purple when he added a lot of U.S. sharks who wanted to operate overseas. But old

Jack couldn't complain; his wild-eyed stepson was adding considerably to the bottom line."

"And you went happily into uniform," said Converse, watching Fitzpatrick's eyes, impressed by the candor he saw in them.

"*Back* into uniform, and very happy—with Press's blessings, legal and otherwise."

"You were fond of him, weren't you?"

Connal lifted his hand off the cannon. "I loved him, Converse. Just as I love my sister. That's why I'm here. That's the contract."

"Incidentally," said Joel kindly, "speaking of your sister, even if I were somebody else I could easily have found out her name was Meagan."

"I'm sure you could have; it was in the papers."

"Then it wasn't much of a test."

"Press never called her Meagen in his life, except for that one phrase in the wedding ceremony. It was always 'Meg.' I would have asked you about that somehow, and if you were lying I'd have known it. I'm very good on direct."

"I believe you. What's the contract between you and . . . Press?"

"Let's walk," said Fitzpatrick, and as they strolled toward the wall with the winding river below and the seven mountains of Westerwald in the distance, Connal began. "Press came to me and said he was into something pretty heavy and he couldn't let it go. He'd come across information that tied a number of well-known men—or once well-known men—together in an organization that could do a lot of harm to a lot of people in a lot of countries. He was going to stop it, stop them, but he had to go outside the usual courtroom ballparks to do it—do it legally.

"I asked the normal questions: Was he involved, culpable, that sort of thing, and he said no, not in any indictable sense, but he couldn't be sure whether or not he was entirely safe. Naturally, I said he was crazy; he should take his information to the authorities and let them handle it."

"Which is exactly what I told him," interrupted Converse.

Fitzpatrick stopped walking and turned to Joel. "He said it was more complicated than that."

"He was right."

"I find that hard to believe."

"He's dead. Believe it."

"That's no answer!"

"You didn't ask a question," said Converse. "Let's walk. Go on. Your contract."

Bewilderment on his face, the naval officer began. "It was very simple," he continued. "He told me he would keep me up to date whenever he traveled, letting me know if he was seeing anyone related to his major concern—that's what we called it, his 'major concern.' Also anything else that could be helpful if . . . if . . . goddamn it, *if!*"

"If what?"

Fitzpatrick stopped again, his voice harsh. "If anything *happened* to him!"

Converse let the emotion of the moment pass. "And he told you he was going to Geneva to see me. The man who knew Avery Preston Fowler

260

Halliday as Avery Fowler roughly twenty-odd years ago in school.''

"Yes. We'd been over that before when I got him the security material on you. He said the time was right, the circumstances right. By the way, he thought you were the best.'' Connal permitted himself a brief uncomfortable smile. "Almost as good as he was.''

"I wasn't,'' said Joel, a half-smile returned. "I'm still trying to figure out his position on some Class B stock in the merger.''

"What?''

"Nothing. What about Lucas Anstett? I want to hear about that.''

"It's in two parts. Press said they'd worked through the judge to spring you if you'd agree to take on the—''

"They? Who's they?''

"I don't know. He never told me.''

"Goddamn it! Sorry, go ahead.''

"That Anstett had talked to your firm's senior partners and they said okay if you said okay. That's part one. Part two is a personal idiosyncrasy; I'm a news freak, and like most of my ilk, I'm tuned into the hourly AFR.''

"Clarification.''

"Armed Forces Radio. Oddly enough, it's probably got the best news coverage on the air; it pools all the networks. I have one of those small transistorized jobs with a couple of shortwave bands I pack when I'm traveling.''

"I used to do that,'' said Converse. "For the BBC, mainly because I don't speak French—or anything else for that matter.''

"They've got good coverage, but they shift bands too much. Anyway, I had AFR on early this morning and heard the story, such as it was."

"What was it?"

"Short on details. His apartment on Central Park South was broken into around two in the morning, New York time. There were signs of a struggle and he was shot in the head."

"That's it?"

"Not quite. According to a housekeeper, nothing was taken, so robbery was ruled out. *That's* it."

"*Jesus.* I'll call Larry Talbot. He may have more information. There wasn't anything else?"

"Only a quick sketch of a brilliant jurist. The point is, nothing was *taken.*"

"I understand that," broke in Joel. "I'll talk to Talbot." They started walking again, south along the wall. "Last night," continued Converse, "why did you tell Dowling you were an embassy man? You must have been at the airport."

"I'd been at that airport for seven hours going from counter to counter asking for passenger information, trying to find out what plane you were on."

"You knew I was on my way to Bonn?"

"Beale thought you were."

"*Beale?*" asked Joel, startled. "Mykonos?"

"Press gave me his name and the number but said I wasn't to use either unless the worst happened." Fitzpatrick paused. "The worst happened," he added.

"What did Beale tell you?"

"That you went to Paris, and as he understood

it, you were going to Bonn next."

"What else?"

"Nothing. He said he accepted my credentials, as he called them, because I had his name and knew how to reach him; only Press could have given me that information. But anything else I'd have to learn from you, if you felt there was something to tell me. He was pretty damned cold."

"He had no choice."

"Although he did say that in case I couldn't find you, he wanted to see me on Mykonos before I began raising my voice . . . 'for everything Mr. Halliday stood for.' That's the way he put it. I was going to give you two more days to get here, if I could hold up."

"Then what? Mykonos?"

"I'm not sure. I figured I'd call Beale again, but he'd have to tell me a lot more than he did to convince me."

"And if he didn't? Or couldn't?"

"Then I'd have flown straight to Washington and gone to whomever the top floor of the Navy Department suggested. If you think for one goddamned minute I'm going to let this thing pass for what it isn't, you're wrong and so is Beale."

"If you'd have made that clear to him, he would have come up with something. You'd have gone to Mykonos." Converse reached into his shirt pocket for his cigarettes; he offered one to Fitzpatrick, who shook his head. "Avery didn't smoke either," said Joel aimlessly as he snapped his lighter. "Sorry . . . Press." He inhaled.

"It's okay; that name's how I got you to see me."

"Let's go back to that a minute. There's a slight inconsistency in your testimony, counselor. Let's clear it up—just so neither one of us makes a mistake."

"I don't know what you think you're crowding in on, but go ahead."

"You said you were going to give me two more days to get here, is that right?"

"Yes, if I could make arrangements, get some sleep and hold up."

"How did you know I didn't get here two days *before* you did?"

Fitzpatrick glanced at Joel. "I've been a legal officer in the Navy for the past eight years, both as defense counsel and as judge advocate in any number of situations—not always courts-martial. They've taken me to most of the countries where Washington has reciprocal legal agreements."

"That's a mouthful, but I'm not in the Navy."

"You were, but I wasn't going to use it if I didn't have to, and I didn't. I flew into Düsseldorf, showed my naval papers to the *Inspektor* of immigration, and asked for his cooperation. There are seven international airports in West Germany. It took roughly five minutes with the computers to find out that you hadn't entered any of them during the past *three* days, which was all I was concerned about."

"But then you had to get to Cologne-Bonn."

"I was there in forty minutes and called him back. No Converse had been admitted, and unless you were crossing the border incognito—which I suspect I know more about than you do—you had to fly in sooner or later."

"You're tenacious."

"I've given you my reasons."

"What about Dowling and that embassy routine at the hotel."

"Lufthansa had you listed on the passenger manifest from Hamburg—you'll never know how relieved I was. I hung around the counter in case there was a delay or anything like that when these three embassy guys showed up flashing their ID's, the head man speaking rotten German."

"You could tell?"

"I speak German—and French, Italian, and Spanish. I have to deal with different nationalities."

"I'll let that pass."

"I suppose that's why I'm a lieutenant commander at thirty-four. They move me around a lot."

"Pass again. What caught you about the embassy people?"

"Your name, naturally. They wanted confirmation that you were on flight Eight-seventeen. The clerk sort of glanced at me and I shook my head; he cooperated without a break in his conversation. You see, I'd given him a few deutsche marks but that wasn't it. These people don't really dig the official U.S. over here."

"I heard that last night. From Dowling. How did he come up?"

"Dowling himself, but later. When the plane arrived I stood at the rear of the baggage claim; the embassy boys were by the entrance to the gates about fifty feet away. We all waited until there was only one piece of luggage on the conveyor belt. It was yours, but you never showed up. Finally a woman came out and the embassy contingent surrounded her, everyone excited, upset. I heard your name mentioned, but that's all I heard because by that time I had decided to go back and speak to the clerk."

"To see if I'd really been on the plane?" asked Converse. "Or whether I turned out to be a no-show."

"Yes," agreed Fitzpatrick. "He was cute; he made me feel like I was suborning a juror. I paid him, and he told me this Caleb Dowling—whom I think I was expected to know—had stopped at the desk before going out to the platform."

"Where he left instructions," said Joel, interrupting quietly.

"How did you know?"

"I picked up a set at the hotel."

"That was it, the *hotel*. Dowling told him he'd met this lawyer on the plane, a fellow American named Converse who'd sat with him since Copenhagen. He was worried that his new friend might not have accommodations in Bonn, and if he asked Lufthansa for suggestions, the clerk should send him to the Königshof Hotel."

"So you totaled up the figures and decided to become one of the embassy people who'd lost me," said Converse, smiling. "To confront Dowling. Who among us hasn't taken advantage of a hostile witness?"

"Exactly. I showed him my naval ID and told

him I was an attaché. Frankly, he wasn't very cooperative."

"And you weren't very convincing, according to his theatrical critique. Neither was I. Strangely enough, that's why he got us together." Joel stopped, crushed out his cigarette against the wall and threw it over the stone. "All right, Commander, you've passed muster or roster or whatever the hell you call it. Where do we stand? You speak the language and you've got government connections I don't have. You could help."

The naval officer stood motionless; he looked hard at Joel, his eyes blinking in the glare of the sunlight, but not from any lack of concentration. "I'll do whatever I can," he began slowly, "as long as it makes sense to me. But you and I have to understand each other, Converse. I'm not backing away from the two days. That's all you've got—*we've* got if I come on board."

"Who made the deadline?"

"I did. I do now."

"It can't work that way."

"Who says?"

"I did. I do now." Converse started walking along the wall.

"You're in Bonn," said Fitzpatrick, catching up, neither impatience nor supplication in his gait or in his voice, only control. "You've been to Paris and you came to *Bonn.* That means you have names, areas of evidence, both concrete or hearsay. I want it all."

"You'll have to do better than that, Commander."

"I made a *promise.*"

267

"To whom?"

"My sister! You think she doesn't know? It was tearing Press apart! For a whole goddamned year he'd get up in the middle of the night and wander around the house, talking to himself but shutting her out. He was obsessed and she couldn't crack the shell. You'd have to know them to appreciate this, but they were good, I mean *good* together. I know it's not very fashionable these days to have two people with a passel of kids who really like each other, who can't wait to be with each other when they're apart, but that's the way they were."

"Are you married?" asked Joel without breaking his stride.

"No," answered the Navy man, obviously confused by the question. "I expect to be. Perhaps. I told you, I move around a lot."

"So did Press . . . Avery."

"What's your point, *counselor?*"

"Respect what he was doing. He knew the dangers and he understood what he could lose. His life."

"That's why I want the facts! His body was flown back yesterday. The funeral's tomorrow and I'm not there because I gave Meagen a promise! I'm coming back too, but with everything I need to blow this whole fucking thing apart!"

"You'll only *implode* it, sending it way down deep if you're not stopped before that."

"That's *your* judgment."

"It's all I've got."

"I don't buy it!"

"Don't. Go back and talk about rumors, about a killing in Geneva that nobody will admit was anything but a robbery, or a murder in New York that remains and probably will remain something it wasn't. If you mention a man on Mykonos, believe me, he'll disappear. Where are you, Commander? Are you just a freak, after all, a philosophical blood brother of Press Halliday who stormed the Presidio and burned his draft card in the good old days of muscatel and grass?"

"That's a crock of shit!"

"It's on the record, Commander. By the way, as a judge advocate, how many officers did you prosecute?"

"What?"

"And as defense counsel, how many cases did you lose?"

"I've had my share of wins and losses, mostly wins, frankly."

"Mostly? Frankly? You know there are certain people who can take fifteen numbers, insert what they call variables, and make the statistics say anything they want them to say."

"What's that got to do with anything? How is it connected to Press's death, his *murder?*"

"Oh, you'd be surprised, Commander Fitzpatrick. Beneath that brass could be a very successful infiltrator, perhaps even an agent provocateur in a uniform you shouldn't be wearing."

"What the *hell* are you talking about? . . . Forget it, I don't want to know. I don't have to listen to you, but you have to listen to me! You've got two days, Converse. Am I on board or not?"

Joel stopped and studied the intense young face beside him—young and not so young, there were hints of creases around the angry eyes. "You're not even in the same fleet," said Converse wearily. "Old Beale was right. It's my decision and I choose to tell you nothing. I don't want you on board, sailor. You're a hotheaded piss ant and you bore me."

Joel turned and walked away.

"All right, *cut!* That's a print! Nice work, Cal, I almost believed that drivel." The director, Roger Blynn, checked the clipboard thrust in front of him by a script girl and issued instructions to the camera crew's interpreter before heading over to the production table.

Caleb Dowling remained seated on the large rock on the slope of the hill above the Rhine; he patted the head of an odoriferous goat, which had just defecated on the toe of his boot. "I'd like to kick the rest of the shit out of you, li'l partner," he said quietly, "but it wouldn't fit my well-developed image."

The actor got up and stretched, aware that the onlookers beyond the roped-off set were staring at him, chattering away like tourists in a zoo. In a few minutes he would walk over—no, not walk, amble over—and pull the rope off the carriage of an arc light so he could mingle with the fans. He never tired of it, probably because it came so late in his life and was, after all, symbolic of what he and his wife currently could afford. Also every now and then there was a bonus: the appearance of one of his former students, who usually

270

approached him cautiously, obviously wondering if the good-natured rapport he had established in the classroom had survived the onslaught of national recognition or been drowned in the tidal wave of so-called stardom. Cal was good at remembering faces, and not too bad with at least one of a person's two names, so when these occasions arose, he invariably would eye his former charge and ask him if he had completed yesterday's assignment. Or would walk up to him—or her—and pedagogically inquire something like "Of the chronicles Shakespeare drew from for his histories, which had the greatest impact on his language, Daniel, Holinshed, or Froissart?" If the answer came back naming the last, he would slap his thigh and exclaim words akin to "Hot damn, li'l wrangler, you busted a tough bronc there!" Laughter would follow, and frequently drinks and reminiscences later.

It was a good life these days, almost perfect. If only some sunlight would reach into the painfully dark corners of his wife's mind. If it could, she'd be here on a hillside in Bonn chatting in her quietly vivacious way with the people beyond the rope—mostly women, mostly those around her age—telling them that her husband was really quite like their own. He never picked up his socks and was a disaster in the kitchen; people liked to hear that even if they didn't believe it. But the sunlight did not reach those far, dark corners. Instead, his Frieda remained in Copenhagen, walking along the beaches of Sjaelland Island, having tea in the botanical gardens, and waiting for a call from her husband saying that he had a few days off and would come out of hated Germany. Dowling looked around at the efficient, enthusiastic crew and the curious spectators; laughter punctuated their conversations, a certain respect as well. These were not hateful people.

"Cal?" the voice belonged to Blynn, the film's director, who was walking rapidly across the slope of the hill. "There's someone here to see you."

"I hope more than one, Roger. Otherwise the men who go under the dubious title of our employers are grossly overpaying me."

"Not for this pile of kitsch." The director's smile disappeared, as he approached the actor. "Are you in any trouble, Cal?"

"Constantly, but not so it's noticeable."

"I'm serious. There's a man here from the German police—the Bonn police. He says he has to talk to you, claims it's urgent."

"What about?" Dowling felt a rush of pain in his stomach; it was the fear he lived with.

"He wouldn't tell me. Just that it was an emergency and he had to see you alone."

"Oh, *Christ!*" whispered the actor. "Freddie! . . . where is he?"

"Over in your trailer."

"*In* my—"

"Rest easy," said Blynn. "That stunt jock Moose Rosenberg's with him. If he moved an ashtray, I think that gorilla would throw him through the wall."

"Thanks, Roger."

"He meant it when he said 'alone'!"

Dowling did not hear this; he had started running across the hill toward the small camper he used for brief periods of relaxation. He prayed to no one in particular for the best, preparing himself for the worst.

It was neither, simply another complication in an enigma. Frieda Dowling was not the subject; instead it was Joel Converse, an American attorney-at-law. The stunt man climbed out of the trailer, leaving Caleb and the police officer alone. The man was in civilian clothes, his English fluent, his manner vaguely officious yet courteous.

"I'm sorry to have upset you, Herr Dowling," said the German in response to Caleb's initial, intense inquiry about his wife. "We know nothing of Frau Dowling. Is she ill, perhaps?"

"She's had a few spells lately, that's all. She's in Copenhagen."

"Yes, so we understand. You fly there frequently, don't you?"

"Whenever I can."

"She does not care to join you here in Bonn?"

"Her name was Oppenfeld, and the last time she was in Germany she wasn't considered much of a human being. Her memories are, let's say, memorable in the extreme. They come back with a lot of acid."

"Yes," said the police officer, his eyes as steady as Caleb's. "We will live with that for generations."

"I hope so," said the actor.

"I wasn't alive, Herr Dowling. I'm very happy she survived, I mean that."

Dowling was not sure why but he lowered his voice, the words nearly inaudible, if not involuntary. "Germans helped her."

"I would hope so," said the German quietly. "My business, however, concerns a man who sat next to you last night on the planes from Copenhagen to Hamburg and from Hamburg to Bonn. His name is Joel Converse, an American attorney."

"What about him? By the way, may I see your identification?"

"Certainly." The police officer reached into his pocket, removed his plastic ID case, and handed it to the actor, who had his glasses firmly in place. "I trust everything is in order," added the man.

"What's this *Sonder Dezernat?*" asked Dowling, squinting at the small print on the card.

"It is best translated as 'special'—'branch' or 'department.' We are a unit of the Bundespolizei, the federal police. It is our job to look into matters the government feels are more sensitive than the normal jurisdictional complaints."

"That doesn't say a damn thing, and you know it," said the actor. "We can use lines like that in movies and get away with it because we write in all those reactions, but you're not Helmut Dantine or Martin Kosleck and I'm not Elissa Landi. Spell it out."

"Very well, I shall spell it out. Interpol. A man died in a Paris hospital as a result of head injuries inflicted by the American, Joel Converse. His condition was diagnosed as improving, but unfortunately it was only temporary; he was found dead this morning. The death is attributed to an unprovoked attack by Herr Converse. We know he flew into Köln-Bonn, and according to the

274

airline stewardesses, you sat with him for three and a half hours. We want to know where he is. Perhaps you can help us.''

Dowling removed his glasses, lowering his chin and swallowing as he did so. ''And you think I know?''

''We have no idea, but you talked with him. And we hope you *do* know that there are severe penalties for withholding information about a fugitive, especially one sought for a killing.''

The actor fingered the stems of his glasses, his instincts in conflict, erupting. He walked over to the cot against the wall and sat down, looking up at the police officer. ''Why don't I trust you?'' he asked.

''Because you think of your wife and will trust no German,'' replied the German. ''I am a man of law and *peace,* Herr Dowling. Order is something the people decide for themselves, myself among them. The report we have received states clearly that this Converse may be a very disturbed man.''

''He didn't sound disturbed to me. In fact, I thought he had a damned good head on his shoulders. He said a lot of very perceptive things.''

''That you wanted to hear?''

''Not all of them.''

''But a good percentage, leading *up* to all of them.''

''What does that mean?''

''A madman is convincing; he plays on all sides, eventually weighing everything in his favor. It's the essence of his madness, his psychosis, his *own* convictions."

Dowling dropped the glasses on the cot, exhaling audibly, feeling the pain of fear again in his stomach. "A madman?" he said without conviction. "I don't believe that."

"Then let us have a chance to disprove it. Do you know where he is?"

The actor squinted at the German. "Give me a card or a number where I can reach you. He may get in touch with me."

"Who was responsible?" The man in the red silk robe behind the large desk sat in semi-darkness, a brass lamp serving to throw a harsh circle of light on the surface in front of him. The glow was sufficient to reveal the outlines of a huge map centered on the wall behind the man and the desk. It was a strange map, not of the global world but of fragments of the world. The shapes of nations were clearly defined yet oddly shadowed, eerily colored, as if an attempt had been made to create a single landmass out of disparate geographical areas. They included all of Europe, most of the Mediterranean and selected portions of Africa. And as if the wide expanse of the Atlantic Ocean were merely a pale blue connector, Canada and the United States of America were part of this arcane entity.

The man stared straight ahead. His lined, square-jawed face, with its aquiline nose and thin, stretched lips, seemed molded from parchment; his close-cropped salt-and-pepper hair was singularly appropriate for a man with such a rigidly framed torso. He spoke again; his voice was rather high, with no resonance but with a secure sense of command. One could easily imagine this voice raised in volume—even to fever pitch—like a tomcat screeching across a frozen lake. It was not raised now, however; it was the essence of quiet urgency. "Who was responsible?" he repeated. "Are you still on the line, London?"

"Yes," replied the caller from Great Britain. "Yes, of course. I'm trying to think, trying to be fair."

"I admire that, but decisions have to be made. In all likelihood the responsibility will be shared, we simply have to know the sequence." The man paused; when he continued, his voice suddenly took on an intensity that was a complete departure from his previous tone. It was the shrill call of the cat across the ice-bound lake. "How was *Interpol* involved?"

Startled, the Englishman answered quickly, his phrases clipped, the words rushing headlong over one another. "Bertholdier's aide was found dead at four in the morning, Paris time. Apparently he was to receive hospital medication at that hour. The nurse called the Sûreté—"

"The Sûreté?" shouted the man behind the desk in front of the fragmented map. "Why the Sûreté? Why not Bertholdier? It was *his* employee, not the Sûreté's!"

"That was the lapse," said the Britisher. "No one realized instructions to that effect had been left at the hospital desk—apparently by an inspector named Prudhomme, who was awakened and told of the man's death."

"And *he* was the one who called in Interpol?"

"Yes, but too late to intercept Converse at German immigration."

"For which we can be profoundly grateful," said the man, lowering his voice.

"Normally, of course, the hospital would have waited and reached Bertholdier in the morning, telling him what happened. As you say, the patient was an employee, not a member of the family. After that, undoubtedly the *arrondissement* police would have been informed and finally the Sûreté. By then our people would have been in place and fully capable of preventing Interpol's involvement. We can still stop them, but it will take several days. Personnel transfers, new evidence, amendments to the case file; we need time."

"Then don't waste any."

"It was those *damned* instructions."

"Which no one had the brains to look for," said the man in front of the shadowed map. "This Prudhomme's instincts were aroused. Too many rich people, too much influence, the circumstances too bizarre. He smells something."

"We'll get him off the case, just a few days," said the Englishman. "Converse is in Bonn, we know that. We're closing in."

"So possibly are Interpol and the German police. I don't have to tell you how tragic that would be."

"We have certain controls through the American embassy. The fugitive is American."

"The *fugitive* has information!" insisted the man behind the desk, his fist clenched in the circle of light. "How much and supplied by whom we don't know and we *must* know."

"Nothing was learned in New York? The judge?"

"Only what Bertholdier suspected and what I knew the moment I heard his name. After forty years Anstett came back, still hounding me, still wanting my neck. The man was a bull, but only a go-between; he hated me as much as I hated him, and up to the end he shielded those behind him. Well, he's gone and his holy righteousness with him. The point is, Converse is *not* what he pretends to be. Now, *find* him!"

"As I say, we're closing in. We have more sources, more informers than Interpol. He's an American fugitive in Bonn who, we understand, doesn't speak the language. There are only so many places he can hide. We'll find him; we'll break him and learn where he comes from. After which, we'll terminate immediately, of course."

"*No!*" The sleek male cat again shrieked across the frozen lake. "We play *his* game! We welcome him, embrace him. In Paris he talked about Bonn, Tel Aviv, Johannesburg; therefore you'll accommodate him. Bring him to Leifhelm—even better, have Leifhelm go to him. Fly in Abrahms from Israel, Van Headmer from Africa, and, yes, Bertholdier from Paris. He obviously knows who they are anyway. He claims ultimately to want a council meeting, to be a part of us. So we'll hold a conference and listen to his lies. He'll tell us more with his lies than he can with the truth."

"I really don't understand."

"Converse is a *point,* but *only* a point. He's

exploring, studying the forward terrain, trying to understand the tactical forces ahead of him. If he were anything else, he'd deal directly through legitimate authorities and legitimate methods. There'd be no reason for him to use a false name or give false information—or to run away, forcibly overcoming a man he thinks is trying to stop him. He's an infantry point who has certain information but doesn't know where he's going. Well, a point can be sucked into a trap, the advancing company ambushed. Oh, yes, we must give him his conference!''

"I submit that's extraordinarily dangerous. He *has* to know who recruited him, who gave him the names, his sources. We can break him physically or chemically and get that information.''

"He probably doesn't have it,'' explained the man patiently. "Infantry points are not privileged to know command decisions; frankly, if they were, they might turn back. We have to know more about this Converse, and by six o'clock tonight I'll have every report, every résumé, every word ever written about him. There's something here we can't see.''

"We already know he's resourceful,'' said the Britisher. "From what we can piece together in Paris, he's considered an outstanding attorney. If he sees through us or gets away from us, it could be catastrophic. He will have met with our people, *spoken* with them.''

"Then once you find him don't let him out of your sight. By tomorrow I'll have other instructions for you.''

"Oh?''

"Those records that are being gathered from all over the country. For a man to do what Converse is doing, he had to be manipulated very carefully, very thoroughly, a driving intensity instilled in him. It's the manipulators we have to find. They're not even who we think they are. I'll be in touch tomorrow."

George Marcus Delavane replaced the telephone in its cradle and slowly, awkwardly twisted his upper body around in the chair. He gazed at the strange, fragmented map as the first light of dawn fired the eastern sky, its orange glow filling the windows. Then, with effort, his hands gripping the arms of the steel chair, he pivoted himself around again, his eyes on the stark pool of light on the desk. He moved his hands to his waist and carefully, trembling, unbuttoned his dark-red velvet jacket, forcing his gaze downward, ordering himself to observe the terrible truth once more. He stared past the five-inch-wide leather strap that diagonally held him in place, now commanding his eyes to focus, to accept with loathing what had been done to him.

There was nothing to see but the edge of the thick steel seat and, below it, the polished wood of the floor. The long, sturdy legs that had carried his trained, muscular body through battles in the snow and the mud, through triumphant parades in the sunlight, through ceremonies of honor and defiance, had been stolen from him. The doctors had told him that his diseased legs were instruments of death that would kill the rest of him. He clenched his fists and pressed them slowly down on the desk, his throat filled with a silent scream.

9

"*Goddamn you,* Converse, who do you think you are?" cried Connal Fitzpatrick, his voice low, furious, as he caught up with Joel, who was walking rapidly between the tall trees near the Alter Zoll.

"Someone who knew Avery Fowler as a boy and watched a man named Press Halliday die a couple of hundred years later in Geneva," replied Converse, quickening his pace, heading toward the gates of the national landmark where there were taxis.

"Don't pull that crap on me! I knew Press far better and far longer than you *ever* did. For Christ's sake, he was married to my sister! We were close friends for fifteen years!"

"You sound like a kid playing one-upmanship. Get lost."

Fitzpatrick rushed forward, pivoting in front of Joel, blocking him. "It's true! Please, I can help, I *want* to help! I know the language; you don't! I have connections here; you don't."

"You also have your own idea about a deadline, which *I* don't. Get out of my way, sailor."

"*Come* on," pleaded the naval officer. "So I didn't get everything I wanted. Don't crowd me out."

"I beg your pardon?"

Fitzpatrick shifted his weight awkwardly. "You've come on strong before yourself, haven't you, counselor?"

"Not if I didn't know the circumstances."

"Sometimes it's a way of finding them out."

"Not with me, it isn't."

"Then my error was in not knowing you; the circumstances were beyond that scope. With someone else it might have worked."

"Now you're talking tactics, but you meant it when you said 'two days.' "

"You're damned right I did," agreed Connal, nodding. "Because I want whatever it is exposed, I want *whoever* it is to *pay!* I'm mad, Converse, I'm mad as hell. I don't want this thing to linger and die away. The longer nothing is done the less people care; you know that as well as I do and probably better. Have you ever tried to reopen an old case? I have with a few courts-martial where I thought things had been screwed up. Well, I learned something: the system doesn't like it! You know why?"

"Yes I do," said Joel. "There are too many new cases in the dockets, too many rewards in going after the current ones."

"*Bingo,* counselor. Press deserves better than that. Meagen deserves better."

"Yes, he does—they do. But there's a complication that Press Halliday understood better than either of us. Put simply—and cruelly—his life wasn't terribly important compared with what he was going after."

"That's pretty damned cruel," said the officer.

"It's very damned accurate," said Converse.

"Your brother-in-law would have wrestled you to the mat, burns and all, for walking into this and trying to call the shots. Back off, Commander. Go back to the funeral."

"*No.* I want to come on board. I withdraw the deadline."

"How considerate of you."

"You call the shots," said Fitzpatrick, nodding again, exhaling in defeat. "I'll do what you tell me to do."

"Why?" asked Joel, their eyes locked.

The Navy lawyer did not flinch; he spoke simply. "Because Press trusted you. He said you were the best."

"Except for him," Converse added, permitting his expression to relax slightly, with a hint of a smile. "All right, I believe you, but there are ground rules. You either accept them or, as you put it, on board you're not."

"Let's hear them. I'll wince inside so you can't see it."

"Yes," agreed Joel, "you'll wince. To begin with, I'll tell you only what I think you have to know in a given situation. Whatever you develop will be on your own; that way it's freewheeling, no way can you tip the evidence we've compiled."

"That's rough."

"That's the way it is. I'll give you a name now and then when I think it will open a door, but it will *always* be a name you heard second or third hand. You're inventive; figure out your own unidentifiable sources so as to protect yourself."

"I've done that on quite a few waterfronts."

"You have? How good are you at playacting?"

284

"What?"

"Never mind, I think you just answered that. You didn't go down to those waterfronts in your dress whites as a lieutenant commander."

"Hell, no."

"You'll do."

"You've got to tell me *something.*"

"I'll give you an overview, a lot of abstractions and a few facts. As we progress—*if* we progress—you'll learn more. If you think you've put it together, tell me. That's essential. We can't risk blowing everything while you operate under wrong assumptions."

"Who's 'we'?"

"I wish to hell I knew."

"That's comforting."

"Yes, isn't it."

"Why don't you tell me everything now?" asked Fitzpatrick.

"Because Meagen Halliday lost a husband. I don't want to see her lose a brother."

"I'll accept that."

"By the way, how long have you got? I mean you're on active duty."

"My initial leave is thirty days, with extensions as warranted. Christ, an only sister with five kids and her husband is killed. I could probably write my own ticket."

"We'll stick to the thirty days, Commander. It's more than we're allowed. We may not have even two weeks."

"Start talking, Converse."

"Let's walk," said Joel, heading back to the Alter Zoll wall and the view of the Rhine below.

The "overview" delivered by Converse described a current situation in which like-minded individuals in various countries were coming together and using their considerable influence to get around the laws and ship armaments and technology to hostile governments and organizations.

"For what purpose?" asked Fitzpatrick.

"I could say 'profits,' but you'd see through it."

"As the only motive, yes," said the Navy lawyer pensively. "Influential people—as I understand the word 'influential' as related to existing laws—would operate singly or at best in small groups within their own countries. That is, if profits were the primary objective. They wouldn't coordinate outside; it isn't necessary. It's a sellers' market; they'd only water down the profits."

"Bingo, counselor."

"So?" Fitzpatrick looked at Joel, as they strolled toward a break in the stone wall where a bronzed cannon was in place.

"Destabilization," said Converse. "Mass destabilization. A series of flash points in highly volatile areas that will call into question the ability of democratic governments to cope with the violence."

"I've got to ask you again, for what purpose?"

"You're quick," said Joel, "so I'll let you answer that. What happens when an existing political structure is crippled by disorder, when it can no longer function, when things are out of control?"

The two men stopped by the cannon, the naval officer's eyes following the line of the huge, threatening barrel. "It's restructured or replaced," he said, turning to look at Converse.

"Bingo again," said Converse softly. "That's the overview."

"It doesn't make sense." Fitzpatrick creased his eyes in the sunlight, as well as in thought. "Let me recap. Am I allowed?"

"You're allowed."

" 'Influential individuals' connotes people in pretty good standing in very high places. Assuming we're not talking about an out-and-out criminal element—which the lack of a pure profit motive would seem to eliminate—we're talking about reasonably respectable citizens. Is there another definition I'm not aware of?"

"If there is, I'm not aware of it, either."

"Then why would they want to destabilize the political structures that guarantee them their influence? It *doesn't* make sense."

"Ever hear of the phrase 'Everything's relative'?"

"To a fare-thee-well. So what?"

"So think."

"About what?"

"Influence." Joel took out his cigarettes, shook one to his lips and lighted it. The younger man stared at the Seven Mountains of the Westerwald in the distance.

"They want *more,*" said Fitzgerald slowly, turning back to Converse.

"They want it all," said Joel. "And the only way they can get it is to prove that their solutions

287

are the only solutions, all others having proved worthless against the eruption of chaos suddenly everywhere."

Connal's expression was fixed, immobile, as he absorbed Converse's words. "Holy *Mary . . .*" he began, his voice a whisper, yet still a cry. "An international plebiscite—the peoples' will—for the almighty state. Fascism. It's multinational *fascism.*"

"I'm sick of saying 'Bingo,' so I'll say 'Right on,' counselor. You've just said it better than any of us."

"Us? Which is *'we,'* but you don't know who you are!" added Fitzpatrick, both bewildered and angry.

"Live with it," said Joel. "As I have."

"Why?"

"Avery Fowler. Remember him?"

"Oh, *Jesus!*"

"And an old man on the island of Mykonos. That's all we have. But what they said is true. It's real. I've seen it, and that's all I need to know. In Geneva, Avery said there was very little time left. Beale refined it; he called it a countdown. Whatever's going to happen will happen before your leave is up—two weeks and four days is the earliest report. That's what I meant before."

"Oh my God," whispered Fitzpatrick. "What else can you tell me—*will* you tell me?"

"Very little."

"The embassy," Connal interrupted. "It's been a couple of years, but I *was there.* I worked with the military attaché. I don't need any introductions. We can get help there."

"We can also get killed there."

"*What?*"

"It's not clean. Those three men you saw at the airport, the ones from the embassy—"

"What about them?"

"They're on the other side."

"I don't believe you!"

"Why do you think they were at the airport?"

"To meet you, talk to you. There could be a dozen different reasons. Whether you know it or not, you're considered a hotshot lawyer on the international scene. Foreign service personnel frequently want to touch base with guys like you."

"I've had this conversation before," said Converse, irritated.

"What does *that* mean?"

"If they wanted to see me, why didn't they go to the gate?"

"Because they thought you'd come into the terminal like everybody else."

"And when I didn't—according to you—they were upset, angry. That's what you said."

"They were."

"All the more reason to meet me at the gate."

Fitzpatrick frowned. "Still, that's kind of flimsy—"

"The woman. Do you remember the woman?"

"Of course."

"She spotted me in Copenhagen. She followed me. Also, there's something else. Later, on the platform, all four were picked up by a car belonging to a man we know—we *know*—is part of everything I've described to you. They drove to

289

the embassy, and you'll have to take my word for that. I saw them.''

Connal fixed his gaze on Joel, accepting what he had heard. ''Oh, *Jesus,*'' he said. ''Okay, no embassy. What about Brussels, SHAPE? There's a Navy intelligence unit; I've dealt with those people before.''

''Not yet. Maybe not at all.''

''I thought you wanted to use the uniform, my connections.''

''Maybe I will. It's nice to know they're there.''

''Well, what do you want me to do? I've got to do *something.*''

''Are you really fluent in German?''

''*Hochdeutsch, Schwäbisch, Bayerisch,* and several dialects in between. I told you, I can handle five languages—''

''You've made it obnoxiously clear,'' interrupted Converse. ''There's a woman named Fishbein here in Bonn. That's the first name I'm going to give you. She's involved; we're not sure how, but she's suspected of being a conduit—a relayer of information. I want you to meet her, talk with her, establish a relationship. We'll have to think of something that'll be convincing in order for you to do it. She's in her forties, and she's the youngest daughter of Hermann Göring. She married a survivor of the holocaust for obvious reasons; he's long gone. Any ideas?''

''Sure,'' said Fitzpatrick without hesitating. ''Inheritance. There are a couple of thousand last wills and testaments every year that the deceased want processed through the military. They're from crazies who leave everything they've got to

290

the *other* survivors. The true Aryan Germanic stock and all that horseshit. We bounce them back to the civil courts, which don't know what to do with them, so they end up in limbo and eventually in the Treasury Department's coffers."

"No kidding?"

"*Eins, zwei, drei.* Believe me, those people mean it."

"Can you use the device?"

"How about a million-plus legacy from a small Midwest brewer of lager beer?"

"You'll do," said Joel. "You're on board."

Converse did not mention Aquitaine or George Marcus Delavane or Jacques-Louis Bertholdier or Erich Leifhelm, or twenty-odd names at the State Department and the Pentagon. Nor did he describe the network as it appeared in the dossiers, or as described by Dr. Edward Beale on Mykonos. He gave Connal Fitzpatrick the barest bones of the body of information. Joel's reasoning was far less benign than he had stated: if the Navy lawyer was taken and interrogated —no matter how brutally—there was little of substance he could reveal.

"You're not really telling me a hell of a lot," said Fitzpatrick.

"I've told you enough to get your head blown off, and that's not a phrase normally in my lexicon."

"Nor mine."

"Then consider me a nice fellow," said Converse, as the two men headed for the entrance gate of the Alter Zoll.

"On the other hand," continued Halliday's

brother-in-law, "you've been through a lot more than I ever have. I read that stuff about you in the security files—files, not file—they were cross-correlated with the files of a lot of other prisoners. You were something else. According to most of the men in those camps, you held them together—until they put you into solitary."

"They were wrong, sailor. I was shaking and scared to death and would have fucked a Peking duck to save my skin."

"That's not what the files say. They say—"

"I'm really not interested, Commander," said Joel as they passed through the ornate gate, "but I've got an immediate problem you can help solve."

"What is it?"

"I gave my word I'd call Dowling on some mobile phone line. I wouldn't know how to ask for it."

"There's a booth over there," said Connal, pointing to a white plastic bubble that protruded from a concrete pylon on the pavement abutting the drive. "Do you have the number?"

"It's here somewhere," replied Converse, rummaging through various pockets. "Here it is," he said as he separated the scrap of paper from several credit-card charges.

"*Vermittlung, bitte.*" The naval officer sounded authentic as he spoke crisply into the telephone. "*Sieben, drei, vier, zwei, zwei. Bitte, Fräulein.*" Fitzpatrick then inserted a series of coins into the metal box and turned to Joel. "Here you are. They're ringing."

"Stay there. Ask for him—say it's his lawyer

calling, the one at the hotel."

"Guten Tag, Fräulein. Ist Herr—Oh, no I speak English. Do you speak English? No, I'm not calling from California, but it's an emergency. . . . Dowling, I have to reach—"

"Caleb," said Joel quickly.

"Caleb Dowling." The Navy man covered the mouthpiece. "What kind of name is that?"

"Something to do with Gucci shoes."

"What? . . . *Ja*—yes, thanks." Fitzpatrick handed the phone to Converse. "They're getting him."

"Joe?"

"Yes, Cal. I said I'd call you after I met with Fowler. Everything's okay."

"No, it's not, Mr. Lawyer," said the actor quietly. "You and I had better have a very serious talk, and I don't mind telling you a hunk of beef named Rosenberg will be just a few feet away."

"I don't understand."

"A man died in Paris. Does that clear things up for you?"

"Oh, *God.*" Converse felt the blood draining from his head and a hollowness in his throat. For a moment he thought he was going to be sick. "They came to you?" he whispered.

"A man from the German police a little over an hour ago, and this time I didn't have any doubts about my visitor. He was the real item."

"I don't know what to say," stammered Joel.

"Did you do it?"

"I . . . I guess I did." Converse stared at the telephone dial, seeing the bloodied face of the man in the alleyway, feeling the blood on his own fingers.

"You *guess?* That's not something you guess about."

"Then yes. . . . The answer is yes. I did it."

"Did you have a reason?"

"I thought I did."

"I want to hear it, but not now. I'll tell you where to meet me."

"No!" exclaimed Joel, confused but emphatic. "I can't involve you. You can't be involved!"

"This fellow gave me a card and wants me to call him if you got in touch with me. He was very specific about withholding information, how it's considered aiding a fugitive."

"He was right, *absolutely* right! For God's sake, tell him everything, Cal! The truth. You got me a room for the night because you thought I might not have a reservation and we had a pleasant few hours on the plane. You put it in your name because you didn't want me to pay. Don't hide *anything!* Not even this call."

"Why didn't I tell him before?"

"That's all right, you're telling him now. It was a shock and I'm a fellow American and you're in a foreign country. You wanted time to think, to reflect. My phone call shook you into behaving rationally. Tell him you confronted me with the accusation and I didn't deny it. Be honest with him, Cal."

"How honest? Should I include my session with Fowler?"

"That's all right, too, but it's not necessary. Let me back up and clarify. Fowler's a false name and he's not relevant to Paris, I give you my word. Bringing him in is only volunteering an unnecessary complication."

"Should I tell him you're at the Alter Zoll?"

"It's where I'm calling you from. I just admitted it."

"You won't be able to go back to the Königshof."

"It doesn't matter," said Joel, speaking rapidly, wanting to get off the phone and start thinking. "My luggage is at the airport and I can't go back there either."

"You had a briefcase."

"I've taken care of that. It's where I can get it."

The actor paused, then spoke slowly. "So your advice to me is to level with the police, to tell them the truth."

"Without volunteering extraneous and un-related material. Yes, that's my advice, Cal. It's the way you can stay clean and you *are* clean."

"It sounds like fine advice, Joe—Joel, and I certainly wish I could take it, but I'm afraid I can't."

"What? *Why?*"

"Because bad men like thieves and killers don't give advice like that. It's not in any script I ever read."

"That's nonsense! For Christ's sake, do as I tell you!"

"Sorry, pardner, it's not good dramaturgy. So you do as I tell *you.* There's a big stone building at the university—beautiful place, a restored palace actually—with a layout of gardens you don't see very often. They're on the south side with benches here and there on the main path. It's a nice place on a summer's night, kind of out of the way and not too crowded. Be there at ten o'clock."

"Cal, I won't involve you in this!"

"I'm already involved. I've withheld information and I've aided a fugitive." Dowling paused again. "There's someone I want you to meet," he said.

"*No.*"

There was a click and the line went dead.

10

Converse hung up the phone and braced himself on the sides of the plastic booth, trying to clear his head. He had killed a man, not in a war anyone knew about, and not in the heat of survival in a Southeast Asian jungle, but in a Paris alleyway because he had to make an instant decision based on probabilities. Rightly or wrongly the act had been done and he could not dwell on it. The German police were looking for him, which meant that Interpol had entered the picture, transmitting the information from Paris somehow supplied by Jacques-Louis Bertholdier, who remained out of sight, beyond the scope of the hunt. Joel recalled his own words spoken only minutes ago. If Press Halliday's life was not terribly important compared with what he was going after, neither was the life of a minion who worked for Bertholdier, Delavane's disciple, Aquitaine's arm in France. There were no options, thought Converse. He had to go on; he had to stay free.

"What's the matter?" asked Fitzpatrick, standing anxiously near him. "You look like you got kicked by a mule."

"I got kicked," agreed Converse.

"What happened to Dowling? Is he in trouble?"

"He *will* be!" exploded Joel. "Because he's a misguided idiot who thinks he's in some kind of goddamned movie!"

"That wasn't your opinion a little while ago."

"We met; it came out all right. This can't, not for him." Converse pushed himself away from the booth and looked at the Navy lawyer, his mind now trying desperately to concentrate on the immediate. "I may tell you and I may not," he said, glancing around for an available taxi. "Come on, we're going to put your awesome linguistic abilities to work. We need shelter, expensive but not showy, especially *not* a place where the well-heeled tourists go who don't speak German. If there's one thing they'll spread about me, it's that I can't talk my way through the five boroughs of New York. I want a rich hotel that doesn't need foreigners, doesn't cater to them. Do you know the kind of place I mean?"

Fitzpatrick nodded. "Exclusive, clubby, German business-oriented. Every large city has hotels like that, and they're always twenty times my per diem for breakfast."

"That's okay, I've got money here in Bonn. I

might as well try to get it out."

"You're full of surprises," said Connal. "I mean *real* surprises."

"Do you think you can handle it? Find a hotel like that?"

"I can explain what I want to a cabdriver; he'll probably know. Bonn's small, nothing like New York or London or Paris. . . . There's a taxi letting people out." The two men hurried to the curb, where the cab was discharging a quartet of passengers balancing camera equipment and out-sized Louis Vuitton handbags.

"How will you do it?" asked Converse as they nodded to the tourists, two couples in the midst of an argument, male versus female, Nikon versus Vuitton.

"A combination of what we both said," answered Fitzpatrick. "A quiet, nice hotel away from the *Ausländerlärm.*"

"What?"

"The clamor of tourists—and worse. I'll tell him we're calling on some very important German businessmen—bankers, say—and we'd like a place they'd be most comfortable in for confidential meetings. He'll get the drift."

"He'll see we don't have any lugguage," objected Joel.

"He'll see the money in my hand first," said the naval officer, holding the door for Converse.

Lieutenant Commander Connal Fitzpatrick, USN, member of the military bar and limited thereby, impressed Joel Converse, vaunted international attorney, to the point where the

298

latter felt foolish. Effortlessly the Navy lawyer got them in a two-bedroom suite at an inn on the banks of the Rhine called Das Rektorat. It was one of those converted prewar estates where most of the guests seemed to have at least a nodding acquaintance with several others and the clerks rarely looked anyone in the eye, as if tacitly confirming their subservience—or the fact that they would certainly not acknowledge having seen Herr So-and-So should someone ask them.

Fitzpatrick had begun his campaign with the taxi driver by leaning forward in the seat and speaking rapidly and quietly. Their exchanges seemed to grow more confidential as the cab sped toward the heart of the city; then it abruptly veered away, crossing the railroad tracks that intersected the capital, and entered a smooth road paralleling the river north. Joel had started to speak, to ask what was happening, but the Navy lawyer had held up his hand, telling Converse to be quiet.

Once they had stopped at the entrance of an inn, reached by an interminably long, manicured drive, Fitzpatrick got out.

"Stay here," he said to Joel. "I'll see if I can get us a couple of rooms. And don't say anything."

Twelve minutes later Connal returned, his demeanor stern, his eyes, however, lively. "Come on, Chairman of the Board, we're going straight up." He paid the driver handsomely and once again held the door for Converse—now a touch more deferentially, thought Joel.

The lobby of Das Rektorat was unmistakably

German, with oddly delicate Victorian overtones; thick heavy wood and sturdy leather chairs were beside and below filigrees of brass ornamentation forming arches over doorways, elegant borders for large mirrors, and valances above thick bay windows where none were required. One's first impression was of a quiet, expensive spa from decades ago, its solemnity lightened by flashes of reflecting metal and glass. It was a strange mixture of the old and the very old. It smelled of money.

Fitzpatrick led Converse to a paneled elevator recessed in the paneled corridor; no bellboy or manservant was in attendance. It was a small enclosure, room for no more than four people, the walls of tinted, marbled glass, which vibrated as the elevator ascended two stories.

"I think you'll approve of the accommodations," said Connal. "I checked them out; that's why it took me so long."

"We're back in the nineteenth century, you know," countered Joel. "I trust they have telephones and not just the Hessian express."

"All the most modern communications, I made sure of that, too." The elevator door opened. "This way," said Fitzpatrick, gesturing to the right. "The suite's at the end of the hall."

"The suite?"

"You said you had money in Bonn."

Two bedrooms flanked a tastefully furnished sitting room, with French doors that opened onto a small balcony overlooking the Rhine. The rooms were sunlit and airy, the décor of the walls again an odd mixture: a reproduction of an Impressionist floral arrangement was beside dramatic prints of past champion horses from the leading German tracks and breeding farms.

"All right, wonder boy," said Converse, looking out the open French doors, then turning back to Connal Fitzpatrick, who stood in the middle of the room, the key still in his hand. "How did you do it?"

"It wasn't hard," replied the Navy lawyer, smiling. "You'd be surprised what a set of military papers will do for a person in this country. The older guys sort of stiffen up and look like boxer puppies smelling a pot roast, and there aren't that many people here much under sixty."

"That doesn't tell me anything unless you're enlisting us."

"It does when I combine it with the fact that I'm an aide assigned by the U.S. Navy to accompany an important American financier over here to hold confidential meetings with his German counterparts. While in Bonn, naturally, incognito is the best means for my eccentric financier to travel. Everything's in *my* name."

"What about reservations?"

"I told the manager that you'd rejected the hotel reserved for us as having too many people you might know. I also hinted that those countrymen of his you're going to meet might be most appreciative of his cooperation. He agreed that I might have a point there."

"How did we hear about this place?" asked Joel, still suspicious.

"Simple. I remembered it from several

301

conversations I had at the International Economic Conference in Düsseldorf last year."

"You were *there?*"

"I didn't know there was one," said Fitzpatrick, heading for the door on the left. "I'll take this bedroom, okay? It's not as large as the other one and that's the way it should be, since I'm an aide—which Jesus, Mary, and Joseph all know is the truth."

"Wait a minute," Converse broke in, stepping forward. "What about our luggage? Since we don't have any, didn't that strike your friend downstairs as a little odd for such important characters?"

"Not at all," said Connal, turning. "It's still in the city at that unnamed hotel you rejected so emphatically after twenty minutes. But only I can pick it up."

"Why?"

Fitzpatrick brought his index finger to his lips. "You also have a compulsion for secrecy. Remember, you're eccentric."

"The manager *bought* all that swill?"

"He calls me *Kommandant.*"

"You're quite a bullshitter, sailor."

"I remind you, sir, that in the land of *Erin go bragh* it's called good healthy blarney. And although you lack certain qualifications, Press said you were a master of it in negotiations." Connal's expression became serious. "He meant it in the best way, counselor, and that's not bullshit."

As the Navy lawyer began walking to the bedroom, Joel felt an odd sense of recognition but could not define it. What was it about the younger man that struck a chord in him? Fitzpatrick had that boldness that came with the untried, that lack of fear in small things that caution would later teach him often led to larger things. He tested waters bravely; he had never come close to drowning.

Suddenly Converse understood the recognition. What he saw in Connal Fitzpatrick was himself—before things had happened. Before he had learned the meaning of fear, raw fear. And finally of loneliness.

It was agreed that Connal would return to the Cologne-Bonn airport, not for Joel's luggage but for his own, which was stored in a locker in the baggage-claim area. He would then go into Bonn proper, buy an expensive suitcase and fill it with a half-dozen shirts, underwear, socks and best off-the-rack clothing he could find in Joel's sizes—namely, three pairs of trousers, a jacket or two and a raincoat. It was further agreed that casual clothes were the most appropriate; an eccentric financier was permitted such lapses of sartorial taste, and also such attire more successfully concealed their non-custom-made origins. Finally, the last stop he would make before returning to Das Rektorat was at a second locker in the railroad station where Converse had left his attaché case. Once the case was in the Navy lawyer's possession and the taxi waiting outside had picked up its passenger, there were to be no further stops. The cab was to drive directly to the countryside inn.

"I wanted to ask you something," said Fitzpatrick just before leaving. "Back at the Alter Zoll you said something about how 'they' would spread the word that you couldn't talk your way through the five boroughs of New York. I gathered that referred to the fact that you don't speak German."

"That's right. Or any other language, adequate English excepted. I tried but it never took. I was married to a girl who spoke fluent French and German, and even she gave up. I don't have the ear, I guess."

"Who did *they* refer to?" asked Connal, barely listening to Converse's explanation. "The embassy men?"

Joel hesitated. "A little wider, I'm afraid," he said, choosing his words carefully. "You'll have to know but not now, not yet. Later."

"Why later? Why not now?"

"Because it wouldn't do you a damned bit of good, and it might raise questions you wouldn't want raised under, shall we say, adverse circumstances."

"That's elliptical."

"It certainly is."

"Is that it? Is that all you'll say?"

"No. There's one other thing. I want my briefcase."

Fitzpatrick had assured him that the switchboard of Das Rektorat was capable of handling telephone calls in English—as well as at least six other languages, including Arabic—and he should have no qualms about placing a call to Lawrence

Talbot in New York.

"Christ, where *are* you, Joel?" Talbot shouted into the phone.

"Amsterdam," replied Converse, not wanting to say Bonn and having had the presence of mind to make the call station-to-station. "I want to know what happened to Judge Anstett, Larry. Can you tell me anything?"

"I want to know what's happened to *you!* René called last night. . . ."

"Mattilon?"

"You told him you were flying to London."

"I changed my mind."

"What the hell *happened?* The police were with him; he had no choice. He had to tell them who you were." Talbot suddenly paused, then spoke in a calmer voice, a false voice. "Are you all right, Joel? Is there something you want to tell me, something bothering you?"

"Something bothering me?"

"Listen to me, Joel. We all know what you went through, and we admire you, *respect* you. You're the finest we've got in the international division—"

"I'm the *only* one you've got," Converse broke in, trying to think, trying to buy time as well as information. "What did René say? Why did he call you?"

"You sound like your old self, fella."

"I *am* my old self, Larry. What did René call you about? Why were the police with him?" Joel could feel the slippage; he was entering another sphere and he knew it, accepted it. The lies would follow, guile joining deceit, because time and freedom of movement were paramount. He had to stay free; there was so much to do, so little time.

"He called me back after the police left to fill me in—incidentally, they were from the Sûreté. As he understood it, the driver of a limousine was assaulted outside the George Cinq's service entrance—"

"The driver of a limousine?" interrupted Converse involuntarily. "They said he was a *chauffeur?*"

"From one of those high-priced services that ferry around people who make odd stops at odd hours. Very posh and very confidential. Apparently the fellow was pretty well smashed up and they say you did it. No one knows why, but you were identified and they say the man may not live."

"Larry, this is preposterous!" objected Joel, his protestation accompanied by feigned outrage. "Yes, I *was* there—in the area—but it had nothing to do with *me!* Two hotheads got into a fight, and since I couldn't stop them, I wasn't going to get my head handed to me. I got out of there, and before I found a taxi I yelled at the doorman to call for help. The last thing I saw he was blowing his whistle and running toward the alley."

"You weren't even involved, then," said Talbot. The statement was a lawyer's positive fact.

"Of course not! Why would I be?"

"That's what we couldn't understand. It didn't make sense."

"It *doesn't* make sense. I'll call René and fly back to Paris, if I have to."

"Yes, do that," agreed Talbot haltingly. "I should tell you I may have aggravated the situation."

"You? How?"

"I told Mattilon that perhaps you were . . . . well, not yourself. When I spoke with you in Geneva, you sounded awful, Joel. Just plain *awful.*"

"Good God, how did you think I'd feel? A man I was negotiating with dies in front of me bleeding from a dozen bullet wounds. How would *you* feel?"

"I understand," said the lawyer in New York, "but then René thought he saw something in you—heard something—that disturbed him, too."

"Oh, come on, will you people get off it!" Converse's thoughts raced; every word he spoke had to be credible, his now diminished "outrage" rooted in believability. "Mattilon saw me after I'd been flying in and out of airports for damn near fourteen hours. Christ, I was exhausted!"

"Joel?" Talbot began, obviously not quite ready to get off it. "Why did you tell René you were in Paris for the firm?"

Converse paused, not for lack of a response but for effect. He was ready for the question; he had been ready when he first approached Mattilon. "A white lie, Larry, and no harm to anyone. I wanted some information, and it seemed the best way to get it."

"About this Bertholdier? He's the general, isn't he?"

"He turned out to be the wrong source. I told René as much, and he couldn't agree with me more." Joel lightened his tone of voice. "Also it would have appeared strange if I'd said I was in Paris for somebody else, wouldn't it? I don't think it would have done the firm any good. Rumors and speculation run rampant down our corridors; you told me that once."

"Yes, and it's true. You did the right thing. . . . Damn it, Joel, why the *hell* did you leave the hotel the way you did? From the basement, or wherever it was."

It was the moment for expressing with total conviction a small inconsequential untruth that if not carried off would lead to the larger, far more dangerous lie. Connal Fitzpatrick could do it well, reflected Converse. The Navy lawyer had not learned to fear the small things; he did not know they were spoors that could lead one back to a rat cage in the Mekong River.

"Bubba, my friend and sole support," said Joel, as cavalierly as he could muster. "I owe you many things, but not the intimacies of my private life."

"The what of your *what?*"

"I am approaching middle age—at least it's not far off—and I have no matrimonial encumbrances or guilt about fidelity."

"You were avoiding a *woman?*"

"Fortunately for the firm, not a man."

"Jee-*sus!* I'm so well into middle age I don't think about those things. Sorry, young fella."

"Young and not so young, Larry."

"We were all off base then. You'd better call

308

René right away and get this thing cleared up. I can't tell you how relieved I am."

"You can tell me about Anstett. That's why I called you."

"Of course." Talbot lowered his voice. "A terrible thing, a tragedy. What did the papers over there say?"

Converse was caught; he had not anticipated the question. "Very little," he replied, trying to remember what Fitzpatrick had told him. "Just that he was shot and apparently nothing was taken from his apartment."

"That's right. Naturally, the first thing Nathan and I thought of was you, and whatever the hell you're involved with, but that wasn't the case. It was a Mafia vendetta, pure and simple. You know how rough Anstett was on appeals from those people; he'd throw them out as fast as he'd call their attorneys a disgrace to the profession."

"It was a confirmed Mafia killing?"

"It will be, and that's straight from O'Neil down at the commissioner's office. They know their man; he's an executioner for the Delvecchio family and last month Anstett threw the key away on Delvecchio's oldest son. He's in for twelve years with no appeals left; the Supreme Court won't touch him."

"They *know* the man?"

"It's only a matter of picking him up."

"How come it's so clear-cut?" asked Joe, confused.

"The usual way," said Talbot. "An informer who needs a favor. And since everything's happened so fast and so quietly, it's assumed that the ballistics will prove out."

"So fast? So quietly?"

"The informer reached the police first thing this morning. A special unit was dispatched and only they know the man's identity. They figure the gun will still be in his possession. He'll be picked up anytime now; he lives in Syosset."

Something was wrong, thought Converse. There was an inconsistency, but he could not spot the flaw. Then it came to him. "Larry, if everything's so quiet, how do you know about it?"

"I was afraid you'd ask that," said Talbot uneasily. "I might as well tell you; it'll probably be in the newspaper follow-ups anyway. O'Neil's keeping me posted; call it courtesy, and also because I'm nervous."

"Why?"

"Except for the man who killed him, I was the last person to see Anstett alive."

"*You?*"

"Yes. After René's second call I decided to phone the judge, after conferring with Nathan, of course. When I finally reached Anstett, I said I had to see him. He wasn't happy about it but I was adamant. I explained that it concerned you. All I knew was that you were in terrible trouble and something had to be done. I went over to his apartment on Central Park South and we talked. I told him what had happened and how frightened I was for you, frankly letting him know that I held him responsible. He didn't say much, but I think he was frightened, too. He said he'd get in touch with me in the morning. I left, and according to the coroner's report, he was killed approximately three hours later."

Joel's breath was short, his head splitting. His concentration was absolute. "Let me get this straight, Larry. You went over to Anstett's apartment after René's call—his second call. *After* he told the Sûreté who I was."

"That's right."

"How long was it?"

"How long was what?"

"Before you left for Anstett's. After you spoke with Mattilon."

"Well, let me see. Naturally, I wanted to talk to Nathan first, but he was out to dinner, so I waited. Incidentally, he concurred and offered to join me—"

"How *long*, Larry?"

"An hour and a half, two hours at the outside."

Two hours plus three hours totaled five hours. More than enough time for the killer puppets to be put in place. Converse did not know how it had been done, only that it *had* been done. Things had suddenly erupted in Paris, and in New York an agitated Lawrence Talbot had been followed to an apartment on Central Park South, where someone, somewhere, recognized a name and a man and the part he had played against Aquitaine. Were it otherwise, Talbot would be the corpse, not Lucas Anstett. All the rest was a smoke screen behind which the disciples of George Marcus Delavane manipulated the puppets.

"—and the courts owed so much to him, the country owed so much." Talbot was speaking, but Joel could no longer listen.

"I have to go, Larry," he said, hanging up.

The killing was obscene. That it was carried out so quickly, so efficiently and with such precise deception was as frightening as anything Converse could imagine.

Joseph (Joey the Nice) Albanese drove his Pontiac down the quiet, tree-lined street in Syosset, Long Island, waving to a couple in a front yard. The husband was trimming a hedge under his wife's guidance. They stopped what they were doing, smiled and waved back. Very nice. His neighbors liked him, thought Joey. They considered him a sweet guy and very generous, what with letting the kids use his pool and serving their parents only the best booze when they dropped over and the biggest steaks money could buy when he had weekend barbecues—which he did often, rotating the neighbors so no one should feel left out.

He *was* a sweet guy, mused Joey. He was always pleasant and never raised his voice in anger to anyone, offering only a glad hand, a nice word and a happy smile to everybody, no matter how lousy he really felt. That was it, *goddamn it!* thought Joey. Irra—fuckin'—gardless of how upset he was, he never let it show! Joey the Nice was what they called him and they were right. Sometimes he figured he had to be some kind of saint—may Jesus Christ forgive him for having such thoughts. He had just waved to neighbors, but in truth he felt like smashing his fist through the windshield and shoving the glass down their throats.

It wasn't them, it was last *night* that did it! A crazy night, a crazy *hit,* everything *crazy!* And that *gumba* they brought in from the West Coast, the one they called Major, he was the nuttiest fruitcake of them all! And a sadist to boot, the way he beat the shit out of that old man and the crazy questions he asked, and shouting all the time. *Tutti pazzi!*

One minute he's playing cards in the Bronx, and the next the phone is ringing. Get down to Manhattan fast! A bad heat is needed *attualmente!* So he goes and what does he find? It's that iron-balled judge, the one who closed the steel doors on Delvecchio's boy! What craziness! They'll trace it back to the old man for sure. He'll know such *afflizione* from the cops and the courts he'll be lucky to own a small whorehouse in Palermo—if he ever got back.

Then maybe—just maybe—thought Joey at the time, there was a turning muscle in the organization. Old Delvecchio was losing his grip; just maybe it was being called for, this *afflizione* that surely would follow. And possibly—just possibly —Joey himself was being tested. Maybe he was *too* nice, too *soave,* to put the bad heat on someone like the old judge who gave them all such a hard time. Well, he wasn't. No sirree, the nice stopped with the handle of a gun. It was his job, his profession. The Lord Jesus decided who should live and who should die, only He spoke through mortal men on earth who told people like Joey whom to hit. There was no moral dilemma for Joey the Nice. It was important, however, that the orders always come from a man with respect;

that was necessary.

They did last night; the order came from a man with great respect. Although Joey did not know him personally, he had heard for years about the powerful *padrone* in Washington, D.C. The name was whispered, never spoken out loud.

Joey touched the brakes of his car, slowing down so as to swing into his driveway. His wife, Angie, would be pissed off at him, maybe shout a little because he didn't come home last night. One more irritation on top of all the craziness, but what the hell was he going to say? Sorry, Angie, but I was gainfully employed throwing six bullets into an old guy who definitely discriminated against Italians. So, you see, Angie, I had to stay across the the bridge in Jersey where one of the paesans I played cards with and who'll swear I was there all night happens to be the chief of police.

But, of course, he would never go into such details with his wife. That was his own law. No matter how aggravated he was he never brought the job home. More husbands should be like him and there would be happier households in Syosset.

Shit! One of the fucking kids had left a bicycle in front of the attached garage; he wouldn't be able to open the automatic door and drive inside. He'd have to get out. Shit! One more aggravation. He couldn't even park by the Millers' curb next door; some creep's car was there but it wasn't the Millers' Buick. Double shit!

Joey brought the Pontiac to a stop halfway into the sloping driveway and got out. He went up to the bike and leaned down. The rotten kid didn't even use the kickstand and Joey hated bending over, what with his heavy gut and all.

"Joseph Albanese!"

Joey the Nice spun around, crouching, reaching under his jacket. That tone of voice was used by only one type of slime! He pulled out his .38 and dove toward the grille of his car.

The explosions reverberated throughout the neighborhood. Birds fluttered out of trees and there were screams along the block in the bright afternoon sunlight. Joseph Albanese was sprawled against the grille of the Pontiac, rivulets of blood slowly rolling down the shiny chrome. Joey the Nice had been caught in the fire, and gripped in his hand was the gun he had used so effectively the night before. Ballistics would prove out. The killer of Lucas Anstett was dead. The judge had been the victim of a gangland assassination, and as far as the world was concerned, it had nothing to do with events taking place six thousand miles away in Bonn, Germany.

Converse stood on the small balcony, his hands on the railing, looking down at the majestic river beyond the forest of trees that formed the banks of the Rhine. It was past seven o'clock; the sun was going below the mountains in the west, its orange rays shooting up, creating blocks of shadows over the earth—moving shadows that floated across the waters in the descending distance. The vibrant colors were hypnotic, the breezes cooling, but nothing could stop the pounding echo in his chest. *Where was Fitzpatrick? Where was his attaché case? The dossiers?* He tried to stop thinking, to stop his imagination from catapulting into frightening possibilities. . . .

There was a sudden harsh echo, not from his chest but from inside the room. He turned quickly as the door opened and Connal Fitzpatrick stood there, removing his key from the lock. He stepped aside, letting a uniformed porter enter with two suitcases, instructing the man to leave them on the floor while he reached into his pocket for a tip. The porter left and the Navy lawyer stared at Joel. There was no attaché case in his hand.

"Where is it?" said Converse, afraid to breathe, afraid to move.

"I didn't pick it up."

"Why *not?*" cried Joel, rushing forward.

"I couldn't be sure . . . maybe it was just a feeling, I don't know."

"What are you talking about?"

"I was at the airport for seven hours yesterday, going from counter to counter asking about you," said Connal softly. "This afternoon I passed the Lufthansa desk and the same clerk was there. When I said hello, he didn't seem to want to acknowledge me; he looked nervous, and I couldn't understand. I came back out of the baggage claim with my suitcase and watched him. I remembered how he had glanced at me last night, and as I passed him I swore his eyes kept shooting to the center of the terminal, but there were so many people, so much confusion, I couldn't be certain."

"You think you were picked up? *Followed?*"

"That's just it, I don't *know.* When I was shopping in Bonn, I went from store to store and

316

every now and then I'd turn around, or shift my head, to see if I could spot anyone. A couple of times I thought I saw the same people twice, but then again, it was always crowded, and—again— I couldn't be sure. But I kept thinking about that Lufthansa clerk; something *was* wrong.''

"What about when you were in the taxi? Did you—''

"Naturally. I kept looking out the rear window. Even during the drive out here. Several cars made the same turns we did, but I told the driver to slow down and they passed us.''

"Did you watch where they went after they passed you?''

"What was the point?''

"There is one,'' said Joel, recalling a clever driver who followed a deep-red Mercedes limousine.

"All I knew was that you're pretty uptight about that attaché case. I don't know what's in it and I figure you don't want anyone else to know, either.''

"Bingo, counselor.''

There was a knocking at the door, and although it was soft, it had the effect of a staccato burst of thunder. Both men stood motionless, their eyes riveted on the door.

"Ask who it is,'' whispered Converse.

"Wer ist da, bitte?'' said Fitzpatrick, loud enough to be heard. There was a brief reply in German and Connal breathed again. "It's okay. It's a message for me from the manager. He probably wants to sell us a conference room.'' The Navy lawyer went to the door and opened it.

However, it was not the manager, or a bellboy, or a porter bringing a message from the manager. Instead, standing there, was a slender, elderly man in a dark suit with erect posture and very broad shoulders. He glanced first at Fitzpatrick, then looked beyond at Converse.

"Excuse me, please, Commander," he said courteously, walking through the door, and approached Joel, his hand outstretched. "Herr Converse, may I introduce myself? The name is Leifhelm. Erich Leifhelm."

11

Joel took the German's hand, too stunned to do anything else. "Field Marshal . . . ?" he uttered, instantly regretting it—he could at least have had the presence of mind to say "General." The pages of Leifhelm's dossier flashed across Converse's mind as he looked at the man—his straight hair, still more blond than white, his pale-blue eyes glacial, his pinkish skin lined, waxen, as if preserved for decades to come.

"An old title and one, thankfully, I have not heard in many years. But you flatter me. You were sufficiently interested to learn something of my past."

"Not very much."

"I suspect enough." Leifhelm turned to Fitzpatrick. "I apologize for my little ruse, Commander. I felt it was best."

Fitzpatrick shrugged, bewildered. "You know

318

each other, apparently.''

"Of one another,'' corrected the German. ''Mr. Converse came to Bonn to meet with me, but I imagine he's told you that.''

''No, I haven't told him that,'' said Joel.

Leifhelm turned back, studying Converse's eyes. ''I see. Perhaps we should talk privately.''

''I think so.'' Joel looked over at Fitzpatrick. ''Commander, I've taken up too much of your time. Why not go downstairs to dinner and I'll join you in a while?''

''Whatever you say, sir,'' said Connal, an officer assuming the status of an aide. He nodded and left, closing the door firmly behind him.

''A lovely room,'' said Leifhelm, taking several steps toward the open French doors. ''And with such a lovely view.''

''How did you find me?'' asked Converse.

''Him,'' replied the former field marshal, looking at Joel. *''Ein Offizier,* according to the front desk. Who is he?''

''How?'' repeated Converse.

''He spent hours last night at the airport inquiring about you; many remembered him. He was obviously a friend.''

''And you knew he'd checked his luggage? That he'd be back for it?''

''Frankly, no. We thought he might come for yours. We knew you wouldn't. Now, please, who is he?''

Joel understood it was vital that he maintain a level of arrogance, as he had done with Bertholdier in Paris. It was the only route he could take with such men; to be accepted by them, they had to see something of themselves in him. "He's not important and he knows nothing. He's a legal officer in the Navy who's worked in Bonn before and is over here now, I gather, on personal business. A prospective fiancée, I think he mentioned. I saw him the other week; we chatted, and I told him I was flying in today or tomorrow and he said he'd make it a point to meet me. He's obsequious, and persistent. I'm sure he has delusions of a civilian practice. Naturally—under the circumstances—I used him. As you did."

"Naturally." Leifhelm smiled; he *was* polished. "You gave him no arrival time?"

"Paris changed any possibility of that, didn't it?"

"Oh, yes, Paris. We must discuss Paris."

"I spoke to a friend who deals with the Sûreté. The man died."

"Such men do. Frequently."

"They said he was a driver, a chauffeur. He wasn't."

"Would it have been wiser to say he was a trusted associate of General Jacques-Louis Bertholdier?"

"Obviously not. They say I killed him."

"You did. We gather it was an uncontrollable miscalculation, no doubt brought on by the man himself."

"Interpol's after me."

"We, too, have friends; the situation will change. You have nothing to fear—as long as *we* have nothing to fear." The German paused, glancing around the room. "May I sit down?"

320

"Please. Shall I ring for a drink?"

"I drink only light wine and very sparingly. Unless you wish . . . it's not necessary."

"It's not necessary," said Converse as Leifhelm sat in a chair nearest the balcony doors. Joel would sit when he felt the moment was right, not before.

"You took extraordinary measures at the airport to avoid us," continued Hitler's youngest field marshal.

"I was followed from Copenhagen."

"Very observant of you. You understand no harm was intended."

"I didn't understand anything. I just didn't like it. I didn't know what effect Paris would have on my arrival in Bonn, what it meant to you."

"What Paris meant?" asked Leifhelm rhetorically. "Paris meant that a man, an attorney using a false name, said some very alarming things to a most distinguished and brilliant statesman. This attorney, who called himself Simon, said he was flying to Bonn to see me. On his way—and I'm sure with provocation—he kills a man, which tells us something; he's quite ruthless and very capable. But that is all we know; we would like to know more. Where he goes, whom he meets. In our position, would you have done otherwise?"

It was the moment to sit down. "I would have done it better."

"Perhaps if we'd known how resourceful you were, we might have been less obvious. Incidentally, what happened in Paris? What did that man do to provoke you?"

"He tried to stop me from leaving."

"Those were not his orders."

"Then he grossly misunderstood them. I've a few bruises on my chest and neck to prove it. I'm not in the habit of physically defending myself, and I certainly had no intention of killing him. In fact, I didn't know I had. It was an accident purely in self-defense."

"Obviously. Who would want such complications?"

"Exactly," agreed Converse bluntly. "As soon as I can rearrange my last hours in Paris so as to eliminate any mention of my seeing General Bertholdier, I'll return and explain what happened to the police."

"As the adage goes, that may be easier said than done. You were seen talking together at L'Etalon Blanc. Undoubtedly, the general was recognized later when he came to the hotel; he's a celebrated man. No, I think you'd be wiser to let us handle it. We *can,* you know."

Joel looked hard at the German, his eyes cold yet questioning. "I admit there are risks doing it my way. I don't like them and neither would my client. On the other hand, I can't go around being hunted by the police."

"The hunt will be called off. It will be necessary for you to remain out of sight for a few days, but by then new instructions will be issued from Paris. Your name will disappear from the Interpol lists; you'll no longer be sought."

"I'll want assurances, guarantees."

"What better could you have than my word? I tell you nothing when I tell you that we could

322

have far more to lose than you.''

Converse controlled his astonishment. Leifhelm had just told him a great deal, whether he knew it or not. The German had as much as admitted he was part of a covert organization that could not take any chance of exposure. It was the first concrete evidence Joel had heard. Somehow it was too easy. Or were these elders of Aquitaine simply frightened old men?

''I'll concede that,'' said Converse, crossing his legs. ''Well, General, you found me before I found you, but then, as we agreed, my movements are restricted. Where do we go from here?''

''Precisely where you wanted to go, Mr. Converse. When you were in Paris, you spoke of Bonn, Tel Aviv, Johannesburg. You knew whom to reach in Paris and whom to look for in Bonn. That impresses us greatly; we must assume you know more.''

''I've spent months in detailed research—on behalf of my client, of course.''

''But who are you? Where do you come from?''

Joel felt a sharp, sickening ache in his chest. He had felt it many times before; it was his physical response to imminent danger and very real fear. ''I am who I want people to think I am, General Leifhelm. I'm sure you can understand that.''

''I see,'' said the German, watching him closely. ''A sworn companion of the prevailing winds, but with the power beneath to carry you to your own destination.''

''That's a little heavy, but I guess it says it. As

323

to where I come from, I'm sure you know that by now.''

Five hours. More than enough time to put the puppets in place. A killing in New York; it had to be dealt with.

"Only bits and pieces, Mr. Converse. And even if we knew more, how could we be certain it's true? What people think you are you may not be.''

"Are you, General?''

"Ausqezeichnet!'' said Leifhelm, slapping his knee and laughing. It was a genuine laugh, the man's waxen face creasing with humor. "You are a fine lawyer, *mein Herr.* You answer—as they say in English—a pointed question with another question that is both an answer and an indictment.''

"Under the circumstances, it's merely the truth. Nothing more.''

"Also modest. Very commendable, very attractive.''

Joel uncrossed his legs, then crossed them again impatiently. "I don't like compliments, General. I don't trust them—under the circumstances. You were saying before about where I wanted to go, about Bonn, Tel Aviv, and Johannesburg. What did you mean?''

"Only that we have complied with your wishes,'' said Leifhelm, spreading his hands in front of him. "Rather than your making such tedious trips, we have asked our representatives in Tel Aviv and Johannesburg, as well as Bertholdier, of course, to fly to Bonn for a conference. With you, Mr. Converse.''

He had done it! thought Joel. They *were* frightened—panicked was perhaps the better description. Despite the pounding and the pain in his chest, he spoke slowly, quietly. "I appreciate your consideration, but in all frankness, my client isn't ready for a summit. He wanted to understand the parts before he looked further at the whole. The spokes support the wheel, sir. I was to report how strong they were—how strong they appeared to me."

"Oh, yes, your client. Who is he, Mr. Converse?"

"I'm sure General Bertholdier told you I'm not at liberty to say."

"You were in San Francisco, California—"

"Where a great deal of my research was done," interrupted Joel. "It's not where my client lives. Although I readily admit there's a man in San Francisco—Palo Alto, to be exact—whom I'd like very much to *be* my client."

"Yes, yes, I see." Leifhelm put the ends of his fingers together as he continued, "Am I to understand that you reject the conference here in Bonn?"

Converse had taken a thousand such questions in opening gambits with attorneys seeking accommodations between corporate adversaries. Both parties wanted the same thing; it was simply a question of flattening out the responsibility so that no one party would be the petitioner.

"Well, you've gone to a lot of trouble," Joel began. "And as long as it's understood that I have the option of speaking to each man individually should I wish to do so, I can't see any

325

harm." Converse permitted himself a strained smile, as he had done a thousand times. "In the interests of my client, of course."

"Of course," said the German. "Tomorrow —say, four o'clock in the afternoon. I'll send a car for you. I assure you, I set an excellent table."

"A table?"

"Dinner, naturally. After we have our talk." Leifhelm rose from the chair. "I wouldn't think of your coming to Bonn and forgoing the experience. I'm known for my dinner parties, Mr. Converse. And if it concerns you, make whatever —security arrangements you like. A platoon of personal guards, if you wish. You'll be perfectly safe. *Mein Haus ist dein Haus.*"

"I don't speak German."

"Actually, it's an old Spanish saying. *Mi casa, su casa.* 'My house is your house.' Your comfort and well-being are my most urgent concerns."

"Mine, too," said Joel, rising. "I wouldn't think of having anyone accompany me, *or* follow me. It'd be counterproductive. Of course, I'll inform my client as to my whereabouts, telling him approximately when he can expect my subsequent call. He'll be anxious to hear from me."

"I should think so." Leifheim and Converse walked to the door; the German turned and once more offered his hand. "Until tomorrow, then. And may I again suggest while you're here that you be careful, at least for several days."

"I understand."

The puppets in New York. The killing that had to be dealt with—the first of two obstacles, two

326

sharp, sickening aches in his chest.

"By the way," said Joel, releasing the field marshal's hand. "There was a news item on the BBC this morning that interested me—so much that I phoned an associate. A man was killed in New York, a judge. They say it was a revenge killing, a contract put out by organized crime. Did you happen to hear anything about it?"

"*I?*" asked Leifhelm, his blond-white eyebrows raised, his waxlike lips parted. "It seems people are killed by the dozens every day in New York, judges included, I presume. Why should I know anything about it? The answer, obviously, is no."

"I just wondered. Thank you."

"But . . . but you. You must have a . . ."

"Yes, General?"

"Why does this judge interest you? Why did you think I would know him?"

Converse smiled, but without a trace of humor. "I won't be telling you anything when I tell you he was our mutual adversary—enemy, if you like."

"Our? You really must explain yourself!"

"As you—and as I—said, I am what I want people to think I am. This man knew the truth. I'm on leave of absence from my firm, working confidentially for a personal client. He tried to stop me, tried to get the senior partner to cancel my leave and call me back."

"By giving him *reasons?*"

"No, just veiled threats of corruption and impropriety. He wouldn't go any further; he's on the bench and couldn't back it up; his own conduct would be suspect. My employer is

327

completely ignorant—angry as hell and confused—but I've calmed him down. It's a closed issue; the less it's explored, the better for us all." Joel opened the door for Leifhelm. "Till tomorrow—" He paused for a brief moment, loathing the man standing in front of him but showing only respect in his eyes. "Field Marshal," he added.

"Gute Nacht," said Erich Leifhelm, nodding his head sharply once in military acknowledgment.

Converse persuaded the switchboard operator to send someone into the dining room for the American, Commander Fitzpatrick. The task of finding the naval officer was not easy, for he was not in the dining room or the bar but outside on the *Spanische Terrasse* having a drink with friends, watching the Rhine at twilight.

"What goddamned friends?" demanded Joel over the phone.

"Just a couple I met out there. He's a nice guy—an executive type, pretty much into his seventies, I think."

"And she?" asked Converse, his lawyer's antenna struck by a signal.

"Maybe—thirty, forty years younger," replied Connal with less elaboration.

"Get up here, sailor!"

Fitzpatrick leaned forward on the couch, his elbows on his knees, his expression a mixture of concern and astonishment as he looked over at Joel, who was smoking a cigarette in front of the

328

open balcony doors. "Let me run this again," he said warily. "You want me to stop someone from getting your service record?"

"Not all of it, just part of it."

"Who the hell do you think I am?"

"You did it for Avery—for *Press*. You can do it for me. You *have* to!"

"That's backwards. I *opened* those files for him, I didn't keep them closed."

"Either way it's control. You've got access; you've got a key."

"I'm *here,* not there. I can't scissor something out you don't like ten thousand miles away. Be reasonable!"

"Somebody can, somebody *has* to! It's only a short segment, and it's got to be at the end. The final interview."

"An *interview?*" said Connal, startled, getting to his feet. "In a service record? You mean some kind of operational report? Because if you do, it wouldn't be—"

"Not a report," interrupted Converse, shaking his head. "The discharge—my *discharge* interview. That stuff Press Halliday quoted to me."

"Wait a minute, *wait* a minute!" Fitzpatrick held up his hands. "Are you referring to the remarks made at your discharge *hearing?*"

"Yes, that's it. The hearing!"

"Well, relax. They're not part of your service record, or anyone else's."

"Halliday had them—*Avery* had them! I just told you, he quoted my words verbatim!" Joel walked to a table where there was an ashtray; he crushed out his cigarette. "If they're not part of the record, how did he get them? How did *you* get them for him?"

"That's different," said Connal, obviously remembering as he spoke. "You were a POW, and a lot of those hearings were put under a debriefing classification, and I *do* mean classified. Even after all these years, many of those sessions are still touchy. A lot of things were talked about that no one to this day wants made public—for everyone's good, not just the military's."

"But *you* got them! I heard my own words, goddamn it!"

"Yes, I got them," admitted the Navy lawyer without enthusiasm. "I got the transcript, and I'd be busted to seaman third class if anyone knew about it. You see, I believed Press. He swore to me he needed it, needed everything. He couldn't make any mistakes."

"How did you do it? You weren't even in San Diego at the time, that's what you said!"

"By calling the vaults and using my legal-release number to have a photostat made. I said it was a Four Zero emergency and I'd take responsibility. The next morning when the authorization came in by pouch for counter-signature, I had the chief legal officer at the base sign it with a lot of other things. It simply got buried in the paper work."

"But how did you know about it in the first place?"

"Selected POW records have flags on their discharge sheets."

"Clarification, please?"

"Just what I said, flags. Small blue seals that denote additional information still held under tight security. No flags, everything's clean; but if there is one, that means there's something else. I told Press, and he said he had to have whatever it was, so I went after it."

"Then anyone else could, too."

"No, not anyone. You need an officer with a legal-release number, and there aren't that many of us. Also there's a minimum forty-eight-hour delay so the material can be vetted. That's almost always in the area of weapons and technology data that still might be classified."

"Forty-eight?" Converse swallowed as he tried to count the hours since Paris, since the first moment his name had surfaced. "There's still time!" he said, his voice taut, his words clipped. "If you can do it there's still *time.* And if you can, I'll tell you everything I know because you'll deserve it. No one will deserve it more."

"Spell it out."

Joel turned aimlessly, shaking his head. "That's funny. I said the same thing to Avery. I said 'Spell it out, Avery.' . . . Sorry, his name was Press." Converse turned back to the Navy lawyer, a military lawyer with a mystifying military privilege called a legal-release number. "Listen to me and hear me clearly. A few minutes ago something happened that I wasn't sure would or *could* happen—something your brother-in-law was killed to prevent. Tomorrow at four o'clock in the afternoon I'm going to walk into the midst of that group of men who've come together to promote a kind of violence that'll stun this world, toppling governments, allowing these same men to step in and fill the voids. They'll run things their way, shape the *laws* their way. One big Supreme Court, each chair owned by a fanatic with specific convictions as to who and what has value and who and what doesn't, and those who don't can go to hell, no appeals on the agenda. . . . I'm going to meet them face-to-face! I'm going to *talk* with them, *hear* their *words!* I admit I'm the most amateurish fox you've ever heard of in a chicken coop—only, in this case it's a vultures' nest, and I mean the type that swoops down and tears the flesh off your back with one pass. But I've got something going for me: I'm one hell of a good lawyer, and I'll learn things they won't know I've learned. Maybe enough to piece together a couple of cases that will blow it all apart—blow *them* apart. I told you before that I rejected your deadline. I still reject it, but *now* it doesn't seem so out of the question. Certainly not two days, but perhaps not ten! You see, I thought I was going to have to fly to Tel Aviv, then Johannesburg. Prime everyone, frighten them. Now I don't have to! We've already done it! They're coming to me because they're the ones who are frightened *now!* They don't know what to think, and that means they've panicked." Converse paused, sweat forming on his hairline; then he added, "I don't have to tell you what a good lawyer can do with panicked hostile witnesses. The materials he can collect for evidence."

"Your plea's accepted, counselor," said Fitzpatrick, not without awe. "You're convincing.

Now, tell me why my intercession can help? What does it accomplish?''

"I want those men to think I'm *one* of them! I can live with everything they can put together about me—I'm not proud of it all; I've made my compromises—but I *can't* live with that transcript of my discharge! Don't you *see?* It's what Avery—Press—understood! I understand now. He knew me nearly twenty-five years ago, and when I think back we were actually pretty damned good friends. And no matter what happened to us individually, he was banking on the fact that I hadn't really changed that much, not in the deeper things. By the time we reach the voting age we're pretty well set, all of us. The real changes come later, much later, dictated by such things as acceptance or rejection and the state of our wallets—the prices we pay for our convictions, or to support our talents, defending success or explaining failure. That transcript confirmed what Halliday believed, at least enough to make him want to meet me, talk with me, and finally to recruit me. Only, he did it—finally—by dying as I held his head. I couldn't walk away after that.''

Connal Fitzpatrick was silent as he walked out on the balcony. He leaned over and gripped the railing as Converse watched him. Then he stood up, raised both his hands, and pulled back the sleeve of his left wrist. "It's twelve-fifteen in San Diego. No one in legal goes to lunch before one o'clock; the Coronado's bar doesn't begin to jump until then.''

"Can you *do* it?''

"I can try,'' said the naval officer, crossing

333

through the French doors toward the telephone. "No, damn it, if you've got your times straight, I can do better than try, I can issue an order. That's what rank's all about."

The first five minutes were excruciating for Joel. There were delays on all overseas calls, but somehow the bi-, tri-, or quadri-lingual Fitzpatrick, speaking urgently, unctuously, in German, managed to get through, the word *dringend* repeated frequently.

"Lieutenant Senior Grade Remington, David. Legal Division, SAND PAC. This is an emergency, sailor, Commander Fitzpatrick calling. Break in if the lines are occupied." Connal covered the mouthpiece and turned to Converse. "If you'll open my suitcase, there's a bottle of bourbon in the middle."

"I'll open your suitcase, Commander."

"Remington? . . . Hello, David, it's Connal. . . . Yes, thanks very much, I'll tell Meagen. . . . No, I'm not in San Francisco, don't call me there. But something's come up I want you to handle, something on my calendar that I didn't get to. For openers, it's a Four Zero emergency. I'll fill you in when I get back, but until I do you have to take care of it. Got a pencil? . . . There's a POW service record under the name of Converse, Joel, Lieutenant, one and a half stripes, Air Arm, pilot—carrier-based, Vietnam duty. He was discharged in the sixties"—Fitzpatrick looked down at Converse, who held up his right hand and three fingers of his left—"nineteen sixty-eight, to be exact." Joel stepped forward, his spread right hand still raised, his left now showing

334

only the index finger. "June of '68," added the Navy lawyer, nodding. "Point of separation our old hometown, San Diego. Have you got all that? Read it back to me, please, David."

Connal nodded sporadically, as he listened. "C-O-N-V-E-R-S-E, that's right. . . . June, '68, Air Arm, pilot, Vietnam, POW section, San Diego separation; that's it, you've got it. Now here's the wicket, David. This Converse's SR is flag status; the flag pertains to his discharge hearing, no weapons or high tech involved. . . . Listen carefully, David. It's my understanding that there may be a request pending accompanied by a legal-release code for the discharge transcript. Under *no* circumstances is that transcript to be released. The flag stays fixed and can't be removed by anyone without my authorization. And if the release *has* been processed it'll still be within the forty-eight-hour vet-delay. *Kill* it. Understood?"

Again Fitzpatrick listened, but instead of nodding, he shook his head. "No, not under any circumstances. I don't care if the secretaries of State, Defense, and the Navy all sign a joint petition on White House stationery, the answer is no. If anyone questions the decision, tell him I'm exercising my authority as Chief Legal Officer of SAND PAC. There's some goddamned article in the 'shoals' that says a station CLO can impound materials on the basis of conceivably privileged information relative to the security of the sector, et cetera, et cetera. I don't recall the time element— seventy-two hours or five days or something like that—but find that statute. You may need it."

Connal listened further, his brows creasing, his eyes straying to Joel. He spoke slowly as Converse felt the sickening ache again in his chest. "Where can you reach me . . . ?" said the naval officer, perplexed. Then suddenly he was no longer bewildered. "I take back what I said before; call Meagen in San Francisco. If I'm not with her and the kids, she'll know where to reach me. . . . Thanks again, David. Sweep your decks and get right on this, okay? Thanks . . . I'll tell Meg." Fitzpatrick hung up the phone and exhaled audibly. "There," he said, slouched in relief, pushing his hand through his loose light-brown hair. "I'll phone Meagen and give her this number, tell her to say I've gone up to the Sonoma hills, if Remington calls—Press had some property there."

"Give her the telephone number," said Joel, "but don't tell her anything else."

"Don't worry, she's got enough on her mind." The naval officer looked at Converse, frowning. "If your hourly count is right, you've got your time now."

"My count's all right. Is Lieutenant Remington? I mean that only in the sense that he wouldn't let anyone override your order, would he?"

"Don't mistake my officiousness where he's concerned," replied Connal. "David isn't easily pushed around. The reason I chose him and not one of the four other senior lawyers in the department is that he's got a reputation for being a stickler prick. He'll find that statute and nail it to the forehead of any four-striper who tries to countermand that order. I like Remington; he's very useful. He scares the hell out of people.''

"We all have case partners like that. It's called the good guy-bad guy routine.''

"David fits. He's got an eye that keeps straying to the right." Fitzpatrick suddenly stood erect, his bearing military. "I thought you were going to get the bourbon, *Lieutenant?*''

"Yes, *sir,* Commander!" shot back Joel, heading for Fitzpatrick's suitcase.

"And if I remember correctly, after you pour us a drink, you're going to tell me a story I want very much to hear.''

"Aye, aye, sir!" said Converse, lifting the suitcase off the floor and putting it on the couch. "And if I may suggest, sir," continued Joel, "a room-service dinner might be in order. I'm sure the Commander needs nourishment after his trying day at the wheel.''

"Good thinking, Lieutenant. I'll phone down to the *Empfang.*''

"Before calling your bookie, may I also suggest that you first call your sister?''

"Oh, Christ, I forgot!''

Chaim Abrahms walked down the dark street in Tel Aviv, his stocky frame draped in his usual safari jacket, boots beneath his khaki trousers, and a beret covering his nearly bald head. The beret was the only concession he made to the night's purpose; normally he enjoyed being recognized, accepting the adulation with well-rehearsed humility. In daylight, his head uncovered and held erect, and wearing his familiar jacket, he would acknowledge the homage with a nod, his eyes boring in on his followers.

"First a Jew!" was the phrase with which he was always greeted, whether in Tel Aviv or Jerusalem, in sections of Paris and most of New York.

The phrase had been born years ago when as a young terrorist for the Irgun he had been condemned to death *in absentia* by the British for the slaughter of a Palestinian village, with the Arab corpses put on display for *Nakama!* He had then issued a cry heard around the world: "I am first a Jew, a son of Abraham! All else follows, and rivers of blood will follow if the children of Abraham are denied!"

The British, in 1948, not caring to create another martyr, commuted his sentence and gave him a large *moshav*. Yet the acreage of the settlement could not confine the militant sabra. Three wars had broken his agricultural shackles as well as unleashing his ferocity—and his brilliance in the field. It was a brilliance developed and refined through the early years of racing with a fugitive, fragmented army, for which the tactics of surprise, shock, hit and melt away were constant, when being outmanned and outgunned were the accepted odds but only victory was the acceptable outcome. He later applied the strategies and the philosophy of those years to the ever-expanding war machine that became the Army, Navy, and Air Force of a mighty Israel. Mars was in the heavens of Chaim Abrahm's vision and, the prophets aside, the god of war was his strength, his reason for being. From Ramat

Aviv to Har Hazeytim, from Rehovot to Masada of the Negev, *Nakama!* was the cry. *Retribution* to the enemies of Abraham's children!

If only the Poles and the Czechs, the Hungarians and the Romanies, as well as the haughty Germans and the impossible Russians, had not immigrated to his country by such tens of thousands. They arrived and the complications came with them. Faction against faction, culture against culture, each group trying to prove it was more entitled to the name *Jew* than the others. It was all nonsense! They were there because they had to be; they had succumbed to Abraham's enemies, permitted—yes, *permitted*—the slaughter of millions rather than rising as millions and slaughtering in return. Well, they found out what their *civilized* ways could bring them, and how much their Talmudic convolutions could earn them. So they came to the Holy Land—*their* Holy Land, so they proclaimed. Well, it wasn't theirs. Where were they when it was being clawed out of rock and arid desert by strong hands with primitive tools—Biblical tools? Where were they when the hated Arab and the despised English first felt the wrath of the tribal Jew? They were in the capitals of Europe, in their banks and their fancy drawing rooms, making money and drinking expensive brandy out of crystal goblets. No, they came here because they had to; they came to the Holy Land of the *sabra*.

They brought with them money and dandy ways and elegant words and confusing arguments and influence and the guilt of the world. But it was the sabra who taught them how to fight. And it was a sabra who would bring all Israel into the orbit of a mighty new alliance.

Abrahms reached the intersection of Ibn Gabirol and Arlosoroff streets; the streetlamps were haloed, their light hazy. It was just as well; he should not be seen. He had another block to go, to an address on Jabotinsky, an unprepossessing apartment house where there was an undistinguished flat leased by a man who appeared to be no more than an unimportant bureaucrat. What few realized, however, was that this man, this specialist who operated sophisticated computer equipment with communications throughout most of the world, was intrinsic to the global operations of the Mossad, Israel's intelligence service, which many considered the finest on earth. He, too, was a sabra. He was one of them.

Abrahms spoke his name quietly into the mouthpiece above the mail slot in the outer lobby; he heard the click in the lock of the heavy door and walked inside. He began the climb up the three flights of steps that would take him to the flat.

"Some wine, Chaim?"

"Whisky," was the curt reply.

"Always the same question and always the same answer," said the specialist. "I say 'Some wine, Chaim?' and you say one word. 'Whisky,' you say. You would drink whisky at the Seder, if you could get away with it."

"I can and I do." Abrahms sat in a cracked leather chair, looking around the plain, disheveled room with books everywhere, wondering, as he always did, why a man with such influence lived this way. It was rumored that the Mossad officer did not like company, and larger, more attractive quarters might invite it. "I gathered from your grunts and coughs over the telephone that you have what I need."

"Yes, I have it," said the specialist, bringing a glass of very good Scotch to his guest. "I have it, but I don't think you're going to like it."

"Why not?" asked Abrahms, drinking, his eyes alert over the rim of the glass and fixed on his host as the latter sat down opposite him.

"Basically because it's confusing, and what's confusing in this business is to be approached delicately. You are not a delicate man, Chaim Abrahms, forgive the indelicacy of my saying it. You tell me this Converse is your enemy, a would-be infiltrator, and I tell you I find nothing to support the conclusion. Before anything else, there must be a deep personal motive for a nonprofessional to engage in this kind of deception, this kind of behavior, if you will. There has to be a driving compulsion to strike out at an image of a cause he loathes. Well, there is a motive, and there is an enemy for which he must have great hatred, but neither is compatible with what you suggest. The information, incidentally, is completely reliable. It comes from the Quang Dinh—"

"What in hell is that?" interrupted the general.

"A specialized branch of North Vietnamese —now, of course, Vietnamese—intelligence."

"You have sources *there?*"

"We fed them for years—nothing terribly vital, but sufficient to gain a few ears, and voices. There were things we had to know, weapons we had to understand; they could be turned against us."

"This Converse was in North Vietnam?"

"For several years as a prisoner of war; there's an extensive file on him. At first, his captors thought he could be used for propaganda, radio broadcasts, television—imploring his brutal government to withdraw and stop the bombing, all the usual garbage. He spoke well, presented a good picture, and was obviously very American. Initially they televised him as a murderer from the skies, saved from the angry mobs by humane troops, then later while eating and exercising; you see, they were programming him for a violently sudden reversal. They thought he was a soft, privileged young man who could be broken rather easily to do their bidding in exchange for more comfortable treatment—after having experienced a period of harsh deprivation. What they learned, however, was quite different. Under that soft shell the inner lining was made of hard metal, and the odd thing was that as the months went by it grew harder, until they realized they had created —created was their word—a hellhound of sorts, somehow forged in steel."

"Hellhound? Was that their word, too?"

"No, they called him an ugly troublemaker, which, considering the source, is not without irony. The point is, they recognized the fact that they *had* created him. The harsher the treatment, the more volatile he became, the more resilient."

"Why not?" said Abrahms sharply. "He was angry. Prod a desert snake and watch him strike."

"I can assure you, Chaim, it is not the normal human response under such conditions. A man can go mad and strike in crazed fury, or he can become reclusive to the point of catatonia, or fall apart weeping, willing to compromise anything and everything for the smallest kindness. He did none of these things. His was a calculated and inventive series of responses drawing on his own inner resources to survive. He led two escapes—the first lasting three days and the second five—before the groups were recaptured. As the leader, he was placed in a cage in the Mekong River, but he devised a way to kill the water rats by grabbing them from beneath the surface like a shark. He was then thrown into solitary confinement, a pit in the ground twelve feet deep with barbed wire anchored across the top. It was from there, during a heavy rainstorm at night, that he clawed his way up, bent the wire back and escaped alone. He made his way south through the jungles and in the river streams for over a hundred miles until he reached the American lines. It was no easy feat. They created a savagely obsessed man who won his own personal war."

"Why didn't they simply kill him before that?"

"I wondered myself," said the specialist, "so I phoned my source in Hanoi, the one who provided the information. He said a strange thing, something quite profound in its way. He said he wasn't there, of course, but he thought it was probably respect.''

"For an ugly troublemaker?''

"Captivity in war does odd things, Chaim, to both the captured and the captors. There are so many factors at work in a vicious game. Aggression, resistance, bravery, fear, and—not the least—curiosity, especially when the players come from such diverse cultures as the Occident and the Orient. An abnormal bond is often formed, as much from the weariness of the testing game as from anything else, perhaps. It doesn't lessen the national animosities, but a subtle recognition sets in that tells these men, these players, that they are not really in the game by their own choosing. In-depth analyses further show us that it is the captors, not the captured, who first perceive this commonality. The latter are obsessed with freedom and survival, while the former begin to question their absolute authority over the lives and conditions of other men. They start to wonder what it would be like to be in the other player's shoes. It's all part of what the psychiatrists call the Stockholm syndrome.''

"What in the name of *God* are you trying to say? You sound like one of those bores in the Knesset reading a position paper. A little of this, a little of that and a lot of wind!''

"You are definitely not delicate, Chaim. I'm trying to explain to you that while this Converse nurtured his hatreds and his obsessions, his captors wearied of the game, and as our source in Hanoi suggests, they grudgingly spared his life out of respect, before he made his final and successful escape.''

To Abrahm's bewilderment the specialist had apparently finished. "And?" said the sabra.

"Well, there it is. There is the motive and the enemy, but they are also *your* motive and *your* enemy—arrived at from different routes, of course. Ultimately, you wish to smash insurgence wherever it erupts, curb the spread of Third World revolutions, especially Islamic, because you know they're being fostered by the Marxists—read Soviets—and are a direct threat to Israel. One way or another it's the global threat that's brought you all together, and in my judgment rightfully so. There is a time and a place for a military-industrial complex, and it is now. It must run the governments of the free world before that world is buried by its enemies."

Chaim Abrahms squinted and tried not to shout. *"And?"*

"Can't you see? This Converse is one of you. Everything supports it. He has the motive and an enemy he's seen in the harshest light. He is a highly regarded attorney who makes a great deal of money with a very conservative firm, and his clients are among the wealthiest corporations and conglomerates. Everything he's been and everything he stands for can only benefit from your efforts. The confusion lies in his unorthodox methods, and I can't explain them except to say that perhaps they are *not* unorthodox in the specialized work he does. Markets can plummet on rumors; concealment and diversion are surely respected. Regardless, he doesn't want to destroy you, he wants to join you."

The sabra put his glass down on the floor and

struggled out of the chair. With his chin tucked into his breastbone and his hands clasped behind his back, Abrahms paced back and forth in silence. He stopped and looked down at the specialist.

"Suppose, just *suppose,*" he said, "the almighty Mossad has made a mistake, that there's something you didn't find."

"I would find that hard to accept."

"But it's a possibility!"

"In light of the information we've gathered, I doubt it. Why?"

"Because I have a sense of smell, *that's* why!"

The man from the Mossad kept his eyes on Abrahms, as if studying the soldier's face—or thinking from a different viewpoint. "There is only one other possibility, Chaim. If this Converse is not who and what I've described, which would be contrary to all the data we've compiled, then he is an agent of his government."

"That's—what I smell," said the sabra softly.

It was the specialist's turn to be silent. He breathed deeply, then responded. "I respect your nostrils, old friend. Not always your conduct but certainly your sense of smell. What do the others think?"

"Only that he's lying, that he's covering for others he may or may not know, who are using him as a scout—an 'infantry point' was the term used by Palo Alto."

The Mossad officer continued to stare at the sabra, but his eyes were no longer focused; he was seeing abstract, twisted patterns, convolutions few men would comprehend. They came from a lifetime of analyzing seen and unseen, legitimate and racial enemies, parrying dagger thrusts with counterthrusts in the blackest darkness. "It's possible," he whispered, as if replying to an unspoken question heard only by himself. "Almost inconceivable, but possible."

"What is? That Washington is behind him?"

"Yes."

"Why?"

"As an outrageous alternative I do not subscribe to, but the only one left that has the slightest plausibility. Simply put, he has too much information."

"And?"

"Not Washington in the usual sense, not the government in the broader sense, but within a *branch* of the government a *section* that has heard whispers about an organization but cannot be sure. They believe that if there is such an organization, they must invade it to expose it. So they choose a man with the right history, the right memories, even the right profession to do the job. He might even believe everything he says."

The sabra was transfixed but impatient. "That has too many complications for me," he said bluntly.

"Try it my way first. Try to accept him; he may be genuine. He'll have to give you *something* concrete; you can force that. Then again he may not because he cannot."

"And?"

"And if he can't, you'll know you're right. Then put as much distance between him and his sponsors as is humanly and brutally possible. He must become a pariah, a man hunted for crimes so insane his madness is unquestioned."

"Why not just kill him?"

"By all means, but not before he's been labeled so mad that no one will step forward to claim him. It will buy you the time you need. The final phase of Aquitaine is when? Three, four weeks away?"

"That's when it begins, yes."

The specialist got up from the chair and stood pensively in front of the soldier. "I repeat, first try to accept him, see if what I said before is true. But if that sense of smell of yours is provoked further, if there's the slightest possibility he has been willingly or unwillingly, wittingly or unwittingly, made a provocateur by men in Washington, then build your case against him and throw him to the wolves. Create that pariah as the North Vietnamese created a hellhound. Then kill him quickly, before anyone else reaches him."

"A sabra of the Mossad speaks?"

"As clearly as I can."

The young Army captain and the older civilian came out of the Pentagon from adjacent glass doors and glanced briefly at each other with no recognition. They walked separately down the short bank of steps and turned left on the cement path that led to the enormous parking lot; the Army officer was perhaps ten feet ahead of the civilian. Upon reaching the huge asphalt area, each veered in a different direction toward his car. If these two men had been the subjects of photographic surveillance during the past fifty seconds, there was no indication whatsoever that they knew each other.

The green Buick coupe turned right in the middle of the block, going through the open chasm that was the entrance to the hotel's underground parking lot. At the bottom of the ramp the driver showed his room key to the attendant, who raised the yellow barrier and waved him along. There was an empty space in the third column of stationary automobiles. The Buick eased into it and the Army captain got out.

He circled through the revolving door and walked to a bank of elevators in the hotel's lower lobby. The panels of the second elevator opened, revealing two couples who had not intended to reach the underground level; they laughed as one of the men repeatedly pressed the lobby button. The officer, in turn, touched the button for the fourteenth floor. Sixty seconds later he walked out into the corridor toward the exit staircase. He was heading for the eleventh floor.

The blue Toyota station wagon came down the ramp, the driver's hand extended, a room key held out, the number visible. Inside the parking area the driver found an empty space and carefully steered the small station wagon into it.

The civilian stepped out and looked at his watch. Satisfied, he started toward the revolving door and the elevators. The second elevator was empty, and the civilian was tempted to press the button for the eleventh floor; he was tired and did not relish the thought of the additional walk.

However, there would be other occupants on the way up, so he held to the rules and placed his index finger over the button beside the number 9.

Standing in front of the hotel-room door, the civilian raised his hand, rapped once, waited several beats, then rapped twice more. Seconds later the door was opened by the Army captain. Beyond him was a third man, also in uniform, the color and the insignia denoting a lieutenant, junior grade, in the Navy. He stood by a desk with a telephone on it.

"Glad you got here on time," said the Army officer. "The traffic was rotten. Our call should be coming through in a few minutes."

The civilian entered, nodding to the Navy man as he spoke. "What did you find out about Fitzpatrick?" he asked.

"He's where he shouldn't be," replied the lieutenant.

"Can you bring him back?"

"I'm working on it, but I don't know where to begin. I'm a very low man on a very big totem pole."

"Aren't we all?" said the captain.

"Who'd have thought Halliday would have gone to him?" asked the naval officer, frustration in his voice. "Or if he was going to bring him in, why didn't he go to him *first?* Or tell him about us?"

"I can answer the last two questions," said the Army man. "He was protecting him from a Pentagon backlash. If we go down, his brother-in-law stays clean."

"And I can answer the first question," said the civilian. "Halliday went to Fitzpatrick because in the final analysis, he didn't trust us. Geneva proved he was right."

"How?" asked the captain defensively, but without apology. "We couldn't have prevented it."

"No, we couldn't," agreed the civilian. "But we couldn't do anything about it afterwards, either. That was part of the trust, and there was no way we could live up to it. We couldn't afford to."

The telephone rang. The lieutenant picked it up and listened. "It's Mykonos," he said.

PART TWO

PART TWO

12

Connal Fitzpatrick sat opposite Joel at the room-service table drinking the last of his coffee. The dinner was finished, the story completed, and all the questions the Navy lawyer could raise had been answered by Converse because he had given his word; he needed a complete ally.

"Except for a few identities and some dossier material," said Connal, "I don't know an awful lot more than I did before. Maybe I will when I see those Pentagon names. You say you don't know who supplied them?"

"No. Like Topsy, they're just there. Beale said a number of them are probably mistakes, but others aren't; they have to be linked to Delavane."

"They had to be supplied by someone too. There had to be reasons why they were listed."

"Beale called them 'decision makers' in military procurements."

"Then I *have* to see them. I've dealt with those people."

"*You?*"

"Yes. Not very often, but enough to know my way around."

"Why you?"

"Basically translating legal nuances from language to language where Navy tech was involved. I think I mentioned that I speak—"

"You did," Joel broke in.

"*Goddamn* it!" cried Fitzpatrick, crushing his napkin in a fist.

"What's the matter?"

"Press *knew* I had dealings with those committees, with the technology and armaments boys! He even asked me about them. Who I saw, who I liked—who I trusted. *Jesus!* Why didn't he come to *me?* Of all the people he knew, I was the logical one! I'm down the pike and his closest friend."

"That's why he didn't come to you," said Converse.

"Stupid *bastard!*" Connal raised his eyes. "And I hope you hear that, Press. You might still be around to see Connal Two win the Bay Regatta."

"I think you really believe he might hear you."

Fitzpatrick looked across the table at Joel. "Yes, I do. You see, I believe, counselor. I know all the reasons why I shouldn't—Press enumerated them to a fare-thee-well when we were in our cups—but I believe. I answered him once with a quote from one of his laid-back Protestant forebears."

"What was that?" asked Joel, smiling kindly.

" 'There's more faith in honest doubt than is held by all the archangels in the mind of God.' "

"It's very nice. I've never heard it before."

"Maybe I didn't get it right. . . . Joel, I've got to see those names!"

"And I have to get my attaché case, but I can't go myself."

"Then I'm elected," said the Navy man. "Do

you think Leifhelm's right? You think he can really call off Interpol?''

"I'm of two thoughts about it. For my immediate maneuverability I hope he can. But if he does, it'll scare the hell out of me.''

"I'm on your side about that,'' agreed Connal, getting out of the chair. "I'll call the desk and get a taxi. Give me the key to the locker.''

Converse reached into his pocket and pulled out the small, rounded key. "Leifhelm's seen you. He could have you followed; he did before.''

"I'll be ten times more careful. If I see the same pair of headlights twice, I'll go to a *Bierkeller*. I know a few here.''

Joel looked at his watch. "It's twenty minutes to ten. Do you think you could swing around to the university first?''

"Dowling?''

"He said he had someone he wanted me to meet. Just walk by him—or them—and say everything's under control, nothing else. I owe him that much.''

"Suppose he tries to stop me?''

"Then pull out your ID and say it's high priority, or ultrasecret, or whatever bullshit security phrases that come to that very inventive mind of yours.''

"Do I sense a touch of legal envy?''

"No, just recognition. I know where you're coming from. I've been there.''

Fitzpatrick walked slowly along the wide path on the south façade of the immense university building, once the great palace of the all-powerful archbishops of Cologne. The unimpeded moonlight swelled over the area, reflecting off the myriad rows of cathedral windows and lending a luminous dimension to the light stone walls of the majestic structure. Beyond the path the winding gardens of August possessed an eerie elegance—circles of sleeping flowers, their beauty heightened by the moonlight. Connal was so struck by the tranquil loveliness of the nocturnal setting that he nearly forgot why he was there.

The reason was brought sharply back into focus when he saw a slender figure slouched alone on a bench. The man's legs were extended and crossed at the ankles, his head covered by a soft cloth hat, but not sufficiently to hide the flowing gray-blond hair that protruded slightly over his temples and the back of his neck. So this Caleb Dowling was an actor, thought the Navy lawyer, amused by the fact that Dowling had feigned shock when he realized Connal did not recognize him. But then, neither had Converse; they were obviously a minority in a world of television addicts. A college professor who had fulfilled the fantasies of youth, a risk-taker, according to Joel, who had won a battle against astronomical odds, was a nice thing to think about; the only sad note was the haunted life of his wife, whom he loved dearly. Also, a marine who had fought in the bloody mess that was Kwajalein was a man to be reckoned with.

Fitzpatrick walked over to the bench and sat down several feet away from Dowling. The actor glanced at him, then did a perfectly natural double take, his head snapping. *"You?"*

"I'm sorry about last night," said Connal. "I

gather I wasn't very convincing.''

"You lacked a certain finish, young fella. Where the hell is Converse?''

"Sorry again. He couldn't make it, but not to worry. Everything's A-okay and under control.''

"Whose okay and whose control?'' countered the actor, annoyed. "I told Joel to come here, not a cub-scout interlocutor.''

"I resent that. I'm a lieutenant commander in the United States Navy and the chief legal officer at a major naval base. Mr. Converse accepted an assignment from us which has an element of personal risk for him and the highest priority of classification for us. Back off, Mr. Dowling. We appreciate—and I speak for Converse as well as myself—your interest and your generosity, but it's time for you to recede. For your own benefit, incidentally.''

"What about Interpol? He killed a man.''

"Who tried to kill *him,*'' added Fitzpatrick quickly, a lawyer rejoining a negative statement by a witness on the stand. "That will be clarified internally and the charges dropped.''

"You're pretty smooth, Commander,'' said Dowling, sitting up. "Better than you were last night—this morning, actually.''

"I was upset. I'd lost him and I had to find him. I had to deliver vital information.''

The actor now crossed his legs at the knees and leaned back, his arm slung casually over the slatted rim of the bench. "So this thing Converse and you are involved with is a real hush-hush operation?''

"It's highly classified, yes.''

359

"And you and he being lawyers, it's got something to do with legal irregularities over here that somehow reach into the military, is that right?"

"In the broadest sense, again yes. I'm afraid I can't be any more specific. Converse mentioned that there was someone you wanted him to meet."

"Yes, there is. I said a couple of harsh things about him, but I take them back; he was doing his thing. He didn't know who the hell I was any more than you did. He's one smart man, tough but fair."

"I hope you understand that under the circumstances Converse can't comply with your request."

"You'll do," said Dowling calmly, removing his arm from the back of the bench.

Connal was suddenly alarmed. There was movement behind him in the shadowed moonlight; he whipped his head around, peering over his shoulder. Out of the protective darkness of the building from within the pitch-black cover of a doorway the figure of a man began walking across the dark green lawn. An arm thrown casually over the rim of the bench, then just as casually removed. Both movements had been signals! Identity confirmed; move in.

"What the hell have you *done?*" asked the Navy lawyer harshly.

"Bringing you two bucks to your senses," replied Dowling. "If my celebrated instincts are valid, I did the right thing. If they're wrong, I still did the right thing."

"*What?*"

The man crossing the lawn entered the spill of clear moonlight. He was heavyset and wore a dark suit and tie; his scowling, late-middle-aged face and straight gray hair gave him the air of a prosperous businessman. It was clear that at the moment he was intensely angry.

Dowling spoke as he got up from the bench. "Commander, may I introduce the Honorable Walter Peregrine, United States ambassador to the Federal Republic of Germany."

Lieutenant David Remington wiped his steel-rimmed glasses with a silicone-treated tissue, then threw the tissue into a wastebasket and got up from his desk. Returning the glasses to his face, he walked to a mirror secured to the back of his office door and checked his appearance. He smoothed his hair, shoved the knot of his tie in place, and looked down at the failing crease of his trousers. All things considered—it was 1730 hours and he had been harassed at his desk since 0800 in the morning, including that crazy Four Zero emergency from Fitzpatrick—he looked quite presentable. And anyway, Rear Admiral Hickman was not a stickler for spit and polish where the desk corps was concerned. He knew damn well that most of the legal execs would bolt in a minute for much higher paying jobs in the civilian sector if the dress and other disposable codes were taken too seriously. Well, David Remington wouldn't. Where the hell else could a man travel all over the world, housing a wife and three kids in some of the nicest quarters imaginable, with all the medical and dental bills paid for, and not have the terrible pressures of rising in private or corporate practice. His father had been an attorney for one of the biggest insurance companies in Hartford, Connecticut, and his father had had ulcers at forty-three, a nervous breakdown at forty-eight, his first stroke at fifty-one, and a final, massive coronary at fifty-six; everyone had said he was so terrific at his job he might even be in line for the presidency. But then, people always said things like that when a man died in the line of corporate duty—which men did too goddamned frequently.

None of that for David Remington, no sir! He was simply going to be one of the best lawyers in the U.S. Navy, serve his thirty years, get out at fifty-five with a generous pension, and become a well-paid legal-military consultant at fifty-six. At the precise age when his father died, he would start living very nicely, indeed. It was simply a matter of building a reputation as a man who knew more about naval and maritime law—and who stuck to it—than any other lawyer in the Navy. If he stepped on toes in his performance, so be it; it could only enhance that reputation. He didn't give a damn about being popular; he cared only about being right. And he never made a decision until he was certain of its correct legal position. Consultants like that were prized commodities in civilian practice.

Remington wondered why Admiral Hickman wanted to see him, especially at this hour when most of the desk corps had gone for the day. There was a court-martial pending that could become a sensitive issue. A black officer, an

Annapolis graduate, had been caught selling cocaine off a destroyer berthed in the Philippines; that was probably it. Remington had pre-prepared the case for the judge advocate, who frankly did not care to prosecute; the amount was not that large, and others were certainly selling far more, and they were probably white. That was not the point, Remington had insisted. If there were others, they had not been caught; if there was evidence, it had not been found. The law was color-blind.

He would say the same thing to Hickman. The "stickler prick," a derisive nickname Remington knew was used behind his back, would stand firm. Well, at fifty-six—the age at which his father had been killed by company policy—a stickler prick would have all the comforts of an exclusive country club without paying the corporate price. Lieutenant Remington opened the door, walked out into the gray hallway, and started for the elevator that would take him to the office of the highest ranking man at the San Diego naval base.

"Sit down, Remington," said Rear Admiral Brian Hickman, shaking the lieutenant's hand and indicating a chair in front of the large desk. "I don't know about you, but this has been what I used to call at your age one fucked-up day. Sometimes I wish Congress wouldn't appropriate so damn much money down here. Everyone gets on such a high you'd think they'd smoked everything in Tijuana. They forget they're supposed to have architects before they start bribing the contractors."

"Yes, sir, I know what you mean, sir," said

Remington, sitting down with proper deference as Hickman stood several feet to his left. The mere reference to Tijuana and drugs confirmed his suspicions; the admiral was about to launch into the everybody-does-it routine, which would lead to "Why should the Navy stir up a racial controversy with something that took place in the Philippines?" Well, he was prepared. The law —naval law—was color-blind.

"I'm going to have a well-deserved drink, Lieutenant," said Hickman, heading for a copper dry bar against the wall. "Can I get you something?"

"No, thank you, sir."

"Hey, look, Remington, I appreciate your staying late for this—conference, I guess you'd call it, but I don't expect any version of corporate military behavior. Frankly, I'd feel foolish drinking by myself, and what we've got to talk about isn't so almighty important. I just want to ask you a couple of questions."

"Corporate behavior, sir? I'll have some white wine, if you have it, sir."

"I always have it," said the admiral with resignation. "It's usually for personnel who are about to get divorced."

"I'm happily married, sir."

"Glad to hear it. I'm on my third wife—should have stuck with the first."

The drinks poured, the seating arrangements in order, Hickman spoke from behind the desk, his tie loosened, his voice casual. But what he said evoked anything but casualness in David Remington.

"Who the hell is Joel Converse?" asked the admiral.

"I beg your pardon, sir?"

The admiral sighed, the sound indicating that he would begin again. "At twelve hundred hours, twenty-one minutes today, you placed a CLO negative on all inquiries regarding a flag on one Lieutenant Joel Converse's service record. He was a pilot in the Vietnam action."

"I know what he was, sir," said Remington.

"And at fifteen hundred hours, two minutes," continued Hickman, looking at a note on his desk. "I get a teletype from the Fifth Naval District requesting that the flag be removed in their favor and the material released immediately. The basis for their request was—as it always is—national security." The admiral paused to sip his drink; he appeared to be in no hurry, simply weary. "I ordered my adjutant to call you and ask why you did it."

"And I answered him completely, sir," Remington broke in. "It was at the instructions of the chief legal officer of SAND PAC, and I cited the specific regulation that states clearly that the CLO of a naval base can withhold files on the basis that his own inquiries can be compromised by the entrance of a third party. It's standard in civil law, sir. The Federal Bureau of Investigation rarely gives a local or metropolitan police force the information it's collected in an investigation for the simple reason that the investigation could be compromised by leaks or corrupt practices."

"And our chief legal officer, Lieutenant Commander Fitzpatrick, is currently carrying out an investigation of an officer who left the service eighteen *years* ago?"

"I don't know, sir," said Remington, his eyes noncommittal. "I only know those were his orders. They're in force for seventy-two hours. After that, you, of course, can sign the order of release. And the President, naturally, can do so anytime in a national emergency."

"I thought it was forty-eight hours," said Hickman.

"No, sir. The forty-eight hours is standard with the release of every flag regardless of who asks for it—except, of course, the President. It's called the vet delay. Naval intelligence cross-checks with the CIA, the NSA, and G-Two to make sure there's no material being released that's still considered classified. That procedure has nothing to do with the prerogatives of a chief legal officer."

"You know your law, don't you?"

"I believe as well as any attorney in the United States Navy, sir."

"I see." The admiral leaned back in his upholstered swivel chair and placed his legs on the corner of the desk. "Commander Fitzpatrick's off the base, isn't he? Emergency leave, if I recall."

"Yes, sir. He's in San Francisco with his sister and her children. Her husband was killed in a robbery in Geneva; the funeral's tomorrow morning, I believe."

"Yes, I read about it. Goddamned lousy. . . . But you know where to reach him."

"I have the telephone number, yes, sir. Do you want me to call him, Admiral? Apprise him of the Fifth Naval request."

"No, no," said Hickman, shaking his head. "Not at a time like this. They can dry their mops at least until tomorrow afternoon. I've got to assume they also know the regulations; if security's so damned jeopardized, they know where the Pentagon is—and the latest rumor out of Arlington is that they found out where the White House is." The Admiral stopped, frowned, and looked over at the lieutenant. "Suppose you didn't know where to reach Fitzpatrick?"

"But I do, sir."

"Yes, but suppose you didn't? And a legitimate request was received—below presidential involvement, but still pretty damned urgent—*you* could release that flag, couldn't you?"

"Theoretically, as next in authority, yes I could. As long as I accepted the legal responsibility for my judgment."

"The what?"

"That I believed the request was sufficiently urgent to override the chief legal officer's prior order, which granted him seventy-two hours for whatever action he deemed necessary. He was adamant, sir. Frankly, short of presidential intervention, I'm legally bound to uphold the CLO's privilege."

"I'd say morally, too," agreed Hickman.

"Morality has nothing to do with it, sir. It's a clear legal position. Now, shall I make that call, Admiral?"

"No, the hell with it." Hickman removed his feet from the desk. "I was just curious and, frankly, you've convinced me. Fitz wouldn't have given you the order unless he had a reason. The

Fifth D can wait three days, unless those boys want to run up telephone bills to Washington."

"May I ask, sir, who specifically made the request?"

The admiral looked pointedly at Remington. "I'll tell you in three days. You see, I've got a man's privilege to uphold too. You'll know then anyway, because in Fitz's absence you'll have to countersign the transfer." Hickman finished his drink and the lieutenant understood. The conference was over.

Remington got up and returned the half-filled wineglass to the copper bar; he stood at attention and spoke. "Will that be all, sir?"

"Yes, that's it," said the admiral, his gaze straying to the window and the ocean beyond.

The lieutenant saluted sharply as Hickman brought a casual hand to his forehead. The lawyer then did an about-face and started for the door.

"Remington?"

"Yes, sir?" replied the lieutenant, turning.

"Who the hell *is* this Converse?"

"I don't know, sir. But Commander Fitzpatrick said the status of the flag was a Four Zero emergency."

"Jesus . . ."

Hickman picked up his phone and touched a combination of buttons on the console. Moments later he was speaking to a fellow ranking officer in the Fifth Naval District.

"I'm afraid you'll have to wait three days, Scanlon."

"Why is that?" asked the admiral named Scanlon.

"The CLO negative holds on the Converse flag as far as SAND PAC is concerned. If you want to go the D.C. route, be my guest. We'll cooperate."

"I told you, Brian, my people don't want to go through Washington. You've had these things happen before. D.C. makes waves, and we don't want waves."

"Well then, why don't you tell me why you want the Converse flag? Who is he?"

"I'd tell you if I could, you know that. Frankly, I'm not all that clear on it myself, and what I do know I've sworn to keep secure."

"Then go to Washington, I'm standing behind my Chief Legal, who, incidentally, isn't even here."

"He isn't? But you talked to him."

"No, to his next in line, a lieutenant named Remington. He took the direct order from the CLO. Believe me, Remington won't budge. I gave him the chance and he covered himself with legalities. Around here he's known as a stickler prick."

"Did he say why the negative was put out?"

"He didn't have any idea. Why don't you call him yourself? He's probably still downstairs and maybe you can—"

"You didn't use my *name,* did you?" interrupted Scanlon, apparently agitated.

"No, you asked me not to, but he'll know it in three days. He'll have to sign the release and I'll have to tell him who requested it." Hickman paused, then without warning exploded. "What the *hell* is this all about, Admiral? Some pilot who was discharged over eighteen years ago is suddenly on everybody's most-wanted list. I get a departmental priority teletype from the big Fifth D and you follow it up with a personal call, playing the old Annapolis memory game, but you won't tell me anything. Then I find out my own CLO without my knowing about it has put a negative on this Converse flag and labeled it a Four Zero emergency status! Now, I know he's got personal problems and I won't bother him until tomorrow, and I realize you've given your word to stay secure, but goddamn it, somebody had better start telling me *something!*"

There was no response from the other end of the line. But there was the sound of breathing; and it was tremulous.

"Scanlon!"

"What did you just say?" said the voice of the admiral thirty-six hundred miles away.

"I'm going to find out anyway—"

"No, the status. The status of the flag." Scanlon could barely be heard.

"Four-Zero emergency, that's what I said!"

The interruption was abrupt; there was only an echoing click. Admiral Scanlon had hung up the phone.

Walter Peregrine, United States ambassador to the Federal Republic of Germany, confronted Fitzpatrick. "What's your name, Commander?"

"Fowler, sir," answered the Navy lawyer, glancing briefly but hard at Dowling. "Lieutenant Commander Avery Fowler, United States Navy."

Again Connal looked at the actor, who stared at him through the moonlight.

"I understand there's some question about that," said Peregrine, his glare as hostile as Dowling's. "May I see your identification, please?"

"I'm not carrying identification, sir. It's the nature of my assignment not to do so, sir." Fitzpatrick's words were rapid, precise, his posture squared and erect.

"I want verification of your name, your rank, and your branch of service! *Now!*"

"The name I've given you is the name I was instructed to give should anyone beyond the scope of the assignment inquire."

"*Whose* instructions?" barked the diplomat.

"My superior officers, sir."

"Am I to infer that Fowler is not your correct name?"

"With respect, Mr. Ambassador. My name is Fowler, my rank is lieutenant commander, my branch of the service is the United States Navy."

"Where the *hell* do you think you are? Behind the lines, captured by the enemy? 'Name, rank, and serial number—that's all I'm required to say under the rules of the Geneva Convention'!"

"It's all I'm *permitted* to say, sir."

"We'll damn well find out about that, Commander—if you *are* a commander. Also about this Converse, who appears to be a very odd liar—one minute the soul of propriety, the next a very strange man on the run."

"Please try to understand, Mr. Ambassador, our assignment is classified. In no way does it involve diplomacy, nor will it impair your efforts as the chief American representative of our government. But it *is* classified. I will report this conversation to my superiors and you will undoubtedly hear from them. Now, if you gentlemen will forgive me, I'll be on my way.''

"I don't think so, Commander—or whoever you are. But if you are who you say, nothing's compromised. I'm not a damn fool. Nothing will be said to anyone on the embassy staff. Mr. Dowling insisted on that and I accepted the condition. You and I will be locked in a communications room with a phone on a scrambler and you're going to place a call to Washington. I didn't take this job at a loss of three-quarters of a million a year to find shoe clerks running an investigation of my own company without my knowing about it. If I want an outside audit, I'll damn well order it myself!''

"I wish I could comply, sir; it sounds like a reasonable request. But I'm afraid I can't.''

"I'm afraid you will!''

"Sorry.''

"Do as he says, Commander,'' interjected Dowling. "As he told you, nothing's been said to anyone, and nothing will be. But Converse needs protection; he's a wanted man in a foreign country and he doesn't even speak the language. Take Ambassador Peregrine's offer. He'll keep his word.''

"With respect, sirs, the answer is negative.'' Connal turned away and started up the wide path.

"*Major!*'' shouted the ambassador, his voice furious. "*Stop* him! *Stop* that man!''

372

Fitzpatrick looked behind him; for reasons he could not explain to himself he saw what he never expected to see, and the instant he did, he knew he should have expected it. From out of the distant shadows of the immense, majestic building a man rushed forward, a man who was obviously a military aide to the ambassador—a member of the *embassy staff!* Connal froze, Joel's words coming back to him. *Those men you saw at the airport, the ones from the embassy . . . they're on the other side.*

Under almost any other circumstances, Fitzpatrick would have remained where he was and weathered it out. He hadn't actually done anything wrong; there was nothing illegal, no laws broken of which he was cognizant, and no one could force him to discuss personal matters where no law had been violated. Then he realized how wrong he was! The generals of George Marcus Delavane would force him, *could* force him! He spun around and ran.

Suddenly gunfire erupted. Two earsplitting shots above him! He dove to the ground and rolled into the shadows of the bushes as a man's voice roared over the stillness of the night and the sleeping gardens.

"You goddamned son of a *bitch!* What do you think you're *doing!*"

There were further shouts, a further barrage of obscenities, and the sounds of struggle filled the quiet enclave of the university.

"You don't *kill* a man! Besides, you *bastard,* there could be other people! Don't say a *word,* Mr. Ambassador!"

Connal scrambled across the graveled path and spread apart the bordering foliage. In the clear moonlight of the distant bench, the actor Caleb Dowling—the former marine from Kwajalein—stood over the body of the major who had run out of the shadow, his boot on the supine man's throat, his hand grasping the man's extended arm to wrench the weapon free.

"You are one dumb son of a bitch, Major! Or, goddamn you, maybe you're something else!"

Fitzpatrick got to his knees, then to his feet, and, crouching, raced into the receding darkness of the wide path toward the exit.

13

"I didn't have any choice!" said Connal. He had dropped the attaché case on the couch and was sitting in an adjacent chair, leaning forward, still shaking.

"Calm down; try to relax." Converse walked to the elegant antique hunt table against the wall where there was a large silver tray with whisky, ice and glasses. Joel had learned to make use of room service in English. "You need a drink," he said, pouring Fitzpatrick's bourbon.

"Do I *ever!* I've never been shot at. You have. Christ, is that what it's like?"

"That's what it's like. You can't believe it. It's unreal, just mind-blowing sounds that can't really have anything to do with you, until—until you see the evidence for yourself. It's real, it's meant for you, and you're sick. There's no swelling music, no brass horns, just vomit." Converse brought the naval officer his drink.

"You're omitting something," said Connal, taking the glass and looking up at Joel.

"No, I'm not. Let's think about tonight. If you heard Dowling right, the ambassador won't say anything around the embassy—"

"I remember," interrupted Fitzpatrick, taking several swallows of the bourbon, his eyes still on Converse. "It was in one of the other flags. During your second escape a man got killed; it was sundown. You reached him when it happened, and the flag said you went crazy for a couple of minutes. Somehow, according to this guy—a sergeant, I think—you circled around in the jungle, caught the North Vietnamese, killed him with his own knife and got his repeating rifle. Then you blew away three other Viets in the area."

Joel held his place in front of the Navy lawyer. He answered the younger man, his voice quiet, his look angry. "I hate descriptions like that," he said flatly. "It raises all the images I loathe. . . . Let me tell you the way it was—like it was, counselor. A kid, no more than nineteen, had to relieve himself, and although we stuck together he had the dignity to go ten or fifteen feet away to take care of his private functions, using leaves because squeezable toilet paper wasn't available. The maniac—I won't use the word 'soldier'—who killed him waited for the precise moment, then fired off a burst that cut that kid's face apart. When I reached him, half of that face in my hands, I heard the cackle, the obscene laughter of an obscene man who personified for me everything I found despicable—whether North Vietnamese or American. If you want to know the truth, whatever I did I did against both—because both were guilty, all of us turned into animals, myself included. Those other three men, those enemies, those uniformed robots, probably with wives and children back in villages somewhere up north, had no idea I got behind them. I shot them in the back, counselor. What would Johnny Ringo say about that? Or John Wayne?''

Connal was silent as Joel walked over to the hunt table to pour himself a whisky. The Navy lawyer drank, then spoke. ''A few hours ago you said you knew where I was coming from because you'd been there. Well, I haven't been where you were, but I'm beginning to see where *you're* coming from. You really hate everything that Aquitaine stands for, don't you? Especially those running it.''

Converse turned. ''With everything that's in me,'' he said. ''That's why we've got to talk about tonight.''

''I told you, I had no choice. You said the embassy people I saw at the airport were with Delavane. I couldn't take the chance.''

''I know. Now we're both running, hunted by our own people and protected by the men we want to trap. We've got to *think,* Commander.''

The telephone rang twice abrasively. Fitzpatrick leaped from the chair, his initial reaction one of shock. Joel watched him, calming him with his look. ''Sorry,'' said Connal. ''I'm still edgy. I'll get it; I'll be all right." The Navy lawyer crossed to the phone and picked it up. *"Ja?"* He listened for several seconds, covered the mouthpiece and looked at Converse. "It's the overseas operator. San Francisco. It's Meagen."

"Which means Remington," said Joel, his throat suddenly dry, his pulse accelerating.

"Meagen? Yes, I'm here. What is it?" Fitzpatrick stared straight ahead as his sister talked; he nodded frequently, the muscles of his jaw working as he concentrated. "Oh, *Christ!* . . . No, it's all right. I *mean* it, everything's okay. Do you have the number?" Connal looked down at the small telephone table; there was a message pad but no pencil. He glanced over at Joel, who had already started for the desk and a hotel pen. Fitzpatrick held out his hand, took the pen and wrote out a series of numbers. Converse stood aside, conscious that he was barely breathing, his fingers gripping the glass. "Thanks, Meagen. I know it's a hell of a time for you; you don't need this, but if you have to call again, make it station-to-station, okay? . . . I will, Meg, I give you my word. Good-bye." The Navy lawyer hung up, his hand for a moment remaining on the telephone.

"Remington called, didn't he?" said Joel.

"Yes."

"What *happened?*"

"Someone tried to get the flag on your service record released," said Fitzpatrick, turning, looking at Converse. "It's okay. Remington stopped it."

"Who was it?"

"I don't know, I'll have to reach David.

Meagen doesn't have any idea what a flag is, much less who you are. The message was only that 'a release was sought for the flag,' but he stopped it."

"Then everything's all right."

"That's what I said, but it's not."

"Clarification, goddamn it!"

"There's a time limit on how long my order stands. It's only a day or two after the vetting process—"

"Which is forty-eight hours," interrupted Joel.

"Yes, I'm sure of that; it's *after* that. You see, you thought this would happen, but frankly I didn't. Whoever's asking for that flag isn't small potatoes. You could walk out of that meeting and a few hours later your new associates could have that stuff in their hands. Converse the Delavane-hater. Is he now the Delavane-*hunter?*"

"Call Remington." Joel went to the French doors, opened them, and walked out on the small balcony. Drifting wisps of clouds filtered the moonlight, and far to the east there were flashes of heat lightning reminding Converse of the silent artillery fire he and the other escaping prisoners would see in the hills, knowing it was sanctuary but unreachable. He could hear Fitzpatrick inside; from the sound of his voice he was getting a line through to San Diego. Joel reached into a pocket for his cigarettes; he lighted one. Whether it was the bright glow of the flame that illuminated the movement he did not know, but he looked in the direction of that movement. Two balconies away, about thirty feet to his right, a man stood watching him. The figure was a silhouette in the dim light; he nodded and went back inside. Was the man simply another guest who had coincidentally gone outside for a breath of air? Or had Aquitaine posted a guard? Converse could hear the Navy lawyer talking conversationally; he turned and walked back into the room.

Connal was seated in the chair on the other side of the table. He held the phone to his ear with his left hand; his right held the pen above the message pad. He made a note, then said quickly. "Wait a minute. You say Hickman told you to let it ride but he wouldn't tell you who specifically made the request? . . . I see. All right, David, thanks very much. Are you going out tonight? . . . So if I need you I can reach you at this number. . . . Yes, I know, it's these damn phones up in Sonoma. One heavy rain in the hills and you're lucky to get a line, forget a clear one. Thanks again, David. Good-bye." Fitzpatrick hung up the phone and looked strangely, almost guiltily, at Joel. Instead of speaking, he shook his head, breathing out and frowning.

"What is it? What's the matter?"

"You'd better get everything you can at that meeting tomorrow. Or is it today?"

"It's past midnight. It's today. Why?"

"Because twenty-four hours later that flag will be released to a section in the Fifth Naval District—that's Norfolk, and it's powerful. They'll know everything you don't want them to know about you. The time limit is seventy-two hours."

"Get an extension!"

Connal stood up, helplessness in his expression.

"On what basis?"

"What else? National security."

"I'd have to spell out the reasons, you know that."

"I *don't* know that. Extensions are granted for all sorts of contingencies. You need more time to prepare. A source or a witness has been postponed—illness or an injury. Or personal matters —goddamn it, your brother-in-law's funeral, your sister's grief—they've delayed your progress!"

"Forget it, Joel. If I tried that, they'd tie you in with Press and good-bye Charlie. They killed him, remember?"

"No," said Converse firmly. "It's the other way around. It separates us further."

"What are you talking about?"

"I've thought about this, tried to put myself in Avery's shoes. He knew his every move was being watched, his telephone probably tapped. He said the geography, the Comm Tech-Bern merger, the breakfast, Geneva itself, everything had to be logical; it couldn't be any other way. At the end of that breakfast he said if I agreed we'd talk later."

"So?"

"He knew we'd be seen together—it was unavoidable—and I think he was going to give me the words to say if someone in Aquitaine asked me about him. He was going to turn everything around and give me the push I needed to reach these men."

"What the hell are you talking about?"

"Avery was going to stamp me with the label I

had to wear to get inside Delavane's network. We'll never know, but I have an idea he was going to tell me to say that he, A. Preston Halliday, suspected me of being one of *them,* that he had inserted himself in the Comm Tech-Bern merger to threaten me with exposure, to *stop* me.''

''Wait a minute.'' Connal shook his head. ''Press didn't know what you were going to do or how you were going to do it.''

''There was only one way *to* do it, he knew that! He also knew I'd reach the same conclusion once I understood the particulars. The only way to stop Delavane and his field marshals is to infiltrate Aquitaine. Why do you think all that money was put up front? I don't need it and he knew he couldn't buy me. But he knew it could be used—would *have* to be used to get inside and start talking, start gathering evidence. . . . Call Remington again. Tell him to prepare an extension.''

''It's not Remington, it's the commander of SAND PAC, an admiral named Hickman. David said I could expect a call from him tomorrow. I'll have to figure that one out and phone Meagen back. Hickman's uptight; he wants to know who you are and why all the interest.''

''How well do you know this Hickman?''

''Fairly well. I was with him in New London and Galveston. He requested me as his CLO in San Diego; that's what gave me the stripe.''

Converse studied Fitzpatrick's face, then without saying anything he turned and walked to the open balcony doors. Connal did not interrupt;

381

he understood. He had seen too many attorneys, himself included, struck by a thought they had to define for themselves, an idea upon which a case might hinge. Joel turned around slowly, haltingly, the dim, abstract shadows of a possibility coming into focus.

"Do it," he began. "Do what I think your brother-in-law might have done. Finish what he might have said but never got a chance to say it. Assume he and I had that meeting after the merger conference. Give me the springboard I need."

"As you would say, clarification, please, counselor."

"Present Hickman with a scenario as it might have been written by A. Preston Halliday. Tell him that flag's got to remain in place because you have reason to believe I was connected with your brother-in-law's murder. Explain that before Halliday flew to Geneva he came to see you—as he did—and told you he was meeting me, an opposing attorney he suspected of being involved with corrupt export licensing, a legal front for some boardroom profiteers. Say he said he was going to confront me. Preston Halliday had a history of causes."

"Not for the past ten or twelve years, he didn't," corrected Fitzpatrick. "He joined the establishment with a vengeance and with a healthy respect for the dollar."

"It's the history that counts. He knew that; it was one of the reasons he came to me. Say you're convinced he did confront me, and since millions are made out of that business, you think I methodically had him removed, covering myself by being there when he died. I have a certain reputation for being methodical.''

Connal lowered his head and ran his hand through his hair, then walked in thought toward the hunt table. He stopped, raised his gaze to one of the racehorse prints and turned back to Converse. ''Do you know what you're asking me to do?''

''Yes. Give me the springboard that'll catapult me right in the middle of those would-be Genghis Khans. To do it you'll have to go further with Hickman. Because you're so personally involved and so goddamned angry—which again is the truth—tell him to explain your position to whoever wants the flag released. It's a nonmilitary matter, so you're taking what you know to the civilian authorities.''

''I understand all that,'' said Fitzpatrick. ''Everything I say *is* the truth, as I saw it when I flew over here to find you. Except that I reverse the targets. Instead of being the one who can help me, you're now the one I want nailed.''

''Right on, counselor. And I'm met by a welcoming committee at Leifhelm's estate.''

''Then I guess you don't see.''

''What?''

''You're asking me to go on record implicating you in first-degree murder. I'll be branding you as a killer. Once I say it, I can't take the words back.''

''I know that. Do it.''

George Marcus Delavane twisted his torso in his

chair behind the desk in front of the strangely colored fragmented map on the wall. It was not a controlled movement; it was an action in search of control. Delavane did not care for obstructions and one was being explained to him now by an admiral in the Fifth Naval District.

"The status of the flag is Four Zero," said Scanlon. "To get it released we'd have to go through Pentagon procedures, and I don't have to tell you what that means. Two senior officers, one from naval intelligence, plus a supporting signature from the National Security Agency; all would have to appear on the request sheet, the level of the inquiry stated, thus escalating the request to a sector demand. Now, General, we can do all this, but we run the risk—"

"I know the risk," interrupted Delavane. "The signatures are the risk, the identities a risk. Why the Four Zero? Who placed it and *why?*"

"The chief legal officer of SAND PAC. I checked him out. He's a lieutenant commander named Fitzpatrick, and there's nothing in his record to give us any indication as to why he did it."

"I'll tell you why," said the warlord of Saigon. "He's hiding something. He's protecting this Converse."

"Why would a chief legal officer in the Navy protect a civilian under these circumstances? There's no connection. Furthermore, why would he exercise a Four Zero condition? It only calls attention to his action."

"It also clamps a lid down on that flag." Delavane paused, then continued before the admiral could interrupt. "This Fitzpatrick," he said. "You've checked the master list?"

"He's not one of us."

"Has he ever been considered? Or approached?"

"I haven't had time to find out." There was the sound of a buzzer, not part of the line over which the two men spoke. Scanlon could be heard punching a button, his voice clear, officious. "Yes?" Silence followed, and seconds later the admiral returned to Palo Alto. "It's Hickman again."

"Maybe he has something for us. Call me back."

"Hickman wouldn't give us anything if he had the slightest idea we existed," said Scanlon. "In a few weeks, he'll be one of the first to go. If it were up to me he'd be shot."

"Call me back," said George Marcus Delavane, looking at the map of the new Aquitaine on the wall.

Chaim Abrahms sat at the kitchen table in his small stone Mediterranean villa in Tzahala, a suburb of Tel Aviv favored by the retired military and those with sufficient income or influence to live there. The windows were open and the breezes from the garden stirred the oppressive summer's night air. There was air conditioning in two other rooms and ceiling fans in three more, but Chaim liked the kitchen. In the old days he and his men would sit in primitive kitchens and plan raids; in the Negev, ammunition was often passed about while desert chicken boiled on a wood stove. The kitchen was the soul of the house. It gave warmth and sustenance to the body, clearing the mind for tactics—as long as the women left after performing their chores and did not interrupt the men with their incessant trivialities. His wife was asleep upstairs; so be it. He had little to say to her anymore, or she to him; she could not help him now. And if she could, she would not. They had lost a son in Lebanon, *her* son she said, a teacher, a scholar, not a soldier, not a killer by choice. Too many sons were lost on both sides, she said. Old men, she said, old men infected the young with their hatreds and used Biblical legends to justify death in the pursuit of questionable real estate. Death, she cried. Death before talk that might avert it! She had forgotten the early days; too many forgot too quickly. Chaim Abrahms did not forget, nor would he ever.

And his sense of smell was as acute as ever. This lawyer, this Converse, this talk! It was all too clever; it had the stench of cold, analytical minds, not the heat of believers. The Mossad specialist was the best, but even the Mossad made mistakes. The specialist looked for a motive, as if one could dissect the human brain and say this action caused that reaction; this punishment that commitment to vengeance. Too damned *clever!* A believer was fueled by the heat of his convictions. They were his only motive, and they did not call for clever manipulations.

Chaim knew he was a plainspoken man, a direct man, but it was not because he was unintelligent or lacked subtle perceptions; his prowess on the battlefield proved otherwise. He

386

was direct because he knew what he wanted, and it was a waste of time to pretend and be clever. In all the years he had lived with his convictions he had never met a fellow believer who allowed himself to waste time.

This Converse knew enough to reach Bertholdier in Paris. He showed how much more he knew when he mentioned Leifhelm in Bonn and specifically named the cities of Tel Aviv and Johannesburg. What more did he have to prove? *Why* should he prove it if his belief was there? Why did he not plead his case with his first connection and not waste time? . . . No, this lawyer, this Converse, was from somewhere else. The Mossad specialist said the motive was there for affiliation. He was wrong. The red-hot heat of the believer was *not* there. Only cleverness, only talk.

And the specialist had not dismissed Chaim's sense of smell. As well he should not, as the two sabras had fought together for years, as often as not against the Europeans and their conniving ways—those immigrants who held up the Old Testament as if they had written it, calling the true inhabitants of Israel uneducated ruffians or clowns. The Mossad specialist respected his sabra brother; it was in his look, that respect. No one could dismiss the instincts of Chaim Abrahms, son of Abraham, archangel of darkness to the enemies of Abraham's children. Thank God his wife was asleep.

It was time to call Palo Alto.

"My general, my friend."

"*Shalom,* Chaim," said the warlord of Saigon.

"Are you on your way to Bonn?"

"I'm leaving in the morning—we're leaving. Van Headmer is in the air now. He'll arrive at Ben Gurion at eight-thirty, and together we'll take the ten o'clock flight to Frankfurt, where Leifhelm's pilot will meet us with the Cessna."

"Good. You can talk."

"*We* must talk now," said the Israeli. "What more have you learned about this Converse?"

"He becomes more of an enigma, Chaim."

"I smell a fraud."

"So do I, but perhaps not the fraud I thought. You know what my assessment was. I thought he was no more than an infantry point, someone being used by more knowledgeable men—Lucas Anstett among them—to learn far more than they knew or heard rumors about. I don't discount a degree of minor leaks; they're to be anticipated and managed, scoffed at as paranoia."

"Get to the point, Marcus," said the impatient Abrahms, who always called Delavane by his middle name. He considered it a Hebrew name, in spite of the fact that Delavane's father had insisted on it for his first son in honor of the Roman Caesar—the philosopher Marcus Aurelius, a proselytizer of moderation.

"Three things happened today," continued the former general in Palo Alto. "The first infuriated me because I could not understand it, and frankly disturbed me because it portended a far greater penetration than I thought possible from a sector I thought *impossible*."

"What was it?" the Israeli broke in.

"A firm prohibition was placed on getting part

of Converse's service record."

"Yes!" cried Abrahms, in his voice the sound of triumph.

"What?"

"Go on, Marcus! I'll tell you when you're finished. What was the second calamity?"

"Not a calamity, Chaim. An explanation so blatantly offered it can't be turned aside. Leifhelm called me and said Converse himself brought up Anstett's death, claiming to be relieved, but saying little else except that Anstett was his enemy—that was the word he used."

"So instructed!" Abrahms' voice reverberated around the kitchen. "What was the third gift, my general?"

"The most bewildering as well as enlightening—and, Chaim, do not shout into the phone. You are not at one of your stadium rallies or provoking the Knesset."

"I am in the field, Marcus. Right *now!* Please continue, my friend."

"The man who clamped the lid down on Converse's military record is a naval officer who was the brother-in-law of Preston Halliday."

"Geneva! Yes!"

"Stop that!"

"My apologies, my dear friend. It's just all so perfect!"

"Whatever you have in mind," said Delavane "may be negated by the man's reason. This naval officer, this brother-in-law, believes Converse engineered Halliday's murder."

"Of course! *Perfect!"*

"You *will* keep your *voice* down!" The cry of

389

the cat on a frozen lake was heard.

"Again my deepest and most sincere apologies, my general. Was that all this naval officer said?"

"No, he made it clear to the commander of his base in San Diego that Halliday had come to him and told him he was meeting a man in Geneva he believed was involved with illegal exports to illegal destinations. An attorney for profiteers in armaments. He intended to confront this man, this international lawyer named Converse, and threaten to expose him. What do we have?"

"A *fraud!*"

"But on whose *side,* sabra? The volume of your voice doesn't convince me."

"Be convinced! I'm right. This Converse is the desert scorpion!"

"What does that mean?"

"Don't you *see?* The Mossad sees!"

"The Mossad?"

"Yes! I talked with our specialist and he senses what I smell—he admits the possibility! I grant you, my general, my honored warrior, that he has information that led him to think this Converse might be genuine, that he wanted truly to be with us, but when I said I smelled bad meat, he granted one other, exceptional possibility. Converse may or may not be programmed, but he could be an agent for his government!"

"A provocateur?"

"Who knows, Marcus? But the pattern is so perfect. First, a prohibition is placed on his military record—it will tell us something, we know that. Then he responds in the negative about the death of an enemy—not his, but *ours,* and claims

390

he was his enemy too—so simple, so instructable. Finally, it is insinuated that this Converse was the killer in Geneva—so orderly, so precisely to his advantage. We are dealing with very analytical minds that watch every move in the chess game, and match every pawn with a king."

"Yet everything you say can be reversed. He could be—"

"He *can't* be!" cried Abrahms.

"Why, Chaim? Tell me why?"

"There is no *heat,* no *fire* in him! It is not the way of a believer! We are not clever, we are adamant!"

George Marcus Delavane said nothing for several moments, and the Israeli knew better than to speak. He waited until the quiet cold voice came back on the line. "Have your meeting tomorrow, General. Listen to him and be courteous; play the game he plays. But he must not leave that house until I give the order. He may never leave it."

"*Shalom,* my friend."

"*Shalom,* Chaim."

14

Valerie approached the glass doors of her studio—identical with the doors of her balcony upstairs—and looked out at the calm, sun-washed waters of Cape Ann. She thought briefly of the boat that had dropped anchor so frighteningly in front of her house several nights ago. It had not been back; whatever had happened was past, leaving questions but no answers. If she closed her eyes she could still see the figure of a man crawling up out of the cabin light, and the glow of the cigarette, and she still wondered what that man was doing, what he was thinking. Then she remembered the sight of the two men in the early light, framed by the dark rims of her binoculars —staring back at her with far more powerful lenses. Were they novices finding a safe harbor? Amateurs navigating the dark waters of a coastline at night? Questions, no answers.

Whatever, it was past. A brief, disturbing interlude that gave rise to black imaginings —demons in search of logic, as Joel would say.

She tossed her long, dark hair aside and returned to her easel, picking up a brush and putting the final dabs of burnt umber beneath the shadowed sand dunes of wild grass. She stepped back, studied her work, and swore to herself for the fifth time that the oil painting was finished. It was another seascape; she never tired of them, and fortunately she was beginning to get a fair share of the market. Of course there were those painters in the Boston-Boothbay axis who claimed she had virtually cornered the market, but that was rubbish. Indeed her prices had risen satisfactorily as a result of the critical approval accorded her two showings at the Copley Galleries, but the truth was that she could hardly afford to live where she lived and the way she lived without at least a part of Joel's check every month.

Then again, not too many artists had a house

on the beach with an attached twenty-by-thirty-foot studio enclosed by full-length glass doors and with a ceiling that was literally one entire skylight. The rest of the house, the original house, on the northern border of Cape Ann was more rambling-quaint than functional. The initial architecture was early-coast-confusion, with lots of heavy bleached wood and curliques, a balustraded second-story balcony, and outsized bay windows in the front room that were charming to look at and look out but leaked fiercely when the winter winds came off the ocean. No amount of putty or sashing compound seemed to work; nature was extracting a price for observing her beauty.

Still, it was Val's dream house, the one she had promised herself years ago she would someday be able to afford. She had come back from the Ecole des Beaux Arts in Paris prepared to assault New York's art world via the Greenwich Village-Woodstock route only to have stark reality alter her plans. The family circumstances had always been sufficiently healthy for her to live comfortably, albeit not lavishly, throughout three years in college and two more in Paris. Her father was a passably good if excessively enthusiastic amateur painter who always complained that he had not taken the risks and gone totally into the fine arts rather than architecture. As a result, he supported his only child both morally and financially, in a very real sense living through her progress and devoted to her determination. And her mother—slightly mad, always loving, always supportive in anything and everything—would take terrible photographs of Val's crudest work and send the pictures back to her sister and cousins in Germany, writing outrageous lies that spoke of museums and galleries and insane commissions.

"The crazy Berlinerin," her father would say fondly in his heavy Gallic accent. "You should have seen her during the war. She frightened us all to death! We half expected she would return to headquarters some night with a drunken Goebbels or a doped-up Göring in tow, then tell us if we wanted Hitler to give her the word!"

Her father had been the Free French liaison between the Allies and the German underground in Berlin. A rather stiff Parisian autocrat who happened to speak German had been assigned to the cell in the Charlottenburg, which coordinated all the activities of Berlin's underground. He frequently said that he had more trouble with the wild Fräulein with the impetuous ideas than he had avoiding the Nazis. Nevertheless they married each other two months after the armistice. In Berlin. Where neither his family would talk to hers, nor hers to his. "We had two small orchestras," her mother would say. "One played pure, beautiful Viennese *Schnitzel,* the other some white cream sauce with deer droppings."

Whether family animosities had anything to do with it neither ever said, but the Parisian and the Berlinerin immigrated to St. Louis, Missouri, in the United States of America, where the Berlinerin had distant relations.

The stark reality. Nine years ago, after she had settled in New York from Paris, a frightened, tearful father had flown in to see her and had told

Val a terrible truth. His beloved crazy Berlinerin had been ill for years; it was cancer and it was about to kill her. In desperation, he had spent nearly all the money he had, including unpaid second and third mortgages on the rambling house in Bellefontaine, to stem the disease. Among the profiteers were clinics in Mexico; there was nothing else he could say. He could only weep, and his losses had nothing to do with his tears. And she could only hold her father and ask him why he had not told her before.

"It was not your battle, *ma chérie*. It was ours. Since Berlin, it was always we two. We fought then together; we fight now as always—as one."

Her mother died six days later, and six months after that her father lit a Gauloise on the screened-in porch and mercifully fell asleep, not to wake up. Valerie could not cry. It was a shock but not a tragedy. Wherever he was he wanted to be there.

So Valerie Charpentier looked for a job, a paying job that did not rely on the sales of an unknown artist. What astonished her was not that employment was so easy to find, but that it had very little to do with the thick portfolio of sketches and line drawings she presented. The second advertising agency she applied to seemed more interested in the fact that she spoke both German and French fluently. It was the time of corporate takeovers, of multinational alliances where profits could be made on both sides of the Atlantic by the same single entities. Valerie Charpentier, artist-in-residence inside, became a company hack on the outside. Someone who could draw and sketch rapidly and make presentations and speak the languages and she hated it. Still, it was a remarkable living for a woman who had anticipated a period of years before her name on a canvas would mean something.

Then a man came into her life who made whatever affairs she had had totally forgettable. A nice man, a *decent* man—even an exciting man— who had his own problems but did not talk about them, *would* not talk about them, and that should have given her a clue. Joel, her Joel, effusive one moment, withdrawn the next, but always with that shield, that façade of quick humor which was often as biting as it was amusing. For a while they had been good for each other. Both were ambitious for entirely different reasons—she for the independence that came with recognition, he for the wasted years he could never reclaim—and each acted as a buffer when the other faced disappointment or delay. But it all began to fall apart. The reasons were painfully clear to her but not to him. He became mesmerized by his own progress, by his own determination, to the exclusion of everything else, starting with her. He never raised his voice or made demands, but the words were ice and the demands were increasingly there. If there was a specific point when she recognized the downhill slide, it was a Friday night in November. The agency had wanted her to fly to West Berlin; a Telefunken account required some fast personal service and she was elected to calm the churning waters. She had been packing when Joel came home from work. He had walked into the bedroom of their apartment and asked her what she was doing, where she was going. When she told him, he had said, "You can't. We're expected at Brooks' house in Larchmont tomorrow night. Talbot and Simon'll be there too. I'm sure they'll talk international. You've got to be there."

She had looked at him, at the quiet desperation in his eyes. She did not go to Germany. It was the turning point; the downhill race had begun, and within a brief few months she knew it was quickening to its finish. She quit the agency, giving up authority for the dog days of free-lancing, hoping the extra time she had to devote to him might help. It did not; he seemed to resent any overt act of sacrifice, no matter how hard she tried to conceal it. His periods of withdrawal multiplied, and in a way she felt sorry for him. His furies were driving him and it was obvious that he disliked what was happening; he disliked what he was but could not help himself. He was on his way to a burnout and she could not help him, either.

If there had been another woman, she could have fought, staking out her claim and fiercely insisting on the right to compete, but there was no one else, only himself and his compulsions. Finally, she realized she could not penetrate his shield; he had nothing left for anyone else emotionally. That was what she had hurled at him: "Emotional burn-out!" He had agreed in that quiet, kind voice and the next day he was gone.

So she took him. Four years, she demanded,

the exact amount of time he had taken from her. Those four years of heady generosity were about to come to an end, Val reflected, as she cleaned her brushes and scraped the palette. In January they were over, the last check, as always, posted by the fifteenth. Five weeks ago, during lunch at the Ritz in Boston, Joel had offered to continue the payments. He claimed he was used to them and was making more in salary and bonuses than he could spend soberly. The money was no hardship, and besides it gave him a certain stature among his peers and was a marvelous ploy to avoid prolonged entanglements. She had declined, borrowing words from her father or more likely her mother, saying that things were far better than they were. He had smiled that half-sad yet still infectious smile and said, "If they turn out otherwise, I'm here."

Goddamn him!

Poor Joel. Sad Joel. He was a good man caught in the vortex of his own conflicts. And Val had gone as far as she could go—to go further was to deny her own identity. She would not do that; she had not done it.

She placed her brushes in the tray and walked to the glass doors that looked over the dunes and the ocean. He was out there, far away, still somewhere in Europe. Valerie wondered if he had given a thought to the day. It was the anniversary of their marriage.

To summarize, Chaim Abrahms was molded in the stress and chaos of fighting for daily survival. They were years of never-ending violent skirmishes, of outthinking and outliving enemies bent on killing not only whole sabra settlements but the desert Jews' aspirations for a homeland as well as political freedom and religious expression. It is not difficult to understand where Abrahms came from and why he is what he is, but it is frightening to think about where he is going. He is a fanatic with no sense of balance or compromise where other peoples with identical aspirations are concerned. If a man has a different stripe, whether of the same species or not, he is the enemy. Armed force takes precedence over negotiations in all matters, and even those in Israel who plead for more moderate stands based on totally secure borders are branded as traitors. Abrahms is an imperialist who sees an ever-expanding Israel as the ruling kingdom of the entire Middle East. An appropriate ending to this report is a comment he made after the well-known statement issued by the Prime Minister during the Lebanon invasion: "We covet not one inch of Lebanon." Abrahms' reply in the field to his troops—the majority by no means sympathetic—was the following.

"Certainly not an inch: The whole damned country: Then Gaza, the Golan, and the West Bank! And why not Jordan, then Syria, and Iraq! We have the means and we have the will! We are the mighty children of Abraham!"

He is Delavane's key in the volatile Middle East.

It was nearly noon, the overhead sun beating

down on the small balcony beyond the French doors. The late-breakfast remnants had been cleared away by room service; only a silver pot remained on the hunt table. They had been reading for hours since the first coffee was brought to the suite at six-thirty. Converse put down the dossier, and reached for his cigarettes on the table by the armchair. *It is not difficult to understand where Abrahms came from . . . but it is frightening to think about where he is going.* Joel looked over at Connal Fitzpatrick, who was seated on the couch, leaning forward over the coffee table and reading a single page while making notes on the telephone message pad; the Bertholdier and Leifhelm dossiers were in two neat piles on his left. The Navy lawyer had said practically the same words to him, thought Converse, lighting a cigarette. *I'm beginning to see where you're coming from. . . .* The inherent question put to Joel's legal mind was simple: Where was he himself going? He hoped to hell he knew. Was he an inept gladiator marching into a Roman arena facing far stronger, better-armed and superior talent? Or were the demons from his own past turning him into his own sacrifice, leading him into the arena's hot sand where angry, half-starved cats waited, ready to pounce and tear him apart? So many questions, so many variables he was incapable of addressing. He only knew he could not turn back.

Fitzpatrick looked up. "What's the matter?" he asked, obviously aware that Converse was staring in his direction. "You worried about the admiral?"

"Who?"

"Hickman, San Diego."

"Among other things. In the clear light of day, you're sure he bought the extension?"

"No guarantees, but I told you he said he'll call me if any emergency heat came down. I'm damn sure he won't do anything before consulting me. If he tries to reach me, Meagen knows what to do and I'll lean harder. If need be, I'll claim point of personal privilege and demand a meeting with those unnamed people in the Fifth District, maybe go so far as to imply they could be part of Geneva. *That'd* be a full circle. We could end up with a standoff—the release of that flag only with a full-scale investigation of the circumstances. Irony and standoff."

"You won't have a standoff if he's with them. He'll override you."

"If he was *with* them, he wouldn't have told Remington he was going to call me. He wouldn't have said anything; he'd have waited the extra day and let it go. I know him. He wasn't just nonplussed, he was mad. He stands by his people and he doesn't like outside pressures, especially Navy pressures. We're on hold, and as long as it's hold, the flag's in place. I told you, he's a lot angrier with Norfolk than with me. They won't even *give* him a reason; they claim they can't."

Converse nodded. "All right," he said. "Call it a case of nerves on my part. I just finished the Abrahms dossier. That maniac could blow up the whole Middle East all by himself and drag the rest of us in with him. . . . What did you think of Leifhelm and Bertholdier?"

"As far as the information goes, they're everything you said and then some. They're more than just influential ex-generals with fistfuls of money, they're powerful rallying symbols for what a lot of people think are justifiable extremes. That's as far as the information goes—but the operative word for *me* is the information itself. Where did it come from?"

"That's a step back. It's there."

"It sure is, but how? You say Beale gave it to you, that Press used the phrase 'we'—'the ones *we're* after,' 'the tools *we* can give you,' 'the connections as *we* think they are.' "

"And we went over this," insisted Joel. "The man in San Francisco, the one he went to who provided the five hundred thousand and told him to build cases against these people legally, and together they'd turn them into plain and simple profiteers. It's the ultimate ridicule for super-patriots. It's sound reasoning, counselor, and that's the *we.*"

"Press and this unknown man in San Francisco?"

"Yes."

"And they could pick up a phone and hire someone to put together *these?*" Fitzpatrick gestured at the two dossiers on his left.

"Why not? This is in the age of the computer. Nobody today lives on an unmapped island or in an undiscovered cave."

"These," said Connal, "are not computer printouts. They're well-researched, detailed, in-depth dossiers that take in the importance of political nuances and personal idiosyncrasies."

"You have a way with words, sailor. Yes, they are. A man who can forward half a million dollars to the right bank on an Aegean island can hire just about anyone he likes."

"He can't hire these."

"What does that mean?"

"Let me take a real step back," said the Navy lawyer, getting to his feet and reaching down for the single page he had been reading. "I won't reiterate the details of my relationship with Press because right now it hurts a little to think about it." Fitzpatrick paused, seeing the look in Converse's eyes that rejected this kind of sentimentality in their discussion. "Don't mistake me," he continued. "It's not his death, not the funeral; it's the other way around. It's not the Press Halliday I knew. You see, I don't think he told us the truth, either you or me."

"Then you know something I don't know," said Converse quietly.

"I know there's no man in San Francisco that even vaguely fits the description of the image he gave you. I've lived there all my life, including Berkeley and Stanford, just like Press. I knew everyone he knew, especially the wealthiest and the more exotic ones; we never held back on those with each other. I was legal worlds away, and he always filled me in if new ones came along. It was part of the fun for him."

"That's tenuous, counselor. I'm sure he kept certain associations to himself."

"Not those kinds," said Connal. "It wouldn't be like him. Not with me."

"Well, I—"

403

"Now let me step forward," interrupted Fitzpatrick. "These dossiers—I haven't seen them before, but I've seen hundreds like them, maybe a couple of thousand on their way to becoming full-fledged versions of them."

Joel sat up. "Please explain that, Commander."

"You just hit it, Lieutenant. The rank says it."

"Says *what?*"

"Those dossiers are the reworked, finished products of intelligence probes utilizing heavy shots of military data. They've been bounced around the community, each branch contributing its input—from straight biographical data to past surveillances to psychiatric evaluation—and put together by teams of specialists. Those were taken from way down in the government vaults and rewritten with current additions and conclusions, then shaped to appear as the work of an outside, nongovernment authority. But they're not. They've got *Classified, Top Secret,* and *Eyes Only* written all over them."

Converse leaned forward. "That could be a subjective judgment based on limited familiarity. I've seen some very detailed, very in-depth reports put together by high-priced firms specializing in that sort of thing."

"Describing precise military incidents during the time of war? Pinpointing bombing raids and specifying regiments and battalions and the current strategies employed? Detailing through *interviews* the internal conflicts of ranking enemy officers and the tactical reasons for shifting military personnel into civilian positions after the

404

cessation of hostilities? No firm would have access to those materials."

"They could be researched," said Joel, suddenly not convinced himself.

"Well, *these* couldn't," Connal broke in, holding up the page of typewritten names, his thumb on the lower two columns listing the "decision makers" from the Pentagon and the State Department. "Maybe five or six—three from each side at maximum—but not the rest. These are people *above* the ones I've dealt with, men who do their jobs under a variety of titles so they can't be reached—bribed, blackmailed, or threatened. When you said you had names, I assumed I'd recognize most of them, or at least half of them. I don't. I only know the departmental execs, upper-echelon personnel who have to go even higher, who obviously report to these people. Press couldn't have gotten these names himself or through others on the outside. He wouldn't know where to look and they wouldn't know where to look—*I* wouldn't know."

Converse rose. "Are you sure you know what you're talking about?"

"Yes. Someone—probably more than one—deep in the Washington cellars provided these names just as he or they provided the material for those dossiers."

"Do you know what you're saying?"

Connal stood still and nodded. "It's not easy for me to say," he began grimly. "Press lied to us. He lied to you by what he said, and to me by what he didn't say. You're tied to a string and it goes right back to Washington. And I wasn't to know anything about it.''

''The puppet's in place. . . .'' Joel spoke so softly he could barely be heard as he walked aimlessly across the room toward the bright sunlight streaming through the balcony doors.

''What?'' asked Fitzpatrick.

''Nothing, just a phrase that kept running through my head when I heard about Anstett.'' Converse turned. ''But if there's a string, why have they hidden it? Why did *Avery* hide it? For what purpose?''

The Navy lawyer remained motionless, his face without expression. ''I don't think I have to answer that. You answered it yourself yesterday afternoon when we were talking about me—and don't kid yourself, Lieutenant, I knew exactly what you were saying. 'I'll give you a name now and then that may open a door . . . but that's all.' Those were your words. Freely translated, you were telling yourself that the sailor you took on board might stumble on to something, but in case he was taken by the wrong people, they couldn't beat out of him what he didn't know.''

Joel accepted the rebuke, not merely because it was justified, but because it made clear a larger truth, one he had not understood on Mykonos. Beale had told him that among those raising questions in Washington were military men who for one reason or another had not pursued their inquiries; they had kept silent. They had kept silent where they might be overheard, perhaps, but they had not totally kept their silence. They had talked in quiet voices until another quiet voice from San Francisco—a man who knew whom to reach courtesy of a brother-in-law in San Diego —made contact. They had talked together, and out of their secret conversations had come a plan. They needed an infiltrator, a man with the expertise who had a loathing they could fuel and, once fired, send out into the labyrinth.

The realization was a shock, but oddly enough, Joel could not fault the strategy. He did not even fault the silence that remained after Preston Halliday's murder; loud accusing voices would have rendered that death meaningless. Instead, they had stayed quiet, knowing that their puppet had the tools to make his way through the maze of illegalities and do the job they could not do themselves. He understood that, too. But there was one thing Converse could not accept, and that was his own expendability as the puppet. He had tolerated being left unprotected under the conditions outlined by Avery Fowler-Preston Halliday, not under these. If he was on a string, he wanted the puppeteers to know he knew it. He also wanted the name of someone in Bonn he could call, someone who was a part of them. The old rules did not apply any longer, a new dimension had been added.

In four hours he would be driven through the iron gates of Erich Leifhelm's estate; he wanted someone on the outside, a man Fitzpatrick could reach if he did not come out by midnight. The demons were pressing hard, thought Joel. Still, he could not turn back. He was so close to trapping the warlord of Saigon, so close to making up for so much that had warped his life in ways no one would ever understand. . . . No, not 'no one,' he

407

reflected. One person did, and she had said she could not help him any longer. Nor had it been fair any longer to seek her help.

"What's your decision?" said Connal.

"Decision?" asked Joel, startled.

"You don't have to go this afternoon. Throw it all *back!* This belongs Stateside with the FBI in conjunction with the Central Intelligence Agency overseas. I'm appalled they didn't take that route."

Converse breathed the start of a reply, then stopped. It had to be clear, not only to Fitzpatrick but to himself. He thought he understood. He had seen the look of profound panic in Avery Fowler's eyes—Preston Halliday's eyes—and he had heard the cry in his voice. The lies were his strategy, but the look and the cry were his innermost feelings.

"Has it occurred to you, Commander, that they can't take that route? That, perhaps, we're not talking about men who can pick up a phone—as you said before—and put those wheels in motion? Or if they tried, they'd have their heads cut off, perhaps literally, with an official rebuke and a bullet in the back of their skulls? Let me add that I don't think they're afraid for themselves any more than I believe they chose the best man for the job, but I *do* think they came to a persuasive conclusion. They couldn't work from the inside because they didn't know whom they could trust."

"Christ, you're a cold son of a bitch."

"Ice, Commander. We're dealing with a paranoid fantasy called Aquitaine, and it's controlled by proven, committed, highly intelligent and resourceful men, who if they achieve what they've set out to do will appear as the voices of strength and reason in a world gone mad. They'll control that world—our world—because all other options will pale beside their stability. *Stability,* counselor, as opposed to chaos. What would you choose if you were an everyday nine-to-fiver with a wife and kids, and you could never be sure when you went home at night whether or not your house had been broken into, your wife raped, your kids strangled? You'd opt for tanks in the street."

"With justification," said the Navy lawyer, the two words spiraling quietly off into the air of the sunlit room.

"Believe that, sailor. They're banking on it, and that's just what they're planning to do on an international scale. It's only a few days or a few weeks away—whatever it is, wherever it is. If I can just get an inkling . . ." Converse turned and started for the door of his bedroom.

"Where are you going?" asked Connal.

"Beale's telephone number on Mykonos; it's in my briefcase. He's my only contact and I want to talk to him. I want him to know the puppet has just been granted some unexpected free will."

Three minutes later Joel stood at the table, the phone to his ear as the Greek operator in Athens routed his call to the island of Mykonos. Fitzpatrick sat on the couch, Chaim Abrahms' dossier in front of him on the coffee table, his eyes on Converse.

"Are you getting through all right?" asked

the Navy lawyer.

"It's ringing now." The erratic, stabbing signals kept repeating—four, five, six times. On the seventh the telephone in the Aegean was picked up.

"Herete?"

"Dr. Beale, please. Dr. Edward Beale."

"Tee tha thelete?"

"Beale. The owner of the house. Get him for me, *please!"* Joel turned to Fitzpatrick. "Do you speak Greek?"

"No, but I've been thinking about taking it up."

"You do that." Converse listened again to the male voice in Mykonos. Greek phrases were spoken rapidly, none comprehensible. "Thank you! Good-bye." Joel tapped the telephone bar several times, hoping the overseas line was still open and the English-speaking Greek operator was still there. "Operator? Is this the operator in Athens? . . . Good! I want to call another number on Mykonos, the same billing in Bonn." Converse reached down on the table for the instructions Preston Halliday had given him in Geneva. "It's the Bank of Rhodes. The number is . . ."

Moments later the waterfront banker, Kostas Laskaris, was on the line. *"Herete."*

"Mr. Laskaris, this is Joel Converse. Do you remember me?"

"Of course. . . . Mr. Converse?" The banker sounded distant, somehow strange, as if wary or bewildered.

"I've been trying to call Dr. Beale at the number you gave me, but all I get is a man who can't speak English. I wondered if you could tell me where Beale is.''

A quiet expulsion of breath could be heard over the phone. ''I wondered,'' said Laskaris quietly. ''The man you reached was a police officer, Mr. Converse. I had him placed there myself. A scholar has many valuable things.''

''*Why?* What do you mean?''

''Shortly after sunrise this morning Dr. Beale took his boat out of the harbor, accompanied by another man. Several fishermen saw them. Two hours ago Dr. Beale's boat was found crashed on the rocks beyond the Stephanos. There was no one on board.''

I killed him. With a scaling knife, dropping his body over a cluster of sharks beyond the shoals of the Stephanos.

Joel hung up the phone. Halliday, Anstett, Beale, all of them gone—all his contacts dead. He was a puppet on the loose, his strings gone haywire, leading only to shadows.

15

Erich Leifhelm's waxlike skin paled further as his eyes narrowed and his starched white lips parted. Then blood rushed to his head as he sat forward at the desk in his library and spoke into the telephone. ''What was that name again, London?''

''Admiral Hickman. He's the—''

''*No,*'' interrupted the German sharply. ''The

other one! The officer who has refused to release the information."

"Fitzpatrick, an Irish name. He's the ranking legal officer at the naval base in San Diego."

"A Lieutenant Commander Fitzpatrick?"

"Yes, how did you know?"

"*Unglaublich! Diese Stümper!*"

"*Warum?*" asked the Englishman. "In what sense?"

"He may be what you say he is in San Diego, Englander, but he is not *in* San Diego! He's here in Bonn!"

"Are you mad? No, of course, you're not. Are you *certain?*"

"He's with Converse! I spoke to him myself. The two are registered in *his* name at Das Rektorat! He is how we found Converse!"

"There was no attempt to conceal the name?"

"On the contrary, he used his papers to gain entrance!"

"How bloody third-rate," said London, bewildered. "Or how downright sure of himself," added the Britisher, his tone changing. "A signal? No one dares touch him?"

"*Unsinn!* It's not so."

"Why not?"

"He spoke to Peregrine, the ambassador. Our man was there. Peregrine wanted to take him, wanted him brought forcibly to the embassy. There were complications; he got away."

"Our man wasn't very good, then."

"An obstruction. Some *Schauspieler*—an actor. Peregrine will not discuss the incident. He says nothing."

412

"Which means no one will touch his naval officer from California," concluded London. "There's a very good reason."

"What is it?"

"He's the brother-in-law of Preston Halliday."

"Geneva! *Mein Gott,* they are into us!"

"Someone is, but not anyone with a great deal of information. I agreed with Palo Alto, who also agrees with our specialist in the Mossad—with Abrahms, as well."

"The Jew? What does the Jew say? What does he *say?*"

"He claims this Converse is an agent flying blind out of Washington."

"What more do you *need?*"

"He is not to leave your house. Instructions will follow."

Stunned, Undersecretary of State Brewster Tolland hung up the phone, sank back in his chair, then shot forward and pressed the appropriate buttons on his console.

"Chesapeake," said the female voice. "Code, please?"

"Six thousand," said Tolland. "May I speak with Consular Operations, Station Eight, please?"

"Station Eight requires—"

"Plantagenet," interrupted the Undersecretary.

"Right away, sir."

"What is it, Six thousand?"

"Cut the horseshit, Harry, this is Brew. What have you got running in Bonn we don't know about?"

"Off the top of my head, nothing."

413

"How far off the top is that?"

"No, it's straight. You're current on everything we're doing. There was an FRG review yesterday morning, and I'd remember if there was anything that excluded you."

"You might remember, but if I'm excluded I'm out."

"That's right, and I'd tell you as much if only to keep you out, you know that. What's your problem?"

"I just got off the scrambler with a very angry ambassador, who may just call a very old friend at Sixteen Hundred."

"Peregrine? What's *his* problem?"

"If it's not you, then someone's playing Cons Op. It's supposedly a covert investigation of the embassy—his embassy—somehow connected with the Navy Department."

"The *Navy?* That's crazy—I mean *dumb* crazy! Bonn's a port?"

"Actually, I suppose it is."

"I never heard of the *Bismarck* or the *Graf Spee* steaming around the Rhine. No way, Brew. We don't have anything like that and we wouldn't have. Do you have any names?"

"Yes, one," replied Tolland, looking down at a pad with hastily scribbled notes on it. "An attorney named Joel Converse. Who is he, Harry?"

"For Christ's sake, I never *heard* of him. What's the naval angle?"

"Someone who claims to be the chief legal officer of a major Navy base with the rank of lieutenant commander."

"*Claims* to be?"

"Well, before that he passed himself off as a military attaché working at the embassy."

"Somewhere the inmates broke out of a home."

"This isn't funny, Harry. Peregrine's no fool. He may be a vanity appointment, but he's damned good and he's damned smart. He says these people aren't only real but may know something he doesn't."

"What does he base that on?"

"First, the opinion of a man who's met this Converse—"

"Who?" interrupted Harry of Station Eight.

"He won't say, just that he trusts him, trusts his judgment. This person with no name says Converse is a highly qualified, very troubled man, not a black hat."

"A what?"

"That was the term Peregrine used. Obviously someone who's okay."

"What else?"

"What Peregrine calls isolated odd behavior in his personnel ranks. He wouldn't elaborate; he says he'll discuss it with the Secretary or Sixteen Hundred if I can't satisfy him. He wants answers fast, and we don't want to rock the boat over there."

"I'll try to help," said Harry. "Maybe it's something from Langley or Arlington—the *bastards!* I can run a check on the Navy's chief legals in an hour, and I'm sure the ABA can tell us who Converse is—*if* he is. At least narrow him down if there's more than one."

"Get back to me. I haven't got much time and we don't want the White House raising its voice."

"The last thing ever," agreed the director of Consular Operations, the State Department's branch of foreign clandestine activities.

"Try *that* on for legal size!" shouted Rear Admiral Hickman, standing by the window, angrily addressing a rigid, pale-faced David Remington. "And tell me with as few goddamned details as possible how it fits!"

"I find it impossible to believe, sir. I spoke with him yesterday—at noon—and then again last evening. He was in Sonoma!"

"So did *I,* Lieutenant. And whenever there was a scratching or an echo, what were the words? All that rain in the hills screwed up the telephone lines!"

"Those were the words, sir."

"He passed through Düsseldorf immigration two *days* ago! He's now in Bonn, Germany, with a man he swore to me had something to do with his brother-in-law's death. The *same* man he's protecting by putting a clamp on that flag. This *Converse!*"

"I don't know what to say, sir."

"Well, the State Department does and so do I. They're pushing through that vet-delay or whatever the hell you called it in your legalese."

"It's vetted material, sir. It simply means—"

"I don't want to *hear,* Lieutenant," said Hickman, heading back to his desk, adding under his breath. "Do you know how much you bastards cost me for the two divorces?"

416

"I beg your pardon, sir?"

"Never mind. I want that flag released. I brought Fitz on board here. I gave him his striper and the son of a bitch lied to me. He not only *lied,* he did it ten thousand miles away—lying about where he was when he knew he shouldn't be there without my authorization! He *knew* it! . . . Do you have any objections, Lieutenant? Something you can put into a sentence or two that won't require my bringing in three other legals to translate?"

Lieutenant Remington, one of the finest lawyers in the United States Navy, knew when to put the engines in reverse. Legal ethics had been violated by misinformation; the course was clear. Aggressive retreat with full boilers—or nuclear power, he supposed, although he did not really know. "I'll personally accelerate the vet-delay, Admiral. As the officer responsible for the secondary CLO statute, I'll make it clear that the direct order is now subject to immediate cancellation. No such order can or should originate under questionable circumstances. Legally—"

"*That* will be all, Lieutenant," said the Admiral, cutting off his subordinate and sitting down.

"Yes, sir."

"No, that *isn't* all!" continued Hickman, abruptly leaning forward. "How's that transcript released, and how soon can you expect it?"

"With State's input it'll only be a matter of hours, sir, noon or shortly afterwards, I'd guess. A classified teletype will be sent to those requesting the flag. However, since SAND PAC has only placed a restriction and not a request—"

"*Request* it, Lieutenant. Bring it up to me the minute it gets here and don't leave the base until it does."

"Aye, aye, sir!"

The deep-red Mercedes limousine weaved down the curving road inside the massive gates of Erich Leifhelm's estate. The late-afternoon orange sun filtered diagonally through the tall trees, which not only bordered the road but were everywhere beyond on both sides. The drive might have been restful had it not been for a sight that made the whole scene grotesque: racing alongside the car were at least a half-dozen giant Dobermans, not one of them making a sound. There was something unearthly about their running furiously in silence, black eyes flashing up at the windows, their jaws wide with rapid, erratic breathing, teeth bared, but no sound emerging from their throats. Somehow Converse knew that if he stepped out of the car without the proper commands being issued, the powerful dogs would tear him to pieces.

The limousine pulled into a long circular drive that fronted wide brown marble steps leading to an arched doorway, the heavy panels covered with dark bas-relief—a remnant of some ancient pillaged cathedral. Standing on the lower step was a man with a silver whistle raised to his lips. Again there was no sound a human could hear, but suddenly the animals abandoned the car and ran to him, flanking him, facing forward on their haunches, jaws slack, bodies pulsating.

"Please wait, sir," said the chauffeur as he climbed out and ran around to Joel's door. "If you will step out, please, and take two paces away from the car. Only two paces, sir." The chauffeur now held in his hand a black object with a rounded metal tube extending from the front of the instrument, not unlike a miniaturized electric charcoal starter.

"What's that?" asked Converse.

"Protection, sir. For you, sir. The dogs, sir. They are trained to sense heavy metal."

Joel stood there as the German moved the electronic detector over his clothes, including his shoes, his inner thighs and the back of his waist. "Do you people really think I'd come out here with a gun?"

"I do not think, sir. I do as I am told."

"How original," mumbled Converse as he watched the man on the marble step raise the silver whistle again to his lips. As one, the phalanx of Dobermans suddenly leaped forward. In panic, Joel grabbed the chauffeur, spinning the German in front of him. There was no resistance; the man simply turned his head and grinned as the dogs veered to the right and raced around the circular drive into the approach road cut out of the forest.

"Don't apologize, *mein Herr,*" said the chauffeur. "It happens often."

"I wasn't going to apologize," said Converse flatly as he released the man. "I was going to break your neck." The German moved away, and Joel remained motionless, stunned by his own words. He had not spoken words like that in over eighteen years.

"This way, sir," said the man on the steps, his accent oddly yet distinctly British.

Inside, the great hall was lined with medieval banners hanging down from an interior balcony. The hall led into an immense sitting room, the motif again medieval, made comfortable by soft leather chairs and couches, gaily fringed lamps and silver services everywhere on thin polished tables. The room was also made ugly by the profusion of protruding animals' heads on the upper walls; large cats, elephants and boar looked down in defiant anger. It was a field marshal's lair.

It was not, however, the furnishings that absorbed Converse's attention but the sight of the four men who stood beside four separate chairs facing him.

He knew Bertholdier and Leifhelm; they stood beside each other on the right. It was the two on the left he stared at. The medium-sized, stocky man with the fringe of close-cropped hair on a balding head and wearing a rumpled safari jacket, the ever-present boots below his khaki trousers, could be no one but Chaim Abrahms. His pouched, angry face with its slits of glaring eyes was the face of an avenger. The very tall man with the gaunt, aquiline features and the straight gray hair was General Jan van Headmer, the Slayer of Soweto. Joel had read the Van Headmer dossier quickly; fortunately it was the briefest, the final summary saying it all.

In essence, Van Headmer is a Cape Town aristocrat, an Afrikaner who has never really accepted the British, to say nothing of the tribal blacks. His convictions are rooted in a reality that for him is unshakable. His forebears carved out a savage land under savage conditions and at a great loss of life brutally taken by savages. His thinking is unalterably that of the late-nineteenth and early-twentieth centuries. He will not accept the sociological and political inroads made by the more educated Bantus because he will never consider them anything more than bush primitives. When he orders austere deprivations and mass executions, he thinks he is dealing only with subhuman animals. It is this thinking that led him to be jailed along with Prime Minister Verwoerd and the racist Vorster during World War II. He concurred wholeheartedly with the Nazi concept of superior races. His close association with Chaim Abrahms is the single difference between him and the Nazis, and not a contradiction for him. The sabras carved a land out of a primitive Palestine; their history parallels his country's, and both men take pride in their strength and respective accomplishments. Van Headmer, incidentally, is one of the most charming men one could meet. On the surface, he is cultured, extremely courteous and always willing to listen. Underneath, he is an unfeeling killer, and he is Delavane's key figure in South Africa with its vast resources.

"*Mein Haus ist dein Haus,*" said Leifhelm,

walking toward Joel, his hand outstretched.

Converse stepped forward to accept the German's hand. Their hands clasped. "That was an odd greeting outside for such a warm sentiment," said Joel, abruptly releasing Leifhelm's hand and turning to Bertholdier. "Good to see you again, General. My apologies for the unfortunate incident in Paris the other night. I don't mean to speak lightly of a man's life, but in those few split seconds I didn't think he had much regard for mine."

Joel's boldness had the desired effect. Bertholdier stared at him, momentarily unsure of what to say. And Converse was aware that the other three men were watching him intently, without question struck by his audacity, in both manners and words.

"To be sure, monsieur," said the Frenchman, pointlessly but with composure. "As you know, the man disregarded his orders."

"Really? I was told he misunderstood them."

"It is the same!" The sharp, heavily accented voice came from behind.

Joel turned around. "Is it?" he asked coldly.

"In the field, yes," said Chaim Abrahms. "Either one is an error, and errors are paid for with lives. The man paid with his."

"May I introduce General Abrahms?" Leifhelm broke in, touching Converse's elbow and leading him to the Israeli.

"General Abrahms, it's a privilege," said Joel with convincing sincerity as they shook hands. "Like everyone here, I've admired you tremendously, although perhaps your rhetoric has

422

been excessive at times."

The Israeli's face reddened as soft laughter filled the large room. Suddenly Van Headmer stepped forward, and Converse's eyes were drawn to the strong face, the brows frowning, muscles taut.

"You are addressing one of my closest associates, sir," he said; the rebuke was unmistakable. Then a thin smile creased his gaunt, chiseled face. "And I could not have said it better myself. A pleasure to know you, young man." The Afrikaner's hand was stretched toward Joel, who accepted it amid the subdued laughter.

"I am insulted!" cried Abrahms, his thick eyebrows raised, his head bobbing in mock despair. "By *talkers* I'm insulted! Frankly, Mr. Converse, they agree with you because none of them has had a woman in a quarter of a century. They may tell you otherwise—others may tell you otherwise—but believe me they hire whores to play cards with them or read stories into their old gray ears just to fool their friends!" The laughter grew louder, and the Israeli, now playing to an audience, went on, leaning forward and pretending to speak sotto voce to Joel. "But you see, *I* hire the whores to tell me the truth while I *shtup* them! They tell me these fancy talkers nod off by nine o'clock, whining for warm milk. With the *Ovaltine,* if it's possible!"

"My dear sabra," said Leifhelm, talking through his laughter, "you read your own romantic fiction too assiduously."

"You see what I mean, Converse?" asked Abrahms, shrugging, palms extended. "You hear

423

that? 'Assiduously.' Now you know why the Germans lost the war. They forever spoke so dramatically of the *Blitzkrieg* and the *Angriffe,* but actually they were talking—*assiduously* —about what to do next!''

"They should have given you a commission, Chaim," said Bertholdier, enjoying himself. "You could have changed your name, called Rommel and Von Runstedt Jews and taken over both fronts."

"The High Command could have done worse," agreed the Israeli.

"I wonder, though," continued the Frenchman, "if you would have stopped there? Hitler was a fine orator, as you are a fine orator. Perhaps you would have claimed that he, too, was a Jew and moved into the chancellery."

"Oh, I have it on good authority that he *was* a Jew. But from a *very* bad family. Even we have them; of course, they're all from Europe."

The laughter grew again and then rapidly began to subside. Joel took the cue. "Sometimes I speak too frankly, General," he said. "I should learn better, but, believe me, no insult was intended. I have nothing but admiration for your stated positions, your policies."

"And that's precisely what we shall discuss," said Erich Leifhelm, drawing everyone's attention. "Positions, policies, overall philosophy, if you will. We will stay as far away from specifics as we can, although a few will undoubtedly intrude. However, it is our approach to the larger abstractions that count. Come, Mr. Converse, have a chair. Let us begin our conference, the first of many, I trust."

Rear Admiral Hickman slowly put down the transcript on his desk, and looked aimlessly—past his propped-up feet—out the window at the ocean under a gray sky. He crossed his arms, lowered his head and frowned. He was as bewildered now as he had been when he first read the transcript, as convinced now as he was then that Remington's conclusions—conclusion, really—was off the mark. But then the legal officer was too young to have any real knowledge of the events as they had actually happened; no one who had not been there could really understand. Too many others did; it was the reason for the flag, but it made no sense to apply that reasoning to this Converse eighteen years later. It was exhuming a corpse that had died from a fever, whether the shell of a man lived on or not. It had to be something else.

Hickman looked at his watch, unfolded his arms and removed his feet from the edge of the table. It was three-ten in Norfolk; he reached for the telephone.

"Hello, Brian," said Rear Admiral Scanlon of the Fifth Naval District. "I want you to know how much we appreciate SAND PAC's help in this thing."

"SAND PAC's?" asked Hickman, bemused that no credit was given to the State Department.

"All right, Admiral, *your* help. I owe you one, old Hicky."

"Start paying by dropping that name."

"Hey, come on, don't you remember the hockey games? You'd come racing up the ice and the whole cadet corps would shout: 'Here comes *Hicky!* Here comes *Hicky!*' "

"May I unblock my ears now?"

"I'm just trying to thank you, pal."

"That's just it, I'm not sure for what? Have you read the transcript?"

"Naturally."

"What the hell's *there?*"

"Well," answered Scanlon tentatively. "I read it pretty quickly. It's been an awful day and, frankly, I just passed it on. What do *you* think is there? Between you and me, I'd like to know, because I barely had time to skim through it."

"What do I think is there? Absolutely *nothing.* Oh, sure, we kept flags on stuff like that back then because the White House passed the order to put a lid on officially recorded criticism and we all went along. Also we were pretty sick and tired of it ourselves. But there's nothing in that transcript that hasn't been heard before, or that has any value for anyone but military historians a hundred years from now as a very small footnote."

"Well," said Scanlon, even more tentatively, "this Converse had some pretty harsh things to say about Command-Saigon."

"About *Mad Marcus?* Christ, I said worse during the Force-Tonkin conferences and *my* CO did me ten times better. We ferried in those kids up and down the coast when all they were ready for was a day at the beach with hot dogs and Ferris wheels. . . . I don't get it. You and my legal zero in on the same thing, and I think it's old hat and discredited. Mad Marcus is a relic."

"Your who?"

"My legal exec. I told you about him, Remington."

"Oh, yes. The stickler prick."

"He picked up on the Saigon thing too. 'That's it,' he said. 'It's in those remarks. It's Delavane.' He wasn't around to know Delavane was fair game for every antiwar group in the country. Hell, *we* gave him the name Mad Marcus. No, it's not Delavane, it's something else. Perhaps it's in those escapes, specifically Converse's last escape. Maybe there's some MIA input we don't know about."

"Well," repeated the admiral in Norfolk for the third time, but now far less tentatively. "You may have something there, but it doesn't concern us. Look, I'll be honest with you. I didn't want to say anything because I didn't want you to think you went to a lot of trouble for nothing, but the word I get is that the whole thing is a bust—negative."

"Oh?" said Hickman, suddenly listening very carefully. "How so?"

"It's the wrong man. Apparently an over-enthusiastic JG was doing some digging in the same time period, the same general circumstances. He saw the flag and drew six wrong conclusions. I hope he enjoys taking five A.M. muster."

"And that's it?" asked SAND PAC's admiral, controlling his astonishment.

"That's the feedback we get here. Whatever your CLO had in mind hasn't anything to do with our people."

Hickman could not believe what he was hearing. Of course Scanlon had not mentioned the

State Department's efforts. He knew nothing about them! He was quickly putting as much distance between himself and the Converse flag as he could, lying because he had not been told. State was working quietly—probably through Cons Op—and Scanlon had no reason to think "old Hicky" knew a damn thing about Bonn or Converse or Connal Fitzpatrick's whereabouts. Or about a man named Preston Halliday who had been murdered in Geneva. What was *happening?* He would not find out from Scanlon. Nor did he care to.

"To hell with it, then. My CLO will be back in three or four days and maybe I'll learn something."

"Whatever it is, it's back in your sandbox, Admiral. My people had the wrong man."

"Your people couldn't navigate a row boat in the D.C. Reflecting Pool."

"Can't blame you for that, Hicky."

Hickman hung up the phone and resumed his standard position when in thought, gazing beyond his propped-up shoes at the ocean. The sun was trying to break through the overcast without much success.

He had never liked Scanlon for reasons too petty to examine. Except one; he knew Scanlon was a liar. What he had not known was that he was such a stupid liar.

Lieutenant David Remington was flattered by the call. The well-known four-striper had invited him to lunch—not only invited him but had apologized for the lateness of the invitation and

428

told him that it was perfectly understandable if it was inconvenient. Further, the captain wanted him to know that the call was of a personal nature, having nothing to do with naval business. The high-ranking officer, although a resident of La Jolla, was in port for only a few days and needed legal advice. He had been told that Lieutenant Remington was just about the best lawyer in the United States Navy. Would the lieutenant accept?

Of course Remington had made it perfectly clear that whatever advice he might offer would be offered on the basis of *amicus-amicae;* no remuneration could possibly be considered, as that would be a violation of Statute . . .

"May I buy you lunch, Lieutenant, or do we have to split the check?" the four-striper had asked—somewhat impatiently, thought Remington.

The restaurant was high in the hills above La Jolla, an out-of-the-way roadside inn that apparently catered to diners of the area and those from San Diego and University City who did not care to be seen together in the usual places. Remington had not been too pleased; he would have preferred being seen at the Coronado with the captain than traveling ten miles north so as *not* to be seen in the hills of La Jolla. Nevertheless, the four-striper had been politely adamant; it was where he wanted to meet. David had checked him out. The much decorated captain not only was in line for promotion but was considered a potential candidate for the Joint Chiefs of Staff. Remington would have ridden a bicycle on the exposed Alaskan pipeline to keep the appointment.

Which was exactly what he thought he was doing, as he spun the steering wheel right, then left, then right and right again as he made his way up the steep narrow roads. It was important to keep in mind, he thought, as he whipped the car to the left, that personal advice was nevertheless professional advice, and without payment of any sort whatsoever, it constituted a debt that would one day be acknowledged. And if a man was elevated to the Joint Chiefs . . . Remington could not help it: in a glow of self-importance he had let drop to a fellow legal officer—the one who had coined the name "stickler prick"—that he was lunching with a highly regarded four-striper in La Jolla and might be late returning to the office. Then to drive his point home, he had asked his associate for directions.

Oh, my God! What *was* it? Oh, my *God!*

At the apex of the hairpin curve was an enormous black rig, thirty feet in length, and out of control. It weaved right and left on the narrow incline, its speed gathering with every foot, measured in racing yards, a black behemoth swerving, crashing down on everything in front of it, a wild beast gone mad!

Remington whipped his head to his right as he spun the wheel to avoid impact. There were only thin trunks of young trees and saplings in late-summer bloom; below was a floral abyss. These were the last images he saw as the car careened on its side and began the plunge.

Far above on another hill a man kneeled,

binoculars raised to his face as the explosion below confirmed the kill. His expression was one of neither joy nor sadness, merely acceptance. A mission had been accomplished. After all, it was war.

And Lieutenant David Remington, whose life was so ordered and orderly, who knew exactly where he was going and how in this world, who knew above all that he would never be trapped by the forces that had killed his father in the name of corporate policy, was put to death by the policy of a company he had never heard of. An enterprise called Aquitaine. He had seen the name Delavane.

Their view is that it's the proper evolution of current history, all other ideologies having failed. . . . The words spoken by Preston Halliday in Geneva kept repeating themselves in Converse's inner ear as he listened to the four voices of Aquitaine. The frightening thing was that they believed what they said without equivocation, morally and intellectually, their convictions rooted in observations going back decades, their arguments persuasive as they illuminated past global mistakes of judgment that resulted in horrible suffering and unnecessary loss of life.

The simple objective of their coming together —allies and former enemies alike—was to bring benevolent order to a world in chaos, to permit the industrial states to flourish for the good of all people, spreading the strengths and benefits of multinational trade to the impoverished, uncommitted Third World and, by so doing, secure its commitment. Only in this way, in this coming together, could Communism be stopped—stopped and reversed until it collapsed under the sheer force of superior armed might and financial resources.

To bring all this about required a shift in values and priorities. Industrial decisions everywhere must be coordinated to bring about the total strength of the free states. Government treasuries, multinational corporations and giant conglomerates must look to a stratum of interlocking committees, agree to be directed by these committees, to accept their decisions—which would in effect be their respective governments' decisions—each keeping the others apprised of its current agenda. What was this ultimate stratum of negotiators? Who would be the members of these committees that would in effect speak for the free nations and set their policies?

Throughout history only one class of people remained constant in its excellence, who when called upon in times of crisis performed far beyond human expectations—even in defeat. The reasons for this segment's unique contributions in war—and even in peace, though to a lesser degree —were historically clear: these men were selfless. They belonged to a class trained to serve without thought of reward except for the recognition of excellence. Wealth was irrelevant because their needs were furnished and perquisites granted only through the outstanding performance of duty.

In the new order this class of people would not be subject to the corruptions of the marketplace. In reality it was unusually well equipped to deal with such corruptions, for it could not be touched by them. The mere presence of any illegally gained wealth within its ranks would instantly be recognized and condemned, resulting in courts-martial. This class of society, this novel branch of the human race, was not only incorruptible at the highest levels, it would be the ultimate savior of mankind as we know it today.

It was the military. The world over, even encompassing one's enemies. Together—even as enemies—they best understood the catastrophic results of weakness.

To be sure, certain minor liberties would perforce have to be withheld from the body politic, but these were small sacrifices for survival. Who could argue?

None of the four spokesmen for Aquitaine raised his voice. They were the quiet prophets of reason, each with his own history, his own identity—allies and enemies together in a world gone mad.

Converse responded in the affirmative to everything that was said—this was not difficult to do—and asked abstract questions of philosophy, as he was expected to do. Even the court jester, Chaim Abrahms, became deeply serious and answered Converse's questions quietly.

At one point Abrahms said, "You think we Jews are the only ones in the Diaspora, my friend? You are wrong. The whole human race is dispersed everywhere, all of us locking rams' horns and not knowing where to go. Certain rabbis claim we Jews shall not see salvation until the Messianic era, the time of divine redemption when a god will appear to show us the way to our own promised land. He was far too late arriving; we could not wait for Him any longer. We created Israel. Do you see the lesson? We—we *here*—are now the divine intervention on earth. And I— even *I,* a man of accomplishment and ego—will give up my life in silence so we may succeed."

Jacques-Louis Bertholdier: "You must understand, Mr. Converse, that Voltaire said it best in his *Discours sur l'homme.* Essentially he wrote that man attained his highest freedom only when he understood the parameters of his behavior. We will establish those parameters. Is anything more logical?"

Erich Leifhelm: "Goethe said it perhaps better when he insisted that the *romance* of politics was best used to numb and quell the fears of the uninformed. In his definitive *Aus meinem Leben* he states clearly that all governing classes must be imbued above all with discipline. Where is it more prevalent?"

Jan van Headmer: "My own country, sir, is the living embodiment of the lesson. We took the beast out of the savage and formed a vast, productive nation. The beast returns and my nation is in turmoil."

And so it went for several hours. Quiet dissertations delivered thoughtfully, reflectively, passions apparent only in the deep sincerity of their convictions. Twice Joel was pressed to reveal the name of his client and twice he demurred, stating the legal position of confidentiality—which could change in a matter of days, perhaps less.

"I'd have to offer my client something

concrete. An approach, a strategy that would warrant his immediate involvement, his commitment, if you will."

"Why is that necessary at this juncture?" asked Bertholdier. "You've heard our reasoning. Certainly an approach can be discerned."

"All right, scratch approach. A strategy, then. Not the why but the how."

"You ask for a plan?" said Abrahms. "On what basis?"

"Because you'll be asking for an investment surpassing anything in your experience."

"That's an extraordinary statement," interjected Van Headmer.

"He has extraordinary resources," replied Converse.

"Very well," said Leifhelm, glancing at each of his associates before he continued. Joel understood; permission was being sought based on prior discussions. It was granted. "What would you say to the compromising of certain powerful individuals in specific governments?"

"Blackmail?" asked Joel. "Extortion? It wouldn't work. There are too many checks and balances. A man's threatened, the threat's discovered and he's out anyway. Then the purification rites set in, and where there was once weakness, suddenly there's a great deal of strength."

"That's an extremely narrow interpretation," said Bertholdier.

"You do not take into consideration the time element!" cried Abrahms defiantly, for the first time raising his voice. *"Accumulation,* Converse!

Rapid *acceleration!"*

Suddenly Joel was aware that the three other men were looking at the Israeli, but not simply watching him. In each pair of eyes was a warning. Abrahms shrugged. "It's merely a point."

"Well taken," said Converse, without emphasis.

"I'm not even sure it applies," added the Israeli, compounding his error.

"Well, *I'm* sure it's time for dinner," said Leifhelm, removing his hand from the side of his chair. "I've boasted so much about my table to our guest that I admit to a shortness of breath—concern, of course. I trust the chef has upheld my honor." As if answering a signal —which Joel knew was the case—the British manservant appeared beneath an archway at the far end of the room. "I am clairvoyant!" Leifhelm rose. "Come, come, my friends. Saddle of lamb *à citron,* a dish created by the gods for themselves and stolen by the irrepressible thief who rules my kitchen."

The dinner was indeed superb, each dish the result of an isolated effort to achieve perfection in both taste and presentation. Converse was no gourmet, his culinary education having been forced on him in expensive restaurants where his mind was only mildly distracted by the food, but he instinctively knew when a dish was the best in its class. There was nothing second-rate about Leifhelm's table, including the table itself, an enormous solid mass of mahogany supported by two huge but delicately carved tripods resting on the intricate parquet floor. The deep-red velour walls in the high-ceilinged room were hung with oils of hunting scenes. The low candelabra in front of the silver-mirrored place mats did not obstruct a guest's view of the person opposite, a feat Joel wished could be mastered by most of the hostesses in New York, London and Geneva.

The talk veered away from the serious topics explored in the sitting room. It was as if a recess had been called, a diversion to ease the burdens of statesmanship. If that was the aim, it was eminently successful, and it was the Afrikaner, Van Headmer, who led the way. In his soft-spoken, charming way (the dossier had been accurate—the "unfeeling killer" *was* charming) he described a safari he had taken Chaim Abrahms on in the veld.

"Do you realize, gentlemen, that I bought this poor Hebrew his first jacket at Safarics' in Johannesburg and there's never been a day when I haven't regretted it. It's become our great general's trademark! Of course, you know why he wears it. It absorbs perspiration and requires very little washing, simply large applications of bay rum. This *is* a different jacket, isn't it, great general?"

"Bleach, *bleach,* I tell my wife!" replied the sabra, grimacing. "It takes out the smell of the godless slave traders!"

"Talking of slaves, let me tell you," said the Afrikaner, warming to his story with a glass of wine, changed with each new course.

The story of Chaim Abrahms' first and only safari was worthy of good vaudeville. Apparently the Israeli had been stalking a male lion for hours with his gun bearer, a Bantu he constantly abused, not realizing the black understood and spoke English as well as he. Abrahms had zeroed in each of his four rifles prior to the hunt, but whenever he had the lion in his sights, he missed. This supposedly superb marksman, this celebrated general with the rifle-eye of a hawk, could not hit eight feet of flesh a hundred yards away. At the end of the day an exhausted Chaim Abrahms, using broken English and a multiplicity of hand gestures, bribed the gun bearer not to tell the rest of the safari of his misses. The hunter and the Bantu returned to camp, the hunter lamenting the nonexistence of cats and the stupidity of gun bearers. The native went to Van Headmer's tent, and as the Afrikaner told it in perfectly-mimicked Anglicized Bantu, said the following: "I liked the lion more than the Jew, sir. I altered his sights, sir, but apparently I will be forgiven my indiscretion, sir. Among other enticements, he has offered to have me bar-mitzvahed."

The diners collapsed in laughter—Abrahms, to his credit, loudest of all. Obviously, he had heard the story before and relished the telling. It occurred to Joel that only the most secure could listen to such telling tales about themselves and respond with genuine laughter. The Israeli was a rock in the firmament of his convictions and could easily tolerate a laugh on himself. That, too, was frightening.

The British servant intruded, walking silently on the hard wood floor and spoke into Erich Leifhelm's ear.

"Forgive me, please," said the German, rising

to take the call. "A nervous broker in Munich who consistently picks up rumors from Riyadh. A sheik goes to the toilet and he hears thunder from the east."

The ebullient conversation went on without a break in the flow, the three men of Aquitaine behaving like old comrades sincerely trying to make a stranger feel welcome. This, too, was frightening. Where were the fanatics who wanted to destroy governments, ruthlessly grabbing control and shackling whole societies, channeling the body politic into their vision of the military state? These were men of intellect. They spoke of Voltaire and Goethe, and had compassion for suffering and pain and unnecessary loss of life. They had humor and could even laugh at themselves while speaking calmly of sacrificing their own lives for the betterment of a world gone mad. But Joel understood their true nature. These were interlopers assuming the mantels of statesmen. What had Leifhelm said, quoting Goethe? "The romance of politics was best used to numb and quell the fears of the uninformed."

Frightening.

Leifhelm returned, followed by the British servant carrying two open bottles of wine. If the call from Munich had brought unfavorable news, the German gave no indication of it. His spirits were as before, his waxen smile at the ready and his enthusiasm for the next course unbridled. "And now, my friends, the lamb *à citron—* medallions of ambrosia and, hyperbole aside, actually rather good. Also, in honor of our guest we have a bonus this evening. My astute English friend and companion was in Siegburg the other day and ran across several bottles of Beerenauslese, '71. What could be a more fitting tribute?''

The men of Aquitaine glanced at one another, then Bertholdier spoke. "Certainly a find, Erich. It's one of the more acceptable German varieties.''

"The '82 Mausberg Riesling in Johannesburg promises to be among the finest in years,'' said Van Headmer.

"I doubt it will rival the Richon-le-Zion Carmel,'' added the Israeli.

"You are all impossible!''

A behatted chef rolled in a silver service cart, uncovered the saddle of lamb and, under appreciative looks, proceeded to carve and serve. The Englishman presented the various side dishes to each diner, then poured the wine.

Erich Leifhelm raised his glass, the flickering light of the candles reflecting off the carved crystal and the edges of the silver-mirrored place mats. "To our guest and his unknown client, both of whom we trust will soon be in our fold.''

Converse nodded his head and drank.

He took the glass from his lips, and was suddenly aware that the four men of Aquitaine were staring at him, their own glasses still on the table. None had drunk the wine.

Leifhelm spoke again, his voice nasal, cold, a fury held in check by an intellect in control. " 'General Delavane was the enemy, *our* enemy! Men like that can't be allowed anymore, can't you understand!' Those were the words, were they not, Mr. Converse?''

"*What?*" Joel heard his voice but was not sure it was his. The flames of the candles suddenly erupted; fire filled his eyes and the burning in his throat became an unbearable pain. He grabbed his neck as he struggled out of the chair, hurling it back; he heard the crash, but only as a succession of echoes. He was falling. The pain surged into his stomach; it was intolerable; he clutched his groin, frantically trying to suppress the pain. Then he felt the chill of a hard surface and somehow knew he was writhing wildly on the floor while being held in check by powerful arms.

"The gun. Step back. Hold him." The voice, too, was a series of echoes, though sharply enunciated in a searing British accent. "Now. *Fire!*"

16

The telephone rang, jolting Connal Fitzpatrick out of a deep sleep. He had fallen back on the couch, the Van Headmer dossier in his hand, both feet still planted on the floor. Shaking his head and rapidly blinking and widening his eyes, he tried to orient himself. Where *was* he? What *time* was it? The phone rang again, now a prolonged, shattering sound. He lurched off the couch, his breathing erratic, his exhaustion too complete to shake off in a few seconds. He had not really slept since California; his body and mind could barely function. He grabbed the phone, nearly dropping it as he momentarily lost his balance.

"Yes . . . *hello!*"

"Commander Fitzpatrick, if you please," said a male voice in a clipped British accent.

"This is he."

"Philip Dunstone here, Commander. I'm calling for Mr. Converse. He wanted me to tell you that the conference is going extremely well, far better than he thought possible."

"You're *who?*"

"Dunstone. Major Philip Dunstone. I'm senior aide to General Berkeley-Greene."

"Berkeley-Greene?"

"Yes, Commander. Mr. Converse said to tell you that along with the others he's decided to accept General Leifhelm's hospitality for the night. He'll be in touch with you first thing in the morning."

"Let me talk to him. Now."

"I'm afraid that's not possible. They've all gone out on the motor launch for a spin downriver. Frankly, they're a secretive lot, aren't they? Actually, I'm not permitted to attend their discussions any more than you are."

"I'm not settling for this, Major!"

"Really, Commander, I'm simply relaying a message. . . . Oh yes, Mr. Converse did mention that if you were concerned I should also tell you that if the admiral called, you were to thank him and give him his regards."

Fitzpatrick stared at the wall. Converse would not bring up the Hickman business unless he was sending a message. The request made no sense to anyone but the two of them. Everything *was* all right. Also there could be several reasons why Joel did not care to talk directly on the phone. Among them, thought Connal resentfully, was probably the fact that he didn't trust his "aide" to say the proper words in the event their conversation was being overheard.

"All right, Major . . . what was the name again? Dunstone?"

"That's right, Philip Dunstone. Senior aide to General Berkeley-Greene."

"Leave word for Mr. Converse that I'll expect to hear from him by eight o'clock."

"Isn't that a little harsh, old boy? It's nearly two A.M. now. The breakfast buffet usually starts about nine-thirty out here."

"Nine o'clock, then," said Fitzpatrick firmly.

"I'll tell him myself, Commander. Oh, one final thing. Mr. Converse asked me to apologize for his not having reached you by midnight. They've really been at it hammer and tongs in there."

That was it, thought Connal. Everything was under control. Joel certainly would not have made that remark otherwise. "Thanks, Major, and by the way, I'm sorry I was rude. I was asleep and tried to get it together too fast."

"Lucky chap. You can head back to the pillows while I stand watch. Next time you can take my place."

"If the food's good, you're on."

"It's not, really. A lot of pansy cooking, to tell you the truth. Good night, Commander."

"Good night, Major."

Relieved, Fitzpatrick hung up the phone. He

443

looked over at the couch, thinking briefly of going back to the dossiers but decided against it. He felt hollow all over, hollow legs, hollow chest, a hollow ache in his head. He needed sleep badly.

He gathered up the papers and took them into Converse's room. He placed them in the attaché case, locked it and turned the combination tumblers. Carrying the case, he went back into the sitting room, checked the door, turned off the lights and headed for his own bedroom. He threw the case on the bed and removed his shoes, then his trousers, but that was as far as he got. He collapsed on the pillows, somehow managing to wrap part of the bedspread around him. The darkness was welcome.

"That was hardly necessary," said Erich Leifhelm to the Englishman, as the latter replaced the phone. " 'Pansy cooking' is not the way I would describe my table."

"He undoubtedly would," said the man who had called himself Philip Dunstone. "Let's check the patient."

The two walked out of the library and down the hall to a bedroom. Inside were the three other men of Aquitaine along with a fourth, his black bag and the exposed hypodermic needles denoting a physician. On the bed was Joel Converse, his eyes wide and glasslike, saliva oozing from the sides of his mouth, his head moving back and forth as if in a trance, unintelligible sounds emerging from his lips.

The doctor glanced up and spoke. "There's nothing more he can give us because there *is* nothing more," said the physician. "The chemicals don't lie. Quite simply, he's a blind sent out by men in Washington, but he has no idea who they are. He didn't even know they existed until this naval officer convinced him they had to exist. His only referrals were Anstett and Beale."

"Both dead," interrupted Van Headmer. "Anstett is public, and I can vouch for Beale. My employee on Santorini flew into Mykonos and confirmed the kill. There can be no trace, incidentally. The Greek is back on the chalk cliffs selling laces and inflated whisky in his *taverna*."

"Prepare him for his odyssey," said Chaim Abrahms, looking down at Converse. "As our specialist in the Mossad put it so clearly, distance is now the necessary requirement. A vast separation between this American and those who would send him out."

Fitzpatrick stirred as the bright morning sunlight from the windows pierced the darkness and expanding shades of white forced his eyelids open. He stretched, his shoulder digging into a hard corner of the attaché case, the rest of him constricted by the bedspread, which was tangled about his legs. He kicked it off and flung his arms on both sides of the bed, breathing deeply, feeling the relaxed swelling of his chest. He swung his left hand above his head, twisted his wrist and looked at his watch. It was nine-twenty; he had slept for seven and a half hours, but the uninterrupted sleep seemed much longer. He got out of bed and took several steps; his balance was steady, his mind clearing. He looked at his watch again, remembering. The major named Dunstone had said breakfast at Leifhelm's estate was served from nine-thirty on, and if the conference had moved to a boat on the river at 2:00 A.M. Converse probably would not call before ten o'clock.

Connal walked into the bathroom; there was a phone on the wall by the toilet if he was wrong about the call. A shave followed by a hot and cold shower and he would be fully himself again.

Eighteen minutes later Fitzpatrick walked back into the bedroom, a towel around his waist, his skin still smarting from the harsh sprays of water. He crossed to his open suitcase on a luggage rack and took out his miniaturized radio, placed it on the bureau and, deciding against the Armed Forces band, dialed in what was left of a German newscast. There were the usual threats of strikes in the industrial south, as well as charges and countercharges hurled around the Bundestag, but nothing earthshaking. He selected comfortable clothes—lightweight slacks, a blue oxford shirt and his cord jacket. He got dressed and walked out into the sitting room toward the phone; he would call room service for a small breakfast and a great deal of coffee.

He stopped. Something was wrong. What was it? The pillows on the couch were still rumpled, a glass half filled with stale whisky still on the coffee table, as were pencils and a blank telephone message pad. The balcony doors were closed, the curtains drawn, and across the room the silver ice bucket remained in the center of the silver tray on the antique hunt table. Everything was as he had last seen it, yet there was something. . . . The *door!* The door to Converse's bedroom was shut. Had he closed it? No, he had *not!*

He walked rapidly over and opened the door. He studied the room, conscious of the fact that he had stopped breathing. It was immaculate—cleaned and smoothed to a fare-thee-well. The suitcase was gone; the few articles Converse had left on the bureau were no longer there. Connal rushed to the closet and yanked it open. It was empty. He went into the bathroom; it was spotless, new soap in the receptacles, the glasses wrapped in clinging paper ready for incoming guests. He walked out of the bathroom stunned. There was not the slightest sign that anyone except a maid had been in that bedroom for days.

He ran out to the sitting room and the telephone. Seconds later the manager was on the line; it was the same man Connal had spoken with yesterday. "Yes, indeed, your businessman was even more eccentric than you described, Commander. He checked out at three-thirty this morning, paying all the bills, incidentally."

"He was *here?*"

"Of course."

"You *saw* him?"

"Not personally. I don't come on duty until eight o'clock. He spoke with the night manager and settled your account before going up to pack."

"How could your man know it was *him?* He never saw him before!"

"Really, Commander, he identified himself as

your associate and paid the bill. He also had his key; he left it at the desk.''

Fitzpatrick paused, astonished, then spoke harshly. ''The room was cleaned! Was that also done at three-thirty this morning?''

''No, *mein Herr,* at seven o'clock. By the first housekeeping shift.''

''But not the outer room?''

''The commotion might have disturbed you. Frankly, Commander, that suite must be prepared for an early-afternoon arrival. I'm sure the staff felt it would not bother you if they got a head start on the task. Obviously, it did not.''

''Early afternoon? *I'm* here!''

''And welcome to stay until twelve noon; the bill has been paid. Your friend has departed and the suite has been reserved.''

''And I don't suppose you have another room.''

''I'm afraid there's nothing available, Commander.''

Connal slammed down the phone. *Really, Commander* . . . Those same words had been spoken by another over the same telephone at two o'clock in the morning. There were three directories in a wicker rack by the table; he pulled out the one for Bonn and found the number.

''*Guten Morgen. Hier bei General Leifhelm.*''

''*Herrn Major Dunstone, bitte.*''

''*Wer?*''

''Dunstone,'' he said, then continued in German, ''He's a guest. Philip Dunstone. He's the senior aide to—to a General Berkeley-Greene. They're English.''

"English? There are no Englishmen here, sir. There's no one here—that is to say, there are no guests."

"He was there last night! They both were. I *spoke* with Major Dunstone."

"The general had a small dinner party for a few friends, but no English people, sir."

"Look, I'm trying to reach a man named Converse."

"Oh, yes, Mr. Converse. *He* was here, sir."

"Was?"

"I believe he left."

"Where's *Leifhelm?*" shouted Connal.

There was a pause before the German replied coldly, "Who should I say is calling *General* Leifhelm?"

"Fitzpatrick. Lieutenant Commander Fitzpatrick!"

"I believe he's in the dining room. If you'll stay on the telephone." The line was put on hold; the suspended silence was unnerving.

Finally there was a click and Leifhelm's voice reverberated over the phone. "Good morning, Commander. Bonn has provided a lovely day, no? The Seven Mountains are as clear as in a picture postcard. I believe you can see them—"

"Where's Converse?" interrupted the Navy lawyer.

"I would assume at Das Rektorat."

"He was supposed to be staying at your place."

"No such arrangements were made. They were neither requested nor offered. He left rather late, but he did leave, Commander. My car drove him back."

"That's not what I was told! A Major Dunstone called me around two this morning—"

"I believe Mr. Converse left shortly before then. . . . *Who* did you say called?"

"Dunstone. A Major Philip Dunstone. He's English. He said he was the senior aide to General Berkeley-Greene."

"I don't know this Major Dunstone; there was no such person here. However, I'm familiar with just about every general officer in the British Army and I've never heard of anyone named Berkeley-Greene."

"Stow it, Leifhelm!"

"I beg your pardon."

"I *spoke* to Dunstone! He—he said the right words. He said Converse was staying at your place—with the *others!*"

"I think you should have spoken directly with Herr Converse, because there was no Major Dunstone or General Berkeley-Greene at my home last night. Perhaps you should check with the British embassy; certainly they'd know if these people were in Bonn. Perhaps you heard the words incorrectly; perhaps they met later at a café."

"I *couldn't* speak to him! Dunstone said you were out on the river in a boat." Fitzpatrick's breath was now coming in short gasps.

"Now, that's ridiculous, Commander. It's true I keep a small launch for guests, but it's a well-known fact that I am not partial to the water." The general paused, adding with a short laugh. "The great field marshal gets seasick in a flatboat six feet from shore."

"You're *lying!*"

"I resent that, sir. Especially about the water. I never feared the Russian front, only the Black Sea. And if we had invaded England, I assure you I would have crossed the Channel in a plane." The German was toying with him; he was enjoying himself.

"You know exactly what I mean!" Connal shouted again. "They said Converse checked out of here at three-thirty this morning! I say he never came *back!*"

"And I say this conversation is pointless. If you are truly alarmed, call me back when you can be civil. I have friends in the Staatspolizei." Again a click; the German had hung up.

As Fitzpatrick replaced the phone another thought suddenly struck him. Frightened, he walked quickly into the bedroom, his eyes instantly zeroing in on the attaché case. It was partly under the pillow; oh *God,* he had been in such a sound sleep! He yanked the case out and examined it. Breathing again, he saw that it was the same case, the combination locks secure; no amount of pressure on the small brass buttons would release the plates. He lifted the case and shook it; the weight and the sounds were proof that the papers were inside and intact, proof also that Converse had not returned to the inn and checked out. All other considerations aside and regardless of whatever emergencies that might have arisen, he would never have left without the dossiers and the list of names.

Connal carried the case back into the sitting room trying to collect his thoughts, putting them

451

in alphabetical sequence so as to impose some kind of order. *A:* He had to assume that the flag on Joel's service record had been lifted or the damaging information unearthed in some other way and that Converse was now being held by Leifhelm and the contingent from Aquitaine that had flown in from Paris, Tel Aviv and Johannesburg. *B:* They would not kill him until they had used every means possible to find out what he knew—which was far less than they imagined and could take several days. *C:* The Leifhelm estate, according to his dossier, was a fortress; thus the chances of going in and bringing Converse out were nil. *D:* Fitzpatrick knew he could not appeal to the American embassy. To begin with, Walter Peregrine would place him under territory arrest and those doing the arresting might put a bullet in his head. One had tried. *E:* He could not risk seeking help from Hickman in San Diego, which under different circumstances might be a logical course of action. Everything in the admiral's makeup ruled out any connection with Aquitaine; he was a fiercely independent officer whose conversations were laced with barbed remarks about the Pentagon's policies and mentality. But if that flag had been officially released—whether with his consent or over his objections—Hickman would have no choice but to call him back to the base for a full inquiry. Any contact at all could result in the immediate cancellation of his leave, but if there was no contact and no way to reach him, the order, obviously, could not be given.

Connal sat down on the couch, the attaché case

at his feet, and picked up a pencil; he wrote out two words on the telephone message pad: *Call Meagen.* He would tell his sister to say that after Press's funeral he had left for parts unknown without explanation. It was consistent with what he had said to the admiral, that he was taking his information to "the authorities" investigating Preston Halliday's death.

F: He could go to the Bonn police and tell them the truth. He had every reason to believe that an American colleague was being held against his will inside the gates of General Erich Leifhelm's estate. Then, of course, the inevitable question would arise: Why didn't the Lieutenant Commander contact the American embassy? The unspoken would be just below the surface: General Leifhelm was a prominent figure, and such a serious charge should have diplomatic support. The embassy again. Strike out. Then again, if Leifhelm said he had "friends" in the Staatspolizei, he probably owned key men in the Bonn Police. If he was alarmed, Converse could be moved. Or killed. *G:* . . . was insane, thought the Navy lawyer as a legal phrase crept slowly into his consciousness, suddenly taking on a blurred viability. *Trade-off.* It was a daily occurrence in pretrial examinations, both civilian and military. *We'll drop this if you accept that. We'll stay out of this area if you stay out of that one.* Standard practice. Trade-off. Was it possible? Could it even be considered? It was crazy and it was desperate, but then nothing was sane, nothing held much hope. Since force was out of the question, could an exchange be made? Leifhelm for Converse. A general for a lieutenant.

Connal did not dare analyze; there were too many negatives. He had to act on instinct because there was nothing else left, nowhere he could turn that did not lead to a blank wall or a bullet. He got up from the couch, went to the table with the telephone and and reached for the directory on the floor. What he had in mind was insane, but he could not think about that. He found the name. *Fishbein, Ilse*. The illegitimate daughter of Hermann Göring.

The rendezvous was set: a back table at the Hansa-Keller café on the Kaiserplatz, the reservation in the name of Parnell. Fitzpatrick had had the presence of mind in California to pack a conservative civilian suit; he wore it now as the American attorney, Mr. Parnell, who was fluent in German and sent by his firm in Milwaukee, Wisconsin, to make contact with one Ilse Fishbein in Bonn, West Germany. He also had the presence of mind in Bonn, West Germany, to have managed a single room at the Schlosspark on the Venusbergweg and placed Converse's attaché case where it would be safe for a considerable length of time, a trail left for Converse should everything blow apart. A trail he would recognize—if Joel was alive and able to hunt.

Connal arrived ten minutes early, not merely to secure the table but to familiarize himself with the surroundings and silently practice his approach. He had done the same thing many times before, walking into military courtrooms before a trial, testing the chairs, the height of the tables, the scan of vision of the tribunal on the dais. It all helped.

He knew it was she when the woman arrived and spoke to the maître d' at his lectern. She was tall and heavy, not obese but fleshy in a statuesque way, conscious of her mature sensuality but smart enough not to parade it. She was dressed in a light-gray summer suit, the jacket buttoned above her generous breasts, a wide white collar demurely angled over the fabric. Her face, too, was full but not soft, the high cheekbones lending an appearance of character that might not otherwise have been there; her hair was dark and shoulder-length, with slight streaks of premature gray. She was escorted to the table by the dining room's captain. Fitzpatrick rose as she approached.

"Guten Tag, Frau Fishbein," he said, extending his hand. *"Bitte, setzen Sie sich."*

"It's not necessary for you to speak German, Herr Parnell," said the woman, releasing his hand and sliding into the chair under the guidance of the captain, who bowed and left. "I make my living as a translator."

"Whatever you feel most comfortable with," said Connal.

"I think under the circumstances I should prefer English, and spoken softly, if you please. Now, what is this incredible thing you alluded to over the telephone, Mr. Parnell?"

"Quite simply an inheritance, Mrs. Fishbein," replied Fitzpatrick, his expression sincere, his eyes steady. "If a few technical questions can be settled, and I'm sure they can be, as a rightful legatee you will receive a substantial sum of money."

"From someone in America I never knew?"

"He—knew your father."

"I did not," said Ilse Fishbein quickly, her eyes darting about at the adjacent tables. "Who is this man?"

"He was a member of your father's staff during the war," answered Connal, lowering his voice still further. "With your father's help —certain contacts in Holland—he got out of Germany before the Nuremberg trials with a great deal of money. He came to the United States by way of London, his funds intact, and started a business in the Midwest. It became enormously successful. He died recently, leaving sealed instructions with my firm, his attorneys."

"But why me?"

"A debt. Without your father's influence and assistance our client would probably have withered for years in jail instead of flourishing as he did in America. As far as anyone was concerned, he was a Dutch immigrant from the Netherlands whose family business was destroyed in the war and who sought his future in America. That future included considerable real estate holdings and a very successful meat-packing plant—all in the process of being sold. Your inheritance is in excess of two million American dollars. Would you care for an aperitif, Mrs. Fishbein?"

The woman could not at first reply. Her eyes had grown wide, her full jaw slackened, her stare was trancelike. "I believe I will, Herr Parnell," she said in a monotone, finding her voice. "A large whisky, if you please."

Fitzpatrick signaled the waiter, ordered drinks and tried several times to make idle conversation, commenting on the beautiful weather and asking what sites he should see while in Bonn. It was no use. Ilse Fishbein was as close to being in a catatonic state as Connal could imagine. She had gripped his wrist, clutching it in silence with extremely strong fingers, her lips parted, her eyes two blank glass orbs. The drinks came, the waiter left, and still she would not let go of him. Instead, she drank somewhat awkwardly, lifting the glass with her left hand.

"What are these questions to be settled? Ask anything, *demand* anything. Do you have a place to stay? Things are so crowded in Bonn."

"You're very kind; yes, I do. Try to understand, Mrs. Fishbein, this is an extremely sensitive matter for my firm. As you can well imagine, it's not the sort of legal work American attorneys are too happy with, and, frankly, had our client not made certain provisos connecting the successful completion of this aspect of his last will and testament to the full execution of other aspects, we might have—"

"The questions! What are the *questions?*"

Fitzpatrick paused before answering, the thoughtful lawyer permitting the interruption but still intent on making his point. "Everything will be handled confidentially, the probate court operating *in camera*—"

"With *photographs?*"

"In private, Mrs. Fishbein. For the good of the community, in exchange for specific state and local taxes that might not be paid in the event of confiscation. You see, the higher courts might decide the entire estate is open to question."

"Yes, the questions! What *are* they?"

"Really quite simple. I've prepared certain statements, which you will sign and to which I can swear to your signature. They establish your bloodline. Then there is a short deposition required substantiating the claim. We need only one, but it must be given by a former high-ranking member of the German forces, preferably a man whose name is recognizable, whom the recent history books or war accounts establish as a working colleague of your natural father. Of course, it would be advantageous to have someone known to the American military in the event the judge decides to call the Pentagon and ask 'Who is this fellow?' "

"I know the man!" whispered Ilse Fishbein. "He was a field marshal, a brilliant *General!*"

"Who is he?" asked the Navy lawyer, then instantly shrugging, dispensing with the question of identity as irrelevant. "Never mind. Just tell me why you think he's the right man, this field marshal."

"He is greatly respected, although not everyone agrees with him. He was one of the *grossmächtigen* young commanders, once decorated by my father himself for his brilliance!"

"But would anyone in the American military establishment know him?"

"Mein Gott! He worked for the Allies in Berlin and Vienna after the war!"

"Yes?"

"And at SHAPE Headquarters in Brussels!"

Yes, thought Connal, we're talking about the same man. "Fine," said Fitzpatrick casually but seriously. "Don't bother giving me his name. It doesn't matter, and I probably wouldn't know it anyway. Can you reach him quickly?"

"In minutes! He's here in Bonn."

"Splendid. I should catch the plane back to Milwaukee by tomorrow noon."

"You will come to his house and he will dictate what you need to his secretary."

"I'm sorry I can't do that. The deposition must be countersigned by a notary. I understand you have the same rules over here—and why not, you invented them—and the Schlosspark Hotel has both typing and notary services. Say this evening, or perhaps early in the morning? I should be more than happy to send a taxi for your friend. I don't want this to cost him a pfennig. Any expenses he incurs my firm will be happy to repay."

Ilse Fishbein giggled—a slightly hysterical giggle. "You do not know my friend, *mein Herr.*"

"I'm sure we'll get along. Now, how about lunch?"

"I have to go to the toilet," said the German woman, her eyes glass orbs again. As she rose, Connal rising with her, she whispered, *"Mein Gott! Zwei Millionen Dollar!"*

"He does not even care to know your *name!*"

459

cried Ilse Fishbein into the phone. "He's from a place called Milwaukee, Wisconsin, and is offering me two *million dollars American!*"

"He did not ask who I was?"

"He said it didn't matter! He probably wouldn't know you, in any event. Can you imagine? He offered to send a taxi for you! He said you should not spend a penny!"

"It's true Göring was excessively generous during the last weeks," mused Leifhelm. "Of course, he was more often drugged than not, and those who supplied him with narcotics, which were difficult to obtain, were rewarded with the whereabouts of priceless art treasures. The one who later smuggled him the poisoned suppositories still lives like a Roman emperor in Luxembourg."

"So you see, it's true! Göring *did* these things!"

"Rarely knowing what he was doing, however," agreed the general reluctantly. "This is really most unusual and very inconvenient, Ilse. Did this man show you any documents, any proof of his assignment?"

"Naturally!" lied Fishbein, close to panic, picking remembered words out of the air. "There was a formal page of legal statements and a . . . *deposition*—all to be handled by the courts confidentially! In *private!* You see, there is a question of taxes, which would not be paid if the estate was confiscated—"

"I've heard it all before, Ilse," Leifhelm broke in wearily. "There are no statutes for so-called war criminals and expatriated funds. So the hypocrites choke on their hypocritical rules the instant they cost money, and abandon them."

"You are always so perceptive, my general, and I have always been so loyal. I've never refused you a single request whether it was professional in nature or far more intimate. *Please.* Two million American! It will take but ten or fifteen minutes!"

"You've been like a good niece, I can't deny it, Ilse. And there is no way anyone could know about you in other matters. . . . Very well, this evening then. I'm dining at the Steigenberger at nine o'clock. I'll stop at the Schlosspark at eight-fifteen or thereabouts. You can buy me a gift with your—shall we say—ill-conceived new riches."

"I'll meet you in the lobby."

"My driver will accompany me."

"*Ach,* bring twenty men!"

"He's worth twenty-five," Leifhelm said.

Fitzpatrick sat in the chair in the small conference room on the second floor of the hotel and examined the gun, the manual of instructions on his lap. He tried to match what the clerk had told him to the diagrams and instructions, and was satisfied that he knew enough. There were basic similarities to the standard Navy issue Colt .45, the only handgun he was familiar with, and the technical information was extraneous to his needs. The weapon he had purchased was a Heckler & Koch PGS auto pistol, about six inches long, its caliber nine millimeters, and with a nine-shell magazine clip. The instructions emphasized such points as "polygonal rifling" and "sliding

461

roller lock functions"; he let the manual slip to the floor, and practiced removing the clip and slapping it back into place. He could load the weapon, aim it and fire it; those were all that was necessary and he trusted the last would *not* be necessary.

He glanced at his watch; it was almost eight o'clock. He shoved the automatic into his belt, reached down for the instructions and stood up, looking around the room, mentally checking off the movements and the locations he had designated for himself. As he had expected, the Fishbein woman had told him Leifhelm would be accompanied by someone, a "driver" in this case, and it could be assumed the man had other functions. If so, he would have no chance to perform them.

The room—one of twenty-odd conference rooms in the hotel—that he had reserved under the name of a fictitious company was not large, but there were structural arrangements that could be put to advantage. The usual rectangular table was in the center, three chairs on each side and two at the ends, one with a telephone. There were additional chairs against the walls for stenographers and observers—all this was normal. However, in the center of the left wall was a doorway that led to a very small room apparently used for private conversations. Inside was another telephone, which when off the hook caused a button on the first telephone on the conference table to light up; confidentiality had its limits in Bonn. The hallway door opened onto a small foyer, thus prohibiting those entering from

462

scanning the room while standing in the corridor.

Connal folded the Heckler & Koch instructions, put them in his jacket pocket, and walked over to the table to survey his set pieces. He had gone to an office-supply store and purchased the appropriate items. On the far end of the table by the telephone—which was placed perpendicular to the edge, the buttons in clear view—were several file folders next to an open briefcase (from a distance its dark plastic looked like expensive leather). Scattered about were papers, pencils and a yellow legal pad, the top pages looped over. The setting was familiar to anyone who had ever had an appointment with an attorney, said learned counsel having put his astute observations down on paper prior to the conference.

Fitzpatrick retraced his steps to the chair, moved it forward several feet, and crossed to the door of the small side room. He had turned on the lights—two table lamps flanking a short couch; he went to the one above the telephone and turned it off. He then walked back to the open door and stood between it and the wall, peering through the narrow vertical space broken up by upper and lower hinges. He had a clear view of the foyer's entrance; three people would pass into the conference room and he would come out.

There was a knock on the hallway door—the rapid, impatient tapping of an heiress unable to control herself. He had told the Fishbein woman the location of the room, but nothing else. No name or number, and in her anxiety she had not asked about either. Fitzpatrick went to the telephone table in the small room, lifted the phone out of its cradle and placed it on its side. He returned to his position behind the door, angling himself so as to look through the crack, his body in the shadows. He took the pistol from his belt, held it in front of him and shouted in a friendly voice, loud enough to be heard outside in the hotel corridor. *"Bitte, kommen Sie herein! Die Türe ist offen. Ich telefoniere gerade!"*

The sound of the door as it opened preceded Ilse Fishbein as she walked rapidly into the room, her eyes directed at the conference table. She was followed by Erich Leifhelm, who glanced about and then turned slightly, nodding his head. A third man in the uniform of a chauffeur came into view, his hand in the pocket of his black jacket. Connal then heard the second sound he needed to hear. The hallway door was slammed shut.

He yanked back the small door and quickly stepped around it, the gun extended, aimed directly at the chauffeur.

"You!" he cried in German. "Take your hand out of your pocket! *Slowly!"* The woman gasped, then opened her mouth to scream. Fitzpatrick interrupted harshly. "Be *quiet!* As your friend will tell you, I haven't anything to lose. I can kill the three of you and be out of the country in an hour, leaving the police to look for a Mr. Parnell who doesn't exist."

The chauffeur, the muscles of his jaw rippling, removed his hand from his pocket, his fingers rigid. Leifhelm stared in anger and fear at Connal's gun, his face no longer ashen but flushed. "You *dare?"*

"I dare, Field Marshal," said Fitzpatrick. "Just as you dared forty years ago to rape a young kid and make damned sure that she and her whole family never walked out of the camps. You bet your ass I dare, and if I were you, I wouldn't give me the slightest cause to be any angrier than I am." Connal spoke to the woman. *You.* Inside that briefcase on the table are eight strands of rope. Start with the driver. Bind his hands and feet; I'll tell you how. Now! *Quickly!*"

Four minutes later the chauffeur and Leifhelm sat in two conference chairs, their ankles and wrists bound, the driver's weapon removed from his pocket. Connal checked the ropes, the knots having been tied under his instructions. Everything was secure; the more one writhed, the tighter the knots would become. He ordered the panicked Fishbein woman into a third chair; he lashed her hands to the arms and her feet to the legs.

Rising, Connal picked up the automatic from the table and approached Leifhelm, who was sitting in the chair next to the lighted telephone. "Now," he said, the gun pointed at the German's head. "As soon as I hang up the phone in the other room we're going to make a call from here." He walked quickly into the small side room, hung up the telephone, and returned. He sat down next to the bound Leifhelm and took a scrap of paper out of the open briefcase. On it was written the phone number of the general's estate on the Rhine beyond Bad Godesberg.

"What do you think you'll accomplish?" asked Leifhelm.

"Trade-off," replied Fitzpatrick, the barrel of the gun pressed against the German's temple. "You for Converse."

"*Mein Gott!*" whispered Ilse Fishbein as the chauffeur writhed, his hands straining against the ropes, which were now biting into his wrists.

"You believe anyone will listen to you, much less carry out your orders?"

"They will if they want to see you alive again. You know I'm right, General. This gun isn't so loud—I made sure of that. I can turn on the radio and kill you and be on a plane out of Germany before you're found. This room is reserved for the night with instructions that we're not to be disturbed for any reason whatsoever." Connal shifted the weapon to his left hand, picked up the telephone, and dialed the number written on the scrap of paper.

"*Guten Tag. Hier bei General Leifhelm.*"

"Put someone in authority on this phone," said the Navy lawyer in perfect German. "I have a gun less than a foot away from General Leifhelm's head and I'll kill him right now unless you do as I say."

There were muffled shouts over the line as a hand was held against the mouthpiece. In seconds a crisp British accent was speaking slowly, deliberately in English.

"Who is this and what do you want?"

"Well, what do you know? This sounds like Major Philip Dunstone—that *was* the name, wasn't it? You don't sound half so friendly as you did last night."

"Don't do anything rash, Commander.

466

You'll regret it."

"And don't you do anything stupid, or Leifhelm will regret it sooner—that is, until he can't regret anything any longer. You've got one hour to get Converse to the airport and inside the Lufthansa security gate. He has a reservation on the ten o'clock flight to Washington, D.C., by way of Frankfurt. I've made arrangements. I'll be calling a number in a room where he'll be taken and I'll expect to talk with him. After I do, I'll leave here and call you on another phone, telling you where your employer is. Just get Converse to that security gate. One hour, Major!" Fitzpatrick shoved the phone in front of Leifhelm's face, and pressed the barrel of the gun into the German's temple.

"Do as he says," said the General, choking on the words.

The minutes went by slowly, stretching into a quarter of an hour, then thirty, the silence finally broken by Leifhelm. "So you found her," he said, gesturing his head at Ilse Fishbein, who trembled as tears streaked down her full cheeks.

"Just as we found out about Munich forty years ago, and a hell of a lot of other things. You're all on your way to that great big war room in the sky, Field Marshal, so don't worry about whether I'll go back on my word to your English butler. I wouldn't miss seeing you bastards paraded for everyone to see what you really are. People like you give the military everywhere a goddamned rotten name."

There was a slight commotion from the hallway beyond the door. Connal looked up, raising the gun and holding it directly at Leifhelm's head.

"Was ist?" said the German, shrugging.

"Keine Bewegung!"

From the hotel corridor came the strains of a melody sung by several male voices more off key than on. Another conference in one of the other rooms had broken up, obviously as much from the excessive intake of alcohol as from the completion of a business agenda. Raucous laughter pierced a refrain as harmony was unsuccessfully attempted. Fitzpatrick relaxed, lowering the automatic; no one on the outside knew the name or number of the room.

"You say men like me give your profession —which is my profession as well—a seriously bad name," said Leifhelm. "Has it occurred to you Commander, that we might elevate that profession to one of indispensable greatness in a world that needs us badly?"

"Needs us?" asked Connal. "We need the world first and not your kind of world. You tried it once and blew it, don't you remember?"

"That was one nation led by a madman trying to impose his imprimatur over the globe. This is many nations with one class of self-abnegating professionals coming together for the good of all."

"Whose definition? Yours? You're a funny fellow, General. Somehow I question your benevolent tendencies."

"Indiscretions of a deprived youth whose name and rightful opportunities were stolen from him should not be held against the man a half-century later."

"Deprived or depraved? I think you made up for lost time pretty quickly and as brutally as you could. I don't like your remedies."

"You have no vision."

"Thanks be to Jesus, Mary, and Joseph it's not yours." The singing out in the corridor faded briefly, then swelled again, more discordant and louder than before. "Maybe that's some of your old Dachau playboys having a beer bust."

Leifhelm shrugged.

Suddenly the door burst open, crashing into the wall as three men raced in, spits filling the air as silenced guns fired, hands jerking back and forth, the surface of the table chewed up, splinters of wood flying everywhere. Fitzpatrick felt the repeated stabs of intense pain in his arm as the automatic was blown out of his grip. He looked down and saw the blood drenching the fabric of his right sleeve. Though in shock he glanced about him. Ilse Fishbein was dead, her bleeding skull shattered by a fusillade of bullets; the chauffeur was smiling obscenely. The door was closed as if nothing had happened.

"*Stümper,*" Leifhelm said as one of the invaders cut the ropes around his wrists. "I used that term only yesterday, Commander, but I did not know how right I was. Did you think a single telephone call could not be traced to a single room? It was all too coincidentally symmetrical. Converse is ours and suddenly this poor whore comes into immense riches—*American* riches. I grant you it was entirely possible—such bequests are made frequently by sausage-soaked idiots who don't realize the harm they do, but the timing was too perfect, too—amateurish.''

"You're one son of a bitch.'' Connal shut his eyes, trying to force the pain out of his mind, unable to move his fingers.

"Why, Commander,'' said the general, getting out of the chair, "do I sense the bravado of fear? Do you think I'm going to have you killed?''

"You sense it. I won't give you any more than that.''

"You're quite wrong. Considering the nature of your military leave, you can be of minor but unique service to us. One more statistic to disrupt a pattern. You'll be our guest, Commander, but not in Germany proper. You are going on a trip.''

17

Converse slowly opened his eyes, a dead, iron weight on his lids and nausea in his throat—blurred darkness everywhere—and a terrible stinging at his side, on his arm, flesh separated from flesh, stretched and inflamed. Blindly he tried to touch the offending spot, then gasping, pulled back in pain. Somewhere light was creeping around the dark space above him, picking its way through moving obstructions, peering into the shadows. Objects slowly came into focus—the metal rim of the cot next to his face, two wooden chairs opposite each other at a small table in the distance, a door also in the distance, but farther away and shut . . . then another door, this one open, a white sink with a pair of dull-metal faucets on the left in a far-away cubicle. The light? It was still moving, now dancing, flickering. Where was it?

He found it: high in the wall on either side of the closed door were two rectangular windows, the short curtains billowing in the breeze. The windows were open, but oddly not open, not clear, the spaces interrupted. Joel raised his head, supporting himself on his forearm and squinted, trying to see more clearly. He focused on the interruptions behind the swelling curtains—thin black metal shafts vertically connecting the window frames. They were bars. He was in a cell.

He fell back on the cot, swallowing repeatedly to lessen the burning in his throat, and moved his arm in circles trying to lessen the pain of the . . . wound? Yes, a wound, a gunshot! The realization jarred his memory; a dinner party had turned into a battleground filled with hysteria. Blinding lights and sudden jolts of pain had been accompanied by strident voices bombarding him, incessant echoes pounding in his ears as he tried desperately to repel the piercing assaults. Then there had been moments of calm, the drone of a single voice in the mists. Converse closed his eyes, pressing his lids tightly together with all his strength as another realization struck him and disturbed him deeply. That voice in the swirling mists was *his* voice; he had been drugged, and he knew he had given up secrets.

He had been drugged before, a number of times in the North Vietnamese camps, and as always there was the sickening feeling of numbed outrage. His mind had been stripped and violated, his voice made to perform obscenities against the last vestiges of his will.

And, again as always, there was the empty hole in his stomach, a vacuum that ran deep and produced only weakness. He felt starved and probably was. The chemicals usually induced vomiting as the intestines rejected the unnatural substance. It was strange, he reflected, opening his eyes and following the moving shafts of light, but those memories from years ago evoked the same self-protective instincts that had helped him then—so many years ago. He could not waste energy; he had to conserve what strength he had. Regain new strength. Otherwise there was nothing but the numbed outrage and neither his mind nor his body could do anything about it.

There was a sound across the room! Then another and another after that! The grating sound of sliding metal told him that a bolt was being released; the sharp sound of a key followed by the twisting of a knob meant that the door in the far distant wall was about to be opened. It was, and a blinding burst of sunlight filled the cell. Converse shielded his eyes, peering between his fingers. The blurred, frazzled silhouette of a man stood in the doorframe carrying a flat object. The figure walked in and Joel, blinking, saw it was the chauffeur who had electronically searched him in the driveway.

The uniformed driver crossed to the table and deftly lowered the flat object; it was a tray, its contents covered by a cloth. It was only then that Converse's attention was drawn back to the sunlit doorway. Outside, milling about in anxious contempt was the pack of Dobermans, their shining black eyes continually shifting toward the door, their lips curled, teeth bared in unending quiet snarls.

"Guten Morgen, mein Herr," said Leifhelm's chauffeur, then shifting to English, "Another beautiful day on the northern Rhine, no?"

"It's bright out there, if that's what you mean," replied Joel, his hand still cupping his eyes. "I suppose I should be grateful to be able to notice after last night."

"Last night?" The German paused, then added quietly, "It was two nights ago, *Amerikaner.* You've been here for the past thirty-three hours."

"Thirty?" Converse pushed himself up and swung his legs over the side of the cot. Instantly he was overcome by dizziness—too much strength had been drained. *Oh Christ! Don't waste movement. They'll be back. The bastards!* "You bastards," he said out loud but without any real emotion. Then for the first time he realized he was shirtless, and noticed the bandage on his left arm between his elbow and his shoulder. It covered the gunshot wound. "Did somebody miss my head?" he asked.

"I'm told you inflicted the injury yourself. You tried to kill General Leifhelm but shot yourself when the others were taking your gun away."

"I tried to kill? With my nonexistent gun? The one you made sure I didn't *have?"*

"You were too clever for me, *mein Herr."*

"What happens now?"

"Now? Now you eat. I have instructions from the doctor. You begin with the *Hafergrütze*—how do you say?—the porridge."

"Hot mush or cereal," said Joel. "With skimmed or powdered milk. Then some kind of soft-boiled eggs taken with pills. And if it all goes down, a little ground meat, and if *that* stays down, a few spoonfuls of crushed turnips or potatoes or squash. Whatever's available."

"How do you know this?" asked the uniformed man, genuinely surprised.

"It's a basic diet," said Converse cynically. "Variations with the territory and the supplies. I once had some comparatively good meals. . . . You're planning to put me under again."

The German shrugged. "I do what I'm told. I bring you food. Here, let me help you."

Joel looked up as the chauffeur approached the cot. "Under other circumstances I'd spit in your goddamned face. But if I did I wouldn't have that slight, *slight* possibility of spitting in it some other time. You may help me. Be careful of my arm."

"You are a very strange man, *mein Herr.*"

"And you're all perfectly normal citizens catching the early train to Larchmont so you can put down ten martinis before going to the PTA meeting."

"*Was ist?* I know of no such meeting."

"They're keeping it secret; they don't want you to know. If I were you, I'd get out of town before they make you president."

"*Mich? Präsident?*"

"Just help me to the chair, like a good ole Aryan boy, will you?"

"Hah, you are being amusing, *ja?*"

"Probably not," said Converse, easing into the

474

wooden chair. "It's a terrible habit I wish I could break." He looked up at the bewildered German. "You see, I keep trying," he said in utter seriousness.

Three more days passed, his only visitor the chauffeur accompanied by the sullen, high-strung pack of Dobermans. His well-searched suitcase was given to him, scissors and a nail file removed from the traveling kit—his electric razor intact. It was their way of telling him that his presence had been removed from Bonn, leaving him to painfully speculate about the life or death of Connal Fitzpatrick. Yet there was an inconsistency and, as such, the basis for hope. No allusions were made to his attaché case, either with visual evidence—the page of a dossier, perhaps—or through his brief exchanges with Leifhelm's driver. The generals of Aquitaine were men of immense egos; if they had those materials in their possession, they would have let him know it.

As to his conversations with the chauffeur, they were limited to questions on his part and disciplined pleasantries on the German's part, no answers at all—at least, none that made any sense:

"How long is this going to go on? When am I going to see someone other than you?"

"There is no one here, sir, except the staff. General Leifhelm is away—in Essen, I believe. Our instructions are to feed you well and restore your health."

Incommunicado. He was in solitary.

But the food was not like that given to prisoners anywhere else. Roasts of beef and lamb, chops, poultry and fresh fish; vegetables that unquestionably had come directly from a nearby garden. And wine—which at first Joel was reluctant to drink, but when he did, even he knew it was superior.

On the second day, as much to keep from thinking as from anything else, he had begun to perform mild exercises—as he had done so many years ago. By the third day he had actually worked up a sweat during a running-in-place session, a healthy sweat, telling him the drugs had left his body. The wound on his arm was still there, but he thought about it less and less. Curiously, it was not serious.

On the fourth day questions and reflections were no longer good enough. Confinement and the maddening frustration of having no answers forced him to turn elsewhere, to the practical, to the most necessary consideration facing him. Escape. Regardless of the outcome the attempt had to be made. Whatever plans Delavane and his disciples in Aquitaine had for him, they obviously included parading a drugless man—more than likely a dead man with no narcotics in his system. Otherwise they would have killed him at once, disposing of his body in any number of untraceable ways. He had done it before. Could he do it again?

He was not rotting in a rat-infested cell and there was no terrible gunfire in the distant darkness, but it was far more important that he succeed now than it ever was eighteen years ago.

And there was an extraordinary irony: eighteen years ago he had wanted to break out and tell whoever would listen to him about a madman in Saigon who sent countless children to their deaths—or worse, who left those children to suffer broken minds and hollow feelings for the rest of their lives. Now he had to tell the world about that same madman.

He had to get out. He had to tell the world what he knew.

Converse stood on the wooden chair, the short curtain pulled back, and peered between the black metal bars outside. His cabin, or cottage, or jailhouse, whatever it was, seemed to have been lowered from above onto a clearing in the forest. There was a wall of tall trees and thick foliage as far as he could see in either direction, a dirt path angling to the right beneath the window. The clearing itself extended no more than twenty feet in front of the structure before the dense greenery began; he presumed it was the same on all sides—as it was from the other window to the left of the door, except that there was no path below, only a short, coarse stubble of brown grass. The two front windows were the only views he had. The rest of this isolated jailhouse consisted of unbroken walls and a small ceiling vent in the bathroom but no other openings.

All he could be certain of, since the chauffeur and the dogs and the warm meals were proof he was still within the grounds of Leifhelm's estate, was that the river could not be far away. He could not see it, but it was there and it gave him hope—more than hope, a sense of morbid exhilaration rooted in his memory. Once before, the waters of a river had been his friend, his guide, ultimately the lifeline that had taken him through the worst of his journey. A tributary of the Huong Khe south of Duc Tho had rushed him silently at night under bridges and past patrols and the encampments of three battalions. The waters of the Rhine, like the currents of the Huong Khe years ago, would be his way out.

The multiple sounds of animal feet pounding the earth preceded the streaking dark coats of the Dobermans as they raced below the window, instantly stopping and crowding angrily in front of the door. The chauffeur was on his way with a breakfast no prisoner in isolation should expect. Joel climbed off the chair and quickly carried it back to the table, setting it in place and going to his cot. He sat down, kicked off his shoes, and lay back on the pillow, his legs stretched out over the rumpled blanket.

The bolt was slid back, the key inserted and the heavy knob turned; the door opened. As he did every time he entered, the German pushed the center of the door with his right hand as he supported the tray with his left. However, this morning he was gripping a bulging object in his right hand, the blinding sunlight obscuring it for Converse. The man walked in and, more awkwardly than usual, placed the tray on the table.

"I have a pleasant surprise for you, *mein Herr*. I spoke with General Leifhelm on the telephone last night and he asked about you. I told him you were recovering splendidly and that I had changed the bandage on your unfortunate injury. Then it occurred to him that you had nothing to read and he was very upset. So an hour ago I drove into Bonn and purchased three days of the *International Herald Tribune.*" The driver placed the rolled-up newspapers next to the tray on the table.

But it was not the issues of the *Herald Tribune* that Joel stared at. It was the German's neck and the upper outside pocket of his uniform jacket. For looped around that neck and angled over to that pocket was a thin silver chain, with the protruding top of a tubular silver whistle clearly visible against the dark fabric. Converse shifted his eyes to the door; the Dobermans were sitting on their haunches, each breathing noisily and salivating, but, to all intents and purposes, immobile. Converse remembered his arrival at the general's monumental lair and the strange Englishman who had controlled the dogs with a silver whistle.

"Tell Leifhelm I appreciate the reading material, but I'd be even more grateful if I could get out of this place for a few minutes."

"*Ja,* with a plane ticket to the beaches in the south of France, *nein?*"

"For Christ's sake, just to take a walk and stretch my legs! What's the matter? Can't you and that drooling band of mastiffs handle one unarmed man getting a little air? . . . No, you're probably too frightened to try." Joel paused, then added in an insulting mock-German accent. " 'I do vot I am tolt.' "

The driver's smile faded. "The other evening you said you would not apologize but instead break my neck. That was a joke. Do you understand? A joke I find so amusing I can laugh at it.''

"Hey, come on," said Converse, changing his tone as he swung his legs off the cot and sat up. "You're ten years younger than I am and twenty times stronger. I felt insulted and reacted stupidly, but if you think I'd raise a hand against you, you're out of your mind. I'm sorry. You've been decent to me and I was stupid again.''

"Ja, you were stupid," said the German without rancor. "But also you were right. I do as I am told. And why not? It is a privilege to take orders from General Leifhelm. He has been *gut* to me.''

"Have you been with him long?''

"Since Brussels. I was a sergeant in the Federal Republic's border patrols. He heard about my problem and took an interest in my case. I was transferred to the Brabant garrison and made his chauffeur.''

"What was your problem? I'm a lawyer, you know.''

"The charge was that I strangled a man. With my arm.''

"Did you?''

"Ja. He was trying to put a knife in my stomach—and lower. He said I took advantage of his daughter. I took no advantage; it was not necessary. She was a whore—it was in the clothes she wore, the way she walked—*es ist klar!* The father was a pig!''

Joel looked at the man, at the clouded malevolence in his eyes. "I can understand

General Leifhelm's sympathies," he said.

"Now you know why I do as I am told."

"Clearly."

"He is calling for his messages at noon. I shall ask him about your walking. You understand that one word from me and the Dobermans will rip your body from its bones."

"Nice puppies," said Converse, addressing the pack of dogs outside.

Noon came and the privilege was granted. The walk was to take place after lunch when the driver returned to remove the tray. He returned, and after several severe warnings Joel ventured outside, the Dobermans crowding around him, black nostrils flared, white teeth glistening, bluish-red tongues flattened out in anticipation. Converse looked around; for the first time he saw that the small house was made of thick, solid stone. The unique squad began its constitutional up the path, Joel growing bolder as the dogs lost a degree of interest in him under the harsh admonitions of the German's commands. They began racing ahead and regrouping in circles, snapping at one another but always whipping their heads back or across at their master and his prisoner. Converse walked faster.

"I used to jog a lot back home," he lied.

"*Was ist?* 'Jog'?"

"Run. It's good for the circulation."

"You run now, *mein Herr,* you will have no circulation. The Dobermans will see to it."

"I've heard of people getting coronaries from jogging too," said Joel, slowing down, but not reducing the speed with which his eyes darted in all directions. The sun was directly overhead; it was no help in determining direction.

The dirt path was like a marked single line in an intricate network of hidden trails. It was bordered by thick foliage, more often than not roofed by low-hanging branches, then breaking open into short stretches of wild grass that might or might not lead to other paths. They reached a fork, the leg to the right curving sharply into a tunnel of greenery. The dogs instinctively raced into it but were stopped by the chauffeur, who shouted commands in German. The Dobermans spun around, bouncing off each other, and returned to the fork, then raced into the wider path on the left. It was an incline and they started up a steep hill, the trees shorter and less full, the bramble bush wilder, coarser, lower to the ground. Wind, thought Converse. A valley wind; a wind whipping up from a trough, a long narrow slice in the earth, the kind of wind a pilot of a small plane avoided at the first sign of weather. A river.

It was there. To his left; they were traveling east. The Rhine was below, perhaps a mile beyond the lower line of tall trees. He had seen enough. He began breathing audibly. The exhilaration inside him was intense; he could have walked for miles. He was back on the banks of the Huong Khe, the dark watery lifeline that would take him away from the Mekong cages and the cells and the chemicals. He had done it before; he was going to do it again!

"Okay, Field Marshal," he said to Leifhelm's driver, looking at the silver whistle in the German's pocket. "I'm not in as good shape as I thought I was. This is a mountain! Don't you have any flat pastures or grazing fields?''

''I do as I am told, *mein Herr,*'' replied the man, grinning. ''Those are nearer the main *house.* This is where you must walk.''

''This is where I say thank you and no thank you. Take me back to my little grass shack and I'll play you a simple tune.''

''I do not understand.''

''I'm bushed and I haven't finished the newspapers. Seriously, I want to thank you. I really needed the air.''

''*Sehr gut.* You are a pleasant fellow.''

''You have no idea, good ole Aryan boy.''

''*Ach,* so amusing. *Die Juden sind in Israel, nein?* Better than in Germany.''

''Nate Simon would love you. He'd take your case for nothing just to blow it— No, he wouldn't. He'd probably give you the best defense you ever had.''

Converse stood on the wooden chair under the window to the left of the door. All he had to hear and see was the sound and the sight of the dogs; after that he had twenty or thirty seconds. The faucets in the bathroom were turned on, the door open; there was sufficient time to run across the room, flush the toilet, close the door and return to the chair. But he would not be standing on it. Instead, it would be gripped in his hands, laterally. The sun was descending rapidly; in an hour it would be dark. Darkness had been his friend before as the waters of a river had been his friend. They had to be his friends again. They *had* to be!

The sounds came first—racing paws and nasal explosions—then the sight of gleaming dark coats of animal fur rushing in circles in front of the jailhouse. Joel ran to the bathroom, concentrating on the seconds as he waited for the sliding of the bolt. It came; he flushed the toilet, then closed the bathroom door and raced back to the chair. He raised it and stood in place, his legs and feet locked to the floor. The door was opened several inches—only seconds now—then the German's right hand pushed it back.

"Herr Converse? *Wo sind . . . ? Ach, die Toilette.*"

The chauffeur walked in with the tray, and Joel swung the chair with all his strength into the German's head. The driver arched back off his feet, tray and dishes crashing to the floor. He was stunned, nothing more. Converse kicked the door shut and brought the heavy chair repeatedly down on the chauffeur's skull until the man went limp, blood and saliva pouring down his eyes and face.

The phalanx of dogs had lurched as one at the suddenly closed door and began to bark maniacally while clawing at the wood.

Joel grabbed the silver chain, slipped it over the unconscious German's head and pulled the silver whistle out of the pocket. There were four tiny holes on the tube; each meant something. He pulled the remaining chair to the window at the right of the door, climbed up and put the whistle to his lips. He covered the first hole and blew into the mouthpiece. There was no sound, but it had an effect.

The Dobermans went mad! They began to

attack the door in suicidal assaults. He removed his finger, placed it over the second hole and blew.

The dogs were confused; they circled around each other, snapping, yelping, snarling, but still they would not take their concentration off the door. He tried the third tiny hole and blew into the whistle with all the breath he had.

Suddenly, the dogs stopped all movement, their tapered, close-cropped ears upright, shifting—they were waiting for a second signal. He blew again, again with all the breath that was in him. It was the sound they were waiting for, and again, as one, the pack raced to the right beneath the window, pounding to some other place where they were meant to be by command.

Converse leaped down from the chair and knelt by the unconscious German. He went rapidly through the driver's pockets, taking his billfold and all the money he had, as well as his wristwatch—and his gun. For an instant Joel looked at the weapon, loathing the memories it evoked. He shoved it under his belt and went to the door.

Outside, he pulled the heavy door shut, heard the click of the lock and slid the bolt in place. He ran up the dirt path estimating the distance to the fork where the right leg was *verboten* and the left led to the steep hill and the sight of the Rhine below. It was actually no more than two hundred yards away, but the winding curves and the thick bordering foliage made it seem longer. If he remembered accurately—and on the walk back he was like a pilot without instruments relying on sightings—there was a flat stretch of about eighty feet below the fork.

He reached it, the same flat area, the same diverging paths up ahead. He ran faster.

Voices! Angry, questioning? Not far away and coming nearer! He dove into the brush to his right, rolling over the needle-like bushes until he could barely see through the foliage. Two men walked rapidly into his limited view, talking loudly, as if arguing but somehow not with each other.

"Was haben die Hunde?"

"Die sollten bei Heinrich sein!"

Joel had no idea what they were saying; he only knew as they passed him that they were heading for the isolated cabin. He also knew that they would not spend much time trying to raise anyone inside before they took more direct methods. And once they did, all the alarms in Leifhelm's fortress would be activated. Time was measured for him in minutes and he had a great deal of ground to cover. He crept cautiously out of the brush on his hands and feet. The Germans were out of sight, beyond a rounding curve. He got up and raced for the fork and the steep hill to the left.

The three guards at the immense iron gate that was the entrance to Leifhelm's estate were bewildered. The pack of Dobermans were circling around impatiently in the out grass, obviously confused.

"Why are they here?" asked one man.

"It makes no sense!" replied a second.

"Heinrich has let them loose, but why?"

said the third.

"Nobody tells us anything," muttered the first guard, shrugging. "If we don't hear something in the next few minutes, we should call."

"I don't like this!" shouted the second guard. "I'm calling right now!"

The first guard walked into the gatehouse and picked up the telephone.

Converse ran up the steep hill, his breath short, his lips dry, his heartbeat thundering in his chest. There it was! The river! He started running down, gathering speed, the wind whipping his face, stinging him. It was exhilarating. He *was* back! He was racing through the sudden, open clearings of another jungle, no fellow prisoners to worry about, only the outrage within himself to prod him, to make him break through the barriers and somehow, somewhere, strike back at those who had stripped him naked and raped an innocence and—*goddamn it*—turned him into an animal! A reasonably pleasant human being had been turned into a half-man with more hatreds than a person should live with. He would get back at them all, all enemies, all *animals!*

He reached the bottom of the open slope of gnarled grass and bush, the trees and intertwining underbrush once more a wall to be penetrated. But he had his bearings; no matter how dense the woods, he simply had to keep the last rays of the sun on his left, heading due north, and he would reach the river.

Rapid explosions made him spin around. Five gunshots followed one upon the other in the distance. It was easy to imagine the target: a circle of wood around the cylinder of a lock in the door of an isolated cabin in the forest. His jailhouse was being assaulted, entrance gained. The minutes were growing shorter.

And then two distinctly different sounds pierced the twilight, interwoven in dissonance. The first was a series of short, staccato bursts of a high-pitched siren. The second, between and under the repeated blasts, was the hysterical yelping of running dogs. The alarms had been set off; scraps of discarded clothing and slept-on sheets would be pressed onto inflamed nostrils and the Dobermans would come after him, no quarter considered—no cornered prey—only animal teeth ripping human flesh a satisfactory reward.

Converse plunged into the wall of green and ran as fast as he could, dodging, crouching, lurching from one side to the other, his arms outstretched, his hands working furiously against the strong, supple impediment of the woods. His face and body were repeatedly whipped by slashing branches and obstinate limbs, his feet continually tripped by fallen debris and exposed roots. He stumbled more times than he could count, each time bringing an instant of silence that emphasized the sound of the dogs somewhere between the fork and the hill and the lower forest. They were no farther away, perhaps nearer. They *were* nearer, they had entered the woods. All around him were the echoes of their hysteria, punctuated by howling yelps of frustration as one or another or several were caught in the tangled ground cover, straining and roaring to be free to join the pursuit.

The *water!* He could see the water through the trees. Sweat was now rolling down his face, the salt blinding his eyes and stinging the scrapes on his neck and chin. His hands were bleeding from the sharp nettles and the coarse bark everywhere.

He fell, his foot plunging into a hole burrowed by some riverbank animal, his ankle twisted and in pain.

He got up, pulling at his leg, freeing his foot, and, limping badly, tried to resume running. The Dobermans were gaining, the yelping and the harsh barking louder and more furious; they had picked up his direct scent, the trail of undried sweat maddening them, preparing them for the kill.

The riverbank! It was filled with soft mud and floating debris, a webbing of nature's garbage caught in a cavity, whirling slowly, waiting for a strong current to pull it all away. Joel grabbed the handle of the chauffeur's gun, not to pull it out but to secure it as he limped down the bank to look for the quickest way into the water.

He heard nothing until the instant when a massive roar came out of the shadows and the huge body of an animal flew through the air over the riverbank directly at him. The monstrous face of the dog was contorted with fury, the eyes on fire, the enormous jaw wide—all teeth and a gaping, shining black mouth. Converse fell to his knees as the Doberman whipped past his right shoulder, ripping his shirt with its upper eye teeth and flipping over on its back in the mud. The momentary defeat was more than the animal could stand. It writhed furiously, rolling over, snarling, then rising on its hind legs, lunged up from the mud for Joel's groin.

The gun was in his hand. Converse fired, blowing off the top of the attack dog's head; blood and tissue sprayed the shadows, and the slack, shining jaws fell into his crotch.

The rest of the pack was now racing toward the bank, accompanied by ear-shattering crescendos of animal cries. Joel threw himself into the water and swam as rapidly as he could away from the shoreline; the weapon was an impediment but he knew he could not let it go.

Years ago—centuries ago—he had desperately needed a weapon, knowing it could be the difference between survival and death, and for five days none could be had. But on that fifth day he had found one on the banks of the Huong Khe. He had floated half underwater past a squad on patrol, and found the point ten minutes later downriver—too far from the scout's unit to be logical—a man perhaps thinking angry thoughts that made him walk faster, or bored with his job and wanting a few moments to be by himself and out of it all. Whichever, it made no difference to that soldier. Converse had killed him with a rock from the river and had taken his gun. He had fired that gun twice, twice saving his life before he reached an advance unit south of Phu Loc.

As he pushed against the shoreline currents of the Rhine, Joel suddenly remembered. This was the fifth day of his imprisonment in Leifhelm's compound—no jungle cell, to be sure, but no less a prison camp. He had done it! And on the fifth day a weapon was his! There were omens wherever one wished to find them; he did not believe in omens, but for the moment he accepted the possibility.

He was in the shadows of the river now, the surrounding mountains blocking the dying sun. He paddled in place and turned. Back on shore, at the cavity in the bank that had been his plank to the water, the dogs were circling in confused anger, snarling, yelping, as several ventured down to sniff their slain leader, each urinating as it did so—territory and status were being established. The beams of powerful flashlights suddenly broke through the trees. Converse swam farther out; he had survived searchlights in the Mekong. He had no fear of them now; he had been there—here —and he knew when he had won.

He let the outer currents carry him east along the river. Somewhere there would be other lights, lights that would lead him to shelter and a telephone. He had to get everything in place and build his brief quickly, but he could do it. Yet the attorney in him told him that a man with a bandaged gunshot wound in soaked clothing and speaking a foreign language in the streets was no match for the disciples of George Marcus Delavane; they would find him. So it would have to be done another way—with whatever artifices he could muster. He had to get to a telephone. He had to place an overseas call. He could do it; he would do it! The Huong Khe faded; the Rhine was now his lifeline.

Swimming breaststroke, the gun still gripped in his hand, his arm smarting in the water, he saw the lights of a village in the distance.

18

Valerie frowned as she listened on the phone in her studio, the spiraling cord outstretched as she reached over and placed a brush in the track of her easel. Her eyes scanned the sunlit dunes outside the glass doors, but her mind was on the words she was hearing, words that implied things without saying them. "Larry, what's *wrong* with you?" she interrupted, unable to hold herself in check any longer. "Joel's not just an employee or a junior partner, he's your *friend!* You sound like you're trying to build a case against him. What's that term you all use? . . . . Circumstantial, that's it. He was here, he was there; someone said this and somebody else said that."

"I'm trying to *understand,* Val," protested Talbot, who had called from his office in New York. "You've got to try to understand too. There's a great deal I can't tell you because I've been instructed by people whose offices I have to respect to say very little or preferably nothing at all. I'm bending those instructions because Joel *is* my friend and I want to help."

"All right, let's go back," said Valerie. "What exactly were you leading up to?"

"I know it's none of my damned business and I wouldn't ask it if I didn't think I had to—"

"I'll accept that," agreed Val. "Now, what is it?"

"Well, I know you and Joel had your problems," continued the senior partner of Talbot, Brooks and Simon, as though he were referring to an inconsequential spat between children. "But there are problems and there are problems."

"Larry," interrupted Val again. "There were problems. We're divorced. That means the problems were serious."

"Was physical abuse one of them?" asked Talbot quickly in a low voice, the words obviously repugnant to him.

Valerie was stunned; it was a question she would never have expected. *"What?"*

"You know what I mean. In fits of anger did he strike you? Cause you bodily harm?"

"You're not in a courtroom, and the answer is no, of course not. I might have welcomed it—at least the anger."

"I beg your pardon?"

"Nothing," said Valerie, recovering from her astonishment. "I don't know what prompted you to ask, but it couldn't be further from the truth. Joel had far more effective ways to deflate my ego than hitting me. Among them, dear Larry, was his dedication to the career of one Joel Converse in Talbot, Brooks and Simon."

"I'm aware of that, my dear, and I'm sorry. Those complaints are perennial in the divorce courts and I'm not sure there's anything we can do about them—not in this day and age, perhaps not ever. But that's different. I'm talking about his black moods—we knew he had them.''

''Do you know any rational person who doesn't?'' asked the former Mrs. Converse. ''This isn't really the best of all possible worlds, is it?''

''No, it isn't. But then Joel lived through a period of time in a far worse world than most of us will ever know or could imagine. I can't believe he emerged from it without a scar or two.''

Valerie paused, touched by the older man's unadorned directness; it had its basis in concern. ''You're sweet, Larry, and I suspect you're right —in fact, I know it. So I think you should tell me more than you have. The term 'physical abuse' is what you lawyers call a leading something-or-other. It's not fair because it could also be misleading. Come on, Larry, be fair. He's not my husband anymore, but we didn't break apart because he chased girls or bashed my head in. I may not want to be married to him but I respect him. He's got his problems and I've got mine, and now you're implying his are a lot bigger. What's happened?''

Talbot was silent for a moment, then blurted out the words, again quickly, quietly; once more they were obviously repugnant to him. ''They say he assaulted a man in Paris without provocation. The man died.''

''*No,* that's impossible! He didn't, he *couldn't!*'

''That's what he told me, but he lied. He told me he was in Amsterdam, but he wasn't. He said he was going back to Paris to clear things up, but he didn't go. He was in Germany—he's *still* somewhere in Germany. He hasn't left the country and Interpol has a warrant for him; they're searching everywhere. Word reached him to turn himself into the American embassy but he refused. He's disappeared."

"Oh, my *God,* you're all so *wrong!*" exploded Valerie. "You don't *know* him! If what you say happened, he was attacked *first—physically* attacked—and had no choice but to hit back!"

"Not according to an impartial witness who didn't know either man."

"Then he's not impartial, he's lying! Listen to me. I lived with that man for four years and, except for a few trips, all of them in New York City. I've seen him accosted by drunks and street garbage—punks he could have pushed through the pavements, and perhaps some of them he should have—but I never saw him so much as take a step forward. He'd simply raise the palms of his hands and walk away. A few times some damn fools would call him names and he'd just stand there and look at them. And let me tell you, Larry, that look was enough to make you feel cold all over. But that's all he'd do, never anything more."

"Val, I want to believe you. I want to believe it was self-defense, but he ran away, he's disappeared. The embassy can help him, protect him, but he won't come in."

"Then he's frightened. That *can* happen, but it was always for only a few minutes, usually at night when he'd wake up. He'd bolt up, his eyes shut so tight his whole face was a mass of wrinkles. It never lasted long, and he said it was perfectly natural and not to worry about it—he didn't, he said. And I don't think he really did; he wanted all that in the past, none of it was ever mentioned.''

"Perhaps it should have been,'' said Talbot softly.

Valerie replied with equal softness, *"Touché,* Larry. Don't think I haven't thought about that these last couple of years. But whatever's happened he's acting this way only because he's afraid—or you know it's quite possible he's been hurt. Or, oh my *God—*''

"All the hospitals and registered doctors have been checked,'' Talbot broke in.

"Well, damn it, there's got to be a *reason!* This isn't like him and you know it!''

"That's just it, Val. Nothing he's done is like the man I know.''

The ex-Mrs. Converse stiffened. "To use one of Joel's favorite expressions,'' she said apprehensively, "clarification, please?''

"Why not?'' answered Talbot, the question was directed as much at himself as at her. "Perhaps you can shed some light; nobody else can.''

"What about this man in Paris, the one who died?''

"There's not much to tell; apparently he was a chauffeur for one of those limousine services. According to the witness, a basement guard in the hotel, Joel approached him, yelled something at him and pushed him out the door. There were sounds of a scuffle and a few minutes later the man was found severely beaten in an alley.''

"It's *ridiculous!* What did Joel say?''

"That he walked out the door, saw two men fighting and ran to tell the doorman on the way to his taxi.''

"That's what he'd have done," said Val firmly.

"The doorman at the George Cinq says it didn't happen. The police say follicles of hair found on the beaten man matched those in Joel's shower.''

"Utterly unbelievable!''

"Let's say there was provocation we don't know about," Talbot went on rapidly. "It doesn't explain what happened later, but before I tell you, I want to ask you another question. You'll understand.''

"I don't understand a single thing! What is it?''

"During those periods of depression, his dark moods, did Joel ever fantasize? I mean, did he indulge in what psychiatrists call role-playing?''

"You mean did he assume other personalities, other kinds of behavior?''

"Exactly.''

"Absolutely not.''

"Oh.''

"Oh, what? Let's have it, Larry.''

"Talking about what's believable and what isn't, you're in for a jolt, my dear. According to those people who don't want me to say very much—and you'll have to take my word they know—Joel flew into Germany claiming he was involved in an undercover investigation of the embassy in Bonn.''

"Perhaps he was! He was on a leave of absence from T., B. and S., wasn't he?''

"On an unrelated matter in the private sector, that much we know. There *is* no investigation—undercover or otherwise—of the embassy in Bonn. Frankly, the people who reached me were from the State Department."

"Oh, my *God . . .* " Valerie fell silent, but before the lawyer could speak, she whispered, *"Geneva.* That horrible business in Geneva!"

"If there's a connection—and both Nathan and I considered it first—it's so buried it can't be followed."

"It's there. It's where it all started."

"Assuming your husband's rational."

"He's not my husband and he *is* rational!"

"The scars, Val. There had to be scars. You agreed with me."

"Not the kind you're talking about. Not killing, and lying and running away! That's *not* Joel! That isn't—*wasn't*—my husband!"

"The mind is a highly complex and delicate instrument. The stresses of the past can leap forward from years ago—"

"Get off it, Larry!" shouted Valerie. "Save it for a jury, but don't pin that nonsense on Converse!"

"You're upset."

"You're damned right I am! Because you're looking for explanations that don't fit the man! They fit what you've been *told.* By those people you say you have to respect."

"Only in the sense that they're knowledgeable—they have access to information we don't have. Then there's the overriding fact that they hadn't the faintest idea who Joel Converse was until the American Bar Association gave them the address and telephone number of Talbot, Brooks and Simon."

"And you *believed* them? With everything you know about Washington you simply accepted their word? How many times did Joel come back from a trip to Washington and say the same thing to me? 'Larry says they're lying. They don't know what to do, so they're lying.'"

"Valerie," said the attorney sternly. "This isn't a case of bureaucratic clearance, and after all these years I think I can tell the difference between someone playing games and a man who's genuinely angry—angry and frightened, I should add. The man who reached me was an Undersecretary of State, Brewster Tolland—I had a call-back confirmation—and he wasn't putting on an act. He was appalled, furious, and, as I say, a very worried man."

"What did you tell him?"

"The truth, of course. Not only because it was the right thing to do, but it wouldn't help Joel to do anything else. If he's ill he needs help, not complicity."

"And you deal with Washington every week."

"Several times a week, and of course it was a consideration."

"I'm sorry, Larry, that was unfair."

"But realistic, and I meant what I said. It wouldn't help Joel to lie for him. You see, I really believe something's happened. He's not himself."

"Wait a minute," cried Valerie, the obvious striking her. "Maybe it's *not* Joel!"

"It's him," said Talbot simply.

"Why? Just because people you don't know in Washington say it is?"

"No, Val," replied the lawyer. "Because I

499

spoke with René in Paris before Washington entered the picture.''

''*Mattilon?*''

''Joel went to Paris to ask for René's help. He lied to him just as he lied to me, but it was more than the lies—Mattilon and I agreed on that. It was something he saw in Joel's eyes, something I heard in his voice. An unhinging, a form of desperation; René saw it and I heard it. He tried to conceal it from both of us but he couldn't. When I last spoke to him, he hung up before we'd finished talking, in the middle of the sentence, his voice echoing like a zombie's.''

Valerie stared at the harsh, dancing reflections of sunlight off the waters of Cape Ann. ''René agreed with you?'' she asked, barely above a whisper.

''Everything I've just told you we said to each other.''

''Larry, I'm frightened.''

Chaim Abrahms walked into the room, his heavy boots pounding the floor. ''So he did it!'' shouted the Israeli. ''The Mossad was right, he's a hellhound!''

Erich Leifhelm sat behind his desk, the only other person in the book-lined study. ''Patrols, alarms, *dogs!*'' cried the German, slamming his frail hand on the red blotter. ''How did he *do* it?''

''I repeat—a hellhound—that's what our specialist called him. The longer he's restricted, the angrier he gets. It goes back a long time. So our *provocateur* starts his odyssey before we planned. Have you been in touch with the others?"

"I've called London," said Leifhelm, breathing deeply. "He'll reach Paris, and Bertholdier will have the units flown up from Marseilles, one to Brussels, the other here to Bonn. We can't waste an hour."

"You're looking for him now, of course."

"*Natürlich!* Every inch of the shoreline for miles in both directions. Every back road and path that leads up from the river and into the city."

"He can elude you; he's proven it."

"Where can he go, sabra? To his own embassy? There he's a dead man. To the Bonn police or the Staatspolizei? He'll be put in an armored van and brought back here. He goes nowhere."

"I heard that when he left Paris, and I heard it again when he flew into Bonn. Errors were made in both places, both costing a great *many* hours. I tell you I'm more concerned now than at any moment in three wars and a lifetime of skirmishes."

"Be reasonable, Chaim, and try to be calm. He has no clothes but what he wears in the river and the mud; he possesses no identification, no passport, no money. He doesn't speak the language—"

"He *has* money!" yelled Abrahms, suddenly remembering. "When he was under the needle, he spoke of a large sum of money promised in Geneva and delivered on Mykonos."

"And where is it?" asked Leifhelm. "In this desk, *that's* where it is. Nearly seventy thousand

American dollars. He hasn't got a deutsche mark in his pocket, or a watch or a piece of jewelry. A man in filthy, soaked clothing, with no identification, no money, no coherent use of the language, and telling an outlandish tale of imprisonment involving *der General* Leifhelm, would undoubtedly be put in jail as a vagrant or a psychopath or both. In which case, we shall be informed instantly and our people will bring him to us. And bear in mind, sabra, by ten o'clock tomorrow morning it won't make any difference. That was *your* contribution, the Mossad's ingenuity. We simply had the resources to make it come to pass—as is said in the Old Testament.''

Abrahms stood in front of the enormous desk, arms akimbo above the pockets of his safari jacket. ''So the Jew and the *field marshal* set it all in motion. Ironical, isn't it, Nazi?''

''Not as much as you think, *Jude*. Impurity, as with beauty, is in the eye of the frightened beholder. You are not my enemy; you never were. If more of us in the old days had your commitment, your audacity, we never would have lost the war.''

''I know that,'' said the sabra. ''I watched and listened when you reached the English Channel. You lost it then. You were weak.''

''It was not *us!* It was the frightened *Debutanten* in Berlin!''

''Then keep them away when we create a *truly* new order, German. We can't afford weakness.''

''You do try me, Chaim.''

''I mean to.''

502

The chauffeur felt the bandages on his face, the swelling around his eyes and his lips painful to the touch. He was in his own room, where the doctor had turned on the television—probably as an insult, as he could barely see it.

He was disgraced. The prisoner had escaped in spite of his own formidable talents and the supposedly impassable pack of Dobermans. The American had used the silver whistle, that much the other guards had told him, and the fact that it had been removed from his neck was a further embarrassment.

He would not add to his disgrace. With blurred vision he had gone through his pockets—which no one in the panic of the chase had thought to do—and found that his billfold, his expensive Swiss watch, and all his money had been taken. He would say nothing about them. He was embarrassed enough, and any such revelations might be cause for dismissal—or conceivably his death.

Joel headed for the shoreline as fast as he could, submerging his head underwater whenever the beam of the searchlight swept toward him. The boat was a large motor launch, its bass-toned engines signifying power, its sudden turns and circles evidence of rapid maneuverability. It hugged the overgrown banks, then would sweep out toward the open water at the slightest sign of an object in the river.

Converse felt the soft mud below; he half swam, half trudged toward the darkest spot on the shore, the chauffeur's gun securely in his belt.

The boat approached, its penetrating beam studying every foot, every moving branch or limb or cluster of river weeds. Joel took a deep breath and slowly lowered himself under the water, his face angled up toward the surface, his eyes open, his vision a muddy dark blur. The searchlight grew brighter and seemed to hover above him for an eternity; he inched his way to the left and the beam moved away. He rose to the surface, his lungs bursting, but suddenly realized he could make no sound, he could not fill his chest with gasps of air. For directly above him, less than five feet away loomed the broad stern of the motor launch, bobbing in the water as if idling. The dark figure of a man was peering through very large binoculars at the riverbank.

Converse was bewildered; it was too dark now to see anything even with magnification. Then he remembered, and the memory accounted for the size of the binoculars. The man was focusing through infrared lenses; they had been used by patrols in Southeast Asia and were often the difference, he had been told, between search-and-destroy and search-and-be-destroyed. They revealed objects in the darkness, soldiers in the darkness.

The boat moved forward, but the idle increased only slightly, entering the slowest of trawling speeds. Again Joel was confused. What had brought Leifhelm's searching party to this particular spot on the riverfront? There were several other boats behind and out in the distance, their searchlights sweeping the water, but they kept moving, circling. Why did the huge motor

504

launch concentrate on this stretch of the shore? Could they have spotted him through infrared binoculars? If they had, they were proceeding very strangely; the North Vietnamese had been far swifter—more aggressive, more effective.

Silently, Converse lowered himself beneath the surface and breaststroked out beyond the boat. Seconds later he raised his head above the water, his vision clear, and he began to understand the odd maneuverings of Leifhelm's patrol. Beyond the darkest part of the riverbank into which he had lurched for concealment were the lights he had seen eight or nine minutes ago, before the launch and its searchlight monopolized all his attention. He had thought they were the lights of a small village, but he was in the wrong part of the world. Instead they were the inside lights of four or five small houses, a river colony with a common dock, summer homes perhaps of those fortunate enough to own waterfront property.

If there were houses and a dock, there had to be a drive—an open passage up to the road or roads leading into Bonn and the surrounding towns. Leifhelm's men were combing every inch of the riverbank, cautiously, quietly, the searchlights angled down so as not to alarm the inhabitants or forewarn the fugitive if he had reached the cluster of cottages and was on his way up to the unseen road or roads. A ship's radio would be activated, its frequency aligned to those in cars roaming above, ready to spring the trap. In some ways it was the Huong Khe again for Joel, the obstacles far less primitive but no less lethal. And then as now there was a time to wait, to wait in the black silence and let the hunters make their moves.

They made them quickly. The launch slid into the dock, the powerful twin screws quietly churning in reverse, as a man jumped off the bow with a heavy line and looped it around a piling. Three others followed, instantly racing off the short pier up onto the sloping lawn, one heading diagonally to the right, the other two toward the first house. What they were doing was obvious: one man would position himself in the bordering woods of the downhill entrance drive while his colleagues checked the houses, looking for signs of entry.

Converse's arms and legs began to feel like weights, each an anvil he could barely support, much less keep moving, but there was no choice. The beam of the searchlight kept moving up and down the base of the riverbank, its spill illuminating everything in its vicinity. A head surfacing at the wrong moment would be blown out of the water. *Huong Khe. Tread water in the reeds. Do it! Don't die!*

He knew the waiting was no longer than thirty minutes, but it seemed more like thirty hours or thirty days suspended in a floating torture rack. His arms and legs were now in agony; sharp pains shot through his body everywhere; muscles formed cramps that he dispersed by holding his breath and floating in a fetal position, his thumbs pressing relentlessly into the cores of the knotted muscles. Twice while gasping for air he swallowed water, coughing it out below the surface, his nostrils drowning, and twice found the air again.

There were moments when it crossed his inner consciousness that it would be so simple just to drift away. *Huong Khe. Don't do it! Don't die!*

Finally through waterlogged eyes he saw the men returning. One, two . . . three? . . . They ran down to the dock, to the man with the rope. *No!* The man with the rope had rushed forward! His eyes were playing tricks! Only two men had run onto the dock, the first man joining them, asking questions. The line man returned to the piling and released the rope; the other two jumped on board. The first man once again joined his companions, now on the bow of the launch—leaving another on shore, a lone observer somewhere unseen between the riverbank and the road above. *Huong Khe. An infantry scout separated from his patrol.*

The motor launch swung away from the dock and sped within a few feet past Joel, who was buffeted underwater by its wake. Once more the boat veered toward the shoreline and slowed down, its searchlight peering into the dense foliage of the bank, heading west, back toward Leifhelm's estate. Converse held his head above the surface, his mouth wide open, swallowing all the air he could as he made his way slowly—very slowly—into the mud. He pulled himself up through the wet reeds and branches until he felt dry ground. *Huong Khe.* He pulled the underbrush over him as best he could, finally covering his upturned face. He would rest until he felt the blood flowing steadily if painfully through his limbs, until the muscles of his neck lost their tension—it was always the neck; the neck was the warning signal—and then he would consider the man on the dark hill above him.

He dozed, until a slapping wave below woke him. He pushed the branches and the leaves away from his face and looked at the chauffeur's watch on his wrist, squinting at the weak radium dial. He had slept for nearly an hour—fitfully, to be sure, the slightest sounds forcing his eyelids briefly open, but he had rested. He rolled his neck back and forth, then moved his arms and legs. Everything still hurt, but the excruciating pain was gone. And now he faced a man on a hill above him. He tried to examine his thoughts. He was frightened, of course, but his anger would control that terrible fear; it had done so before, it would do so now. The objective was all that mattered —some kind of sanctuary, a place where he could think and put things together and somehow make the most important telephone call in his life. To Larry Talbot and Nathan Simon in New York. Unless he could do these things he was dead—as Connal Fitzpatrick was undoubtedly dead. *Jesus!* What had they done to him? A man with the purity of vengeance purely sought caught in a diseased web called Aquitaine! It was an unfair world. . . . But he could not think about it; he had to concentrate on a man on the hill.

He crept on his hands and knees. Stretch by stretch he crawled through the woods bordering the dirt road that wound up the hill from the lawn and the riverbank. Whenever a twig crunched or a rock was displaced he stopped, waiting for the moment to dissolve back into the sounds of the forest. He kept telling himself he had the advantage; he was the unexpected. It helped

508

counteract the fear of the darkness and the knowledge that a physical confrontation was before him. Like the patrol scout years ago in the Huong Khe, that man above him now had things he needed. The combat could not be avoided, so it was best not to think about it but to simply force himself into a mind-set empty of any feeling, and do it. But do it well, his mind had to understand that, too. There could be no hesitation, no intrusions of conscience—and no sound of a gun, only the use of the steel.

He saw him, oddly enough, silhouetted in the distant glare of a single streetlamp far above on a road. The man was leaning against the trunk of a tree and facing down, his sweep of vision taking in everything below. As Joel crept up the slope the space between his hands and knees became inches, the stops more frequent, silence more vital. He made his way in an arc above the tree and the man and then started down, like a large cat descending on its prey. He was the predator he had once been long ago, everything blocked out but the requirement of the lifeline.

He was within six feet; he could hear the man's breathing. There was a snap beneath him. A branch! The scout turned, his eyes alive in the glare of light. Converse lunged, the barrel of the gun gripped in his hand. He crashed the steel handle into the German's temple and then into his throat. The man fell backward, dazed but not unconscious; he started to scream. Joel sprang for his enemy's neck and half choked him before bringing the steel handle down with all his strength on the German's forehead; instantly there was an eruption of blood and crushed tissue.

Silence. No movement. Another scout separated from his patrol had been taken out. And as he had years ago, Converse permitted himself no feeling. It was done, and he had to go on.

The man's dry clothes, including the dark leather jacket, fit reasonably well. Like most small or medium-sized commanders, Leifhelm surrounded himself with tall men, as much to protect himself as to proclaim his superiority over his larger compatriots.

There was also another gun; Joel struggled with the clip, removed it, and threw it along with the weapon into the woods. The bonus came with the German's billfold; it contained a sizable sum of money as well as a frayed, much stamped passport. Apparently, this trusted employee of Leifhelm traveled widely for Aquitaine—probably knowing nothing and being very expendable, but always available at the moment of decision. The man's shoes did not fit; they were too small. So Converse used his drenched clothing to wipe his own, and the German's dry socks helped to absorb some of the moisture of the leather inside. He covered the man with branches and walked up the hill to the road.

He stayed out of sight between the trees as five cars passed by, all sedans, all possibly belonging to Erich Leifhelm. Then he saw a bright-yellow Volkswagen come into view, weaving slightly. He stepped out and held up his hands, the gesture of a man in trouble.

The small car stopped—a blond girl in the passenger seat, the driver no more than eighteen or twenty, another young man in back, also blond, who looked as though he might be the girl's brother.

"*Was ist los, Opa?*" asked the driver.

"I'm afraid I don't speak German. Can you speak any English?"

"I speak some English," said the boy in back, slurring his words. "Better than these two! All they want to do is get to our place and make love. See! I do speak English?"

"You certainly do, and very well, indeed. Would you explain to them, please? Frankly, I've had a fight with my wife at a party down there— you know, at those cottages—and I want to get back to Bonn. I'll pay you, of course."

"*Ein Streit mit seiner Frau! Er will nach Bonn. Er wird uns bezahlen.*"

"*Warum nicht? Sie hat mich heute sowieso schon zu viel gekostet,*" said the driver.

"*Nicht fuer was du kriegst, du Drecksack!*" cried the girl, laughing.

"Get in, *mein Herr!* We are your chauffeurs. Just pray he stays on the road, *ja!* What hotel are you staying at?"

"Actually, I'd rather not go back there. I'm really very angry. I'd like to teach her a lesson by staying away tonight. Do you think you could find me a room? I'll pay you even more, of course. Frankly, I've been drinking a bit myself."

"*Ein betrunkener Tourist! Er will ein Hotel. Fahren wir ihn ins Rosencafé?*"

"*Dort sind mehr Nutten als der alte knacker schafft.*"

"We are your guides, *Amerikaner,*" said the

511

young man beside Converse. "We are students from the university who will not only find you a room, but with excellent prospects of getting back at your wife with some pleasure! There's also a café. You'll buy us a lager or six, *ja?*"

"All you want. But I'd also like to make a telephone call. To the United States—it's business. Will I be able to?"

"Most everyone in Bonn speaks English. If they don't at this Rosencafé, I, myself, will take care of it. Six lagers, though, remember that!"

"Twelve, if you like."

"Da wird es im Pissoir eine Überschwemmung geben!"

He knew the rate of exchange, and once inside the raucous café—actually a run-down bar favored by the university crowd—he counted the money he had taken from the two Germans. It was roughly five hundred dollars, over three from the man on the hill. The seedy clerk at the registration desk explained in convoluted English that, indeed, the switchboard could place a call to America, but it might take several minutes. Joel left fifty dollars in deutsche marks for his youthful Good Samaritans, excused himself and headed for his room—such as it was. An hour later the call came through.

"Larry?"

"Joel?"

"Thank *God* you're there!" cried Converse in relief. "You'll never know how I kept hoping you weren't out of town. Getting a call through from here is a bitch!"

"I'm here," said Talbot, his voice suddenly calm and in control. "Where are *you,* Joel?" he asked quietly.

"Some poor excuse for a hotel in Bonn. I just got here. I didn't get the name."

"You're in a hotel in Bonn but you don't know which one?"

"It doesn't matter, Larry! Get Simon on the line. I want to talk to you both. Quickly."

"Nathan's in court. He should be back here by four o'clock—our time. That's about an hour from now."

"*Goddamn* it!"

"Take it easy, Joel. Don't upset yourself."

"Don't *upset* . . . ? For Christ's sake, I've been locked up in a stone cabin with bars in the windows for five days! I broke out a couple of hours ago, and ran like hell through the woods with a pack of dogs and lunatics carrying guns chasing me. I spent an hour in the water damn near drowning before I could reach land without getting my head shot off, and then I had to—I had to—"

"You had to what, Joel?" asked Talbot, a strange passivity in his voice. "What did you have to do?"

"Goddamn it, Larry, I may have *killed* a man to get out of there!"

"You had to kill someone, Joel? Why did you think you had to do that?"

"He was waiting for me! They were searching for me! On the land, in the woods along the riverbanks—he was a scout separated from his patrol. *Scouts, patrols!* I had to get out, get *away!*

And you tell me not to be upset!''

"Calm down, Joel, try to get hold of yourself. . . . You escaped before, didn't you? A long time ago—''

"What's that got to do with anything?'' Converse broke in.

"You had to kill people then, didn't you? Those memories must always be with you.''

"Larry, that's bullshit! Listen to me and take down everything I say—the names I give you, the facts—get it all down.''

"Perhaps I should bring Janet on the line. Her shorthand—''

"No! Only you, no one else! They can trace people, anyone who knows anything. It's not that complicated. Are you ready?''

"Of course.''

Joel sat down on the narrow bed and took a deep breath. "The best way to put it—as it was put to me, but you don't have to write this down, just understand—is that they've come back.''

"Who?''

"The generals—field marshals, admirals, colonels—allies and enemies, all field and fleet commanders and above. They've come together from everywhere to change things, change governments and laws and foreign policies, everything to be based on military priorities and decisions. It's crazy, but they could do it. We'd live out their fantasies because they'd be in control, believing they're right and selfless and dedicated—as they've always believed.''

"Who are these people, Joel?''

"Yes, write this down. The organization is

514

called Aquitaine. It's based on a historical theory that the region in France once known as Aquitaine might have become all of Europe and by extension—as colonies—the North American continent as well."

"Whose theory?"

"It doesn't *matter,* it's just a theory. The organization was conceived by General George Delavane—he was known as Mad Marcus in Vietnam—and I saw only a fraction of the damage that son of a bitch did! He's pulled in military personnel from all over the place, all commanders, and they're fanning out recruiting their own kind, fanatics who believe as they do, that theirs is the only way. For the past year or so, they've been shipping illegal weapons and armaments to terrorist groups, encouraging destabilization wherever they can, the ultimate purpose being that they'll be called in to restore order, and when they do, they'll take over. . . . Five days ago I met with Delavane's key men from France and Germany, Israel and South Africa—and, I think, possibly England."

"You met with these people, Joel? Did they invite you to a meeting?"

"They thought I was one of them, that I believed in everything they stood for. You see, Larry, they didn't know how much I hated them. They hadn't been where I'd been, hadn't seen what I saw—as you said, years ago."

"When you *had* to escape," added Talbot sympathetically. "When you had to kill people—times you'll never forget. They must have been terrible for you."

"Yes, they were. Goddamn it, *yes!* Sorry, let's stay on course. I'm so tired—still frightened, too, I think."

"Relax, Joel."

"Sure. Where was I?" Converse rubbed his eyes. "Oh, yes, I remember. They got information on me, information from my service record, my status as a POW, which wasn't actually part of the record, but they got it and they found out what and who I was. They heard the words that told them how much I hated them, hated what Delavane had done, what they all had done. They drugged me, got whatever they could and threw me into a Godforsaken stone house set in the middle of the woods above the Rhine. While under the chemicals I must have told them everything I knew—"

"Chemicals?" asked Talbot, obviously never having heard the term.

"Amytols, Pentothals, scopolamine. I've been the route, Larry. I've been there and back."

"You *have? Where?"*

"In the camps. It's immaterial."

"I'm not sure it is."

"It is! The point is they found out what I know. That means they'll move up their schedule."

"Schedule?"

"We're in the countdown. *Now!* Two weeks, three weeks, four at the outside! No one knows how or where or what the targets are, but there'll be eruptions of violence and terrorism all over the place, giving them the excuse to move in and take over. 'Accumulation,' 'rapid acceleration,' those

516

were the words they used! Right now in Northern Ireland—everything's blown apart, nothing but chaos—whole armored divisions are moving in. *They* did it, Larry! It's a test, a trial run for them! I'm going to give you the names." Converse did so, both surprised and annoyed that Talbot did not react to any of the men of Aquitaine. "Have you got them?"

"Yes, I have."

"Those are the salient facts and the names I can vouch for. There's a lot more—people in the State Department and the Pentagon, but the lists are in my briefcase and it's been stolen, or hidden somewhere. I'll get some rest and start writing out everything I know, then call you in the morning. I have to get out of here. I'm going to need help."

"I agree, so may I talk now?" said the lawyer in New York in that odd flat voice. "First, where are you, Joel? Look on the phone or read the print on an ashtray—or check the desk; there must be stationery."

"There's no desk and the ashtrays are chipped glass. . . . Wait a minute, I picked up some matches from the bar when I bought cigarettes." Converse reached into the pocket of the leather jacket and pulled out the book of matches. "Here it is. 'Riesendrinks.' "

"Look below that. My German is limited, but I think it means 'big drinks' or something."

"Oh? Then it must be this. 'Rosencafé.' "

"That sounds more like it. Spell it for me, Joel."

Converse did, an undefined feeling disturbing him. "Have you got it?" he asked. "Here's a

517

telephone number.'' Joel read off the numbers printed on the cover.

''Good, that's splendid,'' said Talbot. ''But before you get off the line—and I know you need rest badly—I have a couple of questions.''

''I would hope to hell you do!''

''When we spoke after that man was hurt in Paris, after that fight you saw in the alley, you told me you were in Amsterdam. You said you were going to fly back to Paris and see René, straighten everything out. Why didn't you, Joel?''

''For God's sake, Larry, I just told you what I've been through! It took every minute I had to set things up. I was going after these people—this goddamned Aquitaine—and it could only be done one way. I had to work myself in, I couldn't waste time!''

''That man died. Did you have anything to do with his death?''

''Christ, yes, I killed him! He tried to stop me, they all tried to stop me! They found me in Copenhagen and had me followed. They were waiting for me at the airport here. It was a trap!''

''To stop you from reaching these men, these generals and field marshals?''

''Yes!''

''Yet you just told me these same men invited you to meet with them.''

''I'll spell it all out for you in the morning,'' said Converse wearily, the tension of the last hours—days—culminating in exhaustion and a wracking headache. ''By then I'll have everything down on paper, but you may have to come over here to get it—and me. The main thing is we're in touch. You've got the names, the overview, and you know where I am. Talk with Nathan, think about everything I've said and the three of us will figure out what to do. We have contacts in Washington, but we'll have to be careful. We don't know who's with whom. But there's a plus here. Some of the material I have—I *had*—could only have come from people down there. One view is that I was set in motion by them, that men I don't know are watching every move I make because I'm doing what they can't do."

"By yourself," said Talbot, agreeing. "Without Washington's help. Without their help."

"That's right. They can't show themselves; they have to stay in the background until I bring out something concrete. That was the plan. When you and Nathan talk, if you have questions call me. I'm just going to lie down for an hour or so anyway."

"I've got another question now, if you don't mind. You know Interpol has an international warrant for you."

"I do."

"And the American embassy is looking for you."

"I know that, too."

"I was told that word reached you to come into the embassy."

"*You* were told?"

"Why haven't you done it, Joel?"

"Jesus, I *can't!* Don't you think I would if I *could?* The place is crawling with Delavane's people. Well, that's an exaggeration, but I know of three. I saw them."

"It's my understanding that Ambassador Peregrine himself got word to you, guaranteeing you protection, confidentiality. Wasn't that enough?"

"Your *understanding* . . . The answer is *no!* Peregrine hasn't any idea what he's got inside that place. Or maybe he does. I saw Leifhelm's car go through those gates like he had a lifetime pass. At three o'clock in the morning. Leifhelm's a Nazi, Larry, he's never been anything else! So what does that make Peregrine?"

"Come on, Joel. You're maligning a man by implication who doesn't deserve it. Walter Peregrine was one of the heroes of Bastogne. His command at the Battle of the Bulge is a legend of the war. And he was a reserve officer, not part of the regular Army. I doubt that Nazis are his favorite guests."

"His command? Another *commander?* Then maybe he knows *exactly* what he's got in that embassy!"

"That's not fair. His outspoken criticisms of the Pentagon are a documented part of his postwar career. He's called them megalomaniacs with too damn much money feeding their egos at the taxpayers' expense. No, you're not being fair, Joel. I think you should listen to him. Call him on the phone, talk to him."

"Not being fair?" said Converse softly, the undefined feeling coming into focus, now a warning. "Wait a minute! You're the one who's not being fair. *'I* was told.' . . . 'It's *my* understanding?' What oracle have you been in touch with? Who's imparting these pearls of

520

wisdom about me? On what basis and where from?"

"All right, Joel, all right, calm down. Yes, I have talked to people—people who want to help you. A man is dead in Paris, and now you say there's another in Bonn. You talk of scouts and patrols and those horrible chemicals, and how you ran through the woods and had to hide in the river. Don't you understand, son? Nobody's blaming you or even holding you responsible. Something happened; you're living it all over again."

"My God!" broke in Converse, stunned. "You don't believe a word I've *said!*"

"You believe it, and that's all that matters. I saw my share in North Africa and Italy, but nothing to compare with what you went through later. You have a deep, understandable hatred for war and all things military. You wouldn't be human if you didn't, not with the suffering you experienced and the terrible things you endured."

"Larry, everything I've told you is *true!*"

"Fine, splendid. Then reach Peregrine, go to the embassy and tell them. They'll listen to you. *He'll* listen."

"Are you denser than I *think?*" shouted Joel. "I just told you, I can't! I'd never get to *see* Peregrine! I'd get my head blown away!"

"I spoke to your wife—sorry, your ex-wife. She said you'd have these moments at night. . . ."

"You spoke to *Val?* You brought *her* into this! Christ, are you out of your *mind?* Don't you know they trace everyone *down?* It was right under your nose, counselor! *Lucas Anstett!* Stay

521

away from her! Stay away or I'll—I'll—"

"You'll what, son?" asked Talbot quietly. "Kill me, too?"

"Oh, *Jesus!*"

"Do as I say, Joel. Call Peregrine. Everything will be all right."

Suddenly Converse heard an odd sound over the line, odd in context but one he had heard hundreds of times before. It was a short buzz, barely significant but there was significance to it. It was Lawrence Talbot's courteous signal to his secretary to come into his office and pick up a revised letter or a corrected brief or a dictation tape. Joel knew what it was now. The address of a seedy hotel in Bonn.

"All right, Larry," he said, feigning an exhaustion that was all too real. "I'm so *damned* tired. Let me lie down for a while and maybe I will call the embassy. Maybe I should get in touch with Peregrine. Everything's so confused."

"That's the way, son. Everything's going to be fine now. Just splendid."

"Good-bye, Larry."

"Good-bye for now, Joel. See you in a couple of days."

Converse slammed down the phone and looked around the dimly lit room. What was he checking for? He had come with nothing and he would leave with nothing but what was on his back—what he had stolen. And he had to leave quickly. He had to run. In minutes men would be speeding in cars from the embassy, and at least one of those men would have a gun and a bullet meant for him!

What in hell was *happening* to him? The truth was a fantasy bolstered by lies, and the lies were his only means of survival. *Insanity!*

19

He ran past the elevator to the staircase, descending the steps two and three at a time, his hand on the iron railing as he lurched around the landings, and reached the lobby door four stories below. He swung it open, suddenly gripping the edge and slowing his pace so as not to call attention to himself. He need not have been concerned. The small band of people milling about in front of the benches against the wall and wandering around the warm tile floor were the neighborhood elderly, looking for nightly companionship, and a few drunks walking in and out of the neon-lit door to the noisy café. Oh, *Christ!* His mind was in a frenzy. He could walk around in the night, hiding in alleys, but a lone man in unfamiliar streets was too easily spotted by unofficial hunters or by the official police. He had to get inside somewhere, somehow. Out of sight.

The café! His Samaritans! He pulled up the collar of the leather jacket and forced the belt of the trousers lower, inching down the gap around his ankles. He then approached the door casually, feigning a slight stagger as he pushed it open. He was greeted by floating levels of smoke—not all of it tobacco, by any means—and adjusted his stinging eyes to the erratically flashing lights as he tried to block out the offending noise, a combination of guttural roars and disco music blaring from high-tech speakers. His Good Samaritans were gone: he looked for the young blond girl as his focal point, but she was not there. The table they had occupied was taken by another foursome—no, not four different people, only three, who had joined the English-speaking student who had sat beside him in the car. The three were young men who seemed also to be students. Joel approached them, and passing an empty chair in his path, he gripped the back and unobtrusively pulled it behind him to the table. He sat down and smiled at the blond-haired student.

"I didn't know if I'd left enough money for those twelve beers I promised," he said pleasantly.

"*Ach!* I was just talking about you, *Herr Amerikaner!* These are my friends—like me, all dreadful students!" The three newcomers were introduced rapidly, the names lost in the music and the smoke. Everyone nodded; the American was welcome.

"Our other two friends left?"

"I told you," shouted the blond youngster through the noise. "They wished to drive to our house and make love. That's all they *do!* Our parents went to Bayreuth for the music festival, so they shall make their own music on *her* bed and I shall come home late!"

"Nice arrangement," said Converse, trying to think of how to broach the subject that had to be broached quickly. He had very little time.

"Very *good,* sir!" said a dark-haired young

524

man on his right. "Hans would have missed that; his English is understandably inferior. I was an exchange student in the state of Massachusetts for two years. 'Arrangement' is also a musical term. You combined the two! *Very* good, sir!"

"I keep trying," said Joel aimlessly, looking at the student. "You really speak English?" he asked sincerely.

"Very well. My scholarship depends upon it. My friends here are good people, make no mistake, but they are rich and come here for amusement. As a boy, I lived two streets away from this place. But they protect the lads here, and why not? Let them have fun; nobody is hurt and money is spread."

"You're sober," said Converse, the statement bordering on a question.

The young man laughed as he nodded. "Tonight, yes. Tomorrow afternoon I have a difficult exam and need a clear head. The summer-session examinations are the worst. The professors would rather be on holiday."

"I was going to talk to *him*," said Joel, nodding at the blond student, who was arguing with his two companions, his hands waving in the smoke, his voice strident. "But that doesn't make sense. You do."

"In *what* sense, sir, if you will forgive the redundancy of the expression?"

" 'Redundancy'? What's your major?"

"Preliminary law, sir."

"I don't need that."

"It is a difficulty, sir?"

"Not for me. Listen, I haven't much time and I have a problem. I have to get out of here. I need

525

to find another place to stay—just until tomorrow morning. I assure you I've done nothing wrong, nothing illegal—in case my clothes or my appearance gives another impression. It's strictly a personal matter. Can you help me?''

The dark-haired young German hesitated, as if reluctant to answer, but nevertheless did so, leaning forward to be heard. ''Since you bring up the subject, I'm sure you can understand that it would not be seemly for a student of the law to help a man under questionable circumstances.''

''That's exactly why I brought it up,'' said Converse rapidly, speaking into the student's ear. ''I'm an attorney and under these clothes a reasonably respectable one. I simply took on the wrong American client over here and can't wait to get a plane out tomorrow morning.''

The young man listened, studied Joel's face and nodded. ''Then these are not lodgings you would normally seek?''

''To be avoided wherever possible. I just thought it would be a good idea to be inconspicuous for the night.''

''There are very few places such as this in Bonn, sir.''

''To Bonn's credit, counselor.'' Glancing about the café and its predominant clientele, Converse had another thought. ''It's summer!'' he said urgently to the student through the bedlam. ''Are there any youth hostels around here?''

''Those in the vicinity of Bonn or Cologne are filled, sir, mostly with Americans and the Dutch. The others which might have spaces are quite far north toward Hanover. However, there is another solution, I think."

"What?"

"Summer, sir. The rooming houses usually filled by those attending the university have many spaces during the summer months. In the house where I stay there are two empty rooms on the third floor."

"I thought you lived around here."

"That was long ago. My parents are retired and live with my sister in Mannheim."

"I'm in a great hurry. May we go? I'll pay you what I can tonight and more tomorrow morning."

"I thought you said you were taking the plane in the morning."

"I have two stops to make first. You can come with me; you can show me where they are."

The young man and Joel excused themselves, knowing they would not be missed. The student started toward the lobby door, but Converse grabbed his elbow, gesturing at the street entrance.

"Your luggage, sir!" shouted the German through the din and the flashing lights.

"You can lend me a razor in the morning!" Converse yelled back, pulling the young man through the mingling bodies toward the door. Several tables before the entrance was an empty chair, on the seat a soft, rumpled cloth cap. He bent down and picked it up, holding it in front of him as he reached the door and walked outside to the pavement, the student behind him. "Which way?" he asked, pulling the cap over his head.

"This way, sir," replied the young German,

527

pointing beneath the shabby canopy of the adjacent hotel entrance.

"Let's go," said Joel, stepping forward.

They stopped—that is, Converse stopped first, gripping the student's shoulder and turning him into the building. A black sedan had come speeding down the street, swerving into the open space in front of the canopy. Two men got out of the back doors and rushed toward the entrance, the second man running around the trunk to catch up with the first. Joel angled his head as the young German stared at him. He recognized both men; both were Americans. They had been at the Cologne-Bonn airport eight nights ago, hoping to trap him then as they were coming to trap him now. The black car moved forward out of the glare of the lights into the shadows. It pulled into the curb and waited, a hearse prepared to receive its cargo.

"*Was ist los?*" asked the German youth, unable to conceal his fear.

"Nothing, really." Converse removed his hand and gave the student two friendly claps on the shoulder. "Just let this be a lesson to you, counselor. Know who your client is before you get greedy and accept too large a retainer."

"*Ja,*" said the young German, attempting a smile but not succeeding, his eyes on the black sedan.

They walked rapidly past the parked automobile with the driver inside, the glow of a cigarette seen in the darkness of the front seat. Joel pulled down the cloth cap and again angled his head, now away from one of his countrymen.

The truth was a fantasy bolstered by lies. . . . Survival was in running and concealment. Insanity!

The early morning was mercifully uneventful except for his raging thoughts. The student, whose name was Johann, had secured him a room at the boardinghouse, the proprietess delighted with a hundred deutsche marks for the rental. It more than made up for the gauze, tape, and antiseptic she gave him to rebandage his wound. Converse had slept soundly, if intermittently, awakened by fears transposed into macabre dreams. By seven o'clock sleep was impossible.

There was an urgent piece of business that had to be taken care of; he understood the risk, but the money was necessary, now more than ever. On Mykonos, the knowledgeable if serpentine Laskaris had forwarded $100,000 to banks in Paris, London, Bonn and New York, using the accepted practice of written-out numbers as a signature to withdraw the funds. Laskaris further had suggested that Joel should not attempt to carry with him or try to memorize four sets of lengthy and entirely different digits. Instead the banker would wire the American Express travel offices in the four cities to hold for a period of three months a message for—*who, Mr. Converse? It should be a name meaningful to you but not to others. It will be your code, no other identification necessary—as with certain telephone banking facilities in your own country. . . . Make it Charpentier. J. Charpentier.*

Joel understood that he might have revealed the

device while under narcotics. Also, he might not have; his mind was not on money. He had a great deal in his possession, and the chemicals tended to elicit only feverish priorities. He had learned that in the camps a lifetime ago, twice astonished that he had not mentioned far-off tactics down the roads of escape. There was also a backup, ethics notwithstanding. The young German, Johann, would be his intermediary. The risks could not be avoided, only minimized; he had also learned that a lifetime ago. If the boy was taken, his conscience would be stricken, but then, what could be the worst that would happen to him? There was no point in thinking about it.

"Go inside and ask if there's a message for J. Charpentier," said Joel to the student. They were in the backseat of a taxi across the street from the American Express office. "If the answer is yes, say the following words. 'It must be a wire from Mykonos,' " he added, recalling Laskaris' precise instructions.

"That is necessary, sir?" asked the dark-haired Johann, frowning.

"Yes, it is. Without mentioning Mykonos and the fact that the message is a cable, they won't give it to you. Also it identifies you. You won't have to sign anything."

"This is all very strange, sir."

"If you're going to be a lawyer, get used to odd forms of communication. There's nothing illegal, simply a means of protecting your client's and your firm's confidentiality."

"I have much to learn, it seems."

"You're not doing anything wrong," continued

Joel quietly, his eyes level with Johann's. "On the contrary, you're doing something very right, and I'll pay you very well for doing it."

"*Sehr gut,*" said the young man.

Converse waited in the taxi, his eyes scanning the street, concentrating on stationary automobiles and those pedestrians walking too slowly or not at all, or anyone whose glances even seemingly strayed to the American Express office. Johann went inside and Joel swallowed repeatedly, a tightness in his throat; the waiting was awful, made worse by the knowledge that he was using the student in a high-risk situation. Then he thought briefly of Avery Fowler-Halliday and Connal Fitzpatrick; they had lost. The young German had an infinitely far greater chance of living for many years.

The minutes went by as the sweat crawled through Converse's hair and down his neck; time was suspended in fear. Finally, Johann came outside, blinking in the sunlight, innocence personified. He crossed the street and climbed into the taxi.

"What did they say to you?" asked Joel, trying to sound casual, his eyes still roaming the street.

"Only if I had been waiting long for the message. I replied that I expected it was a cablegram from Mykonos. I didn't know what else to say."

"You did fine." Joel tore open the envelope and unfolded the wire. There was an unbroken series of written-out numbers, well over twenty, he judged at a glance. Again he remembered Laskaris' instructions: *Pick every third number beginning with the third and ending with the third from the last. Think merely in terms of three. It's quite simple—these things usually are—and in any event, no one else can sign for you. It's merely a precaution.*

"Is everything all right?" asked Johann.

"So far we're ahead one step and you're one step nearer a bonus, counselor."

"I'm also nearer my examination."

"What time do you take it?"

"Three-thirty this afternoon."

"Good omen. Think in terms of three."

"I beg your pardon?"

"Nothing. Let's find a pay telephone. You've only got one more thing to do, and tonight you can buy your friends the biggest dinner in Bonn."

The taxi waited at the corner while Converse and the young German stood outside the booth, Johann having written down the bank's number from the telephone book. The student was reluctant to go any further; the exotic chores asked of him now were more than he cared to accept.

"All you have to do is tell the truth!" insisted Joel. *"Only* the truth. You met an American attorney who doesn't speak German and he's asked you to make a call for him. This attorney has to withdraw funds for a client from a confidential accounts-transfer and wants to know whom he should see. That's all. No one will ask your name, or mine, either, for that matter."

"And when I do this there will be something else, *mein Herr? Nein,* I think not. You call yourself—"

"I can't make a mistake! I can't misunderstand a word. And there is nothing else. Just wait wherever you like around the bank or near the bank. When I come out I'll give you two thousand deutsche marks, and as far as I'm concerned—as far as *anyone's* concerned—we never met."

"So much for so little, sir. You can understand my fears."

"They're nothing compared to mine," said Converse quietly yet urgently. "Please, do this. I need your help."

As he had done the night before through the noise and the smoke and the flashing lights of the raucous bar, the young German looked hard at Joel, as if trying to see something he could not be sure was there. Finally, he nodded once without enthusiasm. *"Sehr gut,"* he said, stepping into the booth with several coins in his hand.

Converse watched through the glass as the student dialed and obviously had brief conversations with two or three different people before reaching the correct party. The one-sided dialogue as observed by Joel seemed interminable —far too long and too complicated for the simple request of a name in the transferred-accounts department. At one point, as he wrote something down on the scrap of paper with the bank's number on it, Johann appeared to object and Converse had to restrain himself from opening the door and terminating the call. The German youth hung up and came out, his expression confused and angry.

"What happened? Was there a problem?"

"Only with the hour and institutional policy, sir."

"What does that mean?"

"Such accounts are serviced only after twelve noon. I made it clear that you had to be at the airport by then, but Herr Direktor said the bank's policy would stand." Johann handed Converse the slip of paper. "You're to see a man named Lachmann on the second floor."

"I'll catch a later plane." Joel looked at the chauffeur's watch on his wrist. It was ten-thirty-five; an hour and a half to go.

"I was hoping to be at the university library long before noon."

"You can still be there," said Converse sincerely. "We can stop, get a stamped envelope, and you can write out your name and address. I'll mail the money to you."

Johann glanced at the pavement, his hesitation all too obvious. "I think, perhaps . . . the examination is not so difficult for me. It's one of my better subjects."

"Of course," agreed Joel. "There's no reason on earth why you should trust me."

"You mistake me, sir. I believe you would mail the money to me. It's just that I'm not sure it's such a good idea for me to receive the envelope."

Converse smiled; he understood. "Finger-prints?" he asked kindly. "Accepted rules of evidence?"

"It's also one of my better subjects."

"Okay, you're stuck with me for another couple of hours. I've got about seven hundred deutsche marks left until I reach the bank. Do you know some clothing store away from the main shopping district where I can buy a pair of trousers and a jacket?"

"Yes, sir. And if I may suggest, if you are going to withdraw enough funds to give me two thousand deutsche marks, perhaps a clean shirt and a tie might be in order."

"Always check your client's appearance. You may go far, counselor."

The ritual at the Bank aus der Bonner Sparkasse was a study in awkward but adamant efficiency. Joel was ushered into Herr Lachmann's office on the second floor where neither a handshake nor small talk was offered. Only the business at hand was addressed.

"Origin of transfer, please?" asked the blunt, corpulent executive.

"Bank of Rhodes, Mykonos branch, waterfront office. The name of the—'dispatcher,' I guess you'd call him, is Laskaris. I don't recall his first name."

"Even his last is unnecessary," said the German, as though he did not care to hear it. The transaction itself seemed somehow to offend him.

"Sorry, I just wanted to be helpful. As you know, I'm in a great hurry. I have a plane to catch."

"Everything will be done according to the regulations, sir."

"Naturally."

The banker shoved a sheet of paper across the desk. "You will write out your numerical signature five times, one below the other, as I read you the regulations which constitute the policy of the Bank aus der Bonner Sparkasse as they pertain to the laws of the Federal Republic of Germany. You will then be required to sign— again in your numerical signature—an affidavit that you thoroughly understood and accept these prohibitions."

"I thought you said 'regulations.' "

"One and the same, sir."

Converse took the cablegram out of the inside pocket of his newly purchased sport jacket and placed it beside the blank page of stationery. He had underlined the correct numbers and began writing.

" 'You the numerically undersigned, traceable from the origin of transfer,' " droned the obese Lachmann, leaning back in his chair and reading from a single page, " 'swear to the fact that whatever funds withdrawn from the Bank aus der Bonner Sparkasse from this confidential account have been subject to all taxes, individual and corporate, from whatever sources of revenue. That they are not being processed through differing currencies to avoid said taxes, or for the purpose of making unlawful payments to individuals, companies, or corporations traf- ficking in illegal and—"

"Forget it," Joel broke in. "I know it; I'll sign it."

" '—egregious activities outside the laws of the Federal Republic of Germany or the laws of the

536

nation of which the undersigned is a legal resident with full citizenship.' "

"Ever tried half-full or resident alien status?" said Converse, starting the last line of numbers. "I know a law student who could punch holes in that affidavit."

"There is more, but you say you'll sign?"

"I'm sure there's more and of course I'll sign." Joel pushed the page with the handwritten numbers back to the banker. "There. Just get me the money. One hundred thousand American, minus your fee. Split it two thirds and a third. U.S. and German, no bills over six hundred deutsche marks and five hundred American."

"That is quite a bit of paper, sir."

"I'll handle it. Please, as quickly as possible."

"Is that amount the entire account? I would not know, of course, until the scanners verify your 'signature.' "

"It's the entire account."

"It could take several hours, *natürlich.*"

"*What?*"

"The regulations, the *policy.*" The fat man extended his arms in supplication.

"I don't *have* several hours!"

"What can I do?"

"What *can* you do? A thousand American—for *you.*"

"One hour, sir."

"Five thousand?"

"Five minutes, my good friend."

Converse walked out of the elevator. The abrasive newly acquired money belt was far less

537

comfortable than the one he had purchased in Geneva, but it would have been pointless to refuse it. It was a courtesy of the bank, Lachmann had said as the German pocketed nearly twelve thousand deutsche marks for himself. The 'five minutes' had been a persuasive exaggeration, thought Joel as he glanced at the clock on the wall; it was nearly twelve-forty-five. The ritual had taken over half an hour, from his "indoctrination" to the verification of his "signature" by electronic scanners capable of detecting the slightest "fundamental" variation in the writing characteristics. Apparently no one dared make any mistakes in the German banks where questionable practices were concerned. The regulations were followed right to the borders of illegality, with everyone covered by following orders that placed the burden of innocence solely on the recipients.

Converse started for the bronze-bordered doors of the entrance when he saw the student, Johann, sitting on a marble bench, looking out of place but not uncomfortable. The young man was reading some sort of pamphlet put out by the bank. Or more precisely, he was pretending to read it; his eyes, darting above the page, were watching the crowds crisscrossing the marble floor. Converse nodded as Johann saw him; the student got up from the bench and waited until Joel reached the entrance before he began to follow.

Something had happened. Outside on the pavement people were rushing in both directions, but mainly to the right; voices were raised, questions shouted, replies blurred with anger and angry ignorance.

"What the hell is it?" asked Converse.

"I don't know," replied Johann, next to him. "Something ugly, I think. People are running to the kiosk on the corner. The newspapers."

"Let's get one," said Joel, touching the young man's arm, as they started toward the growing crowd on the block.

"*Attentat! Mord! Amerikanische Botschafter ermordet!*"

The newsstand operators were shouting, handing out papers as they grabbed coins and bills with little or no attempt to give change. There was a sense of swelling panic that came with sudden unexplained events that presaged greater disasters. All around them people were snapping papers, their eyes riveted on the headlines and the stories beneath.

"*Mein Gott!*" cried Johann, glancing at a folded newspaper on his left. "The American ambassador has been assassinated!"

"*Christ!* Get one of those!" Converse threw a number of coins into the kiosk as the young German grabbed a paper from the extended hand of a newsstand operator. "Let's get out of here!" yelled Joel, gripping the student's arm.

But Johann did not move. He stood there in the middle of the shouting crowd, staring at the newspaper, his eyes wide, his lips trembling. Converse shoved two men away with his shoulders as he pulled the young man forward, now both of them surrounded by anxious, protesting Germans obsessed with getting to the newsstand.

"You!" Johann's scream was muted by some intolerable fear.

Joel ripped the newspaper from the student's hands. In the upper center of the front page were photographs of two men. On the left was the murdered Walter Peregrine, American ambassador to the Federal Republic. On the right was the face of an American *Rechtsanwalt*—one of the few words in German Converse knew; it meant attorney. The photograph was of himself.

20

"No!" roared Joel crushing the paper in his left fist, his right hand gripping Johann's shoulder. "Whatever it says, it's a *lie!* I'm not any part of this! Don't you see what they're trying to *do?* Come on with me!"

"Nein!" screamed the young German, looking frantically around, realizing his voice was lost in the enveloping bedlam.

"I said *yes!"* Converse shoved the newspaper inside his jacket, and throwing his right arm around Johann's neck, pulled him alongside. "You can think and do what you like, but first you come with *me!* You're going to read me every goddamned word!"

"Da ist er! Der Attentater!" shrieked the young German, reaching out, clutching the trousers of a man in the crowd who cursed and swung his arm down on the offending hand.

Joel wrenched the student's neck to his left, and

shouted into his ear, his words stunning himself as much as they did the young man. "You want it this way, you can *have* it! I've got a gun in my pocket and if I have to use it I will! Two decent men have been killed already—now three—why should you be the exception? Because you're *young?* That's no reason! When you come right down to it, who the hell are we *dying* for?"

Converse yanked the youth back and forth, dragging him out of the crowd. Once on the clear pavement he released his armlock, replacing it with a strong grip on the back of Johann's neck. He propelled the student forward, his eyes roving the street, trying to find a secluded area where they could talk—where Johann could talk, after reading a string of lies put out by the men of Aquitaine. The newspaper slipped down beneath his jacket; he reached in and grabbed it by the edge, pulling the paper out intact. He could not just keep walking, pushing his captive down the pavement; several people had glanced at them, fuel for the curious. Oh, Christ, The photograph—his *face!* Anyone might recognize him, and he was calling attention to himself by keeping the boy in tow.

Up ahead, on the right, there was a bakery or a coffee shop or a combination of both with tables under umbrellas on the sidewalk; several were empty at the far end. He would have preferred a deserted alley or a cobblestoned side street too narrow for vehicles, but he could not keep doing what he was doing—walking so rapidly with a prisoner in his grip.

"Over there! That table in the rear. You sit

facing out. And remember, I wasn't joking about the gun; my hand will be in my pocket."

"*Please,* let me *go!* You've done enough to me! My friends know we left together last night; my landlady knows I got you a room! The police will *question* me!"

"Get in there," said Converse, shoving Johann between the chairs to the table at the rear of the pavement. Both sat down; the young German was no longer trembling, but his eyes were darting in all directions. "Don't even think about it," continued Joel. "And when a waiter comes over, speak in English. *Only* English!"

"There are no waiters. Customers go inside and bring out their own sweet rolls and coffee."

"We'll do without—you can get something later. I owe you money and I pay my debts."

. . . *I always pay my debts. At least during the last four years I have.* Words from a note left by a risk-taker. An actor named Caleb Dowling.

"I want no money from you," said Johann, his English guttural with fear.

"You think it's tainted, makes you a true accessory, is that right?"

"You are the lawyer, I am merely a student."

"Let me set you straight. It's not tainted because I didn't do whatever they said I did, and there's no such thing as an accessory to innocence."

"You are the lawyer, sir."

Converse pushed the newspaper in front of the young German and with his right hand reached into his pocket, where he had put ten thousand deutsche marks in ascending denominations for his immediate use. He counted out seven thousand and reached over, placing it in front of Johann. "Put that away before I shove it down your throat."

"I will not take your money!"

"You'll take it and tell them I gave it to you, if you want to. They'll have to give it back."

"What do you mean?"

"The truth, counselor. You'll find out one day that it's the best shield you've got. Now, read me what the paper says!"

" 'The ambassador was killed sometime last night,' " began the student haltingly as he awkwardly put the deutsche marks in his pocket. ". . . 'The approximate time of death is difficult to establish until further examinations,' " he continued, translating the words in the article in fits and starts, trying to find the appropriate meanings. " '. . . The fatal wound was . . . 'Schädel'—cranial, a head wound—'the body in the water for many hours, washed up on the riverbank in the Plittersdorf and found early this morning. . . . The military chargé d'affaires was quoted as saying that the last person known to have been with the ambassador was an American by the name of Joel Converse. When that name appeared, there were . . .' " The young German squinted, shaking his head nervously. "How do you *say* it?"

"I don't know," said Joel coldly, his voice flat. "What am I trying to say?"

" '. . . very excited'—frantic—'communications between the governments of Switzerland, France and the Federal Republic, all in coordination with

543

the International Criminal Police, otherwise known as Interpol, and the . . . pieces of the tragic . . . *Ratsel* . . . puzzle fell into place,'—became clear, it means. 'Unknown to Ambassador Peregrine, the American Converse has been the object of an Interpol . . . *Suche* . . . search as a result of killings in Geneva and Paris as well as several attempted murders not yet clarified.' " Johann looked up at Converse. There was a throbbing in his throat.

"Go on," ordered Joel. "You don't know how enlightening this is. Go *on!*"

" 'According to the ambassador's office, a confidential meeting was arranged at the request of this man Converse, who claimed to have information injurious to American interests and which has subsequently proven to be false. The two men were to meet at the entrance of the Adenauer Bridge, between seven-thirty and eight o'clock last evening. The chargé d'affaires who accompanied Ambassador Peregrine confirmed that the two men met at seven-fifty-one P.M. and started across the bridge on the pedestrian walkway. It was the last time anyone from the embassy saw the ambassador alive.' " Johann swallowed, his hands trembling. He took several deep breaths and went on, his eyes rushing forward across the print, beads of perspiration breaking out on his hairline. " 'Below are more complete . . . *eingehendere* . . . details as they are known, but a statement issued by Interpol described the suspect, Joel Converse, as an apparently normal man who is in reality a . . . *wandernde.* . . .' " The young German lowered

544

his voice to a whisper. " 'a walking explosive with severe mental disturbances. He is judged by several behavioral experts in the United States to be psychopathically ill as a result of nearly four years as a prisoner of war during the Vietnam conflict. . . .' "

As Johann stammered on, frightened by his own voice, the telling words and damning phrases came with staccato regularity, backed up by hastily contacted departmental "sources" and unnamed, faceless "authorities." The portrait was that of a mentally deranged man who had been thrown back in time, his derangement triggered by some violent event that left him with his intelligence intact but without moral or physical control. In addition, Interpol's search for him was spoken of in clouded terms, implying a secret manhunt that had been in progress for a number of days, if not weeks.

" '. . . His homicidal tendencies are channeled,' " continued the now near-panicked student as the article quoted another "authoritative" source. " '. . . He has a pathological hatred for present or former high-ranking military personnel, especially those who had gained prominent public stature. . . . Ambassador Peregrine was a celebrated battalion commander in World War Two's Bastogne campaign, during which many American lives were lost. . . . Authorities in Washington have speculated that the disturbed man, who after several harrowing attempts finally escaped from a maximum-security camp in North Vietnam years ago, traveling over a hundred miles through enemy . . . *Dschungel*. . . jungle to reach his lines, is reliving his own experiences. . . . . His justification for survival—according to a military psychiatrist—is the killing of superior officers, past or present, who gave orders in combat, or, in the extreme, even civilians who in his imaginings bore some responsibility for the suffering he and others endured. Yet he is outwardly a normal man, as so many like him. . . . Guards have been placed in Washington, London, Brussels, and here in Bonn. . . . As an international lawyer, who is presumed to have access to numerous criminal elements who deal in illegal passports . . .' ''

It was a brilliantly executed trap, the crucial lies supported by truths, half-truths, distortions and complete falsehoods. Even the precise timing of the evening was considered. The chargé d'affaires at the embassy stated unequivocally that he had seen Joel at the Adenauer Bridge ''at 7:51 P.M.,'' approximately twenty-five minutes after he had broken out of the stone jailhouse on Leifhelm's estate, and less than ten minutes after he had plunged into the Rhine. Every fragment of the hour was accounted for. That he was ''officially'' placed at the bridge by ''7:51'' denied his story of capture and escape any credibility.

The incident in Geneva—the death of A. Preston Halliday—was introduced as a possible explanation for the violent act that had hurled him back in time, triggering Joel's maniacal behavior. ''. . . It has been learned that the attorney who was shot to death had been a well-known leader in the American protest movement in the sixties. . . .'' The veiled conclusion was that

Converse might have hired the killers. Even the death of the man in Paris was given a very different and far more important dimension— oddly enough, based in reality. ". . . Initially the victim's true identity was withheld in hopes of aiding the manhunt, as suspicions were aroused as a result of an interview the Sûreté had with a French lawyer who has known the suspect for a number of years. The attorney who had lunched with the suspect that day indicated that his American friend was in 'serious trouble' and needed 'medical attention.' . . ." The dead man in Paris, of course, was an outstanding colonel in the French Army, and an aide successively to several "prominent generals."

Finally, as if to convince any remaining unbelievers in this public trial by "authoritative" journalism, references were made not only to his conduct but to the remarks he made upon his separation from service over a decade and a half ago. These were released by the United States Department of the Navy, Fifth Naval District, which included its own recommendation at the time that one Lieutenant Converse be placed under voluntary psychiatric observation; it was refused. His conduct had been insulting in the extreme to the panel of officers who wished only to help him, and his remarks were nothing short of violent threats against numerous high-ranking military personnel, whom, as a carrier pilot, he could have known nothing about.

It all completed the portrait as painted by the artists of Aquitaine. Johann finished the article, the newspaper now clutched in his hands, his eyes wide and frightened. "That's all there is . . . sir."

"I'd hate to think there's any more," said Joel. "Do you believe it?"

"I have no thoughts. I'm too frightened to think."

"That's an honest answer. Uppermost in your mind is the fact that I might kill you, so you can't face what you think. That's what you're really saying. You're afraid that by a look or a wrong word I could take offense and pull a trigger."

"*Please,* sir, I am not adequate!"

"Neither was I."

"Let me *go.*"

"*Johann.* My hands are on the table. They've been on the table since we sat down."

"*What . . . ?*" The young German blinked and looked at Converse's forearms, both of which were in front of him, his hands clasped on the white metal surface. "You have no gun?"

"Oh, yes, I have a gun. I took it from a man who would have killed me if he'd had the chance." Joel reached into his pocket as Johann stiffened. "Cigarettes," said Converse, taking out a pack and a book of matches. "It's a terrible habit. Don't start if you don't smoke."

"It's very expensive."

"Among other things." Joel struck a match, lighting a cigarette, his eyes remaining on the student. "We've talked off and on since last night. Except for a few moments back there in the crowd when you could have had me lynched, do I look or sound like the man described in that newspaper story?"

"I am no more a doctor than a lawyer."

"Two points for the opposition. The burden of sanity's on me. Besides, it said I appeared perfectly normal."

"It said you suffered a great deal."

"Several hundred years ago, but no more than thousands of others and far, far less than some fifty-eight thousand who never came back. I don't think an insane man is capable of making a rational remark like that under these circumstances, do you?"

"I don't know what you're talking about."

"I'm trying to tell you that everything you just read to me is an example of a man being tried by negative journalism. Truths mixed with half-truths, distortions, and implausible judgments were slanted to support the lies that are meant to convict me. There's not a court in any civilized country that would admit that kind of testimony or permit a jury to hear it."

"Men have been killed," said Johann, again his words whispered. "The ambassador was killed."

"Not by me. I wasn't anywhere near the Adenauer Bridge at eight o'clock last night. I don't even know where it is."

"Where were you?"

"Not where anyone saw me, if that's what you mean. And those who know I couldn't have been at the bridge would be the last people on earth to say so."

"There has to be some evidence of where you were." The young German nodded at the cigarette in Converse's hand. "Perhaps one of those. Perhaps you finished a cigarette."

"Or finger or foot prints? Pieces of clothing?

There's all of that, but they don't tell the time."

"There are methods," corrected Johann. "The advances in the technology of . . . *Forschung* . . . the investigation techniques have been rapid."

"Let me finish that for you. I'm not a criminal lawyer but I know what you're saying. Theoretically, for example, the ground depression of a footprint matched with the scrapings off my shoes could put me where I was within the hour."

"*Ja!*"

"No. I'd be dead before a scrap of evidence reached a laboratory."

"*Why?*"

"I can't tell you. I wish to God I could but I can't."

"Again, I must ask why?" The fear in the young man's eyes was joined by disappointment, the last glimpse of believability, perhaps, gone with Joel's refusal to explain.

"Because I can't, I won't. You said a few minutes ago that I'd done enough to you, and without meaning to, I have. But I won't do this. You're not in a position to do anything but get yourself killed. That's as frankly as I can put it, Johann."

"I see."

"No you don't, but I wish there was a way to convince you that I have to reach others. People who *can* do something. They're not here; they're not in Bonn, but I'll reach them if I can get away."

"There's something else? You would have me do something *else?*" The young German stiffened again, and again his hands trembled.

"No. I don't want you to do anything. I'm asking you *not* to do anything—at least for a while. Nothing. Give me a chance to get out of here and somehow get in touch with people who can help me—help all of us."

"All of us?"

"I mean that, and it's all I'll say."

"These people are not to be found in your own embassy, *Amerikaner?*"

Converse looked hard at Johann, his eyes as steady as he could manage. "Ambassador Walter Peregrine was killed by one or more men at that embassy. They came to kill me last night at the hotel."

Johann breathed deeply, taking his eyes off Joel and staring down at the table. "Back at the kiosk, in the crowd, when you threatened me . . . you said three men had been killed already—three decent men."

"I'm sorry. I was desperate."

"It wasn't simply that, it was what you said right afterward. You said why should I be the exception. Because I was young? That was no reason, you claimed, and then you shouted very strange words—I remember them precisely. You said, 'When you come right down to it, who the hell are we dying for?' It was more than a question, I think."

"I won't discuss the implications of that remark, counselor. And I can't tell you what to do. I can only tell you what I've told dozens of clients over the years. When a decision is reduced to several strong opposing arguments—mine included—and you've listened to them all, put

551

them behind you and follow your own gut instinct. Depending upon who and what you are, it'll be the right one for you." Converse paused, pushing back his chair. "Now I'm going to get up and walk out of here. If you start screaming, I'll run and try to hide somewhere where I'll be safe before anyone recognizes me. Then I'll do whatever I can do. If you don't set off an alarm, I'll have a better chance, and that in my view would be best—for all of us. You could go to the university library and come out in an hour or so, buy a paper, and go to the police. I'd expect you to do that, if you felt you had to. That's my view. I don't know what yours is. Good-bye, Johann."

Joel rose from the table, bringing his hand instantly to his face, his fingers spread, touching his eyebrows. He turned and walked through the tables to the pavement, veering right, heading for the first intersection. He barely took a breath; his lungs were bursting for air but he dared not let even a breath impair his hearing. He waited as he walked, his pulse accelerating, his ears so keenly tuned that the slightest dissonance would have burned them.

There were only the sounds of the excited street conversations in counterpoint with the blaring horns of taxis—not the screams of a young male voice raising an alarm. He walked faster, entering the flow of pedestrians crossing the square —faster, *faster*—passing strollers who saw no need to rush. He reached the curb of the opposite pavement and slowed down—a rapidly walking man called attention to himself. Yet the impulse to break into a run was almost uncontrollable the farther he distanced himself from the tables of the sidewalk bakery-café. His ear had picked up no alarm and every split second of that absence told him to race into whatever secluded side streets he could find.

Nothing. Nothing broke the discordant sounds of the square, but there *was* a change, a discernible change, and it had nothing to do with strident alarms provoked by a single screaming voice. The discordant sounds themselves had become subdued, replaced by shrugs and relaxed gestures indicating inability to comprehend. The word *Amerikaner* was repeated everywhere. The panic initially ignited by the news had passed. An American had killed an American; it was not a German assassin, or a Communist, or even a terrorist who had eluded the Federal Republic's security arrangements. Life could go on; Deutschland could not be held responsible for the death—and the citizens of Bonn breathed a sigh of relief.

Converse spun around the corner of a brick building and stared across the square at the tables of the bakery-café. The student, Johann, remained in his chair, his head bowed, supported by both hands, reading the newspaper. Then he got up and walked into the bakery itself. *Was there a telephone inside? Would he talk to someone?*

How long can I wait? thought Converse, prepared to run, as instinct held him back.

Johann came out of the bakery carrying a tray of coffee and rolls. He sat down and meticulously separated the plates from the tray and once again stared at the newspaper in front of him. Then he looked up at nothing in particular—as if he knew he was being watched by unseen eyes—and nodded once.

Another risk-taker, thought Joel, as he turned and looked and listened to the unfamiliar sights and sounds of the side street he had entered. He had been given a few hours; he wished he knew how to use them—he wished he knew what to *do*.

Valerie ran to the phone. If it was another reporter, she would say the same thing she had said to the last five. *I don't believe a word of it and I've nothing more to say!* And if it was one more person from Washington—from the FBI or the CIA or the VA or any other combinations of the alphabet—she would scream! She had spent three hours being interviewed that morning until she had literally ordered the crucifiers out of the house. They were liars trying to force her to support their lies. It would be far easier to take the phone off the hook, but she could not do that. She had called Lawrence Talbot in New York twice, telling his office to trace him wherever he was and have him call her back. It was all madness. *Insanity!* as Joel used to say with such quiet intensity she thought his voice was a wild roar of protest.

"Hello?"

"*Valley?* It's Roger."

"*Dad!*" Only one person had ever called her by that name and that man was her former father-in-law. The fact that she was no longer married to his son had made no difference in their relationship. She adored the old pilot and knew he felt the same about her. "Where *are* you? Ginny didn't know and she's frantic. You forgot to turn on your answering machine."

"I didn't forget, Valley. Too damned many people to call back. I just flew in from Hong Kong, and when I got off the plane I was upwinded by fifty or sixty screaming newspaper people and so many lights and cameras I won't be able to see or hear for a week."

"Some enterprising airline clerk let out the word you were on board. Whoever it was will eat for a week off a generous expense account. Where are you?"

"Still at the airport—in the traffic manager's office. I'll say this for 'em, they got me out of there. . . . Valley, I just read the papers. They got me the latest editions. What the *hell* is this all about?"

"I don't know, Dad, but I do know it's a lie."

"That boy's the sanest thing I ever had anything to do with! They're twisting everything, making the good things he did into something . . . I don't know, sinister or something. He's too damned *up-front* to be crazy!"

"He's not crazy, Roger. He's being taken, he's being put through a wringer."

"What *for?*"

"I don't know. But I think Larry Talbot does—at least more than he's told me."

"What *has* he told you?"

"Not now, Dad. Later."

"Why?"

"I'm not sure. . . . Something I feel, perhaps."

"You're not making sense, Valley."

"I'm sorry."

"What did Ginny say? I'll call her, of course."

"She's hysterical."

"She always was—a little bit."

"No, not that way. She's blaming herself. She thinks people are striking out at her brother for the things *she* did in the sixties. I tried to tell her that was nonsense, but I'm afraid I made it worse. She asked me perfectly calmly if I believed what was being said about Joel. I told her of course I didn't."

"The old paranoia. Three kids and an accountant for a husband and it still comes back. I never could handle that girl. Damned good pilot, though. Soloed before Joel, and she was two years younger. I'll phone her."

"You may not be able to reach her."

"Oh?"

"She's having her number changed, and I think you should do the same thing. I know I'm going to the minute I hear from Larry."

"Valley . . ." Roger Converse paused. "Don't do that."

"Why not? Have you any idea what it's been *like* here?"

"Look, you know I've never asked what happened between you and Joel, but I usually have dinner with that piss ant lawyer once a week when I'm in town. He thinks it's some kind of filial necessity, but I'd knock it off in a minute if I didn't like him. I mean he's a likable guy, kind of funny sometimes."

"I know all that, Roger. What are you

trying to say?"

"*They* say he disappeared, that no one can find him."

"And?"

"He may call you. I can't think of anyone else he would call."

Valerie closed her eyes; the afternoon sun through the skylight was blinding. "Is that based on your weekly dinner conversations?"

"It's not intuition. I never had any except in the air. . . . Of course it is. It was never said outright, but it was always just below the cloud cover."

"You're impossible, Dad."

"Pilot error's like any other. There are times when you can't afford it. . . . Don't change your number, Valley."

"I won't."

"Now, what about me?"

"Ginny's husband had a good idea. They're referring all questions to their attorney. Maybe you should do the same. Do you have one?"

"Sure," said Roger Converse. "I got three. Talbot, Brooks and Simon. Nate's the best, if you want to know the truth. Did you know that at the age of sixty-seven that son of a bitch took up flying? He's qualified in multiengines now—can you imagine?"

"*Dad!*" Valerie broke in suddenly. "You're at the airport?"

"That's what I said. Kennedy."

"Don't go home. Don't go to your apartment. Take the first plane you can to Boston. Use another name. Call me back and let me know

557

what flight you're on. I'll pick you up."

"*Why?*"

"Just do as I say, Roger. *Please!*"

"What for?"

"You're staying here. I'm leaving."

21

Converse hurried out of the clothing store on the crowded Bornheimer Strasse and studied his reflection in the window. He surveyed the overall effect of his purchases, not as a customer inside in front of the full-length mirror for fit and appearance, but as one of the strolling pedestrians on the sidewalk. He was satisfied; there was nothing about the clothes that called attention to him. The photograph in the papers—the only one in the past fifteen years that would be in a wire service or newspaper file—was taken about a year ago when he was one of several merger attorneys interviewed by Reuters. It was a head-and-shoulders shot, showing him in his lawyer's clothes—a dark suit and vest, white shirt and striped tie—the image of a rising international specialist. It was also the image everyone who read the papers had of him, and since it would not change but only spread with later editions, then he was the one who had to change.

Also, he could not continue to wear the clothes he had worn to the bank. A panicked Lachmann would undoubtedly give a complete description to the police, but even if his panic rendered him silent, he had seen him in a dark jacket, white shirt and striped tie. Unconsciously or not, thought Joel, he had sought a patina of respectability. Perhaps all men running for their lives did so because their essential dignity had been stolen from them. Regardless, dressed in those clothes he was the man in the newspaper photograph.

The appearance he had in mind belonged to a history professor he had known in college, a man whose various articles of clothing were all related. His jackets were subdued tweeds with elbow patches, the trousers gray—heavy or light flannel, never anything else—and his shirts were blue buttoned-down oxford, again without exception. Above his thick horn-rimmed glasses was perched a soft Irish walking hat, the brim sloped downward front and back. Wherever that man went, whether down a street in Boston or New York's Fifth Avenue or Beverly Hills' Rodeo Drive—the last a place that Joel was sure he never saw—one would know he belonged to academic New England.

Converse had managed to duplicate the outward appearance of the man in his memory, except for the tinted glasses, which he would have to replace with horn rims. He had passed a large variety store, Bonn's equivalent of an American five-and-dime, and he knew that there would be a counter with glasses of different sizes and shapes, a few slightly magnified for reading, others clear.

For reasons that were only beginning to come into focus, those glasses were now vital to him. Then he understood. He was preoccupied with what he knew he *could* do—change his appearance. He was procrastinating, uncertain what to do next, not sure he was capable of doing anything.

He looked at his face in the oval mirror of the variety store, again satisfied with what he saw. The ersatz tortoiseshell rims were thick, the glass clear; the effect was owlish, scholarly. He was no longer the man in the newspaper photograph, and equally important, the concentration he had devoted to his appearance had begun to clear his mind. He could think again, sit down somewhere and sort things out. He also needed food and a drink.

The café was crowded, the stained-glass windows muting the summer sunlight into shafts of blue and red piercing the smoke. He was shown to a table against the black-leather upholstered banquette, assured by the maître d', or whoever he was, that all he had to do was request a menu in English; the items were numbered. Whisky on the Continent, however, was universally accepted as Scotch; he ordered a double, and took out the pad and ball-point pen he had picked up at the variety store. His drink came and he proceeded to write.

> *Connal Fitzpatrick?*
> *Briefcase?*
> *$93,000 plus*
> *Embassy out*
> *No Larry Talbot et al.*
> *No Beale*
> *No Anstett*

560

No man in San Francisco
Men in Washington. Who?
Caleb Dowling? No.
Hickman, Navy, San Diego? Possible.
. . . Mattilon?

René! Why hadn't he thought of Mattilon before? He understood why the Frenchman made the remarks attributed to him anonymously in the newspaper story. René was trying to be protective. If there was no defense, or if it was so weak so as not to be viable, the most logical backup was temporary insanity. Joel circled Mattilon's name and wrote the number 1 on the left, circling it also. He would find a telephone exchange in the streets, the kind where operators assigned booths to bewildered tourists, and call René in Paris. He took two swallows of whisky, relaxing as the warmth spread through him, then went back to his list, starting at the top.

Connal . . . ? The presumption that he had been killed was inevitable, but it was not conclusive. If he was alive, he was being held for whatever information could be pried out of him. As the chief legal officer of the West Coast's largest and most powerful naval base, and a man who had a history of meetings with the State Department's Office of Munitions Control as well as its counterparts at the Pentagon, Fitzpatrick could be an asset to the men of Aquitaine. Yet to call attention to him was to guarantee his execution, if he had not been killed already. If he was still alive, the only way to save him was to find him, but not in any orthodox or official manner; it had to be done secretly. Connal had to be rescued secretly.

Suddenly, Joel saw the figure of a man in the uniform of the United States Army across the room talking with two civilians at the bar. He did not know the man. It was the uniform that struck him. It brought to mind the military chargé d'affaires at the embassy, that extraordinarily observant and precise officer who was capable of seeing a man who was not at a bridge at the exact moment he was not there. A liar for Aquitaine, someone whose lies identified him. If that liar did not know where Fitzpatrick was, he could be made to find out. Perhaps there was a way, after all. Converse drew a line on the right side of his list, connecting Connal Fitzpatrick with Admiral Hickman in San Diego. He did not give it a number; there was too much to consider.

Briefcase? He was still convinced that Leifhelm's men had not found it. If the generals of Aquitaine had that attaché case, they would have let him know. It was not like those men to conceal such a prize, not from the prisoner who had thought he was a match for them. No, they would have told him one way or another, if only to make clear to him how totally he had failed. If he was right, Connal had hidden it. At the inn called Das Rektorat? It was worth a try. Joel circled the word *Briefcase* and numbered it 2.

"Speisekarte, mein Herr?" said a waiter before Converse knew he was standing there.

"English, please?"

"Certainly, sir." The waiter separated his menus as though they were an outsized deck of cards. He selected one and handed it to Joel as he spoke. "The *Spezialität* for today is *Wiener-schnitzel*—it is the same in English."

"That's fine. Keep the menu, I'll take it."

"Danke." The man swept away before Joel could order another drink. It was just as well, he thought.

$93,000 plus. There was nothing more to be said; the irritating bulge around his waist said it all. He had the money; it was to be used.

Embassy out . . . No Larry Talbot et al. . . . No Beale . . . No Anstett . . . No man in San Francisco. Throughout the meal he thought about each item, each statement, wondering how it all could have happened. Every step had been considered carefully, facts absorbed, dossiers memorized, caution uppermost. But everything had been blown away by complications far beyond the simple facts provided by Preston Halliday in Geneva.

Build just two or three cases that are tied to Delavane—even circumstantially—and it'll be enough.

In light of the revelations on Mykonos, then in Paris, Copenhagen and Bonn, the simplicity of that remark was almost criminal. Halliday would have been appalled at the depth and the breadth of influence Delavane's legions had attained, at the penetrations they had made at the highest levels of the military, the police, Interpol and, obviously, now those who controlled the flow of news from so-called authoritative sources in Western governments.

Converse abruptly checked his racing thoughts.

He suddenly realized that he was thinking about Halliday in the context of a man who saw only a pair of eyes at night in the jungle, unaware of the size or the ferocity of the unseen animal in the darkness. That was wrong. Halliday knew the materials Beale was handing over to him on an island in the Aegean; he knew about the connections between Paris, Bonn, Tel Aviv and Johannesburg; he knew about the decision makers in the State Department and the Pentagon—he knew it *all!* He had arranged it all with unknown men in Washington! Halliday had lied in Geneva. A California wrestler he had befriended years ago in school named Avery Fowler was the manipulator, and in the name of A. Preston Halliday, he had lied.

Where were those subterranean men in Washington who had the audacity to raise half a million dollars for an incredible gamble but were too frightened to come out in the open? What kind of men *were* they? Their scout had been killed, their puppet accused of being a psychopathic assassin. How long could they *wait? What* were they?

The questions disturbed Converse so much that he tried not to pursue them—they would lead only to rage, which would blind his reason. He needed reason and, above all, the strength that came with awareness.

It was time to find a telephone exchange and reach Mattilon in Paris. René would believe him, René would help him. It was unthinkable that his old friend would do anything else.

The civilian walked in silence to the hotel window, knowing he was expected to deliver a pronouncement that would form the basis of a miracle—not a solution but a miracle, and there were no such things in the business he knew so well. Peter Stone was by all the rules a relic, a castaway who had seen it all, and in the final years of seeing had finally fallen apart. Alcohol had taken the place of true audacity, at the end rendering him a professional mutant, a part of him still proud of past accomplishments, another part sickened by the waste, by the knowledge of wasted lives, wasted strategies—morality thrown into a gargantuan wastebasket of a collective nonconscience.

Still, he had once been one of the best—he could not forget that. And when he knew it was all over, he had faced the fact that he was killing himself with a plethora of bourbon and self-pity. He had pulled out. But not before he had gained the enmity of his past employers in the Central Intelligence Agency, not for speaking out publicly but for telling them privately who and what they were. Fortunately, as sobriety returned he learned that his past employers had other enemies in Washington, enemies having nothing to do with foreign entanglements or competition. Simply men and women serving the republic who wanted to know what the hell was going on when Langley wouldn't tell them. He had survived—was surviving. He thought about these things, knowing that the two other men in the room believed he was concentrating on the issue at hand.

There was no issue. The file was closed, the border rimmed in black. The two who were with him were so young—God, so *damned* young!— they would find it too terrible to accept. He remembered, vaguely, when such a conclusion would have appalled him. But that was nearly forty years ago; he was almost sixty now, and he had heard such conclusions repeated too often to shed tears of regret. The regret—the sadness was there—but time and repetition had dulled his senses; clear evaluation was everything.

Stone turned and said with quiet authority, "We can't *do anything.*" The Army captain and the Navy lieutenant were visibly upset. Peter Stone continued, "I spent twenty-three years in the tunnels, including a decade with Angleton, and I'm telling you there's absolutely nothing we can do. We have to let him hang out, we can't touch him."

"Because we can't *afford* to?" asked the naval officer scathingly. "That's what you said when Halliday was killed in Geneva. We can't *afford* to!"

"We can't. We were outmaneuvered."

"That's a *man* out there," insisted the lieutenant. *"We sent* him out—"

"And they set him up," the civilian broke in, his voice calm, his eyes sadly knowledgeable. "He's as good as dead. We'll have to start looking elsewhere."

"Why is that?" asked the Army captain. "Why is he as good as dead?"

"They have too many controls, we can see that now. If they don't have him locked up in a cellar, they know pretty much where he is. Whoever finds him will kill him. A riddled body of a crazed killer is delivered up and there's a collective sigh of relief. That's the scenario."

"And that's the most cold-blooded analysis of a murder I've ever heard! *Murder,* an unwarranted execution!"

"Look, Lieutenant," said Stone, stepping away from the window, "you asked me to come with you—convinced me I should—because you wanted some experience in this room. With that experience comes the moment when you recognize and accept the fact that you've been beaten. It doesn't mean you're finished, but you've been punched out of the round. We've been punched out, and it's my guess the punches haven't stopped yet."

"Maybe . . ." began the captain haltingly. "Maybe we should go to the Agency, tell them everything we know—everything we *think* we know—and what we've done. It might get Converse out alive."

"Sorry," countered the former CIA man. "They want his head and they'll get it. They wouldn't have gone to all this trouble if 'dead' wasn't written all over him. He found out something, or they found out something about him. That's the way it works."

"What kind of world do you live in?" asked the naval officer quietly, shaking his head.

"I don't live in it anymore, Lieutenant, you know that. I think it's one of the reasons you came to me. I did what you two—and whoever else is with you—are doing now. I blew a whistle—only, I did it with two months of bourbon in my veins and ten years of disgust in my head. You say you might go to the Company? Good, go ahead, but you'll do it without me. No one worth a quarter in Langley will touch me."

"We can't go to G-Two or naval intelligence," said the Army officer. "We know that, we've all agreed. Delavane's people are there; they'd shoot us down."

"Aptly put, Captain. Would you believe with real bullets?"

"*I* do now," said the Navy man, nodding at Stone. "The report out of San Diego is that the legal, Remington, was killed in an automobile accident in La Jolla. He's the one who last spoke to Fitzpatrick, and before he left the base, he asked another legal the directions to a restaurant in the hills. He'd never been there—and I don't think it was an accident."

"Neither do I," agreed the civilian. "But it takes us to the somewhere else we can look."

"What do you mean?" said the Army captain.

"Fitzpatrick. SAND PAC can't find him, right?"

"He's on leave," interjected the naval officer. "He's got another twenty days or so. He wasn't ordered to list his itinerary."

"Still, they've tried to find him but they can't."

"And I still don't understand," objected the captain.

"We go after Fitzpatrick," said Stone. "Out of San Diego, not Washington. We find a reason to *really* want him back. A SAND PAC emergency, routed strictly through Eyes Only, a base problem—nobody else's."

"I hate to repeat myself," said the Army man, "but you've lost me. Where do we start? Whom do we start with?"

"With one of your own, Captain. Right now he's a very important person. The chargé d'affaires at the Mehlemer House."

"The what?"

"The American embassy in Bonn. He's one of them. He lied when it counted most," said Stone. "His name is Washburn. Major Norman Anthony Washburn, the Fourth."

The telephone complex was off the lobby of an office building. It was a large square room with five enclosed booths built into three walls and a high, squared counter in the center where four operators sat in front of consoles, each woman obviously capable of speaking two or more languages. Telephone directories of the major European cities and their suburbs were on racks to the left and right of the entrance; small pads with attached ball-point pens had been placed on the ledges above for the convenience of those seeking numbers. The routine was familiar: a caller delivered a written-out number to an operator, specified the manner of payment—cash, credit card or collect—and was assigned a booth. There were no lines; a half-dozen booths were empty.

Joel found the number of Mattilon's law firm in the Paris directory. He wrote it out, brought it to an operator and said he would pay in cash. He was told to go to booth number seven and wait for the ring. He entered it quickly, the soft cloth brim of his hat falling over his forehead above the tortoiseshell glasses. Any enclosure, whether a toilet stall or a glass booth, was preferable to being out in the open. He felt his pulse accelerating; it seemed to explode when the bell rang.

"*Saint-Pierre, Nelli, et Mattilon,*" said the female voice in Paris.

"Monsieur Mattilon, please—*s'il vous plaît.*"

"*Votre* . . . ?" The woman stopped, undoubtedly recognizing an American's abysmal attempt at French. "Who may I say is calling, please?"

"His friend from New York. He'll know. I'm a client."

René did know. After several clicks his strained voice came on the line. "Joel?" he whispered. "I don't *believe* it!"

"Don't," said Converse. "It's not true—not what they say about Geneva or Bonn, not even what *you* said. I had nothing to do with those killings, and Paris was an accident. I had every reason to think—I *did* think—that man was reaching for a gun."

"Why didn't you stay where you *were*, then, my friend?"

"Because they wanted to stop me from going on. It's what I honestly believed, and I couldn't let them do that. Let me talk. . . . At the George Cinq you asked me questions and I gave you evasive answers and I think you saw through me. But you were kind and went along. You have nothing to be sorry about, take my word for

570

it—my very *sane* word. Bertholdier came to me that evening in my room; we talked and he panicked. Six days ago I saw him again here in Bonn—only, this time it was different. He was ordered to be there, along with three other very powerful men, two generals and a former field marshal. It's a cabal, René, an international cabal, and they can pull it off. Everything's secret and moving fast. They've recruited key military personnel all over Europe, the Mediterranean, Canada, and the U.S. There's no way to tell who's with them and who isn't—and there isn't time to make a mistake. They've got millions at their disposal, warehouses all over filled with munitions ready to ship to their people when the moment comes."

"The moment?" Mattilon broke in. "What moment?"

"Please," insisted Joel, rushing ahead. "They've been funneling weapons and explosives to maniacs everywhere—terrorists, provos, certified lunatics—with one purpose only: destabilization through violence. It's their excuse to move in. Right now they're blowing up Northern Ireland."

"The madness in *Ulster?*" interrupted the Frenchman again. "The horrors going on—"

"It's *their* horror! It's a trial run. They did it with one massive shipment from the States—to prove they *can* do it! But Ireland's only a test, a minor exercise. The big explosion's coming in a matter of days, a few weeks at most. I've got to reach the people who can stop them, and I can't do that if I'm dead!" Converse paused, only to

571

catch his breath, giving Mattilon no chance to speak. "These are the men I was after, René —after *legally,* to build a few cases against them, expose them in the courts before they got anywhere. But then, I found out. They're already there. I was too late."

"But why *you?*"

"It started in Geneva—with Halliday, the man who was shot to death. He was killed by their gunmen, but not before he recruited me. You asked me about Geneva and I lied to you, but that's the truth. Now, you'll either help me, or try to help me, or you won't. Not for me—I'm insignificant—but what I got roped into isn't. And I *was* roped into it, I know that now. But I've seen them, *talked* to them, and they're so goddamned logical, so fucking persuasive, they'll turn all Europe fascist; they'll set up a military federation with my country the progenitor. Because it started in my country; it started in San Francisco with a man named Delavane."

"Saigon? The Mad Marcus of *Saigon?*"

"Alive and well and living in Palo Alto, pushing his military buttons all over the place. He's still a magnet and they're drawn to him like flies to a pig."

"Joel, are you . . . are you . . . all *right?*"

"Let's put it this way, René. I took a lousy watch off a man who guarded me—a paranoid who nevertheless was nice to me—and it's got a sweep hand. You've got thirty seconds to think about what I've told you, then I'll hang up. *Now,* old friend, twenty-nine seconds."

Ten passed and Mattilon spoke. "An insane

572

man does not deliver such a precise explanation so precisely. Very well, perhaps I am mad, too, but what you speak of—God knows the times are right, what else can I say? *Everything* is crazy!"

"I've got to get back to the States alive, to Washington. I know people there. If I can reach them and show myself for what I am, they'll listen to me. Can you help?"

"I have contacts in the Quai d'Orsay. Let me go to them."

"*No,*" objected Converse. "They know we're friends. One word to the wrong person and you'd be killed. Forgive me, but more important, your talking would set off alarms. We can't afford that."

"Very well," said Mattilon. "There is a man in Amsterdam—don't ask me how I know him—who can arrange such things. I assume you have no passport."

"I have one but it's not mine. It's German. I took it off a guard who was ready to put a bullet in my head."

"Then I'm sure he's not in a position to complain to the authorities."

"He's not."

"In your mind you really did go back, didn't you, my friend?"

"Let's not talk about it, okay?"

"*Bien.* You are you. Keep that passport; it will be useful."

"Amsterdam. How do I get there?"

"You are in Bonn, no?"

"Yes."

"There is a train to Emmerich on the Dutch

border. In Emmerich, switch to local transport
—streetcars, autobuses, whatever. The customs
are lax, especially during the peak hours when
workers go back and forth. No one looks, so just
show the passport you have quickly, partially
covering the photograph, perhaps. It's good that
it's German. You should have no trouble."

"Suppose I do?"

"Then I can't help you, my friend. I'm being
honest. And then I *must* go to the Quai d'Orsay."

"All right. I get across, then what?"

"You'll reach Arnhem. From there you take
the train to Amsterdam."

"And then?"

"The man. His name is on a card in my bottom
drawer. Do you have something to write on
—write with?"

"Go ahead," said Converse, reaching for the
note pad and the ballpoint pen on the ledge
beneath the telephone.

"Here it is. Thorbecke. Cort Thorbecke. The
apartment house is on the southwest corner of
Utrechtsestraat and Kerkstraat. The telephone
number is zero-two-zero, four-one-one-three-zero.
When you call for an appointment, tell him you
are a member of the Tatiana family. Do you have
that? *Tatiana.*"

"René?" said Joel, writing. "I never would
have guessed. How come you know someone like
this?"

"I told you not to ask, but on the other hand
he may probe and you should have at least vague
answers—everything was always vague. Tatiana is
a Russian name, one of the Czar's daughters

574

reputedly executed at Ekaterinburg in 1918. I say 'reputedly' because many believe she was spared along with her sister Anastasia and smuggled out with a nurse who had a fortune in jewels on her. The nurse favored Tatiana and, once free, gave everything to the child and nothing to her sister. It's said she lived anonymously in great wealth—may even be living today—but no one knows where."

"That's what I have to know?" asked Converse.

"No, it's merely the origins of its present meaning. Today it is a symbol of trust given to very few people in recent years, people who themselves are trusted by the most suspicious men on earth, men who cannot afford to make mistakes."

"Good Lord, who?"

"Russians, powerful Soviet commissars who have a fondness for Western banking, who broker money out of Moscow for investments. You can understand why the circle is small. Few are called and fewer chosen. Thorbecke is one of them, and he does an extensive business in passports. I'll reach him and tell him to expect your call. Remember, no name, just Tatiana. He'll have you on a KLM to Washington in short order. You'll need money, however, so we must think how I can—"

"Money's one thing I don't need," interrupted Converse. "Just a passport and a plane ticket to Dulles Airport without being picked up."

"Get to Amsterdam. Thorbecke will help."

"Thank you, René. I wanted to count on you

and you came through. It means a lot to me. It means my life.''

"You're not in Washington yet, my friend. But call me when you get there, no matter the hour.''

"I will. Thanks, again.''

Joel hung up, put the note pad and the pen into his pocket, and went out of the booth to the counter. He asked for his charges, and while the English-speaking operator was getting them he remembered the item he had marked 2 on his list. His attaché case with the dossiers and the names of the decision makers at the Pentagon and the State Department. Das Rektorat. Through some extraordinary oversight on Leifhelm's part, had Connal managed to hide it somewhere? Could it have been found perhaps by an employee at the country inn? Converse spoke to the operator who was handing him his bill.

"There's a place called Das Rektorat. It's a hotel in the countryside—where I'm not sure, but I'd like to call it and reach the manager. I'm told he speaks English.''

"Yes, sir. Das Rektorat has splendid accommodations, if they are available.''

"I'm not looking for a reservation. A friend of mine stayed there last week and thinks he may have left a valuable item in his room. He called me and asked me to check for him, to speak with the manager. If I find the number, would you place the call for me and get him on the line? I'm sorry to say I don't speak German; I'd probably reach the chef.''

"Certainly, sir,'' replied the woman, smiling. "It would be easier for me to get the number.

Return to booth seven and I'll ring you. You can pay for both calls when you are finished.''

Inside the glass enclosure Joel lit a cigarette, thinking about what he was going to say. He barely had time to formulate his words when the ring came.

"This is the *Vorsteher*—the manager—of Das Rektorat, sir," said the operator. "And he does speak English."

"Thank you." The operator broke off her connection. "Hello?"

"Yes, may I help you, sir?"

"I hope so. I'm an American friend of Commander Connal Fitzpatrick, chief legal officer of the San Diego Naval Base in California. I understand he stayed there last week."

"Indeed he did, sir. We were so sorry we could not have extended his visit with us, but there was a prior reservation."

"Oh? He left unexpectedly?"

"I shouldn't put it that way. We spoke in the morning and I believe he understood our situation. I myself made arrangements for a taxi."

"He was alone when he left?"

"Yes, sir."

"Oh. Then if you'll tell me which hotel he went to, I can check there as well."

"Check, sir?"

"The Commander misplaced one of his briefcases, a flat leather type with two combination locks. The contents are of no value except to him, but he very much wants to find it. It was a present from his wife, I think. Have you come across it?"

"No, sir."

"Are you *sure?* The commander has a habit of concealing his legal papers, sometimes under a bed or in the back of a closet."

"He left nothing here, sir. The room was thoroughly examined and cleaned by our staff."

"Perhaps someone came to see him and took the wrong case." Converse knew he was pressing but there was no reason not to.

"He had no visitors." The German paused. "Just one moment, I do recall now."

"Yes?"

"You say a flat briefcase, what is generally referred to as an attaché case?"

"Yes!"

"He carried it with him. It was in his hand when he left."

"Oh . . ." Joel tried to recover quickly. "Then if you'll just tell me what forwarding address he left, what hotel he went to."

"I'm sorry, sir. There were no such instructions."

"Somebody had to make a reservation for him! Rooms are tight in Bonn!"

"Please, sir. I myself offered to try, but he refused my aid—somewhat discourteously, I might add."

"I'm sorry." Joel was annoyed that he had lost control. "Those legal papers were important. Then you have no idea where he went?"

"But I do, sir, if one wishes to be humored. I made a point of asking. He said he was going to the *Bahnhof,* the train station. If anyone asked for him, we were to say he was sleeping in a

578

baggage locker. I'm afraid it was also meant discourteously."

The *train* station? A locker! It was a *message!* Fitzpatrick was telling him where to look! Without speaking further, Converse hung up the phone, left the booth, and went to the counter. He paid for both calls and thanked the operator, wanting to leave her a tip but knowing it would only call attention to him. "You've been very kind and, if I may, one last favor."

"Sir?"

"Where is the train station?"

"You can't miss it. Turn left out of the building and walk four streets, then left again for two more. It is one of the more uncertain prides of Bonn."

"You've been very kind."

Joel hurried down the pavement, constantly reminding himself to check his speed. Everything depended on control now, *everything*. Every move he made had to be normal, even casual, nothing to cause anyone to take a second glance at him. Mattilon had told him to take a train; Fitzpatrick had told him to go to the train station—a locker! It was another omen! He was beginning to think that such a thing *did* exist.

He walked through the large open doors of the entrance and turned to his right toward the row of lockers where he had left the attaché case before heading out to the Alter Zoll to meet "Avery Fowler." He reached the locker itself; there was a key in it, nothing inside. He began scrutinizing the lockers around it, on both sides, below, not at all sure what he was looking for but knowing there would be *something*. He found it! Two rows above on the left! The initials were small but clear, scratched into the metal by a strong, precise hand: *C.F.* Connal Fitzpatrick!

The Navy lawyer had done it! He had put the explosive papers back where only the two of them knew where they would be. Suddenly Converse felt sick. How could he get them out? How could he get *inside?* He looked around the station at the summer crowds. The huge clock read two-thirty; in two and a half hours the offices would be closed, the business day over, the crowds fuller. Mattilon had told him to reach Emmerich during the busiest time, when workers traveled back and forth across the border at the end of the day, and it took nearly two hours to reach Emmerich, *if* there was a train. He had less than a half hour to get inside the locker.

There was an information booth at the far end of the cavernous station. He walked toward it, his mind again racing, choosing words that might produce a key. The abrasive weight of the money belt around his waist gave him a glimpse of hope.

"Thank you very much," he said to the clerk, his tortoiseshell glasses perched on his nose, the cloth hat falling over his forehead. He had been assigned an English-speaking, middle-aged information dispenser with a pinched face and a bored, irritated expression. "Quite simply I've lost the key to the locker in which I stored my luggage and I have to get a train to Emmerich. By the way, when is the next one?"

"*Ach,* it is always ze case," replied the clerk, thumbing a schedule. "Nozzing but trouble wiz zer sommer people. You lose ziss, you lose zat; and you expect everyone to help you! Zer train for Emmerich left twenty-seven minutes ago. Zer iss another in nineteen *minuten,* but nozzing after that for an hour.''

''Thank you. I have to be on it. Now, about the locker?'' Joel removed a hundred-deutsche-mark note below the counter and raised it slowly above the ledge. ''It's very important that I get my luggage and take that train. May I shake your hand for helping me?''

''It will be done!'' exclaimed the clerk quietly, looking to his right and left, as he grasped Converse's hand and the money. He picked up the phone at his side and dialed abusively. *''Schnell! Wir müssen ein Schliessfach offnen. Standort zehn Auskunft!''* He slammed down the phone and looked up at Joel, a smile sculpted onto his rigid lips. ''A man will be here instantly to be of service. We are always eager to be of service. The *Amerikanen,* so thoughtful.''

The man came, bulging out of his railroad uniform, his eyes dull, his authority questionable. *''Was ist?''*

The clerk explained in German, then looked again at Converse. ''He speaks some English, not well, of course, but adequately, and he will assist you.''

''Zer are our regulations,'' said the official keeper of the locker keys. ''Come, show me.''

''Happy birthday,'' said Joel to the clerk behind the information booth.

''It is not my birthday, sir.''

''How would you know?'' asked Converse,

smiling, taking the fat man's arm.

"Zer are procedures," said the railroad bureaucrat, opening the locker with a master key. "You will sign for zer contents at zer office."

It was *there!* His attaché case was on its side, nothing broken or slashed. He reached into his pocket and took out his money. "I'm in a great hurry," he said as he slipped out first a hundred-deutsche-mark note, then, with hesitation, another. "My train leaves in a few minutes." He shook the German's hand, passing the money, and asked calmly but with cheerful friendliness in his eyes. "Couldn't you say it was a mistake?"

"It *vas* a mistake!" answered the uniformed man enthusiastically. "You must catch a train!"

"Thank you. You're a nice person. Happy birthday."

"*Was?*"

"I know, don't bother. Thank you again."

Glancing around rapidly but subtly, hoping against hope that no one was watching him, Joel walked to an unoccupied wooden bench against the wall, sat down, and opened the attaché case—everything was there. But he could not keep it. Again he looked around the station, knowing what he had to find; he saw it. A drugstore or its equivalent; there would be envelopes somewhere inside. He closed the briefcase and got up, trusting someone in the store would speak English.

"Nearly all of us speak English," said the matronly woman behind the counter near the stationery section. "It is practically a requirement,

582

especially during the summer months. What are your needs?''

''I have to send a business report back to the United States,'' answered Converse, a large, thick envelope and a roll of tape in his right hand, the attaché case in his left, ''but my train leaves in a few minutes and I don't have time to get to a post office.''

''There are several post-collection boxes in the *Bahnhof,* sir.''

''I need stamps, postage. I don't know how much,'' said Joel helplessly.

''If you will put your materials in the envelope, seal it and address it, I shall weigh the package and suggest the appropriate amount of stamping. We keep sheets here for convenience, but they are more expensive than in the post office.''

''It doesn't matter. I'd like it to go air-mail, with more postage rather than less.'' Five minutes later Converse handed the accommodating clerk the heavily sealed package for weighing. He had written a note on the top of the first dossier and printed the address clearly on the front of the envelope. The woman returned with the appropriate postage. He paid her and placed the envelope on the counter in front of him.

''Thank you,'' he said, looking at his watch, as he began frantically licking the stamps and securing them. ''Would you by any chance know where I can buy a ticket to . . . Emmerich, or Arnhem, I guess?''

''Emmerich is German, Arnhem is Dutch. Any stall, sir.''

"I may not have time," said Joel, on the last three stamps. "I suppose I could buy one on the train."

"They will not stop it if you have money."

"There." He had finished. "Where's the nearest mailbox—collection box?"

"At the other end of the *Bahnhof.*"

Again Joel looked at his watch, and again his chest began to pound as he ran out into the station; then instantly checking himself, he watched the crowds for anyone who might be watching him. He had less than eight minutes to mail the envelope, buy a ticket and find the train. Depending on the complications, perhaps he could eliminate the second step. But to pay his fare on board would mean engaging in conversation, conceivably having to find someone to translate —the possibilities and the possible consequences were frightening.

As he feverishly looked for the mailbox, he kept repeating to himself the exact words he had scribbled on the top of the first dossier's cover: *Do not—repeat, do not—let anyone know you have this. If you don't hear from me within five days, send it to Nathan S. I'll call him if I can. Your once and obedient husband. Love, J.* He then looked down at the name and the address he had written on the envelope in his hand and wondered, stricken by a dull, sickening pain—how could he do this to her?

Ms. Valerie Charpentier
R.F.D. 16
Dunes Ridge

Three minutes later he found a mailbox and deposited the envelope, opening and closing the slot several times to make sure it had fallen inside. He looked around at the signs everywhere, the German script confusing him, the lines in front of the windows discouraging him. He felt helpless, wanting to ask questions but afraid of stopping anyone, afraid that someone would study his face.

There was a window across the station, far away on the other side; two couples had left the line—four people with a sudden change of plans. Only one person was left. Converse hurried through the crowds, once again trying to hold himself in check and minimizing his movements.

"Emmerich, please," he said to the clerk, as the lone customer finally left the window. "Netherlands." he added, enunciating clearly.

The attendant briefly turned and looked at the clock on the wall behind him. Then he spoke in German, the phrases fast and guttural. *"Verstehen?"* he asked.

"Nein . . . Here!" Converse put three hundred-deutsche-mark notes on the ledge of the counter, shaking his head, shrugging. "Please, a ticket! I know, I've only got a few minutes."

The man took two of the bills, shoving the third back. He made change and pressed several buttons beneath him; a ticket spewed out and he handed it to Joel. *"Danke. Zwei Minuten!"*

"The track. What *track?* Can you understand? Where?"

"Wo?"

"Yes, yes that's it! Where?"

"Acht."

"What?" Then Converse held up his right hand, raising and lowering the fingers to indicate numbers.

The attendant responded by holding up both hands, a five-finger spread and three middle fingers. *"Acht,"* he repeated, pointing across the station to Joel's left.

"Eight! Thank you." Converse began walking as fast as possible without breaking into a run. He saw the gate through the throngs of people; a conductor was making an announcement while looking at his watch and backing into the archway.

A woman carrying packages collided with him, careening into his left shoulder, the bundles plummeting out of her arms, scattering on the floor. He tried to apologize through the abuse she hurled at him, loud words that caused the surrounding travelers to stop and gape. He picked up several shopping bags as the woman's barking voice reached a crescendo.

"Up yours, lady," he mumbled, dropping the packages and turning, now running to the closing gate. The conductor saw him and pushed it open.

He got to his seat, gasping, his soft hat pulled down over his forehead. The wound in his left arm was aching sharply, and he thought he might have ripped it open in the collision. He felt under his jacket, past the handle of the gun he had taken from Leifhelm's chauffeur. There was no blood and he closed his eyes briefly in relief.

He was oblivious of the man across the aisle who was staring at him.

In Paris, the secretary sat at her desk speaking on the telephone in a low voice that was muted further by her cupped hand over the mouthpiece. Her Parisian French was cultured if not aristocratic.

"That is everything," she said quietly. "Do you have it?"

"Yes," said the man on the other end of the line. "It's extraordinary."

"Why? It's the reason I'm here."

"Of course. I should say *you're* extraordinary."

"Of course. What are your instructions?"

"The gravest. I'm afraid."

"I thought so. You have no choice."

"Can you?"

"It's done. I'll see you at Taillevent. Eight o'clock?"

"Wear your black Galanos. I adore it so."

"The Great Spike anticipates."

"It is ever so, my dearest. Eight o'clock."

The secretary hung up the phone, rose from the chair and smoothed her dress. She opened a drawer and took out a purse with long straps; she slipped it over her shoulder and walked to her employer's closed door. She knocked.

"Yes?" asked Mattilon inside.

"It is Suzanne, monsieur."

"Come in, come *in,*" said René, leaning back in his chair as the woman entered. "The last letter is filled with incomprehensible language, no?"

"Not at all, monsieur. It's just that I . . . well, I'm not sure it's proper to say."

"What could be improper? And if it is, at my age I'd be so flattered I'd probably tell my wife."

"Oh, monsieur . . ."

"No, really, Suzanne, you've been here—what now?—a week, ten days? One would think you had been here for months. Your work is excellent and I appreciate your filling in."

"Your secretary is a dear friend, monsieur. I could do no less."

"Well, I thank you. I hope the good Lord sees His way to pull her through. Young people today, they drive so fast—so terribly fast and so dangerously. I'm sorry, what is it, Suzanne?"

"I've had no lunch, sir. I was wondering—"

"My *God* I'm inconsiderate! I'm afraid it goes with two partners who take August seriously and go on holiday! Please, as long as you like, and I insist you bring the bill to me and let me reimburse you."

"That's not necessary, but thank you for the offer."

"Not an offer, Suzanne, an order. Have lots of wine and let's both of us make messes of my partners' clients. Now, off you go."

"Thank you, monsieur." Suzanne went to the door, opened it slightly and then stopped. She turned her head and saw that Mattilon was absorbed in reading. She closed the door silently, reached into her purse and withdrew a large pistol with the perforated cylinder of a silencer attached to the barrel. She pivoted slowly and walked toward the desk.

The lawyer looked up as she approached. *"What?"*

Suzanne fired four times in rapid succession. René Mattilon sprang back in his chair, his skull pierced from his right eye to his left forehead. Blood streaked down his face and over his white shirt.

22

"Where in God's name have you been?" cried Valerie into the phone. "I've been trying to reach you since early this morning!"

"Early this morning," said Lawrence Talbot, "when the news broke, I knew I had to get the first plane to Washington."

"You don't *believe* what they're saying? You *can't!*"

"I do, and worse, I feel responsible. I feel as if I'd unwittingly pulled the trigger myself, and in a way that's exactly what happened."

"Goddamn you, Larry, explain that."

"Joel called me from a hotel in Bonn—only, he didn't know which one. He wasn't rational, Val. He was calm one moment, shouting the next, finally admitting to me that he was confused and frightened. He rambled on—most of the time incoherently—telling some incredible story of having been captured and thrown into a stone house in the woods, and how he escaped, hiding in the river, eluding guards and patrols and killing a man he called a 'scout.' He kept screaming that he had to get away, that men were searching for him, in the woods, along the riverbank. . . . Something's happened to him. He's gone back to those terrible days when he was a prisoner of war. Everything he says, everything he describes, is a variation of those experiences—the pain, the stress, the tensions of running for his life through the jungles and down rivers. He's sick, my dear, and this morning was the horrible proof.''

Valerie felt the hollowness in her throat, the sudden, awful vacuum below. She was beyond thinking; she could only react to words. "Why did you say you were responsible, that in some way you pulled the trigger?"

"I told him to go to Peregrine. I tried to convince him that Peregrine would listen to him, that he wasn't the man Joel thought he was."

" 'Thought he was'? What did Joel say?"

"Very little that made sense. He ranted about generals and field marshals and some obscure historical theory that brought all the commanders from various wars and armies together in a combined effort to take control of governments. He wasn't lucid. He'd pretend to be, but the minute I questioned a statement he made or a point in his story, he'd blow up and tell me it didn't matter, or I wasn't listening, or I was too dense to understand. But at the end he admitted he was terribly tired and confused and how badly he needed sleep. That was when I made my last pitch about Peregrine, but Joel didn't trust him. He was actually hostile toward him because he said he saw a former German general's car go through the embassy gates, and as you may or may not know, Peregrine was an outstanding officer during the Second World War. I explained as patiently and as firmly as I could that Peregrine was not one of 'them,' that he was no friend of the military. . . . Obviously, I failed. Joel reached him, set up a rendezvous and killed him. I had no *idea* how sick he was.''

"Larry," began Valerie slowly, her voice weak. "I hear everything you say, but it doesn't ring true. It isn't that I don't believe you—Joel once said you were an embarrassingly honest man—but something's missing. The Converse I know and lived with for four years never bent the facts to support abstractions he wanted to believe. Even when he was angry as hell, he couldn't do that. I told him he'd make a lousy painter because he couldn't bend a shape to fit a concept. It wasn't in him, and I think he explained it. At five hundred miles an hour, he said, you can mistake a shadow on the ocean for a carrier if your instruments are out.''

"You're telling me he doesn't lie.''

"I'm sure he does—I'm sure he did—but never about important things. It simply isn't in him.''

"That was before he became ill, violently ill. He killed that man in Paris, he admitted it to me.''

Valerie gasped. *"No!"*

"Yes, I'm afraid. Just as he killed Walter Peregrine.''

"Because of some obscure historical *theory?* It's all wrong, Larry!''

"Two psychiatrists at the State Department explained it, but in phrases I'm sure I'd mangle if

I tried to repeat them. 'Progressive latent retrogression,' I think, was one of them."

"Bullshit!"

"But you may be right about one thing. Geneva. Remember you said it all had something to do with Geneva?"

"I remember. What about Geneva?"

"It's where it started, everyone in Washington agrees with that. I don't know if you've read the papers—"

"Only the *Globe;* it's delivered. I haven't left the phone."

"It was Jack Halliday's son—stepson, actually. He was the lawyer who was killed in Geneva. It seems he was a prominent leader of the antiwar movement in the sixties and he was Converse's opponent in the merger. It was established that they met for breakfast before the conference. The theory is that he baited Joel, and we can assume it was brutal, as he had a reputation for going for the jugular."

"Why would he *do* that?" asked Val, her frayed nerves now suddenly alert.

"To throw Joel off. To distract him. Remember, they were dealing in millions, and the attorney who came off best could do very well for himself—clients lining up all over Wall Street to retain him. There's even evidence that Halliday succeeded."

"What evidence?"

"The first part's technical, so I won't try to explain it except to say that there was a subtle transfer of voting stock which under certain isolated market conditions might give Halliday's clients more say in management than the merger intended. Joel accepted it; I don't think he would have normally."

"Normally? What's the other part?"

"Joel's behavior at the conference itself. According to the reports—interviews with everyone in that room—he wasn't himself, he *was* distracted, some said agitated. Several lawyers on both sides commented on the fact that he kept to himself, standing by a window most of the time, looking out as if he expected something. His concentration was so lax that questions addressed to him had to be repeated, and when they were, he appeared as though he didn't understand them. His mind was somewhere else, on something that consumed him."

"Larry!" shouted Valerie. "What are you *saying?* That Joel had something to do with this Halliday being *killed?*"

"It can't be ruled out," said Talbot sadly. "Either psychologically or in light of what people saw in the anteroom when Halliday died."

"What they *saw?*" whispered Valerie. "The paper said he died with Joel holding his head."

"I'm afraid there's more, my dear. I've read the reports. According to a receptionist and two other attorneys, there was a violent exchange between them just before Halliday died. No one's sure what was said, but they all agree it seemed vicious, with Halliday clutching Joel's lapels, as though accusing him. Later, when questioned by the Geneva police, Joel claimed there was no coherent conversation, only the hysterical words of a dying man. The police report added that he was not a cooperative witness."

"My God, he was probably in *shock!* You know what he went through—the sight of that man dying literally in his arms must have been traumatic for him!"

"Admittedly, this is hindsight, Valerie, but everything must be examined—above all, his behavior."

"What do they think he did? What's the theory *now?* That Joel went out into the street, saw someone who fit the bill and hired him to *kill* a man? Really, Larry, this is ludicrous."

"There are more questions, than there are answers, certainly, but what's happened—what we know has happened—isn't ludicrous at all. It's tragic."

"All right, all right," said Valerie, her words rushed. "But why would he do it? Why would he want Halliday killed? *Why?"*

"I think that's obvious. How he must have despised someone like Halliday. A man who stayed safely at home, who condemned and ridiculed everything men like Joel went through, calling them goons and murderers and lackeys —and unnecessary sacrifices. Along with his hated 'commanders,' the Hallidays of this world must have stood for everything else he loathed. One group ordering men into battle, to be maimed, killed, captured . . . tortured, the other making a mockery of everything they endured. Whatever Halliday said at that breakfast table must have made something snap in Joel's head."

"And you think," said Valerie quietly, the words echoing in her throat, "that's why he wanted Halliday dead?"

"Latent vengeance. It's the prevalent theory, the consensus, if you will."

"I don't 'will.' Because it's not true, it couldn't be true."

"These are highly qualified experts, Val, doctors in the behavioral sciences. They've analyzed everything in the records and they feel the pattern is there. Shock-induced, instant pathological schizophrenia."

"That's very impressive. They should embroider it on their Snoopy baseball caps because that's where it belongs."

"I don't think you're in a position to dispute—"

"I'm in a hell of a position," interrupted the ex-Mrs. Converse. "But nobody bothered to ask me, or Joel's father, or his sister—who just happened to have been one of those wild-eyed protesters you all speak of. There's no way Halliday could have provoked Joel the way they say he did—at breakfast, lunch *or* dinner."

"You can't make such a statement, my dear. You simply don't know that."

"I *do* know, Larry. Because Joel thought the Hallidays of this world, as you put it, were *right.* He wasn't always crazy about the way they did things, but he thought they *were right!"*

"I don't believe that. Not after what he went through."

"Then go to another source—if that's what you call it. To some of those records your high priests of the behavioral sciences conveniently overlooked. When Joel came back, there was a parade for him at Travis Air Force Base in California, where he was given everything but the keys to every starlet's apartment in Los Angeles. Am I right?"

"I recall there was a military welcome for a man who had escaped under extraordinary circumstances. The Secretary of State greeted him at the plane, in fact."

"In absolute fact, Larry. Then what? Where else was he paraded?"

"I don't know what you mean?"

"Look at the records. Nowhere. He wouldn't do it. How many invitations did he get? From how many towns and cities and companies and organizations—all pushed like *hell* by the White House? A hundred, five hundred, five *thousand?* At least that many, Larry. And do you know how many he accepted? Tell me, Larry, do you know? Did those high priests talk about this?"

"It wasn't an issue."

"Of course it wasn't. It warped the pattern; it bent the shapes Joel Converse wouldn't bend! The answer is *zero,* Larry. He wouldn't *do* it, any of it! He thought one day more of that war was one more day in hell too long. He refused to lend his name."

"What are you trying to say?" said Talbot sternly.

"Halliday wasn't his enemy, not the way you're trying to paint him. The brushstrokes aren't there. They're not on the canvas."

"Your metaphors are more than I can handle, Val. What are you trying to tell me?"

"That something smells, Larry. It's so rotten I

can hardly breathe, but the stench isn't coming from my former husband. It's coming from all of you."

"I have to take exception to that. All I want to do is help, I thought you knew that."

"I do, really I do. It's not your fault. Good-bye, Larry."

"I'll call you the minute I learn anything."

"Do that. Good-bye." Valerie hung up the phone and looked at her watch. It was time to get down to Logan Airport in Boston to pick up Roger Converse.

"Köln in zehn Minuten!" shouted the voice over the loudspeaker.

Converse sat by the window, his face next to the glass, as the towns sped by on the way to Cologne—Bornheim, Wesel, Brühl. The train was perhaps three-quarters full, which was to say that each double seat had at least one occupant. When they pulled out of the station a woman had been sitting where he sat now, a fashionably dressed suburbanite. Several seats behind them another woman—a friend—spotted her. His seatmate spoke to Joel. The brief attention she had called to both of them when he could not reply unnerved him. He shrugged and shook his head; she exhaled impatiently, got up in irritation and joined her friend.

She had left a newspaper behind, the same newspaper with his photograph on the front page, which remained flat out on the seat. He stared at it until he realized what he was doing and instantly shifted seats, picking up the paper and folding it so that the picture would be out of sight. He glanced around cautiously, holding his hand casually above his lips, frowning, pensive, trying to seem like a man in thought whose eyes saw nothing. But he had seen another pair of eyes and they were studying him—staring at him while the owner was engaged in what appeared to be a lively conversation with an elderly woman next to him. The man had looked away, and Converse had a brief half-second to observe the face before he turned to the window. He knew that face; he had talked to that man, but he could not remember where it was or when it was, only that they had spoken. The realization was as maddening as it was frightening. *Where* was it? *When* was it? Did the man know him, know his *name?*

If the man did, he had done nothing about it. He had returned his concentration to the woman, the conversation still lively. Joel tried to picture the whole man; perhaps it would help. He was large, not so much in height as in girth, and on the surface jovial, but Converse sensed a meanness in him. Was that now or before? When was before? *Where?* Ten minutes or so had passed since the exchange of looks, and Joel was no further ahead in peeling away the layers of memory. He was stymied and afraid.

"Wir kommen in zwei Minuten in Köln an. Bitte achten Sie auf Ihr Gepäck!"

A number of passengers got up from their seats, tugging at their jackets and skirts, reaching for luggage. As the train began to slow down, Converse pressed his forehead against the cool glass of the window. He let his mind go slack, unfocused, expecting the next few minutes to tell him what to do.

The minutes passed, the suspension on hold, his mind blank as passengers got off and others got in, many carrying attaché cases, several very much like his own, which he had left in a trash can in Bonn. He had wanted to keep it but he could not. It had been a gift from Valerie, as his gold pen was a gift, both initialed in those better days. . . . No, not better, he told himself, simply different. Nothing was better or worse; there were no comparisons where commitments were concerned. They either stuck or they did not. Theirs came unstuck.

Then why, he asked himself, as the train ground to a stop at Cologne, had he sent the contents of his briefcase to Val? His answer was the essence of logic, he thought. She would know what to do; the others would not. Talbot, Brooks and Simon were out. His sister, Virginia, was even further out. His father? The fly-boy with a sense of responsibility that went as far as his last wing dip? It could not be the pilot. He loved old Roger, more than he suspected Roger loved him, but the pilot could never come to grips with the ground. Hard earth meant relationships, and old Roger never knew how to handle them, even with a wife he claimed to have loved dearly. The doctors said she had died of a coronary occlusion; her son thought it was from neglect. Roger was not on the scene, had not been for several weeks. So that left Valerie . . . his once and former Valerie.

"Entschuldigen Sie. Ist dieser Platz frei?" The intruding voice came from a man about his own age, carrying an attaché case.

Joel nodded, assuming the words referred to the empty seat beside him.

"Danke," said the man, sitting down, the attaché case at his feet. He withdrew a newspaper from under his left arm and snapped it open. Converse tensed as he saw his photograph, his own serious face staring at him. He turned again to the window, pulling the soft brim of the hat lower, his face down, hoping he looked like an exhausted traveler wishing only to catch a few minutes' sleep. Moments later, as the train started forward, he had an inkling that he had succeeded.

"Verrückt, nicht wahr?" said the man with the attaché case reading the newspaper.

Joel stirred and blinked open his eyes beneath the brim of the hat. "Umm?"

"Schade," added the man, his right hand separated from the paper in a gesture of apology.

Converse settled back against the window, the coolness of the glass an anchor, his eyes closed, the darkness more welcome than he could ever remember. . . . No, that was not true; he remembered to the contrary. In the camps there were moments when he was not sure he could keep up the façade of strength and revolt, when everything in him wanted to capitulate, to hear even a few kind words, to see a smile that had meaning. Then the darkness would come and he would cry, the tears drenching his face. And when they stopped, the anger would be inexplicably restored. Somehow the tears had cleansed him,

600

purged the doubts and the fears and made him whole again. And angry again.

"Wir kommen in fünf Minuten in Düsseldorf an!"

Joel bolted forward, his neck painfully stiff, his head cold. He had dozed for a considerable length of time, judging from the stiffness above his shoulder blades. The man beside him was reading and marking a report of some kind, the attaché case on his lap, the newspaper folded neatly between himself and Converse, folded maddeningly with his photograph in clear view. The man opened his case, put the report inside, and snapped it shut. He turned to Converse.

"Der Zug ist pünklich," he said, nodding his head.

Joel nodded back, suddenly aware that the passenger across the aisle had gotten up with the elderly woman, shaking her hand and replying to something she had said. But he was not looking at her; his eyes had strayed over to Converse. Joel slumped back into the seat and the window, resuming the appearance of a weary traveler, the soft brim of his hat pulled down to the rims of his glasses. Who *was* that man? If they knew each other, how could he be silent under the circumstances? How could he simply look over now and then and casually return to his conversation with the woman? At the very least, he would have to betray some sense of alarm or fear, or, at the minimum, excited recognition.

The train began to slow down, the metallic grinding of the steel plates against the huge wheels swelling; soon the whistles would commence for their arrival in Düsseldorf. Converse wondered if the German next to him would get off. He had closed his attaché case but made no preliminary moves to rise and join the line forming at the forward door. Instead, he picked up the newspaper, opening it, mercifully, to an inside page.

The train stopped, passengers disembarked and others got on board—mostly women with shopping boxes and plastic bags emblazoned with the logos of expensive boutiques and recognizable names in the fashion industry. The train to Emmerich was a suburban "mink run," as Val used to call the afternoon trains from New York to Westchester and Connecticut. Joel saw that the man from across the aisle had walked the elderly woman up to the rear of the line, again shaking her hand solicitously before sidestepping his way back toward his seat. Converse turned his face to the glass, his head bowed, and closed his eyes.

"Bitte, können wir die Plätze tauschen? Dieser Herr ist ein Bekannter. Ich sitze in der nächsten Reihe."

"Sicher, aber er schläft ja doch nur."

"Ich wecke ihn," said Converse's seatmate, laughing and getting up. The man from across the aisle had changed seats. He sat down next to Joel.

Converse stretched, covering a yawn with his left hand, his right slipping under his jacket to the handle of the gun he had taken from Leifhelm's chauffeur. If it became necessary, he would show that gun to his new yet familiar companion. The train started, the noise below growing in volume; it was the moment. Joel turned to the man, his eyes knowing but conveying nothing.

"I *figured* it was you," said the man, obviously an American, grinning broadly but not attractively.

Converse had been right, there was a meanness about the obese man; he heard it in the voice as he had heard it before—but where he did not remember. "Are you sure?" asked Joel.

"Sure I'm sure. But I'll bet you're not, are you?"

"Frankly, no."

"I'll give you a hint. I can always spot a good ole Yank! Only made a couple of mistakes in all the years of hopping around selling my li'l ole line of look-alike, almost originals."

"Copenhagen," said Converse, remembering with distaste waiting for his luggage with the man. "And one of your mistakes was in Rome when you thought an Italian was a Hispanic from Florida."

"You got it! That guinea bastard had me buffaloed, figured him for a spik with a lot of bread—probably from running dope, you know what I mean? You know how they are, how they cornered the market from the Keys up. . . . Say, what's your name again?"

"Rogers," replied Joel for no other reason than the fact that he had been thinking about his father a while ago. "You speak German," he added, making a statement.

"Shit, I'd better. West Germany's just about our biggest market. My old man was a Kraut; it's all he spoke."

"What do you sell?"

"The best imitations on Seventh Avenue, but

don't get me wrong, I'm not one of the Jew boys. You take a Balenciaga, right? You change a few buttons and a few pleats, put a ruffle maybe where the Latino doesn't have one. Then farm the patterns out to the Bronx and Jersey, lower Miami and Pennsylvania, where they sew in a label like 'Valenciana.' Then you wholesale the batch at a third of the price and everybody's happy—except the Latino. But there's not a fucking thing he can do that'd be worth his time in court because for the most part it's legal.''

"I wouldn't be so sure about that."

"Well, a guy would have to plow through a road of *chazzerai* to prove it *wasn't* legal."

"Sadly, that's true."

"Hey, don't get me wrong! We provide the merchandise and a service for thousands of nice li'l ole housewives who can't afford that Paris crap. And I earn my bread, ole Yankee Doodle. Take that wrinkled old broad I was with; she owns a half-dozen specialty shops in Cologne and Düsseldorf, and now she's looking into Bonn. Let me tell you, I waltz her. . . ."

The towns and small cities went by. Leverkusen . . . Lagenfeld . . . Hilden, and still the salesman went on, one tasteless anecdote leading to the next, his voice grating, his comments repetitive.

"Wir kommen in fünf Minuten in Essen an!"

It happened in Essen.

The commotion came first but it was not sudden. Instead, it grew in volume as an immense rolling wave gathers force approaching a ragged coastline, a sustained crescendo culminating in the crash over the rocks. The embarking passengers

604

all seemed to be talking excitedly, with one another, heads turned, necks craned to listen to the voices coming from several transistor radios. Some were held against the ear, others with the volume turned up at the request of those nearby. The more crowded the train became, the louder everyone talked as the conversations were almost drowned out by the shrill, metallic voices of the newscasters. A thin young girl in the uniform of a private school, her books in a canvas beach bag and a blaring radio in her left hand, sat down in the seat in front of Joel and the salesman. Passengers gathered around, shouting, apparently asking the girl if she could make the radio louder.

"What's it all about?" asked Converse, turning to the obese man.

"Wait a minute!" replied the salesman, leaning forward with difficulty and in greater discomfort rising partially from the seat. "Let me listen."

There was a perceptible lull, but only among the crowd around the girl, who now held up the radio. Suddenly there was a burst of static and Converse could hear two voices, in addition to that of the newscaster, a remote report from somewhere away from the radio. And then Joel heard the words spoken in English; they were nearly impossible to pick out, as an interpreter kept rushing in to give the German translation. "A full inquiry . . . *Eine vollständiges Verhör* . . . entailing all security forces . . . *sie erfordert alle Sicherheitskräfte* . . . has been ordered . . . *wurde veranlasst.*"

Converse grabbed the salesman's coat. "What is it—tell me what happened?" he asked rapidly.

"That *nut* hit again! . . . Wait, they're going back. Lemme hear this." Again there was a short burst of static and the excited newscaster came back on the air. A terrible sense of dread spread through Joel as the onslaught of German crackled out of the small radio, each phrase more breathless than the last. Finally the guttural recitation ended. The passengers straightened their backs. Some stood up, turning to one another, their voices raised in counterpoint, excited conversations resumed. The salesman lowered himself into the seat, breathing hard not, apparently, because of the alarming news he had heard but because of sheer physical discomfort.

"Would you *please* tell me what this is all about?" asked Converse, controlling his anxiety.

"Yeah, sure," said the heavyset man, taking a handkerchief from his breast pocket and mopping his forehead. "This mother-loving world is full of crazies, you know what I mean? For Christ's sake, you can't tell who the fuck you're talking to! If it was up to me, every kid who was born cross-eyed or couldn't find a tit would be buried in dirt. I'm just sick of the weirdos, you know what I mean?"

"That's very enlightening—now, what *happened?*"

"Yeah, okay." The salesman put the handkerchief back in his pocket, then loosened his belt and undid the buttons above his zippered fly. "The soldier boy, the one who runs the headquarters in Brussels—"

"The supreme commander of NATO," said Joel, his dread complete.

"Yeah, that one. He was shot, his head blown off right in the goddamned street when he was leaving some little restaurant in the old section. He was in civilian clothes, too."

"When?"

"A couple of hours ago."

"Who do they say did it?"

"The same creep who knocked off that ambassador in Bonn. The *nut!*"

"How do they know that?"

"They got the gun."

"The what?"

"The gun. It's why they didn't release the news right away; they wanted to check the fingerprints with Washington. It's his, and they figure the ballistics will show it's the same gun that was used to kill what's-his-name."

"Peregrine," said Converse quietly, aware that his dread was not complete. The worst part was only coming into focus. "How did they get the gun?"

"Yeah, well, that's where they've marked the bastard. The soldier boy had a guard with him who shot at the nut and hit him—they think on the left arm. When the weirdo grabbed his arm, the gun dropped out of his hand. The hospitals and the doctors have been alerted and all the borders all over the place are being checked, every fucking American male passport made to roll up his sleeves, and anyone looking anywhere's near like him hauled off to a customs tank."

"They're being thorough," said Joel, not knowing what else to say, feeling only the pain of his wound.

"I'll say this for the creep," continued the salesman, eyes wide and nodding his head in some obscene gesture of respect. "He's got 'em chasing their asses from the North Sea to the Mediterranean. They got reports he was seen on planes in Antwerp, Rotterdam, and back there in Düsseldorf. It only takes forty-five minutes to get from 'Düssel' to Brussels, you know. I got a friend in Munich who flies a couple times a week to have lunch in Venice. Every place over here's a short hop. Sometimes we forget that, you know what I mean?"

"Yes, I do. Short flights . . . Did you hear anything else?"

"They said he could be heading for Paris or London or maybe even Moscow—he could be a Commie, you know. They're checking the private airfields, too, figuring he's got friends who are helping him—some friends, huh? A regular happy group of drooling psychos. They're even comparing him to that Carlos, the one they call 'the jackal,' what do you think of that? They say if he does go to Paris, the two of them might link up and there could be a few more executions. This Converse, though, he's got his own regular trademark. He puts bullets in their heads. Some kind of Boy Scout, huh?"

Joel stiffened, feeling the tension throughout his slumped body, a sharp hollow pain in the center of his chest. It was the first time he had heard his name spoken casually by a stranger, identifying him as the psychopathic killer, an assassin hunted by governments whose border patrols were scrutinizing everyone at every checkpoint—private airfields watched, a dragnet in progress. The generals of Aquitaine had done their job with precision, right down to his fingerprints on a gun and a flesh wound in his arm. But the timing—how could they *dare?* How did they know he was not in an embassy somewhere asking for temporary asylum until he could make a case for himself? How could they take the *chance?*

Then the realization came to him, and he had to dig his fingers into his wrist to control himself, to contain his panic. The call to *Mattilon!* How easily René's phone could have been tapped, by either the Sûreté or Interpol, and how quickly Aquitaine's informers would have spread the word! Oh, *Christ!* Neither one of them had thought of it! They *did* know where he was, and no matter where he went he was trapped! As the offensive salesman had accurately phrased it, "Every place over here's a short hop." A man could fly from Munich to Venice for lunch and be back in his office for a three-thirty appointment. Another man could kill in Brussels and be on a train in Düsseldorf forty-five minutes later. Distances were measured in half-hours. From ground-zero in Brussels, "a couple of hours ago" covered a wide circle of cities and a great many borders. Were his hunters on the train? They might be, but there was no way they could know which train he had taken. It would be easier and far less time-consuming to wait for him in Emmerich. He had to think, he had to *move.*

"Excuse me," said Converse, getting up. "I have to use the men's room."

"You're lucky." The salesman moved his heavy legs, holding his trousers as he let Joel pass. "I can hardly squeeze into those boxes. I always take a leak before . . ."

Joel made his way up the aisle. He stopped abruptly, swallowing, trying to decide whether to continue or turn back. He had left the newspaper on his seat, the photograph easily revealed by unfolding the top page. He had to continue; any change of movement, however minor, might attract attention. His objective was not the men's room but the passageway between the cars; he had to see it. A number of people had opened the door and gone through, several apparently looking for someone they expected to find on the train. He would look down at the lock on the bathroom door and proceed.

He stood in the swerving, vibrating passageway studying the metal door. It was a standard two-tiered exit; the top had to be opened first before the lower part could be unlocked and pulled back, revealing the steps. It was all he had to know.

He returned to his seat, and to his relief the salesman was splayed back, his thick lips parted, his eyes closed, a high-pitched wheeze emanating from his throat. Converse cautiously lifted one foot after the other over the fat man's legs and maneuvered himself into his seat. The newspaper had not been touched. Another relief.

Diagonally above and in front of him, he saw a small receptacle in the curved wall with what appeared to be a sheaf of railroad schedules fanned out by disuse. Limp, bent pieces of paper ignored because these commuters knew where they were going. Joel raised himself off the seat, reached out, and took one, apologizing with several nods of his head to the young girl below. She giggled.

Oberhausen . . . Dinslaken . . . Voerde . . . Wesel . . . Emmerich.

Wesel. The last stop before Emmerich. He had no idea how many miles Wesel was from Emmerich, but he had no choice. He would get off the train at Wesel, not with departing passengers but by himself. He would disappear in Wesel.

He felt a slight deceleration beneath him, his pilot's instincts telling him it was the outer perimeter of an approach, the final path to touchdown in the scope. He stood up and carefully maneuvered between the fat man's legs to reach the aisle; at the last second the salesman snorted, shifting his position. Squinting under the brim of his hat, Joel casually glanced around, as if he were momentarily unsure of which way to go. He moved his head slowly; as far as he could see, no one was paying the slightest attention to him.

He walked with carefully weary steps up the aisle, a tired passenger in search of relief. He reached the toilet door and was greeted by an ironic sign of true relief. The white slot below the handle spelled out BESETZT. His first maneuver had its basis in credibility; the toilet was in use. He turned toward the heavy passageway door, pulled it open and, stepping outside, crossed the vibrating, narrow coupling area to the opposite door. He pushed it open, but instead of going inside he took a single stride forward, then lowered his body, turning as he did so, and stepped back into the passageway, into the shadows. He stood up, his back against the external bulkhead, and inched his way to the edge of the thick glass window. Ahead was the inside of the rear car, and by turning he had a clear view of the car in front. He waited, watching, turning, at any moment expecting to see someone lowering a newspaper or breaking off a conversation and looking over at his empty seat.

None did. The excitement over the news of the assassination in Brussels had tapered off, as had the rush of near panic in Bonn when the streets learned that an ambassador had been killed. A number of people were obviously still talking about both incidents, shaking their heads and grappling with the implications and the future possibilities, but their voices were lowered; the crisis of the first reports had passed. After all, it was not fundamentally the concern of these citizens. It was American against American. There was even a certain gloating in the air; the gunfight at O.K. Corral had new significance. The colonists were, indeed, a violent breed.

"Wir kommen in . . . " The rapid clacking of the wheels below, echoing in the metal chamber, obscured the distant announcement over the loudspeakers. Only moments now, thought Converse as he turned and looked at the exit door. When the train slowed sufficiently and the lines began to form at both inner doors, he would make his move.

"Wir kommen in drei Minuten in Wesel an!"

612

Several passengers in both cars got out of their seats, adjusted their briefcases and shopping bags and started up the aisle. The grinding of the giant wheels underneath signified the approach to touchdown. *Now.*

Joel turned to the exit door and, finding the upper latch, snapped it open, pulling the upper section back; the rush of air was deafening. He spotted the handle of the lower release and gripped it, prepared to yank it up as soon as the ground beyond slowed down. It would be in only seconds. The sounds below grew louder and the sunlight outside created a racing silhouette of the train. Then the abrasive words broke through the dissonance and he froze.

"*Very* well thought out, Herr Converse! Some win, some lose. You *lost.*"

Joel spun around. The man yelling at him in the metal chamber was the passenger who had gotten on the train at Düsseldorf, the apologetic commuter who had sat next to him until the obese salesman had asked him to exchange seats. In his left hand was a gun held far below his waist, in his right the ever-respectable attaché case.

"You're a surprise," said Converse.

"I would hope so. I barely made the train in Düsseldorf. *Ach,* three cars I walked through like a madman—but not the madman you are, *ja?*"

"What happens now? You fire that gun and save the world from a madman?"

"Nothing so simplistic, pilot."

"Pilot."

"Names are immaterial, but I am a colonel in the West German Luftwaffe. Pilots only kill one another in the air. It is embarrassing on the ground."

"You're comforting."

"I also exaggerate. One disconcerting move on your part and I shall be a hero of the Fatherland, having cornered a crazed assassin and killed him before he killed me."

" 'Fatherland'? You still call it that?"

"*Natürlich.* Most of us do. From the father comes the strength; the female is the vessel."

"They'd love you in a Vassar biology class."

"Is that meant to be amusing?"

"No, just disconcerting—in a very minor way, nothing serious." Joel had moved imperceptibly until his back was against the bulkhead, his whole mind, his entire thinking process, on pre-set. He had no choice except to die, now or in a matter of hours from now. "I suppose you have an itinerary for me," he asked as he swung his left arm forward with the question.

"Quite definitely, pilot. We will get off the train at Wesel, and you and I will share a telephone, my gun firmly against your chest. Within a short time a car will meet us and you will be taken—"

Converse slammed his concealed right elbow into the bulkhead, his left arm in plain sight. The German glanced at the door of the forward car. *Now!*

Joel lunged for the gun, both hands surging for the black barrel as he crashed his right knee with all the force he could command into the man's testicles. As the German fell back he grabbed his hair and smashed the man's head down onto a protruding hinge of the opposite door.

It was over. The German's eyes were wide, alarmed, glassy. Another scout was dead, but this man was no ignorant conscript from an impersonal government, this was a soldier of Aquitaine.

A stout woman screamed in the window, her mouth opened wide with her screams, her face hysterical.

"*Wesel* . . . *!*"

The train had slowed down and other excited faces appeared at the window, the frenzied crowd now blocking those who tried to open the door.

Converse lunged across the vibrating metal enclosure to the exit panel. He grasped the latch and pulled it open, crashing the door into the bulkhead. The steps were below, gravel and tar beyond. He took a deep breath and plunged outside, curling his body to lessen the impact of the hard ground, and when he made contact he rolled over, and over, and over.

23

He careened off a rock and into a cluster of bushes. Nettles and coarse tendrils enveloped him, scraping his face and hands. His body was a mass of bruises, the wound in his left arm moist and stinging, but there was no time even to acknowledge pain. He had to get away; in minutes the whole area would be swarming with men searching for him, hunting for the murderer of an officer in the Federal Republic's air arm. It took no imagination to foresee what would happen next. The passengers would be questioned—including the salesman—and suddenly a newspaper would be in someone's hand, a photograph studied, the connection made. A crazed killer last seen in a back street in Brussels was not on his way to Paris or London or Moscow. He was on a train out of Bonn, passing through Cologne, Essen and Düsseldorf—and he killed again in a town called Wesel.

Suddenly he heard the high-pitched wail of a horn. He looked up the small hill toward the tracks; a south-bound train was gathering speed out of the station several thousand feet away. Then he saw his hat; it was on the hill, halfway down. Joel crept out of the tangling brush, staggered to his feet, and ran to it, refusing to listen to that part of his mind which told him he could barely walk. He grabbed the hat and began running to his right. The south-bound train passed; he raced up the hill and across the tracks, heading for an old building, apparently deserted. More of its windows were shattered than intact. He might rest there for a few moments but no longer; it was too obvious a hiding place. In ten or fifteen minutes it would be surrounded by men with guns aimed at every exit, every window.

He tried desperately to remember. How had he done it before? How had he eluded the patrols in the jungles north of Phu Loc? . . . Vantage points! Get where you can see them but they can't see you! But there were tall trees then and he was younger and stronger and could climb them, concealing himself behind green screens of full branches on firm limbs. There was nothing like that here on the outskirts of a railroad yard . . . or maybe there was! To the right of the building was a landfill dump, tons of earth and debris piled high in several pyramids; it was his only choice.

Gasping, his arms and legs aching, his wound inflamed, he ran toward the last of the pyramids. He reached it, propelled his way around the mass, and started climbing the rear side, his feet slipping into soft earth, and wood and cardboard and patches of garbage, where it had been layered. The sickening smells took his mind off the pain. He kept crawling, clawing with each slipping foot. If he had to, he could burrow himself into the stinking mess. There were no rules for survival, and if sinking himself into the putrid hill kept a spray of bullets from ending his life, so be it.

He reached the top and lay prone below the ridge, dirt and protruding debris all around him. Sweat rolled down his face, stinging the scrapes on his face; his legs and arms were heavy with pain, and his breathing was erratic from the trembling caused not only by unused muscles but by fear. He looked down at the outskirts of the railroad yard, then up ahead at the station. The train had stopped, and the platform was filled with people milling around, bewildered. Several uniformed men were shouting orders, trying to separate passengers—apparently those in the two cars flanking the scene of the killing or anyone else who knew anything. In the parking lot surrounding the station house was a blue-and-white-striped police car, its red roof light spinning, the signal of emergency. There was a rapid clanging in the distance, and seconds later a long white ambulance streaked into the lot, whipped into a horseshoe turn and plunged back, stopping close to the platform. As the rear doors opened, two attendants jumped out carrying a stretcher; a police officer above them on the steps shouted at them, gesturing with his arm. They ran up the metal staircase and followed him.

A second patrol car swerved into the lot, tires screeching as it stopped next to the ambulance. Two police officers got out and walked up the steps; the officer who had directed the ambulance attendants joined them, with two civilians, a man and a woman, beside him. The five talked, and moments later the two patrolmen returned to their vehicle. The driver backed up and spun to his left, gunning the engine, heading for the south end of the parking lot, directly toward Converse. Again they stopped and got out, now with weapons drawn; they raced across the tracks and down the slope of gravel and tar into the wild grass. They would be coming back in minutes, thought Joel, absently clawing the ragged surface by his shoulders. They would stop and check out the deserted building, perhaps call for assistance, but sooner or later they would examine the huge mounds of landfill.

Converse looked behind him; there was a dirt road marked with the tracks of heavy trucks leading to a tall link fence, the gate held in place with a thick chain. A man running up that road and climbing that fence would be seen; he had to stay where he was, hidden in the putrid rubble.

Another sound interrupted his frantic calculations—a sound like one he had heard only moments before. On his right, in the parking lot. A third patrol car came speeding in, its claxon howling, but instead of heading for the ambulance and the first police vehicle by the platform, it veered to its left, racing over to join the striped car at the south end of the lot. The two policemen in the field had radioed for assistance, and Joel felt a numbing sense of despair. He was looking at his own executioners. Executioner. The newly arrived patrol car contained only the driver—or did it? Did the policeman turn his head and speak? No, he was disengaging something, a seat belt probably.

A gray-haired uniformed man got out, looked around, then started walking rapidly toward the tracks. He crossed them and stood on the top of the slope, shouting down at the police officers in the sun-drenched brown grass. Converse had no idea what the man was saying, but the scene appeared strangely out of place.

The two policemen came racing into view, their guns no longer in their hands but holstered. There was a brief heated conversation. The older officer was pointing to a distant area south of the land-fill; his words, to judge by their volume, were commands. Joel looked back at his patrol car; on the panel of the front door was an insignia that was absent on the other car. The man held a rank superior to those of his young associates; he was issuing orders.

The younger policemen ran back across the

tracks to their vehicle, their superior following but not running. They swung back the doors, literally jumped in and, in a burst of the engine's roar, swerved to the right and sped out of the parking lot. The older man reached his patrol car, but he made no movement to open the door or get inside. Instead, he spoke—at least his lips moved—and five seconds later the rear doors opened and two men emerged. One man Converse knew well. His gun was in Joel's pocket. It was Leifhelm's chauffeur, a taped bandage across his forehead, another on the ridge of his nose. He pulled out a gun and barked a command to the other man; in his voice was the vengeful fury of a soldier dishonored in combat.

Peter Stone left the hotel in Washington. He had told the young Navy lieutenant and the slightly older Army captain that he would contact them in the morning. *Children,* he thought. Idealistic amateurs were the worst, because their righteousness was usually as valid as their actions were impractical. Their childish disdain for duplicity and deceit did not countenance the fact that to rip out the maniacal bastards frequently required greater malevolence and far more deception than they could imagine.

Stone got into a taxi—leaving his car in the basement parking area—and gave the driver the address of an apartment building on Nebraska Avenue. It was a lovely apartment, but it did not belong to him; it was leased by an Albanian diplomat at the United Nations who was rarely there—naturally, because he was based in New

York. But the former intelligence officer had worked hard and turned the Albanian several years ago, not merely with ideological pleas to a fine scholar's conscience but also with photographs of this same scholar in all manner of sexual indulgences with very strange women—women in their sixties and seventies, bag ladies off the streets, who after carnal abuse were subject to sheer physical abuse. He was a winner, the scholar-diplomat. A psychiatrist in Langley had said something about wish-fulfillment—sexually repressed matricide. Stone did not need that nonsense; he had the photographs of a son-of-a-bitch sadist. But it was the children that occupied his mind now, not the excesses of a fool that permitted him access to a luxury apartment far beyond his consultation fees.

The *children. Jesus!* They were so right, their sensibilities so correctly on target, but they did not understand that when they took on the George Marcus Delavanes of today's world it was war in all its worst forms of brutality, because that was the way these men fought. Righteousness had to join with a commitment to crawl in the gutter if necessary, no quarter sought, for none would be given. This was the last fifth of the twentieth century and the generals were going for it all; the paranoia of their disgust and frustrations had come to the end of endurance.

Stone had seen it coming for years, and there were times when he had come close to applauding, throwing his hands up in frustration, willing to sell what was left of his soul. Strategies had been aborted—men *lost*—because of the maddening bureaucratic restraints that led back to laws and a constitution that were never written with anything like Moscow in mind. The Mad Marcuses of this planet—this part of the planet—had a number of very plausible points. There were those in the Company years ago who were adamant and not squirrelly about it. They said, *"Bomb* the nuclear plants in Tashkent and Tselinograd! Blow them the hell up in Chengdu and Shenyang! Don't let them begin! We are responsible and they are *not!"*

Who knew? Would the world have been better off?

Then Peter would wake up in the morning and that part of his soul he had not sold would tell him, no, we cannot do that. There had to be another way, a way without confrontation and wholesale death. He still clung to that alternative, but he could not dismiss the Delavanes as megabomb off-the-wallers. Where were we heading now?

He knew where *he* was heading—had been heading for years. It was why he had joined the children. Their righteousness was justified, their indignation valid. He had seen it all before in too many places, always at the extremes of the political spectrum. The Delavanes of the planet would turn everyone into robots. In many ways, death was preferable.

Stone unlocked the door of the apartment, closed it, took off his jacket and made himself the only drink he would permit himself for the evening. He walked to the leather chair by the telephone and sat down, taking several swallows before putting the glass on the table beneath the floor lamp. He picked up the phone and dialed seven digits, then three more, and one more after that. A very faint dial tone replaced the original, and he dialed again. Everything was in order. The call was being routed through a KGB diplomatic scrambler cable on an island in the Cabot Strait southwest of Newfoundland. Only Dzerzhinsky Square would be confused. Peter had paid six negatives for the service. Five rings preceded the sound of a male voice in Bern, Switzerland.

"Allo?"

"This is your old friend from Bahrain, also the vendor in Lisbon and a buyer in the Dardanelles. Do I have to sing 'Dixie'?"

"Well, *mah wuhd,*" said the man in Bern stretching out the phrase in a dialect bred in the American Deep South, the French pretense dropped. "You go back a long time, don't you, suh?"

"I do, sir."

"I hear you're one of the bad guys now."

"Unloved, mistrusted, but still appreciated," said Stone. "That's more accurate. The Company won't touch me, but it's got its share of unfriendlies in town who throw me consultations pretty regularly. I wasn't as smart as you. No deposits from Uncle No-Name in Swiss accounts."

"I was told you had a little juice problem."

"A big one, but it's over."

"Never negotiate a release from people worse than you if you can't pass a Breathalyzer test. You've got to scare them, not make 'em laugh."

"I found that out. I hear you do some

623

consulting yourself."

"On a limited basis and only with clients who could pass Uncle No-Name's muster. That's the agreement and I stick to it. Either I do or some Boom Boom Botticelli is flown over and Massa's in de cole, cole ground."

"Where the threats don't do you any good," said the civilian.

"That's the stand-off, Pearlie May. It's our little *détente.*"

"Would I pass muster? I give you my word I'm working with good people. They're young and they're on to something and they haven't got an evil thought in their heads, which under the circumstances is no recommendation. But I can't tell you anything substantive. For your sake as well as mine and theirs. Is that good enough?"

"If the consultation doesn't take place in outer space, it's more than enough, and you know it. You saved Johnny Reb's ass three times, only y'awl got the sequence backwards. In the Dardanelles and Lisbon you got me out before the guns came in. Over in Bahrain you rewrote a report about a little matter of missing contingency funds that probably kept me from five years in a Leavenworth stockade."

"You were too valuable to lose over a minor indiscretion. Besides, you weren't the only one, you merely got caught—or nearly did."

"Regardless, Johnny Reb owes. What is it?"

Stone reached for his glass and took a drink. He spoke, choosing his words carefully. "One of our commanders is missing. It's a Navy problem, SAND PAC-based, and the people I'm with want to keep it contained. No Washington input at this stage."

"Which is part of what you can't tell me," said the Southerner. "Okay. SAND PAC—that's San Diego and points west and wet until the date line, right?"

"Yes, but it's not relevant. He's the chief legal out there—maybe *was,* by now. If he's not past tense, *if* he's alive, he's nearer you than me. Also if I get on a plane, my passport ignites the computers and things can't go that way."

"Which is also part of what you can't tell me."

"Check."

"What *can* you tell me?"

"You know the embassy in Bonn?"

"I know it's in trouble. Just like the security units in Brussels. That psycho's cutting one hell of a path. What about Bonn?"

"It's all related. Our commander was last seen there."

"He's got something to do with this *Converse?*"

Steve paused. "You can probably fill in more spaces than is good for any of us, but the bones of the scenario are as follows. Our commander was a very upset man. His brother-in-law—who, incidentally, was his closest friend—was killed in Geneva—"

"Down the road from here," interrupted the expatriate in Bonn. "The American lawyer whose demise was engineered by Converse, at least that's what I've read."

"That's what our commander believed. How or from whom he got the information no one knows, but apparently he found out that Converse was heading for Bonn. He went on leave to go after him.''

''Commendable but dumb,'' said the Southerner. ''A one-man lynching mob?''

''Actually, no. By simple equations we can assume he went to the embassy—at least he met someone *from* the embassy to explain why he was there, perhaps to warn them, who knows? But the rest speaks for itself. This Converse struck and our commander disappeared. We'd like to find out whether he's alive or dead.''

It was the Southerner's turn to pause, but his breathing was clearly heard on the line. Finally: ''Brer Rabbit, you've simply *got* to put a little flesh on those bones.''

''I'm about to, General Lee.''

''Much obliged, Yankee.''

''It's also related. If you were a lieutenant commander in the United States Navy and wanted to reach someone at the embassy in Bonn, someone who would accord you the attention your rank deserved, who would you call?''

''The military chargé d'affaires, who else?''

''That's the man, Uncle Remus. Among other things, he's a liar, but I can't go into that. It's our thinking that the commander spoke with him and the chargé dismissed him as a fringe case, probably didn't even give him an appointment with Ambassador Peregrine. And when it happened, to save his ass and his career—well, people do strange things.''

''What you're suggesting is awful damned strange.''

"I won't back away from it," said the civilian.

"Okay, what's his name?"

"Washburn. He's a—"

"*Norman* Washburn? Major Norman Anthony Washburn, the Third, Fifth, or Sixth?"

"That's the one."

"*Don't* back away. You left the field too early. Washburn was in Beirut, then Athens and, after that, Madrid. He gave every Company flack in the territories the business! He'd nail his Park Avenue mama to a velvet wall for a good evaluation report. He figures by forty-five he'll be heading the Joint Chiefs—and he intends to."

"By forty-five?"

"I've been out of touch for a couple of years, but he can't be any more than thirty-six, thirty-seven. The last I heard they were going to jump the light-colonel status and make him a full bird, then a brigadier soon after that. He is *loved,* Yankee!"

"He's a liar," said the civilian in the dimly lit apartment on Nebraska Avenue.

"Sure 'nuff," agreed the man in Bern, "but I never figured anything this radical. I mean, he's got to be scratchin' mule shit for oil to do something so far out."

"I still won't back away," repeated the civilian, drinking his bourbon.

"Which means you know."

"Check."

"And you can't talk about that, either." A statement.

"Check again."

"Are you firm?"

"No room for error. He knows where the commander is—if he's alive."

"Holy *Jesus!* What *are* you Northern boys *into?*"

"Will you track? Starting yesterday?"

"With pleasure, Yankee. How do you want it?"

"In the twilight zone. Only words that come with needles—that's important. He has to wake up thinking he ate a bad piece of meat."

"Women?"

"I don't know. You probably have a better fix on that than I do. Would he risk his image?"

"With two or three Fräuleins I've got in Bonn, Jesuits would risk the papacy, suh. The name of the commander, please?"

"Fitzpatrick. Lieutenant Commander Connal Fitzpatrick. And, Uncle Remus, whatever you hear under the needles, give only to me. No one else. *No one.*"

"Which is the last part of what you can't tell me, right?"

"Check."

"My blinders are in place. One objective only with only one target. No side trips and no curiosity, just a tape recorder in my head or my hand."

Again Stone paused, filling the silence with a tentative whisper. *"Tape . . . ?"* Then he continued. "The latter's not a bad idea. Mini-micro, of course."

"Naturally. Those little mothers are so small you can hide them in the most embarrassing places. Where do I reach you? My quill is poised."

"All right, the area code's eight-zero-four." The former CIA man gave the expatriate in Bern a telephone number in Charlotte, North Carolina. "A woman will answer. Tell her you're from the Tatiana family and leave a number."

Their brief good-byes concluded, Peter hung up the phone, got out of the chair and carried his drink to the window. It was a hot, still night in Washington, the air outside barely moving, the hint of a summer storm. If the rains came they would wash the streets and cleanse at least part of the pollution.

The former deep-cover agent wished there were some balm on earth or from the skies that could wash his hands and cleanse that part of his soul he had not put on the auction block—or for a disastrous period of time into a bottle of bourbon. Maybe all he had done was hammer another nail in Converse's coffin, one more scrap of credibility that labeled the lawyer something he was not. Stone realized that instead of casting reasonable doubts based on his own certain knowledge, he had compounded the fiction that Converse was the psychopathic killer the international media described. Worse, he had attributed that credibility to a responsible missing man, a naval officer who was most likely dead. There were two justifications for the lie, and only one was remotely feasible; the other, however, was probably the most productive move they could make. The first assumed that Fitzpatrick *might* be alive, a weak premise. But if he was dead, the missing commander provided the reason to call in an old debt and go after a chargé d'affaires named Washburn and do so without any connection to George Marcus Delavane. Even if "Johnny Reb" was caught—and every man in a gray to black operation had to assume the possibility—no mention could be made of an international conspiracy of generals. . . . Major Norman Washburn, IV, might or might not know the fate of Connal Fitzpatrick, but everything else he might say under the needles—especially about the commander—would be of value.

What surprised the civilian was Converse himself in the matter of the lying military attaché. If Converse was running and not under lock and key, he certainly had to have learned about the lie that had condemned him. If so, why hadn't the attorney done something about it? The major's lie was the chain's weakest link; it could be snapped with a minimum of effort—the man's a liar. *I was here or there, or anywhere except where he placed me when he placed me.* Stone drank sparingly from the glass; he knew the futility of speculating because he knew the answer. It was why he did not feel that yet another part of his soul had been clipped away. Converse was not in a position to do anything. He was either trapped or taken, soon to be offered up as a sacrificial corpse by the generals. There was nothing anyone could do for him. He was a dead man, a sacrifice in the truest sense of the word—given up even by his own.

Peter walked back to the chair and sat down, loosening his tie and kicking off his shoes. He had learned years ago to cut losses in the field wherever possible. If it meant disowning pawns or plants or blinds, one took the statistical approach and let the executions follow. It was better than losing more. But what was even better was to make significant progress with whatever the loss. He was doing that now with Converse's death and "Johnny Reb" in Bern—and a liar named Washburn.

Oh, *Christ!* He was playing God again with charts and diagrams—pluses and minuses of human value! Yet the objective was worth more than anything he had ever faced before. Delavane and his legions had to be stopped, and they would not be stopped in Washington. There were too many watchful eyes, too many ears, too many men in unknown corners who believed in the myth—men who had nothing else. The children were right about that. And there would be no empty bottles of bourbon on the floor now, or blurred memories of nights past, or words passed. Despite advancing age, he was ready; he was primed.

It was odd, thought the civilian. He had not used the Tatiana family in years.

Joel watched from the ridge of the landfill as Leifhelm's chauffeur and his companion approached the deserted building. Both were experienced; one raced before the other, stopping behind displaced rocks from the fill and barrels used for early-morning fires. Almost simultaneously they reached separate doors, each door off its hinges, angling into the dirt. The chauffeur gestured with his weapon, and both men disappeared inside.

Converse again looked behind him. The fence

was about two hundred yards away. Could he slide down the stinking hill, race to the inter-woven wire and climb over the fence before his executioners came out of the decrepit building? Why *not?* He could try! He raised himself off his stomach, hands sinking into the debris, spun to his right and plunged downward.

A distant crash came first and then a scream. He spun around again and scrambled up the ten-odd feet his lunge had carried him. The chauffeur was racing out of his door, around the corner to where his companion had entered, his gun leveled, prepared to fire. He approached cautiously, then seeing something, exploded in disgust as he entered the shadows. Seconds later he emerged holding the other man; obviously a staircase or a floorboard had collapsed. The second man held his leg and limped.

Two piercing blasts came from the station; the platform was empty, the milling passengers back on board. The panic had subsided and the train would make a Teutonic effort to be on time. The last police car and the ambulance were gone.

Below, the chauffeur slapped his companion repeatedly in fury, shoving him backwards to the ground. The man got up, gesturing, pleading for no more, and the chauffeur relented, ordering his subordinate to a position between the building, the landfill and the fence, and when the man was in place, the chauffeur went back into the deserted building.

The minutes passed, the descending sun intercepted by low-flying clouds in the west, creating long, lateral shadows over the outskirts of the railroad yard. Finally the chauffeur came into view, emerging from an unseen exit on another side of the building. He stood for a moment and looked west across the tracks to the expanse of wild grass and marshland beyond. Then he turned and stared at the mounds of landfill and made up his mind.

"Rechts über Ihnen!" he screamed at his companion, pointing to the second mound. *"Hinter Ihnen! Er schiesst."*

Joel crawled, racing down the debris like a panicked sand crab. Halfway to the bottom his left hand was snared; he yanked at the looping entrapment, pulled it free and was about to fling it away when he saw it was a length of ordinary electric cord. He bunched it up in his hand and frantically continued downward. When he was within six feet of the ground, he whipped his whole body into a frenzy and clawed at the dirt and garbage. He stabbed his legs repeatedly into the rubbish and loose earth, and sank his body into the mass, pulling debris around his head. The stench was overpowering, and he could feel the insects penetrating his clothes, crawling over his skin. But he was hidden, of that he was certain. He began to comprehend what his fragmented mind was trying to tell him. He was back in the jungle, about to spring on a scout from an unseen place.

Again minutes passed, and the shadows became longer, then permanent, as the sun's trajectory dropped below the top of the landfill. Converse remained immobile, straining every muscle, grinding his teeth to stop himself from thrashing his arms and scratching his clothes and his exposed skin to rip away the maddening insects. But he knew he could not move. It would happen any moment, any second.

The prelude came. The limping man was in view, peering up at the hill of refuse and dirt, squinting against the residue of sunlight at the top, his gun held out, angled diagonally, prepared to fire. He sidestepped slowly, cautiously, apprehensive of what he could not see. He passed directly in front of Joel, the extended gun no more than three feet away from Converse's face. Another step and the line of contact could be clear.

Now! Joel lunged out, grabbing the barrel of the gun, instantly and violently twisting it clockwise and downward. As the German fell forward Converse crashed his knee up into the bridge of the man's nose, stunning him before he could scream. The weapon spiraled off into the debris. The man staggered, and was about to find his voice when Joel lunged again, a section of the wire cord stretched out in both hands; he whipped it over the scout's head, pulling it taut around the scout's throat.

The man went limp, and Converse bent over the body, about to roll it into the base of the landfill and conceal it, but then he stopped. There had to be another way because there was another option, one he had taken a hundred years ago with another scout in a jungle. He looked around; there was a pile of carelessly dumped railroad ties thirty-odd yards away on his right—old ties, several broken, forming a low wall. A *wall.*

It was a risk. If Leifhelm's chauffeur finished his examination of the first mound of landfill and stepped out toward the second one at any three of the four angles, he would have a clear line of sight. The man had been sent to the Emmerich train for two reasons—one, he knew the quarry by sight, and, two, the quarry had disgraced him; Joel's corpse would be his redemption. Such a man was an expert with weapons—which the quarry was not. What was the point of thinking! Since Geneva, *everything* was a risk, a gamble against death.

He gripped the German's body under the armpits, and breathing hard—for some reason foolishly counting off "One, two, three"—he lurched backwards, hauling the dead man across a dead man's zone.

He reached the railroad ties and swung the corpse around them, the heels of its shoes digging an arc into the dirt as he dragged the dead German into the base of the wall. Then without thinking, acting only on instinct, Converse did what he had been wanting to do for the last hour. Concealed by the ties, he ripped off his jacket and shirt and rolled on the ground, scattering the insects like an infested dog in a field, scratching them out of his hair, away from his face. It was all he could do for the moment. He crawled into the bank of railroad ties and found a space between two separated logs.

"Werner! Wo sind Sie?"

The shouts preceded the figure of Leifhelm's chauffeur. He appeared at the far end of the second mound, moving slowly, his gun raised,

635

each step taken cautiously, his head shifting in all directions, a soldier experienced in combat patrol. Converse thought how much better off the world would be if he were an expert shot. He was not. In pilot training he had gone through the obligatory small-arms course, and at twenty-five feet had rarely hit the target. This second soldier of Aquitaine had to be sucked in much closer.

"Werner! Antworten Sie doch!"

Silence.

The chauffeur was alarmed; he walked backward, now crouching, scanning the hill of refuse, kicking away any object in his backward path, his head pivoting. Joel knew what he had to do; he had done it before. Divert the killer's attention, pulling him closer to the encounter, then move away.

"Auughh . . . !" Converse let the wail come out of his throat. Then added in clear English, "Oh, my *God!*" Instantly he crawled to the far end of the wall of railroad ties. He peered around the side, his head in shadows.

"Werner! Wo sind—!" The German stood erect, his eyes following his line of hearing. Suddenly he broke into a run, his weapon thrust in front of him—a man cornering a hated object, the sound of English leading him to the loathed enemy.

The chauffeur threw himself prone across the railroad ties, his expression alert, his gun in front of him. He fired into the shadowed corpse below, a roar of vengeance accompanying the explosions.

Joel got to his knees, aimed his automatic, and pulled the trigger twice. The German spun off the ties, blood erupting in his chest.

"Some win," whispered Converse rising to his feet, remembering the man on the train to Emmerich.

He was down in the marshlands, the clothes in his arms. He had scrambled across the railroad tracks, down through the wild grass into the swampy dampness of the marsh. It was water, and that was all he had to know. Water was a benefit, whether as an escape route or as a purifying agent for a wracked body—also lessons he had learned years ago. He sat naked on a sloping marsh bank, taking off his inhibiting money belt, wondering if the paper bills inside were soaked but not caring enough to examine them.

He did, however, examine every pocket of the clothes he had stripped from his would-be executioners. He was not sure what was of value and what was not. The money was irrelevant, except for the small bills; and the driver's licenses had photographs embedded in plastic—neither was worth the risk of scrutiny. There was an ominous-looking knife, the long blade released through the head by the touch of a button on the handle; he kept it. Also a cheap butane lighter and a comb—and, for the drinking man, two breath fresheners. The rest were personal effects—keys, a four-leaf-clover good-luck charm, photographs in the wallets—he did not care to look at them. Death was death, enemy and friend fundamentally equalized. The only things he was interested in were the clothes. *They* were the option, the option he had used in the jungle a lifetime ago. He had crammed himself inside a scout's tattered uniform, and twice across a narrow riverbank he had not been shot by the enemy who had spotted him. Instead, they had waved.

He selected the articles of clothing that fit best and put them on; the rest he threw into the marsh. Whatever he looked like, there was little or no resemblance to the tweedy academic he had tried to be in Bonn. If anything, he could be mistaken for a man who worked on the Rhine, a roughhewn mate or a foreman of a barge crew. He had chosen the chauffeur's coat, a dark, coarse-woven jacket cut to the hips, with the man's blue denim shirt underneath—both bullet holes washed clean of blood. The trousers were those of the subordinate executioner; brown creaseless corduroys, flared slightly at the ankles, which, thankfully, they reached. Neither man had worn a hat, and his was somewhere in the landfill; he would find one or buy one or steal one. He had to; without a hat or a cap covering part of his face, he felt as naked, as exposed and as frightened as he would have felt without clothes.

He lay back in the dry wild grass as the sun disappeared over an unseen horizon and stared up at the sky.

24

"Well, *Ahh'l be . . . !*" exclaimed the distinguished-looking man with the flowing mane of white hair, his full, nearly white eyebrows arched in astonishment. "You're Molly Washburn's boy?"

"I beg your pardon?" said the Army officer at the adjacent table along the banquette in Bonn's Am Tulpenfeld restaurant. "Have we met, sir?"

"Not so's you'd remember, Major. . . . Please forgive my intruding." The Southerner addressed the apology to the officer's companion across the table, a balding middle-aged man who had been speaking English with a pronounced German accent. "But Molly would never forgive this pore old Georgia cracker if he didn't say hello to her son and insist on buyin' him a drink."

"I'm afraid I'm at a loss," said Washburn pleasantly but without enthusiasm.

"I would be, too, young fella. I know it sounds cornpone, but you were just barely in long pants back then. The last time I saw you, you were in a blue blazer jacket and madder 'n hell at losing a soccer game. I think you blamed it on your left wing, which in my opinion then and now is a logical place to blame *anything.*"

The major and his companion laughed appreciatively. "Good Lord, that does go back a long time—to when I was at Dalton."

"And captain of the team, as I recall."

"How did you ever recognize me?"

"I dropped in on your momma the other week at the house in Southampton. Proud girl that she is, there were a few real handsome photographs of you in the living room."

"Of course, on the piano."

"That's where they were, silver frames and all."

"I'm afraid I've forgotten your name."

"Thayer. Thomas Thayer, or just plain old T.T. as your momma calls me." The two shook hands.

"Good to see you again, sir," said Washburn, gesturing at his companion. "This is Herr Stammler. He handles a great deal of our press relations with the West German media."

"How do you do, Mr. Stammler."

"A pleasure, Herr Thayer."

"Speakin' of the embassy and I assume you were, I promised Molly I'd ring you up over there when I got here. Mah word on it, I was goin' to do just that tomorrow—I'm fightin' jet lag today. One hell of a coincidence, isn't it? You bein' here and my bein' here, right *next* to each other!"

"Major," interrupted the German courteously. "Two people who go back so many years must have a great deal to reminisce about. And since our business is fundamentally concluded, I think I shall press on."

"Now, hold on, Mr. Stammler," objected Thayer. "Ah simply couldn't allow you to do that!"

"No, really, it's perfectly all right." The

German smiled. "Truthfully, Major Washburn felt he should insist on taking me to dinner this evening after the terrible things we've had to deal with during the past few days—he far more than I—but to be quite honest, I'm exhausted. Also I am far older than my young friend and nowhere near as resilient. The bed cries out, Herr Thayer. Believe me when I tell you that."

"Hey, Mr. Stammler, Ah've got an idea. You're fanned out and I'm droppin' from the jet stream, so why don't we leave the young skunk here and *both* hit the pillows?"

"But *I* couldn't allow *you* to do that." The German got up from the table and extended his hand to Thayer. They shook, and Stammler turned to Washburn, shaking his hand also. "I'll call you in the morning, Norman."

"All right, Gerhard. . . . Why didn't you just say you were tired?"

"And conceivably offend one of my largest clients? Be reasonable, Norman. Good night, gentlemen." The German smiled again, and walked away.

"Ah guess we're stuck with each other, young man," said the Southerner. "Why not move over here and let me save the embassy a couple of dollars?"

"All right," replied Washburn, getting up with his drink and sidling between the tables to the chair opposite Thayer. He sat down. "How is Mother? I haven't called her in a couple of weeks."

"Molly is always Molly, my boy. She came forth and they broke the mold, but I don't have to tell *you* that. She looks the same as she did twenty years ago. I swear I don't know how she *does* it!''

"And she's not going to tell you, either.''

Both men laughed as the Southerner raised his glass and brought it forward for the touch. The glasses met, a gentle ring was heard. It was the beginning.

Converse waited, watching from a dark storefront on the shabby street in Emmerich. Across the way were the dim lights of a cheap hotel, the entrance uninviting, sleazy. Yet with any luck he would have a bed there in the next few minutes. A bed with a sink in the corner of the room and, with even more luck, hot water with which he could bathe his wound and change the bandage again. During the last two nights he had learned that such places were his only possibilities for refuge. No questions would be asked and a false name on a registration card expected. But even the most sullen greeting was a menace for him. He had only to open his mouth and whatever came out identified him as an American who could not speak German.

He felt like a deaf-mute running a gauntlet, careening off walls of people. He was helpless, so goddamned helpless! The killings in Bonn, Brussels and Wesel had made every American male over thirty and under fifty suspect. The melodramatic suspicions were compounded by speculations that the obsessed man was being aided, perhaps manipulated, by terrorist organizations—Baader-Meinhof, the PLO, Libyan splinter groups, even KGB destabilization teams sent out by the dreaded Voennaya. He was being hunted everywhere, and as of yesterday, the *International Herald Tribune* had printed further reports that the assassin was heading for Paris—which meant that the generals of Aquitaine wanted the concentration to be *on* Paris, not where they knew he was, where their soldiers could run him down, take him, kill him.

To get off the streets he had to move with the flotsam and jetsam and he needed a run-down hotel like the one across the street. He knew he had to get off the streets; there were too many traps outside. So on the first night in Wesel he remembered the student Johann, and looked for ways to re-create similar circumstances. Young people were less prone to be suspicious and more receptive to the promise of financial reward for a friendly service.

It was odd, but that first night in Wesel was both the most difficult and the easiest. Difficult because he had no idea where to look, easy because it happened so rapidly, so logically.

First he stopped at a drugstore, buying gauze, adhesive tape, antiseptic and an inexpensive cap with a visor. Then he went to a café, to the men's room, where he washed his face and the wound, which he bound tight, skin joining skin, the bandage firmly in place. Suddenly, as he finished his ministrations, he heard the familiar words and emphatic melody, young raucous voices in song: *"On, Wisconsin. . . . On, Wisconsin . . . on to victoreee . . ."*

The singers were a group of students from the

German Society at the University of Wisconsin, as he later found out, who were bicycling through the northern Rhineland. Casually approaching a young man getting more beers from the bar and introducing himself as a fellow American, he told an outrageous story of having been taken by a whore and rolled by her pimp, who stole his passport but never thought of a money belt. He was a respected businessman who had to sleep it off, gather his wits, and reach his firm back in New York. However, he spoke no German; would the student consider the payment of $100 for helping him out?

He would and did. Down the block was a dingy hotel where no questions were asked; the young man paid for a room and brought Converse, who was waiting outside, his receipt and his key.

All yesterday he had walked, following the roads in sight of the railroad tracks until he reached a town named Halden. It was smaller than Wesel, but there was a run-down, industrial section east of the railroad yards. The only "hotel" he could find, however, was a large, shoddy house at the end of a row of shoddy houses with signs saying ZIMMER, 20 MARK in two first-floor windows and a larger one over the front door. It was a boardinghouse, and several doors beyond in the spill of the streetlamps a heated argument was taking place between an older woman and a young man. Above, a few neighbors sat in their windows, arms on the sills, obviously listening. Joel also listened to the sporadic words shouted in heavily accented English.

". . . 'I hate it here!' *Das habe ich ihm gesagt.* 'I do not care to stay, *Onkel!* I vill go back to Germany! Maybe join Baader-Meinhof!' *Das habe ich ihm gesagt.*"

"*Narr!*" screamed the woman, turning and going up the steps. "*Schweinehund!*" she roared, as she opened the door, went inside and slammed it shut behind her.

The young man had looked up at his audience in the windows and shrugged. A few clapped, so he made an exaggerated, elaborate bow. Converse approached; there was no harm in trying, he thought. "You speak very good English," he said.

"Vye not?" replied the German. "They spend bags of groceries for five years to give me lessons. I must go to her brother in America. I say *Nein!* They say *Ja!* I go. I *hate* it!"

"I'm sorry to hear that. I'm an American and I like the German people. Where were you?"

"In Yorktown."

"Virginia?"

"*Nein!* The city of New York."

"Oh, *that* Yorktown."

"*Ja,* my uncle has two butcher shops in New York, in what they call Yorktown. *Shit,* as you say in America!"

"I'm sorry. Why?"

"The *Schwarzen* and the *Juden!* If you speak like me, the black people steal from you with knives, and the Jews steal from you with their cash registers. *Heinie,* they call me, and *Nazi.* I told a Jew he cheated me—I vas nice, I vas not impolite—and he told me to get out of his shop or he call the 'cops'! I vas *shit,* he said! . . . You vear a good German suit and spend good German money, they don't say those things. You are a delivery boy trying to learn, they kick the shit out of you! What do *I* know! My father vas only a fourteen-year-old soldier. *Shit!*"

"Again, I'm telling you I'm sorry. I mean it. It's not in our nature to blame children."

"*Shit!*"

"Perhaps I can make up for a little of what you went through. I'm in trouble—because I was a *stupid* American. But I'll pay you a hundred American dollars . . ."

The young German happily got him a room at the boardinghouse. It was no better than the one in Wesel, but the water was hotter, the toilet nearer his door.

Tonight was different from the other nights he had spent in Germany, thought Joel, as he looked across the street at the decrepit hotel in Emmerich. Tonight could lead to his passage into Holland. To Cort Thorbecke and a plane to Washington. The man Joel had recruited was somewhat older than the others who had helped him. He was a merchant seaman out of Bremerhaven, in Emmerich to make a duty call on his family, with whom he felt ill at ease. He had made the obligatory call, been soundly rebuked by his mother and father, and had returned to the place and the people he loved best—a bar at the bend of the riverbank.

Again, as it had been in Wesel, it was the English lyrics of a song that had caught Joel's attention. He stared at the young seaman standing at the bar and playing a guitar. This time it was not a college football song but an odd, haunting mixture of slow biting rock and a sad madrigal: ". . . When you finally came down, when your feet hit the ground, did you know where you were? When you finally were real, could you touch what you feel, were you there in the know? . . ."

The men around the bar were caught up by the precise beat of the minor-key music. When the seaman finished there was respectful applause, followed by a resumption of fast talk and faster refilling of mugs of beer. Minutes later Converse was standing next to the seagoing troubador, the guitar now slung over his shoulder and held in place by a wide strap like a weapon. Joel wondered if the man really knew English or only lyrics. He would find out in seconds. The seaman laughed at a companion's remark; when the laughter subsided, Converse said, "I'd like to buy you a drink for reminding me of home. It was a nice song."

The man looked at him quizzically. Joel stammered, thinking that the seaman had no idea what he was talking about. Then, to Converse's relief, the man answered. *"Danke.* It is a good song. Sad but good, like some of ours. You are *Amerikaner?"*

"Yes. And you speak English."

"Okay. I don't read no good, *aber* I speak okay. I'm on merchant ship. We sail Boston, New York, Baltimore—sometimes ports, Florida."

"What'll you have?"

"Ein Bier," said the seaman, shrugging.

"Why not whisky?"

"*Ja?*"

"Certainly."

"*Ja.*"

Minutes later they were at a table. Joel told his story about a nonexistent whore and a fictional pimp. He told it slowly, not because he felt he had to pace the narrative to his listener's understanding, but because another option was coming sharply into focus. The guitar-playing merchantman was young, but there was a patina about him that indicated he knew the docks and the waterfront and the various businesses that flourished in that very special world.

"You should go to the *Polizei,*" said the man when Converse had finished. "They know the whores and they will not print your name." The German smiled. "We want you back to spend more money."

"I can't take the chance. In spite of the way I look, I deal with a lot of important people—here and in America."

"Which makes *you* important, *ja?*"

"And very stupid. If I could just get over into Holland, I could handle everything."

"*Die Niederlande?* Vat is problem?"

"I told you, my passport was taken. And it's just my luck that every American crossing any border is looked at very carefully. You know, that crazy bastard who killed the ambassador in Bonn and the NATO commander."

"*Ja,* and in Wesel two, three days ago," said the German. "They say he goes to Paris."

"I'm afraid that doesn't help me. . . . Look,

you know the river people, the men who have boats going out every day. I told you I'd pay you a hundred dollars for the hotel. . . ."

"I agreed. You are generous."

"I'll pay you a great deal more if you can somehow get me over into Holland. You see, my company has an office in Amsterdam. They can help me. Will *you* help me?"

The German grimaced and looked at his watch. "Is too late for such arrangements tonight and I leave for Bremerhaven on the morning train. My ship sails at fifteen hundred."

"That was the amount I had in mind. Fifteen hundred."

"Deutsche marks?"

"Dollars."

"You are more crazy than your *Landsmann* who kills soldiers. If you knew the language, it cost no more than fifty."

"I don't know the language. Fifteen hundred American dollars—for you if you can arrange it."

The young man looked hard at Converse, then moved back his chair. "Wait here. I will make phone call."

"Send over more whisky on your way."

"Danke."

The waiting was spent in a vacuum of anxiety. Joel looked at the weathered guitar lying across an extra chair. What were the words? . . . *When you finally came down, when your feet hit the ground . . . did you know where you were? When you finally were real, could you touch . . . what you feel, were you there in the know? . . .*

"I will stop for you at five o'clock in the

morning," announced the merchant seaman, who sat down with two glasses of whisky. "The captain will accept two hundred dollars, *aber* only if there are no drugs. If there are drugs, you don't come on board."

"I have no drugs," said Converse, smiling, controlling his elation. "That's done and you've earned your money. I'll pay you at the dock or pier or whatever it is."

"Natürlich."

It had all happened less than an hour ago, thought Joel, watching the hotel entrance across the street. At five o'clock in the morning he would be on his way to Holland, to Amsterdam, to a man named Cort Thorbecke, Mattilon's broker of illegal passports. All the passenger manifests on all aircraft heading for the United States would be watched by Aquitaine, but a hundred years ago he had learned that there were ways to elude the watchers. He had done it before from a deep, cold shaft in the ground and despite a barbed-wire fence in the darkness. He could do it again.

A figure emerged under the dimly lit marquee of the hotel. It was the young merchant seaman. Grinning, he beckoned Converse to join him.

"Hell's fire and Jeesus *H,* what *is* it, Norman?" cried the Southerner, as Washburn suddenly went into an erratic series of convulsions, his lips trembling as he gasped for air.

"I . . . don't . . . know." The major's eyes

650

grew wide, the pupils now dancing and out of control.

"Maybe it's that Heimlich thing!" said Thomas Thayer, rising from the banquette and quickly moving toward Washburn. "Hell no, it *can't* be! Our food's not here; you haven't *eaten!*"

The couples near by expressed alarm, talking loudly, rapidly in German. At a remark made by one of the diners, the Southerner turned and spoke to the man. *"Das glaube ich nicht,"* said Johnny Reb in flawless German. *"Mein Wagen steht draussen. Ich weiss einen Arzt."*

The maître d' came rushing over and, seeing that the commotion involved the Americans, addressed his concern in English. "Is the major ill, sir? Shall I ask if there is . . ."

"No doctor I'm not familiar with, thanks," interrupted Thayer, bent over the embassy's chargé d'affaires, who was now inhaling deeply, his eyes half closed, his head swaying back and forth. "This here is Molly Washburn's boy and I'll see he gets the best! My car's outside. Maybe if a couple of your waiters will give a hand we can put him in the limo and I'll take him right over to my man. He's a specialist. At my age you gotta have 'em everywhere."

"Bestimmt. Certainly!" The maître d' snapped his fingers; three busboys responded instantly.

"The embassy . . . the *embassy!*" choked Washburn as the three men half carried the officer to the door of the restaurant.

"Don't you worry, Norman-boy!" said the Southerner, hearing the plea, walking behind with the maître d'. "I'll phone 'em from the car, tell 'em to meet us at Rudi's place." Thayer turned to the German beside him. "You know what Ah think? Ah think this fine soldier is jest plumb wore out. He's been workin' from sunrise to sunrise with nary a break. I mean, can you imagine everything he's had to contend with these last couple of days? That crazy mongrel goin' around shootin' up a feud, killin' the ambassador, then that honcho in Brussels! You know, Molly's boy here is the char-jay d'affaires."

"Yes, the major is our guest frequently—an honored guest."

"Well, even the most honorable among us has a right and a time to say 'The hell with it, I'll sit this one out.' "

"I'm not sure I understand?"

"Ah have an idea this fine young man who I knew as a mere saplin' lad never learned about the quantitative effects of old demon whisky."

"Ohh?" The maître d' looked at Johnny Reb—a fashionable gossipmonger relishing a new rumor.

"He had several mites too much, that's all—and *that's* jest between *us.*"

"He vas not in focus. . . ."

"He started bustin' corks before the sun hit the whites of the west cotton." They reached the front entrance, the unit of busboys maneuvering Washburn out the door. "Who was more entitled? That's what I say." Thayer removed his wallet.

"Ja, I agree."

"Here," said the Southerner, removing bills. "I haven't had time to convert, so there's a hundred

652

American—that should cover the tab and plenty for the boys outside. . . . And here's a hundred for you—for not talkin' too much, *verstehen?"*

"Completely, *mein Herr!"* The German pocketed both $100 bills, smiling and nodding his head obsequiously. "I vill say absolutely nozzing!"

"Well, I wouldn't go that far. It might be a good thing for Molly's boy to learn that it ain't the end of the world if a few people know he's had a drink or two. Might loosen him up a bit, and in mah Georgia judgment, he needs a little loosenin'. Maybe you might wink at him when he next comes in."

"Vink?"

"Give him a friendly smile, like you know and it's okay. *Verstehen?"*

"*Ja,* I agree! He vas entitled!"

Outside at the curb, Johnny Reb instructed the busboys just how to place Major Norman Anthony Washburn IV into the backseat. Stretched out, facing up, supine. The Southerner gave each man a $20 American bill and dismissed them. He then spoke to the two men in front, pressing a button so they could hear his voice beyond the glass partition.

"Ah got the jump seats down," he said, pulling the velvet backs out of the velvet wall. "He's out. Come on and join me, Witch Doctor. And you, Klaus, you entertain us with a long drive in your beautiful countryside."

Minutes later, as the limousine entered a backcountry road, the overhead light switched on, the doctor unbuckled Washburn's belt, slid the trousers down, and rolled the chargé d'affaires over and into the seat. He found the area he wanted at the base of the spine, the needle held above in his steady hand.

"Ready, chap?" asked the dark-skinned Palestinian, yanking down the elastic top of the unconscious man's shorts.

"You got it, Pookie," answered Johnny Reb, holding a small recorder over the edge of the jump seat. "Right where he won't find it for a week, if he ever does. Take him up, Arab. I want him to *fly*."

The doctor inserted the long hypodermic needle, slowly pressing his thumb on the plunger. "It will be quick," said the Palestinian. "It is a heavy dose and I've seen it happen when the patient began babbling before the interrogator was ready."

"I'm ready."

"Put him on track instantly. Ask direct questions, center his concentration immediately."

"Oh, Ah will, indeed. This is a bad man, Pookie. A nasty little boy who tells tall tales that ain't got nothin' to do with a big catfish that broke off a hook." The Southerner gripped the unconscious Washburn's left shoulder and yanked him forward, face up on the seat. "All right, Molly's boy, let's you and me talk. How come you got the *audacity* to mess around with an officer of the United States Navy named Fitzpatrick? Connal Fitzpatrick, boy! Fitzpatrick, Fitzpatrick, *Fitzpatrick!* C'mon, baby, talk to Daddy, 'cause you've got nobody else *but* Daddy! Everyone you think you got is gone! They set you up, Molly's boy! They made you lie in print so the whole world *knows* you lied! But Daddy can make it right. Daddy can straighten it all out and put you on top—right on the very *top!* The Joint Chiefs—the *big* chief! Daddy's your tit, boy! Grab it or suck air! Where'd you put Fitzpatrick? Fitzpatrick, *Fitzpatrick!*"

The whisper came as Washburn's body writhed on the seat, his head whipping back and forth, saliva oozing out of the edges of his mouth. "Scharhörn, the isle of Scharhörn. . . . The Heligoland Bight."

Caleb Dowling was not only angry but bewildered. Despite a thousand doubts he could not let it go; too many things did not make sense, not the least of which was the fact that for three days he had been unable to get an appointment with the acting ambassador. The scheduling attaché claimed there was too much confusion resulting from Walter Peregrine's assassination to permit an audience at this time. Perhaps in a week . . . In short words, actor, get lost, we have important things to do and you're not one of them. He was being checked, shoved into a corner and given the lip service one gives to a well-known but insignificant person. His motives as well as his intelligence were undoubtedly being questioned out loud by arrogant, harried diplomats. Or someone else.

Which was why he was sitting now at a back table in the dimly lit bar of the Königshof Hotel. He had learned the name of Peregrine's secretary, one Enid Heathley, and had sent the stunt man, Moose Rosenberg, to the embassy with a sealed

letter purportedly from a close friend of Miss
Heathley's in the States. Moose's instructions had
been to deliver the envelope personally, and as
Rosenberg's size was formidable, no one in the
reception room had argued. Heathley had come
down in person. The message was short and to the
point.

Dear Miss Heathley:
   I believe it to be of the utmost importance
that we talk as soon as possible. I will be in
the bar of the Königshof at 7:30 this evening.
If it is convenient, please have a drink with
me, but I urge you not to speak to anyone
about our meeting. Please, no one.
                                    Sincerely,
                                    C. Dowling

It was seven-thirty-eight and Caleb was growing
anxious. For the past several years he was used to
people being on time for appointments and
interviews; it was one of the minor perks of being
Pa Ratchet. But there could be several reasons
why the secretary might not wish to meet with
him. She knew that Peregrine and he had become
friends of sorts and also that there were actors
who were known to seek publicity from events
they had nothing to do with, posturing with
statesmen and politicians when they couldn't spell
out a position on slavery. He hoped to hell . . .
   There she *was*. The middle-aged woman had
come through the door, squinting in the dim light.
The maître d' approached her, and moments later
she was escorted to Dowling's table.

"Thank you for coming," said Caleb, rising as Enid Heathley took her chair. "I wouldn't have asked you if I didn't think it was important," he added, sitting down again.

"I gathered that from your note," said the pleasant-faced woman with signs of gray in her hair and very intelligent eyes. Her drink ordered, casual talk covered its arrival.

"I imagine it's been very difficult for you," said Dowling.

"It hasn't been easy," agreed Miss Heathley. "I was Mr. Peregrine's secretary for nearly twenty years. He used to call us a team, and Jane and I—Mrs. Peregrine—are quite close. I should be with her now, but I told her I had some last-minute things to do at the office."

"How is she?"

"Still in shock, of course. But she'll make it. She's strong. Walter wanted the women around him strong. He thought they were worthwhile and they shouldn't hide their worth."

"I like that kind of thinking, Miss Heathley."

Her drink came, the waiter left, and the secretary looked quizzically at Caleb. "Forgive me, Mr. Dowling, I can't say I'm a devoted follower of your television show, but, of course, I've seen it a number of times. It seems that whenever I'm asked to dinner and the magic hour arrives, meals are suspended."

"I'd suggest those people upgrade their kitchens."

The woman smiled. "You're too modest, but that's not what I mean. You don't sound at all like the man on the television screen."

"Because I'm not he, Miss Heathley," said the former university professor, his expression serious, his intelligent eyes level with hers. "I assume we share certain traits because I've the physical instrument through which his fictions are filtered, but that's the extent of any similarity."

"I see. That's very well put."

"I've had practice saying it. But I didn't ask you here to expound on theories of acting. It's a subject with limited appeal."

"Why did you ask me?"

"Because I don't know whom else to go to. Well, I do, but I can't get near him."

"Who's that?"

"The acting ambassador, the one who flew over from Washington."

"He's up to his ears—"

"He should be told," interrupted Caleb. "Warned."

"Warned?" The woman's eyes grew wide. "An attempt on his *life?* Another killing—that maniac, *Converse?*"

"Miss Heathley," began the actor, his posture rigid, his voice quiet. "What I'm about to say may shock you, even offend you, but as I said, I don't know another person I can go to at the embassy. However, I *do* know there are people over there I *can't* go to."

"What are you talking about?"

"I'm not convinced that Converse is either a maniac or that he killed Walter Peregrine."

"*What?* You can't be serious! You've heard what they say about him, how unbalanced he is. He was the last person *with* Mr. Peregrine. Major

658

Washburn established that!"

"Major Washburn is one of those people I'd rather not see."

"He's considered one of the finest officers in the United States Army," objected the secretary.

"Then, for an officer he has a strange concept of taking orders from a superior. Last week I brought Peregrine to meet someone. The man ran and Walter told the major to stop him. Instead, Washburn tried to kill him."

"Oh, *now* I understand," said Enid Heathley, her tone unpleasant. "That was the night you arranged a meeting with Converse—it *was* you, I remember now! Mr. Peregrine told me. What *is* this, Mr. Dowling? A Hollywood actor protecting his image? Afraid he'll be held responsible and his ratings, or whatever they are, will plummet—that *is* the word, isn't it? This conversation is despicable." The woman moved her chair back, prepared to leave.

"Walter Peregrine was a man of his word, Miss Heathley," said Caleb, still immobile, staring at the secretary. "I think you'll agree with that."

"*And?*"

"He made a promise to me. He told me that if Converse reached him and asked to meet with him, I'd come along. *Me,* Miss Heathley. Specifically *not* Major Washburn, whose actions that night at the university were as bewildering to him as they were to me."

The middle-aged woman held her place, her eyes narrowed, concerned. "He *was* upset the next morning," she said softly.

"Damned angry better describes him, I think.

The man who ran away wasn't Converse—and he also wasn't crazy. He was dead serious, with the speech of someone used to authority. There was—or is—some kind of confidential investigation going on involving the embassy. Peregrine didn't know what it was, but he intended to find out. He mentioned that he was going to call Washington on a scrambler phone. I'm not up on the technology, but I don't think a person places a call like that unless he's worried that someone might try to tap the line."

"He *did* place a scrambler call. He told you that?"

"Yes, he did. And there's something else, Miss Heathley. As you correctly stated, I'm the one responsible for Walter Peregrine ever having heard of Converse, and I don't feel very good about it. But isn't it odd that in spite of the fact that it wasn't a secret—*you* knew, Washburn knew—nobody has come to question me since Walter was killed?"

"No one?" asked the woman incredulously. "But I included your name in my report."

"Whom did you give it to?"

"Well, Norman was handling everything. . . ." Enid Heathley stopped.

"Washburn?"

"Yes."

"Didn't you speak to anyone else? Weren't you questioned?"

"Yes, of course. An inspector from the Bonn police. I'm sure I mentioned your name—I'm *positive* I did."

"Was anybody else in the room?"

"Yes," said the murdered ambassador's secretary. "Norman," she whispered.

"Strange behavior for a police department, isn't it?" Caleb leaned forward, but only slightly. "Let me reemphasize something you just said, Miss Heathley. You asked me if I was a Hollywood actor trying to protect his image. It's a logical question, and if you ever saw the unemployment lines in Los Angeles you'd understand just how logical it is. Don't you think other people believe the same thing? I haven't been questioned because *specific* people here in Bonn think I'm shaking in Pa Ratchet's boots, keeping silent so as to protect that image and the ratings that make it possible. Oddly enough, that reasoning is my best physical protection. You don't kill off a Pa Ratchet unless you want the wrath of millions of viewers who, in my judgment, would latch on to the flimsiest connection to raise hysterical questions. *National Enquirer,* you are there."

"But you're not keeping silent," said Enid Heathley.

"I'm not talking loudly, either," corrected the actor. "But not for the reasons I've described. I owe Walter Peregrine—I know that better than anyone else. And I can't pay that debt if a man I think is innocent is hanged for his murder. But here's where I step back into my own confusion. I can't be certain. I could be wrong."

The woman returned Dowling's stare, then slowly frowned, keeping her eyes on him. "I'm going to leave now, but I'd like you to stay here for a while, if you wouldn't mind. I'm going to

661

call someone I think you should see. You'll understand. He'll reach you here—no paging, of course. Do as he says, go where he wants you to go."

"Can I trust him?"

"Mr. Peregrine did," said Enid Heathley, nodding. "And he didn't like him."

"That's trust," said the actor.

The phone call came and Caleb wrote out the address. The doorman at the Königshof secured him a taxi, and eight minutes later he got out in front of an ornate Victorian house on the outskirts of Bonn. He walked up to the door and rang the bell.

Two minutes later he was ushered into a large room—once a library, perhaps—but now with shades covering the obvious bookshelves. Shades that were detailed maps of East and West Germany. A man wearing glasses got up from behind a desk. He nodded perfunctorily and spoke. "Mr. Dowling?"

"Yes."

"I appreciate your coming out here, sir. My name is not important—why not call me George?"

"All right, George."

"But for your own confidential information —and I must stress *confidential*—I am the station chief for the Central Intelligence Agency here in Bonn."

"All right, George."

"What do you do, Mr. Dowling? What's your line of work?"

"*Ciao,* baby," said the actor, shaking his head.

25

The first indefinite light of dawn crept up the lower wall of the eastern sky, and along the river pier boats bobbed in their slips, straining their lines, creating an eerie symphony of creaks and thumps. Joel walked beside the young merchant seaman, his hand unconsciously straying to his face, to the new soft hair that was the outgrowth of a stubble. He had not shaved in four days, not since Bonn, and now he had the beginnings of a short, neat beard, not yet full but no longer an unkempt bristle. One more day and he would have to begin clipping it, shaping it, another plane of removal from the photograph in the newspapers.

And in one more day he would have to decide whether or not to phone Val at Cape Ann. Actually, he had made his decision—negative. His instructions had been clear enough, and the possibility that her telephone was tapped was more than he could handle. Yet he wanted so terribly to hear her voice, to hear the support he knew he would find in it. Negative. To hear it was to involve her. *Negative!*

"It is the last boat on the right," said the seaman, slowing his pace. "I must ask you again, because I gave my word. You carry no drugs."

"I carry no drugs."

"He may want to search you."

"I can't permit that," Converse broke in, thinking of his money belt. What could be mistaken for a cache of narcotics would reveal many times the amount of money for which most of the dregs on the riverfront would kill.

"Maybe he want to know why. Drugs bring bad penalty, long time in prison."

"I'll explain to him privately," said Joel, thinking again. He would do so with his gun in one hand and an additional $500 bill in the other. "But I give you my word, no drugs."

"It is not my boat."

"But you made the arrangements, and you know enough about me to come after me if they came after you."

"*Ja,* I remember. Connect-teecut—I been to visit friends in Bridge*port.* A broker house, a vice-president. I find you, if I have to."

"I wouldn't want that. You're a nice fellow who's helping me out and I'm grateful. I won't get you in trouble."

"*Ja,*" said the young German, nodding his head. "I believe you. I believe you last night. You talk very good, very high class, but you were stupid. You did a stupid thing and your face is red. A red face costs more than you want to pay, so you pay much more to make it go away."

"Your homilies are getting to me."

"*Was ist?*"

"Nothing. You're right. It's the story of upper-level management. Here." Joel had the bills in his left-hand pocket; he pulled them out. "I promised you fifteen hundred dollars. Count it, if you like."

"Vye? If is not there I talk loud and you stay here. You are too afraid to risk that."

"You're a natural-born lawyer."

"Come, I bring you to the captain. To you, he is only 'captain.' You will be dropped off where he says. . . . And be careful. Watch the men on the boat. They will think you have money."

"That's why I don't want to be searched," admitted Converse.

"I know. I do my best for you."

The seaman's best was not quite good enough. The captain of the filthy barge, a short hulk of a man with very poor teeth, brought Joel up to the wheelhouse, where he told him in broken but perfectly clear English to remove his jacket.

"I explained to my friend on the dock that I can't do that."

"Two hundred dollars *Amerikaner,*" said the captain.

Converse had the money in his right-hand pocket. He reached down for it, his eyes briefly glancing at the portside window where he saw two other men climb on board below in the dim light. They did not glance up; they had not seen him in the wheelhouse shadows.

The blow came suddenly, without warning, the impact such that Joel doubled over, his breath knocked out of him, and gripped his stomach. In front of him the surly bull of a captain was shaking his right hand, the grimace on his face indicating sharp pain. The German's fist had crashed into the gun lodged in Converse's belt. Joel staggered back into the bulkhead, leaned against it, and lowered himself to the floor as he reached under his jacket and took out the weapon. On his haunches, his legs bracing him against the wall, he aimed the automatic at the captain's huge chest.

"That was a rotten thing to do," said Converse, breathing hard, still holding his stomach. "Now, you bastard, *your* jacket!"

"*Was. . . ?*"

"You heard me! Take it off, hold it upside down, and shake the goddamned thing!"

The German slowly, reluctantly, slid off his waist-length coat, twice darting his eyes to the left of Joel, toward the wheelhouse door. "I look only for drugs."

"I'm not carrying any, and if I were, I suspect whoever sold them to me would have a better way to get across the river than with you. Turn it upside down! *Shake* it!"

The captain held his coat by the bottom edge and let it fall away. A short, ugly revolver plummeted to the floor, clacking on the wood, followed by the lighter sound of a long knife encased in a flat bone handle, flared at the end. As it struck the deck the blade shot out.

"This is the river," said the German without elaboration.

"And I just want to cross it without any trouble—and trouble to someone as nervous as I am is anyone walking through that door." Converse angled his head, gesturing at the wheelhouse entrance on his left. "In my state of mind, I'd fire this gun. I'd probably kill you and whoever else came in here. I'm not as strong as you, Captain, but I'm afraid, and that makes me much more dangerous. Can you understand that?"

"*Ja*. I not hurt you. I look only for drugs."

"You hurt me plenty," corrected Joel. "And that frightens me."

"*Nein. Bitte* . . . please."

"When do you take the boat out?"

"When I say."

"How many crew?"

"One man, that is all."

"*Liar!*" whispered Converse sharply, the gun thrust forward.

"*Zwei*. Two men . . . *today*. We pick up heavy crates in Elten. On my word, is normal only one man. I can't pay more."

"Start the engine," ordered Joel. "Or engines. I only know Chris-Crafts and Bertrams, which is a silly fucking thing to say."

"What?"

"*Do* it!"

"*Die Mannschaft*. The . . . crew. I must give orders."

"Wait!" Converse crawled sideways past the wheelhouse door, glancing above to his left at the thick wooden paneling of the pilot's window, his gun never once wavering from its line of fire into the German's chest. Again, he used the bulkhead and his braced legs to shinny himself up the wall; he was in shadows, with a clear view of the bow and, through both wheelhouse windows behind him, the stern of the boat. In sight were the fore and aft pilings on both sides, the lines looped around the thick protrusions of weather-beaten logs. The two crewmen were sitting on a storage

667

hatchway, smoking cigarettes, one drinking from a can of beer. "All right," said Joel, clicking the hammer back on the automatic—a weapon he was not sure he could use accurately within ten feet. "Open that door and give your orders. And if either of those men down there does anything but free those ropes, I'll kill you. Can you understand that?"

"I understand . . . everything you say, but you do not understand me. I search you for drugs —not a *grosse Mann*—the *Polizei* do not go after such people, they leave them alone. They go after the small people who use the riverboats. It makes them look good, you see. I would not hurt you. I only protect myself. I want to believe what my *Neffe*—nephew—told me, but I must be sure."

"Your *nephew?*"

"The seaman from Bremerhaven. How you think he got his job? *Ach, mein Bruder* sells flowers! It is his Frau's shop! He once sailed the oceans as I did. Now, he is a *Blumenhändler!*

"I swear to Christ I don't understand anything," said Joel, partially lowering his gun.

"Maybe you understand if I tell you he offered to pay me one half of the fifteen hundred dollars you pay him."

"A consortium of thieves."

"*Nein,* I not take. I tell him buy a new *Gitarre.*"

Converse sighed. "I have no drugs. Do you believe me?"

"*Ja,* you are only a fool, he told me. Rich fools pay more. They cannot tell people how foolish they are. The poor do not care."

"Do those little bromides run in the family?"

"What?"

"Forget it. Give the orders. Let's get out of here."

"*Ja*. Watch through the windows, please. I do not want you to be more afraid. You are right. A man afraid is much more dangerous."

Joel leaned back against the bulkhead as the captain shouted his orders. The engines started and the lines were released from their pilings. It was so contrary, he thought. Hostile, belligerent men who struck out in anger were not always his enemies, while pleasant, seemingly friendly people wanted to kill him. It was a world he knew nothing about, a long stretch from a courtroom or a boardroom where courtesy and "killing" could mean a variety of things. There were no such gray areas a hundred years ago in the camps and the jungles. One knew who the enemy was; the definition was clear on all sides. But during the past four days he had learned that there were no defined lines for him now. Converse stared out the window, at the pockets of mist rising out of the water, a few spiraling up to catch the early light in their clouds of vapor. His mind went blank. He did not care to think for a while. . . .

"Five, perhaps six minutes," said the captain, swinging the wheel to his left.

Joel blinked; he had been in a peaceful, rest-filled void, for how long he was not sure. "What are the procedures?" he asked, conscious of the rising orange sun firing what was left of the river mists. "I mean, what do I do?"

"As little as you can," answered the German.

669

"Just walk like you walk the pier every morning and go through the repair yard to the street. You will be in the south part of the town of Lobith. You will be in *die Niederlande* and we never saw each other."

"I understand that, but how?"

"You see that *Bootshafen?*" said the captain, pointing to a complex of docks with heavy winch machinery and hoisting devices across the water.

"It's a marina."

"*Ja,* marina. My second petrol tank is empty—I say I test. I stall the engines three hundred meters offshore and go in. I yell at the Dutchman's price but I pay, because I do not buy from the *deutsche* thief this far downriver. You get off with one of my crew, have a cigarette and laugh at your stupid captain—then you walk away."

"Just like that?"

"*Ja.*"

"It's so easy."

"*Ja.* No one said it was difficult. You only have to keep your eyes clear."

"For the police?"

"*Nein,*" said the captain, shrugging. "If there is *Polizei* they come to boat, you stay on board."

"Then who am I looking for?"

"Men who may watch you, may see you walk away."

"What men?"

"*Gesindel, Gauner*—what you call scum. They come each morning to the piers and look for work, most still drunk. Watch for such men. They will think you have drugs or money. They will break your head and steal."

"Your nephew told me to watch the men on your own boat."

"Only the new man, he is a *Gauner*. He chokes on his beer hoping it will clear his head. He thinks he fools me but he does not. I keep him on board, tell him to scrape the rail, something. The other is no problem for you. He is loyal to me, an *Idiot* with a strong back and no head. The riverboats do not hire him. I do. *Verstehen?*"

"I think so. By the way, I have to get to Amsterdam. Is there a train here?"

"No train in Lobith. You take the omnibus to Arnhem. The train to Amsterdam is in Arnhem. I use it many times when my ships dock in *die Niederlande*. The omnibus stops at the railroad station. Not long ride."

"Ships? Large ships?" asked Joel, struck by the captain's words.

"I once sailed the oceans, not a stinking river. Fifteen years of age I ship out with *mein Bruder*. By twenty-three I am *Obermaat*—'petit' officer—good money, good life. . . . Very happy." The German lowered his voice as he throttled back the engines and spun the wheel starboard; the boat skidded on the water. "Why talk? It is over," he added angrily.

"What happened?"

"It is not for you, *Amerikaner*." The captain pushed the throttle forward; the engines coughed.

"I'm interested."

"*Warum?* Why?"

"I don't know. Maybe it takes my mind off my own problems," said Converse honestly.

The German looked briefly at him. "You ask? Okay. We never see each other. . . . I stole money, much money. It took the company purser nine months to find me. *Aber, ach,* he *find* me! It was many years ago. No more oceans, only the river."

"But you said you were making good money. Why did you steal?"

"Why do most men steal?"

"They need it—the money—or they want things they can't have normally, or they're just basically dishonest, which I don't think you are."

"Go back. Adam stole the apple, *Amerikaner.*"

"Not exactly. You mean a woman?"

"Many years ago. She was with child and she did not want her man on the seas and the ships. She wanted more." The captain permitted himself the slightest glint in his eyes and a touch of a smile on his lips. "She wanted a flower shop."

From the core of his stomach, his pain momentarily forgotten, Joel laughed. "You're quite a guy, Captain."

"I never see you again."

"Then your nephew—"

"Never *see* you again!" the German broke in, now laughing out loud himself, his eyes on the water as he headed into the Dutch marina.

Converse leaned against a piling smoking a cigarette, the visor of his cheap cap angled over his forehead, his eyes roaming up and down the pier and beyond to the repair yard in the Dutch marina. The men milling about the huge machinery were mechanically going about their

672

tasks while those around the boats seemed more intent on inspecting than doing, shaking their heads solemnly. The captain argued with the dispenser of fuel, making obscene gestures at the rapidly climbing figures on the glass-encased face of the pump while his softheaded deckhand grinned several feet away. On board, the *Gauner* alternately leaned over the railing, a large wire brush in his hands, and abruptly turned back to his scraping whenever his employer glanced over at him.

The time was right, thought Joel as he pushed himself away from the piling. No one anywhere had the slightest interest in him; the dismal chores and the early-morning dissatisfactions took precedence over the insignificant and unfamiliar.

He started walking up the pier, his pace casual to the point of being slovenly but his eyes alert. He proceeded to the edge of the repair yard approaching a row of hulls in dry dock. Beyond the last elevated boat, no more than three hundred feet away, was an inordinately tall hurricane fence and an open gate. A uniformed guard sat on the left drinking coffee and reading a newspaper, his chair angled back into the crisscrossing wire mesh. Seeing him, Joel stopped, his breath suspended, an internal alarm going off—for no reason. Men passed back and forth through the gate, but the guard did not so much as glance at anyone, his eyes devouring only the tabloid on his lap.

Converse turned, a last look at the river. Suddenly he became aware of the captain. The German had run to the base of the pier and was gesturing wildly, pressing his hands forward in short, rapid strokes. He was trying to warn Converse. Then he shouted at the top of his lungs; men stared at him and turned away, none caring to be involved. They had seen too much in the early hours on the waterfront, the slashing with hooks too frequently the language of the docks.

"*Lauf!* Run! *Get out!*"

Joel was mystified; he looked around. Then he saw them. Two—no *three*—burly men were lurching up from the pier, their glassy eyes focused on him. The first man staggered forward to the left of the captain. The German grabbed his shoulder, swinging him around, stopping him, but only for seconds as the other two men crashed their fists into the captain's neck and spine. They were animals—*Gauner*—their nostrils inflamed by the scent of a trapped fat quarry who might keep them in food and drink for days.

Converse dove under the row of dry-docked boats, smashing his head on several hulls as he scrambled toward the other side and the shafts of light beyond. He could see frantic legs pounding the earth behind him; they were gaining on him; they were running, he was crawling. He reached the end of the suspended row of hulls, sprang out and started for the gate. He pulled out his shirt, tore off the lower section and held it against the cuts on his head as he walked rapidly past the guard and through the gate. He looked around. The three men were arguing furiously, drunkenly, among themselves, two crouching and peering unsteadily under the boats. Then the man standing saw him. He shouted to the others; they stood up and started after Joel. He ran faster, until he could see them no longer; the animals had given up.

He was in the Netherlands; the welcome was less than gracious, but he was there, one step closer to Amsterdam. On the other hand he had no idea where he was right now except that the town was named Lobith. He had to catch his breath and think. He stepped into a deserted storefront, where a dark shade behind the entrance made the glass a dim mirror; it was enough. He was a mess. Think. For God's sake, *think!*

Mattilon had told him to take the train from Arnhem to Amsterdam, he remembered that clearly. And the captain of the barge had said he had to take an "omnibus" from Lobith to Arnhem; there was no train in Lobith. The first thing he had to do was reach the railroad station in Arnhem, clean himself up, then study the crowds and judge whether to risk becoming part of them. And relative to this consideration, his mind darted in several directions at once. The plain-lensed glasses had long since disappeared, undoubtedly during the insane events in Wesel; he would replace them with dark glasses. There was little he could do about the scrapes on his face, but they would appear less menacing after soap and water, and certainly in or around a railroad station something could be done about his torn clothing. . . . And a *map*. Goddamn it, he was a pilot! He could reach Point A from Point B—and he had to do so quickly. He had to reach Amsterdam and find a way to make contact with a man named Cort Thorbecke—and call Nathan Simon in New York. There was so much to do!

As he walked out of the storefront he was suddenly aware of what was happening to him. It had happened before—a lifetime ago, in the jungles—when the fear of the night sounds had passed and he could watch the dawn and accurately plot his directions, his lines of march, his survival. He was thinking, his mind functioning again. All things considered, he was far less the man than what he had been, but he could be better than he was—he *had* to be. Every day that passed brought the generals of Aquitaine closer to whatever madness they were planning. Everywhere. He and they had to reverse roles. The hunted had to become the hunter. Delavane's disciples had convinced the world he was a psychopathic assassin, and so they had to find him, take him, kill him and hold him up as one more example of the spreading insanity that could be contained only with *their* solutions. Aquitaine had to be exposed and destroyed before it was too late. The countdown was in progress, the commanders surely, inexorably, moving into their positions, consolidating their powers.

Move! shouted Converse silently to himself as he walked faster down the pavement.

He sat in the last car of the train, still wary but satisfied by the progress he had made. He had done everything cautiously but without wasting motion, his concentration absolute, aware of a dozen possible dangers—eyes that stared at him, a man or a woman seen twice in too short a time, a clerk delaying him by being more helpful than the hour and the crowds would normally permit. These calculated possibilities were his readouts, his dials, his gauges; without clearance he would abort all forward motion, takeoff canceled, the escape hatch sprung, safety found in the streets. His equipment was not an aircraft that was an extension of himself, it was *himself,* and he had never flown with such precision in his life.

ENGLISH SPOKE had been the sign tacked to the roof of the busy corner newsstand in Lobith. He had asked directions to the "omnibus" to Arnhem while buying a map and a newspaper, holding both close to his face. The owner was too preoccupied with customers to notice his appearance and shouted rapid instructions, more useful in the pointed finger than in the words. Joel found the bus stop some four blocks away. He sat in the crowded vehicle, his face buried in a newspaper he could not read, and forty-odd minutes later he got off at the railroad station in Arnhem.

First on his checklist was a trip to the farthest washbasin in the men's room, where he cleaned himself up. He had brushed his clothes as best he could and looked in the mirror. He was still a mess, but somehow he looked more like a man who had been injured than one who had been beaten; there was a difference.

Next, outside in the station, he converted his deutsche marks and five hundred American dollars into florins and guilders. He then bought a pair of wide-rimmed dark glasses at a pharmacy several doors from the currency exchange. As he got into the cashier's line, his hand casually covering the bruises on his face, his eyes fell on a cosmetics counter across the far aisle. It triggered a memory.

Shortly after their marriage, in one of those maddening accidents that only happen at the most inopportune times, Valerie had slipped on a foyer rug and fell, hitting her head against the corner of an antique hallway table. By seven that night she had what Joel had described as "one hell of a mouse"; the black eye was an almost perfect oval, arcing from the bridge of her nose to the edge of her left temple. At ten the next morning she was scheduled to lead a bilingual presentation for agency clients from Stuttgart. She had sent him out to the drugstore for a small bottle of liquid makeup, which, except at close range, had concealed the bruise remarkably well.

"I don't want people to think my brand-new husband beat the hell out of me for not fulfilling his wildest sexual fantasies."

"Which one did you miss?" he had asked.

He stepped out of the cashier's line and made his way around the cases to the display of creams and colognes, shampoos, and nail polish. He recognized the bottle, chose a darker shade, and returned to the line.

A second trip to a washbasin had taken ten minutes, but the results justified the time. He applied the makeup carefully; the scrapes and bruises faded. Unless someone stood very close to him, he was no longer a battered brawler but a man who had perhaps suffered a not too serious fall. Converse congratulated himself in that men's room in the railroad station. Under other circumstances, he might not have dressed a client so well before a trial for assault and battery.

The checklist continued. It had taken him to where he was now, in the last car on the straight-through train from Arnhem to Amsterdam. After buying his ticket on what he inferred was a low-priced excursion train that made numerous stops, he had walked out on the platform prepared to run back at the slightest negative readout, the first steady glance that held him in focus. Instead he saw a group of men and women, couples around his own age, talking and laughing together, friends more than likely off for a short summer's holiday, perhaps leaving the river for the sea. The men carried worn, dented suitcases, most held together with rope, while a number of the women held wicker baskets looped over their arms. Their luggage and their clothing denoted working class—factories for the men, home and children or the less demanding clerical jobs for the women—all within that part of the spectrum that suited Joel's own appearance. He had walked behind them, laughing quietly when they laughed, climbing on board as though he were part of the group, sitting in an aisle seat across from a burly man with a slender woman, who, despite her thin frame, proudly bore a pair of enormous breasts. Converse's eyes could hardly avoid them and the man grinned at Joel, no malice in his look as he raised a bottle of beer to his lips.

Somewhere Converse had read or heard that in the northern countries people going on summer vacations—or on holiday, as was the term—

gravitated to the last cars in the Trans-Europe-Express. It was a custom that somehow signified their status, producing a general camaraderie that enlivened the working man's junket. Joel observed the none too subtle transformation. Men and women got out of their seats and walked up and down the aisle talking to friends and strangers alike, cans and bottles in their hands. From the front of the car a few people broke into song, obviously a familiar country song; others took it up only to be drowned out by Converse's group, who raised their voices in an entirely different chorus until the singing of both camps dwindled away into laughter. Conviviality, indeed, was the order of the morning in the last car on the train to Amsterdam. The stations went by, a few passengers getting off at each, more getting on, with suitcases, baskets, and broad smiles, and being welcomed on board with boisterous greetings. A number of men wore T-shirts emblazoned with the names of town and district teams—soccer, Converse assumed. Catcalls and amiably derisive shouts were hurled at them by age-old competitors. The railroad car was turning into an odd Dutch version of a trainload of suddenly freed adults going off to a summer camp. The volume grew.

The towns were announced, the brief stops made as Joel remained in his seat, motionless and unobtrusive, now and then glancing at his adopted group, half smiling or laughing softly when it seemed appropriate. Otherwise he looked like someone of limited intelligence poring over a map as a child might, equal parts wonderment and confusion. He was studying the streets and canals of Amsterdam. There was a man who lived on the southwest corner of Utrechtsestraat and Kerkstraat, a man he had to identify by sight, isolate and make contact with . . . his springboard to Washington would be as a "member of the Tatiana family." He had to pull Cort Thorbecke away from his base of operations without alerting the hunters of Aquitaine. He would pay an English-speaking intermediary to get to a telephone and use words sufficiently plausible to draw the broker out to some other location, with no mention of the Tatiana connection or its source in Paris. Those words would have to be found; he would find them somehow, he *had* to. He was psychologically on his way back toward friendly fire—in terms of actual time less than seven hours from Washington—and men who would listen to him with Nathan Simon's help and an extraordinary file that would persuade them to hide him and protect him until the soldiers of Aquitaine were exposed. It was not the way envisioned by a man he had once known in Connecticut as Avery Fowler, hardly the legal tactics whose roots were in ridicule as prescribed by A. Preston Halliday in Geneva, but there was no time now. Time was running out for manipulated webs of legality.

The train slowed down, jerking as it did so, as if the engineer far up ahead was trying to send another kind of message to a rowdy car in the rear, which felt the shocks most severely. If that was his intent, it, too, backfired. The pitching motion served only to accelerate the laughter and provoke insults shouted at an unseen incompetent.

"Amstel!" screamed a conductor, opening the forward door between the cars. "Amsterdam! Amst—!" The poor man could not finish the call —he had to pull the door shut to avoid a barrage of rolled-up newspapers thrown at him. Summer camp in the Netherlands.

The train pulled into the station and a contingent of T-shirted chests and breasts announced their arrival with shouts of recognition. Five or six people at the front of Joel's group rose as one to welcome their friends; again cans and bottles were held in the air and laughter bounced off the narrow walls, nearly drowning out the whistles of departure outside. Bodies fell over bodies, hugs were exchanged, breasts playfully grabbed at.

Beyond the new arrivals, walking unsteadily, was the illogically logical capstone for the juvenile antics taking place in front of Converse. An old woman, obviously drunk, made her way down the aisle, her disheveled clothes matching the large, tattered canvas bag she clutched in her left hand while she steadied herself with her right on the edge of the seats as the train accelerated. Grinning, she accepted a bottle of beer as another was thrown into her satchel, followed by several sandwiches wrapped in waxed paper. Again, there were greetings of welcome as two men in the aisle bowed to the waist as if to a queen. A third slapped her behind and whistled. For several minutes the ritual continued, a new mechanical toy for the children off to summer camp. The old woman drank and danced a jig and made playfully suggestive gestures at men and women alike, sticking out her tongue and rolling it around, her ancient eyes bulging, rolling, her ragged shawl twirling in circles like the ballet of some macabre Scheherazade. She amused everyone with her drunken antics as she accepted all that was dropped into her offering cloth, including coins. The Dutch vacationers were kind, thought Joel; they took care of someone less fortunate than themselves, someone who would be barred from another class of car on another train. The woman approached him, her canvas bag now held in front of her so as to accept alms from both sides. Converse reached into his pocket for a few guilders, letting them slip from his hand into the bag.

"*Goedemorgen,*" said the old woman, weaving. "*Dank u wel, beste man, erg vriendelijk van u!*"

Joel nodded, returning to his map, but the bag lady remained.

"*Uw hoofd! Ach, heb je een ongeluk gehad, jongen?*"

Again Converse nodded, reaching again into his pocket and giving the inebriated old hag more money. He pointed to his map and waved her away, as yet another raucous chorus erupted.

"*Spreekt u Engels?*" shouted the bag lady, leaning over unsteadily.

Joel shrugged, sinking back into the seat, his eyes riveted on the map.

"I think you *do.*" The old woman spoke hoarsely, clearly, soberly, her right hand no longer on the edge of the seat but instead in the canvas bag. "We've been looking for you every day, on every train. Don't *move!* The gun is equipped with a silencer. With all this noise, if I pull the trigger no one would know the difference, including the man beside you who wants only to join the party and the big-breasted women. I think we shall let him. We *have* you, *Meneer* Converse!"

There was no summer camp, after all. Only death minutes away from Amsterdam.

26

"Mag ik u even lastig vallen?" shouted the old woman, once more weaving unsteadily as she spoke to the passenger beside Converse. The man took his eyes off the raucous festivities in the aisle and glanced up at the harridan. She shouted again, her right hand still in the bag, her mass of disheveled gray hair springing back and forth as she nodded to her right, toward the front of the car. *"Zou ik op uw plaats mogen zitten?"*

"Mij best!" The man got up grinning, as Joel instinctively moved his legs to let him pass. *"Dank u wel,"* the man added, heading for a single empty seat beyond a couple dancing in the aisle.

"Move over!" commanded the old woman harshly, swaying with the rhythm of the racing train.

If it was going to happen, thought Converse, it was going to happen *now*. He started to rise, his eyes straight ahead, his right elbow on the armrest inches from the bulging bag. Suddenly he plunged his hand into the open canvas bag and gripped the fat wrist of the woman's hand that held the unseen gun. Straining, pressing farther down, clutching flesh and metal, he swung violently to his left and yanked the old woman through the narrow space, twisting her, crashing her down into the seat next to the window. There was a sharp spit as the gun exploded, burning a hole in the heavy cloth, smoke billowing, the bullet embedding itself somewhere below. The hag's strength was maniacal, unlike anything he might have imagined. She fought viciously, clawing at his face until he pulled her arm above her head, twisting it, clamping it behind her, their two hands still struggling below in the bag. She would not let go of the weapon and he could not pry it loose; he could only hold it downward, his grip immobilizing her fingers, force against force, her contorted face telling him she would not surrender.

The midmorning revels of the railroad car reached a crescendo; a cacophony of voices raised in jumbled song competed with the swelling echoes of laughter. And no one paid the slightest attention to the savage struggle that was taking place in the narrow seat. Suddenly, within the panic of that struggle, within the violent impasse, Joel was aware that the train was slowing down, if only imperceptibly. Once again his pilot's instincts told him a descent was imminent. He jammed his elbow into the old woman's right breast to jolt her into freeing the gun. Still she held on, bracing herself against the seat, her arm pinned, her fat legs stretched below, angled like thick pylons anchored beneath the forward seat, her obese body twisted, locking his own arm in place so he could not dislodge the weapon from her grip.

"Let go!" he whispered hoarsely. "I won't hurt you—I won't kill you. Whatever you're being paid, I'll pay you more!"

"Nee! I would be found at the bottom of a canal! You can't escape, *Meneer!* They wait for you in Amsterdam, they wait for the *train!"* Grimacing, the old woman kicked out, briefly freeing her left arm. She swung her hand around, clawing his face, her nails sliding down his beard until he grabbed her wrist, pulling her arm across the seat and cracking it into her own knee, twisting her hand clockwise, forcing her to be still. It made no difference. Her right hand had the strength of an aging lioness protecting its pride; she would not release the gun below.

"You're lying!" cried Converse. "No one knows I'm on this train! *You* just got on twenty minutes ago!"

"Wrong, *Amerikaan!* I've been on since Arnhem—I start in the front, walk back. I found you out at Utrecht and a telephone call was made."

"Liar!"

"You will see."

"Who hired you?"

"Men."

"Who?"

"You will see."

"Goddamn you, you're not part of them! You *can't* be!"

"They pay. Up and down the railroad they pay. On the piers, in the airports. They say you speak nothing but English."

"What else do they say?"

"Why should I tell you? You're caught. It is you who should let *me* go. It could be easier for you."

"How? A quick bullet in the head instead of a Hanoi rack?"

"Whatever it is, the bullet could be better. You are too young to know, *Meneer*. You were never under occupation."

"And you're too old to be so goddamned strong, I'll give you that."

"*Ja,* I learn that, too."

"Let *go!*"

The train was braking and the drunken crowd in the car roared its approval as men grabbed suitcases from the upper racks. The passenger who had been sitting next to Joel hastily yanked his from above the seat, his stomach pressing into Converse's shoulder. Joel tried to appear as though he were in deep conversation with his grimacing half-prisoner; the man fell back, suitcase in hand, laughing.

The old woman lurched forward, sinking her mouth into Converse's upper arm, millimeters from his wound. She bit him viciously, her yellow teeth penetrating his flesh, blood bursting out of his skin, trickling down the woman's gray chin.

He pulled back in pain. She freed her hand from his grip in the canvas bag; the gun was hers! She fired; the muted spit was followed by a shattering of a section of the floor in the aisle, missing Joel's feet by inches. He grabbed the unseen barrel, twisted it, pulled it, trying with all his strength to wrench it away. She fired again.

Her eyes grew wide as she arched back into the seat. They remained open as she slumped into the window, blood spreading quickly through the thin fabric of her dress in the upper section of her stomach. She was dead, and Joel felt ill, nauseated—he had to swallow air to keep from vomiting. Trembling, he wondered who this old woman was, why she was—what she had lived through that made her become what she was. *You were too young to know. . . . You were never under occupation.*

No time to think about all this! She had wanted to kill him, that was all he had to know, and men were waiting for him only minutes away. He had to think, *move!*

Twisting the gun from her rigid fingers inside the canvas bag, he quickly lifted it up and shoved it under his coarse jacket, inserting it under his belt, feeling the weight of the other weapon in his pocket. He reached over and bunched the woman's dress in folds, then layered her shawl over the bloodstains and pushed her mass of disheveled hair over her right cheek, concealing the wide dead eyes. Experience in the camps told him not to try to close the eyes; too often they would not respond. The action might only call attention to him—to her. The last thing he did was to pull a can of beer out of the bag, open it, and place it on her lap; the liquid spilled out, drenching her lap.

"*Amsterdam! De volgende halte is Amsterdam-Centraal!*"

A roar went up from the vacationing crowd as the line began to form toward the door. Oh, *Christ!* thought Converse. *How?* The old woman had said a telephone call had been made. A telephone call, which implied she had not made it herself. It was logical; there was too little time. She had undoubtedly paid one of her sister bag ladies who plied the trains at the station in Utrecht to make it. The information therefore would be minimum, simply because there *was* no time. She was a special employee, one who had been researched as only Aquitaine could research, an old woman who was strong and who could use a weapon and who would not shrink from taking a life—who would not say too much to anyone. She would merely give a telephone number and instruct the hired caller to repeat the time of the train's arrival. Again . . . therefore . . . he had a chance. Every male passenger would be scrutinized, every face matched against the face in the newspapers. But he was and he was *not* that face! And he did not speak any language but English—that information had been spread with emphasis.

Think!

"*Ze is dronken!*" The words were shouted by the burly man with the enormously endowed wife at his side as he pointed to the dead woman. Both were laughing, and Joel did not need an interpreter to understand. Converse nodded, grinning broadly as he shrugged. He had found his way out of the station in Amsterdam.

For Converse understood there was a universal language employed when the decibel of noise was such that one could neither hear nor be heard. It was also used when one was bored at cocktail parties, or when one watched football games on television with clowns who were convinced they knew a great deal more than coaches or quarterbacks, or when one was gathered and trapped into an evening in New York with the "beautiful people"—most of whom qualified as neither in the most rudimentary sense, egos far outdistancing either talent or humanity. In such situations one nodded; one smiled; one occasionally placed a friendly hand on a shoulder, the touch signifying communication—but one said nothing.

Joel did all of these things as he got off the train with the burly man and his wife. He became almost manic, playing the role as one who knew there was nothing left between death and survival but a certain kind of controlled madness. The lawyer in him provided the control; the child pilot tested the winds, knowing his aircraft would respond to the elemental pressures because it was sound and he was good and he enjoyed the craziness of a stall forced by a downdraft; he could easily pull out.

He had removed his dark glasses and pulled his cap far down over his forehead. His hand was on the burly man's shoulder as they walked up the platform, the Dutchman laughing as he spoke, Joel nodding, slapping his companion's shoulder, laughing in return whenever there was a break in the man's monologue. Since the couple had been drinking, neither took much notice of his incomprehensible replies; he seemed like a nice

690

person, and in their state nothing else really mattered.

As they walked up out of the platform toward the terminal Converse's constantly roving eyes were drawn to a man standing in a crowd of welcomers beyond the archway at the end of the ramp. Joel first noticed him because unlike those around him—whose faces were lit up in varying degrees of anticipation—this man's expression was serious to the point of being solemn. He was not there to offer welcome. Then suddenly Converse knew there was another reason why this man had caught his attention. The moment he recognized the face he knew exactly where he had seen it—walking rapidly down a path surrounded by thick foliage with another man, another guard. The man up ahead was one of the patrols from Erich Leifhelm's compound above the Rhine.

As they approached the arch, Joel laughed a little louder and made it a point to clap the Dutchman's shoulder a little harder, his cap still angled down over his forehead. He followed several nods with a shrug or two and then with a good-humored shaking of the head; with brows furrowed and lips constantly moving, he was obviously in fluent conversation. Through narrowed eyes Converse saw that Leifhelm's guard was staring at him; then the man looked away. They passed through the arch and in the corner of his vision Joel was abruptly aware of a head whipping around, then of a figure pushing other figures out of his path. Converse turned, looking over the Dutchman's shoulder. It happened. His eyes locked with those of

Leifhelm's guard. The recognition was instant, and for that instant the German panicked, turning his head back toward the ramp. He started to shout, then stopped. He reached under his jacket and moved forward.

Joel broke away from the couple and began racing, threading his way through succeeding walls of bodies, heading for a series of archlike ascending exits through which sunlight streamed into the ornate terminal. Twice he looked behind him as he ran; the first time he could not see the man, the second time he did. Leifhelm's guard was screaming orders to someone across the way, rising on the balls of his feet to see and be seen, gesturing at the exit doors in the distance. Converse ran faster, pulling his way through the crowd toward the steps that led to the massive exit. He climbed the staircase swiftly but within the rhythm of the most harried departing passengers, holding to the center, trying to call as little attention to himself as possible.

He bolted through a door into the sunlight, into total confusion. Below was water and piers and glass-covered boats bobbing up and down, people rushing past them, others ushered on board under the watchful eyes of men in white-and-blue uniforms. He had come off a train only to emerge on some kind of strange waterfront. Then he remembered: the railroad station in Amsterdam was built on an island facing the center of the city; thus it was known as the Centraal. Yet there was a street—two streets, *three* streets bridging the water toward other streets and trees and buildings . . . no *time!* He was out in the open and those

692

streets in the distance were his caves of survival; they were the ravines and the thick, impenetrable acres of bush and swamp that would hide him from the enemy! He ran as fast as he could along the wide boulevard bordered by water and reached an even wider thoroughfare clogged with traffic, buses, trams, and automobiles, all at their own starting gates, anxious for bells to release them. He saw a dwindling line at the door of an electric tramway, the final two passengers climbing on board; he raced ahead and, just before the door swung shut, he stepped up into the tram—the last fare.

Spotting an empty seat in the last row, he walked quickly to the back of the huge vehicle. He sat down, breathing hard, desperately, the sweat matting his hairline and his temples and rolling down his face, the shirt under his jacket drenched. It was only then that he realized how exhausted he was, how loud and rapid the tattoo in his chest, how blurred his vision and his thoughts. Fear and pain had combined into a form of hysteria. The desire to stay alive and the hatred of Aquitaine had kept him going. Pain? He was suddenly aware of the ache in his arm above his wound, an old woman's last act of vengeance—against what? For what? An enemy? Money? No time!

The tram started up and he turned in his seat to look out the rear window. He saw what he wanted to see. Leifhelm's guard was racing across the intersection, a second man running to join him from the waterfront quai. They met, and the words they exchanged were obviously exchanged in near panic. Another joined them, from where Joel could not see; he was suddenly just there. The three men spoke rapidly, Leifhelm's guard apparently the leader; he pointed in several directions, issuing orders. One man ran down the street, below the curb, and began checking the half-dozen or so taxis in the traffic jam; a second stayed on the pavement, slowly making his way around the tables of a sidewalk café, then going inside. Finally, Leifhelm's guard ran back across the intersection, dodging cars, and reaching the curb, he signaled. A woman walked out of a store and met him at the corner.

No one had thought of the tram. It was his first cave of survival. He sat back and tried to collect his thoughts, knowing they would be difficult to face. Aquitaine would penetrate all of Amsterdam, canvass it, tear it apart until they found him. Was there conceivably a way to reach Thorbecke or had he been fooling himself, reaching into the past where too often accidents and misplaced arrogance led to success? No, he could not think for a while. He had to lie down in the cave and rest, and if sleep came, he hoped the nightmares did not come with it. He looked out the window and saw a sign. It read DAMRAK.

He remained on the electric conveyance for well over an hour. The lively streets, the lovely architecture of the centuries-old buildings and the endless canals calmed him. His arm still ached from the old woman's teeth but not severely, and thoughts of cleansing the wound faded. He could not weep for the old woman, but as with certain, strange witnesses at a trial, he wished he knew her story.

Hotels were out. The foot soldiers of Aquitaine would scour them, offering large sums for any information about any American of his general description—which they now specifically had. Thorbecke would be watched, his telephone tapped, his every move and conversation scrutinized. Even the embassy, or consulate —whichever it was in Amsterdam—would have another military chargé d'affaires or his equivalent on the prowl for a signal that a non-assassin wanted to come in and start the process of rectification. If his perceptions were right, that left him with only one escape hatch. Nathan Simon.

Nathan the Wise, Joel had dubbed him once, only to be told that a Gentile with his intelligence should certainly come up with something more original. Then after a particularly long session at the office in which Nate detailed in excruciating detail why they should not take on a client named Liebowitz, who in his opinion would put too great a burden on the obligation to respect a client's confidence, and during which Lawrence Talbot had dozed off, Converse suggested that he alter his sobriquet to Nathan the Talmudic-pain-in-the-ass. Nate had roared, shocking Talbot awake, and proclaiming, "I love it! And Sylvia will love it better!"

Joel had learned more about the law from Nathan Simon than from anyone else, but there was always a distance between them. It was as though Nate never really wanted them to be too close in spite of the obvious affection the older man had for the younger. Converse thought he understood; it was a question of loyalty. Simon had two sons, who, in the properly guarded phrase, "were in business for themselves in California and Florida." One sold insurance in Santa Barbara, and the other ran a bar in Key West. Nate Simon was a tough act to follow, and Joel was given a hint of just how hard it was one late afternoon when Simon offered to buy him a drink at "21" after a harrowing conference on Fifth Avenue.

"I like your father, Converse. I like Roger. He has minimal legal requirements, of course, but he's a good man."

"He has *no* legal requirements, and I tried to stop him from coming to us."

"You couldn't. It was the gesture he had to make. Put some business where the son is. Very touching."

"With an unnecessary will that you much too generously charged him only two hundred dollars for, and some crazy disposition of his war medals to three different institutions—for which you refused to bill him on patriotic grounds?"

"We were in the same theater of operations."

"Where?"

"Europe."

"Come on, Nate. He's my father and I love him but I also know he's off the wall. Take him out of a vintage prop and he's not sure where he is. Pan Am got their money's worth, not in any administrative sense, but because he was a pistol at conventions."

Nathan Simon had gripped his glass that late afternoon at "21," and when he spoke, the quiet thunder of a deeply troubled man poured forth. "You have respect for your father, do you hear me, Joel? My friend Roger offered a gesture to his son, for it was all he had, all he could imagine. I had a great deal more and I didn't know how to make such gestures. I only gave commands. . . . He said I could still do it. I'm going to take up flying."

Simon would help him only if he was convinced there was substance to his case. But he would legally lean over backwards in the negative if he thought a relationship or personal sentimentality was being used to manipulate him. Of course, if an indictment followed, he would rush in for the defense after the fact. That was professional; those were his ethics. And by now Valerie would have sent him the envelope with the dossiers and their awesome implications. *They* were the substance Simon required. Knowing Val, she would have sent them down by car, the great American postal service having given rise to a score of competitors who eschewed the taxpayer's dollar. Joel's decision was made. Since there was a five-hour time difference, he would wait until early evening and then call Nathan Simon. He was functioning again.

The tram came to the last stop before its return run. At least he was the only one left on board; he walked up the aisle, got off and saw another. He got on. Sanctuary.

A hundred streets and a dozen crisscrossed canals later, he looked out the window, encouraged by the seedy neighborhood he saw, washed clean on the surface but with the promise of far more interesting bacteria below. There was a row of pornography shops, their wares in magnified displays in the storefronts. Above, in open windows, garishly painted girls stood provocatively, brassieres slipped on and off lethargically, faces bored but pelvises churning. The crowds in the streets were animated, some curious, some feigning shock, others interested in buying. There was a carnival atmosphere, one into which he could melt, thought Converse, as he got out of his seat and went to the door.

He wandered around the streets, astonished, even embarrassed, as he always was when sex was paraded so publicly. He enjoyed sexual encounters and never lacked for them, but for him the privacy of the acts was intrinsic to their fulfillment. He could no more walk through one of those neon-lit doors up-to-heaven than he could have performed a bowel movement on the curb.

There was a café across the street; it was above a canal, tables on the sidewalk, dark within. What struck him was the crowd that hovered around the doorway, many people simply glancing in and going on, drawn briefly to some curious oddity inside. Regardless, it was the crowd that attracted him; there was anonymity in numbers. He crossed the thoroughfare, weaved his way through the crowd and went inside. Sleep might be out of the question, but he needed food. He had not eaten a real meal in nearly three days. He found a small empty table in the back of the room, and was stunned that a television set, clamped above on the wall, was blaring inanities. He could not understand. There *was* no television in the Netherlands during the afternoons! How many times had he heard colleagues and friends remark that one of the most civilized aspects of traveling in Holland was the absence of the idiot box until seven o'clock in the evening? Conversely, there were those sports enthusiasts who bemoaned the fact that certain events were not shown, but on the whole the verdict came down in favor of Dutch civility and restraint. Yet *here* was a television set in full operation. It undoubtedly accounted for those curious passersby on the street who glanced inside, shaking their heads in bewilderment as they went on their way.

Then Joel saw the folded card on the table, the announcement in four languages, English first.

In accord with the advances in teknology we are pleased to bring our patrons and visitors from outside the Netherlands rekordings of our national programs.

Video tapes! It was a come-on, an innovative ploy to lure customers; this was the district for it. And he understood why the English language was first: *e pluribus unum*. Let's not lose touch with the tube. At least the tapes were in Dutch; it helped, but not much.

Straight whisky helped, too, but again not much. The anxiety of the hunted came back and he kept turning his head toward the entrance, at any moment expecting to see one of the foot soldiers of Aquitaine walk through the door, out of the sunlight and into the cave to find him. He went to the men's room at the rear of the café, removed his jacket, placed the gun with the silencer in the inside pocket, and tore his left sleeve. He filled one of the two basins with cold water, and then he plunged his face into it, pouring the water through his hair over the back of his neck. He felt a vibration, a sound! He whipped his head up, gasping, frightened, his hand instinctively reaching for his coat on a hook. A portly middle-aged man nodded and went to a urinal. Quickly Joel looked at the teeth marks on his arm; they were like a dog bite. He drained the sink, turned on the hot water faucet, and with a paper towel squeezed and blotted the painful area until blood emerged from the broken skin. It was the best he could do; he had done much the same thing a lifetime ago when attacking water rats swam through the bars of his bamboo cage. Then in another kind of panic, he had learned that rats could be frightened. And killed. The man at the urinal turned and went out the door, glancing uncomfortably at Converse.

Joel layered a paper towel over the teeth marks, put on his coat and combed his hair. He opened the door and went back to his table, once again annoyed by the blaring television on the wall.

The menu, like the announcement about the television, was in four languages, the last Oriental, undoubtedly Japanese. He was tempted to go for the largest, rarest piece of meat he could find, but here his pilot's control dictated otherwise. He'd had no solid sleep in days—oddly enough, since his imprisonment at Leifhelm's compound, where the sleep itself had been greatly induced by the huge quantities of very decent food, all part of the healing process for a deflecting pawn. A heavy meal would make him drowsy, and one did not fly a jet going six hundred miles an hour in that condition. At the moment his air speed was approaching Mach I. He ordered filet of sole and rice; he could always order twice. And one more whisky.

The voice! Oh, Christ. The *voice!* He was hallucinating! He was going mad! He was hearing a voice—an echo of a voice—he could not possibly be hearing!

". . . Actually, I think it's a national disgrace, but like so many others, I speak only English."

"Frau Converse—"

"Miss—Fräulein—I think that's right—Charpentier, if you don't mind."

"Dames en heren . . ." a third voice broke in quietly, authoritatively, speaking Dutch.

Converse gasped for the air he could not find, gripping his wrist, closing his eyes with such intensity that every muscle in his face was in pain, twisting his neck away from the source of the terrible, horrible hallucination.

"I'm in Berlin on business—I'm a consultant for a firm in New York—"

"Mevrouw Converse, of juffrouw Charpentier, zoals we . . ."

Joel was now sure that he *was* mad, *insane!* He was hearing the impossible. *Hearing!* He spun around and looked up. The television screen! It was *Valerie!* She was *there!*

"Whatever you say, Fräulein Charpentier, will be accurately translated, I can assure you."

"*Zoals juffrouw Charpentier zojuist zei . . .*"
The third voice, the voice in Dutch.

"I haven't seen my former husband in several years—three or four, I'd say. Actually, we're strangers. I can only express the shock my whole country feels. . . ."

"*Juffrouw Charpentier, de vroegere mevrouw Converse . . .*"

". . . he was a deeply disturbed man, subject to extreme depressions, but I never imagined anything like this."

"*Hij moet mentaal gestoord zijn . . .*"

"There's no connection between us, and I'm surprised you learned I was flying to Berlin. But I appreciate the chance to clear the air, as we say."

"*Mevrouw Converse gelooft . . .*"

"In spite of the dreadful circumstances over which, of course, I had no control, I'm delighted to be in your beautiful city. Half-city, I guess, but yours is the beautiful part. And I hear the Bristol-Kempinski. . . . I'm terribly sorry, that's what we call a 'plug' and I shouldn't."

"It is a landmark, Fräulein Charpentier. It is not *verboten* over here. Do you feel at all threatened?"

"*Mevrouw Converse, voelt u zich bedreigd?*"

"No, not really. We've had nothing to do with each other for so long."

My God! Val had come over to find him! She was sending him a signal—signals! She spoke every bit as fluent German as the interviewer! They kept in touch every month; they had lunch

702

together six weeks ago in Boston! Everything she was saying was a lie and in those lies was the code. Their code! *Reach me!*

PART THREE

PART THREE

27

Joel was stunned, but he had to control his panic and try to isolate the words, the phrases. The message was in them! The Bristol-Kempinski was a hotel in West Berlin, he knew that. It was something else she had said, something that should trigger a memory—one of *their* memories. What *was* it?

I haven't seen my former husband in years. . . . No, only one of the lies. *He was a deeply disturbed man . . . .* Less a lie, but not what she was trying to tell him. *Actually, we're strangers. . . . There's no connection between us. . . .* Another lie, but with some truth in it. . . . *Stop it!* What *was* it! . . . Before, earlier. . . . *I'm a consultant. . . .* That was it!

"May I speak with Miss Charpentier, please? My name is Mr. Whistletoe, Bruce Whistletoe. I'm the confidential consultant for Springtime antiperspirant for which your agency is doing some artwork, and it's urgent, *most* urgent!" *Con molta forza.*

Val's secretary had been a talker, a marvelous spreader of in-house gossip, and whenever Joel and Valerie had wanted an extra hour for lunch or even a day, he would make such a phone call. It never failed. If a demanding vice-president (one of dozens) wanted to know where she was, the excitable secretary would tell of an urgent call from one of those outside watchdogs of a *very* large account. It was enough for any ulcer-prone executive, and Valerie's understated professionalism took care of the rest. She would say "things" were under control and rarely did a relieved account man pursue what might give him an acid attack.

She was telling him to use the tactic in case the police were monitoring her calls. He would have done so in any event; she was simply reminding him, warning him.

The interview was over, the last few minutes obviously a recap in Dutch, the camera frozen on a still frame of Valerie's face. When had the tape been made? How long had she been in Berlin? *Goddamn* it, why couldn't he understand anything unless it was spoken in English? When she lied about her inability to speak German, Val had said it was a national disgrace. She was right, but she might have gone further; it was a national disorder rooted in arrogance. He looked around the café for a telephone; there was one on the rear wall several feet from the door to the men's room, but he hadn't the vaguest idea of how to use it! His frustrations grew, swirling into circles of panic. Suddenly he heard his name.

"*De Amerikaanase moordenaar Converse is advocaat. Hij is een ex-piloot uit de Vietnamese oorlog. Een ander advocaat, een Fransman, en een vriend van Converse . . .*"

Joel looked up at the screen bewildered, at once shocked, then paralyzed. There was a film clip, a hand-held camera entered an office door and focused on a body slumped over a desk, streams

708

of blood spreading from the head like a hideous Medusa wig. Oh, Christ! It was René!

As the recognition came an insert appeared on the upper left of the screen. It was a photograph of Mattilon—then another photograph was suddenly inserted on the right. It was he, the *moordenaar Amerikaans,* Joel Converse. The Dutch newscast had connected two events, the interview with Val and a death in France. Neither language nor diagrams were necessary. René had been killed and he had been named the killer. It answered the question; it was the reason Aquitaine had put out the word that an assassin was heading for Paris.

He was a giver of death; it was his gift to new and old friends. René Mattilon, Edward Beale . . . Avery Fowler. And to enemies he did not know, could not evaluate, either as enemies or as individuals—a man in a tan overcoat in a Paris cellar, a guard above a riverbank on the Rhine, a pilot on a train, a memorably unmemorable face at the base of a landfill pyramid, a chauffeur moments later who had actually befriended him in a stone house with bars in the windows . . . an old woman who had played her role brilliantly in a raucous railway car. *Death.* He was either the distant observer or the executioner, all in the unholy name of Aquitaine. He was back, back in the camps and the jungles that he had sworn never to return to. He could only survive and hope that someone better than himself would provide the solutions. But at the moment, death was both his closest ally and his most hostile adversary. He wanted to collapse into nothingness—let someone else take up the cause no one knew had been given him in Geneva.

Jesus! The tape! If it was even twelve or twenty-four hours old, Val probably had not received the envelope he had sent from Bonn! She could not have. She would not have flown to Europe if she had!

Oh, my God! thought Joel, swallowing the last of the whisky as he rubbed his forehead, his confusion complete. Without the envelope in Nathan Simon's hands, no plea to him made sense! No call to him would evoke anything but a demand that Joel turn himself in and a telephone trace would be put on the line. Nate would not disobey the law; he would fight violently for a client afterward, but not before that client obeyed the law. It was his religion, far more important to him than his temple, for the law allowed mistakes; it was essentially human, not esoterically metaphysical. Converse's hands began to tremble; he *had* to find out!

"Your filet of sole, *Meneer.*"

"*What?*"

"Your sole, sir," repeated the waiter.

"You speak English?"

"But of course," said the gaunt, bald-headed man with detached courtesy. "We spoke before, but you were very excited. This district can do that to a man, I understand."

"Listen—to—me." Joel brought his hand across his lips, emphasizing each word. "I will pay you a lot of money if you will place a phone call for me. I don't speak Dutch, or French, or German or anything but English. Can you understand that?''

"I understand."

"To West Berlin."

"It is not difficult, sir."

"Will you do it for me?"

"But of course, *Meneer*. You have a telephone credit card?"

"Yes . . . no. I don't want to use it."

"Of course."

"I mean I don't—I don't want it recorded anywhere. I have money."

"I understand. In a few minutes I shall be off my shift. I shall come for you. We shall place your call and I shall know the amount from the operator. You shall pay."

"Absolutely."

"And 'a lot of money,' *ja?* Fifty guilder, *ja?*"

"You're on. Yes."

Twenty minutes later Converse sat behind a small desk in a very small office. The waiter handed him the phone. "They speak English, *Meneer.*"

"Miss Charpentier, please," said Joel, his voice choking, overwhelmed by a kind of paralysis. If he heard her voice he was not sure he could handle his own reaction. For an instant he thought about slamming down the phone. He could not involve her!

"Hello?"

It was she, and as a part of him died another part came alive. A thousand pictures flashed across his mind, memories of happiness and anger, of love and of hate. He could not speak.

"Hello? Who's this?"

"Oh . . . there you are. Sorry, it's a lousy connection. This is Jack Talbot from . . . Boston Graphics. How are you, Val?"

"Fine . . . Jack. How are you? It's been a couple of months. Since lunch at the Four Seasons, if I remember."

"That's right. When did you get in?"

"Last night."

"Staying long?"

"Just for the day. I've been in crisis meetings all morning, with another one this afternoon. If I'm not too bushed I'll catch the plane back tonight. When did you get to Berlin?"

"Actually, I'm not in Berlin. I saw you on a Belgian broadcast. I'm in . . . Antwerp, but I'm going to Amsterdam this afternoon. Christ, I'm sorry about all that crap you had to take. Who would ever have guessed it? About Joel, I mean."

"I should have guessed it, Jack. It's all so horrible. He's so very sick. I hope they catch him quickly for everyone's sake. He needs help."

"He needs a firing squad, if you don't mind my saying so."

"I'd rather not discuss it."

"Did you get the sketches I sent you when we lost the Gillette account? I figured it was a way to your sack?"

"Sketches? . . . No, Jack, I never got anything like that. But thanks for the thought, the sack notwithstanding."

Christ! "Oh? I thought you might have looked at your mail."

"I did . . . until the day before yesterday. It doesn't matter—you'll be in Amsterdam?"

"For a week. I wondered if you were going to check any of the agency's accounts up there before heading back to New York."

"I should, but I don't think so. There's no time. If I do, I'll be at the Amstel Hotel. If not, I'll see you back in New York. You can buy me lunch at Lutèce, and we'll swap trade secrets."

"I've got more of them. You buy. Take care, youngster."

"Take care . . . Jack."

She was *magnificent*. And she had not received the envelope from Bonn.

He roamed the streets, afraid of walking too fast, afraid of staying in one place too long, knowing only that he had to keep moving, watching, finding the shadows and letting them envelope him. She would be in Amsterdam by evening; he knew that, it was in her voice, and she had told him to reach her at the Amstel Hotel. *Why?* Why had she come? What did she think she was *doing?* Suddenly, the face of René Mattilon came to him. It was in sharp focus, filling his inner eye, surrounded by sunlight, the face a mask—a death mask. René had been killed by Aquitaine for sending him to Amsterdam. Valerie would not be spared if the disciples of George Marcus Delavane thought she had flown over to find him, to help him.

He would not reach her! He could not! It was signing another death warrant! *Her* death warrant. He had taken so much from her, given so little. The last gift could not be the taking of her life. Yet . . . yet there was Aquitaine and he meant what he had said to Larry Talbot on the phone. He, one Joel Converse, was inconsequential where the gathering of the generals was concerned. So were A. Preston Halliday and Edward Beale and Connal Fitzpatrick. If Val could help, he had no right to let his feelings stop her—the lawyer in him told him that, the outraged man confirmed it. And it was possible she *could* help, do the things he could not do himself. She could fly back, get the envelope and go to Nathan Simon herself, saying that she had seen him, talked to him, *believed* him.

It was three-thirty; it would be dark by eight o'clock or so. He had roughly five hours to remain unseen and stay alive. And somehow find a car.

He stopped on the pavement and looked up at an overly made-up, extremely bored whore in a window on the third floor of a colorful brick house. Their eyes made contact and she smiled a bored smile at him, the thumb and forefinger of her right hand meeting, the wrist motion leaving little to the imagination.

Why not? thought Converse. The only certain thing in a very uncertain world was the fact that there was a bed beyond that window.

The ''concierge'' was a clerk, a man in his middle fifties with the pink face of an aging cherub, who explained in perfectly fluent English that payment was based on twenty-minute sessions, two sessions paid in advance, one to be refunded should the guest come downstairs during the final five minutes of the first period. It was a loan shark's dream, thought Converse, glancing at the various clocks placed on numbered squares on the counter. As an elderly man walked down the staircase the clerk hastily grabbed one of the clocks and pushed the second hand forward.

Joel calculated rapidly, converting guilders to dollars, the rate of acceleration based on roughly $30 per session. He gave the astonished "concierge" the equivalent of $275, accepted his number and headed for the staircase.

"She is a friend, sir?" asked the stunned custodian of the revels as Converse reached the first step. "An old lover, perhaps?"

"She's a Dutch cousin I haven't seen in years," replied Joel sadly. "We have to have a long talk." With heavy shoulders, he continued up the staircase.

"*Slapen?*" exclaimed the woman with the spangled dark hair and heavily rouged cheeks. She was as astonished as her keeper below. "You want *slapen?*"

"It doesn't translate well, but yes," said Converse, removing his glasses and his cap and sitting on the bed. "I'm very tired and sleep would be terrific, but I suspect I'll just rest. Read one of your magazines, I won't bother you."

"What is the matter? You think I am not pretty? Not clean? You yourself are no fine picture, *Meneer!* Cuts on your face, a bruise here and there, red eyes. Perhaps it is you who are not clean!"

"I fell down. Come on, I think you're adorable and I love your deep-purple eye shadow but I really want to rest."

"Why here?"

715

"I don't want to go back to the hotel. My wife's lover is there. He's my boss."

"*Amerikaans!*"

"You speak our language very well." Joel took off his shoes and stretched out on the bed.

"Ach, I start with *Amerikaan* college boys. All talk, most are too afraid for nothing but talk. Those who get on the bed—*poof!*—is over. Then talk, too goddamn much talk. Then your soldiers and your sailors and your businessmen. Most drunk; they behave like giggle-children. All talk. Twelve years, *I* learn."

"Don't write a book. They're probably all senators and congressmen and priests by now." Converse placed his hands behind his head and stared at the ceiling. There was a glimmer of peace. He softly whistled the tune first, then found the words: " 'Yankee Doodle' came to Holland/ nothing in his pistol . . .' "

"You are amusing, *Meneer,*" said the whore, laughing coarsely and picking up a thin blanket off a chair. She carried it to the bed and spread it over him. "You don't tell the truth but you are amusing."

"How do you know I'm not telling you the truth?"

"If your wife had a lover, you would kill him."

"Not so."

"Then she would not be your wife. I see many men, *Meneer*. It's in your face. You are a good man, perhaps, but you would kill."

"I'll have to think about that," said Joel uncomfortably.

"Sleep, if you wish. You paid. I am here." The

woman walked to the chair against the wall and sat down with a magazine.

"What's your name?" asked Converse.

"Emma," replied the whore.

"You're a nice person, Emma."

"No, *Meneer,* I am not."

He awoke, startled by the touch, and bolted upright on the bed, his hand instinctively rushing to his waist to make sure his money belt was in place. He had been so deep in sleep that for a moment he had no idea where he was, then he saw the garishly made-up woman standing beside him, her hand on his shoulder as she spoke.

"Meneer, are you hiding from people?" she asked softly.

"What?"

"Word goes up and down the Leidseplein. Men are asking questions."

"What?" Converse whipped the blanket off the bed and swung his legs to the floor. "What men? Up and down *where?"*

"Het Leidseplein— This district. Men ask questions. They look for an American."

"Why *here?"* Joel moved his right hand from the money belt up to the outline of the weapon above.

"People who wish not to be seen often come down to the Leidseplein."

Why not? thought Converse. If he thought of it, why wouldn't the enemy? "Do they have a description?"

"It is you," answered the whore frankly.

"And?" Joel looked into the woman's eyes.

"Nothing was said."

"I can't believe our friend downstairs felt so charitable toward me. I'm sure they offered money."

"It was given," corrected the whore. "More promised with additional information. A man remains behind down the street. In a café next to a telephone. He is to be called and will bring back the others. Our . . . friend downstairs thought you might want to match the funds."

"I see. An auction. One head on the block."

"I do not understand."

"What are we talking about? How much?"

"A thousand guilder. Much more if you are taken."

"Our friend still sounds too charitable. I'd think he'd grab it and close up shop."

"He owns the building. Also, the man was German and spoke like a soldier giving orders, that's what our friend downstairs said."

"He was right. The man is a soldier but not in any army Bonn knows about."

"Zo?"

"Nothing. Find out if our friend will take American money."

"Of course he will."

"Then I'll match the offer and double it."

The whore hesitated. "Now it is my turn."

"I beg your pardon?"

"*En?* As you say—*'and'?*"

"Oh. You?"

"*Ja.*"

"I have something special for you. Can you drive a car, or do you know someone who can?"

"I do myself, *natuurlijk*. In bad weather I drive my children to school."

"Oh, Jesus. . . . I mean, that's good."

"Without my face like *zo*, of course."

The stories. Oh, God, the stories! thought Converse. "I want you to rent a car and bring it around here to the front door. Then get out and leave the keys inside. Can you do that?"

"*Ja*, but nothing is for nothing."

"Three hundred dollars—eight hundred guilders, give or take."

"Five hundred—fourteen hundred, take or give," countered the woman. "And the money to rent the automobile."

Joel nodded as he unbuttoned his jacket and pulled out his shirt. The handle of the gun with the short barrel and the extended silencer was clearly visible beneath the wide canvas belt. The whore saw it and gasped. "It's not mine," said Converse quickly. "Whether you believe it or not doesn't matter to me, but I took it from someone who tried to kill me."

The woman stared at him, her look partially one of fear but it was not hostile, only curious. "The man—this soldier from no German army —the others who ask questions in the street. They wish to kill you?"

"Yes." Joel unzipped the belt and counted off the money with his thumb. He pulled out the bills and closed the pocket.

"You have done them much harm?"

"Not yet, but I hope to." Converse held out the money. "There's enough for our friend downstairs and the rest is for you. Just bring me the car, along with one of those tourist maps of Amsterdam that show where all the major stores and hotels and restaurants are.''

"Perhaps I can tell you where it is you wish to go.''

"No, thank you.''

"*Ja.*'' The whore nodded knowingly and took the money. "These people are bad people?'' she asked, counting out the bills.

"The pits, lady.''

"They do those things to your face?''

"Yes. Mostly.''

"Go to the *politie.*''

"The police? It's not practical. They wouldn't understand.''

"They want you also,'' concluded the woman.

"Not for anything I did.''

The whore shrugged. "It is no problem for me,'' she said, going to the door. "I will say the auto is stolen. There is a *Tromp* garage twelve blocks from here; they know me. I have rented there when my Peugeot has troubles and I must get home. *Ach, kinderen!* Recitals, dance classes! Be downstairs in twenty minutes.''

"Recitals?''

"Don't look so, *Meneer.* I do my job and call it what it is. Most people do the same and call it something else. Twenty minutes.'' The spangled-haired woman went out the door, closing it behind her.

Joel approached the sink against the wall without enthusiasm, then saw it was spotless, a can of cleanser and a bottle of bleach below on the floor next to a roll of paper towels. Naturally.

Dance lessons and recitals were part of the whore's life, as well as a car that often gave her trouble, just like any other commuter. Converse looked in the mirror; the woman was right, he was "no fine picture," but one had to be quite close to him to notice the severity of the bruises. He splashed water on his face, then blotted it, put on the dark glasses and made himself as presentable as possible.

It had happened. Val had come to find him, and despite the horrors surrounding their seeing each other again, a part of him wanted to sing —silently—or shout silently into the mists of his imagination. He wanted so much to look at her, to touch her, hear her voice close to him—and he knew it was for all the wrong reasons. He was the hunted and in pain and vulnerable, all the things he had never been when they were together, and because he was what he had become, he permitted her to find him. It was hardly admirable. He did not care to be a hungry dog in a cold rain; it did not fit his part of their past dual image, the *de suite,* as René Mattilon had phrased it . . . René. A telephone call had signed the order for his execution. *Aquitaine.* How in God's name could he let Val even come near him? thought Joel, a terrible pain in his throat. The answer was the same: Aquitaine. And the fact that he thought he knew what he was doing. Every move he made in the streets, and on the trains, and in the cafés, was as carefully thought out as the steps he had taken in the jungles—in the routes he had chosen, in the rivers and streams he had forded and used as watery tunnels to bypass an enemy time and again. He would use an automobile in Amsterdam, and a map of Amsterdam.

He looked at his watch: it was almost five-thirty. He had roughly two and a half hours to find the Amstel Hotel and drive around again and again until he knew every foot of the area, every stoplight, every side street and canal. And then the route to one other place—the American embassy or the consulate. It was part of his plan, the only protection he could give her—if she followed his instructions. And somewhere an airlines schedule; that, too, was part of the plan.

Twelve minutes had passed, and he wanted to be at the doorway when Emma, the honest commuter, drove up in front of the house on the crowded street. If there was no place to park at the curb, he would walk out on the pavement, signal to her to leave the car and quickly replace her behind the wheel so as not to hold up traffic. He left the small room, went to the staircase and started down, aware of the feigned groans of ecstasy behind several closed doors. He wondered briefly if the girls had thought of using cassette recorders; they could push buttons while reading magazines. He reached the second landing; below in clear view was the cherub-faced, middle-aged owner of the establishment behind his counter. He was on the telephone. Joel continued down the steps, in his hand a $100 bill he had decided to give the man—an additional gratuity in exchange for his life.

As he set foot on the lobby floor he suddenly was not at all sure he should let the "concierge" have anything but a cage in the Mekong River.

722

The pink-faced man looked over at Converse, his eyes wide, staring fixedly, the blood draining from his cherubic cheeks. He trembled as he hung up the phone, attempted a smile, then spoke in a high-pitched voice. "Problems! There are always problems, sir. Scheduling is so difficult I should buy a computer."

The bastard had done it! He had made the call to a man down the street in a café! "Keep your hands on the counter!" shouted Joel.

The command did not come in time; the Dutchman raised a gun from below. Converse lunged forward, his hand tearing at the buttons of his jacket, finding the handle of the revolver in his belt. The "concierge" fired wildly as Joel crashed his left shoulder up into the flimsy counter; it collapsed and Converse saw the extended arm, the hand holding the gun. He swung the barrel of his own weapon onto the Dutchman's wrist; the gun went flying, clattering over the lobby floor.

"You bastard!" cried Joel, grabbing the man by the front of his shirt, pulling him up. "You *bastard! I paid you!*"

"Don't kill me! *Please!* I am a poor man in much debt! They said they only wished to talk to you! What harm is there in that? *Please!* Don't do this!"

"You're not worth the price—to me, you son of a bitch." Converse crashed the barrel of the gun down on the Dutchman's head and ran to the door. The street was crowded with traffic, then suddenly there was a break and the cars and buses and open tourist vans lurched forward. Where *was* she? Where was Emma the Practical?

"Theodoor! Deze kerel is onmogelijk! Hij wil . . . !" The hysterical words came from a bare-breasted woman rushing down the staircase, a thin, short slip covering the essentials of her trade. She stopped on the next to last step, saw the carnage and the unconscious Theodoor and screamed. Joel ran to her and clamped his left hand over her mouth; his right—with the gun—pressed against her shoulder, pushing her into the railing.

"Be quiet!" Converse could not restrain himself from shouting. "Shut up!" He slammed his elbow into the prostitute's neck, the weapon now in front of her face. She screamed again and kicked viciously at his groin, gouging his nostrils with two fingers, scratching, pushing him away. He could do nothing else but to pummel the handle of the gun into the base of her jaw. Her red lips parted and remained open; she went limp.

Doors crashed everywhere above, beyond the staircase, metal and wood smashing into walls. He heard shouts, angry, frightened, questioning. A horn suddenly intruded, blaring from the street beyond the open front door. He ran to the doorframe, his right arm supporting him, the gun out of sight.

It was Emma the whore, the car in the middle of the street, unable to crawl to the curb. He shoved the weapon under his jacket, under his belt, and ran outside. She understood his gestures and got out of the car; he raced around the hood. "Thank you!" he said.

"It was stolen!" she said, shrugging. "Good fortune, *Meneer*. I think you will need it, but it is

724

not my problem."

He jumped into the seat behind the wheel and studied the panel as if he were approaching Mach I and had to understand the readouts of every dial. It was simple, primitive; he pulled the gear into *D* and started up with the surrounding traffic.

Without warning, the figure of an immense man slammed against the window on his right. Joel lurched and slapped the lock on the window; taking advantage of another break in the traffic, he spurted forward. The killer held on as he yanked out a gun. Converse careened into the side of an automobile parked at the curb, and still the man held on. Joel reached under his jacket as the killer, holding on to God knew what, brought his weapon up and aimed at Converse. Joel ducked, smashing his head into the window frame as the explosion shattered the glass, fragments entering his skin above his eyes. But his gun was free; he pointed it at the figure hugging the window and pulled the trigger. Twice.

Two muted spits echoed in the darkness of the car as two holes appeared in the area of the glass that had not been shattered. Screaming, both hands covering his throat, the man fell away, rolling onto the curb between two trucks. Converse turned right into a wide, empty alleyway. *One man remains behind, down the street. . . He will bring back the others.* He was free again—for a while—thought Joel. A dead man could not identify an automobile. He parked the car in shadows and pulled out a cigarette, trying to steady his hand as he struck the match.

Inhaling deeply, he felt his forehead, and slowly, carefully removed the particles of glass.

He now prowled the streets like a mechanized animal, but with each hesitation, each stop, he used his eyes and nostrils as if he were a primitive thing conscious only of its need to survive in a violently hostile environment. He had made the run four times from the Amstel Hotel on the Tulpplein, across the streets and over the canals to the American consulate on the city square called the Museumplein. He had learned the alternate approaches; he knew the side streets that would bring him back to the main route without interruption. Lastly, he drove east and crossed the Schellingwouder Brug, the bridge over the IJ River and took the road along the coast until he found a stretch of deserted fields above the water. They would do; they were isolated. He turned around and headed back to Amsterdam.

It was eight-thirty, the sky dark; he was ready. He had studied the tourist map, which included a paragraph on the use of pay phones. He had once been a pilot; instructions were second nature. They were the difference between blowing an aircraft apart and landing it on a carrier. He parked the car across the street from the Amstel Hotel and walked into a booth.

"Miss Charpentier, please."

"*Dank u,*" said the operator, shifting instantly to English. "One moment, please. . . . Oh, yes, *Missen* Charpentier arrive only one hour ago. I have her room now."

"Thank you."

"Hello?"

Oh *God,* should he speak? *Could* he speak? *Aquitaine.* "Val, it's Jack Talbot. I took a chance you might fly in. Glad you did. How are you, youngster?"

"Totally exhausted, you awful man. I talked to New York this afternoon and mentioned our accounts in Amsterdam—courtesy of one Jack Talbot. The orders were for me to get to Canal City and spend tomorrow morning holding hands."

"Why not hold mine?"

"They're too cold. You can, however, buy me dinner."

"Be delighted, but first I need a favor. Can you grab a cab and pick me up at the consulate on Museumplein?"

"What . . . ?" The pause was filled with fear. "Why, Jack?" The question was a whisper.

Converse lowered his voice. "I've been here for a couple of hours taking too damn much abuse and I'm afraid I blew my cork."

"What—happened?"

"It was dumb. My passport expired today and I needed a temporary extension. Instead I got a half-dozen lectures and told to come back in the morning. I was very loud and not too benign."

"And now it would be embarrassing for you to ask them to call you a cab, is that it?"

"That's it. If I knew this part of the city I'd walk and try to find one, but I've never been over here before."

"I'll straighten my face and pick you up. Say in about twenty minutes?"

"Thanks, I'll be outside. If I'm not, wait in the cab; I'll only be a few minutes. You've got yourself a good dinner, youngster." Joel hung up the phone, left the booth and went back to the rented car. The waiting had begun, the watching would soon follow.

Ten minutes later he saw her, and the pounding in his chest accelerated. A mist clouded his eyes. She walked out the glass doors of the Amstel, carrying a large, dark cloth bag, her posture erect, her stride long and graceful, bespeaking the dancer she might have been, announcing her presence without pretense, telling anyone who watched her that she was herself; no artifices were necessary. He had once loved her so, as much for the person she appeared to be as for the woman she was. But he had not loved her enough; she had slipped away from him because he had not cared enough. There was not that much love or care in him. "Burn-out!" she had shouted. "Emotional burn-out!"

There had been nothing left to say; he could not dispute her. He had been running so fast, so furiously, wanting it all yet not wanting to remember the reasons why—wanting only to get even. He had concealed the intensity of his feelings with flippancy and a casualness that bordered on disdain, but he was not casual at all, and there was little room for the time consumed in being disdainful. There was also very little room for people, for Val. Being together demanded the responsibility that was part of any relationship, and as the months stretched into a year, then two and three, he knew it was not in him to live up to that responsibility. As much as he profoundly disliked himself for it, he could not be dishonest—with either himself or Valerie. He had nothing left to give; he could only take. It was better to break clean.

The waiting was over; the watching began. The Amstel doorman hailed her a cab and she climbed in, immediately leaning forward in the seat to give instructions. Twenty tense seconds later, during which his eyes scanned the street and the pavements in every direction, he started the car and switched on the headlights. No automobile had crept out from the curb after the taxi; still, he had to be certain. Joel swung the wheel and drove into the street, heading for the most direct route to the consulate. A minute later he saw Val's cab take the correct right turn over a canal. There were two cars behind her; he concentrated on their shapes and sizes; instead of following, he continued straight ahead, pressing down on the accelerator, using an alternate route on the bare chance that he himself had been picked up by a hunter from Aquitaine. Three minutes later, after two right turns and a left, he entered the Museumplein. The taxi was directly ahead, the two other automobiles no longer in sight. His strategy was working. The possibility that Val's phone was being tapped was real—René's had been, and his death was the result—so in Val's case he assumed the worst. If it was relayed that the Charpentier woman was heading over to the American consulate to pick up a business acquaintance, one Joel Converse would be ruled out. The consulate was no place for the fugitive assassin; he would not go near it. He was a killer of Americans.

The taxi pulled into the curb in front of 19 Museumplein, the stone building that was the consulate. Converse remained a half-block behind, waiting again, watching again. Several cars went by, none stopping or even slowing down. A lone cyclist pedaled down the street, an old man who braked and turned around and disappeared in the opposite direction. The tactic *had* worked. Val was alone in the cab thirty yards away and no one had followed her from the Amstel. He could make his final move to her, his hand under his coat, gripping the gun with the perforated silencer attached to the barrel.

He got out of the car and walked up the pavement, his gait slow, casual, a man taking a summer night's stroll in the square. There were perhaps a dozen people—couples mainly—also walking, strolling in both directions. He studied them as a frenzied but rigid cat studies the new mounds of mole holes in a field; no one in the street had the slightest interest in the stationary taxi. He approached the rear door and knocked once on the window. She rolled it down.

They stared at each other for a brief moment, then Val brought her hand to her lips, stifling a gasp. "Oh, my God," she whispered.

"Pay him and walk back to a gray car about two hundred feet behind us. The last three numbers on the license are one, three, six. I'll be there in a few minutes." He tipped his hat, as if he had just answered a question from a bewildered tourist, and proceeded down the pavement. Forty feet past the taxi, at the end of the block, he turned and crossed the square, reaching the other side with his head angled to the left, a pedestrian watching for traffic; in reality he was apprehensively watching a lone woman make her way down the sidewalk toward an automobile. He went swiftly into the shadows of a doorway and stood there watching, breathing erratically, peering into every pocket of darkness along the opposite pavement. Nothing. No one. He walked out of the doorway, suppressing a maddening desire to run, and ambled casually down the block until he was directly across from the rented car. Again he paused, now lighting a cigarette, the flame cupped in his hand, again waiting, watching. . . . No one. He threw the cigarette to the curb and, unable to contain himself any longer, ran across the street, opened the door and climbed in behind the wheel.

She was inches from him, her long, dark hair framing her face in the dim light, that lovely face taut, filled now with anxiety, her wide eyes burning into his.

"*Why,* Val? Why did you *do* it?" he asked, a cry in the question.

"I didn't have a choice," she answered quietly, enigmatically. "Drive away from here, please."

28

They drove for several minutes. Neither of them spoke. Joel was concentrating on the streets, knowing the turns he wanted to make—knowing, too, he wanted to shout. It was all he could do to control himself, to keep from stopping the car and grabbing her, demanding to know why she had done what she did, furiously replying to whatever she said that she was a goddamned *fool!* Why had she come back into his life? He was *death!* . . . Above all, he wanted to hold her in his arms, his face against hers, and thank her and tell her how sorry he was—for so much, for now.

"Do you know where you're going?" asked Val, breaking the silence.

"I've had the car since six o'clock. A map of the city came with it and I've spent the time driving around, learning what I thought I had to learn."

"Yes, you'd do that. You were always methodical."

"I thought I *should,*" he said defensively. "I followed you from the hotel just in case anybody else did. Also I'm better off in a car than on the streets."

"I wasn't insulting you."

Converse glanced at her; she was studying him, her eyes roving over his face in the erratic progressions of light and shadow. "Sorry. I guess I'm a little sensitive these days. Can't imagine why."

"Neither can I. You're only wanted on two continents and in some eight countries. They say you're the most talented assassin since that maniac they call Carlos."

"Do I have to tell you it's all a lie? All a huge lie with a very clear motive—purpose is better."

"No," replied Valerie simply. "You don't have to tell me that because I know it. But you've got to tell me everything else. *Everything.*"

He looked at her again, searching her eyes in the flashes of light, trying to penetrate, trying to peel away the layers of clouded glass that held her thoughts, her reasons. Once he had been able to do that, in love and in anger. He could not do it now; what she felt was too deep inside her, but it was not love, he knew that. It was something else, and the lawyer in him was cautious, oblique. "What made you think I'd see you on television? I almost missed you."

"I didn't think about television, I was counting on the newspapers. I knew my face would be on the front pages all over Europe. I assumed your memory was not so dulled that you wouldn't recognize me, and reporters always pick up on hotels or addresses—it lends authenticity."

"I can't read anything but English."

"Your memory *is* dulled. I made three trips with you to Europe, two to Geneva and one to Paris. You wouldn't have coffee in the morning unless the *Herald Tribune* was on the room-service table. Even when we went skiing in Chamonix—from Geneva—you made an awful fuss until the waiter brought the *Tribune.*"

"You were in the *Tribune?*"

"Class acts aside, it's their kind of story. With all the details. I assumed you'd pick one up and realize what I was doing."

"Because we were strangers and hadn't seen each other in years, and, of course, you couldn't speak German or French or anything else."

"Yes. It was an acceptable explanation for those who knew I did. A cover, I guess. A lot of people who speak several languages do it all the time. It's common practice; it cuts conversations short or at least keeps them to basic statements, and you always know if you're misquoted."

"I forgot, that's your business in a way."

"It's not where the idea came from. It came from Roger."

"Dad?"

"Yes. He flew in from Hong Kong a few days ago and some hungry clerk alerted the newspapers that he was on the flight. When he got into Kennedy it was a media blitz. He hadn't read a newspaper or listened to a radio or seen a television screen in two days. He was in a panic and called me. I simply made sure the wire services in West Berlin knew I was flying in."

"How *is* Dad? He can't handle this."

"He's handling it. So's your sister—less so than your father, but her husband stepped into the breach and took over. He's a better man than you thought, Converse."

"What's happening to them? How *are* they taking it?"

"Confused, angry, bewildered. They've changed their telephone numbers. They speak through attorneys—supporting you, incidentally. You may not realize it but they love you very much, although I'm not sure you gave them much reason to."

"I think we're closer to home," said Joel quietly, as they approached the Schellingwouder Brug. "Our once and former home." They

734

entered the dark span of the bridge, diaphanous lights above, speckled dots far below on the water. Valerie did not respond to his statement; it was not like her to avoid a provocation. He could not stand it. *"Why,* Val?" he cried, "I asked you before, and I have to know! Why did you fly over?"

"I'm sorry, I was thinking," she said, her eyes leaving his face, staring straight ahead through the windshield. "I guess it's better I say it now while you're driving and I don't have to look at you. You look awful, you're a mess, and your face tells me what you've gone through, and I don't *want* to look at you."

"I'm hurt," said Converse gently, trying genuinely to lessen the impact of his appearance. "Helen Gurley Brown called and wants me for *Cosmopolitan's* centerfold."

"Stop that! It's not remotely funny and you know it—worse, you don't even feel like saying it!"

"I retreat. There were times when you never did read me right."

"I always read you right, Joel!" Valerie continued to focus on the road and the beams of the headlights; she did not move her head. "Don't play the serious fool any longer. We haven't time for that; we haven't time for your flip remarks. It was always a little sad to watch you put people off who really wanted to talk to you, but it's finished now."

"Glad to hear it. Then *talk!* Why the hell did you walk into this?"

Their eyes met in anger, in abrupt recognition,

in a love once remembered, perhaps. She turned away as Converse steered the car into the right exit off the bridge, then peeled into the road that ran along the coastline.

"All right," said Valerie, hesitant but in complete control. "I'll spell it out as best I can. I say 'as best I can' because I'm not entirely sure—there are too many complications to be absolutely sure. . . . You may be a rotten husband and careless beyond stoning where another person's feelings are concerned, but you're not what they say you are. You didn't kill those men."

"I know that. You said you knew it, too. Why did you come over here?"

"Because I had to," said Val, her voice firm, still staring straight ahead. "The other night after the news—your picture was on every channel, so different from what it was years ago—I walked along the beach and thought about you. They weren't pleasant thoughts, but they were honest ones. . . . You put me through my own personal hell, Joel. You were driven by terrible things in your past, and I tried to understand because I knew what had happened to you. But you never tried to understand *me*. I, too, had things I wanted to do, but they faded, they weren't important. . . . Okay, I thought. Someday it'll pass and the nightmares will go away for him and he'll stop and look at me and say, 'Hey, you're *you*.' Well, the nightmares went away and it never happened."

"I concede my adversary's logic," said Converse painfully. "I still don't understand."

"I needed you, Joel, but you couldn't respond. You were amusing as hell, even when I knew you didn't feel like it, and you were terrific in bed, but your only real concerns were for you, always you."

"Conceded again, learned counselor. *And?*"

"I remembered something I said to myself that afternoon when you left the apartment, said it silently as I watched you leave. I promised myself that if ever a person I was close to needed me as much as I needed you then, I wouldn't walk away. Call it the one moral commitment I've ever made in my life. Only the irony is that that person turned out to be you. You're not a madman and you're not a killer, but someone wants the world to think you are. And whoever it is has done it very well. Even your friends who've known you for years believe what's being said about you. I don't and I can't walk away."

"Oh *Christ,* Val—"

"No strings, Converse. No playing an old sweet song and hopping into bed. That's out. I came here to help you, not console you. And over here I can. My roots go back several generations. They may be withering underground but they *were* the underground—undergrounds—and they're willing to help. For once you need *me,* and that's a twist, isn't it, friend?"

"A veritable twist," said Joel, understanding her last statement but little else, speeding down the coast road toward the deserted fields. "Only a few minutes," he added. "I can't be seen in the city and neither can you—and you not a chance with me."

"I wouldn't worry so much. We're being watched by friends."

"*What?* What—'friends'?"

"Keep your eyes on the road. There were people in front of the Amstel, didn't you see them?"

"I suppose so. No one got in a car and went after you."

"Why should they? There were others on the streets and over the canals to the consulate."

"What the hell are you talking about?"

"And an old man on a bicycle in the Museumplein."

"I saw *him*. Was *he* . . . ?"

"Later," said Valerie, shifting the large cloth bag at her feet into another position and stretching her long legs. "They may follow us out here but they'll stay out of sight."

"Who *are* you, lady?"

"The niece of Hermione Geyner, my mother's sister. You never knew my father, of course, but if you had he would have regaled you with tales of Mom during the war, but he would have choked at the mention of my aunt. Even according to the French she went too far. The Dutch and German undergrounds worked together. I'll tell you all about it later."

"You'll tell me *later? Following* us?"

"You're new at this. You won't see them."

"Shit!"

"That's expressive."

"All right, all right! . . . What about Dad?"

"He's weathering it. He's staying at my place."

"Cape Ann?"

738

"Yes."

"I sent the envelope there! The 'sketches' I mentioned on the phone. It's everything! Everything about what's happened. It names the names, gives the reasons. Everything!"

"I left three days ago. It hadn't arrived by then. But Roger's there." Valerie's face paled. "Oh, my God!"

"What?"

"I've been trying to call him! Two days ago, then yesterday and again today!"

"Goddamn it!" In the distance there were the lights of a bay-front café. Joel spoke rapidly, giving an order that could not be disobeyed. "I don't care how you do it, but you call Cape Ann! You come back here and tell me my father's all right, do you understand?"

"Yes. Because I want to hear it, too."

Converse skidded to a stop in front of the café, knowing he should not have done so, but not caring. Valerie rushed out of the car, her purse open, her telephone credit card in her hand. If there was a phone on the premises, she would use it; no one could stop her. Joel lit a cigarette; the smoke was acrid, stinging his throat; it was no relief. He stared out at the dark water, at the lights spanning the bridge in the distance, trying not to think. It was no use. What had he done? His father knew his handwriting, and the instant he recognized it he would rip open the envelope. He would be looking for exculpation for his son and he would find it. He would undoubtedly call Nathan Simon immediately—and therein was the horrible possibility. Val would know enough from the material itself to say little or nothing on the phone, but not his father, not Roger. He would blurt out everything in a frenzy of anger and defense of his son. And if others were listening on that line. . . . Where was Val? She was taking too long!

Converse could not stop himself. He cracked the handle of the door and leaped out of the car. He raced toward the entrance of the café, then stopped abruptly on the gravel. Valerie walked out, gesturing for him to back away. He could see the tears rolling down her cheeks.

"Get in the car," she said, approaching him.

"No. Tell me what happened. *Now.*"

"Please, Joel, get back in the car. Two men in there kept watching me while I was on the phone. I spoke German, but they knew I was placing a call to the States, and they saw I was upset. I think they recognized me. We have to get out of here."

"Tell me what *happened!*"

"In the car." Valerie tossed her head to the side, her dark hair flying over her shoulder as she brushed away her tears, and walked past Converse to the automobile. She opened the door and got in, sitting motionless in the seat.

"*Goddamn* you!" Trembling, Converse ran to the car, jumped in behind the wheel and started the engine, slamming the door shut as he pulled on the gearshift. Turning the wheel, he backed up, then shot forward into the road, the tires spinning on the border of gravel. He kept his foot on the accelerator until the dark scenery outside was a racing blur.

"Slow down," said Val simply, without emphasis. "You'll only call attention to us."

He could barely hear her through his panic, but he heard the order. He eased his foot off the pedal. "He's dead, isn't he?"

"Yes."

"Oh, *Christ!* What happened? What did they tell you? Whom did you talk to?"

"A neighbor, the name's not important. We have keys to each other's house. She volunteered to take in the newspapers and check the place until the police reached me. She happened to be there when I called. I asked her if there was a large envelope sent from Germany in the pile of mail. She said there wasn't."

"The police? What *happened?*"

"You know my house is on the beach. There's a jetty of rocks about a hundred yards up-water. It's not large or long really, just some kind of marking from years ago—"

"Tell me!" shouted Joel, gripping the wheel.

"They say he must have gone for a walk last night, went out on the jetty and slipped on the wet rocks. There was a large bruise on his head. His body was washed up onshore and found this morning."

"Lies! *Lies!* They heard him! They went after him!"

"My telephone? On the plane over here I thought about that."

"You would, he *wouldn't!* I killed him. Goddamn it, I *killed* him!"

"No more than I did, Joel," insisted the ex-Mrs. Converse, touching his arm, wincing at the

741

sight of tears in his eyes. "And I loved him very much. You and I left each other, but he was still a very close friend, perhaps my closest."

"He called you 'Valley,' " said Joel, choking, trying to push back the pain. "The bastards! *Bastards!*"

"Do you want me to drive?"

"No!"

"The telephone. I have to ask you—I thought the police or the FBI or people like that might get a court order."

"Of course they would! It's why I knew I couldn't call you. I was going to call Nate Simon."

"But you're not talking about the police or the FBI. You're talking about someone else, some *thing* else."

"Yes. No one knows who they are—where they are. But they're there. And they can do whatever they want to do. Jesus! Even *Dad!* That's what's so goddamned frightening."

"And that's what you're going to tell me about, isn't it?" said Valerie, gripping his arm.

"Yes. A few minutes ago I was going to hold back and *not* tell you everything, instead try to convince you to get Nate to fly over here so we could meet and he could see I wasn't crazy. But not now. There's no time now; they're cutting off every outlet. They've got the envelope—it was all I had! . . . I'm sorry, Val, but I *am* going to tell you everything. I wish to God I didn't have to—for your sake—but like you, I don't have a choice anymore."

"I didn't come over here to give you a choice."

He drove into the field near the water's edge and stopped the car. The grass was high, the moon a bright crescent over the bay, the lights of Amsterdam in the distance. They got out and he led her to the darkest spot he could find, holding her hand, suddenly realizing that he had not held her hand in years—the touch, the grip, so comfortable, so much a part of them. He repelled the thought; he was a provider of death.

"Here, I guess," he said, releasing her hand.

"All right." She lowered herself gracefully, like a dancer, and sat down on the soft grass, pushing the reeds aside. "How do you feel?" she asked.

"Awful," said Joel, looking up at the dark sky. "I meant what I said. I killed him. All the years of trying—his trying, my trying—and I end up killing him. If I'd only let him alone, let him be himself, not someone I wanted him to be, he'd probably be drinking up a storm somewhere thousands of miles away, telling his crazy stories, making everyone laugh. But not in your house at Cape Ann yesterday."

"You didn't force him to fly back from Hong Kong, Joel."

"Oh, hell, not by pleading or giving him an order, if that's what you mean. But the order was there nevertheless. After Mother died it was the unspoken words between us. 'Grow *up,* Dad! Have your little trips but don't stay away so long, people worry. Be responsible, father mine.' Christ, I was so *fucking* holier than thou! And I end up killing him."

"You didn't kill him! Others did! Now, tell

me about them.''

Converse swallowed, brushing the tears from his eyes. ''Yes, you're right—there isn't time, even for old Roger.''

''There'll be time later.''

''If there's a later,'' said Joel, breathing deeply, finding control. ''You know about René, don't you?''

''Yes, I read about it yesterday. I was sick. . . . Larry Talbot told me that you saw him in Paris. How even René thought you were disturbed, as Larry did when you talked to him. And René was killed for seeing you. Larry must be going out of his mind.''

''That's not the reason René was killed. Let's talk about Larry. The first time I reached him I needed information without asking him directly. He was being used because of me, followed, and he didn't know it. If I'd told him, the jock in him would have reacted, and he'd have been shot down in the street. But the last time I spoke with him I walked into it. I'd broken away from the people who'd caught me—I was exhausted, still frightened, and I was open with him. I told him everything.''

''He mentioned it to me,'' interrupted Val. ''He said you were reliving your experiences in North Vietnam. There was a psychiatric term for it.''

Converse shook his head, a short, derisive laugh emerging from his throat. ''Isn't there always? I suppose there were similarities and I'm sure I alluded to them, but that's all they were, similarities. . . . Larry didn't hear what I was saying. He was listening for words that confirmed what others had said about me, what he believed was true. He pretended to be the friend I knew but he wasn't. He was a lawyer trying to convince a client that he was sick, that for everyone's safety the client should turn himself in. When I realized what he was doing and that I'd told him where I was, I knew he'd spread the word, thinking he was doing the right thing. I just wanted to get out of there, so I halfway agreed with him, hung up, and ran. . . . I was lucky. Twenty minutes later I saw a car drive up in front of the hotel with two of my would-be executioners.''

"You're sure of that?''

Joel nodded. "The next day one of them stated for the record that he'd seen me at the Adenauer Bridge with Walter Peregrine. I wasn't anywhere near that bridge—at least I don't think so, I don't know where it is.''

"I read that story in the *Times*. The man was an Army officer, a major from the embassy named Washburn.''

"That's right.'' Converse broke off a long blade of grass, twisting it, tearing it in his fingers. "They're great at manipulating the media—newspapers, radio, television. Every word they put out is cleansed through channels, branded authentic, official. They take out lives as if people were pieces in a chess game, including their own. They don't care; they only want to win. And it's the biggest game in modern history. The terrifying thing is that they can win it.''

"Joel, do you know what you're *saying?* An American ambassador, the supreme commander of NATO, René, your father . . . *you.* Then killers in the embassy, a manipulated press, lies out of Washington, Paris, Bonn—all given official status. You're describing some kind of *Anschluss,* some demonic, political takeover!''

Converse looked at her in the moonlight, the breezes off the water bending the tall grass. ''That's exactly what it is, conceived by one man and run by a handful of others, all completely sincere in their beliefs and as persuasive as any group of professionals I've ever heard. But the bottom line is that they're fanatics, killers in a quest they consider nothing less than holy. They've recruited—*are* recruiting—like-minded men everywhere, other frustrated professionals who think there's nowhere else to turn. They grab at the theories and the promises, accepting —accepting, hell, *extolling*—the myths of efficiency and discipline and self-sacrifice, because they know it leads to power. Power to replace the inefficient, the undisciplined, the corrupters and the corrupted. They're blind; they can't see beyond their own distorted image of themselves. . . . If that sounds like a summation it probably is. I haven't slept much, but I do a lot of thinking.''

''The jury's still in place, Joel,'' said Valerie, her eyes alive, again leveled at his. ''I don't want a summation, I want it all. I think you should begin at the beginning—where it began for you.''

''Okay. It started in Geneva—''

''I *knew* it,'' interrupted Val, whispering.

''What?''

''Nothing. Go on.''

''With a man I hadn't seen in twenty-three

years. I knew him by one name then, but in Geneva he was using another. He explained it and it didn't matter. Except that it was a little eerie. I didn't know how eerie it was, or how much he didn't explain, or how many lies he told me in order to manipulate me. The hell of it is he did what he did for all the right reasons. I was the man they needed. *They.* And I don't know who they are, only that they're there, somewhere. . . . As long as I live—however long I'm permitted —I'll never forget the words he used when he reached the core of why he had come to Geneva. 'They're back,' he said. 'The generals are back.' "

He told her everything, allowing his mind and his thoughts to wander, to include every detail he could recall. The countdown was in progress. In a matter of days or at best a week or two there would be eruptions of violence everywhere—like what was taking place in Northern Ireland right now. 'Accumulations,' they said. 'Rapid acceleration!' Only, no one knew who or what or where the targets were. George Marcus Delavane was the madman who conceived it all, and other powerful madmen were listening to him, following his orders, moving into positions from which they would leap for the controls. *Everywhere.*

Finally he was finished, a part of him in anguish, knowing that if she was caught by the soldiers of Aquitaine, the narcotics inserted in her body would reveal the information that would result in her death. He said as much when he had finished, wanting desperately to breach the space between them and hold her, telling her how much he hated himself for doing what he knew he had to do. But he made no move toward her; her eyes told him not to; she was evaluating, thinking things out for herself.

"Sometimes," she said quietly, "when the dreams would come, or you drank too much, you'd talk about this Delavane. You'd become so panicked you'd tremble and close your eyes and every now and then you'd scream. You hated that man so. You were also frightened to death of him."

"He caused a lot of death, unnecessary death. Kids . . . children in grown-up uniforms who didn't know that *gung ho* meant search and destroy and get blown apart."

"There's no way you could be—what do they call it—transferring your emotions?"

"If you believe that, I'll drive you back to the Amstel and you can fly home in the morning and go back to your easels. I'm not crazy, Val. I'm here and it's happening."

"All right, I had to ask. You didn't live through some of those nights, I did. You were either crashing into the bed or so scratched by a bottle you didn't know where you were."

"It didn't happen often."

"I'll grant you that; but when it did you were *there*. And hurting."

"Which is exactly why I was reached in Geneva—recruited in Geneva."

"And this Fowler, or Halliday, knew the exact words to use. Your own."

"Fitzpatrick got it all for him. He thought he was doing the right thing too."

748

"Yes, I know, you told me. What do you think happened to him? Fitzpatrick, I mean."

"For days I've tried to come up with a reason for them to keep him alive. I can't. He's more dangerous to them than I am. He's worked the streets they're undermining; he knows his way around Pentagon procurements and export clearances so well he could nail them with half the evidence. They've killed him."

"You liked him, didn't you?"

"Yes, I did, and just as important, I was almost in awe of that mind of his. He was quick and perceptive and had one hell of an imagination, which he wasn't afraid to use."

"He sounds like someone I was married to," said Val gently.

Converse kept his eyes on her for a moment, then looked away at the water. "If I get out of this alive—and I don't really think I will—I'm going hunting. I'm going to find out who did it, who pulled the trigger. There won't be any trial, no witnesses for the prosecution or the defense, no circumstances, mitigating or otherwise. Just me—and a gun."

"Sorry to hear that, Joel. I always admired your principles. They were a constant, like your attraction—your reverence, I think—for the law. It wasn't all conceit and ambition, I knew that. It gave you the only real roots you ever had. You could look at the law and argue, as a child does with a parent, knowing the parent is some kind of absolute. . . . Your father never gave you that—by his own admission, incidentally."

"I think that's pretty tasteless."

"I'm sorry. He brought it up once. I *am* sorry."

"It's all right. We're talking. We didn't do much of that the last year or so together, did we?"

"I didn't think you wanted to."

"You're on target. Forget it. There's now."

"And there's so much you can deny! All they have is words against you! I said the same thing to Larry—they say you were here, you were there, you did this and you did that, but you *weren't* where they said you were and you *didn't* do what they say! You're the lawyer, Converse. For God's sake, stand up and defend yourself!"

"I'd never get near a courtroom, can't you understand that? Wherever and whenever I showed up, someone would be there, someone ordered to kill me even if it meant losing his own life—considering the consequences, an insignificant sacrifice. My idea was to use the envelope—the dossiers and all the information they contained, the information that could only have come from government sources, which means I have partners somewhere in Washington. With all of that I could reach people I knew—the firm knew—and with Nathan's help get them to listen to me, see I wasn't crazy. Hear from *me* what I saw, what I heard, what I *learned*. But without that envelope, even Nate couldn't help. Besides, he'd insist I go by the book and come *in,* telling me he had guarantees of full protection. There *is* no protection, not from them. They're in embassies and naval stations and Army bases; in the Pentagon, police departments, Interpol, and

750

the Department of State. They're bag ladies on a train and commuters with attaché cases—you don't know who they are but they're there. And they can't afford to let me live. I've heard their almighty credo firsthand."

"Checkmate," said Val softly.

"Check," agreed Converse.

"Then we have to find somebody else."

"What?"

"Someone those people you want to reach would listen to. Someone whose presence might force those men in Washington who sent you out from Geneva to say who they are—to show themselves."

"Who are you thinking of? John the Baptist?"

"Not John. Sam. Sam Abbott."

"*Sam?* I thought about him that night in Paris! How did you—?"

"Like you, I've had a lot of time to think. In New York, on the plane, last night after I saw my aunt in Berlin."

"Your aunt?"

"I'll get to that. . . . I knew that if you were alive there had to be a reason why you stayed in hiding, why you didn't come out shouting, denying all those insane things they were saying about you. It didn't make sense; it wasn't *you*. And if you'd been killed or captured it would have been on the front pages everywhere, on all the broadcasts. Since there was no such story, I assumed you had to be alive. But why did you keep running, hiding? Then I thought, My God, if Larry Talbot doesn't believe him, who will? And if Larry didn't, it meant that the people around him, men like him, all your friends and those so-called contacts you had had been reached and convinced that you were the maniac everyone in Europe was talking about. No one would touch you and you needed someone. Not me, heaven knows. I'm your ex-wife and I don't carry any weight and you needed someone who did. . . . So I thought about everyone you'd ever talked about, everyone we knew. One name kept on coming back to me. Sam Abbott. Brigadier General Abbott now, according to the papers about six months ago.''

" 'Sam the Man,' " said Joel, shaking his head in approval. "He was shot down three days after I was, and we were both shoved around from one camp to another. Once he was in the cell next to mine and we'd tap out Morse on the walls until they moved me. He stayed in the Air Force for all the right reasons. He knew he could be his best there.''

"He thought the world of you," said Val, her voice a mixture of conviction and quiet enthusiasm. "He said you did more for morale than anyone in the camps, that your last escape gave everyone hope.''

"That's a crock. I was a troublemaker—that's what they called me—who could afford to take chances. Sam had the roughest job. He could have done what I did, but he was the ranking officer. He knew there'd be reprisals if he ever tried. He held everyone together, I didn't.''

"He said otherwise. I think he's the reason you never thought much of your sister's husband. Remember when Sam flew into New York and you tried to match him up with Ginny? We all had dinner at that restaurant we couldn't afford."

"Ginny scared the hell out of him. He told me later that if she'd been drafted and put in charge of Command-Saigon it never would have fallen. He wasn't going to refight that war for the rest of his life."

"And you lost a desirable brother-in-law." Valerie smiled; then the smile faded and she leaned forward. "I can reach him, Joel. I'll find him and talk to him, tell him everything you've told me. Above all, that you're no more insane than I am, than he is. That you were manipulated by people you don't know, men who lied to you so you'd do the work they either couldn't do or were afraid to do."

"That's unfair," said Converse. "If they started digging around State and the Pentagon, there could be a rash of accidents—very fatal and very dead. . . . No, they were right. It had to start over here and be traced back. It was the only way."

"If you can say that after all you've been through, you're saner than any of us. Sam will know that. He'll help."

"He *could,*" said Joel slowly, pensively, breaking off another reed of grass. "He'd have to be careful—none of the usual channels—but he could do it. Three or four years ago, after you and I broke up, he found out I was in Washington for a few days and called me. We had dinner and later too many drinks; he ended up spending the night on the sofa in my hotel room. We talked—both of us too much. Me

753

about me—and you—and Sam about his newest monumental frustration."

"Then you're still close. It wasn't that long ago."

"That isn't my point. It's what he was doing. He'd worked his ass off to get into the NASA program, but they turned him down. They said he was too valuable where he was. No one was in his class when it came to all-altitude, sub-mach maneuvers. He designed more patterns in the sky than any designer on Seventh Avenue ever did on the ground. He could look at an aircraft—specs aside—and tell you what it could do."

"I don't understand."

"Oh, sorry. He'd been brought to Washington from wherever he was stationed as a consultant to the National Security Agency, cross-pollinating with the CIA. It was his job to evaluate the capabilities of the new Soviet and Chinese equipment."

"What?"

"Airplanes, Val. He worked over at Langley and at a dozen different safe houses in Virginia and Maryland, appraising photographs brought out by agents, questioning defectors—especially pilots, mechanics and technicians. He knows the people I have to reach, he's *worked* with them."

"You're talking about the intelligence service, or services, I gather."

"Not just services," corrected Joel. "Men who crawl around in the shadows of those paintings of yours. People trained to cut down bastards like Delavane and his tribe, cut them out silently by using methods and techniques you and I know

754

nothing about—drugs and whores and little boys. They should have been brought in at the beginning! Not Geneva, not me. They kill when it's the pragmatic thing to do, and justify the killing because it's in the ultimate interests of the country. And Lord, how I railed against them, the righteous attorney in me demanding that they be held accountable. Well, Mr. Naïve has changed —been changed—because I've seen the enemy and he isn't us, not the us I think we are. If it takes a garrote to choke off a cancer when legal medicine can't do it, hand me the wire, pal, and I'll read the manual."

"I thought you loathed fanatics."

"I do. I . . . do."

"Sam," persisted Valerie. "I'll go home tomorrow and find him."

"No," said Converse. "I want you to fly back tonight. You always carried your passport in your purse—still the same?"

"Of course. But I have—"

"I don't want you going back to the Amstel. You've got to get out of Amsterdam. There's a KLM night flight to New York at eleven-forty-five."

"But my things—"

"They're not worth it. Call the hotel when you get back. Wire them money and say it was an emergency. They'll mail everything to you."

"You're serious, aren't you?"

"Never more so in my life. I think you should know the truth about René. He wasn't killed because we met in Paris; nothing had happened then. I called him from Bonn four days ago and

755

we talked. He believed me. He was shot to death because he sent me to Amsterdam, to reach a man who might have gotten me on a plane to Washington. That's out now and it doesn't matter. You do. You came here and you found me, and the people who are looking for me all over the city will know it soon if they don't know it already."

"I never said I was going to Amsterdam," Valerie broke in. "I specifically left word at the Kempinski that I was flying directly home, that if I got any calls to refer them to New York."

"Did you have a reservation on the plane?"

"Naturally. I just never showed up."

"Good, but not good enough. Delavane's people are efficient. Leifhelm has connections at every airport and immigration point in Germany. They'll find out otherwise. We might have fooled them once tonight, not twice. My guess is there's a German waiting for you at the Amstel now, probably in your room. I want him to think you're coming back, that you're still here."

"If someone like that goes to my room—*into* my room—he's in for a shock."

"What do you mean?"

"Someone else is there. An old man with a long memory, who's been given instructions I'd rather not repeat."

"Your aunt's doing?"

"She sees things in black and white, no grays. There *is* the enemy and there is *not* the enemy. And anyone who would harm her sister's daughter is very definitely the enemy. You don't know these people, Joel. They live in the past;

they never forget. They're old now and not what they once were, but they remember what they were and why they did the things they did. It was so simple for them. Good and evil. They live with those memories—frankly, it's a little scary, *they're* a little scary, to tell you the truth. Nothing in their lives since has been so alive, so important to them. I honestly think they'd all prefer going back to those days, the horror and all.''

"What about your aunt, though? After everything that's been said about me in the newspapers and on television, she went along with you? She didn't ask any questions? The fact that you were her sister's daughter was *enough?*''

"Oh, no, she asked one very specific question and I answered it. *That* was enough. I must tell you, though. She's odd—very odd—but she can do what has to be done and that's all that matters.''

"Okay. . . . You will go back tonight?''

"Yes," said Val, nodding. "It's reasonable and I can do more from New York in the morning than from here. From everything you've said, every hour's important.''

"Vital. Thanks. . . . Also you may have trouble reaching Sam. I don't have any idea where he is and the services aren't cooperative when it comes to a woman trying to locate an officer—especially one with high rank. It's too complicated—an overseas love affair, a child the man never knew about, probably not his—they're very circumspect.''

"Then I won't ask them to tell me where he is. I'll say I'm a relative *he's* been trying to reach, that I travel a great deal and if he wishes to call me, I'll be at the such-and-such hotel for the next twenty-four hours. Certainly they have to relay that kind of message to a general."

"Certainly," agreed Joel. "But if you leave your name, you're risking too much. For you *and* Sam."

"I'll use a variation, one he'll recognize." Valerie blinked, staring at the ground. "Like Parquet—only, I'll feminize it—Parquette. A floor, wood—something associated with a Charpentier a carpenter. Then I'll add Virginia— he'd remember Ginny because of you. Virginia Parquette, he'll figure it out."

"He probably will. So might others. When you don't show up tonight, Leifhelm will have the airports checked. They could pick you up at Kennedy."

"Then I'll lose them at LaGuardia. I'll go to a motel where I stay when I take the plane to Boston. I'll check in and get out without their knowing it."

"You're very quick."

"I told you, my roots go back; I've heard the stories. . . . Now, what about you?"

"I'll stay out of sight. I'm getting pretty good at it and I can pay for anything I need."

"Your words, Converse: 'Not good enough.' The more money you spread, the more of a trail you leave. They'll find you. You have to get out of Amsterdam too."

"Well, I could slip across a few borders and head down to Paris for my old suite at the George Cinq. Of course, it might be a little obvious, but then if I tipped high enough—they *are* French."

"Don't try to be funny."

"I don't feel remotely amusing. Also, I'd like a private toilet and a shower—even a secondhand bath. The rooms I find you *can't* find in the most esoteric travel guides."

"You haven't had a shower in God knows how long, that much I can tell you in the open air."

"Oh, beware the wife who's offended by her husband's hygiene. It's a sign of something."

"Cut it out, Joel, I'm not your wife. . . . I've got to be able to reach you."

"Let me think, I'm also getting very inventive. I'll figure out something. I could—"

"I've already figured it out," interrupted Val firmly. "Before I flew over I talked with my aunt."

"From your house?"

"From the midtown hotel in New York where I registered under a different name."

"You *were* thinking about your phone."

"Not the way you were. I told her what I thought had happened, what I was going to try to do. She came to see me in Berlin last night. She talked up a storm—how she could do this, do that—but it all boiled down to the fact that she'll help. She'll hide you. So will others."

"In *Germany?*"

"Yes. She lives in the countryside, on the outskirts of Osnabrück. It's the safest place you could go, the last place those people would think to look for you."

"How do I get *back* into Germany? It was rough enough getting out! Delavane's people aside, every border's on the alert, my photograph on every wall."

"I talked to Hermione this afternoon, after you called—from a pay phone; she was staying with a friend. She started making arrangements right away, and when I flew in here a few hours ago, an old man met me at the airport, the same man you'll be staying with tonight. You don't know him but you've seen him; he was riding the bicycle in the Museumplein. I was taken to a house on the Lindengracht where I was to call my aunt; the phone was what they term *'unberührt,'* clean, untouched."

"My God, they are back in the forties."

"Not much has changed, has it?"

"No, I guess not. What did she say?"

"Only your instructions. Late tomorrow afternoon, when the terminal's full, you're to go to the Central Station here in Amsterdam and walk around by the information booth. A woman will come up to you and say hello, saying she recognized you as someone she met in Los Angeles. Respond to her, and during the conversation she'll hand you an envelope. Inside will be a passport, a letter, and a train ticket."

"A passport? *How?*"

"All they needed was a photograph. I knew that much when I left your father in Cape Ann."

"You *knew?*"

"I told you, I've heard the stories all my life. How they got Jews and Gypsies and all the men who parachuted down from planes out of Germany and into neutral or occupied countries. The false papers, the photographs, they became an art form."

"And you brought a photograph?"

"It seemed logical. Roger thought so, too. Remember, he was in that war."

"Logical . . . a photograph."

"Yes. I found one in an album. Do you remember when we went to the Virgin Islands and you scorched yourself that first day in the sun?"

"Sure. You made me wear a tie to dinner and my neck was killing me."

"I was trying to teach you a lesson. That picture's a close-up. I wanted your sunburn in all its agony."

"It's still my *face,* Val."

"That photograph was taken eight years ago and the burn softened your features. It'll do."

"Don't I have to *know* anything?"

"If you're detained for that kind of questioning, you'll probably be caught. My aunt doesn't think you will be."

"Why is she so confident?"

"The letter. It spells out what you're doing."

"Which is?"

"A pilgrimage to Bergen-Belsen, later to Auschwitz in Poland. It's written in German and you're to hand it to anyone who stops you because you speak only English."

"But why would that—?"

"You're a priest," interrupted Valerie. "The pilgrimage was financed by an organization in Los Angeles called the Coalition of Christians and Jews for World Peace and Repentance. Only a German very sure of himself will call attention to you. I've got a dark suit in your size in my tote bag, along with a black hat, shoes, and a clerical collar. The instructions will be with your ticket. You'll take the northern express to Hanover where you're supposed to switch trains for Celle and be driven to Bergen-Belsen in the morning, but of course you won't. When you reach Osnabrück, get off. My aunt will be waiting for her priest. And by then I'll be back in New York getting in touch with Sam."

Converse shook his head. "Val, it's all very impressive, but you weren't listening to me. Leifhelm's men have seen me—*in* that station, as a matter of fact. They know what I look like."

"They saw a pale-faced man with a beard and a battered face. Shave off the beard tonight."

"And apply for cosmetic surgery?"

"No, apply a generous amount of lotion called Instant Sun—it's with the clothes I brought you. It'll darken your face more like the photograph on the passport and also cover the bruises—they won't be that noticeable. The black hat and the clerical collar will take care of the rest."

"Omens," said Joel, touching the bruises on his face and noting that they were less painful. "Do you remember when you fell and hit the table in the foyer, the black eye?"

"I was in a panic; I had a presentation the next day. You went out and got the makeup for me."

"I bought the same stuff this morning. It helped."

"I'm glad."

They looked at each other across the short distance between them in the moonlit field. "I'm sorry about everything, Val. I wish you weren't part of this. If there was any other way I wouldn't let you be, you know that.''

"I know it, but it doesn't matter to me one way or the other. I came over here because of a promise I made to myself—a promise I meant. Not you. I'm *over* you, Joel, believe that.''

"The promise you made to yourself was provoked by me. Since I was the offending party of the second part, that should have canceled it.''

"That's probably a rotten legal opinion,'' said Val, shifting her legs and looking away. "There's also the obvious. Everything you've told me terrifies me—not fact A and fact B, or who's conspiring with whom; I'm a landscape painter; I can't deal with such things. But I'm so terribly afraid because I can personalize. I can see how these people—this Aquitaine—*can* win, can take control of our lives, turning us all into complacent flocks of sheep. Good God, Joel, we'd *welcome* them!''

"I missed something.''

"Then you're blind. I don't think it's just women, or women who live alone like me, I think it's most of the people walking around in the streets, trying to earn a living, trying to make the rent or a mortgage or a car payment, trying to make it through *life*. We're *sick* of everything around us! We're told one minute we may be blown up in a nuclear war unless we're taxed out of our houses to pay for bigger bombs, and that our water's contaminated, or that we can't buy this or that because it might be poisoned. Children disappear, and people are killed walking into a store for a quart of milk, and addicts and muggers with guns and knives cut people down on the streets. I live in a small town and I won't go there after dark, and if I'm in the city—any city—I look behind me in broad daylight, and I'll be damned if I'll get into an elevator unless it's crowded. . . . I couldn't afford it but I put in a burglar alarm system in a house I don't own because there was a boat out in the water one day that stayed there overnight. In my mind I saw men crawling up the beach to my windows. We all see such things, whether out on the water, or down city blocks, or in a field like this. We're frightened; we're sick of the problems, sick of the *violence.* We want someone strong to *stop* it—and I'm not sure it even matters who they are. And if the men you're talking about push things any further—believe me, they know what they're doing. They can walk in and be crowned, no votes required. . . . And in spite of everything I've said, that's even more frightening. Which is why you're going to take me to the airport."

"Why did I ever let you go?" whispered Joel, more to himself than to her.

"Cut it out, Converse. It's over. *We're* over."

He watched from the darkest area of the parking lot at Amsterdam's Schilphol Airport as the plane sped down the runway and lifted off into the night sky. He had driven up to a crowded platform where Val had gotten out, giving him the scrap of paper with the address that was to be his refuge for the night. So that he would know she had been able to get on board the flight, she was to come out the glass doors, look at her watch

764

and go back inside. If the plane was overbooked, she was to continue on the pedestrian walk to the temporary lot a hundred yards away from the entrance where he would be waiting for her. She had come outside, glanced at her watch and returned to the terminal. A part of him had felt relief, another part a quiet, hollow emptiness.

He watched the huge silver plane bank to the left and disappear, its fading lights a trajectory in the dark sky.

He stood naked in front of the mirror in the small bathroom in the house on the Lindengracht. The car was some twenty streets away. He had made the return journey cautiously on foot. The old man who owned the flat was pleasant and spoke in haltingly clear English, but his eyes were far away and never really made contact. His mind was in another place, another time.

Joel had shaved carefully, showered far longer than a guest should, and had finished applying the deep red lotion to his face, neck and hands. In moments his skin was bronzed. The result was far more authentic than it used to be with the earlier products he remembered, when anyone who used them stood out—the mask of sickly brown was too smooth and cosmeticized to be anything but unnatural. The new coloring further concealed the bruises on his face; he looked almost normal. He would discard the tinted glasses; they would only call attention to him, especially from anyone who had seen him or had been given his description. He washed his hands repeatedly, kneading them together to remove the stains from his fingertips.

He stiffened. From somewhere beyond the door came the sound of an erratic bell. He quickly turned off the water and listened, his breathing suspended, his eyes on the gun he had placed on the narrow windowsill. He heard the sound again; it stopped. Then he heard a single voice, a man on a telephone. He dried his hands and slipped on the short cotton bathrobe that had been left on the bed in his small, immaculate room. He put the gun in his pocket, went out the door and down the dark, narrow hallway that led to the old man's "study." It was a former bedroom filled with old magazines, a few books, and tabloid newspapers on tables and chairs opened to the bloodiest sections, with red crayon marks circling articles and pictures. On the walls were prints and photographs of long-past wartime accomplishments—including corpses in various poses of death. In an odd way it reminded Converse of L'Etalon Blanc in Paris, except that here there were no glories of war, only the ugliness of death. It was more honest, he thought, if nothing else.

"Ah, *Meneer,*" said the old man, sitting forward in a huge leather chair that engulfed his frail body, the telephone beside him. "You are safe, *quite* safe! That was Kabel—code name, Kabel, *natuurlijk.* He has left the hotel and reports his progress." Fragile, in his seventies, the Dutchman struggled out of the chair and stood erect, his thin shoulders back, his body rigid—a foolish old man playing soldier. "Operation Osnabrück proceeds!" he said, as if reporting to a commanding officer. "As contemplated by underground intelligence reports, the enemy infiltrated the area and he has been compromised.''

"He's been what?''

"Executed, *Meneer*. A wire around the throat, taken from behind. The blood stays on the clothes as the neck is pulled back, thus there are no signs of combat and the enemy is removed from the place of compromise.''

"*What* did you say?''

"Kabel is strong for one of his age,'' said the old man, grinning, his weathered face a thousand creases, his posture now relaxed. "He took the body from the room, dragged it to the fire exit, and down into the alley. From there he gained access to the cellars and put the corpse back by the furnaces. It is summer; the man may not be found for days—unless the stench becomes too much.''

Converse heard the words, but his concentration was only on one. *Compromise*. In this odd language of another time it meant . . . execution. Execution . . . murder . . . assassination!

What would you say to compromising certain powerful individuals in specific governments . . . ? Leifhelm's words.

It wouldn't work. His own.

You do not take into consideration the time element! Accumulation! Rapid acceleration! Chaim Abrahms.

Good *Christ!* thought Joel. Was that what the generals of Aquitaine meant? *Assassinations?* Was it the reason for the glaring, disapproving looks directed at the Israeli and Abrahms' sudden retreat into qualification, then dismissal: *It's*

767

merely a point . . . I'm not sure it even applies.

Accumulation, rapid acceleration, one after another—national leaders cut down *everywhere.* Presidents and prime ministers; ministers of state and vice-presidents, powerful men and women from all shades of the narrow, acceptable political spectrums violently eliminated—governments in chaos. All to take place in a matter of hours, savagery erupting in the streets, fueled by hysteria, victims and violators blurred until the commanders were summoned to restore order, not to leave until the controls were theirs. The climate was established, the day was coming. *Assassinations!*

He had to get back into Germany. He had to reach Osnabrück and be there when Val called. Sam Abbott had to be told.

29

His hands manacled and chained, his wounded right forearm encased in a filthy bandage, Connal Fitzpatrick gripped the ledge of the small window and peered out beyond the bars at the strange, violent activity taking place on the huge concrete parade ground. That it was a parade ground had been clear on the second morning of his capture when, along with the other prisoners, he was granted an hour's exercise outside the concrete barracks—and they *were* barracks—once part of an old refueling station for submarines was his guess. The slips along the water as well as the winching machinery were far too small and too obsolete for today's nuclear marauders—no Trident could fit in any space along the concrete and steel piers—but once, he judged, the base had served the German undersea Navy well.

Now, however, it was being used to the great disservice of the Federal Republic of Germany and of free governments everywhere. It was Aquitaine's training ground, the place where strategies were being refined, maneuvers perfected, and the final preparations made for the massive assaults that would propel Delavane's military commanders to power over paralyzed civilian authorities. Everything was reduced to killing—swift and brutal, the shock of the acts themselves intrinsic to the wave of violence.

Beyond the window, units of four and five men raced separately and in succession around and between a crowd of perhaps a hundred others, taking their turns at the sickening exercise they were perfecting. For at the end of the parade ground was a concrete platform, seven feet high and perhaps thirty feet long, where mannequins were lined up in a row—some standing, others in chairs—their inanimate figures rigid, their lifeless glass eyes staring straight ahead. They were the targets. At the center of each clothed chest, "male" and "female," was an encased circle of bullet-proof wire mesh; within each was a high-intensity orange light, seen clearly in the afternoon sun. At the discretion of the compound's trainer, it flashed on. It was the signal that this particular mannequin was the particular unit's specific target or, if more than one,

769

targets. Hits were recorded electronically by other lights on the high stone wall above each figure on the platform. Red was a kill, blue merely a wound. Red was acceptable, blue was not.

The screaming admonitions over the loudspeakers were delivered in nine languages, four of which Connal understood. The words were the same:

Thirteen days to ground-zero! Accuracy is uppermost! Escape is with the diversion of a kill! Otherwise there is only death!

Eleven days to ground-zero! Accuracy is uppermost . . . !

Eight days to ground-zero! Accuracy is . . . !

Individual members of the killer teams fired at their targets, exploding stuffed skulls and pulverizing chests and stomachs, sometimes by themselves, other times in unison with their comrades. Each "kill" was greeted with exuberant shouts as the men raced through the crowd, melting into it, finally becoming part of it as their maneuver was completed. Another team was then instantly formed from within the ranks of the spectators; and another exercise in assassination was mounted, executed swiftly. And so it went, hour after hour, the crowd reacting to the "kills" with roars of approval as weapons were reloaded for upcoming assaults against the mannequins. Every twenty minutes or so, as sections of the lifeless figures on the platform were progressively blown apart, they would be replaced with fresh heads and torsos. All that was missing were rivers of blood and mass hysteria.

In anger and frustration, Connal spread his manacled wrists apart, pulling at the unbreakable chain and yanking with all his might as the rusted, circular braces dug into his flesh and bruised his wrist bones. There was nothing he could do, no way to get out! He knew the secret of Aquitaine; the evidence of its ultimate strategy was right there before his eyes. The mass killing of political figures in nine different nations—eight days away!

He turned from the window, arms aching, wrists stinging, and looked around at the barracks full of prisoners—forty-three men trying not to fail but failing fast. Many were lying listlessly on their cots, others stared forlornly out various windows; a number talked quietly in small groups against the blank walls. All were manacled as he was. The abysmally short rations and the prolonged, brutal periods of "exercise" had weakened them all in both body and mind. Whispering among themselves, they had come to several erroneous conclusions about their captors' goal, but their own captivity eluded reason. They were part of a strategy they could not understand. In unwatched corners Connal tried to explain, only to be met with blank stares and bewilderment.

Several points were established—for whatever they signified. To begin with, they were all military officers ranging in rank from the middle to the higher echelons. Secondly, all were bachelors or divorced, none with children or currently involved in serious relationships that demanded constant communications. Lastly, all were on 30- to 45-day leaves, only one other—like

Connal—with emergency status, the rest on normal summer holidays. There was a pattern, but what did it mean?

There *was* a clue to that meaning, but it, too, was beyond understanding. Every other day or so the prisoners were brought postcards from widely diverse locations—resort areas in Europe and North America—and instructed to write specific messages to specific individuals they all recognized as various fellow officers at the posts or bases from which they were on leave. The messages were always in the vein of *Having wonderful time; wish you were here; off to——* To refuse to write these peripatetic greetings was to be denied the scant food they were given and to be driven out to the parade ground, where they were forced to run as fast as they could in laps, with guns pointed at them, until they dropped.

They agreed among themselves that the reason behind the near-starvation level of daily rations had a purpose. They were all trained, competent officers. Such men in decent physical and mental condition were capable of attempting escape or, at the least, of creating serious disturbances. But that was all they could understand. All but Connal had been there for a minimum of twenty-two to a maximum of thirty-four days. They were in a concentration camp somewhere on some indeterminate coastline, not knowing their crimes, real or imagined by their captors.

"*Qué pasa?*" asked a prisoner named Enrique from Madrid.

"*Es lo mismo afuera en el campo de maniobras,*" replied Fitzpatrick, nodding his head

772

at the window, and continued in Spanish, "They're killing stuffed dummies out there, figuring each hit makes them heroes or martyrs or both."

"It's crazy!" cried the Spaniard. "It's crazy and it's sick in the head! What do they accomplish? Why this madness?"

"They're going to cut down a lot of important people eight days from now. They're going to kill them during some kind of international holiday or celebration or something like that. What the *hell* is happening eight days from now? Have you any idea?"

"I am only a major at the garrison at Zaragoza. I make my reports on the Basque provisionals, and read my books. What do I know of such things? Whatever it is, it would not reach Zaragoza—barbarous country, but I would wear corporal's stripes to return to it."

"Vite! Contre la muraille!"

"Schnell! Gegen die Mauer!"

"Move! Against the wall!"

"Fa presto! Contro il muro."

Four guards burst through the barracks doors, others following, repeating the same order in different languages. It was a manacles-and-chain inspection, carried out at whim day and night, never less than once an hour during the daylight, as frequently as four times at night. The slightest evidence of any prisoner having attempted to break or weaken his chain or crack his manacles by filing them against the concrete or smashing them into rock was met with immediate punishment, which meant running naked—

preferably in the rain—until collapse, and remaining in chains where he fell with no food or water for thirty-six hours. Of the forty-three men, twenty-nine of the strongest among them had been so punished, a number more than two and three times until they had little strength left. Connal had run the gauntlet only once, thanks apparently to his bilingual guard, an Italian who seemed to appreciate the fact that his *americano* had taken the trouble to learn *italiano*. The man from Genoa was a bitter, cynical former paratrooper —and probably a convict—who referred to himself as an outcast but predicted he would come into his own when he was rewarded for his work. But like most men from his part of the world, he instinctively responded to a foreigner's praise of *bella Italia, bellissima Roma.*

It was from their short, whispered conversations that Fitzpatrick had learned as much as he had, his legal military mind operating on the level of addressing a malcontented military client. He had pushed the buttons he had pushed so often before.

"What's in it for *you?* They *know* you're garbage!"

"They promise me. They pay me much money to teach what I know. Without people like me—many of us here—they will not accomplish."

"Accomplish what?"

"That is for them to say. I am, as *you* say, employed."

"To show them how to kill?"

"And to run and not be seen. That is our life—the lives of many of us here."

"You could lose everything."

"Most of us have nothing. We were used and discarded."

"These men will do the same to you."

"Then we will kill again. We are experienced."

"Suppose their enemies find this place?"

"They will not. They cannot."

"Why not?"

"It's an island no one thinks of."

"They know that."

"Impossible! No planes fly over, no boats come. We would know if they did."

"Why don't you think about what *was* here?"

"What do you mean?"

"Submarines. Surrounding your island."

"If that was true, *americano,* the—how you say?—the *custode* . . ."

"The warden."

"He would explode everything away. Everything on this side of the island would be *fumo*—smoke, nothing. It is part of our *contratto.* We understand."

"The warden—the *custode*—he's the big German with the short gray hair, isn't he?"

"Enough talk. Have your drink of water."

"I have information for you," whispered Connal, as the guard checked his manacles and chain. "Information that will guarantee you a big reward and might possibly save my life."

"What kind of information?"

"Not here. Not now. There isn't time. Come back tonight; everyone's so exhausted they're asleep before they reach their cots. I'll stay awake.

775

Come and get me, but come alone. You don't want to share this."

"My head is filled with *zucchini?* I come alone to a barracks filled with condemned men?"

"What can any of us do? What can *I* do? I'll stay by the door; you open it and I'll step out, your gun no doubt at my head. I don't want to die, that's why I'm talking to you!"

"You will die. May you go with God."

"You're a fool, a *buffone!* You could have a fortune instead of a bullet in your chest."

The Italian looked guardedly at Fitzpatrick, then around at the others; the inspections were nearly finished. "For me to do such a thing, I need more than what you have told me."

"Two of your guards are traitors," whispered Connal.

"Che cosa?"

"That's all you get until tonight."

Fitzpatrick lay on the cot in the darkness, waiting, listening for the sound of footsteps, the sweat of anxiety drenching his face. All around him were the sleep-induced moans of hungry, physically abused men. He pushed his own pains out of his mind; he had other things to think about. If he could reach the water, the manacles would slow him down but not stop him, he could sidestroke nearly indefinitely—and somewhere down the coastline, away from "this side of the island," there would be a beach or a dock, a place where he could crawl out of the sea. There was nothing else left; he had to try it. He also had to make sure his Italian guard could raise no alarms.

The bolt in the door was quietly sliding back! He had missed the footsteps; his thoughts had distracted him. He got up silently and started down the aisle on the balls of his feet, flexing his hands but keeping the chain taut. He could not make any noise whatsoever, because several prisoners had begun to have violent nightmares when there was the slightest disturbance. He reached the door and somehow understood he was to push it open, not wait for it to be opened; the guard would stay back, his weapon aimed at him.

It was so. The Italian gestured with his gun for Connal to move forward as he sidestepped to the door and secured the bolt. He then pointed with the barrel of his weapon, ordering Fitzpatrick to walk ahead. Moments later both men stood in the shadows in front of the barracks, the old refueling station still visible in the darkness, the ocean waves lapping at the pilings.

"Now we talk," said the guard. "Who are these traitors and why should I believe you?"

"I want your word that you'll tell your superiors I turned them in. I don't say anything until I have your word!"

"My *word, americano?*" said the Italian, laughing softly. "Very well, *amico,* you have my word."

The guard's quiet, cynical laughter covered the seconds. Connal suddenly whipped out the chain and crashed it down on the man's weapon; grabbing the barrel of the gun with his right hand, he wrenched it free; it fell to the grass below. He then raised the chain as he kicked the guard in the groin, and slammed the heavy links into the man's face, smashing the manacles into the Italian's skull until the guard's eyes grew wide and then closed in unconsciousness. Fitzpatrick crouched, finding his bearings.

It was directly ahead—an old submarine slip, its long pier extending out to the middle water. He got up and ran. The air was exhilarating, the breezes from the sea told him to run faster, *faster*. Escape was seconds away.

He plunged over the dock into the water, knowing he would find the strength to do anything, swim anywhere! He was *free!*

Suddenly, he was blinded by the floodlights everywhere. Then a fusillade of bullets exploded from all sides, ripping up the water around him, cracking the air overhead, but none entering his body or blowing apart his head. And words over a loudspeaker filled the night: "You are most fortunate, Prisoner Number Forty-three, that we still might have need of you. Otherwise, your corpse would be food for the North Sea fishes."

30

Joel walked out of the bright afternoon sun into Amsterdam's cavernous Centraal station. The dark suit and hat fit comfortably; the clerical collar and the black shoes pinched but were bearable, and the small suitcase was an impediment he could discard at any time, although it was a correct accessory and held odd bits of clothing, none of which was likely to fit.

Since a déjà vu would be no illusion for those he had encountered before, he walked cautiously, alert to every sudden movement—no matter how inconsequential. He expected at any instant to see men rushing toward him, their eyes filled with purpose and the intent to kill.

No such men came, but even if they had come, he would have had some comfort in knowing he had done his best. He had written the most complete brief of his legal career, written it with painstakingly clear handwriting, organizing the material, pulling together the facts to support his judgments and conjectures. He had recalled the salient points of each dossier to lend credibility to his own conclusions. Regarding his own painful experiences and firsthand observations, he had weighed every statement, discarding those that might seem too emotional, reshaping the rest to reflect the cold objectivity of a trained, *sane,* legal mind. He had lain awake for hours during the night, allowing the organizational blocks to fall into place, then started writing in the early morning, ending with a personal letter that dispelled any misconceptions about his sanity. He was a pawn who had been manipulated by frightened, invisible men who had supplied the tools and knew exactly what they were doing. In spite of everything that had happened he understood, and felt that perhaps there had not been any other way to do it. He had finished it all an hour ago and sealed the pages in a large envelope supplied by the old man who said he would post it on the Damrak after dropping Converse off. Joel had sent it to Nathan Simon.

"*Pastoor* Wilcrist! It is *you,* is it not?"

Converse spun around at the touch on his arm. He saw that the shrill greeting came from a gaunt, slightly bent woman in her late seventies. Her wizened face was dominated by intense eyes, her head framed by a nun's crown, her slender body encased in a black habit. "Yes," he said, startled. "Hello, Sister?"

"I can tell you don't remember me, *Pastoor,*" exclaimed the woman, her English heavily— loudly—accented. "No, don't fib, I can see you have no idea who I am!"

"I might if you'd keep your voice down, Sister." Joel spoke softly, leaning down and trying to smile. "You'll call attention to us, lady."

"The religious always greet each other *so,*" said the old woman confidentially, her eyes wide and direct, too direct. "They wish to appear like normal people."

"Shall we walk over here so we can talk quietly?" Converse took the woman by the arm and led her toward a crowded area of a gate. "You have something for me?"

"Where are you from?"

"Where am I from? What do you mean?"

"You know the rules. I have to be certain."

"Of what?"

"That you are the proper contact. There can be no substitutes, no deviations. We are not fools, *Meneer.* Now, where are you *from?* Quickly! Hesitation itself is a lie."

"Wait a minute! You were told to meet me here; you were given a description. What more do you want?"

"To know where you're from."

"*Christ,* how many sunburned priests did you expect to see at the information booth?"

"They are not *zo* un-normal. Some swim, I am told. Others play tennis. The Pope himself once skied in the mountain sun! You see I am a good Catholic, I know these things."

"You were given a description! Am I that man?"

"You all look alike. The Father last week at confession was not a good man. He told me I had too many sins for my age and he had others waiting. He was not a patient man of God."

"Neither am I."

"All alike."

"*Please,*" said Joel, looking at the thick, narrow envelope in the woman's hands, knowing that if he took it forcibly from her she would scream. "I have to reach Osnabrück, you know that!"

"You are from *Osnabrück?*" The "nun" clutched the envelope to her chest, her body bent further, protecting a holy thing.

"No, not Osnabrück!" Converse tried to remember Val's words. He was a priest on a pilgrimage . . . to Auschwitz and Bergen-Belsen . . . from, from . . . "*Los Angeles!*" he whispered harshly.

"*Ja, goed.* What country?"

"Jesus!"

"*Wat?*"

"The United States of America."

"*Goed!* Here you are, *Meneer.*" The old woman handed him the envelope, now smiling

781

sweetly. "We all must do our jobs, must we not? Go with God, my fellow servant of the Lord. . . . I do like this costume. I was on the stage, you know. I don't think I'll give it back. Everyone smiles, and a gentleman who came out of one of those dirty houses stopped and gave me fifty guilder."

The old woman walked away, turning once and smiling again, discreetly showing him a pint of whisky she had taken from under her habit.

It might have been the same platform, he could not tell, but his fears were the same as when he arrived in Amsterdam twenty-four hours ago. He had come to the city as an innocuous-looking laborer with a beard and a pale, bruised face. He was leaving as a priest, erect, clean-shaven, sunburned, a properly dressed man of the cloth on a pilgrimage for repentance and reaffirmation. Gone was the outraged lawyer in Geneva, the manipulating supplicant in Paris, the captured dupe in Bonn. What remained was the hunted man, and to survive he had to be able to stalk the hunters before they could stalk him; that meant spotting them before they spotted him. It was a lesson he had learned eighteen years ago when his eyes were sharper and his body more resilient. To compensate, he had to use whatever other talents he had developed; all were reduced to his ability to concentrate—without appearing to concentrate. Which was how and why Joel saw the man.

He was standing by a concrete pillar up ahead on the platform reading an unfolded train schedule in the dim light. Converse glanced at him—as, indeed, he glanced briefly at nearly everyone in sight—then seconds later he looked again. Something was odd, incongruous. There could be several reasons why a man remained outside a well-lit railroad car to read a schedule—a last cigarette in the open air, waiting for someone—but that same man could hardly read the very small print while casually holding the schedule midway between his head and his waist without any evidence of a squint. It was like trying to read a page from a telephone directory in a car stuck in traffic in the Lincoln Tunnel; it took observable effort.

Converse continued down the platform, approaching the two open doors that signified the end of one railway car and the beginning of the next. He purposely let his suitcase catch on a protruding window ledge, pivoting as it did so, and apologized to a couple behind him. Courteously he let them pass and courteously, as each saw his collar, they smiled and nodded. But while he remained facing them, his eyes strayed to the man diagonally to the left by the pillar. The man still clutched the schedule in his hand but was concentrating now on Joel. It was enough.

Converse entered the second door, his gait casual again, but the instant he could no longer see the man by the pillar he rushed inside the railroad car. He tripped, falling to the floor by the first seat, and again apologized to those behind him—a divine undone by profane luggage. He looked out the window, past the two passengers in the seat, both of whom paid attention to his collar before looking at his face.

The man by the pillar had dropped the schedule

and was now frantically signaling with quick beckoning gestures. In seconds he was joined by another man; their conversation was rapid, then they separated, with one going to the door at the front of the car, the other heading for the entrance Joel had just passed through.

They had found him. He was trapped.

Valerie paid the driver and climbed out of the cab, thanking the doorman, who greeted her. It was the second hotel reservation she had made in the space of two hours, having left a dead-end trail in case anyone was following her. She had taken a cab from Kennedy to LaGuardia, bought a ticket to Boston on a midmorning shuttle, then registered at the airport motel, both under the name of Charpentier. She had left the motel thirty minutes later, having paid the cabdriver to return for her at a side exit and calling the hotel in Manhattan to see if a reservation was possible at that hour. It was. The St. Regis would welcome Mrs. DePinna, who had flown in from Tulsa, Oklahoma, on a sudden emergency.

At the all-night Travelers Shop in Schilphol Airport, Val had purchased a carry-on bag, filling it with toiletries and whatever more inconspicuous articles of clothing she could find among the all too colorful garments on the racks. It was still the height of the summer, and depending upon the circumstances, such clothes might come in handy. Also she needed something to show customs.

She registered at the hotel desk, using a "Cherrywood Lane"—but without a number —she remembered from her childhood in St.

Louis. Indeed, the name DePinna came from those early days as well, a neighbor down the street, the face a blur now, only the memory of a sad, vituperative woman who loathed all things foreign, including Val's parents. "Mrs. R. DePinna," she had written; she had no idea where the "R" came from—possibly Roger for balance.

In the room she turned on the radio to the all-news station, a habit she had inherited from her marriage, and proceeded to unpack. She undressed, took a shower, washed out her underthings, and slipped into the outsized T-shirt. This last was another habit; "T-sacks," as she called them, had replaced bathrobes and morning coats on her patio in Cape Ann, although none had a sunburst emblazoned on the front with words above and below heralding TOT ZIENS —AMSTERDAM!

She resisted calling room service for a pot of tea; it would be calming, but it was an unnecessary act that at three o'clock in the morning would certainly call attention, however minor, to the woman in 714. She sat in the chair staring absently at the window, wishing she hadn't given up cigarettes—it would give her something to do while thinking, and she had to think. She had to rest, too, but first she had to think, organize herself. She looked around the room, and then at her purse, which she had placed on a bedside table. She was rich, if nothing else. Joel had insisted she take the risk of getting through customs with more than the $5,000 legal limit. So she had rolled up an additional twenty $500 bills and shoved them into her brassiere. He had been right; she could not use credit cards or anything that carried her name.

She saw two telephone directories on the shelf of the table. Sitting on the edge of the bed, she removed both volumes. The cover of one read, *New York County, Business to Business;* the other, *Manhattan*—and in the upper left-hand corner, printed across a blue diagonal strip: *Government Listings See Blue Pages.* It was a place to start. She returned the business directory to the shelf and carried the Manhattan book over to the desk. She sat down, opened to the blue pages and found *Department of the Air Force . . . Command Post ARPC.* It was an 800 number, the address on York Street in Denver, Colorado. If it was not the number she needed, whoever she reached could supply the correct one. She wrote it down on a page of St. Regis stationery.

Suddenly Val heard the words. She snapped her head around toward the television set, her eyes on the vertical radio dial.

". . . And now the latest update on the search for the American attorney, Joel Converse, one of the most tragic stories of the decade. The former Navy pilot, once honored for outstanding bravery in the Vietnam war, whose dramatic escape electrified the nation, and whose subsequent tactical reports shocked the military, leading, many believed, to basic changes in Washington's Southeast Asian policies, is still at large, hunted not for the man he was, but for the homicidal killer he has become. Reports are that he may still be in Paris. Although not official, word has been leaked from unnamed but authoritative sources

786

within the Sûreté that fingerprints found on the premises where the French lawyer, René Mattilon, was slain are definitely those of Converse, thus confirming what the authorities believed—that Converse killed his French acquaintance for cooperating with Interpol and the Sûreté. The manhunt is spreading out from Paris and this station will bring you . . ."

Valerie sprang from the chair and ran to the television set; she furiously pushed several buttons until the radio was silent. She stood for a moment, trembling with anger—and fear. And something else she could not define—did not care to define. It tore her apart and she had to stay together.

She lay on the bed staring at the ceiling, at the reflections of light from things moving in the street below, and hearing the sounds of the city. None of it was comforting—only abrasive intrusions that kept her mind alert, rejecting sleep. She had not slept on the plane, but had only dozed intermittently, repeatedly jarred awake by half-formed nightmares probably induced by excessive turbulence over the North Atlantic. She needed sleep now . . . she needed Joel now. The first, mercifully, came; the latter was out of reach.

There was a shattering noise accompanied by a burst of sunlight that blinded her as she shot up from the bed, kicking away the sheet and throwing her feet on the floor. It was the telephone. The telephone? She looked at her watch; it was seven-twenty-five. The phone rang once again, piercing the mists of sleep but not clearing them away. The telephone? How . . . ?

Why? She picked it up, gripping it with all her strength, trying to find herself before speaking.

"Hello?"

"Mrs. DePinna?" inquired a male voice.

"Yes."

"We trust everything is satisfactory."

"Are you in the habit of waking up your guests at seven o'clock in the morning to ask if they're comfortable?"

"I'm terribly sorry, but we were anxious for you. This *is* the Mrs. DePinna from Tulsa, Oklahoma, isn't it?"

"Yes."

"We've been looking for you all night . . . since the flight from Amsterdam arrived at one-thirty this morning."

"Who are you?" asked Val, petrified, holding her wrist below the phone.

"Someone who wants to help you, Mrs. Converse," said the voice, now relaxed and friendly. "You've given us quite a runaround. We must have woken up a hundred and fifty women who checked in at hotels since two A.M. . . . the 'flight from Amsterdam' did it; you didn't ask me what I was talking about. Believe me, we want to help, Mrs. Converse. We're both after the same thing."

"Who *are* you?"

"The United States Government covers it. Stay where you are. I'll be over in fifteen minutes."

The hell the United States Government covers it! thought Val, shivering, as she hung up the phone. The United States Government had cleaner ways of identifying itself. . . . She had to get *out!*

788

What did the "fifteen minutes" mean? Was it a trap? Were men downstairs waiting for her now—waiting to see if she would run? She had no *choice!*

She ran to the bathroom, grabbing the carry-on case off a chair and throwing her things into it. She dressed in seconds and stuffed what clothes remained into the bag; snatching the room key off the bureau, she ran to the door, then stopped. Oh, *Lord,* the stationery with the Air Force number! She raced back to the desk, picked up the page beside the open telephone book and shoved it into her purse. She glanced wildly about—was there anything else? No. She left the room and walked rapidly down the hall to the elevators.

Maddeningly, the elevator stopped at nearly every floor, where men and women got on, most of the men with puffed circles under their eyes, a few of the women looking drawn, sheepish. Several apparently knew each other, others nodded absently, gazes straying to plastic name plates worn by most of the passengers. Val realized that some sort of convention was going on.

The doors opened to a crowded bank of elevators; the ornate lobby to the right was swarming with people, voices raised in greetings, questions and instructions. Cautiously Val approached the gilded arch that led to the lobby proper, looking around in controlled panic to see if anyone was looking at her. A large gold-framed sign with block letters arranged in black felt under glass was on the wall: WELCOME: MICMAC

DISTRIBUTORS. There followed a list of meetings and activities.

Buffet Breakfast 7:30-8:30 A.M.
Regional Conferences 8:45-10:00 A.M.
Advertising Symposium Q and A 10:15-11:00 A.M.
Midmorning Break. Make Reservations
for city tours.

"Hey, sweet face," said a burly, red-eyed man standing next to Val. "That's a no-no."

"I beg your pardon?"

"We are *marked,* princess!"

Valerie stopped breathing; she stared at the man, gripping the handles of her carry-on, prepared to smash it into his face and bolt for the glass doors thirty feet away. "I have no idea what you mean."

"The *name,* princess! Where's your Micmac spirit? How can I ask you to have breakfast with me if I don't know your name?"

"Oh . . . the name tag. I'm sorry."

"What's your region, beautiful creature?"

"Region?" Valerie was puzzled but only for a moment. She suddenly smiled. "Actually, I'm new—just hired yesterday. They said my instructions would be at the desk, but it's so crowded I'll never get over there. Of course, with *your* shoulders I might make it before I'm fired."

"Grab hold, princess! These shoulders used to play semi-pro ball." The heavyset salesman was an effective blocking back; they reached the counter and the man growled appropriately, a lion preening before its conquest. "Hey, fella! This lady's been trying to get your attention. Need I say more, *fella?*" The salesman, holding in his stomach, grinned at Val.

"No, sir—yes, ma'am?" said the perplexed clerk, who was not at all busy. The activity was taking place in front of the counter, not at the counter.

Valerie leaned forward, ostensibly to be heard through the noise. She placed her key on the counter and opened her purse, taking out three $50 bills. "This should cover the room. I've been here one night, and there are no charges. What's left is yours."

"Thank *you,* ma'am."

"I need a favor."

"Of course!"

"My name is Mrs. DePinna—but of course the key tells you that."

"What is it you want me to do, ma'am?"

"I'm visiting a friend who's just had an operation. Could you tell me where the—Lebanon Hospital is?"

"The Lebanon? It's in the Bronx, I think. Somewhere on the Grand Concourse. Any cabdriver will know, ma'am."

"Mrs. DePinna's the name."

"Yes, Mrs. DePinna. *Thank* you."

Valerie turned to the heavyset, red-eyed salesman, again smiling. "I'm sorry. Apparently I'm at the wrong hotel, the wrong company, can you imagine? It would have been nice. Thanks for your help." She turned and quickly dodged her way through the crowd toward the revolving doors.

The street was only beginning to come alive. Valerie walked rapidly down the pavement, then stopped almost immediately in front of a small, elegant bookstore and decided to wait in the doorway. The stories she had heard all her life included not only tales of leaving false information but lessons showing the need for knowing what the enemy looked like—it was often the difference.

A taxi drove up in front of the St. Regis, and before it came to a stop the rear door opened. She could see the passenger clearly, he was paying the fare hurriedly without thought of change. He climbed out swiftly and started running toward the glass doors. He was hatless, with unkempt, blondish hair, and dressed in a madras jacket and light-blue summer jeans. He was the enemy, Valerie knew that and accepted it. What she found hard to accept was his youth. He was in his twenties, hardly more than a boy. But the face was hard and set in anger, the eyes cold—distant flashes of steel in the sunlight. *Wie ein Hitlerjunge,* thought Val, walking out of the bookstore doorway.

A car streaked past her, heading west toward the hotel; within seconds she heard screeching tires and expected a crash to follow. Like the other pedestrians, she turned around to look. Fifty feet away a brown sedan had come to a stop; on its door panels and trunk were the clear black letters U.S. ARMY. A uniformed officer got out quickly. He was staring at her.

She broke into a run.

Converse sat in an aisle seat roughly in the middle of the railway car. His palms perspired as he turned the pages of the small black prayer book, which had been placed in the envelope along with his passport, the letter of pilgrimage, and a typewritten sheet of instructions, which included a few basic facts about Father William Wilcrist, should they be necessary. On the bottom of the page was a final order: *Commit to memory, tear up, and flush down toilet before immigration at Oldenzaal.*

The instructions were unnecessary, even distracting. Quite simply, he was to take a stroll through the railway cars twenty minutes out of a station called Rheine, leaving the suitcase behind as if he intended to return to his seat, and get off at Osnabrück. The details of his supposedly changing trains at Hanover for Celle and the subsequent morning drive north to Bergen-Belsen could have been said in one sentence rather than buried in the complicated paragraphs describing the underground's motivations and past successes. The facts about Father William Wilcrist, however, were succinct, and he had memorized them after the second reading. Wilcrist was thirty-eight years old, a graduate of Fordham, with a theological degree from Catholic University in Washington. Ordained at St. Ignatius in New York, he was an "activist priest" and currently assigned to the Church of the Blessed Sacrament in Los Angeles. In Valerie's words, if he was asked to recite more than that he was probably caught.

For all practical purposes he was caught now, thought Joel, gazing at the back of a man's head in the front of the car, the same man who had joined another standing by a pillar on the platform in Amsterdam. Undoubtedly that first man was now looking at the back of *his* head from a seat in the rear, mused Converse, turning another page in the prayer book. On the surface, the odds against him were overwhelming, but there was a fact and a factor just below the surface. The fact was that he knew who his executioners were and they did not know he knew. The factor was a state of mind he had drawn upon in the past.

The train traveled north, then east; there were two stops before Oldenzaal, after which he presumed they would cross the Rhine into West Germany. They had pulled in and out of the Deventer station; that left one more, a city named Hengelo. The announcement came, and Joel got out of his seat before any of the Hengelo commuters rose from theirs; he turned in the aisle and walked back to the rear of the car. As he passed the man who stood by the pillar he saw that Aquitaine's hunter was staring straight ahead, his body so rigid it barely moved with the movement of the train. Converse had seen such postures many times before, at trials and in boardrooms; they invariably belonged to insecure witnesses and unsure negotiators. The man was tense, afraid perhaps of failing an assignment or of the people who had sent him to Amsterdam —whatever it was, his anxiety was showing and Joel would use it. *He was crawling out of a deep shaft in the ground, one tenuous grasp of earth after another, the indentations preformed after nights of preparation. The wire fence was in the distance, the rain falling, the patrols concerned, anxious—frightened by every sound they could not quickly identify. He needed only one to move away and he had it. . . . He could reach the fence!*

Reach *Osnabrück*—alone.

The toilet was unoccupied; he opened the door, went inside, and took out the page of instructions. He folded it, tore it in shreds, and dropped the pieces into the bowl, pressing the foot button as he did so. They disappeared with the flush; he turned back to the door and waited.

A second announcement blared from the speakers outside as the train slowed down; the sound of gathering feet was inches away beyond the door. The train came to a stop; he could feel the vibration of moving bodies, determined commuters thinking of home and relief and undoubtedly the Dutch equivalent of a martini. The vibrations stopped; the sounds faded away. Converse opened the door no more than half an inch. The rigid hunter was not in his seat. *Now.*

Joel slid out of the door and stepped quickly into the open separation between cars, excusing himself between the stragglers getting off from the car behind, and walked rapidly inside and down the aisle. As he approached the last rows he saw an empty seat—two seats, facing the platform —and swung in; he sat down beside the window, his hand in front of his face, peering outside through his fingers.

Aquitaine's hunter raced back and forth, sufficiently aggressive to stop three men who were walking away, their backs to him; rapid apologies followed. The hunter turned to the train, having exhausted the departing possibilities. He got back on board, his face a creased map falling apart.

More, thought Converse. *I want more. I want you stretched, as patrols before you were stretched. Until you can't stand it!*

Oldenzaal arrived, then was left behind. The train crossed the Rhine, the clattering of the bridge below like snare drums. The hunter had crashed the forward door open, too panicked to do anything but quickly look around and return to his companion, or to a lone suitcase perhaps. Joel's head was below the back of the seat in front of him. Minutes later came the Sonderpolizei checking the border, scrutinizing every male of a vague description, dozens of uniformed men walking through the railway cars. They were courteous, to be sure, but nevertheless they gave rise to ugly vestiges of a time past. Converse showed his passport and the letter written in German for the conscience of Germans. A policeman grimaced sadly, then nodded and went on to the next seat. The uniforms left; the minutes became quarter-hours. He could see through the windows into the forward car; the two hunters met several rows behind where he had been sitting. Again they separated; one fore, one aft. *Now.*

Joel got up from his seat and sidestepped into the aisle, pretending to check his schedule and bending down to look out the darkened window. He would stay there for as long as he had to, until one of the hunters spotted him. It took less than ten seconds. As Converse pitched his head down supposedly to see a passing sign outside he caught a glimpse of a figure moving into the upper panel of glass on the forward door. Joel stood up. The man behind the glass spun out of sight. It was the sign he had been waiting for, the moment to move quickly.

He turned and walked to the rear of the car, opened the door and crossed the dark clattering space to the car behind. He went inside and swiftly made his way down the aisle, again to the rear and again into the next car, turning in the intervening darkness to see what he expected to see, what he wanted to see. The man was following him. *A guard was taking himself out of position in the downpour. Only seconds and he could reach the barbed wire.*

As he ran through the third car a number of passengers looked up at him, at a running priest. Most turned in their seats to see if there was an emergency, and seeing none shook their heads in bewilderment. He reached the door, pulled it open, and stepped into the shadows, suddenly startled by what he saw. In front of him, instead of another railroad-car door, the upper part a window, there was a solid panel of heavy wood, the word FRACHT printed across the midsection above a large steel knob. Then he heard the announcement over the loud-speakers:

"Benthelm! Nächste Station, Benthelm!"

The train was slowing down, the first of two stops before Osnabrück. Joel moved forward into the darkest area and inched his head in view of the window behind him, confident that he could not be seen by a man facing light reflected off a panel of glass. What he saw again startled him —not by the activity, but by the inactivity. The hunter made no move toward the door; instead, he sat down facing forward, a commuter finding a more comfortable seat, nothing else on his mind. The train came to a stop; those passengers getting off were forming a line in front . . . in *front*.

There had been a sign above this last door, but since he could not read it, he had simply gone through. He looked now at the exit doors; there were no handles. Obviously that incomprehensible sign was there to inform anyone who approached the door that it was not an exit. If he had been facing a trap before, he was in a cage now, a steel cage that began moving again, as the wheels gathered speed against the tracks. A racing jail from which there was no escape. Converse reached into his shirt pocket and took out his cigarettes. *He had been so close to the barbed wire; he had to think!*

A rattle? A key . . . a *bolt*. the door of a heavy wood with the word FRACHT stenciled on it opened and the figure of a stout man emerged, preceded by his stomach.

"Ein Zigarette für Sei, während ich zum Pinkeln gehe!" said the railroad guard, laughing, as he crossed through the short, dark corridor to the door. *"Dann ein Whisky, ja?"*

The German was going for a drink, and although he had pulled the door of his domain nearly shut, he had not closed it; he was an untroubled man, a guard with nothing he felt worth guarding. Joel pushed the heavy panel open and went inside, knowing what would happen; it *had* to happen the instant the guard walked by the hunter on his way to *"ein Whisky."*

There were half a dozen sealed crates and roughly ten cages holding animals—dogs mostly and several cats, cowering in corners, claws extended at the sound of growls and barks. The only light came from a naked bulb swaying on a thick wire from the ceiling beyond another cage, this one built for man with wire mesh at the end of the freight car. Converse concealed himself behind a crate near the door. He reached under his priestly coat and pulled out the gun with the perforated cylinder, the silencer.

The door opened—cautiously, millimeter by millimeter—the weapon appeared before the hand or the arm. Finally there was the man, the foot soldier from Aquitaine.

Joel fired twice, not trusting a single shot. The arm crashed back into the edge of the half-open door, the gun spinning out of the killer's hand, a single spurt of blood erupting near the executioner's wrist. Converse sprang from behind the crate—*the patrol was his, and so was the stretch of barbed-wire fence! He could climb it and crawl over now! The rock had smashed the window in the barracks! The staccato barrage of machine-gun fire was spraying where he was not! Seconds, only seconds, and he was out!*

Joel pinned the man to the floor, gripping his throat and pressing one knee on his chest—one prolonged squeeze and the soldier from Aquitaine would be dead. He held the barrel of the gun against the man's temple.

"You speak any *English?*"

"*Ja!*" coughed the German. "I . . . speak English."

"What were your orders?"

"Follow you. Only follow you. Don't shoot! I am *Angestellte!* I know nothing!"

"A *what?*"

"A hired man!"

"*Aquitaine!*"

"What?"

The man was not lying; there was too much panic in his eyes. Converse raised the gun and abruptly shoved it into the German's left eye, the perforated cylinder pressed deep into the socket.

"You tell me exactly what you were told to do! The truth—and I'll know a lie—and if you lie, your skull will be all over this wall! Talk to me!"

"To follow you!"

"*And?*"

"If you left the train we were to phone the *Polizei*. Wherever. Then . . . the orders were to kill you before they came. But I would not *do* that! I swear by my *Christ* I would *never* do that! I am a good Christian. I even love the Jews! I am unemployed!"

Joel crashed the weapon into the man's skull—*the patrol had been taken out! He could climb the fence now!* He pulled the German behind a crate and waited. How long it was impossible to tell; time had lost its meaning. The railway guard came back, somewhat more drunk than sober, and took refuge behind his wire-meshed office with the single light bulb.

The other cages were not so serene. The smell of human blood and sweat was more than the dogs could take; they began to react. Within minutes the railway car labeled FRACHT became a madhouse, the animals were now hysterical—the dogs snarling, barking, hurling themselves against their cages; the cats, provoked by the dogs, screeching, hissing, backs arched, fur standing on end. The guard was perplexed and frightened; anchoring himself to the chair in his sanctuary of wire mesh, he poured more whisky down his throat. He stared at the cages, his eyes wide within the folds of puffed flesh. Twice he looked at a glass-encased lever on the wall inches above the desk, above his hand. He had only to lift the casing and pull it.

"Rheine! Nächste Station, Rheine!"

The last stop before Osnabrück. Before long the German would revive, and unless Joel's eyes were on him at that instant the man would scream and an emergency lever would be pulled. Too, there was another man only cars behind who was also hired to follow him, to kill him. To remain where he was any longer was to let the trap close. He had to get off.

The train stopped, and Converse lunged for the door, his movement causing a dozen caged animals to vent their anger and confusion. He pushed back the bolt, opened the heavy door and raced into the forward car. He ran up the aisle—a priest perhaps on an errand of mercy—repeatedly apologizing as he rushed past the departing passengers, intent only on getting off before an unconscious body was found, a lever pulled, an alarm sounded. He reached the exit and leaped from the second step to the platform; he looked

801

around and ran into the shadows of the station.

He was free. He was alive. But he was miles away from an old woman waiting for her priest.

31

Valerie kept running, afraid to look behind, but when she forced herself to turn her head she saw the Army officer arguing with the driver of the Army car. Seconds later she looked again as she reached the corner of Madison Avenue. The officer was now running after her, shortening the distance between them with each stride. She raced across the street just as the light turned, and the blaring of horns signified the anger of several drivers.

Thirty feet away a taxi heading north had pulled to the curb and a gray-haired man was lethargically stretching himself out onto the pavement, tired, unwilling to accept the morning. Val ran back into the street, into the traffic, and raced to the cab's door; she opened it and climbed in as the startled gray-haired man was receiving change.

"Hey, lady, you *crazy?*" yelled the black driver. "You're supposed to use the curb! You'll get flattened by a bus!"

"I'm *sorry!*" cried Val, sinking low and back on the seat. *What the hell?* "My husband is running up the street after me and I *will* not be hit again! I *hurt*. He's—he's an Army officer."

The gray-haired man sprang out of the cab like

a decathlon contender, slamming the door behind him. The taxi driver turned around and looked at her, his large black face suspicious. "You tellin' the truth?"

"I threw up all morning from the punches last night."

"An officer? In the Army?"

"Yes! Will you please get *out* of here?" Val sank lower. "He's at the corner now! He'll cross the street—he'll see me!"

"Fret not, ma'am," said the driver, calmly reaching over the seat and pressing down the locks on the rear doors. "Oh, you were right on! Here he comes runnin' across like a crazy man. And would you look at them ribbons! Would you believe that horseshit—excuse me, ma'am. He's kinda skinny, ain't he? Most of the real bad characters were skinny. They compensated—that's a psychiatric term, you know."

"Get *out* of here!"

"The law's precise, ma'am. It's the duty of every driver of a medallion vehicle to protect the well-being of his fare. . . . And I was an infantry grunt, ma'am, and I've waited a hell of a long time for this particular opportunity. Having a real good reason and all that. I mean, you sure can't deny the words you said to me." The driver climbed out of the cab. He matched his face; he was a very large man, indeed. Val watched in horrified astonishment as the black walked around the hood to the curb and shouted, "Hey, Captain! Over here, on the sidewalk! You lookin' for a very pretty lady? Like maybe your wife?"

"*What?*" The officer ran up on the pavement

to the black man.

"Well, Captain-baby, I'm afraid I can't salute 'cause my uniform's in the attic—if I had an attic—but I want you to know that this search-and-destroy has successfully been completed. Would you step over to my jeep, sir?"

The officer started to run toward the taxi but was suddenly grabbed by the driver, who spun him around and punched him first in the stomach, then brought his knee crashing up into the Army man's groin, and finally completed the "assignment" by hammering a huge fist into the officer's mouth. Val gasped; blood spread over the captain's entire face as he fell to the pavement. The driver ran back to the cab, climbed in, shut the door and pulled the gear; the taxi shot forward in the traffic.

"Lawdy, *lawdy!* said the driver in a caricature of Southern dialect. "That felt *real* good! Is there an address, ma'am? The meter's running."

"I . . . I'm not sure."

"Let's start with the basics. Where do you want to go?"

"To a telephone . . . Why did you *do that?*"

"That's my business, not yours."

"You're sick! You could have been arrested!"

"For what? Protecting a fare from assault? That bad character was actually runnin' toward my cab and the vibes were not good, not good at all. Also, there weren't no cops around."

"I presume you were in Vietnam," said Val, after a period of silence, looking at the large head of black hair in front of her.

"Oh, yes, I was accorded that privilege. Very

scenic, ma'am.''

"What did you think of General Delavane? General George Marcus Delavane?''

The cab suddenly, violently, swerved as the driver gripped the wheel and slammed his heavy foot on the brake, causing the taxi to bolt to a stop, throwing Val against the rim of the front seat. The large black head whipped around, the coal-black eyes filled with fury and loathing and that deep unmistakable core of fear Valerie had seen so many times in Joel's eyes. The driver swallowed, his piercing stare somehow losing strength, turning inward, the fear taking over. He turned back to the wheel and answered simply, "I didn't do much thinking about the General ma'am. What's the address, missus? The meter's running.''

"I don't know. . . . A telephone, I have to get to a telephone. Will you wait?''

"Do you have money? Or did the captain take it all? There are limits to my concern, lady. I don't get no compensation for good deeds.''

"I have money. You'll be well paid.''

"Show me a bill.''

Valerie reached into her purse and pulled out a hundred dollars. "Will that do?'' she asked.

"It's fine, but don't do that with every cab you want in a hurry. You could end up in Bed-Stuy a damn good-lookin' corpse.''

"I don't want to believe that.''

"Oh, my, we have a liberal! Stick to it, ma'am, until they stick it to you. Me, I want 'em all to *fry!* Your kind don't really get it—*we* do. You only get the *periphery,* you *dig?* A couple of rapes

805

in the classy suburbs—and some of *them* might be open to dispute; and a few heists of silver and jewelry—*hell,* you're covered by insurance! Where I come from we're covered by a gun under the pillow, and God help the son of a bitch who tries to take it from me."

"A telephone, please."

"Your meter, lady."

They stopped at a booth on the corner of Madison and Seventy-eighth Street. Valerie got out, and took from her purse the sheet of St. Regis stationery with the Air Force telephone number. She inserted a coin and dialed.

"Air Force, Recruit Command, Denver," announced the female operator.

"I wondered if you could help me, miss," said Val, her eyes darting about at the traffic, looking for a roving brown sedan with U.S. ARMY printed across its doors. "I'm trying to locate an officer, a relative, actually . . ."

"One minute, please. I'll transfer you."

"Personnel, Denver Units," came a second voice, now male. "Sergeant Porter."

"Sergeant, I'm trying to locate an officer," repeated Valerie. "A relative of mine who left word with an aunt that he wanted to reach me."

"Where in Colorado, ma'am?"

"Well, I'm not sure."

"The Springs? The Academy? Lowry Field or possibly Cheyenne Mountain?"

"I don't know that he *is* in Colorado, Sergeant."

"Why did you call Denver, then?"

"You were in the telephone book."

"I see." The Army man paused. "And this officer left word that he wanted to reach you?"

"Yes."

"But he didn't leave an address or a telephone number."

"If he did, my aunt lost it. She's quite elderly."

"The procedure is as follows, miss. If you will write a letter to the MPC—Military Personnel Center—at the Randolph Air Force Base, San Antonio, Texas, stating your request and the officer's name and rank, the letter will be processed."

"I don't have time, Sergeant! I travel a great deal—I'm calling from an airport now, as a matter of fact."

"I'm sorry, miss, those are the regulations."

"I'm not a 'miss' and my cousin's a general and he really does want to speak to me! I just want to know where he is, and if you can't tell me, certainly you can call him and give him my name. I'll call *you* back with a number where he can reach me. That's reasonable, isn't it, Sergeant? Frankly, this is an emergency."

"A general, ma'am?"

"Yes, Sergeant Potter. A General Abbott."

"Sam Abbott? I mean, Brigadier General Samuel Abbott?"

"That's the one, Sergeant Potter."

"Porter, ma'am."

"I'll remember that."

"Well, I can't see any security breach here, miss—ma'am. Everybody knows where General Abbott is stationed. He's a popular officer and in the newspapers a lot."

807

"Where is that, Sergeant? I'll personally tell him you've been most helpful—to both of us."

"Nellis Air Force Base in Nevada, ma'am, just outside Las Vegas. He commands the advanced tactical maneuver squadrons. All the squadron commanders get their final training at Nellis. He's the *man*. . . . May I have your name, please?"

"Oh, good Lord! There's the last boarding call for my plane! Thank you, Sergeant." Valerie hung up the phone, her eyes still scanning the street, trying to decide what to do—whether to call Sam now or wait. Suddenly she realized she could *not* call; it would mean using a credit card, origin of call and destination listed. She went back to the taxi.

"Lady, I'd just as soon get out of here, if you don't mind," said the driver, a quiet urgency in his voice.

"What's the matter?"

"I keep a police scanner in my cab in case there's problems in my neighborhood, and I just heard the word. An Army captain was clobbered on Fifty-fifth and Madison by a black driver of a taxi heading north. Lucky for me they didn't get the license or the company, but the description's pretty good. 'A big black son of a bitch with a size-twelve fist' was the way those mothers put it."

"Let's go," said Val. "I hate to say this, and I mean that, but I can't get involved." The cab sped forward, the driver turning east on Eightieth Street. "Is—my husband pressing charges?" she asked.

"No, I'm off the hook there," replied the

808

driver. "He must have punched you real bad. He just fled and had nuthin' to say. Bless his white heart. Where to?"

"Let me think."

"It's your meter."

She had to get to Las Vegas, but the idea of going back to Kennedy or LaGuardia airports frightened her. They seemed too logical, too easily anticipated. Then she remembered. About five or six years ago she and Joel were weekending with friends in Short Hills, New Jersey, when Joel got a call from Nathan Simon, telling him he had to fly to Los Angeles on Sunday for a Monday-morning meeting. All the legal papers would be sent to the Beverly Hills Hotel by air express. Joel had taken the plane from Newark Airport.

"Can you drive me to Newark?"

"I can drive you to Alaska, lady, but *Newark?*"

"The airport."

"That's better. It's one of the best. I guess Newark's okay, too. I got a brother there and, hell, he's still alive. I'll swing through the park at Sixty-sixth and head down to the Lincoln Tunnel. Do you mind if I turn on the scanner again?"

"No, go right ahead."

The voices went in and out, then the driver pushed a button and they became steady: "Incident at Fifty-fifth and Madison is a negative. Precinct Ten has called it off as the victim refused assistance and did not identify himself. So patrols, onward and upward. We helps them what helps themselves. On, brothers."

"Oh, he's a *brother!*" shouted the driver in

relief as he turned off the radio. "You catch that 'incident is a negative'? They coulda used him in Nam, in those big body-count press conferences. . . . Come to think of it, he was probably there—not with the press, just one of the bodies. They never did get it right."

Valerie leaned forward on the seat. "I asked you about—Nam. About General Delavane. Would you tell me about him?"

It was nearly a minute before the black replied, and when he did so, his voice was soft, even mellifluous. And somewhere at the base of it was abject defeat. "My driver's identification is lookin' at you, lady. I'm drivin' you to Newark Airport—that's what you're payin' for, and that's what you'll get."

The rest of the ride was made in silence, an oppressive sense of fear pervading the cab. *After all these years,* thought Val. *Oh, God.*

They hit heavy traffic at the tunnel and then on the turnpike; it was the start of the weekend and vacationers were heading for the Jersey shore. The airport was worse; it was jammed, cars backed up for a quarter of a mile in the departure lanes. Finally they edged up into a parking space and Valerie got out. She paid the driver a hundred dollars above the fare and thanked him. "You've been much more than helpful, you know that. . . . I'll never really know why but I'll think about it."

"Like I said, it's my business. I got my reasons."

"I wish I could say something, something that could help."

"Don't try, lady. The green is enough."

"No, it's not."

"Sure, it is until something better comes along, and that ain't gonna be in my lifetime. . . . You take care, missus. I think you got bigger problems than most of us. You said too much, which I don't recall, of course."

Valerie turned and went into the terminal. The lines in front of the counters were horrendous, and before joining one she had to know which one. Twenty minutes later she was in the proper line and nearly an hour after that she had a ticket to Las Vegas on American's 12:30 flight, another hour before boarding. It was time to see if it all made sense. If Sam Abbott made sense, or whether she was grasping desperately at a man she once remembered who might not be that man any longer. She had exchanged $20 in bills for two $10 rolls of quarters. She hoped it would be enough. She took an escalator up to the second floor and went to a telephone at the far end of the wide corridor past the shops. Nevada information gave her the number of the main switchboard at Nellis Air Force Base. She dialed and asked to be put through to Brigadier General Samuel Abbott.

"I don't know if he's on the base yet," said the operator.

"Oh?" she had *forgotten*. There was a three-hour time difference.

"Just a minute, he's checked in. Early-morning flight schedule."

"General Abbott's office."

"May I speak to the general, please. The name is Parquette, Mrs. Virginia Parquette."

"May I ask what this is in reference to?" asked

the secretary. "The general's extremely busy and is about to head down to the field."

"I'm a cousin he hasn't seen in a long time, actually. There's been a tragedy in the family."

"Oh, I'm terribly sorry."

"Please tell him I'm on the line. He may not recall my name; it's been so many years. But you might remind him that in the old days we had some wonderful dinners in New York. It's really most urgent. I wish someone else were making this call, but I'm afraid I was elected."

"Yes—yes, of course."

The waiting put Valerie in the last circle of hell. Finally there was a click, followed by the voice she remembered.

"Virginia . . . Parquette?"

"Yes."

"*Ginny*—from New York? *Dinner* in New York?"

"Yes."

"You're the wife, not the sister."

"*Yes!*"

"Give me a number. I'll call you back in ten minutes."

"It's a pay phone."

"*Stay* there. The number."

She gave it to him and hung up, frightened, wondering what she had done, but knowing that she could not have done anything else. She sat in the plastic chair by the phone, watching the escalators, looking at the people going in and out of the various shops, the bar, the fast-food restaurant. She tried not to look at her watch; twelve minutes passed. The phone rang.

"Yes?"

"Valerie?"

"*Yes!*"

"I wanted to get out of the office—too many interruptions. Where are you? I know the area code's New Jersey."

"Newark Airport. I'm on the twelve-thirty flight to Las Vegas. I've got to see you!"

"I tried to call *you*. Talbot's secretary gave me your number—"

"*When?*"

"Starting two days ago. I was in the Mojave on maneuvers and too bushed to turn on a radio—we didn't have newspapers. A man answered, and when he said you weren't there I hung up."

"That was Roger, Joel's father. He's dead."

"I know. They say it was most likely suicide."

"*No!* . . . I've seen him, Sam. I've seen Joel! It's all lies!"

"That's what we have to talk about," said the general. "Call me when you get in. Same name. I don't want to pick you up at the airport; too many people know me over there. I'll figure out a place where we can meet."

"*Thank* you, Sam!" said Valerie. "You're all we have left."

"We?"

"For the time being, yes. I'm all *he* has left."

Converse watched from the far dark corner of the railroad station as the train for Osnabrück started up, its huge wheels pressing into the tracks, groaning for momentum. At any moment he expected whistles to pierce the quiet night and the train to stop, a bewildered half-drunken guard running from the freight car, screaming. None of it happened. Why? Was the man more than half drunk? Had the sounds of the enraged animals driven him further into the bottle, strengthening his resolve to remain in the safety of his cage? Had he seen only a blur racing to the door in the dim light, or perhaps nothing, an unconscious body subsequently not discovered? Then Joel saw that there was another possibility, a brutal one. He could see a figure running forward through the second to last car, twice lunging between the seats, his face pressed against the glass. Moments later the man was leaning out above the lower door of the first exit, the steps below blocked off by the heavy solid gate. In his hand was a gun, held laterally across his forehead as he squinted against the station lights, peering into the shadows.

Suddenly the killer made his decision. He gripped the metal rim and leaped over the guardrail, dropping to the ground, rolling over in the gravel away from the gathering speed of the train. The hunter from Aquitaine was in panic; he dared not lose the quarry, dared not fail to carry out his assignment.

Converse spun around the corner and raced along the dark side of the building to a parking area. The passengers who had gotten off the train were starting their automobiles or climbing into them; two couples were chatting on the near platform, obviously waiting to be picked up. A car came curving in off the road beyond; the men waved, and in moments all four were inside, laughing as the car sped away. The parking area was deserted, the station shut down for the night. A single floodlight from the roof illuminated the emptiness, a border of tall trees beyond the wide expanse of coarse gravel gave the appearance of an immense impenetrable wall.

Staying as best he could in the shadows, Joel darted from one space of darkness to another until he reached a solid, indented arch at the end of the building. He pressed his back against the brick and waited, his hand gripping the gun at his side, wondering if he would have to use it, if he would even have a chance to use it. He had been lucky on the train and he knew it; he was no match for professional killers. And no matter how strongly he tried to convince himself, he was not in the jungles a lifetime ago, not the younger man he had been then. But when he thought about it—as he was thinking about it now—those memories were all he had to guide him. He ducked out of the shadowed arch and quickly dashed to the corner.

The explosion came, blowing out the stone to the left of his head! He lunged to his right, rolling on the gravel, then quickly rose to get away from the spill of the floodlight. Three more shattering explosions tore up the rock and earth around his feet. He reached a dark row of foliage and dove into the bushes, instinctively knowing exactly what he had to do.

"Augh! Aughhh . . . !" His final scream ended on a convincing note of agony.

He then crawled through the underbrush as fast as he could penetrate the tangled nets of prickly green. He was at least ten feet away from where he had shouted; he pivoted on his knees and remained still, facing the floodlit expanse beyond the bushes.

It happened, as it had happened before when three children in official pajamas had killed another child indelicately in the jungle. Anxious men were drawn to the last sounds they heard—as this hunter from Aquitaine was drawn now. The man stalked out of the darkness of the railroad station's rear platform, his gun extended, held steady with both hands. He walked directly, cautiously, to that small section in the overgrowth where the screams had come from.

Converse scratched the ground noiselessly until he found a rock larger than his fist. He gripped it and waited, staring, feeling the drumming in his chest. The killer was within eight feet of the border of greenery. Joel lobbed the rock, arcing it in the air to his right.

The crunching thud was loud. Instantly Aquitaine's soldier crouched and fired one round after another—*two, three, four!* Converse raised his weapon and pulled the trigger twice. The man spun to his left, gasping, as he clutched his stomach and fell to the ground.

There was no time to think or feel or consider what had happened. Joel crawled out to the gravel and raced over to his would-be executioner; he grabbed him by the arms and dragged him back into the bushes. Still, he had to find out. He knelt down and held his fingers against the base of the man's throat. He was dead, another scout taken out in the war of the modern Aquitaine, the military confederation of George Marcus Delavane.

There was no one around—if there had been, the gunshots would have provoked screams and brought running feet; the police would have been summoned; they would have been there by now. How far away was Osnabrück? He had read the schedule and tried to figure out the times, but everything had happened so swiftly, so brutally, he had not absorbed what he read. It was less than an hour, that much he knew. Somehow he had to get word to the station at Osnabrück. Christ, *how?*

He walked out on the platform, glancing up at the sign: RHEINE. It was a start; he had counted only the stops, not the names. Then he saw something in the distance—above the ground, high above—with lights on the inside. A tower! He had seen such towers dozens of times in Switzerland and France—they were signal depots. They dotted the Eurail's landscape, controlling the trains that sped across their sectors. He started running along the tracks, suddenly wondering what he looked like. His hat was gone, his clothes soiled, but his clerical collar was still in place—he was still a priest.

He reached the base of the tower. He brushed off his clothes and tried to smooth his hair; Composing himself, he began climbing the metal steps. At the top he saw that the steel door to the tower itself was bolted, the inch-thick bulletproof glass a sign of the terrorist times—speeding trains were vulnerable targets. He approached the door and rapped on the metal frame. Three men were inside, huddled over electronic consoles; an elderly man turned from the numerous green screens and came to the door. He peered through the glass and crossed himself, but did not open the door. Instead, there was a sudden echoing sound projected into the air, and the man's voice emerged from a speaker: *"Was ist, Hochwürden?"*

"I don't speak German. Do you speak English?"

"Engländer?"

"Yes—*ja."*

The old man turned to his associates and shouted something. Both shook their heads, but one held up his hand and came to the door.

"Ich spreche . . . a little, Mr. *Engländer. Nicht* come enter here, *verstehen?"*

"I have to call Osnabrück! A woman is waiting for me—a *Frau!*

"Ohh? *Hochwürden! Eine Frau?"*

"No, *no!* You don't understand! Can't anybody here speak *English?"*

"Sie sprechen Deutsch?"

"No!"

"Warten Sie," said the third man from the console. There was a rapid exchange between the two men. The one who spoke "a little" turned back to the door.

"Eine Kirche," said the man groping for words. "Church! *Ein Pfarrer*—priest! *Er spricht Englisch. Drei* . . . three *strassen* . . . *there!"* The German pointed to his left; Joel looked down over his shoulder. There was a street in the distance. He understood; there was a church three

blocks away, and a priest who spoke English, presumably a priest who had a telephone.

"The train to Osnabrück. *When?* When does it *get* there?" Converse pointed to his watch. "When? *Osnabrück?*"

The man looked over at the console, then turned back to Joel and smiled. *"Zwölf Minuten, Hochwürden!"*

"How? *What?*"

"Zwölf . . . tvelf."

"Twelve?"

"Ja!"

Converse turned and clattered down the steps; on the ground he ran as fast as he could toward the streetlamps in the distance. Once there, he raced in the middle of the street, clutching his chest, vowing for the five hundredth time to give up cigarettes. He had persuaded Val to throw them away; why hadn't he taken his own advice? He was invulnerable, that's why. Or did he simply care for her more than he cared for himself? *Enough!* Where was the goddamned *church?*

It was there, on the right. A small church with fake spires, a silly-looking church with what looked like a decorated Quonset hut for a rectory beside it. Joel ran up the short path to the door, a door with a hideously bejeweled crucifix in the center—a rhinestone Jesus; rock along with Christ—and knocked. Moments later an overweight, cherubic man with very little white hair, though perfectly groomed, opened the door.

"Ah, Guten Tag, Herr Kollege."

"Forgive me," said Converse, out of breath. "I

don't speak German. I was told you speak English."

"Ah, yes, indeed, I should hope so. I spent my novitiate in the Mother Country—as opposed to the Fatherland—you understand the difference in gender, of course. Come in, come *in!* A visit from a fellow priest calls for a *Schnaps.* 'A touch of wine' sounds better, doesn't it? Again the Mother Country—so soft, so understanding. My, you're an attractive young man!"

"Not so young, Father," said Joel, stepping inside.

"That's relative, isn't it?" The German priest walked unsteadily into what was obviously his living room. Again there were jeweled figures mounted on black velvet on the walls, the cheap stones glittering, the faces of the saints unmistakably feminine. "What would you like? I have sherry and muscatel, and for rare occasions a port I've been saving for very special occasions. . . . Who sent you? That wicked novice from Lengerich?"

"I need *help,* Father."

"Great Jesus, who *doesn't?* Is this to be a confessional? If so, for God's sake give me until morning. I love the Lord my God with all my soul and all my strength—and if there are sins of the flesh, they are *Satan's.* Not I, but the *Archangel of Darkness!*"

The man was drunk; he fell over a hassock and tumbled to the floor. Converse ran to him and lifted him up, then lowered him into a chair—a chair by the only telephone in the room.

"Please understand me, Father. Or don't

*mis*understand me. I have to reach a woman who's waiting for me at Osnabrück. It's *important!*"

"A woman? *Satan!* He is *Lucifer* with the eyes of fire! You think you're better than *me?*"

"Not at all. *Please.* I need *help!*"

It took ten minutes of pleading, but finally the priest calmed down and got on the telephone. He identified himself as a man of God, and moments later Joel heard the name that allowed him to breathe steadily again.

"Frau Geyner? Es tut mir leid . . . " The old priest and the old woman talked for several minutes. He hung up and turned to Converse. "She waited for you," he said, frowning in bewilderment. "She thought you might have gotten off in the freight yards. . . . What freight yards?"

"I understand."

"I do not. But she knows the way here and will pick you up in thirty minutes or so. . . . You have sobered me, Father. Was I disgraceful?"

"Not at all," said Joel. "You welcomed a man in trouble, there's nothing wrong with that."

"Let's have a drink. Forget *Schnaps* and 'a glass of wine'; they're a bore, aren't they? I have some American bourbon in the refrigerator. You *are* American, are you not?"

"Yes, and a glass of bourbon would be just fine."

"Good! Follow me into my humble kitchen. It's right through here, mind the sequined curtain, dear boy. It *is* too much, isn't it? . . . Oh, well, for all of that—whatever it is—I'm a good man. I

821

believe that. I give comfort.''

''I'm sure you do.''

''Where were you schooled, Father?'' asked the priest.

''Catholic University in Washington,'' replied Converse, pleased with himself that he remembered and answered so quickly.

''Good Lord, I was there *myself!*'' exclaimed the German priest. ''They shunted me around, you understand. Do you remember what's his name . . . ?''

Oh, my God! thought Joel.

Frau Hermione Geyner arrived, and took Converse in tow—commandeered him, in fact. She was a small woman, far older than Joel had imagined. Her face was withered, reminding him of the woman in the Amsterdam station, and dominated by wide, intense eyes that seemed to shoot out bolts of electricity. He got in the car and she pushed the lock in place. She climbed behind the wheel and sped up the street, reaching what had to be sixty miles an hour in a matter of seconds.

''I appreciate everything you're doing for me,'' said Converse, bracing his feet against the floorboard.

''It is *nothing!*'' exclaimed the old woman. ''I have myself taken out officers from airplanes that crashed in Bremerhaven and Stuttgart and Mannheim! I spat in *soldiers'* eyes, and crashed through barricades! I never failed! The pigs could not touch me!''

''I only meant that you're saving my life, and I want you to know I'm grateful. I'm aware that

Valerie—your niece, and my . . . my former wife —told you I didn't do the things they said I did, and she was right. I didn't."

"*Ach,* Valerie! A sweet child, but not very reliable, *ja?* You got rid of her, *ja?*"

"That's not exactly the way it happened."

"How *could* she be?" continued Hermione Geyner, as if he had not spoken. "She is an artist, and we all know how unstable they are. And, of course, her father was a Frenchman. I ask you, could she have a greater disadvantage? *Franzose!* The worms of Europe! As untrustworthy as their wine, which is mostly in their stomachs. They're drunkards, you know. It's in their blood."

"But you believed her where I was concerned. You're helping me, you're saving my life."

"Because we *could!* We *knew* we could!"

Joel stared at the road ahead, at the rapidly oncoming curves taken at sixty miles an hour as the tires screeched. Hermione Geyner was not at all what he had expected, but then nothing was anymore. She was so old and it was late at night and she had been through a great deal these last two days; it had to have taken its toll on her. Old prejudices come to the surface when very old people are tired. Perhaps in the morning they could have a clearheaded conversation. The morning—it was the start of the second day, and Valerie had promised to call him in Osnabrück with news of Sam Abbott and the progress she was making to reach the pilot. She *had* to make that call! Sam had to be told about the strange language Joel had heard from an old man in Amsterdam, where a word meaning one thing also meant something else entirely. Assassination! *Val, call me. For God's sake, call me!*

Converse looked out the window. The minutes passed; the countryside was peaceful but the silence awkward.

"Here we are!" shouted Hermione Geyner, turning crazily into the drive that led to a large old three-story house set back off the country road. From what Converse could see, it was a house that had once had a certain majesty, if only by its size and the profusion of roofed windows and gables. In the moonlight now, it looked—like its owner—very old and frayed.

They walked up the worn wooden steps of the enormous porch and crossed to the door. Frau Geyner knocked rapidly, insistently; in seconds an old woman opened it, nodding solemnly as they went inside.

"It's very lovely," began Joel. "I want you to know—"

"Sshh!" Hermione Geyner dropped her car keys in a red laquered bowl on a hall table and held up her hand. *"This way!"*

Converse followed her to a pair of double doors; she opened them and Joel walked in behind her. He stopped, confused and astonished. For in front of them in the large Victorian room with the subdued lighting was a row of high-backed chairs and seated in each was an old woman—nine old women! Mesmerized, he looked closely at them. Some smiled weakly, several trembled with age and infirmity, obviously senile; a few wore stern, intense expressions, and one seemed to be humming to herself.

There was an eruption of fragile applause—
hands thin and veined, others swollen with flesh,
flesh striking flesh with obvious effort. Two
chairs had been placed in front of the women;
Valerie's aunt indicated that they were for Joel
and herself. They sat down as the applause
dwindled off to silence.

"Meine Schwestern Soldaten," cried Hermione
Geyner, rising. *"Heute Nacht . . ."*

The old woman spoke for nearly ten minutes,
interrupted occasionally by scattered applause and
expressions of wonder and respect. Finally, she sat
down. *"Nun. Fragen!"*

The women one after another began to speak
—frail, halting voices for the most part, yet
several were emphatic, almost hostile. And then
Converse realized that most were looking at him.
They were asking him questions, one or two
crossing themselves as they spoke, as if the
fugitive they had saved were actually a priest.

"Come, my friend!" cried Hermione Geyner.
"Answer the ladies. They deserve the courtesy of
your replies."

"I can't answer what I can't understand,"
protested Joel quietly.

Suddenly, without any warning, Valerie's aunt
rose quickly out of the chair and struck him
across the face. "Such evasive tactics will not
serve you *here!"* she screamed, striking him
again, the ring on her finger breaking his skin.
"We know you understand every word that's been
spoken! Why do you Czechs and Poles always
think you can fool us. You *collaborated!* We have
proof!"

825

The old women began to shout, their lined, contorted faces filled with hate. Converse got to his feet; he understood. Hermione Geyner and everyone else in that room were mad or senile or both. They were living in a violent time that was forty years in the past.

And then, as if on some demented cue, a door opened across the room and two men came out. One in a raincoat had his right hand in his pocket and was carrying some kind of package in his left. The second man held a topcoat over one arm, no doubt concealing a weapon. And then a third man appeared, and Joel closed his eyes, pressing them shut tight, the pain in his chest unbearable. The third man had a bandage across his forehead and one arm in a sling. Converse had caused those wounds; he had last seen the man in a freight car filled with frantic animals.

The first man came up to him and held out the package, a thick manila envelope with no stamps on the cover. It was the brief he had sent to Nathan Simon in New York.

"General Leifhelm sends you his regards, even his respects," said the man, pronouncing the word "general" with the hard German *g*.

32

Peter Stone watched as the CIA-approved doctor put the third and final stitch into the corner of the Army officer's mouth as the captain sat straining in the chair.

"The bridge will have to be repaired," said the doctor. "I have a man in the laboratory who'll do it in a few hours, and a dentist on Seventy-second Street, he'll do the rest. I'll call you later when I've made the arrangements."

"Son of a *bitch!*" roared the captain, as loud as he could with half his mouth Novocained. "He was a tank, a fucking black *tank!* He couldn't have been working for her, he was just a goddamned cabdriver! Why the *hell?*"

"Maybe you triggered him," said Stone, walking away as he looked at several pages of notes. "It happens."

"*What* happens?" yelled the officer.

"Cut it out, Captain. You'll break the stitches." The doctor held up a hypodermic needle; it was a threat.

"Okay, okay." The officer spoke in a softer voice. "What does 'trigger' mean in that esoteric language of yours?"

"It's perfectly clear English." Stone turned to the doctor. "You know I'm not employed any longer, so you'd better give me a bill."

"When you're in town a dinner will do. The lab and the dentist are different, though. I'd suggest cash. And get him out of uniform."

"Will do."

"What . . . ?" The captain stopped, seeing Stone's hand held unobtrusively in front of his chest, telling the officer to be quiet.

The doctor put his instruments in the black bag and went to the door. "By the way, Stone," he said to the former CIA agent, "thanks for the Albanian. His wife is spending Moscow's rubles

827

like mad for every ache I can find a name for."

"The ache is her husband. He has an apartment in D.C. she doesn't know about and some very strange sex habits."

"I'll never tell."

The doctor left, and Stone turned back to the captain. "When you're with men like that, don't say any more than you have to, and that includes questions. They don't want to hear and they don't want to know."

"Sorry. What did you mean—*I* triggered that hulk?"

"Come on. An attractive woman being chased down the street by a beribboned Army officer. How many memories—black memories—do you think are out there with less than fondness for your ilk."

"Ilk? I never thought of myself as an ilk, but I see what you mean. . . . You were on the phone when I got here, and then there were two other calls. What is it? Any line on the Converse woman?"

"No." Stone again looked down at his notes, shuffling the pages. "We can assume she came back to reach someone—someone she and her ex-husband trust."

"He knows his way around Washington. Maybe someone on the Hill, or even in the administration, or State."

"I don't think so. If he knew anyone like that and thought his story would get out before his head was shot off, he would have surfaced days ago. Remember, he's been tried, convicted, and condemned. Can you think of anyone in Washington who wouldn't play it—play *him*—strictly by the rules? He's contaminated. Too many 'authoritative sources' have confirmed it, even diagnosed the disease.''

"And by now he's learned what we found out months ago. You don't know where they are or who you're talking to.''

"Or whom they've hired,'' added Stone. "Or whom they've blackmailed into doing what they want without giving away any trade secrets.'' He sat down opposite the Army officer. "But a couple of other things have fallen into place. We're getting a pattern and a few additional names. If we could pull Converse out and combine what he's learned with what we've got—it might just possibly be enough.''

"What?" The captain shot forward in the chair.

"Take it easy. I said just possibly. I've been calling in some old debts, and if we could put it all together, there are one or two left I can trust.''

"That's why we called you in,'' said the officer quietly. "Because you know what to do, we don't. . . . What have you got?''

"To begin with have you ever heard of an actor named Caleb Dowling—actually, it's Calvin, but that's not important except for the computers.''

"I know who he is. He plays the father on a television show called *Santa Fe*. Don't shout it from the rooftops, but my wife and I watch it now and then. What about him?''

Stone looked at his watch. "He'll be here in a few minutes.''

"No kidding? I'm impressed.''

"You may be more impressed after we've talked to him."

"Jesus, fill me in!"

"It's one of those odd breaks we all look for that seem to come out of left field but are perfectly logical. It's the timing that's not logical. . . . Dowling was in Bonn filming a picture and struck up a friendship with Peregrine. American celebrity, *et cetera*. He also met Converse on a plane and got him a hotel room when they were tough to find. Most significant, Dowling was the initial contact between Peregrine and Converse —which didn't work out because Fitzpatrick stepped in."

"So?"

"When Peregrine was killed, Dowling called the embassy a number of times trying to get an appointment with the acting ambassador, but he was put on hold. Finally he sent a note to Peregrine's secretary saying he had to see her, that it was important. The secretary met with him, and this Dowling dropped a bomb on her lap. Apparently he and Peregrine had an agreement that if Converse called the embassy and contact was to be made, Dowling would go along. He didn't think Peregrine would go back on his word. Secondly, Peregrine told Dowling that something was rotten in the embassy ranks, some very odd behavior. One incident Dowling witnessed himself. He said there were too many things that didn't make sense—from Converse's sane and lucid conversations to the fact that he, Dowling, hadn't been officially questioned, as if people were avoiding one of the last people to see

Converse. The bottom line was that he didn't think Converse had anything to do with Peregrine's murder. The secretary damn near fainted but told him he would be contacted. She knew the Agency's station chief in Bonn and called him. So did I, two days ago, telling him I was brought in deep down by State."

"He confirmed all of this?"

"Yes. He called Dowling in, listened to him, and has begun digging himself. He's coming up with names, one of which we know, but there'll be others. I was on the phone with him when you got here. Dowling flew in yesterday; he's at the Pierre and will be here by eleven-thirty."

"That's movement," said the captain, nodding. "Anything else?"

"Two other things. You know how stymied we were when Judge Anstett caught it and how strong the case was made for a mob killing. Hell, we weren't even sure why Halliday used Anstett in the first place. Well, the computer boys at the Army data banks have come up with the answer. It goes back to October of 1944. Anstett was a legal officer in Bradley's First Army, where Delavane held a battalion command. Delavane railroaded a sergeant who'd cracked through a court-martial. The charge was desertion under fire, and Colonel Delavane wanted an example both for his own troops and for the Germans, to let the first know they were being led by a ramrod, and the second that they were fighting one. The verdict was guilty, the sentence execution."

"Oh, my God," exclaimed the Army officer.

"Slovik all over again."

"Exactly. Except that a lowly lieutenant named Anstett heard about it and came rolling in with all his legal barrels smoking. By using psychiatric evaluation reports he not only got the sergeant sent home for treatment but literally turned the proceedings around and put Delavane himself on trial. Using the same kind of psychological evaluations—stress, mainly—he called into question Delavane's fitness for command. It damned near ruined an illustrious military career, and would have if it wasn't for the colonel's friends in the War Department. They buried the report so well it was under another Delavane's name and wasn't picked up until all the records were computerized in the sixties."

"That's one hell of an explanation, Stone."

"It's only part of it. It didn't explain Anstett's killing itself. And make no mistake, it was the Mafia down to the man with the gun." Stone paused and turned a page. "So there had to be a connection somewhere, somehow a link, probably going back years. The boys with the disks looked further, and I think we've got it. Guess who was Colonel Delavane's chief aide in the First Army. No, don't bother, you couldn't. He was a Captain Parelli, Mario Alberto Parelli."

"Good Christ! The senator?"

"The five-term senator, thirty years in that august body. Up-from-the-bootstraps Mario, with a slight push from the G.I. Bill, some early benefactors and a few lucrative legal retainers."

"Wow . . ." said the captain softly, without enthusiasm, as he leaned back in the chair.

"That's heavy, isn't it?"

"It's there. It fits. And I don't mind telling you that in '62 and '63, during the Let's-get-Fidel days, Parelli was a frequent visitor at the White House, courtesy of both the Kennedy boys."

"Even in the Senate. He's one of the biggest cannons on the Hill."

"While you're staring, let me give you the last item. We've found Commander Fitzpatrick."

"What?"

"At least we know where he is," completed Stone. "As to whether we can bring him out, or even want to try, that's another question."

Valerie got in the cab at McCarran Airport in Las Vegas and gave the driver the address of a restaurant on Route 93, repeated twice by Sam Abbott over the phone. The driver, creasing his forehead, looked at her in his rearview mirror. Val was used to men scrutinizing her; she was neither flattered nor annoyed anymore. Frankly, she was just bored by the childishness of it all, by the fantasies of grown-up children abusing themselves with their eyes.

"Are you sure, miss?" asked the driver.

"I beg your pardon?"

"That isn't a restaurant—like I mean a *restaurant*. It's a diner, a pit stop for trucks."

"It's where I wish to go," said Val coolly.

"Sure, okay, fine." The taxi pulled out into the departing traffic.

The driver was right. A half-acre of asphalt surrounded the long, low, L-shaped diner; a dozen huge trucks dwarfed the cars, which were parked at respectful distances from the intimidating rigs. Val paid the driver and went inside; she looked around and walked past the cashier's counter toward the L-shaped section. Sam had told her he would be in one of the booths in that area.

He was, at the rear of the second aisle. As Valerie approached she looked at the man she had not seen in nearly seven years. He had not changed much; the brown hair had a fringe of gray around the temples, but the strong, relaxed face was not very different—perhaps the eyes were a little deeper, a few more lines at the sides and the cheekbones a touch more pronounced. It was a better face for a portrait now, she thought; the character beneath was emerging. Their eyes met, and the brigadier general got out of the booth, his clothes denying his rank and profession. He was dressed in an open sport shirt, tan summer slacks and dark loafers. He was somewhat shorter than Joel, but not by much. His gray eyes said she was a welcome sight.

"*Val.*" Abbott held her briefly, obviously not wanting to call attention to them.

"You look well, Sam," she said, sitting down across from him, putting the carry-on beside her.

"You look merely outstanding, which is military for all those other adjectives." Abbott smiled. "It's funny, but I come out here a lot because no one pays any attention to me, so I thought, hell, it's the perfect place. I should have remembered—you walk through that arcade of gorillas and eggs get put in ears with coffee spoons."

"Thanks. I could use some confidence."

"I could probably use a strong alibi. If someone does recognize me, word will go back that the brigadier's pulling outside duty."

"You're *married,* Sam?"

"Five years ago. Late, but with all the fixings. A lovely bride and two beguiling daughters."

"I'm so happy for you. I hope I get a chance to meet her, meet them—but not this trip. Definitely not this trip."

Abbott paused, looking into her eyes, a touch of sadness in his. "Thank you for understanding," he said.

"There's nothing to understand, or rather, there's everything to understand. The fact that you're willing to meet me after all that's happened is more than we had a right to expect. Both Joel and I know the risks you're taking—legally, as a general, all of it—and if there was any other way, we wouldn't involve you. But after you hear what I have to say, you'll understand why we can't wait any longer, why Joel agreed to let me try to find you. . . . You were my idea, Sam, but Joel wouldn't have heard of it unless he felt he had to—not for himself; he doesn't expect to live. That's what he said and he believes it."

A waitress brought coffee and Abbott thanked her. "We'll order later," he added, staring at Valerie. "You'll have to trust my judgment, you understand that, don't you?"

"Yes. Because I trust you."

"When I couldn't reach you I made a few calls to people I worked with a couple of years ago in Washington. They're men who're deep into these kinds of things, who have answers long before most of us know the questions."

"Those are the people Joel wants you to reach!" interrupted Val. "You saw him then; you spent a night at his hotel, don't you remember? He said you both drank too much."

"We did," agreed Sam. "And talked too much."

"You were evaluating aircraft—'equipment,' Joel called it—with specialists from various intelligence units."

"That's right."

"They're the ones he has to contact! He has to see them, talk to them, tell them everything he knows! I'm getting ahead of myself, Sam, but Joel thinks those people should have come in at the beginning—the beginning for him. He understands why he was chosen and, incredibly, he doesn't even now fault that decision! But *they* should have been there!"

"You're way ahead of yourself."

"I'll go back."

"Let me finish first. I talked to them, telling them I didn't believe what I was reading and hearing; it wasn't the Converse I knew, and to a man they told me to back off. It was hopeless and I could get badly tarnished. It *wasn't* the Converse I knew, they said. He'd psyched out; he was another person. There was too much evidence to support the blow-out."

"But you took *my* call. Why?"

"Two reasons. The first is obvious—I knew Joel; we went through a lot together and none of this makes sense to me, maybe I don't want it to make sense. The second reason is a lot less subjective. I know a lie when I hear one—when I know it can't be the truth—and a lie was fed to me just as it was fed to the people who delivered it." Abbott sipped his coffee, as if telling himself to slow down and be clear. The leader of the squadron was in control; he had to be. "I spoke to three men I knew, men I trust, and each checked with his own sources. They all came back to me, each telling me essentially the same thing but in different language, different viewpoints depending on their priorities—that's the way it works with these people. But one item didn't vary so much as a syllable, and it was the lie. The label is drugs. Narcotics."

"Joel?"

"Their words were practically identical. 'Evidence is pouring in from New York, Geneva, Paris, that Converse was a heavy buyer.' That was one phrase; the other was 'Medical opinion has it that the hypodermics finally blew him up and blew him back.' "

"That's crazy! It's *insane!*" cried Valerie as Abbott grabbed her hand to quiet her down. "I'm sorry, but it's such a *terrible* lie," she whispered. "You don't know—"

"Yes, Val, I do know. Joel was pumped five or six times in the camps with substances sent down from Hanoi, and no one fought it harder or hated it more than he did. The only chemicals he'd allow in his body after that were tobacco and alcohol. I've seen us both with third-degree hangovers and while I tore medicine cabinets apart for a Bromo or an aspirin, he wouldn't touch them."

"Whenever his passport shots came up, he had to have four martinis before he went to the doctor," said Valerie. "Good God, who would spread a thing like that?"

"When I tried to find out I was told that even I couldn't have that information."

The former Mrs. Converse now stared at the brigadier general. "You *have* to find out, Sam, you know that, don't you?"

"Tell me why, Val. Put it together for me."

"It began in Geneva, and for Joel the operative name—the *operative* name—was George Marcus Delavane."

Abbott flinched and shut his eyes; his face became suddenly older.

The cry of the cat on a frozen lake became a scream as the man in the wheelchair fell to the floor, his two stumps that once were legs scissoring maniacally to no avail. With strong arms he pushed his torso up from the rug.

"Adjutant! *Adjutant!*" roared General George Marcus Delavane as the dark-red telephone kept ringing on the desk below the fragmented map.

A large, muscular middle-aged man in full uniform ran out of a door and rushed to his superior. "Let me help you, sir," he said emphatically, pulling the wheelchair toward them both.

"Not me!" yelled Delavane. "The *phone!* Get the phone! Tell whoever it is I'll be right there!" The old soldier began crawling pathetically toward the desk.

"Just one minute, please," said the adjutant into the phone. "The general will be with you in a moment." The lieutenant colonel placed the telephone on the desk and ran first to the chair and then to Delavane. "Please, sir, let me *help* you."

With a look of loathing on his face, the half-man permitted himself to be maneuvered back into the wheelchair. He propelled himself forward and took the phone. "Palo Alto International. You're red! What is the day's code?"

"Charing Cross" was the reply in a clipped British accent.

"What is it, England?"

"Radio relay from Osnabrück. We've got him."

"Kill him!"

Chaim Abrahms sat in his kitchen, tapping his fingers on the table, trying to take his eyes off the telephone and the clock on the wall. It was the fourth time span, and still there was no word from New York. The orders had been clear: the calls were to be placed within thirty-minute periods every six hours commencing twenty-four hours ago, the estimated arrival time of the plane from Amsterdam. Twenty-four hours and nothing! The first omission had not troubled him; rarely were transatlantic flights on schedule. The second he had rationalized; if the woman was in transit, traveling somewhere else either in a car or by plane, the surveillance might find itself in a difficult position to place an overseas call to Israel. The third omission was unacceptable, this fourth lapse intolerable! It was nearly the end of the thirty-minute span, six minutes to go. When in the name of God would it ring?

It rang. Abrahms leaped from the chair and picked it up.

"Yes?"

"We lost her" was the flat statement.

"You *what?*"

"She took a taxi to LaGuardia Airport and bought a ticket for a morning flight to Boston. Then she checked into a motel and must have left minutes later."

"Where were our *people?*"

"One parked in a car outside, the other in a room down the hall. There was no reason to suspect she would leave. She had a ticket to Boston."

"Idiots! *Garbage!*"

"They will be disciplined. Our men in Boston have checked every flight, every train. She hasn't shown up."

"What makes you think she will?"

"The ticket. There was nothing else."

"Imbeciles!"

Valerie had finished; there was nothing more to say. She looked at Sam Abbott, who seemed far older than he had been an hour ago.

"There are so many questions," said the brigadier general. "So much I want to ask Joel. The lousy thing is I'm not qualified, but I know someone who is. I'll talk to him tonight, and tomorrow the three of us will fly to Washington. Like today, I have an early A.M. squadron run,

840

but I'll be finished by ten. I'll take the rest of the day off—one of the kids is sick, but nothing serious, nothing out of the ordinary. Alan will know whom we should go to, whom we can trust."

"Can you trust *him?*"

"Metcalf? With my life."

"Joel says you're to be careful. He warns you that they can be anywhere—where you least expect them."

"But somewhere there's got to be a list. *Somewhere.*"

"Delavane? San Francisco?"

"Probably not. It's too simple, too dangerous. It's the first place anyone would look; he'd consider that. . . . This countdown—Joel thinks it's tied into massive riots taking place in different cities, various capitals?"

"On a vast scale, larger and more violent than anything we can imagine. Eruptions, total destabilization, spreading from one place to another, fueled by the same people who are called in to restore order."

Abbott shook his head. "It doesn't sound right. It's too complicated, and there are too many built-in controls. Police, troops from the National Guard; they have separate commands. The chain would break somewhere."

"It's what he believes. He says they could do it. He's convinced they have warehouses everywhere stocked with weapons and explosives, even armored vehicles and conceivably planes in out-of-the-way airfields."

"Val, that's *crazy*—sorry, wrong word. The

841

logistics are simply too overwhelming."

"Newark, Watts, Miami. They were also overwhelming."

"They were different. They were essentially racial and economic."

"The cities burned, Sam. People were killed and order came with guns. Suppose there were more guns than either of us could count? On both sides. Just like what's happening in Northern Ireland right now."

"Ireland? The slaughter in Belfast? It's a war no one can stop."

"It's *their* war! *They* did it! Joel called it a test, a trial run!"

"It's *wild,*" said the pilot.

" 'Accumulation, rapid acceleration.' Those were the words Abrahms used in Bonn. Joel tried to figure them out. He couldn't buy Leifhelm's statement that they referred to blackmail or extortion. It wouldn't work, he said."

"Extortion?" Abbott frowned. "I don't remember your mentioning that."

"I probably didn't because Joel discounted it. Leifhelm asked him what he thought about powerful figures in various governments being compromised, and Joel said it wouldn't work. The cleansing process was too certain, the reactions too quick."

"Compromised?" Sam Abbott leaned forward in the booth. *"Compromised,* Val?"

"Yes."

"Oh, my God."

"What do you mean?"

"Mean? . . . Meaning, that's what I mean.

'Compromised' has more than one meaning. Like 'neutralize' and 'take out,' and probably a dozen others I don't know about.''

"You're beyond me, Sam."

"In one context, the word 'compromise' means *killing*. Pure and simple murder. Assassination."

Valerie checked into the MGM-Grand Hotel giving the bewildered clerk three days' advance payment for the room in lieu of a credit card. Key in hand, she took the elevator up to the ninth floor and let herself into a room with the kind of pleasantly garish opulence found only in Las Vegas. She stood briefly on the balcony, watching the orange setting sun, thinking about the insanity of everything. She would call Joel first thing in the morning—noon or thereabouts in Osnabrück, West Germany.

She ordered from room service, ate what she could, watched an hour or so of mind-numbing television, and finally lay down on the bed. She had been right about Sam Abbott. Dear Sam, straight-as-the-proverbial-arrow Sam, direct and uncomplicated. If anyone would know what to do, Sam would, and if he did not know, he would find out. For the first time in days, Val felt a degree of relief. Sleep came, and this time there were no horrible dreams.

She awoke to the sight of the early sun firing the mountains beyond the balcony doors in the distance. For a moment or two while she emerged through the layers of vanishing sleep she thought she was back at Cape Ann, the sunlight streaming into her bedroom from the balcony outside, and vaguely recalled a distant nightmare. Then the bold floral drapes came into focus, and then the faraway mountains and the slightly stale odor of thick hotel carpeting, and she knew the nightmare was very much with her.

She got out of the oversized bed, and navigated to the bathroom, stopping on the way to switch on the radio. She reached the door and suddenly stopped, gripping its edge to brace herself, her head detonating with a thousand explosions, her eyes and throat on fire.

She could only scream. And scream again and again as she fell to the floor.

Peter Stone turned up the radio in the New York apartment, then walked quickly to the table where there was an open telephone directory, the pages blue, the book itself having been taken from "Mrs. DePinna's" room in the St. Regis Hotel. Stone listened to the news report as he scanned the opposing blue pages of government listings.

"... *It has now been confirmed that the earlier reports of the crash of an F-18 jet fighter plane at Nellis Air Force Base in Nevada are accurate. The accident took place this morning at seven-forty-two, Pacific time, during first-light maneuvers over the desert thirty-eight miles northwest of the Nellis field. The pilot, Brigadier General Samuel Abbott, was chief of Tactical Operations and considered one of the finest pilots in the Air Force as well as a superb aerial tactician. The press officer at Nellis said a full inquiry will be launched, but stated that according to the other pilots the lead plane of the squadron, flown by*

844

General Abbott, plunged to the ground after executing a relatively low-altitude maneuver. The explosion could be heard as far away as Las Vegas. The press officer's remarks were charged with emotion as he described the downed pilot. 'The death of General Abbott is a tragic loss for the Air Force and the nation,' he told reporters. A few minutes ago the President . . ."

"That's it," said Stone, turning to the Army captain across the room. "That's where she was heading. . . . Shut that damn thing off, will you? I knew Abbott; I worked with him out of Langley a couple of years ago."

The Army officer stared at the civilian as he turned off the radio. "Do you know what you're saying?" he asked.

"Here it is," replied Stone, pointing to the lower left-hand corner of a page in the thick telephone directory. "Blue thirteen, three pages from the end of the book. 'United States Government offices. Air Force, Department of the—' "

"There are dozens of other listings, too, including your former employer. 'Central Intelligence—New York Field Office.' Why not it? Them? It fits better."

"He can't go that route and he knows it."

"He didn't go," corrected the captain. "He sent her."

"*That* doesn't fit—with everything we know about him. She'd be sent to Virginia and come out a basket case. No, she came back here to find a particular person, not a faceless department or a section or an agency. A man they both knew and trusted. Abbott. She found him, told him everything Converse told her and he talked to others—the wrong others. *Goddamn it!*"

"How can you be sure?" pressed the Army man.

"*Christ,* Captain, what do you want, a *diagram?* Sam Abbott was shot down over the coast of the Tonkin Gulf. He was a POW and so was Converse. I have an idea that if we put it through the computers, we'd find out they knew each other. I'm so sure I won't use up another debt. *Fuck it!*"

"You know," said the Army officer. "I've never seen you lose your temper. The cold can get hot, can't it, Stone. I believe you."

The former intelligence officer looked hard at the captain, and when he spoke his voice was flat—and cold. "Abbott was a good man—even an exceptional man for someone in uniform—but don't mistake me, Captain. He was killed—and he *was* killed—because whatever that woman told him was so conclusive he had to be compromised hours later."

"Compromised?"

"Figure it out. . . . I'm angry at Sam's death, yes, you're damned right. But I'm a lot angrier that we don't have the woman. Among other things, with us she has a chance, without us I judge very little and I don't want her on my conscience—what little I've got left. Also to get Converse out we have to find her, there's no other way."

"But if you're right she's somewhere near Nellis, probably Las Vegas."

"Undoubtedly Las Vegas, and by the time we reached anyone who could check around for us, she'll be on her way somewhere else. . . . You know, I'd hate to be her now. The only avenue she had was neutralized. Whom can she turn to, where can she go? It's what Dowling said about Converse yesterday, what he didn't tell Peregrine's secretary. Our man was systematically isolated and more afraid of U.S. embassy personnel than anyone else. He would never have agreed to a meeting with Peregrine because he knew it'd be a trap, therefore he couldn't have killed him. He was set up; everywhere he looked there was another trap to keep him running and out of sight." The civilian paused, then added firmly, "The woman's finished, Captain. She's at the end of a bad road—their road. And that may be the best part of it for us. If she panics, we could find her. But we're going to have to take some risks. How's that neck of yours? Have you made out a will?"

Valerie wept quietly by the glass doors overlooking the gaudy strip of Las Vegas. Her tears were not only for Sam Abbott and his wife and children, but for herself and Joel. It was permitted under the circumstances, and she could not lie to herself. She had no idea what to do next. No matter whom she went to the answer would be the same. *Tell him to come out of hiding and we'll listen to him.* And the minute he did, Joel would be dead, fulfilling his own prophecy. And if through a bureaucratic miracle she was granted a meeting with someone of power and influence, how strong would her case be? What words would she use?

I was married to this man for four years and I divorced him—let's call it incompatibility—but I know him! I know he couldn't have done what they say he did, he didn't kill those men. . . . What proof? I just told you, I know him! . . . What does incompatibility mean? I'm not sure, we didn't get along—he was remote, distant. What difference does it make? What are you implying? Oh, God! You're so wrong! I have no interest in him that way. Yes, he's successful and he's paid me alimony, but I don't need his money. I don't want it! . . . You see, he told me about this . . . this incredible plot to put the military establishments of the United States and the countries of Western Europe in virtual control of their governments, that they could do it by instigating massive rioting in key cities, terrorism, destabilization everywhere. He's met them and talked with them; there's a plan already in progress! They see themselves as a dedicated international organization, as a strong alternative to the weak governments of the West who won't stand up to the Soviet bloc. But they're not a reasonable alternative, they're fanatics! They're killers; they want total control of all of us! . . . My former husband wrote it all up, everything he's learned, and sent it to me, but it was stolen, his own father killed because he read it. No, it was not suicide! . . . He calls it a conspiracy of generals conceived by a general who'd been labeled a madman. General George Delavane— 'Mad Marcus' Delavane. . . . Yes, I know what

*the police in Paris and Bonn and Brussels say,
what Interpol says, what our own embassy has
reported—fingerprints and ballistics and seeing
him in this place and that place, and drugs, and
meeting with Peregrine—but can't you understand, they're all lies! . . . Yes, I know what
happened when he was a prisoner of war—what
he went through, the things he said when he was
discharged. None of that is relevant! His feelings
aren't relevant! He told me that! He told me—he
looks so terrible . . . he's been so hurt.*

Who would believe her?

Tell him to come in. We'll listen.

He can't! He'll be killed! . . . You'll kill him!

The telephone rang, for a moment paralyzing
her. She stared at it, terrified but forcing herself
to stay in control. Sam Abbott was dead, and he
told her only he would call—only he. My God,
thought Val, they'd *found* her, just as they'd
found her in New York. But they would not
repeat the mistakes they had made in New York.
She had to remain calm and think—and outthink
them. The ringing stopped. She approached the
phone and picked it up, then pressed the button
marked *O.* "Operator, this is room nine-one-four.
Please send the security police up here right away.
It's an emergency."

She had to move quickly, be ready to leave the
instant the security men arrived. She had to get
out and find a safe telephone. She had heard the
stories; she knew what to do. She had to reach
Joel in Osnabrück.

Colonel Alan Metcalf, chief intelligence officer,

849

Nellis Air Force Base, walked out of the telephone booth and looked around the shopping mall, his hand in the pocket of his sport jacket, gripping the small revolver inside. He glanced at his watch; his wife and three children would be in Los Angeles soon, then reach Cleveland by late afternoon. The four of them would stay with her parents until he said otherwise. It was better this way—since he had no idea what the "way" would be like.

He only knew that Sam Abbott had run that sub-mach maneuver a thousand times; he knew every stress point and P.S.I. throughout the entire aircraft, and he never flew a jet that had not been scanned electronically. To ascribe that crash to pilot error was ludicrous; instead, someone had lied to that pilot, a circuit and backup shorted. Sam was killed because his friend, Metcalf, had made a terrible mistake. After talking with Abbott for nearly five hours, Metcalf had called a man in Washington, telling him to prepare a conference the following afternoon with two ranking members each from the NSC, G-Two and naval intelligence. The reason-of-record: Brigadier General Samuel Abbott had pertinent and startling information about the fugitive Joel Converse relative to the assassinations of the American ambassador in Bonn and the supreme commander of NATO.

And if they could so readily, so efficiently kill the man who had the information, they might easily go after the messenger, the intelligence officer bringing him in. It was better this way, with Doris and the kids in Cleveland. He had a

850

great deal to do and a terrible debt to repay.

The Converse woman! Oh, Christ, why had she
done it, why had she run so quickly? He had
expected it, of course, but he had hoped against
hope that he would reach her in time, but it had
not been possible. First there was Doris and the
kids and plane reservations and the call to her
folks; they had to get out; he could be next. Then
racing to the field, his revolver beside him in the
car, and ransacking Sam's office—as Nellis'
intelligence officer, a particularly loathsome duty,
but in this case vital—and questioning Abbott's
distraught secretary. A name had emerged:
Parquette.

"I'll pick her up," Sam had said last night.
"She's staying at the Grand and I promised only
I'd phone her. She's a cool lady, but she had a
close call in New York. She wants to hear a voice
she knows and I can't blame her."

Cool lady, thought Alan Metcalf, as he climbed
into his car, *you made the biggest mistake of your
shortened life. With me you had a chance to
live—perhaps—but now as they say in this part of
Nevada, the odds are heavily against.*

Nevertheless she would be on his conscience,
reasoned the intelligence officer, now speeding into the cutoff toward Route 15 and points
south.

Conscience. He wondered if those silent
bastards in Washington had Joel Converse on
their collective conscience. They had sent a man
out and abandoned him, not even having the
grace to make sure he was killed quickly,

mercifully. The programmers of the kamikazes were saints beside such people.

Converse. Where *was* he?

33

Joel stood silently as Leifhelm's man removed his gun and turned to speak to the assembled row of senile old women in the high-backed chairs. He spoke for less than a minute, then grabbed Converse by the arm—his and their trophy —forcing Joel to face Hermione Geyner, whose true prisoner he was. It was a mystical ritual of triumph from a time long past.

"I have just told these brave women of the underground," said the German looking at Converse, "that they have uncovered a traitor to our cause. Frau Geyner will confirm this, *ja, meine Dame?*"

"*Ja!*" spat out the intense old woman, her face alive with the fierce joy of victory. "Betrayal!" she screamed.

"The telephone calls have been made and our instructions received," continued Leifhelm's soldier. "We shall leave now, *Amerikaner.* There's nothing you can do, so let us go quietly."

"If you had this whole thing so organized, why those two men on the train, including that one?" asked Joel, nodding at the man with his arm in the sling, instinctively stalling for time, an attorney allowing an adversary to compliment himself.

"Observed, not organized," answered the German. "We had to be sure you did everything expected of you. Everyone here agrees, *Stimmt das, Frau Geyner?*"

"*Ja!*" exploded Valerie's aunt.

"The other one is dead," said Joel.

"A loss for the cause and we shall mourn him. Come!" The German bowed to the ladies, as did his two companions, and led Converse through the large double doors to the front entrance. Outside on the decrepit porch, Leifhelm's hunter gave the thick envelope to the man with the sling and issued orders. Both nodded and walked rapidly down the steps, the wounded man steadying himself on a rickety railing, and then they hurried to the right of the long circular drive. Down at the far exit, near the country road, Joel could see the shape of a long sedan in the darkness.

The three prison guards led him out of the compound. It was the middle of the night, and he was being transferred either to another camp or to his own execution, the killing ground somewhere in the dense jungle where his screams would be muted. The head guard barked a command to his two subordinates, who bowed and began running down the road toward a captured American Jeep several hundred yards away in the darkness. He was alone with the man, thought Converse, knowing the moment would not come again except as a corpse. If it was going to happen, it had to happen now. He moved his head slightly, lowering his gaze to the dark outline of the gun in the guard's hand. . . .

The German's hand was steady, the weapon it held rigid against Joel's chest. Inside the house, the old women had broken into song; their pathetic frail voices were raised in some victory anthem heard through the large casement windows open for the summer breezes. Converse inched his right foot around the floorboards on the porch, testing several and finding one weaker than the others. He pressed down with his full weight; the resulting creak was loud and sharp. Startled, the German turned at the echoing sound.

Now. Joel grabbed the barrel of the gun, twisting hand and steel back and clockwise; he hammered the man across the porch into the wall while gripping the weapon with all his strength, twisting tighter and shoving it into the man's stomach.

The gunshot was partially muffled by cloth and flesh, by the noise of an engine starting and the excited singing of senile voices that came through the open windows. The German collapsed, his head snapping, his eyes bulging; there was a stench of burnt fabric and intestines—he was dead. Converse crouched, then whipped around to look down at the long U-shaped drive, half expecting to see the two other men racing toward him with guns extended. Instead, he saw the lights of the car in the distance; it was on the country road outside, now turning into the entrance gate on the left. It would be at the porch in moments.

Prying the weapon out of the German's hand, Joel dragged him across the floorboards into the shadows to the right of the steps. Seconds now.

Get the Jeep. Use the Jeep. The nearest vehicle

check was five miles down the road—they had seen it on work details. Get the Jeep! Cover the ground! The Jeep!

The long sedan pulled up in front of the porch and the man with his arm in the sling got out of the right front door. Converse watched him from behind the thick corner pillar as the wounded German stood on the pavement, looking up into the shadows.

"König?" he asked softly, questioning. "König, *was ist?*" He started up the steps, his left hand awkwardly, tentatively, going inside his jacket.

Joel spun around the pillar and rushed down the old staircase. Grabbing the wounded man by the sling, he jammed the pistol into the foot soldier's throat; he turned him around and rushed him back to the car, then crashed his head against the roof as he crouched and thrust the weapon through the open front window.

The astonished driver was quicker than the foot soldier; he was already yanking his gun out of an unseen holster. He fired wildly, shattering the windshield. Converse fired back, blowing the man's head half out of the window.

Take the bodies into the jungle! Don't leave them here near the compound! Every second counts, every minute!

Joel sprang up and pulled the wounded German away from the car as he opened the front door. "You're going to help me, you good Christian!" he whispered, remembering the whining supplication of a killer in a freight car. "You do as I tell you or you'll join your friends. *Capisce,* or is it *verstehen?* Whatever the hell it is, you do as I say, do you understand me? I'm a panicked man, mister—on the *edge,* and I'll argue that position in front of the Supreme Court! . . . What the hell am I *saying?* I've got the gun and I've killed again—it gets easier when you don't want to be killed yourself. *Move!* That lousy son of Gestapo on the porch! Bring him down here! In the back!''

Perhaps a minute later, Joel would never know the time, the wounded man was behind the wheel driving with difficulty, the two corpses in the backseat. A tableau of horror—Converse thought he would vomit. Fighting back the nausea, he watched every landmark in the countryside as he directed the driver to take this turn and that—pilotage indelibly imprinted on the mind for the flight back without a radio or a map or a means to obtain either. They reached what looked like a series of rocky pastures at the base of a mountain, and Converse told the German to get off the road. They clambered over several hundred yards until there was a sharp decline that ended at a dense row of trees. He ordered the driver out.

He had given the last guard a chance. He was a kid in a mismatched uniform; his eyes were intense but his face raised questions. How much was felt, how much indoctrinated? He had given the boy—the child—a simple exam, and a believer had failed the examination.

"Listen to me," said Joel. "You told me on the train that you were *hired* but that you didn't want to kill anybody. You were just unemployed and

856

needed a job, is that right?"

"Yes! I kill *no one!* I only watched, followed!"

"All right. I'll put the gun away and I'm going to walk out of here. You go wherever you want to go, okay?"

"*Ich verstehe!* Yes, of course!"

Converse shoved the weapon in his belt and turned, his fingers still gripping the handle as he started up the slope. A *scratch!* The crunching sound of rocks displaced by moving feet! He pivoted, dropping to his knees as the German lunged.

He fired once at the body above him. The foot soldier screamed as he arced in the air and rolled down the hill. A believer had failed the examination.

Joel walked up the incline with the envelope addressed to Nathan Simon and across the rocky field to the road. He knew the landmarks; the pilot in him would make no mistakes. He knew what he had to do.

He was concealed far back in the bushes on the edge of Hermione Geyner's property, thirty yards from the decaying house, twenty from the U-shaped drive, which was filled with ruts and bordered by brown overgrown grass, dead from the heat and lack of water. He had to stay awake, for if it was going to happen, it would happen soon. Human nature could take only so much anxiety; he had played upon the truism too often as a lawyer. Answers had to be given to anxious men—panicked men. The sun was up, the birds foraging in the early light, myriad noises replacing the stillness of the night. But the house was silent, the large casement windows, through which only hours ago the voices of demented old women had helped muffle gunshots, were closed, many of the panes cracked. And through all the madness, the insanity of violent events, he still wore the clerical collar, still had his priestly passport and the letter of pilgrimage. The next few hours would tell him whether or not they were of any value.

The roar of an engine came first and then the sight of a black Mercedes swerving off the country road into the drive. It sped up to the porch, jolting to a stop; two men climbed out and the driver raced around the trunk to join his companion. They stood for a moment looking up at the porch and the windows of the house, then turned and scanned the grounds, walking over to Hermione Geyner's car and peering inside. The driver nodded and reached under his jacket to pull out a gun; they went back to the steps, taking them rapidly, heading across the porch to the door. Finding no bell, the man without a gun in his hand knocked harshly, repeatedly, finally pounding with a closed fist while twisting the knob to no avail.

Guttural shouts came from inside as the door swung back, revealing an angry Frau Geyner dressed in a tattered bathrobe. Her voice was that of a shrewish teacher lambasting two students for cheating when in fact they had not. Each time one of the men tried to speak her voice became even more shrill. Cowed, the man with the gun put it away, but his companion suddenly grabbed Valerie's aunt by the shoulders and spoke harshly, directly, forcing her to listen.

Hermione Geyner did listen, but when she replied her answers were equally harsh and delivered with authority. She pointed down at the overgrown drive and described what she had apparently witnessed in the dark, early-morning hours—what she herself had accomplished. The men looked at each other, their eyes questioning and afraid, but not questioning what the old woman had told them, only what she could not tell them. They raced across the porch and down the steps to their car. The driver started the engine with a vengeance so pronounced the ignition mechanism flew into a high-pitched, grinding scream. The Mercedes plunged forward, skirting past Frau Geyner's car, and in a sudden attempt to avoid a hole in the overgrown pavement, the driver swung to his left, then to his right, skidding on the surface, the tires sliding on the crawling vine weeds until the side of the car careened into the disintegrating stone gate. Roars of abuse from both men filled the morning air as the Mercedes straightened itself out and raced through the exit. It swung left and sped down the country road as Hermione Geyner slammed the door shut on the porch.

There was nothing any longer without risk, thought Joel, as he crawled out of the foliage, but the risk for him now was one he faced with a degree of confidence. Aquitaine had used up Frau Geyner; there was nothing more it could learn from her. To return to a madwoman held a greater risk for them. Envelope in hand, he walked across the ugly drive, up the creaking steps, and across the sagging porch to the door.

He knocked, and ten seconds later a screeching Hermione Geyner opened it. He then did something so totally unpredictable, so completely out of character, he did not believe it himself as he followed through with the sudden impulse.

He punched the old woman squarely in the center of her lower jaw. It was the beginning of the longest eight hours of his life.

The bewildered security police from the MGM-Grand Hotel reluctantly refused Valerie's offer of a gratuity, especially as she had raised it from $50 to $100, thinking that the economy of Las Vegas was somewhat different from New York's and certainly Cape Ann's. They had driven around the streets of the old and the new city for nearly forty-five minutes, until both men, both professionals in their work, assured her that no one was following their car. And they would put a special patrol on the ninth floor in an attempt to catch the man who had harassed her, who had attempted to gain entrance to the room. They were, of course, naturally chagrined that she took a room across the boulevard at Caesars Palace.

Val tipped the bellman, took her small overnight bag from him, and closed the door. She ran to the phone on the table by the bed.

"I *haff* to go to the toilet!" shouted Hermione Geyner, holding an ice pack under her chin.

"Again?" asked Converse, his eyes barely open, sitting across from the old woman, the envelope and the gun in his lap.

"You make me nervous. You struck me."

"You did the same and a hell of a lot more to me last night," said Joel, getting up from the chair and shoving the gun under his belt, the envelope in his hand.

"I vill see you hanging from a rope! *Betrayer!* How many hours now? You think our operatives in the *Untergrund* will not *miss* me?"

"I think they're probably feeding pigeons in the park, cooing along with the best of them. Go on, I'll follow."

The telephone rang. Converse grabbed the old woman by the back of her neck and propelled her to the antique desk and the phone. "Just as we practiced," he whispered, holding her firmly. *"Do it!"*

"Ja?" said Hermione Geyner into the telephone, Joel's ear next to hers.

"Tante! Ich bin's, Valerie!"

"Val!" shouted Converse, pushing the old woman away. "It's me! I'm not sure the phone's clean; she was set up, *I* was set up! Quickly! Tell Sam I was *wrong—I think* I was wrong! The countdown could be *assassinations*—all over the goddamned place!"

"He knew that!" shouted Valerie in reply. "He's dead, Joel! He's dead! They killed him!"

"Oh, Christ! There's no time, Val, no time! The *phone!"*

"Meet me!" screamed the ex-Mrs. Converse.

"Where? Tell me *where?"*

The pause was less than several seconds, an eternity for both. "Where it began, my darling!" cried Valerie. "Where it began but *not* where it

861

began. . . . The clouds, darling! The patch and the clouds!"

Where it began. Geneva. But not Geneva. Clouds, a patch. A patch!

"Yes, I *know!*"

"Tomorrow! The next day! I'll be there!"

"I have to get out of here. . . . Val . . . I love you so much! *So* much!"

"The clouds, my darling—my only darling —oh, *God,* stay alive!"

Joel ripped the telephone out of the wall as Hermione Geyner came rushing at him, swinging a heavy brass-handled poker from the fireplace. The iron hook glanced off his cheek; he grabbed her arm and shouted, "I haven't got time for you, you crazy bitch! My client doesn't have time!" He spun her around and pushed her forward, picking up the envelope from the table. "You were on your way to the bathroom, remember?"

In the hall Converse saw what he had hoped he would see in the red lacquered bowl on the wall table; the old woman had dropped them there last night—the keys to her car. The bathroom door pulled out—it was the solution. Once she was inside, Joel dragged over a heavy chair from against the wall and jammed the thick rim under the knob, kicking the legs in place, wedging them into the floor. She heard the commotion and tried to open the door; it held. The harder she pressed, the more firmly the legs became embedded.

"We convene again tonight!" she roared. "We will send out our best people! The *best!*"

"God help Eisenhower when you meet,"

muttered Converse, inwardly relieved. If Aquitaine did not have the phone covered, the old woman would be found in a few hours. The envelope under his arm, he took the keys from the lacquered bowl and pulled the gun from his belt. He ran to the front door and opened it cautiously. There was no one, nothing, only Hermione Geyner's car parked on the weed-ridden drive. He went outside and pulled the door shut, leaving it unlocked, and raced down the steps to the automobile. He started the engine; there was half a tank of gas, enough to get him far away from Osnabrück before refilling. Until he could get a map, he would go by the sun heading south.

Valerie made arrangements at the travel office in Caesars Palace, paying cash and using her mother's maiden name, perhaps hoping some of that resourceful woman's wartime expertise might find its way to the daughter. There was a 6:00 P.M. Air France flight to Paris from Los Angeles. She would be on it, the hour's trip to LAX made on a chartered plane to which she would be chauffeured, thus avoiding the terminal at McCarran Airport. Such courtesies were always available, usually for celebrities and casino winners. There was no basic problem with a false name on the Air France passenger manifest—at worst, only embarrassment, in her case easily explained: her former husband, now a stranger, was an infamous man, a hunted man; she preferred anonymity. She would not legally be required to produce her passport until she arrived at immigration in Paris, and once through, she could travel anywhere she wished, under any name she gave, for she would not be leaving the borders of France. It was why she had thought of Chamonix.

She sat in the chair, looking out the window, thinking of those days in Chamonix. She had flown over with Joel to Geneva, where he had three days of conferences with the promise of five days off to go skiing at Mont Blanc, a bonus from John Brooks, the brilliant international negotiator of Talbot, Brooks and Simon, who flatly refused to give up some reunion dinner for what he termed "lizard-shit meetings between idiots—our boy can do it. He'll charm their asses off while emptying their corporate pockets." It was the first time Joel really knew that he was on his way, yet oddly enough he was almost as excited about the skiing. They both enjoyed it so much. Together. Perhaps because they were both good.

But Joel had not enjoyed the skiing at Chamonix that trip. On the second day he had taken a terrible fall and sprained his ankle. The swelling was enormous, the pain as acute in his head as in his foot. She had knighted him "Sir Grump"; he demanded his *Herald Tribune* in the morning, childishly refusing to have his breakfast before the paper arrived, and even more childishly playing the martyr as his wife went off to the slopes. When she had suggested that she really did not care to go without him, it was worse. He had charged her with trying to be some kind of saint. He would be perfectly fine—he had things to read, which artists would not understand.

Reading, that was.

Oh, what a little boy he had been, thought Val. But during the nights it was so different, he was so different. He became the man again, loving and tender, at once the generous lion and the sensitive lamb. They made love, it seemed, for hours on end, the moonlight on the snow outside, finally the hint of the sun's earliest rays on the mountains until they fell—together—into exhausted sleep.

On their last day before heading back to Geneva for the night flight to New York, she had surprised him. Instead of going out for a few final hours of skiing, she had gone downstairs at the hotel and bought him a sweater, to which she sewed a large patch on the sleeve. It read: DOWNHILL RACER—CHAMONIX. She had presented it to him while a porter waited outside the door with a wheelchair—she had made arrangements through the influential manager of the hotel. They were taken to the center of Chamonix, to the cable car that scaled thirteen thousand feet to the top of Mont Blanc—through the clouds to the top of the world, it seemed. When they reached the final apex, where the view was breathtaking, Joel had turned to her, with that silly, oblique look in his eyes that belied everything he was and everything he had been through—again, as always, his way of thanking her.

"Enough of this foolish scenery," he had said. "Take off your clothes. It's not really that cold."

They had hot coffee, sitting on a bench outside, the magnificence of nature all around them. They held hands, and *Christ!* She had felt such love that she had to hold back the tears.

She felt the love now and got out of the chair, rejecting the intrusion of emotion. It was the wrong time. Whatever clarity of mind she could summon was needed now. She had to travel halfway across the world avoiding God knew how many people who were looking for her.

He had said he loved her—"so much." Was it love or was it need . . . support? She had replied with the words "my darling"—no, she had said more than that; she had been far more specific. She had said "my only darling." Was it a response born of the panic?

Not knowing was the worst of it, thought Converse, studying the road signs in the wash of the headlights. He had been driving for nearly seven hours after picking up a map in the city of Hagen while refilling the tank—seven hours, and according to the map he was still a long way from the border crossing he had chosen. The reason lay in his ignorance, in not knowing whether Hermione Geyner's car had been the object of a search in the first few hours out of Osnabrück. It undoubtedly was now—officially by the police —but during those early hours he could have made better time on the highways he dared not use in case Aquitaine had raced to Geyner's house with Val's call. He had traveled circuitous backcountry roads, his pilot's eye on the sun, veering always south until he reached Hagen. Now the back roads were a necessity; whether they were before he would never know. Now, however, Hermione Geyner and her band of lunatics must have gone to the police to report her stolen car. Joel had no idea what they could possibly say that would convince the *Polizei* that Valerie's aunt was an injured party, but a stolen car was a stolen car, whether driven by Saint Francis of Assisi or Jack the Ripper. He would stay on the back roads.

Lennestadt to Kreuztal, crossing the Rhine at Bendorf and following the west bank of the river through Koblenz, Oberwesel, and Bingen, then south to Neustadt and east to Speyer and the Rhine again. And again south through the border towns of Alsace-Lorraine, finally to the city of Kehl. It was where he would cross into France, a decision based on the fact that several years ago John Brooks had sent him to Strasbourg, the French city across the river border, to a terribly dull conference at which eight lawyers argued so continuously with each other over minor aspects of language and translation that nothing of substance was accomplished. As a result, Joel had walked the city and driven out to the countryside, awed by its beauty. He had taken several boat trips up and down the Rhine, and now he remembered the ferries that shuttled back and forth between the piers of Germany and France. Above all, he remembered the crowds in Strasbourg. Always the crowds had helped him—he needed them especially now.

It would take another three to four hours of driving, but somewhere he would have to stop and sleep for a while. He was exhausted; he had not slept for so long he could not accurately remember when he had last closed his eyes. But there was Chamonix and Val ahead. He had told her he loved her—he had *said* it. He had gotten it out after so many years; the relief was incredible, but the response even more incredible. "My darling—my only darling." Did she mean it? Or was she supporting him again, the artist's emotions riding over reason and experience?

Aquitaine! Push everything out of your mind and get into France!

The polar flight from Los Angeles to Paris was uneventful, the moonscapes of ice over the northernmost regions of the world hypnotically peaceful, suspending thought by the sheer expanse of their cold infinity. Nothing seemed to matter to Val as she looked down from the substratosphere. But whatever tranquility the flight produced, it came to an end in Paris.

"Are you in France on business or on holiday, madame?" asked the immigration official, taking Valerie's passport and typing her name into the computer.

"*Un peu de l'un et de l'autre.*"

"*Vous parlez français?*"

"*C'est ma langue préferée. Mes parents étaient parisiens,*" explained Val, and continued in French, "I'm an artist and I'll be talking with several galleries. Naturally, I'll want to travel—" She stopped, seeing the official's eyes glance up from his screen, studying her. "Is anything the matter?" she asked.

"Nothing of concern, madame," said the man, picking up his telephone and talking in a low voice, the words indistinguishable in the hum of the huge customs hall. "There is someone who wishes to speak with you."

"That's of considerable concern to *me,*" objected Valerie, frightened. "I'm not traveling under my own name for a very good reason —which I suspect that machine of yours has told you, and I will *not* be subjected to interrogations or the indignity of the press! I've said all I have to say. Please reach the American embassy for me."

"There is no need for that, madame," said the man, replacing the phone. "It is not an interrogation and no one of the press will know you are in Paris unless you tell them. Also, there is nothing in this machine but the name on your passport—and a request."

A second uniformed official hurriedly entered the roped-off aisle from a nearby office. He bowed politely. "If you will come with me, madame," he said quietly in English, obviously noticing the fear in her eyes and assuming her reluctance. "You may, of course, refuse, as this is in no way official, but I hope you will not. It is a favor between old friends."

"Who are you?"

"Chief inspector of immigrations, madame."

"And who wishes to speak with me?"

"It would be up to him to tell you that—his name does not appear on the request. However, I'm to give you another name. Mattilon. He says you two were old friends and he respected him a great deal."

"*Mattilon?*"

"If you will be so kind as to wait in my office, I will personally clear your luggage."

"This is my luggage," said Val, her thoughts

on someone who would bring up René's name. "I'll want a police officer nearby, one who can watch through a glass door."

"*Pourquoi?* . . . Why, madame?"

"*Une mesure de sûreté,*" replied Valerie.

"*Oui, bien sûr, mais ce n'est pas nécessaire.*"

"*J'insiste ou je pars.*"

"*D'accord.*"

It was explained that the person who wished to speak with her was driving out to De Gaulle Airport from the center of Paris; it would take thirty-five minutes. Waiting, she had coffee and a small glass of Calvados. The man walked through the door. Of late middle age, he was dressed in rumpled clothing, as if his appearance did not matter any longer. His face seemed lined as much from weariness as from age, and when he spoke his voice was tired but nevertheless precise.

"I will keep you but a few minutes, madame. I'm sure you have places to go, people to see."

"As I explained," said Val, looking hard at the Frenchman, "I'm in Paris to talk with several galleries—"

"That is no concern of mine," interrupted the man, holding up his hands. "Forgive me, I do not care to hear. I care to hear nothing unless madame wishes to speak after I've spoken to her."

"Why did you use the name of Mattilon?"

"An introduction. You were friends. May I go back before Monsieur Mattilon?"

"Go back by all means."

"My name is Prudhomme. I am with the Sûreté. A man died in a hospital here in Paris several weeks ago. It is said your former husband, Monsieur Converse, was responsible."

"I'm aware of that."

"It was not possible," said the Frenchman calmly, sitting down and taking out a cigarette. "Have no fear, this office is not 'tapped' or 'bugged.' The chief inspector and I go back to the Resistance."

"That man died after a brutal fight with my former husband," said Val cautiously. "I read it in the newspapers, heard it on the radio. Yet you're telling me he wasn't responsible for his death. How can you say that?"

"The man did not *die* in the hospital, he was killed. Between two-fifteen and two-forty-five in the morning. Your husband was on a flight from Copenhagen to Hamburg during those hours. It has been established."

"You *know* this?"

"Not officially, madame. I was removed from the case. A subordinate, a man with little police experience but with the Army—later in the Foreign Legion, no less—was given the assignment while I was shifted to more 'important' matters. I asked questions; I will not bore you with details, but the man's lungs collapsed—a sudden trauma unrelated to his wounds. The man was suffocated. It was not in the report. It was removed."

Valerie controlled herself, keeping her voice cool and distant despite her anxiety. "Now," she said, "what about Mattilon? My *friend,* Mattilon."

"Fingerprints," replied the Frenchman wearily.

"They suddenly are discovered twelve hours after the *arrondissement* police—who are *very* good—have examined that office. And yet there was a death in Wesel, West Germany, within the rising and the setting of the same sun. Your former husband's countenance was described, his identity all but confirmed. And an old woman on a train to Amsterdam—the same routing—who is found with a gun in her hand—again a description given. Has this Converse wings? Does he fly unobserved over borders by himself? Again it is not possible."

"What are you trying to tell me, Monsieur Prudhomme?"

The man from the Sûreté inhaled on his cigarette as he tore off a page from his note pad and wrote something on it. "I'm not certain, madame, since I am no longer officially privileged in these matters. But if your former husband did not cause the man in Paris to die and could not have shot your old friend Monsieur Mattilon, how many others did he *not* kill, including the American ambassador in Bonn and the supreme commander of NATO? And who are these people who can tell government sources to confirm this and confirm that, to change assignments of senior police personnel at will, to alter medical reports removing—suppressing—evidence? There are things I do not understand, madame, but I am certain those are the very things I am not *meant* to understand. And that is why I'm giving you this telephone number. It is not my office; it is my flat in Paris—my wife will know where to reach me. Simply remember, in an emergency say that

872

you are from the Tatiana family."

Stone sat at the desk, the ever-present telephone in his hand. He was alone—had been alone when the call came from Charlotte, North Carolina, from a woman he had once loved very dearly years ago in the field. She had left the "terrible game," as she called it; he had stayed, their love not strong enough.

The connection was completed to Cuxhaven, West Germany, to a telephone he was sure would be sterile. That certainty was one of the pleasures in dealing with Johnny Reb.

"Bobbie-Jo's Chicken Fry!" was the greeting over the line. "We deliver."

"I gather that. It's Stone."

"*Mah wuhd,* the Tatiana re-route!" exclaimed the Southerner. "Someday you must tell me about this here fascinatin' family of yours, Brer Rabbit."

"Someday I will."

"I seem to recollect having heard the name somewheres around the late sixties, but I didn't know what it meant."

"Trust whoever used it."

"Why should I do that?"

"Because whoever it was was trusted by the hangingest judges in the world."

"Who might that be?"

"The enemy, Rebel."

"If that's a parable, Yankee, you lost me."

"Someday, Johnny, not now. What have you got?"

"Well, let me tell you, I saw the damnedest

little island over here you ever did see. It's not twenty miles off the coast, near the mouth of the Elbe, right where it's supposed to be. In the Heligoland Bight, they call it, which is a section of the North Sea."

"Scharhörn," said Stone, making a statement. "You found it."

"It wasn't tough to find—everybody seems to know about it—but nobody goes near a certain southwest shoreline. It used to be a U-boat refueling station in World War Two. The security was so tight most of the German High Command didn't know about it, and the Allies never got a clue. The old concrete-and-steel structures are still there, and it's supposed to be deserted except for a couple of caretakers, who, I'm told, wouldn't pick you out of the water if your boat crashed into one of the old submarine winches." Johnny Reb paused, then continued softly, "I went out there last night and saw lights, too many lights in too many places. There are people out there on that old base, not just a couple of watchmen, and you can bet a Yankee pot roast your lieutenant commander is one of them. Also around two o'clock in the morning after the lights went out, the tallest mother-lovin' antenna this side of Houston slid up like a bionic cornstalk, but there was no corn on the top. Instead, it bloomed like a regular sunflower. It was a disk, the kind they use for satellite transmissions. . . . You want me to mount a team? I can do it; there's a lot of unemployment these days. Also the cost will be minimal, because the more I think about it, the more I appreciate your swinging me out of the

Dardanelles before those guns got there. That was really more important than getting me off the hook with those contingency funds in Bahrain.''

"Thanks, but not yet. If you go in for him now, we show cards we can't show."

"How long can you wait? Remember I taped that prick Washburn."

"How much did you put together?"

"More than this old brain can absorb, if you want the truth. But not more than I can accept. It's been a long time coming, hasn't it? The eagles think they're gonna catch the goddamned sparrows after all, don't they? 'Cause they're gonna turn everyone *into* sparrows. . . . You know, Stone, I shouldn't say this because in your old age you became a bit softer than I did in mine, but if they get it off the ground, a lot of people everywhere may just lie back in their hammocks or go fishin', and say the hell with it—let the big, uniformed daddies do it. Let'em straighten things out—get the potheads with their guns and switchblades off the streets and out of the parks. Show the Russkies and the oil boys in bathrobes we don't take their crap anymore. Let's show Jesus we're the good guys with a lot of clout. Those soldiers, they got the guts and the guns, the corporations and the conglomerates, so what does it mean to me? Where do *I* change, says the Joe in the hammock, except maybe for the better?"

"Not better," said Stone icily. "Those same people become robots. We all become robots, if we live. Don't you understand that?"

"Yeah, *I* do," answered Johnny Reb. "I guess

875

I always have. I live on a hog-high in Bern while you scratch in D.C. Yes, old buddy, I understand. Maybe better than you do. . . . Forget it, I'm enlisted. But what in all-fire hell are you going to do about this Converse? I don't think he's going to get out.''

"He *has* to. We think he has the answers—the *firsthand* answers—that give us the proof."

"In my opinion he's dead," said the Southerner. "Maybe not now but soon—soon's they find him."

"We have to find him first. Can you help?"

"I started the night I needled Major Norman Anthony Washburn the Fourth, Fifth, or Sixth—I keep losin' track of the numerals. You got the computers—the ones you have access to—and I've got the streets where they sell things you're not supposed to buy. So far, nothing."

"Try to find something, because you were right before—we don't have much time. And, Johnny, do you have the same feeling I have about that island, about Scharhörn?"

"Like Appomattox, way down deep in the stomach. I can taste the bile, Brer Rabbit, which is why I'm going to possum down here for a few days. We found ourselves a beehive, boy, and the drones are restless, I can sense it."

34

Joel put the map and the thick envelope on the grass and began pulling branches down from a small tree in the orchard to cover Hermione Geyner's car. Each yanking of a limb filled him with pain, as much from fatigue as from the strain on his arms. Finally, he bunched together reeds of tall grass and threw them everywhere over the frame. The effect in the moonlight was that of an immense mound of hay. He picked up the map and the envelope and started walking toward the road two hundred yards away. According to the map, he was on the outskirts of a city or town called Appenweier, ten miles from the border at Kehl, directly across the Rhine from Strasbourg.

He walked along the road, running into the grass whenever he saw the headlights of a car in either direction. He had traveled perhaps five or six miles—there was no way to tell—and knew that he could go no farther.

In the jungles he had rested, knowing that rest was as much a weapon as a gun, the eyes and the mind far more lethal when alert than a dozen steel weapons strapped to his body.

He found a short ravine that bordered a brook; the rocks would be his fortress—he fell asleep.

Valerie walked out of the Charles De Gaulle Airport on the arm of the man from the Sûreté, Prudhomme, having accepted the scrap of paper with his telephone number but volunteering nothing. They approached the cabstand on the platform and Prudhomme spoke. "I will make myself clear, madame. You may take a taxi here and I shall bid you *adieu,* or you may permit me to drive you wherever you like—perhaps to another taxi stand in the city, to go wherever you wish—and I will know if anyone is following you."

"You would?"

"In thirty-two years, even a fool learns something. My wife keeps telling me she has no lovers only because I have learned the rudiments of my profession."

"I accept your invitation," interrupted Val, smiling. "I'm terribly tired. A small hotel, perhaps. Le Pont Royal, I know it."

"An excellent choice, but I must say that my wife would welcome you—without any questions."

"My time must be my own, monsieur," said Valerie, climbing into the car.

"D'accord."

"Why are you doing this?" she asked as Prudhomme got behind the wheel. "My husband was a lawyer—*is* a lawyer. The rules can't be that different. Aren't you some kind of accessory —assuming what I know damned well you're assuming?"

"I only wish that you will call me, saying that you are from the Tatiana family. That is my risk and that is my reward."

Converse looked at his watch—a watch taken from a collapsed body so long ago he could not remember when—and saw that it was five-forty-five in the morning, the sun abruptly illuminating his fortress ravine. The stream was below, and so he took care of his necessities downstream and plunged his face into the flow of water upstream.

He had to move; as he remembered, he had five miles to walk to the border.

He reached Kehl. There he bought a razor, reasoning that a priest would maintain his appearance as best he could even under the duress of poor travel accommodations. He shaved at the river depot, then took the ferry across the scenic Rhine to Strasbourg. The customs officials were so deferential to his collar and his passport as well as to his shabby appearance—undoubtedly taken as a sign of the vow of poverty—that he found himself blessing a number of men, and by extension their entire families, as he was passed through the building.

Out on the bustling streets he knew that the first thing he had to do was to get into a hotel room, shower off two days of fear and violence, and have his clothes cleaned or replaced. An impoverished-looking priest would not travel to the expensive wonders of Chamonix; it would be unseemly. But a normally dressed priest would be perfectly acceptable, even desirable, a figure of respectability among the crowds. And a priest he would remain, Converse had decided—the decision here based again on legal experience. Think out—anticipate—what your adversary expects you to do, then do not conform unless you retain the advantage. The hunters of Aquitaine would expect him to shed his priestly habit, as it was his last known means of disguise; he would not do that; there were too many priests in France and too much advantage in being one.

He registered at the Sofitel on the Place Saint-Pierre-le-Jeune and without elaboration explained to the concierge that he had been through a dreadful three days of traveling and would the kind man see to several items he needed rather desperately. He was from a very well-endowed parish in Los Angeles and— An American $100 bill took care of the rest. His suit was cleaned and pressed within the hour, his muddy shoes shined, and two new shirts with clerical collars purchased from a shop "unfortunately quite a distance away on the Quai Kellermann," thus necessitating an additional charge. The gratuities, the expenses and the surcharges for rush service—all were a hotelman's dream. The suntanned priest with a blemish or two on his face, and odd demands based on time, certainly had to come from a "well-endowed" parish. It was worth it. He had checked in at eight-thirty in the morning, and by nine-fifty-five he was ready to make his final arrangements for Chamonix.

He could not risk taking a plane or going by rail; too much had happened to him at airports and on trains—they would be watched. And sooner or later Hermione Geyner's car would be found, and his direction if not his destination would be known. Aquitaine's alarms would go out across the three borders of Germany, France and Switzerland; again the safest way was by automobile. The eagerly accommodating concierge was summoned; a fine rental car was arranged for the youngish monsignor, and a route planned to Geneva, some two hundred thirty-eight miles south.

Of course, he would not cross over into Geneva but would go along the border roads and head for

Chamonix, an hour-plus away. His estimated travel time was between five and six hours; he would reach the base of Mont Blanc by four-thirty in the afternoon, five at the latest. He wasted no time speeding out of Strasbourg on the Alpine Autoroute marked *83* on his map.

Valerie dressed as the first light silhouetted the irregularly shaped buildings of Paris outside her windows on the Boulevard Raspail. She had not been able to sleep, nor had she made any attempt to to do so; she had lain awake pondering the words of the strange Frenchman from the Sûreté who could not speak officially. She had been tempted to tell him the truth but knew she would not, not yet, perhaps not at all, for the possibility of a trap was considerable—revelations based on truth could too easily be employed to corner the hunted. Still, his plea had the ring of truth, his own truth, not someone else's: "Call and say you are from the Tatiana family. That is my wish and my reward."

Joel would have an opinion. If the man was not simply bait put out by Aquitaine, it was a crack in their strategy the generals knew nothing about. She hoped he was his own man, but to trust him at this point was impossible.

She had read the domestic schedules provided by Air France on the plane from Los Angeles and knew the routing she would take to Chamonix. Air Touraine had four flights daily to Annecy, the nearest airport to Chamonix and Mont Blanc. She had hoped to make a reservation on the 7:00 A.M. flight last night but the sudden, unnerving intrusion of Prudhomme had ruled it out, and by the time she called Touraine from the Pont Royal there were no seats—it was summer and Mont Blanc was a tourist attraction. Nevertheless, she was on standby for the eleven o'clock flight. It was better to be at Orly Airport, better to be in the crowds, as Joel insisted.

She took the open, brass-grilled elevator down to the lobby, paid her bill, and asked for a taxi.

"A quelle heure, madame?"

"Maintenant, s'il vous plaît."

"Dans quelques minutes."

"Merci."

The taxi arrived and Val went outside, greeted by a surly, sleepy-eyed driver who had no intention of getting out of the cab to help her in and was only vaguely willing to accept her patronage.

"Orly, s'il vous plaît."

The driver started up, reached the corner and swung his wheel to the left to make a rapid U-turn so as to head back into the Raspail toward the expressway leading to the airport. The intersection appeared to be deserted. It was not.

The crash behind them was close by and sudden—metal striking metal as glass shattered and tires screeched. The driver slammed on his brakes, screaming in shock and fear as the taxi veered into the curb. Val was thrown against the front seat, her knees scraping the floor. Awkwardly she started to get up as the driver leaped from the cab yelling at the offending parties behind.

Suddenly the right rear door opened and the

lined, weary face of Prudhomme was above her, a trickle of blood rolling down from a gash in his forehead. He spoke quickly, quietly. "Go, madame—wherever it is you go. No one will follow you now."

"*You?* . . . You've been here all night! You were waiting for me, watching. It was you who crashed into that car!"

"There is no time. I will send your driver back. I must make out my tedious report while scattering a few items in the man's car, and you must leave. Now—before others learn."

"That name!" cried Val. "It was *Tatiana?*"

"Yes."

"Thank you!"

"*Au revoir. Bonne chance.*" The man from the Sûreté ducked away and ran back to the two Frenchmen shouting at each other behind the taxi.

It was three-twenty in the afternoon when Converse saw the sign: SAINT-JULIEN EN GENEVOIS—15 KM. He had rounded the border of Switzerland, the autoroute to Chamonix directly ahead, east of Geneva, just south of Annemasse. He would reach Mont Blanc in something over an hour; he had done it! He had also driven as he had never before driven in his life, the powerful Citröen responding to his pilot's touch, his pilot's mind oblivious to everything but the sweep in front of him, the equipment around him—the feel of the hard road beneath as he took the Alpine curves. He had stopped to refuel once at Pontarlier, where he drank steaming hot tea from a vending machine. Since he had left the expressway for the shorter distance of the mountain roads, his speed depended on his every reaction being instantaneous and accurate. An hour now. *Be there, Val. Be there, my love!*

Valerie looked at her watch ready to scream —as she had wanted to scream since six-thirty in the morning at Orly Airport. It was four-ten in the afternoon, and the entire day had been filled with one crisis after another, from the crash in the Boulevard Raspail, and Prudhomme's revelation that she was being followed, to her arrival at Annecy on the one o'clock flight from Paris —itself delayed by a malfunctioning luggage door. Her nerves were stretched to the outer limits, but she knew above all that she could not lose her control. Doing so would only rivet attention on her; it briefly had.

There were no seats on the seven o'clock flight and the eleven o'clock plane had been over-booked. Only those with tickets in their hands were permitted through the gate. She had protested so angrily that people began staring at her. Then she had retreated to the soft-spoken bribe, which only served to irritate the clerk—not because he was morally offended but because he could not accommodate her and accept the money. Again passengers behind and on both sides, in both lines, had looked over as the clerk admonished her with true Gallic hauteur. It was no way to get to Chamonix alive, Val had thought, and had accepted a ticket on the one o'clock flight.

The plane landed at Annecy over a half-hour

late, several minutes after three, and the subsequent crush at the taxi platform caused her to behave in a way she generally tried to avoid. Being a relatively tall woman—tall in appearance, certainly—she knew the effect she provoked when she looked down disdainfully at those around her. A genetic preordination had made her privileged, didn't they know? Foolishly, too many people accepted the posturing as proof of innate superiority; the women were intimidated, the men both intimidated and sexually aroused. The tactic had gained her a few forward places in the taxi line, but the line was still long. Then she had happened to glance to her right; at the far end of the platform were glistening limousines, with several chauffeurs leaning against them, smoking cigarettes, picking their teeth and chattering. *What in heaven's name was she doing?* She had broken away from the line, opening her purse as she ran.

Her final frustration now was the result of something she should have remembered. There was a point in the theatrical setting that was the wondrous "village" of Chamonix where automobiles could not pass and only small official vehicles and jitneys for tourists were allowed. She got out of the limousine and walked rapidly down the wide, crowded boulevard. She could see the large red cable-car terminal in the distance. Somewhere above, above the clouds, was Joel. Her Joel. She could not stop herself; she did not try to maintain the control she had imposed on herself all day. She began to run—faster, faster! *Be up there, my darling! Be alive, my darling—my only darling!*

It was ten minutes to five when Converse
screeched into the parking lot; he slammed on the
brakes and leaped out of the car. There had been
traffic on the Mont Blanc autoroute, a holdover
at the new construction over the vast gorge
bridge. Every muscle in his right leg had been
cramped by the exertion of seizing every
opportunity to swing around the lethargic traffic.
He was *here!* He was in Chamonix, the majestic
splendor of the Alps in front of him, the village
below. He started running, taking swallows of
breath from the clear air of the mountains,
forgetting the pain—for she *had* to be there!
*Please, Val, make it! I love you so . . . goddamn
it, I need you so! Be there!*

She stood outside the cable lift looking at the
clouds below on the mountains that formed a wall
of mist hiding all earthly concerns. She shivered in
the Alpine cold but she could not leave. She stood
by the stone railing, by a thick mountain telescope
through which tourists could observe the wonders
of the Alpine world for a few francs. She was
frightened to death that he would not come
—could not come. *Death.*

It was the last cable car, none were permitted
after the sun descended over the western
peaks—cables were suddenly frozen with
shadows. Except for the bartender and several
customers inside the glass doors of the bar, she
was the only one there. *Joel! I told you to stay
alive! Please do what I said, my darling—my only*

darling! My only love!

The cable car laboriously approached, then screechingly came to a stop. There was no one there. It was empty! *Death.*

And then he walked into view, a tall man in a clerical collar, and the top of the world made sense again. He stepped out of the car and she ran to him as he ran to her. They embraced, holding each other as they had never held each other as man and wife.

"I love you!" he whispered. "Oh, *God,* I love you."

She pulled back, holding his shoulders, tears filling her eyes. "You're alive, you're here! You did what I asked you to do."

"What I had to do," he said. "Because it was you."

35

They slept naked, their bodies together, their arms around each other, for a while pushing out the world as they knew it to be, a world they would face in the morning. But for a time there had to be something for themselves, for each other, giving and receiving, precious hours alone, speaking in whispers, trying to understand what they had lost and why, each telling the other it would never be lost again.

When morning came, they wanted to deny its arrival, yet not completely. There *was* the world as they knew it, and there was another world as the generals of Aquitaine would have it.

They ordered Continental breakfasts and an extra pot of coffee. While Val combed her hair Joel went to the window and looked down at the colorful, vibrant town of Chamonix. Hoses pouring out water were seemingly everywhere —the streets were being washed down. The storefronts were splashed until they glistened. Chamonix was preparing for the onslaught of summer tourists—thinking of which, mused Converse, they had been lucky to find rooms. They had gone to three hotels—the first was nearly a disaster before they reached the desk. "For God's sake, get rid of that *collar!*" Valerie had whispered. None of the three had anything available, but the fourth, the Croix Blanche, had just received a cancellation.

"I'll go out and get you some clothes later," said Val, coming up behind him, placing her head on his shoulder.

"I've missed that," he said, turning, putting his arms around her. "I've missed you. So much."

"We've found each other, darling. That's all that matters." There was a knock on the door, the polite knock of a waiter. "That'll be the coffee. Go use my toothbrush."

They sat across from each other at the small marble table in front of the window. It was time, and they both knew it. Joel placed a sheet of hotel stationery beside his coffee and a hotel pen on top.

"I still can't get over my aunt!" said Val suddenly. "How could I have *done* it? How could I not have *known?*"

"A couple of times I asked myself the same question." Converse smiled gently. "About you, I mean."

"I'm surprised you didn't throw me out of the cable car."

"Only crossed my mind twice."

"God, I was *stupid!*"

"No, you were desperate," corrected Joel. "Just as she was desperate. You were grasping at possibilities, for help. She was desperately trying to go back to the only meaningful days of her life. A person can be terribly convincing feeling like that. She had the proper words, all those esoteric phrases you'd heard all your life. You believed her. I would have believed her too."

"You're devastating when you're kind, darling. Go easy, it's morning."

"Tell me about Sam Abbott," he said.

"Yes, of course, but before I do, I want you to know we're not alone. There's a man in Paris, an inspector from the Sûreté, who knows you didn't kill René and you couldn't have killed the one they called a chauffeur at the George Cinq."

Startled, Joel leaned forward over his coffee. "But I did kill that man. God knows I didn't mean to—I thought he was reaching for a gun, not a radio—but I fought him, I smashed his head into the wall; he died from a cranial something-or-other."

"No, he didn't. He was killed in the hospital. He was suffocated; his lungs were collapsed by suffocation. It was unrelated to his injuries, that's what Prudhomme said. As he put it, if you didn't kill the driver and you didn't kill Rene, how many others didn't you kill? He thinks you've been set up; he doesn't know why any more than he can understand why evidence has been suppressed, or suddenly found when it should have been found earlier if it existed—in this case your fingerprints in Mattilon's office. He wants to help; he gave me a telephone number where we can reach him."

"Can we trust him?" asked Joel, writing a note

"I think so. He did something remarkable this morning, but I'll get to that."

"The man at the George Cinq," said Converse softly. "Bertholdier's aide. It's where the running began. It's as though the moment was suddenly seized upon, someone recognizing a possible strategy, not wanting to let the opportunity slip away. 'Brand him a killer now, maybe we can use it, build on it. All it costs is a life.' *Jesus!*" Joel struck a match and lit a cigarette. "Go on," he continued. "Go back. What about Sam?"

She told him everything, starting with the madness at the St. Regis in New York—the frightening telephone call that led to an intense young man racing up the steps and an Army officer running after her down the street.

"The odd thing here," interrupted Converse, "is that those men, that call, might have been legitimate."

"*What?* How? The first one looked like a Hitler youth, and the other was in uniform!"

"Most people in uniform would be the first ones to want the generals of Aquitaine cut loose in a typhoon. Remember, Fitzpatrick said those four dossiers came from way down deep in official vaults, and judging from much of the material, Connal thought there was heavy military input. Maybe my silent partners in Washington are beginning to crawl out of their sewers. Sorry. Go on."

She told him of meeting Sam at the diner in Las Vegas—the married Sam, Sam the father of two young girls. Wincing, Joel listened, all his antennae revolving, catching every turn of phrase, every meaning that might have more than one meaning, trying desperately to find a clue, a way—something, *anything* they might use or act upon. And then he held up his hand, signaling Val to stop.

"The *three* of you were going to Washington?"

"Yes."

"You and Sam and this third person he was going to see, going to talk to—the one he said would know what to do."

"Yes. The man who had Sam killed. He was the *only* one Sam talked to."

"But Abbott said he trusted him. With 'his life,' I think you said."

"Sam said," corrected Valerie. "He was wrong."

"Not necessarily. Sam was easygoing but not easily conned. He chose his friends carefully; he didn't have too many because he knew his rank was vulnerable."

"But he didn't talk with anyone else—"

"I'm sure he didn't, but this other man had to. I know something about crisis conferences in Washington—and that's exactly what Sam meant when he said you were going there. Those meetings don't just happen; some strong words are used to cut a path through the bureaucratic mess. Certainly Sam's name would have been put forward first—he had the status and the rank—and just possibly my name, or yours, or even Delavane's, any of which would have been enough." Converse picked up the pen. "What was his name?"

"Oh, Lord," said Val, closing her eyes, her fingers massaging her forehead. "Let me think. . . . Alan, the first name was Alan. . . . Alan Metzger? Metland . . . ?"

"Was there a rank, a title of some kind?"

"No. *Metcalf!* Alan Metcalf, that was it."

Joel wrote down the name. "Okay, let's get to Paris, the man from the Sûreté."

She began with the odd behavior of the immigration officials, which led to the strange meeting with the weary, rumpled Prudhomme. She reached the end of the Frenchman's startling revelations, repeating herself but filling in all the details she had omitted previously. When she finished, Converse held up his palm for the second time, his mouth open in astonishment, his eyes wide and alive.

"The *Tatiana* family?" he asked incredulously. "Are you certain?"

"Completely. I asked him again this morning."

"This morning? Yes, you said he did something remarkable this morning. What happened?"

"He stayed up all night outside the hotel in his car, and when I left in a taxi shortly after the sun was up he crashed—and I mean crashed—into the car behind us. I was being followed. He told me to hurry up and get out of there. That's when I asked him to repeat the name. It was Tatiana."

"That was the name René told me to use with Cort Thorbecke in Amsterdam. 'Say you're a member of the Tatiana family.' Those were his instructions."

"What does it mean?"

"René didn't go into it too deeply, but I got the drift. Apparently it means some kind of trust, a litmus test that clears someone for a level of information that would be withheld from ninety-nine percent of the people wanting it."

"Why?"

"It sounds crazy, but Mattilon said it was because whoever was part of Tatiana was trusted by the most suspicious people on earth—men who couldn't afford to make a mistake."

"My God, *who?*"

"Russians. Commissars in the Kremlin who float money out to brokers in the West who invest it."

"You're right," said Val. "It's crazy."

"But it works, don't you see? Decent men who for one reason or another found themselves in a world they probably hated, never knowing whom they could trust, figured out a code among themselves. To be a member of the Tatianas is some kind of clearance. It's not only a signal of emergency, it's more than that. It means that whoever sends that signal is all right—in spite of what he may have to do. I'll bet it's one hell of a small circle. René, this Prudhomme, they'd fit into it. And for us it's a key; we can trust it."

"You're in court, aren't you?" said the now and former Mrs. Converse, reaching across the table for his free hand.

"I don't know any other way to do it. Facts, names, tactics; somewhere there's a crack, a road we can take—we *have* to take. Quickly."

"I'd start with Prudhomme," said Val.

"We'll call in his hand but maybe not first. Let's take things in sequence. Are there two phones in here? A certain—ex-wife had me too preoccupied to notice last night."

"She's probably pregnant."

"Wouldn't that be *wonderful?*"

"Down, boy. Yes, there's another phone. It's in the bathroom."

"I want you to call this Metcalf, Alan Metcalf, in Las Vegas. We'll get the number from information. I'll listen."

"What do I say?"

"What name did you and Sam use?"

"The one I told you. Parquette."

"Say that's who's calling, nothing else. Let him make the first move. If it's wrong, I'll know—we'll both know—and I'll hang up. You'll hear me and you hang up, too."

"Suppose he's not there? Suppose I get a wife or a girl friend or a child?"

"Leave your name quickly and say you'll call back in an hour."

Peter Stone sat on the sofa, his feet up on the coffee table. Across, in two armchairs, were the Army captain—out of uniform—and the young Navy lieutenant, also in street clothes.

"We agree, then," said Stone. "We try this Metcalf and hope for the best. If we're wrong—if *I'm* wrong—we could be traced, and don't fool yourselves, you've been seen here, you could be identified. But as I told you before, there comes a time when you have to take a risk you'd rather not take. You're out of safe territory and you hope to Christ you get through it fast. I can't promise that you will. This phone is tapped into another number, a hotel across town, so any trace would be delayed, but only delayed while everyone registered is checked, every room checked. Once that's over with, any experienced telephone repairman could go down in the cellars and find the intercept."

"How much time would that give us?" asked the Army officer.

"It's one of the largest hotels in New York," replied the civilian. "With luck, twenty-four to thirty-six hours."

"Go for it!" ordered the Navy man.

"Oh, for God's sake," said the captain, running his hand through his hair. "Yes, of course, try it, try *him*. But I'm still not sure *why*."

"Scat patterns. It was routine information and easy to get. Abbott wrote out his schedules every day and he was precise about them. There was a preponderance of lunches alone with Metcalf, and dinners with both families at either the Abbott or the Metcalf home. I think he trusted the man, and as a longtime intelligence officer Metcalf was the logical one to go to. Also, there's something else. Along with Converse, all three were prisoners of

895

war in Vietnam.''

"Go for it!'' cried the Navy lieutenant.

"For Christ's sake, find another phrase,'' said the captain.

"It's an answering machine!'' shouted Val, gripping the mouthpiece of the telephone.

Joel came out of the bathroom. "One hour,'' he whispered.

"One hour,'' she said. "Miss Parquette will call back in an hour.'' She hung up.

"And every hour after that,'' added Converse, staring down at the phone. "I don't like this. It's one o'clock in the morning back there, and if there's a wife or children around, someone should have been there.''

"Sam didn't mention a wife or children, except his own.''

"No reason why he would.''

"There could be a dozen explanations, Joel.''

"I just hope it's not the one I keep thinking about.''

"Let me call Prudhomme,'' said Valerie. "Let's use this Tatiana family.''

"Not yet.''

"Why *not?*''

"We need something else—*he* needs something else.'' Suddenly, Converse's gaze fell on the thick envelope addressed to Nathan Simon. It was on the bureau, his false passport on top. "My God, we may *have* it,'' he said quietly. "It's been right there all the time and I didn't see it.''

Val followed his eyes. "The analysis you wrote for Nathan?''

896

"I called it the best brief I ever wrote, but of course it's not a brief at all. It doesn't address points of law except in the widest, most abstract sense, without acceptable evidence to support the accusations. What it does address is the perverted ambitions of powerful men who want to *change* the laws, altering governments, supplanting them with raw military controls, all in the name of *maintaining* the law and preserving the *order* they themselves will be called upon to maintain and preserve. And if 'compromise' means killing—if they intend mounting wholesale assassinations —they can do it."

"What's your *point,* Joel?"

"If I'm going to build a case, I'd better do it the only way I know how—from premise to conclusion based on affidavits, depositions—starting with my own and ending with pretrial examinations."

"What the hell are you talking about?"

"The law, Mrs. Converse," said Joel, picking up the envelope. "And what it's meant to do. I can use most of what's in here—just in a different form. Naturally, I'll want other corroborating depositions, the farther afield the better. That's when you'll call this Prudhomme and join the Tatiana family. Then hopefully we'll reach Sam's friend, Metcalf—goddamn it, he'll have *something* to give us. . . . Finally, I'm going to want to examine at least two of the alleged defendants orally—Leifhelm, for one, and probably Abrahms, maybe Delavane himself."

"You're *mad!*" cried Valerie.

"No, I'm not," said Converse simply. "I'll

need help, I know that. But I've got enough money to hire a couple of squads of miscreants—and once Prudhomme understands, I have an idea he'll know where the union hall is. We've got a lot of work to do, Val. All courts like immaculate manuscripts."

"For Christ's sake, Joel, speak English."

"You're a romantic, Mrs. Converse," he said approaching her. "These are the nuts and bolts you don't find in seascapes."

"They *do* have to be sketched, my darling. And balanced or unbalanced, the colors deliberate— What *are* you talking about?"

"A stenographer—a legal secretary, if you can find one. Someone who's willing to stay here all day and half the night, if need be. Offer three times the going rate."

"Say I find one," said Val. "What in heaven's name are you going to tell her? Or him?"

Joel frowned as he crossed aimlessly to the window. "A novel," he said, turning. "We're writing a novel. The first twenty or thirty pages are to be read as an upcoming court case, a trial."

"Based on real people, men everyone's read about?"

"It's a new kind of fiction, but it's only a novel. That's all it is."

Morning came to New York and Stone was alone again. The Navy lieutenant and the Army captain were back at their desks in Washington. It was better this way; they could not help him, and the less they were seen around the apartment, the more likely they might escape detection if the hammer came down. And the hammer *could* come down, Stone knew it. It was as clear as the fact that Colonel Alan Metcalf was the chord they needed to start the music. "Without him," as Johnny Reb might have said in the old days, "the tune ain't gonna get out of the fiddle—no stompin' unless he shows up." But could he show up? wondered the former operations officer for Central Intelligence. To all intents and purposes he had disappeared, that was the word from Nellis, and the investigating unit did not pretend to understand or appreciate his absence. That, too, was the word and it was delivered harshly.

But Stone understood. Metcalf now knew what he knew—what they knew—and the colonel would not play by any rules written in the regulations, not if he was any good. Not if he was alive. And the ex-agent also understood something else when it came to telephone answering machines and intelligence personnel. The equipment was adaptable and sophisticated, courtesy of the American taxpayer and, considering the extraordinary waste, one of his better investments. Metcalf would play it well—if he was alive and any good. He would use a remote, programming it and reprogramming it, hearing what he wanted to hear, erasing what he wanted to erase, and leaving in certain information, preferably misleading. There would also be a code, probably changed daily, that if not inserted accurately would melt the tape with a ten-second burst of microwaves—all standard. If he was any good. If he was alive.

Stone counted on both—that the colonel was

good and that he was alive. There was no point in thinking otherwise; that only led to staying in Johnny Reb's hammock or "goin' fishin'," doing whatever one did as a robot. Which was why Stone had left a message on Metcalf's machine an hour ago at six-thirty-five. He had chosen a name Converse's wife—former wife—would have to have relayed to the dead Samuel Abbott. *Marcus Aurelius ascending. Respond and erase, please.* Then Stone had given the telephone number at the apartment, which, if traced, would lead the tracers to the Hilton Hotel on Fifty-third Street.

There was only one other person in the world Stone wished he could reach, but that man was "on holiday—we have no means of getting in touch." The words were patently a lie, but to challenge that lie would mean that Peter would have to say more than he wanted to say. The man was Derek Belamy, chief of Clandestine Operations for Britain's M.I.6 and one of the only real friends Stone had ever had in all his years with the Central Intelligence Agency. Belamy was such a good friend that when Peter was station chief in London, the Englishman had told him bluntly to get out for a while before the whisky took over altogether and his ass was nailed to an alcoholic cross: "I have a doctor who'll certify a minor breakdown, Peter. I've a guest cottage on the grounds in Kent. Stay there, get well, old boy."

Stone had refused, and it was the most destructive decision he had ever made. The rest was the drunken nightmare Belamy had predicted.

But it was not Derek's concern for a friend that

made Peter want to reach him. It was Belamy's brilliance, his perceptiveness, quietly concealed behind a pleasant, even prosaic exterior. And the knowledge that Derek Belamy had the pulse of Europe in his head, and given the most basic information, could smell out a Delavane operation. And, in fact, thought Stone hopefully, he was smelling them out now in Ireland—certainly where he was now. Sooner or later—preferably sooner—Belamy would return his call. When he did, a munitions shipment from Beloit, Wisconsin, would be described in full. Derek Belamy loathed the Delavanes of this world. His old friend would become an ally against the generals.

The telephone rang; Stone looked at it and let it ring again. *Metcalf?* He reached over and picked it up. "Yes?"

"Aurelius?"

"Somehow I knew you'd come through, Colonel."

"Who the hell *are* you?"

"The name's Stone and we're on the same side, at least I think we are. However, you wear a uniform and I don't, so I need a little more confidence in you. Can you understand that?"

"You're one of those bastards in D.C. who sent him out!"

"You're warmer, Colonel. I came on late, but yes, I am one of those bastards. What happened to General Abbott?"

"He was killed, you son of a bitch! . . . I assume this phone is clean."

"For at least twenty-four hours. Then we all

disappear, just like you disappeared."

"No remorse? No conscience? Do you know what you've *done?*"

"We don't have time for that, Colonel. Perhaps later, if there's a later for us. . . . Get *off* it, soldier! I've *lived* with this! *Now.* Where do we meet? Where are you?"

"Okay, okay," said the obviously exhausted Air Force officer. "I took a dozen different flights. I'm in—where the hell am I?—in Knoxville, Tennessee. I've got a flight to Washington in twenty minutes."

"Why?"

"To blow this fucking thing out of the air, what *else?*"

"Forget it, you're a dead man. I'd think you'd have learned that by now. You set up something on the information Abbott gave you, right?"

"Yes."

"And *he* was blown out of the air, right?"

"Goddamn you, shut up!"

"You should have learned. They're where you can't see them or find them. But the wrong word to the wrong person and they can find you."

"I *know* that!" shouted Metcalf. "But I've been in this business for twenty years. There's got to be *someone* I can trust!"

"Let's talk about it, Colonel. Scratch D.C. and fly up to New York. I'll get a room at the Algonquin—actually, I've already reserved one."

"What name?"

"What else? Marcus."

"You're on, but as long as we're in this deep I should tell you. The woman's been trying to reach

902

me since one o'clock this morning."

"Converse's *wife?*"

"Yes."

"We need her. We need *him!*"

"I'll reprogram the machine. The Algonquin?"

"That's it."

"He's from New York, isn't he? I mean he's a New Yorker."

"Whatever that means, yes. He's lived here for years."

"I hope he's bright—they're bright."

"Neither of them would be alive now if they weren't *very* bright, Colonel."

"See you in a few hours, Stone."

The civilian hung up the phone, his hands shaking, his eyes on a bottle of bourbon across the room. *No!* There would be no drinks, he had promised himself. He got out of the chair and went to the bed, where his small suitcase was open, a gaping mouth waiting to be filled. He filled it, leaving the bottle of whisky on the table, and went outside to the elevators down the hall.

I, Joel Harrison Converse, an attorney admitted to practice before the bar of the State of New York and employed by the firm of Talbot, Brooks and Simon, 666 Fifth Avenue, New York City, New York, arrived in Geneva, Switzerland, on August 9 for legal conferences on behalf of our client, the Comm Tech Corporation, for the purpose of finalizing a contemplated business association referred to hereafter as the Comm Tech-Bern merger. On the morning of August 10, at approximately eight o'clock, I was contacted by the chief counsel representing the Bern Group, Mr. Avery Preston Halliday of San Francisco, California. As he was an American only recently retained by the Swiss companies, I agreed to meet with him to clarify the existing points of argument and our positions with respect to them. When I arrived at the café on the Quai du Mont Blanc, I recognized Mr. Halliday as a student and close friend I had known years ago at the Taft School in Watertown, Connecticut. His name then was Avery P. Fowler. Mr. Halliday readily confirmed this fact, explaining that his surname had been changed upon the death of his father and the remarriage of his mother to a John Halliday of San Francisco. The explanation was acceptable, the circumstances, however, were not. Mr. Halliday had ample prior time and opportunity to apprise me of his identity—the identity with which I was familiar—but did not do so. There was a reason. On that morning of August 10, Mr. Halliday sought a confidential meeting with the undersigned regarding a matter totally unrelated to the Comm Tech-Bern merger. This meeting was the primary reason for his being in Geneva. It was the first of many disturbing revelations. . . .

If the very proper and distant British stenographer had the slightest interest in the material she was transcribing in segments from dictation to the typewritten page, she did not show it. Her thin lips pursed, her gray hair knotted into a forbidding bun on the top of her head, she performed like a machine, as if everything was accepted in rote and by rote. Valerie's somewhat guarded explanation that her husband was an American novelist intrigued by recent events in Europe was greeted with a cold stare and the gratuitous information that the legal secretary never watched television and rarely read the newspapers. She was a member of the Franco-Italian Alpine Society, whose purpose was to defend the natural endowments being eroded by man; working for the society took up all her time and energy when she was not earning a living to enable her to remain in her beloved mountains. She was an automaton putting in her time; one could dictate the book of Genesis and Val doubted the woman would know what she was typing.

It was the seventh hour and there was still no answer at Alan Metcalf's telephone in Las Vegas. Only a machine. It was time for the eighth call.

"If we don't get him now," said Converse grimly, above the quiet tapping of the typewriter across the room, "go ahead and reach Prudhomme. I wanted to talk to this Metcalf first, but it's possible that—it may not be possible."

"What difference does it make? You need help quickly, and he's willing to help."

"The difference is I know where Prudhomme's coming from, you've told me. I got an idea what he can do and what he can't do, but I don't know anything about Metcalf—except that Sam put him way up on a high priority. Whoever I call first

I've got to make specific statements to him, accusations and observations that'll blow his mind. Those are commitments, Val, and I have to go with the strongest. . . . Try Metcalf again." Joel turned and headed for the telephone in the bathroom as Valerie dialed the international codes for Las Vegas, Nevada.

"Caller C, message received. Please reidentify yourself twice, followed by a slow count to ten. Stay on the line."

Joel put the phone down on the edge of the basin and rushed out to the bedroom-sitting room. He walked over to Val, holding up his hand as he reached for a pencil on the desk. He wrote out the words: "Go ahead. Stay calm. P.S.E."

"This is Miss Parquette speaking," said Valerie, frowning, bewildered. "This is Miss Parquette speaking. One, two, three, four . . ."

Converse returned to the bathroom, picked up the telephone and listened.

". . . eight, nine, ten."

Silence. Finally, there were two sharp clicks and the metallic voice came back on the line. "Confirmed, thank you. This is the second tape and will be microed out when completed. Listen carefully. There is a place on an island well known for its tribal nights. The King will be in his chair. That's it. We are burning."

Joel hung up the phone and studied the half-legible words he had hastily scribbled in soap on the mirror above the basin. The door opened and Valerie walked in, a piece of paper in her hand.

"I wrote it down," she said, handing it to him.

"I wrote it sideways—your way is better. Christ, a *riddle!*"

"No more than the one you gave me. What in heaven's name does 'P.S.E.' mean?"

" 'Psychological Stress Evaluator,' " answered Converse, leaning against the wall and reading Metcalf's message. He looked up at her. "It's a voice scanner you can attach to a phone or a recording machine that supposedly tells you whether the person you're talking to is lying or not. Larry Talbot played around with one for a while but claimed he couldn't find anyone telling the truth, including his ninety-two-year-old mother. He threw it away."

"Does it work?"

"They say it's much more accurate than a lie detector, and I suppose it is if you know how to read it or use it. It worked in your case. Your voice was matched against the other calls you made, which means this Metcalf is into pretty high-tech equipment. That scanner tripped the second tape, and it was all done by remote, from another phone, otherwise he would have answered himself after you passed the test."

"But if I passed, why the riddle? Why an island with tribal nights?"

"Because any machine like that can be beaten. It's why they're not admissible in court. Years ago Willie Sutton was wired into a lie detector, and according to the result, he never even broke into a piggy bank, much less Chase Manhattan. Metcalf was willing to take a risk, but not all the way. He's running too." Converse returned to what Val had written down.

"An island." Val spoke softly, reading the soaped words on the mirror. "Tribes . . . The Caribe tribes; they were all through the Antilles. Or Jamaica—tribal nights, Obeah rituals, voodoo rites in Haiti. Even the Bahamas—the Lucayan Indians—they held puberty rituals, they all did."

"You impress me," said Joel, looking up from the paper. "How come?"

"Art courses," she replied. "Those nuts and bolts you won't grant us that go into the makeup of a culture's visual work. . . . And it doesn't fit. It's too loose."

"Why? It could mean someplace in the Caribbean, some resort that's advertised a lot. The King is an emperor and that has to mean Delavane—Mad Marcus, as in Aurelius. It has to be Marcus; no one's named Aurelius! . . . All those television commercials, the newspaper ads—pictures of people doing the limbo under torches with costumed blacks smiling down benignly, counting the dollars. Which *one?*"

"Too loose," repeated Val. "Too abstract—blocks and geometric shapes without specifics—no representational images."

"Now what the hell are *you* talking about?" objected Converse.

"It's too wide, Joel, too many places to choose from, places you might not know anything about. It has to be closer, more familiar to you or to me, something we can recognize. Like Brueghel or Vermeer, littered with specific detail."

"They sound like dentists."

Valerie took the paper from him. *"Manhattan's*

an island," she said softly, reading and frowning again.

"If there are torches and tribal puberty rites, it's not my part of town."

"Not tribal rites, tribal *nights,"* corrected Val. "Tribal—not Black but Red? 'The King will be in his chair'—chair . . . table. His *table.* Tribal . . . nights. Nights! That's where we're misreading it. *Nights!"*

"How else can you read it?"

"Not nights but *knights!* With a *k!"*

"And a table," broke in Converse. "Knights of the Round Table."

"But *not* the King Arthur legend, not Camelot. Much nearer, much closer. Tribal—*American* natives. American *Indians."*

"Algonquins. The Round Table!"

"The Algonquin Hotel," cried Valerie. "That's it, that's what he meant!"

"We'll know in a few minutes," said Joel. "Go inside and place the call."

The wait was both intolerable and interminable. Converse looked at his face in the mirror; perspiration began to drench his face, the salt stinging his scrapes and burning his eyes. Far more telling, his hand shook and his breath was short. The Algonquin switchboard answered and Val asked for a Mr. Marcus. There was a stretch of silence, and when the operator came back on the line, Joel thought he would smash the telephone into the mirror.

"There are two Marcuses registered, ma'am. Which one did you wish to speak to?"

"Already it's a rotten day!" Val broke in

suddenly over the phone, startling Converse with her words. "My boss, the *clown,* told me to call Mr. Marcus at the Algonquin right away and give him the time and place for lunch. Now the clown's disappeared to a meeting somewhere outside and I'm left holding it. Sorry, dear, I didn't mean to take it out on you."

"It's okay, hon, we got a few like that around here."

"Maybe you can help me. Which Marcus is which? Maybe I'll recognize a first name or a company."

"Sure. Lemme plug into Big Reggie. We all gotta stick together when it comes to the clowns, right? . . . Okay, here they are. Marcus, Myron. Sugarman's Original Replicas, Los Angeles. And Marcus, Peter . . . not much help here, sweetie. Just says Georgetown, Washington, D.C."

"That's the one. Peter. I'm sure of it. Thanks, dear."

"Glad to be of help, hon. I'll ring now."

The folded *New York Times* resting on his knee, Stone inked in the last two words of the crossword puzzle and looked at his watch. It had taken him nine minutes, nine minutes of relief; he wished it had been longer. One of the joys of having been station chief in London was the London *Times* crossword. He could always count on at least a half-hour when he could forget problems in the search for words and meanings.

The telephone rang. Stone stared at it, his pulse accelerating, his throat suddenly dry. No one knew he had checked into the Algonquin under the name of Marcus. *No* one! . . . Yes, there was someone, but he was in the air, flying up from Knoxville, Tennessee. What had gone *wrong?* Or had he been wrong about Metcalf? Was the supposedly angry, sermonizing Air Force intelligence officer one of *them?* Had his own instincts, honed over a thousand years of sorting out garbage, deserted him because he so desperately sought an opening, an escape from a steel net that was dropping down on him? He got out of the chair and walked slowly, in fear, to the bedside table. He picked up the insistently ringing phone.

"Yes?"

"Alan Metcalf?" said the soft, firm voice of a woman.

"Who?" Stone was so thrown by the name he could barely concentrate, barely think!

"I beg your pardon, I have the wrong room."

"Wait! Don't hang up. Metcalf's on his way here."

"I'm sorry."

"Please! Oh Christ, *please!* I was tired, I was *asleep.* We've been up night and day. . . . Metcalf. I talked with him two hours ago—he said he was going to reprogram his machine, that someone was trying to reach him since one o'clock this morning. He had to get *out* of there. A man was killed, a pilot. It was *not* an *accident!* Am I making sense to you?"

"Why should I talk to you?" asked the woman. "So you can trace the call?"

"Listen to me," said Stone, his voice now in total control. "Even if I wanted to—and I

911

don't—this is a hotel, not a private line, and to do what you suggest would take at least three men on the trunk lines and another controlling the switchboard. And even with such a unit it would be at least four minutes before they could isolate the wire and send out a tracer signal—which initially would only give us an area location, not a specific phone. *And* if you were calling from overseas we'd have to have another man, an expert, *in* that specific location to narrow it down to *perhaps* a twenty-mile radius, but only if you stayed on *your* phone for at least six minutes. . . . Now, for God's sake, give me at least *two!*"

"Go on. Quickly!"

"I'm going to assume something. Maybe I shouldn't, but you're a clever woman, Mrs. DePinna, and you could do it."

"DePinna?"

"Yes. You left a telephone book open to the blue pages, the government pages. When the *accident* happened in Nevada, I made a simple connection with a listing, and two hours ago I learned I was right. Metcalf returned my call—from a pay phone at an airport. A pilot, a general, had talked to him at length. He's joining us. You ran from the wrong people, Mrs. DePinna. But as for what I'm thinking, I think the man we want to find is listening on this phone."

"There's no one else here!"

"Please don't interrupt me, I've got to use every second." Stone's voice suddenly became stronger. *"Leifhelm, Bertholdier, Van Headmer, Abrahms.* And a fifth man we can't identify, an

912

Englishman who's down so deep he makes Burgess, Maclean and Blunt look like amateurs. We don't know who he is, but he's there, using warehouses in Ireland and offshore cargo ships, and long-forgotten airfields to transport materials that shouldn't be going out. Those dossiers came from *us, Converse!* We sent them to you! You're a lawyer, and you know that by using your name I'm incriminating myself *or* committing suicide if anyone's taping this. I'll go further. We sent you out through Preston Halliday in Geneva. We sent you out to build a legal case—from left field—so we could abort this thing with a minimum of fallout, sending all those goddamned idiots back to reality. But we were wrong! They were much further ahead than we ever suspected—*we* ever suspected—but not Beale on Mykonos. He was dead right, and he's dead because he was right! Incidentally, he was the 'man from San Francisco.' It was his five hundred thousand dollars; he came from a rich family, which, among other things, bequeathed him a conscience. Think back to Mykonos! To what he told you —what his life was all about. From celebrated soldier to a scholar—to a killing that must have killed a part of him to commit. . . . He said you almost caught him up on a couple of things he didn't mean to say. He said you were a good lawyer, a good choice. Preston Halliday was a student of his at Berkeley, and when this broke a year and a half ago, when Halliday realized what Delavane was doing and how he was being used, he went to Beale, who was about to retire. The rest you can figure out.''

The woman's voice interrupted. "Say what I want to hear you say. *Say* it!"

"Of course I will! Converse didn't kill Peregrine and he didn't kill the commander of NATO. Both of them were marked by Delavane —George Marcus Delavane—because both those men would have taken him and his ilk to the mat! They were convenient, *very* convenient, targets. I don't know about the others—I don't know what you've been through—but we broke a liar in Bad Godesberg, the major from the embassy who put *you, Converse,* at the Adenauer Bridge! He doesn't know it, but we broke him, and we learned something. We think we know where Connal Fitzpatrick is. We think he's alive!"

A male voice intruded. "You *bastards,*" said Joel Converse.

"Thank *God!*" said the civilian, sitting down on the hotel bed. "Now we can talk. We have to talk. Tell me everything you can. This phone is clean."

Twenty minutes later, his hands trembling, Peter Stone hung up the phone.

36

General Jacques-Louis Bertholdier ceased the rushing pelvic thrusts of intercourse, withdrew himself from the moaning dark-haired woman beneath him, and rolled over, grabbing the telephone.

"*Yes?*" he shouted angrily. And then he

listened, his flushed face growing ashen as his organ collapsed. "Where did it happen?" he whispered, not in confidence but in sudden fear. "The Boulevard Raspail? The charges? . . . *Narcotics? Impossible!*"

Holding the phone, the general swung his legs over the side of the bed, listening carefully, concentrating as he stared at the wall. The naked woman rose to her knees and leaned into him, her breasts pressed into his back, her open mouth caressing his ear, her teeth gently biting his lobe.

Bertholdier suddenly, viciously, swung his arm back, cracking the phone into the woman's face, sending her reeling to the other side of the bed, blood erupting from her broken lower lip.

"Repeat that, please," he said into the phone. "It's obvious, then, isn't it? The man cannot be questioned further, can he? There is always the larger strategy to consider, losses to be anticipated in the field, no? It is the hospital all over again, I'm afraid. See to it, then, like the fine officer you are. The Legion's loss was our immense gain. . . . Oh? What is it? The arresting officer was *Prudhomme?*" Bertholdier paused, his breathing steady and audible; then he spoke, rendering a command decision. "A stubborn bureaucrat from the Sûreté will not let go, will he? . . . He is your second assignment to be carried out with your usual expertise before the day is over. Call me when both are accomplishments, and consider yourself the aide to General Jacques-Louis Bertholdier."

The general hung up and turned to the dark-haired woman, who was wiping her lips with a bed sheet, the expression in her eyes an admixture of anger, embarrassment and fear.

"Apologies, my dear," he said courteously. "But you must leave now. I have telephone calls to make, business to attend to."

"I will not come *back!*" cried the woman defiantly.

"You will come back," said the legend of France standing up, his body rigid in its nakedness. "If you are asked."

Erich Leifhelm walked rapidly into his study and directly over to the large desk, where he took the phone from a white-jacketed attendant, dismissing the man with a nod. The instant the door was closed he spoke. "What is it?"

"The Geyner car was found, Herr General."

"Where?"

"Appenweier."

"And what is *that?*"

"A town fifteen or eighteen kilometers from Kehl. In the Alsace."

"Strasbourg! He crossed into France! He *was* a priest!"

"I don't understand, Herr—"

"We never *thought* . . . *!* Never mind! Whom have you got in the sector?"

"Only one man. The man with the police."

"Tell him to hire others. Send them into Strasbourg! Look for a priest!"

"Get *out* of here!" roared Chaim Abrahms as his wife walked through the kitchen door. "This is no place for you now!"

916

"The Testaments say otherwise, my husband —yet not my husband," said the frail woman dressed in black; a circle of soft white hair framed gentle features and her brown eyes were dark, receding mirrors. "Will you deny the Bible you employ so readily when it suits you? It is not all thunder and vengeance. Must I read it to you?"

"Read *nothing! Say* nothing! These are matters for men!"

"Men who kill? Men who use the primitive savagery of the Scriptures to justify the spilling of children's blood? My *son's* blood? I wonder what the mothers of the Masada would have said had they been permitted to speak their hearts. . . . Well, I speak now, *General.* You will not kill anymore. You will not use this house to move your armies of death, to plot your tactics of death—always your holy tactics, Chaim, your holy vengeance."

Abrahms slowly got out of the chair. "What are you talking about?"

"You think I haven't heard you? Phone calls in the middle of the night, calls from men who sound like you, who speak of killing so easily—"

"You *listened!*"

"Several times. You were breathing so hard you heard nothing but the sound of your own voice, your own orders to kill. Whatever you're doing will be done without you now, my husband—yet not my husband. The killing is over for you. It lost its purpose years ago, but you could not stop. You invented new reasons until there was no reason left in you."

The sabra's wife removed her right hand from

the folds of her black dress. She was holding Abrahms' service automatic. The soldier slapped his holster in disbelief, then suddenly lunged toward the woman he had lived with for thirty-eight years and grabbed her wrist, spinning her around. She would not relent! She resisted him, clawing at his face as he crashed her back into the wall, twisting her hand in the attempt to disarm her.

The sound of the explosion filled the kitchen, and the woman who had borne him four children, the last finally a son, fell to the floor at his feet. In horror Chaim Abrahms looked down. Her dark-brown eyes were wide, her black dress drenched with blood, half her chest torn away.

The telephone rang. Abrahms ran to the wall and grabbed it, screaming, "The children of Abraham *will not be denied!* A bloodbath will follow—we will have the land delivered to us by God! Judea, Samaria—they are *ours!*"

"Stop it!" roared the voice over the line. "Stop it, *Jew!*"

"Who calls me *Jew* calls me *righteous!*" yelled Chaim Abrahms, the tears falling down his face, as he stared at the dead woman with the wide brown eyes. "I have sacrificed with *Abraham!* No one could ask *more!*"

"I ask more!" came the cry of the cat. "I ask *always* more!"

"Marcus?" whispered the sabra, closing his eyes and collapsing against the wall, turning away from the corpse. "Is it you . . . my leader, my *conscience?* Is it you?"

"It is I, Chaim, my friend. We have to move

fast. Are the units in place?"

"Yes. Scharhörn. Twelve units in place, all trained, prepared. Death is no consideration."

"That's what I had to know," said Delavane.

"They await your codes, my general." Abrahms gasped, then began to weep uncontrollably.

"What is it, Chaim? Get hold of yourself!"

"She's dead. My wife lies dead at my *feet!*"

"My God, what *happened?*"

"She overheard, she listened . . . she tried to kill me. We fought and she's dead."

"A terrible, terrible loss, my dear friend. You have my deepest affection and condolences in your bereavement."

"Thank you, Marcus."

"You know what you must do, don't you, Chaim?"

"Yes, Marcus. I know."

There was a knock at the door. Stone got out of the chair and picked up his gun awkwardly from the table. In all the years of sorting out garbage, he had fired a weapon only once. He had blown a foot off a KGB informant in Istanbul for the simple reason that the man had been exposed while drunk and had lunged at him with a knife. That one incident was enough. Stone did not like guns.

"Yes?" he said, the automatic at his side.

"Aurelius," replied the voice behind the door.

Stone opened it and greeted his visitor. "Metcalf?"

"Yes. Stone?"

"Come in. And I think we'd better change the code."

"I suppose I could use 'Aquitaine,' " said the intelligence officer, walking into the room.

"Somehow I'd rather you didn't."

"Somehow I don't think I will. Do you have coffee?"

"I'll get some. You look exhausted."

"I've looked better on a beach in Hawaii," said the slender, muscular middle-aged Air Force man. He was dressed in summer slacks and a white Izod jacket, and his thin face matched his short, thinning brown hair; dark circles were prominent under his clear authoritative eyes. "At nine o'clock yesterday morning I drove south out of Las Vegas to Halloran, and from there I began a series of cross-country flights a computer couldn't follow, hopping from airport to airport under more names than I can remember."

"You're a frightened man," said the civilian.

"If you're not, I'm talking to the wrong person."

"I'm not only frightened, Colonel, I'm petrified." Stone went to the phone, ordered coffee, and before hanging up, he turned to Metcalf. "Would you like a drink?" he asked.

"I would. Canadian on the rocks, please."

"I envy you." The civilian gave the order, and both men sat down; for several moments only the sounds of the street outside broke the silence. They looked at each other, neither concealing the fact that he was silently evaluating the other.

"You know who and what I am," said the Colonel. "Who are you? What?"

"CIA. Twenty-nine years. Station chief in London, Athens, Istanbul, and points east and north. A once disciple of Angleton and coordinator of clandestine operations until I was fired. Anything else?"

"No."

"Whatever you did to your answering machine, you did it right. The Converse woman called."

Metcalf shot forward in the chair. *"And?"*

"It was touch and go for a while—I wasn't at my best—but he finally got on the line, or I should say he finally spoke. He was there all the time."

"Your second best must have been pretty good."

"All he wanted to hear was the truth. It wasn't hard."

"Where is he? Where are *they?*"

"The Alps, that's all he'd say—"

"Goddamn it!"

"—for now," completed the civilian. "He wants something from me first."

"What?"

"Affidavits. You could call them depositions."

"What?"

"You heard me. Affidavits from myself and the people I'm working with—working for, actually —stating what we know and what we did."

"He's out to hang you, and I don't blame him."

"That's part of it, and I don't blame him, either, but he says it's secondary and I believe that. He wants Aquitaine. He wants Delavane and his crowd of maniacs nailed to the wall before the

921

whole damn thing erupts—before the killing begins.''

''That was Sam Abbott's judgment. The killing—multiple assassinations, here and throughout Europe, the quickest and surest way to international chaos.''

''The woman told him.''

''No, he pieced it together from things Converse told *her*. Converse didn't understand the words.''

''He does now,'' said Stone. ''Did I say I was petrified? What's a stronger phrase?''

''Whatever it is, it applies to both of us because we both know how simple it would be—so *simple*. We're not dealing with woolly-brained crazies or even your run-of-the-mill terrorists—we've got thirty years' experience and ninety percent of them are in our computers. When the signals break out, we know where they are and usually we can stop them. But here we're dealing with the roughest professionals in our own and in allied ranks, also with years of experience. They're walking around the Pentagon, and on Army and Navy bases—and at an Air Force base in Nevada. *Christ,* where *are* they? You open your mouth and you don't know whom you're talking to, who'll cut you down or program an aircraft to break apart in the sky. How can we stop what we can't *see?*''

''Perhaps Converse's way.''

''With *affidavits?*''

''Maybe. Incidentally, he wants one from you. Your meeting with Abbott, everything he told you, as well as your evaluation of his mental capacities and stability. That means you'll have to stay here tonight. A half-hour ago I reserved three other rooms—I said I'd give the front desk the names later."

"Would you mind answering my question? What the hell are affidavits going to do? We're dealing with an army out there—how large and how widespread we don't know—but it *is* an *army!* At minimum, a couple of battalions, here and in Europe. Professional officers trained to carry out orders, believing in those orders and in the generals who are issuing them. *Affidavits,* depositions, for Christ's sake! Is this some kind of flaky legal handspring that doesn't *mean* anything? Do we have *time* for this?"

"You're not thinking anything I didn't think, Colonel. But then, I'm not a lawyer and neither are you. Converse is, and I had a long conversation with him. He's taking the only route he knows. The legal route. Oddly enough, it's why we sent him out."

"Give me an answer, Stone," said Metcalf coldly.

"Protection," replied Stone. "What Converse wants is instant protection and for all of us to be taken seriously. Not as psychopaths or as cranks or as people with mental aberrations or diminished capacities—I think those were his words."

"Aren't they nice? What in the name of sweet Jesus do they mean? *How?*"

"With formal legal documents. Responsible men setting forth what they know and, in the case of depositions, under qualified examination.

923

Through the courts, Colonel. *A* court—it only takes one, only one judge. On the basis of the affidavits a petition is made to the court—*a* court, *a* judge—that protection be given under seal.''

''Under what?''

''Under seal. It's completely confidential—no press, no divulging of information, simply an order from the court transmitted to the authorities most suited to carry out the order. In this case, all the branches of the Secret Service instructed by the court to provide *extraordinary* service.''

''Extraordinary? For whom?''

''The President of the United States, the Vice-President, the Speaker of the House, the Secretary of Defense, the Secretary of State—right on down the line. The law, Colonel. That's what the law can do—also his words, I think.''

''Jesus!''

There was a rapping on the door. This time Stone covered his automatic with the folded *New York Times.* He got up and admitted a waiter, who rolled in a table with a pot of coffee, two cups, a bottle of Canadian whisky, ice and glasses. He signed the bill and the man left.

''Coffee or a drink first?'' asked Stone.

''My God, a drink. *Please.*''

''I envy you.''

''You're not going to join me?''

''Sorry, I can't. I allow myself one in the evening; I'll join you then. You live in Las Vegas, so you'll understand. I'm trying to beat the odds, Colonel. I intend to beat them. I was fired, remember?'' Stone brought the Air Force officer a drink and sat down.

"You can't beat the odds, don't you know that?"

"I've beaten a few. I'm still here."

"The courts," said Metcalf, shaking his head. "A court! It's an end run. He's using the law to go around the flanks of the government people he should reach but whom he can't trust. Can it *work?*"

"It buys time, a few days perhaps, it's hard to tell. 'Under seal' lasts only so long. The law also calls for full disclosure. But what's most important is that it legitimately tightens the security around potential targets, hopefully screwing up whatever tactics Aquitaine is mounting, forcing the generals to regroup, rethink. Again time."

"But that's only over here in the States."

"Yes. That's why Converse wants the time."

"What for?"

"He won't tell me, and I'm in no position to make demands."

"I see," said the Colonel, his drink to his lips. "You said three rooms. Who are the others?"

"You'll meet them and you won't like them. They're two kids who stumbled into this along with a few others I don't know, and they won't say who they are. After Halliday reached them—or one of them—they provided the dossiers for Converse. They're young, but they're all right, Colonel. If I ever had a son, I'd like to think he'd be one of them."

"I have a son and I expect he would be," said Metcalf. "Otherwise, I blew it. What are the procedures?"

Stone sat rigidly back in the chair and spoke slowly, his voice pitched to the static emphasis of a monotone. He was repeating instructions not of his own making and certainly not to his liking. "At three o'clock this afternoon I'm to call an attorney named Simon, Nathan Simon, one of the senior partners of Converse's firm here in New York. Presumably by then Converse's wife will have reached him, telling him to expect a call from me and to please do as I ask—apparently they believe he will. To be brief about it, Simon will come over here to the hotel accompanied by a stenographer and take all our depositions, along with our credentials, ranks, and current responsibilities. He'll stay until he's finished."

"You were right on the phone," interrupted the military man. "We're dead."

"I said as much to Converse and he asked me how it felt. He was inquiring, of course, from firsthand knowledge."

"He wants all of you."

"But not you," said Stone. "He'd like your testimony—and, by extension, Abbott's—but he won't insist on it. He knows he can't ask you to walk in on this."

"I walked in when that plane went down. Also there's something else. If we can't stop Delavane and his generals, what the hell's left for people like us? . . . Converse wouldn't tell you what he was going to do?"

"Not in terms of what he calls the countdown, but yes, as far as tomorrow is concerned. He's sending over his own affidavit and, he expects, another from a man from the Sûreté who has information showing that most of the official reports out of Paris are lies. . . . And we're not dead yet, Colonel. Converse made it clear that Nathan Simon was the best attorney we could have—as long as he believes us."

"What can a lawyer do?"

"I asked Converse the same thing, and he gave me a strange answer. He said, 'He can use the law, because the law isn't men, it's the law.' "

"That's beyond me," said Metcalf, irritated. "Not in a philosophical context but how it applies now—right goddamned *now!* . . . Hell, it doesn't make any difference—*we* don't make any difference! Once those guns go off and the bodies fall in Washington and London, Paris or Bonn —wherever—they've got the controls and we won't get them back. I know that because I know how long so many people have wanted someone to *take* control. Stop the carnage, make things safe, piss on the Soviets. God help me, there were times I thought that way myself."

"So did I," said the civilian quietly.

"We were wrong."

"I know that. It's why I'm here."

Metcalf drank, holding the cold glass against his warm cheek. "I keep thinking about what Sam said to me. 'There's got to be a list,' he said. 'A master list of everyone in this Aquitaine.' He ruled out all the obvious places—not in a vault, not on paper—probably electronically programmed, flashed on with codes, as his aerial tactics were frequently flashed on a screen inside a jet's cockpit. Someplace no one would ever think of, away from anything official or tied in with anyone remotely military. 'A list. There *has* to be a list!' he kept saying. For a pilot, he had a hell of an imagination. I guess it's why he was so good at that tactical stuff at forty thousand feet in the air. Come out of the sun where they don't expect you, or from a dark horizon where the radar can't pick you up. He knew it all. He was a tactical genius.''

As Metcalf talked, Stone leaned forward in the chair, looking intently at the Air Force officer and absorbing every word he spoke.

''Scharhörn,'' he said, barely above a whisper. ''It's *Scharhörn!*''

The twin-engined Riems 406 circled the private airfield at Saint-Gervais, fifteen miles east of Chamonix, the amber lights of the two runways throwing an orange glow up into the lower night sky. Inside, Prudhomme checked the strap of his seat belt as the pilot on his left received clearance to make his final approach to the north-south strip.

Mon Dieu, what an incredible day! thought the man from the Sûreté as he glanced at his right hand under the spill of the panel lights. The dark bruises on his fingers were at least less noticeable than the blood that had covered his entire hand only hours ago. His would-be executioner had not even bothered to conceal his assignment, such was his arrogance—bred undoubtedly in the Légion étrangère! And the sentence of death had been delivered right inside the car at the far end of the parking area in the Bois de Boulogne! The man had called him at the office and, in truth, it had entered Prudhomme's mind that this man might

928

call him, and so it was less a surprise than it could have been—and certainly gave him cause to be prepared. The man had asked his recent superior to meet him at the Bois, in the parking lot—he had startling news. He would be driving his official Peugeot, and since he could not leave his radio phone, would the inspector mind joining him. Of course not.

But there had been no startling news. Only questions, asked very arrogantly.

"Why did you do what you did this morning?"

"Shave? Go to the toilet? Eat breakfast? Kiss my wife good-bye? What are you talking about?"

"You know what I refer to! Earlier! The man on the Boulevard Raspail. You crashed into his car, stopping him. You threw narcotics inside. You arrested him falsely!"

"I didn't approve of what he was doing. Any more than I approve of this conversation." Prudhomme had awkwardly reached for the handle of the door with his left hand, his right having other business.

"Stop!" his former subordinate had shouted, grabbing his shoulder. "You were protecting the woman!"

"Read my report. Let me go."

"I'll let you go to hell! I'm going to kill you, meddler! Insignificant bureaucrat!"

The former subordinate had yanked a gun from his jacket holster but he was too late. Prudhomme had fired twice the small weapon he gripped under his coat. Unfortunately, it was small caliber and the ex-colonel of the Legion was a very large man; he had lunged at Prudhomme inside the automobile. However, the veteran of the Resistance had gone back to an old wartime habit—just in case: along the lapels of his coat was threaded a long wire—a wire with two braided loops at each end. He had whipped it out, and looping it over his would-be executioner's head with his wrists crossed, he violently yanked it taut until the flesh burst around the throat and blood drenched Prudhomme's hands.

"We're cleared for landing, Inspector," said the pilot, grinning. "I swear to Christ no one would *believe* this! Of course I have no intention of saying a thing, I swear on my mother's grave!"

"She's probably drinking brandy in Montmartre at this moment," interjected Prudhomme dryly. "Say nothing, and you may have another six months flying in your foolish tobacco from Malta."

"Nothing else! *Never* anything else, Inspector. I am a father!"

"You are to be commended. Six months and then get out, do you understand?"

"On my father's grave, I swear!"

"He's very much alive and in jail—he'll be out in sixty days. Tell him to stop his presses. Government relief checks—*really*."

Joel and Valerie listened in silence as the man from the Sûrete told his story. He was finished now; there was nothing left to say. Interpol had been compromised, the *arrondissement* police manipulated, the Sûreté itself corrupted, and official government communiqués issued on the basis of lies—all lies. Why?

"I'll tell you because I want your help—much more help," said Converse, getting out of the chair and going to the desk, where the typewritten pages of his affidavit were in the center of the green blotter. "Better, you can read it yourself, but I'm afraid you'll have to read it here. In the morning I'll have copies made; until then I don't want it to leave this room. By the way, Val got you a reservation, a single—don't ask me how, but a clerk downstairs will have a new wardrobe if not a new house by tomorrow."

"*Merci, madame.*"

"The name is French," added Joel.

"Yes."

"No, I mean the *name* is French."

"*Oui.*"

"No, what I mean is—"

"*Pardon, monsieur,*" interrupted Valerie. "*Le nom sur le registre est 'Monsieur French,' mais 'French,' comme en anglais—French. Arthur French.*"

"But I will have to sign, talk. Surely they will know."

"You sign nothing and you say nothing," said Val, taking a key off the bedside table and handing it to Prudhomme. "The room is paid for—three days, to be precise. After that —before, if possible, if you agree to help—the three of us will be someplace else."

"*Formidable.* I must read."

"*Mon ami—mon époux—est un avocat exceptionnel.*"

"*Je comprends.*"

"There are some forty pages here," said Converse, bringing the papers to Prudhomme. "To absorb it will take you at least an hour. We'll go downstairs and grab a bite to eat and leave you alone."

"*Bien*. There is much I wish to learn."

"What about you?" asked Joel, standing over the Frenchman. "I mean now. They'll find that body in the car."

"Most certainly," agreed Prudhomme. "I left it where it was along with that pig from the Legion. But for the Sûreté there will be no connection to me."

"Fingerprints? The fact that you were away from your office?"

"Another old habit from the war," said the man from the Sûreté, reaching into his pocket. He pulled out a pair of extremely thin rubberized gloves—surgical gloves—cut off at the wrist. "I washed these out at the Bois. The German occupation forces had all our fingerprints in a thousand files. There was no point in asking for our own executions. As for my absence at my desk, it is quite simple. I explained to an assistant that I would be in Calais for several days on a contraband investigation and would call in. My years permit a certain latitude and flexibility."

"That's the Sûreté, not the others. Not where the Legionnaire came from."

"I am aware of that, monsieur. So I must be careful. It will not be the first time."

"Enjoy your reading," said Converse, nodding at Val to join him. "If you want anything, call room service."

"Bon appétit," said Prudhomme.

Chaim Abrahms lifted the stiffening wrist of his dead wife's hand, the weapon gripped fiercely in her white fingers, and angled the gun toward her chest, into the bloody cavern between her breasts.

The wide, brown eyes would not stay closed. They stared up at him, accusing—accusing!

"What do you *want* from me!" he screamed. "I have seen the dead. I have *lived* with the dead! Leave me be, woman! You couldn't *understand!*"

Yet she had, for so many years. She had cooked the meat—the desert chicken and the lamb, caught in the outlying marshes—and fed the units of the Irgun and the Haganah, never questioning death then. Fighting for a hope, a simple hope that was the beginning of a dream. The land was *theirs,* rightfully, Biblically, *logically* theirs! They had fought and they had won! Two thousand years of being outcasts—despised, reviled, and spat upon by the almighty Gentiles until the tribes were burned and gassed and told to eliminate themselves from the face of the earth—and yet they had survived. Now the tribes were strong. They were the *conquerors,* not the conquered.

"It's what we *fought* for! What we prayed for! Why do you insult me with your *eyes!*" Chaim Abrahms roared as he pressed his forehead against the dead flesh of his wife's face.

Hitabdut was among the most heinous crimes committed against the laws of the Talmud. It was *ebude atzmo,* the taking of one's own life against the wishes of Almighty God, in whose image man

933

was created. A Jew who consigned his or her earthly being to *hitabdut* was denied burial in the Hebrew cemetery. It would be so for Chaim Abrahms' wife, the most devout human being he had ever known.

"I have to *do* it!" he screamed, raising his eyes in supplication. "It is for the best, can't you *understand?*"

Prudhomme poured himself a cup of coffee and returned to his chair. Valerie sat opposite him as Converse stood by the window looking over at the man from the Sûreté, listening.

"I cannot think of any other questions," said the Frenchman, his intensely troubled eyes darting about, his lined face looking wearier than before. "Although it's possible I'm still too deep in shock to think at all. To say it's incredible serves no purpose; also it would not be true. It's all *too* credible. The world is so frightened it cries out for stability, for a place to hide, for protection—from the skies, from the streets, from each other. I believe the time has come when it will settle for sheer, absolute strength, no matter the cost."

"The operative word is 'absolute,'" said Joel, "as in controls and power. A confederation of military governments fueling one another, interlocking policies and altering the laws, all in the name of stability—and anyone who disagrees with them is declared unstable and silenced. And if too many disagree, the chaos erupts again —stability wins, Aquitaine wins. All they need is that initial wave of terror, a tidal wave of killing and confusion. 'Key figures' were the words they

used. 'Accumulation' . . . 'rapid acceleration'
—chaos. Powerful men cut down as riots break
out in half a dozen capitals and the generals
march in with their commanders. That's the
scenario, right from their own words.''

"That also is the problem, monsieur. They are
only words, but they are words you can pass
along to very few people, for they could be the
wrong people. You could move up this countdown, as you call it, trigger this holocaust
yourself.''

"The countdown's running out, make no
mistake,'' Converse broke in. "But there *is* a way.
'Accumulation' and 'rapid acceleration' can be
used in another manner, and you're right, it's
only with words—*accumulated* words, *accelerated*
words. I can't come out, not yet. I can't show
myself. There's no protection any court or
government agency or the police could provide
that would stop them from killing me, and then,
once I'm dead, calling whatever I said the ravings
of a psychopath. Don't misunderstand me, I have
no death wish, but my death in itself isn't
important. What is important is that the truth
goes down with me, because I'm the only one
who's talked directly to Delavane's four caesars
over here, and probably the fifth, the Englishman.''

"And these *déclarations*—these affidavits you
speak of—can change that?''

"They can turn things around, maybe just
enough.''

"Why?''

"Because that's a real world out there, a

935

practical, complicated world that has to be penetrated as fast as possible—people have to be reached who can be trusted, who can *do* something. Quickly. It's what I wanted to do a couple of weeks ago, but I was going about it the wrong way. I wanted to get everything I knew to someone I knew. Nathan Simon, the best attorney I've ever met. I wrote it all out—twice—not realizing that I was only tying his hands, probably killing him." Joel stepped away from the window, a lawyer in summation. "Whom could he go to without me, without the presence of an obviously sane man and not simply the words of a 'psychopathic killer'? And if I did come out, as he would have rightfully insisted, we're both dead. Then Val told me about the man in New York who reached her on the phone and the other who chased her down the street and I guessed right. Those aren't the methods of people who want to kill you; they don't announce themselves. They were the men in Washington who had sent me out and were now trying to make contact with me. Then she described her meeting with Sam Abbott and his mentioning this Metcalf, a man he trusted and who had to be some kind of very important person for him to tell the story to. Finally, there was you in Paris—what you said, what you did, and how you offered to help, using the same code as René Mattilon—the Tatiana family. Tatiana, a name or a word I think means trust, even among sharks."

"You are right, monsieur."

"That's when it all came together for me. If I could somehow establish lines of communication and reach *all* of you, there was a way. You people knew the truth—some of you knew all of it; others, like yourself, knew only fragments, but regardless, you understood the immensity, the reality of the generals and their Aquitaine and what they could do, what they're *doing*. Even you, Prudhomme. What did you say? Interpol is compromised, the police manipulated, the Sûreté corrupted—official reports all lies. Added to these, Anstett in New York, Peregrine, the commander of NATO, Mattilon, Beale, Sam Abbott . . . Connal Fitzpatrick—the only question mark—and God knows how many others. All dead. The generals are marching—forget theories, they're *killing!* . . . If I could convince all of you to write out affidavits—or have depositions taken—and get them to Nathan Simon, he'd have the ammunition he needs. I fed legal mumbo jumbo to Stone in New York; some of it applies, most of it doesn't, but he'll do his part and force the others to join him—he has no choice. The main point, the *only* point, is to get this material to Simon. Once he has written testimony, a series of events and observations all sworn to be true by diverse men of experience, he has a *case*. Believe me, he'll treat them like the plans of a neutron bomb. He'll have it all tomorrow, and he'll reach the right people if he has to walk into the Oval Office—which he could do, but may not choose to." Joel paused and looked hard at the man from the Sûreté; he nodded at the pages of his own affidavit on the table beside the Frenchman. "I've made arrangements for that to be flown to New York tomorrow. I'd like one from you."

"Certainly you may have it. But can you trust the courier?"

"The world could blow apart and she'd still be sitting in her house in the mountains and not know it. Or care. How's your English?"

"Adequate, I believe. We've talked for several hours."

"I mean written English. It'd save time if you wrote it out tonight."

"My spelling is probably no better than yours is in French."

"Make that English," said Valerie. "I'll straighten it out and if you're not sure of something, write it in French."

"That would help. I must write it tonight?"

"The secretary will be here first thing in the morning," explained Converse. "She'll type it up. She's the one taking the flight from Geneva to New York tomorrow afternoon."

"She agreed to do this?"

"She agreed to accept a large donation to a nature organization that apparently runs her life."

"Very convenient."

"There's something else," said Joel, sitting on an arm of Valerie's chair and leaning forward. "You know the truth now, and beyond the material that has to reach Simon, there's one last thing I have to do. I've got a lot of money and a banker in Mykonos who'll confirm I have access to a great deal more—but you've read all that. With time to find the personnel and the equipment I might be able to pull it off myself, but we don't have the time. I need your help, I need the resources you have."

"For what, monsieur?"

"The final depositions. The last part of the testimony. I want to kidnap three men."

37

I, Peter Charles Stone, age fifty-eight, a resident of Washington, D. C., was employed by the Central Intelligence Agency for twenty-nine years, during which time I attained the rank of station chief in various European posts and ultimately Second Director of Clandestine Operations, Langley, Virginia. My record is on file at the Central Intelligence Agency and may be obtained pursuant to the regulations governing such procedures. Since separation from the CIA, I have worked as a consultant and analyst for numerous intelligence departments, the specifics therein withheld from this statement pending government clearances should they be deemed pertinent to this document.

On or about last March 15, I was contacted by Captain Andrew Packard, United States Army, who asked if he might come to my apartment to discuss a confidential matter. When he arrived, he stated at the outset that he was speaking for a small group of men from both the military services and the State Department, the number and identities of which he would not divulge. He stated further that they sought professional consultation from an experienced intelligence officer no longer associated (permanently) with any branch of the intelligence community. He said he had certain funds available he believed would be adequate and would I be interested. It should be noted here that Captain Packard and his associates had made a thorough if not exhaustive search of my background—warts and alcohol and all, as is said. . . .

I, Captain Howard NMI Packard, U.S. Army, 507538, age thirty-one, currently residing in Oxon Hill, Maryland, am assigned to Section 27, Department of Technological Controls, the Pentagon, Arlington, Virginia. In December of last year, Mr. A. Preston Halliday, an attorney from San Francisco with whom I had struck up a friendship as a result of his numerous petitions to our section on behalf of clients (all successful and above reproach), asked me to have dinner with him at a small restaurant in Clinton, approximately ten miles from my house. He apologized for not asking my wife, explaining that what he had to say would only disturb her, as, indeed, it would disturb me, but in this case it was my responsibility to be disturbed. He added that there was no conceivable conflict in our meeting, as he had no business pending, only business that should be investigated and stopped. . . .

I, Lieutenant (J.G.) William Michael Landis, U.S. Navy, a bachelor, age twenty-eight; current address, Somerset Garden Apartments, Vienna, Virginia, am a computer programmer for the Department of the Navy, Sea-Armaments Procurements Division, stationed at the Pentagon, Arlington, Virginia. Actually, in all but rank (due within sixty days), I'm in command of most programming for Pentagon-Navy, having received a doctorate in advanced computer technology from the University of Michigan, College of Engineering. . . . I'm probably not saying this right, sir.

Go ahead, young man.

I state this because with the highly sophisticated equipment at my disposal as well as the classified micro-conversion codes available to me, I'm able to tap into a great many restricted computers with a tracing capacity that can circumvent—or penetrate, if you like—closures placed on extremely sensitive information.

Last February, Captain Howard Packard, United States Army, and three other men— two from the Department of State, Office of Munitions Controls, and the third a Marine Corps officer I knew from the Amphibious Section, Navy Procurements—came out to see me on a Sunday morning. They said they were alarmed over a series of weapons and high-tech transfers that appeared to violate D.O.D. and State Department sanctions. They gave me the data they had concerning nine such incidents, impressing upon me the confidentiality of the inquiry.

The next afternoon I went to the maximum-security computers and with the conversion codes inserted the data for the nine transfers. The initial entries were confirmed—those numbers never change so as to eliminate the possibilities of duplication—but in each case, after confirmation, the remaining information was erased, wiped off

*the computer tapes. Six of those nine transfers
were traced through the initial entries to a firm
called Palo Alto International, owned by a retired
Army general named Delavane. This was my first
involvement, sir.*

Who were the three other men, Lieutenant?

*It wouldn't do any good to give their names,
sir. It could only hurt their families.*

I'm not sure I understand—can possibly
understand.

*They're dead. They went back and asked
questions and they're dead, sir. Two supposedly
in automobile accidents involving trucks—on back
roads they never took home—and the third
indiscriminately shot by a deranged sniper while
jogging in Rock Creek Park. All those joggers
and he was the one who got it. . . .*

[Captain Packard]

*As an Army captain with full security clearance
and frequently dealing in top-secret procedures, I
was able to set up a sterile telephone (i.e., one
that is constantly scanned for taps or intercepts)
so Mr. Halliday could reach me at any time of
day or night without fear of being overheard.
Also in concert with Mr. Stone and Lieutenant
Landis, we pooled our sources and obtained in-
depth intelligence dossiers on the well-known
names Halliday found among General Delavane's
notes. Specifically, Generals Bertholdier,
Leifhelm, Abrahms, and Van Headmer. Using
funds provided by Dr. Edward Beale, we secured
the services of private firms in Paris, Bonn, Tel
Aviv, and Johannesburg to up-date the dossiers*

with all available current information about the subjects.

By now we had uncovered ninety-seven additional computer erasures directly related to export licensing and military transfers involving an estimated $45 million. A great many were initiated by Palo Alto International, but without further data there was nothing to trace. It was like a series of blips disappearing from a radar screen. . . .

[Stone]

My years in the CIA's Clandestine Operations taught me that the larger the pattern, the greater the numbers, and that those areas with the heaviest concentration of activity invariably held the tightest and most ruthless security. Nothing terribly original here but the reverse application is frequently overlooked. Since Washington was the clearinghouse for illegal exports totaling millions upon millions in American merchandise and matériel, it stood to reason that there would be a range of safeguards, scores of Delavane's informants—both knowing and unknowing, that is, ideologically involved or simply hired or threatened—in the government agencies and departments related to the activities of Palo Alto International. Without going into specifics, Captain Packard confirmed this judgment by telling me that an incident had recently taken place that cost the lives of three men who tried to follow up on a number of computer erasures. We had moved from the realm of ideological extremists into one of fanatics and killers.

Therefore it was my contention—and I hereby assume full responsibility for the decision—that safer and more rapid progress could be made by sending a man out into the peripheral sectors of Delavane's operation with enough information to trace connections back to Palo Alto International. By the very nature of illegal export licensing itself there is more open territory at the receiving ends. The obvious place to start was with the four generals whose names were found in Delavane's notes. I had no candidate with the expertise I felt was necessary for the assignment. . . .

[Captain Packard]

On or about July 10, Mr. Halliday called me on the sterile phone I'd set up for him and said he believed he'd found the proper candidate for the assignment as outlined by Mr. Stone. An attorney whose field was international law, a man he had known years ago and a former prisoner of war in Vietnam who conceivably had the motivation to go after someone like General Delavane. His name was Joel Converse. . . .

I, Alan Bruce Metcalf, age forty-eight, am an officer in the United States Air Force, holding the rank of colonel and currently stationed at the Nellis Air Force Base, Clark County, Nevada, as chief intelligence officer. Thirty-six hours ago, as I dictate this statement, on August 25 at four o'clock in the afternoon, I received a telephone call from Brigadier General Samuel Abbott, commanding officer, Tactical Operations, Nellis A.F.B. The general said it was urgent that we meet, preferably off base, as soon as possible. He had new and extraordinary information regarding the recent assassinations of the supreme commander of NATO and the American ambassador to Bonn, West Germany. He insisted that we be in civilian clothes and suggested the library at the University of Nevada, Las Vegas campus. We met at approximately 5:30 P.M. and talked for five hours. I will be as accurate as possible, and that will be very accurate, as the conversation is still fresh in my mind, engraved there by the tragic death of General Abbott, a close friend for many years and a man I admired greatly. . . .

The above, then, are the events as told to General Abbott by the former Mrs. Converse, and as he related them to me, and the subsequent actions I took to convene an emergency meeting of the highest-level intelligence personnel in Washington. General Abbott believed what he had been told because of his knowledge and perceptions of the individuals involved. He was a brilliant and stable man, not given to bias where judgments were concerned. In my opinion, he was deliberately murdered because he had "new and extraordinary information" about a fellow prisoner of war, one Joel Converse.

Nathan Simon, tall, portly, sitting well back in his chair, removed the tortoiseshell glasses from his tired face and tugged at the Vandyke beard that covered the scars of shrapnel embedded at Anzio years ago. His thick salt-and-pepper eyebrows were arched above his hazel eyes and sharp, straight nose. The only other person in the room was Peter Stone. The stenographer had been dismissed; Metcalf, exhausted, had retired to his room, and the two other officers, Packard and Landis, had opted to return to Washington—on separate planes. Simon carefully placed the typewritten affidavits on the table beside his chair.

"There was *no one* else, Mr. Stone?" he asked, his deep voice gentle, far gentler than his eyes.

"No one I knew, Mr. Simon," replied the former intelligence officer. "Everyone I've used since—what we call pulling in old debts—was lower-level with access to upper-level equipment, not decisions. Please remember, three men were killed when this thing barely started."

"Yes, I know."

"Can you do what Converse said? Can you get something 'under seal' and move some mountains we can't move?"

"He told you that?"

"Yes. It's why I agreed to all of this."

"He had his reasons. And I have to think."

"There's no time to *think*. We have to act, we have to *do* something! Time's running out!"

"To be sure, but we cannot do the wrong thing, can we?"

"Converse said you had access to powerful people in Washington. I could trust you to reach them."

"But you've just told me I don't know whom to trust, isn't that right?"

"Oh, *Christ!*"

"A lovely and inspired prophet." Simon looked at his watch as he gathered up the papers and rose from the chair. "It's two-thirty in the morning,

Mr. Stone, and this weary body has come to the end of its endurance. I'll be in touch with you later in the day. Don't try to reach me. I'll be in touch."

"In *touch?* The package from Converse is on its way here. I'm picking it up at Kennedy Airport on the Geneva flight at two-forty-five this afternoon. He wants you to have it right away. *I* want you to have it!"

"You'll be at the airport?" asked the lawyer.

"Yes, meeting our courier. I'll be back here by four or four-thirty, depending on when the plane gets in and traffic, of course."

"No, don't do that, Mr. Stone, stay at the airport. I'll want everything Joel has compiled for us in my hands as soon as possible, of course. Just as there is a courier from Geneva, you may be the courier from New York."

"Where are you going? Washington?"

"Perhaps, perhaps not. At this moment I'm going home to my apartment and think. Also, I hope to sleep, which is doubtful. Give me a name I can use to have you paged at the airport."

Johnny Reb sat low in the small boat, the motor idling, the waves slapping the sides of the shallow hull in the darkness. He was dressed in black trousers, a black turtleneck sweater and a black knit hat, and he was as close as he dared drift into the southwest coast of the island of Scharhörn. He had spotted the bobbing green glows on the series of buoys the first night; they were trip lights, beams intersecting one another above the water, ringing the approach to the old

U-boat base. They formed an unseen wall—to penetrate it would set off alarms. This was the third night, and he was beginning to feel vindicated.

Trust the gut, trust the stomach and the bile that crept up into the mouth. The bellies of the old-time whores of the community knew when things were going to happen—partly out of dread, partly because a score was near that would enlarge an account in Bern. There was no account in the offing now, of course—only a succession of outlays to pay back a considerable debt, but there was a score to be made. Against the Delavanes and the Washburns, and those German and French and Jewish catfish who would sweep the ponds and make it impossible for gentlemen like Johnny Reb to make a high-hog living. He didn't know much about the South African, except that those nigger-haters had better the hell wise up. The coloreds were coming along just fine, and that was fine by Johnny; his current girlfriend was a lovely black singer from Tallahassee, who just happened to be in Switzerland for silly reasons involving a little cocaine—and a good-sized account in Bern.

But the other catfish were *bad. Real* bad. Johnny Reb had it in for men who would make it jailhouse for people to think the way they wanted to. *No sir,* those people had to go! Johnny Reb was very seriously committed to that proposition.

It was happening! He focused his infrared binoculars on the old concrete piers of the sub base. It was also flat-out crazy! The seventy-foot motor launch had pulled into a dock, and moving out on the pier was a long, double line of men—forty, sixty, eighty . . . nearly 100—preparing to board. What was crazy was the way they were dressed. Dark suits and conservative summer jackets and ties; a number wore hats and every damned one of them carried luggage and a *briefcase*. They looked like a convention of bankers or a parade of lace-pants from the diplomatic corps. *Or*—thought the Rebel as he inched his binoculars backward along the line of passengers—ordinary businessmen, executives, men seen every day standing on railroad platforms and getting out of taxis and flying in planes. It was the very ordinariness of their collective appearance contrasted with the exotically macabre dark outlines of the old U-boat refueling station that gnawed at Johnny's imagination. These men could go unnoticed almost anywhere, yet they did not *come* from anywhere. They came from Scharhörn, from what was undoubtedly a highly sophisticated cell of this multinational military collusion that could put the goddamned catfish generals in the catbird seats. Ordinary people going wherever they were ordered to go—looking like everyone else, behaving like everyone else, opening their attaché cases on planes and trains, reading company reports, sipping drinks but not too many, skimming an occasional paperback novel ostensibly to ease the strain of business—*going wherever they were ordered to go.*

That was it, thought the Rebel, as he lowered the binoculars. *That was it!* These were the hit teams! The stomach never lied; the bile was sent up for a reason, its acrid, sickening taste an ugly alarm that came to those privileged enough to have survived. Johnny Reb turned and fingered the motor, cautiously pushing the rudder to the right and inching the throttle forward. The small boat spun around in the water, and the rogue intelligence officer—former intelligence officer—headed back to his berth in Cuxhaven, accelerating the engine with each fifty feet of distance.

Twenty-five minutes later he pulled into the slip, lashed the lines to the cleats, grabbed his small waterproof case, and with effort climbed up onto the pier. He had to move quickly, but very, *very* cautiously. He knew vaguely the area of the Cuxhaven waterfront where the motor launch would return, for he had watched the lights of the vessel as it bobbed its way out of the harbor toward the island. Once in the vicinity he could determine the specific dock as the boat headed into port, and then he would have only minutes to scout the area and get into position. Carrying his waterproof case, he hurried to the base of the pier and turned left, walking rapidly through the shadows toward the area where he judged the launch had departed. He passed a huge warehouse and reached an open space beyond; there were five short piers, one after the other, extending no more than two hundred feet out into the water. It was dockage for small and medium-sized craft; several trawlers and a few antiquated pleasure boats were lashed to the pilings on each of the piers except one. The fourth pier was empty. The Rebel knew it belonged to the launch; he could taste the bitterness in his mouth. He started out across the space; he would find a place to conceal himself.

"*Halt—stehenbleiben!*" shot out the guttural command as a man walked out of the darkness from around the hull of a trawler at the third pier. "*Was machen Sie hier? Wer sind Sie?*"

Johnny Reb knew when to use his age; he stooped his shoulders and hung his head slightly forward. "*Passen Sie auf diese alten Kästen auf?*" he asked, and continued in German, "I'm a fisherman on one of these relics and I lost my billfold this afternoon. Is it a crime to look for it?"

"Come back later, old man. You can't look for it now."

"*Eh?* What?" The Rebel raised his right hand to his ear, twisting the ring on his middle finger as he did so and pressing a catch on the band. "My hearing's not what it was, Mr. Watchman. What did you say?"

The man stepped forward, first looking out at the water, as the sound of a powerful engine was heard in the distance. "Get out of here!" he shouted, his lips close to Johnny's ear. "*Now!*"

"Good heavens, you're Hans!"

"Who?"

"*Hans!* It's so good to *see* you!" The Rebel slapped his hand around the German's neck —prelude to an affectionate embrace—and plunged the surface of his ring into the man's flesh, deeply embedding the needle.

"Get your hands off me, you stinking old man! My name's not Hans and I never saw you before.

Get out of here or I'll put a . . . a bullet . . . in your . . . *head!*'' The German's hand plunged inside his jacket but there it remained as he collapsed.

"You younger catfish really ought to have more respect for your elders,'' mumbled Johnny as he dragged the unconscious body into the shadows to the left of the trawler on the third pier. "'Cause you don't know the flies we use. Your daddies do, but you little pricks don't. And I *want* your daddies, those mind-suckers!''

The Rebel climbed aboard the trawler and dashed across the deck to the gunwale. The motor launch was heading directly into the fourth pier. He opened his waterproof case into which he had snapped the binoculars in place, and adjusted his eyes to the dim light, studying the tools of his trade. He unlatched a camera and then a lens, a Zeiss-Ikon telescopic, developed by conscientious Germans during World War II for photographing Allied installations at night; it was the best. He inserted it into the lens mount, locked it into position and switched on the camera's motor, noting with satisfaction that the battery was at full capacity, but then he knew it would be. He had been too long in the deadly game to make amateurish mistakes.

The huge motor launch slid into the pier like a mammoth black whale, a killer whale. The lines were secured, and as the passengers disembarked, Johnny Reb began taking pictures.

"Honeychile, this is Tatiana. I've got to reach my boy.''

"The Algonquin Hotel in New York City," said the calm female voice. "The number is Area Code two-one-two, eight-four-zero, six-eight-zero-zero. Ask for Peter Marcus."

"Subtle son of a bitch, isn't he?" said Johnny Reb. "Pardon my language, ma'am."

"I've heard it before, Rebel. This is Anne."

"Goddamn, little lady, why didn't you tell me *before!* How *are* you, sweet child?"

"Doing fine in my dotage, Johnny. I'm out, you know. This is just a courtesy for an old friend."

"An old *friend?* Fair girl, if it wasn't for Petey, I'd have made one hell of a play for you!"

"You should have, Reb. I wasn't in his cards, his terribly important cards. And you were one of the nicest—a little more subterranean than most, but a nice person. What was it? 'Gentleman Johnny Reb'?"

"I've always tried to keep up appearances, Annie. May I request the privilege of calling you one day, if we ever get out of this mess?"

"I don't know what the mess is, Reb, but I do know you have my telephone number."

"You give me heart, fair girl!"

"We're older now, Johnny, but I guess you wouldn't understand that."

"Never, child. Never."

"Stay well, Reb. You're too good to lose."

The operator at the Algonquin Hotel was adamant. "I'm sorry, sir, Mr. Marcus is not in his room and does not answer the page."

"I'll call back," said the Rebel.

"Sorry, sir. There's no answer in Mr. Marcus's room and no response to the page."

"I believe we spoke several hours ago, sir. There's still no answer in Mr. Marcus's room, so I took the liberty of calling the desk. He hasn't checked out and he didn't list an alternate number. Why not leave a message?"

"I believe I will. As follows, please. 'Stay put until I reach you. Or you reach me. Imperative. Signed, Z. Tatiana. That's T-a-t-i-a—"

"Yes, sir. Thank you, sir. Z, sir?"

"As in zero, miss." Johnny Reb hung up the phone in the flat in Cuxhaven. The taste in his mouth was overpoweringly sour.

Erich Leifhelm entertained his luncheon guests at his favorite table at the Ambassador restaurant on the eighteenth floor of the Steigenberger Hotel in Bonn. The spacious, elegant room had a magnificent view not only of the city and the river but also of the mountains beyond, and this particular table was positioned to take advantage of that view. It was a bright, cloudless afternoon, and the natural wonders of the northern Rhineland were there for the fortunate to observe.

"I never tire of it," said the former field marshal, addressing the three men at his table, gesturing with masculine grace at the enormous window behind him. "I wanted you to see it before returning to Buenos Aires—indeed, one of the most beautiful cities in the world, I must add."

954

The maître d' intruded with deference, bowing as he spoke softly to Leifhelm. "Herr General, there is a telephone call for you."

"An aide is dining at table fifty-five," said Leifhelm casually, in spite of his racing pulse. Perhaps there was word of a priest in Strasbourg! "I'm sure he can take it for me."

"The gentleman on the line specifically requested that I speak with you personally. He said to tell you he was calling from California."

"I see. Very well." Leifhelm got out of his chair, apologizing to his guests. "No surcease from the vagaries of commerce, is there? Forgive me, I shall only be a moment or two. Please, more wine."

The maître d' nodded, adding, "I've had the call put through to my private office, Herr General. It's right inside the foyer."

"That pleases me. Thank you."

Erich Leifhelm shook his head subtly as he passed table 55 near the entrance. The lone diner acknowledged the dismissal with a nod of his head. In all the years of strategies and tactics, military and political, that dismissal would prove to be one of the field marshal's gravest errors.

Two men stood in the foyer, one looking at his watch, the other looking annoyed. To judge by their expensive clothes they belonged to the Ambassador's regular clientele and were obviously waiting for late luncheon companions, probably their wives, as they had not gone to their table. A third man stood outside the glass doors in the corridor; he was dressed in the maintenance uniform of the hotel and watched the two men inside.

Leifhelm thanked the maître d' as the latter held open the door to his modest office. The restaurateur closed the door and returned to the dining room. The two men—swiftly, as one —raced inside after the old soldier, who was at that moment picking up the telephone.

"Was geht hier vor? Wer ist . . . !"

The first man lunged across the desk and gripped Leifhelm's head, clamping the general's mouth with very strong hands. The second man pulled a hypodermic needle from his pocket and removed the rubber shield as he tore at Leifhelm's jacket and then the collar of his shirt. He plunged the needle into the base of the general's throat, released the serum, pulled out the syringe and immediately began massaging the flesh as he restored the collar and pulled the jacket back in place.

"He'll be mobile for about five minutes," said the doctor in German. "But he can neither speak nor reason. His motor controls are now mechanical and have to be guided."

"And after five minutes?" asked the first man.

"He collapses, probably vomiting."

"A nice picture. Hurry! Get him up and *guide* him, for God's sake! I'll check outside and knock once."

Seconds later the knock came, and the doctor, with Leifhelm firmly in his grip, propelled the general out of the office and through the glass doors into the hotel corridor.

"This way!" ordered the third man in the

maintenance uniform, heading to the right.

"Quickly!" added the doctor.

Among the strollers in the plush hallway and the diners heading for the restaurant, a number recognized the legendary old soldier and stared at his pale face with the lips trembling, trying to speak. Or scream.

"The great man has had terrible news," said the doctor repeatedly and reverentially. "It's terrible, simply terrible!"

They reached a service elevator, which was on HOLD, and went inside. A stretcher on wheels stood against the padded back wall. The third man took a key from his pocket, inserted it in the HOLD lock to release the controls and pressed the nonstop switch for the basement. The other two lifted Leifhelm up on the stretcher and covered his entire body with a sheet.

"They'll start talking up there," said the first man. "His bulls will come running. They're never far away."

"The ambulance is downstairs now by the elevator door," said the man in the maintenance uniform. "The plane is waiting at the airfield."

The once great field marshal of the Third Reich threw up under the sheet.

Jacques-Louis Bertholdier let himself into the apartment on the Boulevard Montaigne and removed his silk jacket. He walked over to the mirrored bar against the wall, poured a vodka, threw in two cubes of ice from a sterling-silver bucket, and strolled to the window beyond the elegantly upholstered couch. The tree-lined boulevard was so peaceful at midafternoon, so spotlessly clean, and somehow so pastoral although very much a part of the city. There were times when he thought it was the essence of the Paris he loved, the Paris of influence and wealth, whose inhabitants never had to soil their hands. It was why he had purchased the extravagant flat and installed his most extravagant and desirable mistress. He needed her now. My *God,* how he needed release!

The Legionnaire shot and garroted in his own automobile! In the parking lot of the Bois de Bologne! And Prudhomme, the filthy bureaucrat, supposedly in Calais! No fingerprints! *Nothing!* The once and foremost general of France needed an hour or so of tranquility.

"Janine! Where *are* you? Come out, Egyptian! I trust you're wearing what I instructed you to wear. If you need reminding, it's the short black Givenchy, nothing underneath, you understand! Absolutely *nothing."*

"Of course, my general," came the words, strangely hesitant, from behind the bedroom door.

Bertholdier laughed silently to himself as he turned and walked back to the couch. Le Grand Machin was still an event to be reckoned with, even by highly sexual twenty-five-year-olds who loved money and fast cars and elegant apartments as much as they adored having their bodies penetrated. Well, he was too upset to disrobe, his nerves too frayed to go through any prolonged preliminary nonsense. He had something else in mind—release without effort.

958

The sound of the turning knob broke off his thoughts. The door opened and a raven-haired girl emerged, her elongated, perfectly proportioned face set in anticipation, her brown eyes wide in a distant wonder. Perhaps she had been smoking marijuana, thought Bertholdier. She was dressed in a short negligee of black lace, her breasts wreathed in gray, her hips revolving in sexual provocation as she approached the couch.

"Exquisite, you whore of the Nile. Sit down. It's been a dreadful day, a *horrible* day, and it is not over. My driver will return in two hours, and until then I need rest—and release. Give it to me, *Egyptian.*" Bertholdier zipped down the fly of his trousers and reached for the girl. "Fondle it, as I will fondle you, and then do what you can do." He grabbed her breasts and pulled her head down into his groin. "Now. *Now. Do* it!"

A blinding flash filled the room, and two men walked out of the bedroom. The girl sprang back onto the couch as Bertholdier looked up in shock. The man in front put the camera in his pocket; his companion, a short, middle-aged heavyset man with a gun in his hand, walked slowly toward the legend of France.

"I admire your taste, General," he said in a gruff voice. "But then, I suppose I've always admired you, even when I disagreed with you. You don't remember me, but you court-martialed me in Algiers, sending me to the stockade for thirty-six months because I struck an officer. I was a sergeant major and he had brutally abused my men with excessive penalties for minor offenses. Three years for hitting a Paris-tailored pig. Three years in those filthy barracks for taking care of my men."

"Sergeant Major Lefèvre," said Bertholdier with authority, calmly zipping up his fly. "I remember. I never forget. You were guilty of treasonous conduct: assaulting an officer. I should have had you shot."

"There were moments during those three years when I would have welcomed the execution. But I'm not here to discuss Algiers—it's when I knew you were all crazy. I'm here to tell you you're coming with me. You'll be returned unharmed to Paris in several days."

"Preposterous!" spat out the general. "You think your weapon frightens me?"

"No, it's merely to protect myself from you, from the last gesture of a brave and famous soldier. I know you too well to think that threats of bodily harm, or even death, could move you. I have another persuasion, however, one you've just made quite irresistible." The ex-sergeant major withdrew a second, oddly shaped gun from his pocket. "This weapon does not hold bullets. Instead it fires darts containing a chemical that accelerates the heart to the bursting point. My thoughts were to threaten you with fielding the photograph after your death, showing that the great general died ignominiously at what he did best. Now, perhaps, there is another approach. The angle was advantageous for certain expert brush-work—your position and the expression on your face would not be touched, of course—but your companion might easily become a *he* rather than a she, a little boy rather than a girl. There were rumors of your excesses once, and a hastily arranged marriage few could understand. Was this the secret Le Grand Machin ran from all his life? Was it the threat the great De Gaulle held over the head of his popular but all too ambitious and rebellious colonel? That the appetites of this pretender, this would-be successor, were so extensive they included anything he could get his hands on, his body on, the gender making no difference. Small boys when there were no women. The whispers of corrupted young lieutenants and captains, of rapes, conveniently called interrogations in your quarters—"

"Enough!" cried Bertholdier, shooting up from the couch. "Further conversation is pointless. Regardless of how absurd and unfounded your accusations are, I will not permit my name to be dragged through filth! I want that film!"

"My God, it's true," said the ex-infantry sergeant. "All of it."

"The *film!*" shouted the general. "Give it to me!"

"You shall have it," replied Lefèvre. "On the plane."

Chaim Yakov Abrahms walked with a bowed head out of the Ihud Shivat Zion synagogue on the Ben Yehuda in Tel Aviv. The solemn crowds outside formed two deep flanks of devoted followers, men and women who wept openly at the terrible suffering this great man, this patriot-soldier of Israel, had been forced to endure at the hands of his wife. *"Hitabdut,"* they said in hushed voices. *"Ebude atzmo,"* they whispered to one another, cupping mouths to ears, out of Chaim's hearing. The rabbis would not relent; the sins of a despicable woman were visited upon this son of sabras, this fierce child of Abraham, this Biblical warrior who loved the land and the Talmud with equal fervor. The woman had been refused burial in a holy place; she was to remain outside the gates of the *beht hakvahroht,* her soul left to struggle with the wrath of Almighty God, the pain of that knowledge an unbearable burden for the one left behind.

It was said she did it out of vengeance and a diseased mind. She had her daughters. It was the father's son—always the *father's* son—who had been slain on the father's battlefield. Who would weep more, who *could* weep more, or be in greater anguish than the father? And now this, the further agony of knowing that the woman he had given his life to had most heinously violated God's Talmud. The shame of it, the *shame!* Oh, Chaim, our brother, father, son and leader, we weep with you. For you! Tell us what to do and we will do it. You are our *king!* King of Eretz Yisrael, of Judea and Samaria, and all the lands you seek for our protection! Show us the way and we shall follow, O *King!*

"She's done more for him in death than she could ever have done alive," said a man on the outskirts of the crowd and not part of it.

"What do you think really happened?" asked the man's companion.

"An accident. Or worse, far worse. She came to our temple frequently, and I can tell you this. She never would have considered *hitabdut.* . . ."

We must watch him carefully before these fools and thousands like them crown him emperor of the Mediterranean and he marches us to oblivion."

An Army staff car, two flags of blue and white on either side of the hood, made its way up the street to the curb in front of the synagogue. Abrahms, wearing his bereavement like a heavy mantle of sorrow only his extraordinary strength could endure, kept bowing his lowered head to the crowds, his eyes opening and closing, his hands reaching out to touch and be touched. At his side a young soldier said, "Your car, General."

"Thank you, my son," said the legend of Israel as he climbed inside and sank back in the seat, his eyes shut in anguish while weeping faces pressed against the windows. The door closed, and when he spoke, his eyes still closed, there was anything but anguish in his harsh voice. "Get me *out* of here! Take me to my house in the country. We'll all have whisky and forget this *crap*. Holy rabbinical bastards! They had the temerity to *lecture* me! The next war, I'll call up the rabbis and put those Talmudic chicken-shits in the front lines! Let them lecture while the shrapnel flies up their asses!"

No one spoke as the car gathered speed and left the crowds behind. Moments later Chaim opened his eyes and pulled his thick back from the seat; he stretched his barrel-chested frame and reclined again in a more comfortable position. Then slowly, as if aware of the stares of the two soldiers beside him, he looked at both men, his head whipping back and forth.

"Who *are* you?" he shouted. "You're not my men, not my *aides!*"

"They'll wake up in an hour or so," said the man in the front seat beside the driver. He turned to face Abrahms. "Good afternoon, General."

"You!"

"Yes, it is I, Chaim. Your goons couldn't stop me from testifying before the Lebanon tribunal, and nothing on earth could stop me from what I'm doing today. I told you about the slaughter of women and children and quivering old men as they pleaded for their lives and watched you laugh. You call yourself a Jew? You can't begin to understand. You're just a man filled with hate, and I don't care for you to claim to be any part of what I am or what I believe. You're shit, Abrahms. But you'll be brought back to Tel Aviv in several days."

One by one the planes landed, the propeller-driven aircraft from Bonn and Paris having flown at low altitudes, the jet from Israel, a Dassault-Breguet Mystère 10/100, dropping swiftly from twenty-eight thousand feet to the private airfield at Saint-Gervais. And as each taxied to a stop at the end of the runway, there was the same dark-blue sedan waiting to drive the "guest" and his escort to an Alpine chateau fifteen miles east in the mountains. It had been rented for two weeks from a real estate firm in Chamonix.

The arrivals had been scheduled carefully, as none of the three visitors was to know that the others were there. The planes from Bonn and Paris landed at 4:30 and 5:45, respectively, the jet

964

from the Mediterranean nearly three hours later at 8:27. And to each stunned guest Joel Converse said the identical words: "As I was offered hospitality in Bonn, I offer you mine here. Your accommodations will be better than I was given, although I doubt the food will be as good. However, I know one thing—your departure will be far less dramatic than mine."

But not your stay, thought Converse, as he spoke to each man. *Not your stay.* It was part of the plan.

38

The first light floated up into the dark sky above the trees in Central Park. Nathan Simon sat in his study and watched the new day's arrival from the large, soft leather chair facing the huge window. It was his thinking seat, as he called it. Recently he had used it as much for dozing as for thought. But there were no brief interludes of sleep tonight—this morning. His mind was on fire; he had to explore and reexplore the options, stretching the limits of his perception of the dangers within each. To choose the wrong one would send out alarms that would force the generals to act immediately, and once under way, events would race swiftly out of control; the control of events would be solely in the hands of the generals—everywhere. Of course, they might decide within hours to begin the onslaught, but Nathan did not think so—they were not fools. All chaos had its visual beginnings, the initial turbulence that would give credibility to subsequent violence. If nothing else, confusion had to be established as the players moved into place without being seen. And the concept of military control over governments was a timeworn idea since the age of the Pharaohs. It bore early fruit in the Peloponnesus and Sparta's conquest of Athens, later with the Caesars, and, later still, was exercised by the emperors of the Holy Roman Empire, then by the Renaissance princes, and finally brought to its apotheosis by the Soviets and the Germans in the twentieth century. Unrest preceded violence, and violence preceded takeover, whether it was a revolution sparked by hundreds of thousands of oppressed Russians or the strangling inequities of a Versailles treaty.

Therein lay the weakness of the generals' strategy: the unrest had to exist before the violence erupted. It required mobs of malcontented people—ordinary people—who could be worked into a frenzy, but for that to happen the mobs had to be there in the first place. The people's discontent would be the sign, the prelude, as it were, but where, *when?* And what could he do, what moves could he make that would escape the attention of Delavane's informers? He was the employer and friend of Joel Converse, the "psychopathic assassin" the generals had created. He had to presume he was being watched—at the very least any overt action he took would be scrutinized, and if he became suspect he would be thwarted. His life was immaterial. In a sense he was trapped, as he and others like him had been trapped on the beaches of Anzio. They had realized that there was a degree of safety in the foxholes behind the dunes, that to emerge from them was to face unending mortar fire. Yet they had known, too, that nothing would be accomplished if they remained where they were.

Contrary to what he had told Peter Stone, Nathan knew precisely whom he had to see—not one man, but three. The President, the Speaker of the House, and the Attorney General. The apex of the executive branch, the leader of the legislative, and the nation's chief law-enforcement officer. He would see no one of lesser stature, and it was far more advantageous to see them all together rather than individually. He had to see them, whether separately or as a group, and there was his dilemma; it was the trap. One did not simply pick up a telephone and make appointments with such men. There were procedures, formalities, and screening processes to ensure the validity of the requests; men with their responsibilities could not waste time. The trap. The minute his name was mentioned, the word would go out. Delavane himself would know within a matter of hours, if not minutes.

Despite Joel's gratuitous and highly dubious statements to Peter Stone, it was not easy to reach powerful government figures any more than it was logical to have a judge issue a court order under seal that somehow miraculously, *legally,* guaranteed extraordinary protection for those same people without informing the entire security apparatus as to why the protection was deemed vital. Ridiculous! Such court orders were reasonable where intimidated witnesses were concerned before a criminal trial and even afterward in terms of fabricated rehabilitation, but that process hardly applied to the White House, the Congress, or the Justice Department. Joel had taken a legal maneuver, ballooned it way out of probability, and scaled it up into orbit—for a reason, of course. Stone and his colleagues had provided depositions.

And yet, thought Simon, there was an odd logic in Converse's misapplied exaggerations. Not in any way Joel had considered but as a means to reach these men. "A court, a single judge . . ." Converse had said to Stone. That was the logic, the rest was nonsense. *The Supreme Court,* a justice of that court. Not a request from one Nathan Simon who would have to be screened, if only in terms of content, not character, but an urgent message to the President from a venerated justice of the Supreme Court! No one would dare question such a man if he pronounced his business to be between the President and himself. Presidents were far more solicitous of the Court than of Congress, and with good reason. The latter was a political battleground, the former an arena of moral judgment. Nathan Simon knew the man he could call *and* see, a justice in his late seventies. The Court was not in session; October was a month away. The justice was somewhere in New England; his private number was at the office.

Nathan blinked, then brought his hand up to shield his eyes. For a brief moment the fireball of the early sun had careened a blinding ray through a geometric maze of glass and steel across the park and entered his window before being blocked by a distant building. And suddenly, at that instant of blindness, he was given the answer to the terrifying question of *where* and *when*—the unrest that had to be the prelude for the eruption of violence. There was scheduled throughout Free Europe, Great Britain, Canada, and the United States an internationally coordinated week-long series of antinuclear protests. Millions of concerned people joining hands and snarling traffic in the streets of the major cities and capitals, making their voices heard at the expense of normalcy. Rallies to be held in the parks and in the squares and in front of government buildings. Politicians and statesmen, perceiving as always the power of ground swells, had promised to address huge crowds everywhere—in Paris and Bonn, Rome and Madrid, Brussels and London, Toronto, Ottawa, New York, and Washington. And again, as always, both the sincere advocates and the posturing sycophants of the bodies politic would blame the lack of arms-control progress on the intransigence of evil adversaries, not on their own deficiencies. The genuine and the phony would walk hand in hand across the many podiums, none sure of the other's stripes.

Crowds everywhere would espouse deeply felt, deeply divisive issues: the believers of universal restraint would be pitted against those who intensely believe in the effectiveness of raw power, and the latter would surely be heard. No one thought the massive demonstrations would be without incidents, yet how far might these minor confrontations escalate if the incidents *themselves* were massive? Units of terrorist fanatics financed anonymously, convinced of their mission to infiltrate and savagely disrupt so as to get their messages across, messages of real and or imagined grievances that had nothing to do with the protests, creating chaos primarily because the crowds were not of their world or their fevers. Crowds—everywhere. These were the hordes of people who could be galvanized by sudden violence and worked into a state of madness. It would be the prelude. Everywhere.

The demonstrations were scheduled to begin in three days.

Peter Stone walked down the wide dirt path toward the lake behind the A-frame house somewhere in lower New Hampshire—he did not know precisely where, only that it was twenty minutes from the airport. It was close to dusk, the end of a day filled with surprises, and apparently more were to come. Ten hours ago, in his room at the Algonquin, he had called Swissair to see if the flight from Geneva was on schedule; he had been told it was thirty-four minutes ahead of schedule and, barring landing delays, was expected a half-hour early. It was the first surprise and an inconsequential one. The second was not. He had arrived at Kennedy shortly before two o'clock, and within a few minutes he heard the page over the public address system for a "Mr. Lackland," the name he had given Nathan Simon.

"Take Pilgrim Airlines to Manchester, New

Hampshire," the lawyer had said. "There's a reservation for Mr. Lackland on the three-fifteen plane. Can you make it?"

"Easily. The flight from Geneva's early. I assume that's LaGuardia?"

"Yes. You'll be met in Manchester by a man with red hair. I've described you to him. See you around five-thirty."

Manchester, New Hampshire? Stone had been so sure Simon would ask him to fly to Washington that he had not even bothered to put a toothbrush in his pocket.

Surprise number three was the courier from Geneva. A prim, gaunt Englishwoman with a face of pale granite and the most uncommunicative pair of eyes he had seen outside of Dzerzhinsky Square. As arranged, she had met him in front of the Swissair lounge, a copy of the *Economist* in her left hand. After studying the wrong side of his out-of-date government identification, she had given him the attaché case and made the following statement—in high dudgeon. "I don't like New York, I never have. I don't like flying either, but everyone's been so lovely and it's better to get the whole whack-a-doo over all at once, righto? They've arranged for me to take the next plane back to Geneva. I miss my mountains. They need me and I do try to give them my *very* all, righto?"

With that abstruse bit of information she had smiled wanly and started back somewhat uncertainly toward the escalator. It was then that Stone had begun to understand. The woman's eyes did not reveal her condition but the whole person did. She was drunk—or, perhaps, "pickled"—having overcome her fear of flying with liquid courage. Converse had made a strange choice of a courier, Stone had thought, but had instantly changed his mind. Who could be less suspect?

The fourth surprise came at the Manchester airport. An ebullient, middle-aged redheaded man had greeted him as though they were long-lost fraternity brothers from some Midwestern university in the late thirties, when such fraternal ties were deemed far deeper than blood. He was effusive to the point where Stone was not only embarrassed by the display of camaraderie but seriously concerned that unwarranted attention would be drawn to them. But once in the parking lot, the redhead had suddenly slammed him into the doorframe of the car and shoved the barrel of a gun into the back of his neck while the man's free hand stabbed his clothes for a weapon.

"I wouldn't take the risk of going through metal detectors with a gun, *damn* it!" protested the ex-CIA agent.

"Just making sure, spook. I've dealt with you assholes, you think you're something else. Me, I was Federal."

"Which explains a great deal," said Stone, meaning it.

"You drive."

"Is that a question or an order?"

"An order. All spooks drive," replied the redhead.

Surprise number five came in the car as Stone took the sudden turns commanded by the redheaded man, who casually replaced the gun in his jacket holster.

"Sorry about the horseshit," he had said in a voice far less hostile than it had been in the parking lot, but nowhere near the false ebullience in the terminal. "I had to be careful, piss you off, see where you stood, you know what I mean? And I was never Federal—I hated those turkeys. They always wanted you to know they were better than you were just because they came from D.C. I was a cop in Cleveland, name's Gary Frazier. How are you?"

"Somewhat more comfortable," Stone had said. "Where are we going?"

"Sorry, pal. If he wants you to know, he'll tell you."

Surprise number six awaited Stone when he drove the car up through the New Hampshire hills to an isolated house of wood and glass, surrounded by forests, the structure an inverted V, two narrowing stories looking out in all directions on woods and water. Nathan Simon had walked down the stone steps from the front door.

"You've brought it?" he asked.

"Here it is," said Stone, handing the attaché case to the lawyer through the open window. "Where are we? Who are you seeing?"

"It's an unlisted residence, but if everything is in order we'll call you. There are guest quarters attached to the boathouse down at the lake. Why not freshen up after your trip? The driver will point the way. If we need you for anything, we'll ring you on the phone. It's a separate number from the house, so just pick it up."

973

And now Peter Stone was walking down the wide dirt path that led to the boathouse by the lake, aware that eyes were following him. Surprise number six: he had no idea where he was and Simon wasn't going to tell him unless "everything was in order," whatever that meant.

The guest quarters alluded to by the attorney was a three-room cottage on the edge of the lake with an entrance to the adjacent boathouse, in which was berthed a small sleek motorboat and a nondescript catamaran that looked more like a raft with two canvas seats and fishing equipment for drift trawling. Stone wandered about trying to find some clue as to the owner's identity but there was nothing. Even the names on the boats were meaningless, but not lacking in humor. The cumbersome, raftlike sail was named *Hawk,* while the aggressive-looking little speedboat was *Dove.*

The former deep-cover intelligence officer sat on the porch and looked out at the peaceful waters of the lake and the rolling, darkening green hills of New Hampshire. Everything *was* peaceful. Even the cries of the loons seemed to proclaim the permanence of tranquility in this special place. But Stone's insides were not peaceful; his stomach churned and he remembered what Johnny Reb used to say in the field. "Trust the stomach, Brer Rabbit, trust the bile. They never lie." He wondered what the Rebel was doing, what he was learning.

The phone inside the cottage rang, accompanied by a strident, unnerving clanging of the porch bell. As if jolted by an electric prod, Stone sprang from the chair, swung back the door and walked rapidly across the room to the telephone.

"Come up to the house, please," said Nathan Simon, adding, "If you were out on the porch, I apologize for not telling you about that damned bell."

"I accept your apology. I was."

"It's for guests who expect calls and may be out in one of the boats."

"The loons are quiet. I'll be right there."

Stone walked up the dirt path and saw the lawyer standing by a screen door that was the lake-side entrance to the house; it was on a patio reached by curving brick steps. He started climbing, prepared for surprise number seven.

Supreme Court Justice Andrew Wellfleet, his thinning unkempt white hair falling in strands over his wide forehead, sat behind the large desk in his library. Converse's thick affidavit was in front of him, and a floor lamp on his left threw light on the pages. It was several moments before he looked up and removed his steel-rimmed glasses. His eyes were stern and disapproving, matching the nickname given him over two decades ago when he was summoned to the Court. "Irascible Andy" was the sobriquet the clerks had given him, but no one ever questioned his awesome intelligence, his fairness, or his devotion to the law. All things considered, surprise number seven was as welcome a shock as Stone could imagine.

"Have you read this?" asked Wellfleet, offering neither his hand nor a chair.

"Yes, sir," replied Stone. "On the plane. It's essentially what he told me over the phone, in far greater detail, of course. The affidavit from the Frenchman, Prudhomme, was a bonus. It tells us how they operate—how they're *capable* of operating."

"And what in hell did you think you were going to do with all of this?" The elderly justice waved his hand over the desk, on which were scattered the other affidavits. "Petition the courts here and in Europe to please, if they'd be so kind, to issue injunctions restricting the activities of all military personnel above a certain rank on the conceivable possibility that they may be part of this?"

"I'm not a lawyer, sir, the courts never entered my mind. But I did think that once we had Converse's own words—along with what we knew —they'd be sufficient to reach the right people in the highest places who *could* do something. Obviously, Converse thought the same thing insofar as he called in Mr. Simon, and if you'll forgive me, Mr. Justice, you're reading it all now."

"It isn't enough," said the Supreme Court justice. "And damn the courts, I shouldn't have to tell you that, Mr. Former CIA Man. You need names, a lot more names, not just five generals, three of whom are retired and one of them, the so-called instigator, a man who had an operation several months ago that left him without legs."

"Delavane?" asked Simon, stepping away from the window.

"That's right," said Wellfleet. "Kind of pathetic, huh? Not exactly the picture of a very imposing threat, is he?"

976

"It could drive him into being an extraordinary threat."

"I'm not denying that, Nate. I'm just looking at the collection you've got here. Abrahms? As anyone worth his kosher salt in Israel will tell you, he's a strutting, bombastic hothead—a brilliant soldier but with ten screws loose. Besides, his only real concerns are for Israel. Van Headmer? He's a relic of the nineteenth century, pretty fast with a hangman's rope but his voice doesn't mean doodly-shit outside of South Africa."

"Mr. Justice," said Stone, speaking more firmly than he had before, "are you implying that we're wrong? Because if you are, there are other names—and I don't just mean a couple of attachés at the embassy in Bonn—names of men who have been killed because they tried to find answers."

"You weren't listening!" snapped Wellfleet. "I just told Nate I wasn't denying anything. How in hell could I? Forty-five *million* in untraceable, *illegal* exports! An apparatus that can shape the news media here and in Europe, that can corrupt government agencies, and as Nate here puts it, 'create a psychopathic assassin' so they can find *you,* or make you back *down.* Oh, no, mister, I'm not saying you're wrong. I'm saying you better damn well do what I'm told you're pretty good at, and you'd better do it quickly. Haul in this Washburn and any others you can find in Bonn; pick a cross section of those people at State and the Pentagon and fill 'em full of dope or whatever the hell you use and get *names!* And if you ever mention that I suggested such wanton measures that violate our most sacred human rights, I'll say you're full of shit. Talk to Nate here. You don't have time for niceties, mister."

"We don't have the resources, either," said Stone. "As I explained to Mr. Simon, there are a few friends I can call upon for information but nothing like what you suggest—like what you didn't suggest. I simply don't have the leverage, the men or the equipment. I'm not even employed by the government any longer."

"I can help you there." Wellfleet made a note. "You'll get whatever you need."

"There's the other problem," continued Stone. "No matter how careful we are, we'd send out alarms. These people are *believers,* not just mindless extremists. They're orchestrated; they have lines of fallbacks and know exactly what they're doing. It's a progression, a logical capitalizing on sequences until we're all forced to accept them—or accept the unacceptable, the continuation of violence, of wholesale rioting, of the killing."

"Very nice, mister. And what are *you* going to do? *Nothing?*"

"Of course not. Rightly or wrongly, I believed Converse when he told me that with our affidavits—with all the evidence we provided him—Mr. Simon could reach people we couldn't reach. Why shouldn't I have believed him? It was an extension of my own thinking *without* a Nathan Simon but with Converse himself. Only, my way would take longer. The precautions would be far more elaborate, but it *could* be done. We'd reach the right people and start

978

the counterattack.''

"Who'd you have in mind?'' asked Wellfleet sharply.

"The President first, obviously. Then, because we're dealing with half a dozen other countries, the Secretary of State. A maximum-security screening process would be set up immediately—one undoubtedly using those chemicals you didn't speak of—until we had unblemished personnel, men and women we were certain beyond doubt had no connections to this Aquitaine. We create cells, command posts here and abroad. Incidentally, there's a man who can help us immeasurably in this, a man named Belamy in Britain's M.I.6. I've worked with him and he's the best—knows the best—and he's done this sort of thing before. Once our cells are in place and in deep cover, we then pull in Washburn and at least two others we know of by description in Bonn. Prudhomme can furnish us with the names of those in the Sûreté who approve transfers, and who furnished evidence against Converse when it didn't exist. And as you know from my own affidavit, we've got the island of Scharhörn under surveillance now—we think it's a nerve center or a communications relay. With the proper equipment we could tap in. The whole point is we widen the circles of information. Once you know a strategy, you can mount a counterstrategy without setting off alarms.'' Stone paused and looked at both men. "Mr. Justice, Mr. Simon. I was station chief in five vital posts in Great Britain and the Continent. I *know* it can be done.''

"I don't doubt you," said Nathan Simon. "How long would it take?"

"If Justice Wellfleet can get me the cooperation and the equipment I need, with the people I select—here and abroad—Derek Belamy and I can mount a crash program. We'd be operational in eight to ten days."

Simon looked at the Supreme Court justice then back at Stone. "We don't have eight or ten days," he said. "We have three—less than three days now."

Peter Stone stared at the tall, portly attorney with the sad, penetrating eyes. He could feel the blood draining from his face.

The cry of the cat was muted in fury. General George Marcus Delavane slowly replaced the telephone on the console. His half-body was propped into the wheelchair, his waist strapped to the steel poles, his arms as heavy as his breath was short, the veins in his neck distended. He brought his hands together, entwining his fingers and pressing the knuckles against each other until the surrounding flesh was white. He raised his large head, his cold, angry eyes narrowing as he looked up at the uniformed aide standing in front of the desk.

"They've disappeared," he said, his high-pitched voice icily controlled. "Leifhelm was taken from a restaurant in Bonn. They say there was an ambulance that raced away, no one knows where. Abrahms' guards were drugged. Others took their places. He was driven off in his own staff car, picked up in front of a synagogue.

Bertholdier did not come down from his apartment on the Montaigne, so the driver went up to discreetly remind him of the time. The woman was bound naked on the bed, the word 'whore' written in lipstick across her breasts. She said two men took him away at gunpoint. There was talk of a plane, she said."

"What about Van Headmer?" asked the aide.

"Nothing. Our charming and oblivious Afrikaner dines at the Johannesburg Military Club and says he will put himself under extra guard. He's not part of the orbit; he's too far away to matter."

"What do you mean, General? What happened?"

"What happened? This *Converse* happened! We created our own most accomplished enemy, Colonel—and I can't say we weren't warned. Chaim said it, our man in the Mossad made it clear. The North Vietnamese created a hell-hound—the Mossad's words—and we created a monster. He should have been killed in Paris, certainly in Bonn."

"You couldn't have ordered it then," said the aide, shaking his head. "You had to know where he came from, and if you couldn't find out, you had to isolate him, make him—what was it?—a pariah, so no one would come forth to claim him. It was sound strategy, General. It still remains sound. No one's come forth—no one's *coming* forth. You held them back, and now it's too late."

Delavane's eyes widened as he appraised the colonel's face. "You've always been the best of adjutants, Paul. You tactfully remind a superior that regardless of periodic setbacks, his decisions were based on sound reasons, and that those reasons will prevail.''

''I've disagreed when I thought it was necessary, General, because whatever I learned I learned from you, so I merely reminded you of yourself. Right now, at this moment, I'm right. *You* were right.''

''Yes, I was—I am. Nothing matters now. Everything's set in motion and nothing can stop it. This Converse—this bold, resourceful enemy— was also held in check by having to keep running. And now *he's* too late. In any event, the men he's taken are merely symbols, magnets to attract others. That's the beauty of clean strategy, Colonel. Once it's set in motion, it rolls like the ocean wave. The power underneath is unseen, but it is relentless. Events will dictate the only acceptable solutions. It's my legacy, Colonel.''

Nathan Simon had nearly finished his explanation. It had taken less than three minutes, during which time Peter Stone remained motionless, his eyes riveted on the older man, his face ashen, the taste in his mouth unbearable.

''You can see the pattern, can't you?'' concluded the attorney. ''The protests begin in the Middle East and follow the sun and the time zones across the Mediterranean, up through Europe, and over the Atlantic, culminating in Canada and the United States. They start with the Peace Now movement in Jerusalem, then Beirut, Rome, Paris, Bonn, London, Toronto, Washing-

982

ton, New York, Chicago, *et cetera*. Gigantic rallies in the major cities and capitals, covering every nation and government Delavane and his people have infiltrated. Confrontations occur —the initial unrest—growing into major disruptions with the infusion of terrorist units. Bombs wired into cars, or under the streets in sewers, or simply rolled into the crowds—the second wave of greater violence—all leading to the mass confusion and disorder they require to put their leading players in position. Or more precisely, once in position to exercise their assignments.''

''The final assaults,'' said Stone quietly. ''Selected assassinations.''

''Chaos,'' agreed Simon. ''World leaders suddenly dead, the descending mantles of authority unclear, too many men protesting, fighting one another, screaming that *they* are in charge. Total chaos.''

''*Scharhörn!*'' said the former intelligence officer. ''We have no other choice now. We have to go in! May I use your telephone, Mr. Justice?'' Without waiting for a reply, Stone walked to Wellfleet's desk as he removed his billfold and pulled out the small piece of paper with a number in Cuxhaven, West Germany, written on it. He turned the phone around under the harsh gaze of the Supreme Court justice, picked it up and dialed. The sequence of transatlantic relays was intolerable. It rang.

''Rebel?''

The explosive invective over the line from half a world away could be heard even by Simon and

Wellfleet. Stone broke it off. *"Stop* it, Johnny! I haven't been near the hotel in hours and I haven't time for this! . . . You *what?"* The CIA man listened, holding his breath, his eyes growing wide. He covered the mouthpiece and turned to Nathan Simon. "My God, there's a breakthrough!" he whispered. "Photographs. Infrared, taken last night and developed this morning—all clear. Ninety-seven men from Scharhörn getting off a boat, heading for the airport and train station. He thinks they're the hit teams."

"Get those photographs to Brussels and flown to Washington on the fastest goddamned military transport you can find!" ordered the venerated justice of the Supreme Court.

39

"Preposterous!" shouted General Jacques-Louis Bertholdier from the brocaded wing chair in the spacious study of the Alpine chateau. "I don't believe you for a minute!"

"That's a favorite word of yours, isn't it?" said Converse, standing by the open cathedral window across the room, the mountain fields beyond. He was dressed in a dark suit, white shirt and a regimental tie, all purchased in Chamonix. "The word 'preposterous,' I mean," he continued. "You used it at least twice when we spoke in Paris, I think. It's as though whatever information you don't like is preposterous—absurd, unwarranted—not only the information itself but also the person who gives you the information. Is that the way you look at people who don't accommodate you?''

"Certainly not! It is the way I treat liars.'' The legend of France began to rise. "And I see no reason—''

"Stay in that chair!'' Joel commanded. "Or only your corpse will get back to Paris,'' he added simply, without hostility. "I told you, all I wanted was this conversation with you. It won't take long, and then you'll be free to go. That's more charity than any of you showed me.''

"You were expendable. I apologize for being so blunt, but it is the truth.''

"If I was so expendable, why didn't you just kill me? Why the elaborate buildup, all that trouble to make me a killer, an assassin, a man hunted all over Europe.''

"The Jew gave us that.''

"The Jew? Chaim Abrahms?''

"It makes no difference now,'' said Bertholdier. "Our man in the Mossad—incidentally, a brilliant analyst—made it clear that if we could not find out where you came from, if you yourself did not know, then we had to put you in 'forbidden territory'—I believe that was the expression. And that was not preposterous. No one claims you. You were—you *are*—indeed, untouchable.''

"Why doesn't it make any difference now—the fact that you've told me what you presume I already know?''

"You've lost, Monsieur Converse.''

"I have?''

"Yes, and if you have delusions about drugging me—as we drugged you—let me spare you and me the discomfort of such procedures. I do not have the information. Actually, no one does. Only a machine that is set in motion and issues commands."

"To other machines?"

"Of course not. To men—men who will do what they have been trained to do, who believe in what they're doing. I have no idea who they are."

"That's the killing, isn't it? They're the killers."

"All war is reduced to killing, young man. And make no mistake. This *is* war. The world has had enough. We will put it to rights, as the English say. You will see; we will not be opposed. We are not only needed, we are wanted."

" 'Accumulation, rapid acceleration,' those were the words, weren't they?"

"The Jew was precipitate. He talks too much."

"He says you're the pompous asshole of creation. He told me that he and Van Headmer were going to put you in a glass room with little boys and girls and watch you screw yourself into a coronary."

"His conversations were always tasteless. . . . But no, I *don't* believe you."

"So we're back to my original statement." Joel walked away from the window and sat down in an armchair diagonally opposite Bertholdier. "Why do you find it so difficult to believe? Because you didn't think of it?"

"No, monsieur. Because it's unthinkable."

Converse pointed to a telephone on the desk.

"You know their private numbers," he said. "Call them. Call Leifhelm in Bonn and Abrahms in Tel Aviv. Also Van Headmer, if you like, although I'm told he's in the States, probably California."

"California?"

"Ask each of them if he came to see me at that little stone house on Leifhelm's property. Ask them what we talked about. Go on, the phone's right over there."

Bertholdier looked sharply at the telephone as Joel held his breath. Then the soldier turned back to Converse, reluctance winning out over inclination. "What are you trying to do? What sort of trick is this?"

"What trick? There's the phone. I can't rig it, I can't make it dial numbers or hire people hundreds or thousands of miles away to impersonate those men."

The Frenchman looked again at the telephone. "What could I say?" he asked quietly, the question directed more at himself than at Joel.

"Try the truth. You're very big on the truth as you see it, as it pertains to large global concepts, and this is only a small matter of several minor omissions. *They're* omitting to tell you that each one of them came to see *me*. Or perhaps the omissions weren't so minor."

"How would I know they came to see you?"

"You weren't listening to me. I said 'Try the truth.' I had you kidnapped, no one else. I did it because I didn't understand, and if push comes to shove, I want to save my life. There's a huge world out there, General. Large parts of it you'll leave intact, and I could live very nicely as long as I didn't have to worry about someone coming out of a doorway to blow my head off."

"You're not the man I thought you were—we thought you were."

"We're all what circumstances make us. I've had my share of sweat. I'm bowing out of the crusading business, or the lid-blowing business, or whatever you want to call it. Would you like to know why?"

"Very much so," said Bertholdier, staring at Joel, confusion and curiosity fighting each other in his eyes.

"Because I listened to you in Bonn. Maybe you're right, or maybe I just don't care anymore because I was left way out in the cold. Maybe the world really does need you arrogant bastards right now."

"It *does!* There's no other *way!*"

"It's the year of the generals then, isn't it?"

"No, not simply the *generals!* We are the consolidators, the symbols of strength and discipline and lawful order. Surely what follows in the aggregate—in the international marketplaces, in joint foreign policies, and yes, in the legal processes themselves—will reflect our leadership, our example, and out of it all will come what is most lacking in today's world. *Stability,* Monsieur Converse! No more madmen like the senile Khomeini or the hollow braggard Qaddafi, or the insane Palestinians. Such men and such nations and would-be nations will be pincered by truly international forces, crushed by the overwhelming might of like-minded governments. Retribution will be swift and total. I am a military strategist of some reputation, so let me assure you the Russians will stand aside, appalled, not daring to interfere—knowing at last that they cannot divide us any longer. They cannot rattle their sabers, frightening one segment while appeasing others, for we are all one!''

"Aquitaine," said Joel softly.

"An adequate code name, yes," agreed Bertholdier.

"You're as convincing as you were in Bonn," added Converse. "And maybe it could all work, but not this way, not with you people."

"I beg your pardon?"

"Nobody has to divide *you*—you're already oceans apart."

"I don't understand."

"Place those calls, General. Make it easy on yourself. Reach Leifhelm first. Tell him you just heard from Abrahms in Tel Aviv and you're appalled. Say Abrahms wants to meet with you because he has information about me, that he admitted he and Van Headmer came to see me alone in Bonn. You could add that *I* told Abrahms he and his Afrikaner friend were my second and third visitors. Leifhelm was the first."

"Why would I tell him this?"

"Because you're angry as hell. No one told you about these separate meetings with me and you consider them highly improper—which, if you don't you damn well should. A little while ago you said I was expendable. Well, you're in for a shock, General."

"Explain that!"

"No. Use the phone. Listen to what he says, how he reacts, how they all react. You'll know. See if I'm telling you the truth."

Bertholdier placed both his hands on the arms of the brocaded chair and started to rise, his eyes on the telephone. Converse sat motionless, watching the Frenchman closely, barely breathing, his pulse racing. Suddenly the general pushed himself violently back into the chair and gripped its arms. "All *right!*" he shouted. "What was *said?* What did they *say?*"

"I think you should use that phone first."

"Pointless!" snapped Bertholdier. "As you say, you cannot make it dial other numbers—well, I suppose you could, but to what end? Impostors? Ridiculous! I could ask any of several hundred questions and know they were merely playactors."

"All the more reason to call them," said Joel calmly. "You'd know I was telling the truth."

"And give an advantage where none was shown to *me.*"

Converse breathed normally again. "It's up to you, General. I'm just looking for a safe way out."

"Then tell me what was said to you."

"Each asked me the obvious—as if he didn't trust the drugs or the one who administered them or each other. Whom did I really represent?" Joel paused; he was about to fish with a witness, but knew he had to pull back instantly if the pond was barren. "I guess I mentioned Beale on Mykonos," he offered hesitantly.

"You did," confirmed the general. "He was reached several months ago, but our contact never returned. You explained that also."

"You thought he might be one of you, didn't you?"

"We thought he threw away a brilliant military career out of disgust. Apparently it was a different disgust, the very weakness we abhorred. But these are not the things I want to hear. You made reference to some aspect of expendability. That is what I want to hear. *Now.*"

"You want it straight? Without the frills?"

"No frills, monsieur."

"Leifhelm said you'll be out in a matter of months, if not sooner. You give too many orders; the others are sick of them—and you want too much for France."

"*Leifhelm?* The hypocritical *weasel* who sold his very soul to deny everything he espoused? Who betrayed his leaders in the dock at Nuremberg, furnishing the court with all manner of evidence so as to worm his way into the Allies' *bowels!* Everywhere, whatever our commitments, we cringed! He brought dishonor on the most honorable profession in this world. Let me tell you, monsieur, it is not *I* who will be out, it is *he!*"

"Abrahms said you were a sexual embarrassment," continued Converse, as though Bertholdier's response was irrelevant. "That was the phrase he used, 'a sexual embarrassment.' He mentioned the fact that there was a record—one he obtained, in fact—that spelled out a string of rapes, female and male, that were covered up by the French Army because you were damned good at what you did. But then he asked the question.

Could a bisexual opportunist, one who ravaged women at will and who sodomized young men and boys, who corrupted the word 'interrogations' as well as whole sections of the officer corps, be truly considered the French leader of code-name Aquitaine. He *also* said you wanted too many controls centered in your own government. But by the time there were such controls, you'd be gone."

"*Gone?*" cried the Frenchman, his eyes once more on fire as they had been weeks ago in Paris, his whole body trembling with rage. "Convicted by a *barbarian,* a smelly, uneducated *Jew?*"

"Van Headmer didn't go that far. He said you were simply too vulnerable—"

"Forget Van Headmer!" roared Bertholdier. "He's a fossil! He was courted solely on the basis that he might deliver raw materials. He's of no consequence."

"I didn't think he was," agreed Joel truthfully.

"But the strutting, foul-mouthed Israeli thinks he can move against *me?* Let me tell you, I have been threatened before—by a great man—and nothing ever came of those threats because, as you put it, I was 'damned good' at what I did. I *still* am! And there is another record, one of outstanding and brilliant service, that dwarfs any compilation of filthy rumors and barracks gossip. My record is unmatched by any in code-name Aquitaine, and that includes the legless egomaniac in San Francisco. He believes it was all *his* idea! *Preposterous!* I refined it! He merely gave it a name based on a far-fetched reading of history."

"He also got the ball started by exporting one

hell of a lot of hardware," interrupted Converse.

"Because it was *there!* And there were profits to be made!" The general paused, leaning forward in the chair. "I will be frank with you. As with any elite corps of leadership, one man rises above the others by the sheer strength of his character and his mind. Beside me the others—all others—pale into mediocrity. Delavane is a deformed, hysterical caricature. Leifhelm is a Nazi, and Abrahms is a bombastic polarizer; alone he could set off waves of anti-Semitism, the worst sort of symbol of leadership. When the tribunals rise out of the confusion and the panic, they will look to me. I shall be the true leader of code-name Aquitaine."

Joel got out of the chair and walked back to the window, staring out at the mountain fields, feeling the soft breezes on his face. "This examination is finished, General," he said.

As if on cue the door opened, and a former sergeant major in the French Army based in Algiers stood there waiting to escort the bewildered legend of France out of the room.

Chaim Abrahms sprang out of the brocaded chair, his barrel chest straining the seams of his black safari jacket. "He said those things about *me?* About *himself?*"

"I told you before we got into any of this to use the phone," said Converse, sitting across from the Israeli, a pistol on a table beside his chair. "Don't take my word for it. I've heard it said you've got good gut instincts. Call Bertholdier. You don't have to say where you are—as a matter

993

of fact, I'd put a bullet in your head if you tried. Just tell him one of Leifhelm's guards, a man you bought to keep his eyes open for you because of a certain innate mistrust you have of Germans, told you that he, Bertholdier, came to see me alone on two separate occasions. Since I haven't been found, you want to know why. It'll work. You'll hear enough to know whether I'm telling you the truth or not."

Abrahms stared down at Joel. "But why do you tell me this truth? If it *is* the truth. Why do you abduct me to tell me these things. *Why?*"

"I thought I made that clear. My money's running out, and although I'm not wild about lox or kreplach, I'd be better off living in Israel under a protective cover than being hunted and ultimately killed running around Europe. You can do that for me, but I know I've got to deliver something to you first. I'm delivering it now. Bertholdier intends to take over what he calls code-name Aquitaine. He said you're a foul-mouthed Jew, a destructive symbol, you'll have to go. He said the same about Leifhelm; the specter of a Nazi couldn't be tolerated, and Van Headmer was a 'fossil'—that was the word, 'fossil.' "

"I can hear him," said Abrahms softly, his hands clasped behind his back, pacing toward the window. "Are you sure our military boulevardier with the cock of steel did not say 'smelly Jew'? I've heard our French hero use such words— always, of course, apologizing to me, saying I was exempt."

"He used them."

"But *why?* Why would he say such things to

994

you? I don't deny his logic, for Christ's sake. Leifhelm will be shot once controls are established. A *Nazi* running the goddamned German government? Absurd! Even Delavane understands this, he will be eliminated. And poor old Van Headmer is a relic, we all know that. Still, there is gold in South Africa. He could deliver it. But why *you?* Why would Bertholdier come to *you?*"

"Ask him yourself. There's the phone. Use it."

The Israeli stood motionless, his narrow eyes encased in swells of flesh riveted on Converse. "I *will,*" he said quietly, emphatically. "You are far too clever, Mr. Lawyer. The fire inside you remains in your head—it has not reached your stomach. You think too much. You say you were manipulated? I say *you* manipulate." Abrahms turned and strode like a bulky Coriolanus to the phone. He stood for a moment, squinting, remembering, then picked up the phone and dialed the series of numbers long ago committed to memory.

Joel remained in the chair, every muscle in his body taut, his throat suddenly dry. Slowly he inched his hand over the arm of the chair nearer the pistol. In seconds he might have to use it, his strategy—his *only* strategy—blown apart by a phone call he had never thought would be made. *What was wrong with him? Where were his vaunted examining tactics taking him? Had he forgotten whom he was dealing with?*

"Code Isaiah," said Abrahms into the phone, his angry eyes again staring across the room at Converse. "Patch me through to Verdun-sur-Meuse. *Quickly!"* The Israeli's massive chest heaved with every breath, but it was the only part of his stocky frame that moved. He spoke again, furiously. "Yes, code *Isaiah!* I have no time to waste! Reach Verdun-sur-Meuse! *Now!"* Abrahms' eyes grew wide as he listened. He looked briefly away from Converse, then snapped his head back toward him, his eyes filled with loathing. *"Repeat* that!" he shouted. And then he slammed the telephone down with such force the desk shook. *"Liar!"* he screamed.

"You mean me?" asked Joel, his hand inches from the gun.

"They say he *disappeared!* They cannot *find him!"*

"And?" Converse's throat was now a vacuum. He had lost.

"He *lies!* The cock of steel is no more than a whining coward! He's hiding—he *avoids* me! He will not *face* me!"

Joel swallowed repeatedly as he moved his hand away from the weapon. "Force the issue," he said, somehow managing to keep the tremor out of his voice. "Trace him down. Call Leifhelm, Van Headmer. Say it's imperative you reach Bertholdier."

"Stop it! And let him know I *know?* He had to give you a reason! Why did he come to see you in the first place?"

"I wanted to wait until you'd spoken to him," said Converse, crossing his legs and picking up a pack of cigarettes next to the pistol. "He might have told you himself—then again, he might not. He has this idea that I was sent out by Delavane

996

to test all of you. To see who might betray him."

"*Betray* him? Betray the legless one? *How?* Why? And if our French peacock believed that, again why would he say these things to you?"

"I'm an attorney. I provoked him. Once he understood how I felt about Delavane, what that bastard did to me, he knew I couldn't possibly have anything to do with him. His defenses were down; the rest was easy. And as he talked I saw a way to save my own life." Joel struck a match, lighting a cigarette. "By reaching you," he added.

"At the end you bank on the morality of a Jew, then? His acknowledgment of a debt."

"In part, yes, but not entirely, General. I know something about Leifhelm, about the way he's maneuvered through the years. He'd have me shot, then send his men after the rest of you, leaving himself in the number one position."

"That's exactly what he'd do," agreed the Israeli.

"And I didn't think Van Headmer had any real authority north of Pretoria."

"Right again," said Abrahms, walking back toward Converse. "So the hellhound created in Southeast Asia is a survivor."

"Let's be more specific," countered Joel. "I was sent out by people I don't know who abandoned me without raising the slightest question as to my guilt or innocence. For all I know, they joined in the hunt to kill me to save their own lives. Given these conditions I intend to survive."

"What about the woman? Your woman?"

"She goes with me." Converse put down the

cigarette and picked up the gun. "What's your answer? I can kill you now, or leave that to Bertholdier, or Leifhelm, if he kills the Frenchman first. Or I can bank on your morality, your acknowledgment of a debt. What's it going to be?"

"Put away the gun," said Chaim Abrahms. "You have the word of a sabra."

"What'll you do?" asked Joel, placing the weapon back on the table.

"*Do?*" shouted the Israeli in a sudden burst of anger. "What I've always *intended* to do! You think I give a horse's fart for this abstraction, this Aquitaine's infrastructure? Do you think I care one whit for titles or labels or chains of command? Let them have it all! I only care that it works, and for it to work *respectability* must come out of the chaos *along* with strength. Bertholdier was right. I am too divisive a figure—as well as a Jew—to be so visible on the Euro-American scene. So I will be *invisible*— except in Eretz Yisrael, where my word will be the law of this new order. I, myself, will help the French bull get whatever medals he wants. I will not fight him, I will *control* him."

"How?"

"Because I can destroy his respectability."

Converse sat forward, suppressing his astonishment. "His *sex* life? Those buried scandals?"

"My God, no, you imbecile! You kick a man below his belt in public you ask for trouble. Half the people cry 'Foul,' thinking it could happen to them, and the other half applaud his courage to

998

indulge himself—which they would very much like to do."

"Then how, General? How can you do this, destroy his respectability?"

Abrahms sat down again in the brocaded chair, his thick body squeezed dangerously between the delicately carved mahogany arms. "By exposing the role he played in 'code-name Aquitaine.' The roles we all played in this extraordinary adventure that forced the civilized world to summon us and the strengths of our professional leadership. It's entirely possible that all free Europe will turn to Bertholdier, as France nearly turned to him after De Gaulle. But one must understand a man like Bertholdier. He doesn't merely seek power, he seeks the *glory* of power—the trappings, the adulation, the mysticism. He would rather give up certain intrinsic authority than lose any part of the glory. *Me?* I don't give a shit about the glory. All I want is the power to get what I need, what I command. For the kingdom of Israel and its imprimatur in all of the Middle East."

"You expose him, you expose yourself. How can you win that way?"

"Because he'll blink first. He'll think of the glory and submit. He'll do as I say, give me what I want."

"I think he'll have you shot."

"Not when he's told that if I die several hundred documents will be released describing every meeting we attended, every decision we made. Everything is scrupulously detailed, I assure you."

"You intended this from the beginning?"

"From the beginning."

"You play rough."

"I'm a sabra. I play for the advantage —without it we would have been massacred decades ago."

"Among these documents is there a list of everyone in Aquitaine?"

"No. It has never been my intention to jeopardize the movement. Call it whatever name you will, I believe truly in the concept. There *must* be a unified, international military-industrial complex. The world will not stay sane without it."

"But there is such a list."

"In a machine, a computer, but it must be programmed correctly, the proper codes used."

"Could you do it?"

"Not without help."

"What about Delavane?"

"You have certain perceptions yourself," said the Israeli, nodding. "What about him?"

Again Joel had to control his astonishment. The computer codes that released the master list of Aquitaine were with Delavane. At least the key symbols were. The remainder were provided by the four leaders across the Atlantic. Converse shrugged. "You haven't really mentioned him. You've talked about Bertholdier, about the elimination of Leifhelm, and the impotence of Van Headmer, who could, however, bring in raw materials—"

"I said 'gold,' " corrected Abrahms.

"Bertholdier said 'raw materials." But what about George Marcus Delavane?"

1000

"Marcus is finished," said the Israeli flatly. "He was coddled—we all coddled him—because he brought us the concept and he worked his end in the United States. We have equipment and matériel all over Europe, to say nothing of the contraband we've shipped to insurgents, just to keep them occupied."

"Clarification," interrupted Joel. " 'Occupied' means killing?"

"All is killing. Disingenuous philosophers notwithstanding, the ends *do* justify the means. Ask a man hunted by killers if he will jump into human excrement to conceal himself."

"I've asked him," said Converse. "I'm he, remember? What about Delavane?"

"He's a madman, a maniac. Have you ever heard his voice? He speaks like a man with his testicles in a vise. They cut off his legs, you know, amputated only months ago for diabetes. The great general felled from an excess of *sugar!* He's tried to keep it a secret. He sees no one and no longer goes to his impressive office filled with photographs and flags and a thousand decorations. He operates out of his home, where the servants come only when he's hidden in a darkened bedroom. How he wished it could have been a mortar shell or a bayonet charge, but no. Only sugar. He's become worse, a raving fool, but even fools can have flashes of brilliance. He had it once."

"What *about* him?"

"We have a man with him, an aide with the rank of colonel. When everything begins, when our commands are in place, the colonel will do as instructed. Marcus will be shot for the good of his own concept.''

It was Joel's turn to get out of his chair. Once again he walked to the cathedral window across the room and felt the cool mountain breezes on his face. ''This examination is finished, General,'' he said.

''*What?*'' roared Abrahms. ''You want your life. *I* want guarantees!''

''Finished,'' repeated Converse as the door opened and a captain in the Israeli Army walked inside, his gun leveled at Chaim Abrahms.

''There will be no discussion between us, Herr Converse,'' said Erich Leifhelm, standing by the door of the study. The doctor from Bonn had just left the room. ''You have your prisoner. Execute him. Over many years and in many ways I have been waiting for this moment. In truth, I'm weary of the morbidity.''

''Are you telling me you want to die?'' asked Joel, standing by the table with the pistol on top.

''No one *wants* to die, least of all a soldier in the quiet of a strange room. Drums and sharp commands to a firing squad are preferable—there's a certain meaning in that. But I've seen too much death to go into hysterics. Pick up your pistol and get it over with. I would if I were you.''

Converse studied the German's face, whose strange eyes were noncommittal, expressing only contempt. ''You mean it, don't you?''

''Shall I give orders myself? There was a newsreel years ago. A black man did that against a bloodstained wall in Castro's Cuba. I've always admired that soldier.'' Leifhelm suddenly shouted, *"Achtung! Soldaten! Präsentiert das Gewehr!"*

"For Christ's sake, why not *talk?*'' roared Joel, riding over the fanatical voice.

"Because I have nothing to say. My actions speak, my life has *spoken!* What is it, Herr Converse? You have no stomach for executions? You cannot give the order to yourself? A small, insignificant man's conscience will not permit him to kill? You are laughable!''

"I remind you, General, I've killed several people these past few weeks. Killed with less feeling than I ever thought possible.''

"The lowliest coward running for his life will kill in panic. There is no character in that, merely survival. No, Herr Converse, you *are* insignificant, an impediment even your own forces care nothing about. You abound in this world. There is an odd phrase you have in your country that so readily applies to you, a phrase our associate uses frequently. You are a 'shit-kicker,' Herr Converse, nothing more and probably less.''

"What did you say? What did you call me?''

"You heard me clearly. A shit-kicker. A little man who steps in waste. Shit-kicker, Herr Converse. *Shit-kicker!*''

He was back a lifetime ago, on the bridge of a carrier, the face in front of him contorted, obscene, the voice shrill. Shit-kicker! Shit-kicker, shit-kicker, shit-kicker! Then other explosions followed, and he was blown into the dark clouds, the wind and the rain buffeting him, hammering him as he swung down toward the earth. Down to

*the ground and four years of madness and death
and dying children weeping. Madness! Shit-kicker
. . . shit-kicker . . . shit-kicker!*

Converse reached down for the pistol on the
table. He picked it up and, with his index finger
around the trigger, leveled it at Erich Leifhelm.

And then a sudden shock went through him.
What was he doing? He needed all three men of
Aquitaine. Not one, not two, but three! It was the
basis, the spine of what he had to do! But still
there was something else. He had to kill, he had
to destroy the deadly human virus staring at him,
wanting death. Oh, Jesus! Had Aquitaine won,
after all? Had he become one of them? If he had,
he had lost.

"Your kind of courage is cheap, Leifhelm," he
said softly, lowering the gun. "Better a quick
bullet than other alternatives."

"I live by my code. I die by it gladly."

"Cleanly, you mean. Swiftly. No Dachau, no
Auschwitz."

"You have the gun."

"I thought you had so much to offer."

"My successor has been chosen carefully. He
will carry out details, every nuance of my
agenda."

*The opening was there, a strategy suddenly
revealed. Joel pushed the button.*

"Your successor?"

"*Ja.*"

"You have no successor, Field Marshal."

"What?"

"Any more than you have an agenda. You
don't have anything without me. It's why I

1004

brought you here. Just you.''

"What are you saying?''

"Sit down, General. I've several things to tell you, and for your own sake you'd better be seated. Your own execution might be more preferable to you than what I've got to say.''

"Liar!" screamed Erich Leifhelm four minutes later, his hands gripping the arms of the brocaded chair. "Liar, liar, *liar!"* he roared.

"I didn't expect you to believe me,'' said Joel calmly, standing in the middle of the spacious, book-lined study. "Call Bertholdier in Paris and tell him you just heard some disturbing news and you'd like a clarification. Say it outright; you've learned that while you were in Essen, Bertholdier and Abrahms came to see me at your place in Bonn.''

"How would I *know* that?''

"The truth. They paid a guard to open the door—I don't know which one, I didn't see him—but a guard did unlock the door and let them in.''

"Because they believed you were an *informer,* sent out by Delavane, himself?''

"That's what they told me.''

"You were drugged! There were no such indications!''

"They were suspicious. They didn't know the doctor and they didn't trust the Englishman. I don't have to tell you they don't trust you. They thought the whole thing might be a hoax. They wanted to cover themselves.''

"Incredible!"

"Not when you think about it,'' said Converse,

sitting down opposite the German. "How did I really get the information I had? How did I know the exact people to reach—except through Delavane? That was their thinking."

"That Delavane would do this—*could* do it?" began the astonished Leifhelm.

"I know what that means now," interrupted Joel quickly, seizing on the new opening presented him. "Delavane's finished, they both admitted it when they understood he was the last person on earth I'd work for. Maybe they were throwing me a few crumbs before setting me up for my own execution."

"That had to be done!" exclaimed the Third Reich's once youngest field marshal. "Certainly you can understand. Who *were* you? Where did you come from? You yourself did not know. You spoke of inconsequential names and lists and a great deal of money but nothing that made sense. Who had penetrated us? Since we could not find out, you had to be turned into a pariah. Into something rotten. A thing of rot no one would touch."

"You did it very well."

"For that I must take credit," said Leifhelm, nodding. "It was essentially my organization. Everything was mine."

"I didn't bring you here to discuss your achievements. I brought you here to save my life. You can do that for me—the people who sent me out either can't or won't—but you can. All I have to do is give you a reason."

"By implying that Abrahms and Bertholdier conspire against me?"

"I won't imply anything, I'll give it to you straight in their own words. Remember, neither one of them thought I'd leave your place except as a corpse conveniently shot in the vicinity of some particularly gruesome assassination." Suddenly Converse got out of the chair, shaking his head. *"No!"* he said emphatically. "Call your trusted French and Israeli allies, your fellow Aquitainians. Say anything you like, just listen to their voices—you'll be able to tell. It takes an accomplished liar to spot other liars, and you're the best."

"I find that offensive."

"Oddly enough, I meant it as a compliment. It's why I reached you. I think you're going to be the winner over here, and after what I've been through I want to go with a winner."

"Why do you say that?"

"Oh, come on, let's be honest. Abrahms is hated; he's insulted everyone in Europe, the U.K. and the U.S. who doesn't agree with his expansionist policies for Israel. Even his own countrymen can't shut him up. All they can do is censure him, and he keeps on screaming. He'd never be tolerated in any kind of international federation."

The Nazi quickly, repeatedly shook his head. *"Never!"* he shouted. "He is the most loathsome man to come out of the Middle East. And of course, he's a Jew. But how is Bertholdier to be equated in this manner?"

Joel paused before answering. *"His* manner," he replied thoughtfully. "He's imperious, arrogant. He sees himself not only as a great military figure and a history-making power broker, but also as some sort of god, above other men. There's no room on his Olympus for mortals. Also he's French. The English and the Americans wouldn't give him spit: one De Gaulle in a century is enough for them."

"There's clarity in your thoughts. He's the sort of abominable egotist only the French can suffer. He is, of course, a reflection of the entire country."

"Van Headmer doesn't count except where he can bring South Africa around for raw materials."

"Agreed," said the German.

"But you, on the other hand," Converse went on rapidly, again sitting down, "worked with the Americans and the English in Berlin and Vienna. You helped implement occupation policies, and in good conscience you turned over evidence to both the U.S. and the U.K. prosecution teams in Nuremberg. Finally, you became Bonn's spokesman in NATO. Whatever you were in the past, they like you." Again Joel paused, and when he continued there was a degree of deference in his voice. "Therefore, General, you're the winner, and you can save my life. All you need is a reason."

"Then give it to me."

"Use the phone first."

"Don't be an idiot and don't take *me* for one! You would not insist so unless you were sure of yourself, which means you are telling the truth. And if those *Schweine* conspire against me, I will not inform them that I'm *aware* of it! What did they say?"

"You're to be killed. They can't risk the accusation that an old-line member of the Nazi party has assumed vital controls in West Germany. Even under Aquitaine there'd be too many cries of 'Foul!'—too much fuel for the inevitable dissenters. A younger man or someone who thinks like they do, but with no party affiliations in his past, will take your place. But no one you recommend."

Leifhelm was braced rigidly in the brocaded chair, his aged but still taut body immobile, his pallid face with the piercing light-blue eyes like an alabaster mask. *"They* have made this most *holy* decision?" he said icily through lips that barely moved. "The vulgar Jew and the depraved French prince of maggots *dare* to attempt such a move against me?"

"Not that it matters, but Delavane agrees."

"Delavane! A raging, infantile clump of fantasies! The man we knew two years ago has disintegrated to a point beyond senility! He doesn't know it, but we give *him* orders, couched naturally as suggestions and beneficial possibilities. He has no more powers of reason than Adolf Hitler had in his last years of madness."

"I don't know about that," said Converse. "Abrahms and Bertholdier didn't go into it other than to say he was finished. They talked about you."

"Really? Well, let *me* talk about *me!* Who do you think it was that made Aquitaine feasible throughout all Europe and the Mediterranean? Who fed the terrorists with weapons and millions

1009

of pounds of explosives—from the Baader-Meinhof to the Brigate Rosse to the Palestinians—priming them for their final, let's say their *finest,* hours? *Who?* It was *I!* Why are our conferences always in Bonn? Why are all directives funneled, ultimately *issued,* through *me?* Let me explain. *I* have the organization! *I* have the manpower —dedicated men ready to do my bidding with a single order. *I* have the *money!* I created an advanced, highly sophisticated communications center out of rubble; no one else in Europe could have done that—this I've known all along. Bertholdier has nothing to speak of in Paris other than influence and the aura that hovers about him—in true battle, meaningless. The Jew and the South African are a continent away. When the chaos comes, it is *I* who will be the voice of Aquitaine in Europe. I never thought otherwise! My men will cut down Bertholdier and Abrahms at their toilets!"

"Scharhörn's the communications center, isn't it?" asked Joel with no emphasis whatsoever.

"They told you that?"

"The name was dropped. The master list of Aquitaine's in a computer there, isn't it?"

"That, *also?*"

"It's not important. I don't care anymore. I was abandoned, remember? You must have figured out the computer, too—no one else could."

"A considerable accomplishment," admitted Leifhelm, his humility shining brightly on his waxen face. "I even prepared for the catastrophe of death. There are sixteen letters; we each carry different sets of four, the remaining twelve are with the legless maniac. He thinks no one can activate the codes without his primary set, but in truth a *pre*-coded combination of two sequences doubled will do it."

"That's ingenious," said Converse. "Do the others know?"

"Only my trusted French comrade," answered the German coldly. "The prince of traitors, Bertholdier. But, naturally, I never gave him the accurate combination, and an inaccurate insertion would erase everything."

"That was a winner thinking." Joel nodded approvingly, then frowned with concern. "What would happen, though, if your center was assaulted?"

"Like Hitler's plans for the bunker, it would go up in flames. There are explosives everywhere."

"I see."

"But since you speak of winners, and in my judgment such men are prophets," continued Leifhelm, leaning forward in the chair, his eyes widening with enthusiasm, "let me tell you about the isle of Scharhörn. Years ago, in 1945, out of the ashes of defeat, it was to be the site of the most incredible creation designed by true believers the world has ever known, only to be aborted by cowards and traitors. It was called Operation Sonnenkinder—the children of the sun—infants biologically selected and sent out all over the world to people waiting for them, prepared to guide them through their lives to positions of power and wealth. As adults, the *Sonnenkinder* were to have but one mission across the globe.

The rising of the Fourth Reich! You see now the symbolic choice of Scharhörn? From this inner complex of Aquitaine will come forth the *new order!* We will have *done* it!"

"Stow it," said Converse, getting out of the chair and walking away from Erich Leifhelm. "The examination's finished."

"*What?*"

"You heard me, get out of here. You make me sick." The door opened, and the young doctor from Bonn came in, his eyes on the once celebrated field marshal. "Strip him," ordered Converse. "Search him."

Joel entered the dimly lit room where Valerie and the Sûreté's Prudhomme flanked a man behind a video camera mounted on a tripod. The thick lens of the camera was inserted in the wall and ten feet away was a television monitor, which showed only the deserted study, with the brocaded wing chair in the center of the screen.

"Everything go all right?" he asked.

"Beautifully," said Valerie. "The operator didn't understand a word, but he claimed the lighting was exquisite. *Au bel naturel,* he called it. He can make as many copies as you like; they'll take about thirty-five minutes each."

"Ten and the original print will be enough," said Converse, looking at his watch, then at Prudhomme as Val spoke quietly in French to the cameraman. "You can take the first copy and still make the five o'clock flight to Washington."

"With the greatest of enthusiasm, my friend. I assume one of these prints will be for Paris."

"And every other head of government along with our affidavits. You'll bring back copies of the depositions Simon took in New York?"

"I'll go make arrangements," said Prudhomme. "It is best my name does not appear on the passenger manifest." He turned and left the room, followed by the cameraman, who headed for his duplicating equipment down the hall.

Valerie went to Joel, and taking his face in both her hands, she kissed him lightly on the lips. "For a few minutes in there you had me in knots. I didn't think you were going to make it."

"Neither did I."

"But you did. That was some display, mister. I'm so very proud of you, my darling."

"A lot of lawyers'll cringe. It was the worst sort of entrapment. As an old, bewildering, but very bright law professor of mine would have put it, they were admissions elicited on the basis of false statements, those same admissions forming the basis of further entrapment."

"Stow it, Converse. Let's go for a walk. We used to walk a lot, and I'd like to get back in the habit. It's not much fun alone."

Joel took her in his arms. They kissed, gently at first, feeling the warmth and the comfort that had come back to them. He pulled his head away, his hands sliding to her shoulders, and looked into her wide, vibrant eyes. "Will you marry me, Mrs. Converse?" he said.

"Good Lord, again? Well, why not? As you said once before, I wouldn't even have to change the initials on my lingerie."

"You never had initials on it."

1013

"You found that out long before you made the remark."

"I didn't want you to think I stared."

"Yes, my darling, I'll marry you. But first we have things to do. Even before our walk."

"I know. Peter Stone by way of the Tatiana family in Charlotte, North Carolina. He did terrible things to me, but strange as it seems, I think I like him."

"I don't," said Valerie firmly. "I want to kill him."

40

It was the end of the second day in the countdown of three. The worldwide demonstrations against nuclear war were only ten hours away, to start at the first light halfway across the world. The killings would begin, setting the chaos in motion.

The group of eighteen men and five women sat scattered about in the dark projection room in the underground strategy complex of the White House. Each had a small writing tray attached to his seat with a yellow pad lighted by a Tensor lamp. On the screen was flashed in thirty-second intervals one face after another, each with a number in the upper right-hand corner. The instructions had been terse, in the language best understood by these people, and delivered by Peter Stone who had selected them. *Study the faces, make no audible comments, and mark down by number any you recognize, bearing in mind terminal operations. At the end of the series the lights will be turned on and we'll talk. And, if need be, run the series again and again until we come up with something. Remember, we believe these men are killers. Concentrate on that.*

They were told nothing else. Except M.I.6's Derek Belamy, who had arrived within a half-hour of the extraordinary session, looking haggard from his obviously exhausting journey. When Derek walked through the door, Peter had pulled him aside and each gripped the other's arms. Stone was never so happy or so relieved in his life to see any man. Whatever *he* might have missed, or could miss, Belamy would find it. The British agent had a tenth sense above anyone else's sixth, including Peter's, which, of course, was denied modestly by Derek.

"I need you, old friend," said Peter. "I need you badly."

"It's why I'm here, old friend," replied Belamy warmly. "Can you tell me anything?"

"There's no time now, but I can give you a name. Delavane."

"Mad Marcus?"

"The same. It's his crisis and it's real."

"The *bastard!*" whispered the Englishman. "There's no one I'd rather see at the end of a barbed-wire rope. Talk to you later, Peter. You've got your socializing to do. Incidentally, from what I can see, you've got the best here tonight."

"The best, Derek. We can't afford any less."

Beyond the American military personnel who had initially approached Stone, as well as Colonel

1015

Alan Metcalf, Nathan Simon, Justice Andrew Wellfleet and the Secretary of State, the remaining audience was composed of the most experienced and secure intelligence officers Peter Stone had known in a lifetime of clandestine operations. They had been flown over by military transport from France, Great Britain, West Germany, Israel, Spain and the Netherlands. Among them were, besides the extraordinary Derek Belamy, François Villard, chief of France's highly secretive Organisation Etrangère; Yosef Behrens, the Mossad's leading authority on terrorism; Pablo Amandarez, Madrid's specialist in KGB Mediterranean penetrations, and Hans Vonmeer of the Netherlands' secret state police. The others, including the women, were equally respected in the caverns of deep-cover, beyond-salvage operations. They knew by name, face or reputation the legions of killers for hire, killers by order, and killers by reason of ideology. Above all, each was trusted, each a man or woman Stone had worked with; collectively they were the elite of the shadow world.

A face! He knew the face! It stayed on the screen and he wrote on his pad: "Dobbins. Number 57. Cecil or Cyril Dobbins. British Army. Transferred to British Intelligence. *Personal aide to . . . Derek Belamy!*"

Stone looked over at his friend across the aisle, fully expecting him to be writing on his yellow pad. Instead, the Englishman frowned and sat motionless in his chair, his pencil poised above the paper. The next face appeared on the screen. And the next, and the next, until the series was over.

1016

The lights came on, and the first person to speak was the Mossad's Yosef Behrens. "Number seventeen is an artillery officer in the IDF recently transferred to the Security Branch, Jerusalem. His name is Arnold."

"Number thirty-eight," said François Villard, "is a colonel in the French Army attached to the guard of Invalides. It is the face; the name I do not recall."

"Number twenty-six," said the man from Bonn, "is Oberleutnant Ernst Müller of the Federal Republic's Luftwaffe. He is a highly skilled pilot frequently assigned to fly ministers of state to conferences both within and without West Germany."

"Number forty-four," said a dark-skinned woman with a pronounced Hispanic accent, "has no such credentials as your candidates. He is a drug dealer, suspected of many killings and operates out of Iviza. He was once a paratrooper. Name, Orejo."

"Son of a *gun*, I just don't believe it!" said the young lieutenant William Landis, the computer expert from the Pentagon. "I know number fifty-*one*, I'm almost positive! He's one of the adjutants in Middle East procurements. I've seen him a lot but I don't know his name."

Six other men and two women volunteered twelve additional identities and positions as everyone in the room silently looked for an emerging pattern. There was a preponderance of military personnel, and the umbrella of the rest was puzzling. In the main they were ex-combat soldiers from high-casualty outfits who had drifted into crime—largely violent crime, the sort of men Peter Stone knew the generals of Aquitaine considered human garbage.

Finally Derek Belamy spoke in his hard, clipped distant voice. "There are four or five faces I associate with dossiers, but I'm not making connections." He looked over at Stone. "You'll run them again, won't you, old boy?"

"Of course, Derek," replied the former station chief in London. Stone, who had said nothing, rose from his chair and addressed the gathering. "Everything you've given us will be fed immediately into computers, and we'll see if we come up with any correlations. And to repeat what I said previously, I want to thank you all and apologize again for not giving you the explanations you deserve, not only for your help but for the trouble we've caused you. Speaking personally, my consolation is that you've all been here before and I know you understand. We'll break for fifteen minutes and start again. There are coffee and sandwiches in the next room." Stone nodded his thanks once more and started for the door. Derek Belamy intercepted him in the aisle.

"Peter, I'm dreadfully sorry it took me so long to get back to you. Truth is, the office had a devil of a time tracking me down. I was visiting friends in Scotland."

"I thought you might be in Northern Ireland. It's a hell of a mess, isn't it?"

"You were always better than you thought you were. I was in Belfast, of course. But right now I promise to do better—I'm sure I will—but the fact is I'm bushed; it was a perfectly terrible trip and, of course, no sleep whatsoever. All those faces began to look alike—I either knew them all or I didn't know a damned one!"

"Running them again will help," said Stone.

"Quite so," agreed Belamy. "And Peter, whatever this tangle is with that maniac, Delavane, I couldn't have been more delighted to see you in the control chair. We were all told you were out, rather firmly out."

"I'm back in. Very firmly."

"I can see that, chap. That *is* your Secretary of State in the back row, isn't it?"

"Yes, it is."

"*Congratulations,* old boy. Well, off for coffee, black and hot. See you in a few minutes."

"Across the aisle, old friend."

Stone walked out the door and turned right in the white corridor. He could feel the rapid acceleration of his heartbeat; it was a cousin to Johnny Reb's claims of a churning stomach and an acid taste in his mouth—bile, the Rebel called it. He had to get to a telephone quickly. Converse's courier, the Sûreté's Prudhomme, would be arriving within the hour; a Secret Service escort was waiting for him at Dulles Airport with instructions to bring him directly to the White House. But it was not the Frenchman who concerned Stone now, it was Converse himself. He had to reach him before the session began again. He *had* to!

When the lawyer had contacted him through the Tatiana relay, Peter had been astonished by the sheer audacity of what Converse had done.

Kidnapping the three generals—video-taping the interrogations or the "oral examinations" or whatever the legal terminology was; it was insane! The only thing more insane was the fact that he had carried it off—thanks obviously to the resources of a very determined, very angry man from the Sûreté. The computer *was* in Scharhorn, the master list of Aquitaine buried somewhere in its intricate mechanism, only to be erased by inaccurate codes, the complex itself mined with explosives. *Jesus!*

And now the final insanity. The man no one could find, the source so deeply shrouded they frequently doubted his existence despite the fact that all logic insisted he was there. There *had* to be Aquitaine's man in England, for there could be no Aquitaine without the British. Further, Stone knew he was the conduit, the primary communicator between Palo Alto and the generals overseas, for constant screenings of Delavane's telephone charges showed repeated calls to a number in the Hebrides, and such a relay device was all too familiar to the former intelligence agent. The calls disappeared at that number in the Scottish islands, just as the KGB calls processed through Canada's Prince Edward disappeared, and the Company's communications routed through Key West could not be traced.

Belamy! The man whose face never appeared in any publication—film was destroyed instantly by aides if he was even in the background of a photograph. The most guarded operations officer in England, with access to secrets culled over decades and scores of devices created by the best minds of M.I.6. And yet, was it *possible?* Derek Belamy, the quiet, good-humored chess player, the friend who gave good whisky and a fine ear to an American colleague who had progressively had serious doubts about his calling in life. The *better* friend for having the wisdom and the courage to warn his colleague that he was drinking too much, that perhaps he should take a sabbatical, and if money was a problem, surely some sort of quiet consultation agreement could be worked out with his own organization. Was it possible, this decent man, this *friend?*

Stone reached the door in the hallway marked simply by the number 14, OCCUPIED. He walked inside the small room and went to the desk and the telephone. He did not sit down; his anxiety would not permit it. He picked up the phone and dialed the White House switchboard as he took out the slip of paper in his pocket with Converse's number somewhere in France. He gave it to the operator, adding simply, "This should be scrambled. I'm talking from Strategy Fourteen, confirm by trace."

"Trace confirmed, sir. Scrambler will be in operation. Shall I call you back?"

"No, thanks, I'll stay on the line." Stone remained standing as he heard the hollow echo of numbers being punched and the faint hum of the scrambling machine. And then he heard the sound of a door opening. He turned.

"Put the phone down, Peter," said Derek Belamy quietly as he shut the door. "There's no point to this."

"It *is* you, isn't it?" Stone slowly, awkwardly

1021

replaced the phone in its cradle.

"Yes, it is. And I want everything you want, my old friend. Neither of us could deny ourselves the parting shots, could we? I said I was visiting friends in Scotland and you said you thought I was in Ireland. We've learned over the years, haven't we? The eyes don't lie. Scotland—calls to the Hebrides; the glass fell over your eyes. And earlier, when that face came on the screen, you looked across the aisle a bit too obviously, I think."

"Dobbins. He worked for you."

"You wrote frantically on your pad, yet you said nothing."

"I was waiting for you to say something."

"Yes, of course, but I couldn't, could I?"

"Why, Derek? For Christ's sake, *why?*"

"Because it's right and you know it."

"I *don't* know it! You're a sane, reasonable man. They're *not!*"

"They'll be replaced, naturally. How often have you and I used drones we couldn't abide because their contributions were necessary to the objective?"

"*What* objective? An international totalitarian alliance? A military state without borders? All of us robots marching to the drums of fanatics?"

"Oh, come off it, Peter. Spare us both the liberal drivel. You left this business once, drinking yourself into a stupor because of the waste, the futility, the deceits we all practiced—the people we killed—to maintain what we laughingly called the status quo. *What* status quo, old man? To be continuously harassed by our inferiors the world over? To be held hostage by screaming mullahs and hysterical fools who still live in the Dark Ages and would cut our throats over the price of a barrel of oil? To be manipulated at every turn by Soviet deceptions? No, Peter, there really *is* a better way. The means may be distasteful, but the end result is not only desirable, it's also honorable.''

''Whose definition? George Marcus Delavane's? Erich Leifhelm's? Chaim—''

''They'll be *replaced!*''

''They *can't* be!'' shouted Stone. ''Once it starts, you can't stop it. The image becomes the reality. It's expected, *demanded!* To deviate is to be accused, to oppose is to be ostracized, penalized! It's lockstep and lockjaw, and you damn well *know* that!''

The telephone rang.

''Let it ring,'' ordered the man from M.I.6.

''It doesn't matter now. *You* were the Englishman at Leifhelm's house in Bonn. A brief description of you would have confirmed it for me.''

''That's *Converse?*'' The phone rang again.

''Would you like to talk to him? I understand he's quite a lawyer, although he broke a fundamental rule—he took himself on as a client. He's coming out, Derek, and he's going after you, all of you. We all are—after all of you.''

''You won't!'' cried Belamy. ''You *can't!* As you yourself put it, once it starts you can't *stop* it!''

Without the slightest indication that he was about to move, the Englishman suddenly lunged at Stone, the three middle fingers of his right hand rigid, zeroing in like steel projectiles on the CIA man's throat. Stone took the agonizing blow, gasping for air as the room spiraled out of his vision, a thousand dazzling spots of white light flashing in his eyes. He could hear the door opening and closing as the phone insistently rang again. But Peter could not see it; the white lights had turned into darkness. The ringing stopped as Stone wildly, blindly careened around the room, trying to trace the bell, trying to find the phone. The minutes passed in madness as he smashed into walls and fell over the desk. Then the door crashed open and Colonel Alan Metcalf rushed in.

"Stone! What *happened?*" Racing to Peter, the Air Force officer instantly recognized the effects of the judo chop. He began massaging Stone's throat, pressing his knee into the CIA man's stomach to force up air. "The switchboard reached us, saying that room fourteen had placed a scrambler call but didn't pick up. *Christ,* who *was* it?"

Vague images came back to Stone, but still he could not speak; he was capable only of gasping coughs. He writhed under Metcalf's strong hands, pointing to a note pad that had fallen from the desk. The colonel understood; he reached for it and yanked out a ball-point pen from his pocket. He rolled Stone over and, placing the pen in his hand, guided the hand to the pad.

Struggling for control, Peter wrote: BELMY. STP. AQUTAIN.

"Oh, my *God!*" whispered Metcalf, reaching for the phone and dialing zero. "Operator, this is an emergency. Give me Security. . . . Security? Colonel Alan Metcalf talking from Strategy Fourteen. *Emergency!* There's an Englishman named Belamy who may still be on the premises trying to leave. Stop him! Hold him! Consider him dangerous. And get word to the infirmary. Send a doctor to Strategy Fourteen. *Quickly!''*

The White House staff doctor removed the oxygen mask from Stone's face and placed it on the desk next to the cylinder. He then gently moved Peter's head back in the chair, inserted a tongue depressor and peered into the CIA man's throat with a pencil light.

"It was a nasty shot," he said, "but you'll feel better in a couple of hours. I'll give you some pills for the pain."

"What's in them?" asked Stone hoarsely.

"A mild analgesic with some codeine."

"No thanks, Doctor," said Peter, looking over at Metcalf. "I don't think I like what I see on your face."

"I don't either. Belamy got out. His pass was high priority, and he told the East Gate he was needed urgently at the British embassy."

"Goddamn it!''

"Try not to strain your voice," said the doctor.

"Yes of course " replied Stone. "Thank you very much, and now if you'll excuse us." He got out of the chair as the doctor picked up his medical bag and headed for the door.

The telephone rang as the door closed. Metcalf picked it up. "Yes? Yes it is; he's right here." The colonel listened for several moments then turned to Stone. "Breakthrough," he said. "All those military who were identified have two things in common. Each is on a minimum thirty-day summer leave, and every request was made five months ago, nearly to the day."

"Thus guaranteeing request-granted status because they were first in line," added the CIA man with difficulty. "And the plans for the antinuclear demonstrations were announced in Sweden *six* months ago."

"Clockwork," said Metcalf. "To identify and neutralize the others we'll send out the word. Every officer in half a dozen armies and navies who's currently returning from summer leave is to be restricted to quarters. There'll be errors, but that's rough. We can send out the photographs and correct them."

"It's time for Scharhörn." Stone got out of the chair, massaging his throat. "And I don't mind telling you it scares me to death. A wrong symbol and we erase Aquitaine's master list. Worse, a wrong move and that whole complex is blown away." The CIA man went to the phone.

"Are you going to call the Rebel?" asked the colonel.

"Converse first. He's working on the codes."

The three generals of Aquitaine sat stunned, staring straight ahead, refusing to look at one another. The lights had been turned on, the large television screen turned off. Behind each general was a man with a gun and concise instructions: "If he gets up, kill him."

"You know what I want," said Converse,

1026

walking in front of the three. "And as you've just seen, there's really no reason why any of you shouldn't give it to me. Four little numbers or letters each of you has memorized in sequence. Of course, if you refuse, there's a doctor here who I'm told has a bag of magic—the same sort of magic you administered to me in Bonn. What'll it be, gentlemen?"

Silence.

"Four, three, L, one," said Chaim Abrahms, looking down at the floor. "They're *filth,*" he added quietly.

"Thank you, General." Joel wrote in a small note pad. "You're free to go now. You can get out of the chair."

"Go?" said the Israeli, getting up. *"Where?"*

"Wherever you like," replied Converse. "I'm sure you'll have no trouble at the airport in Annecy. You'll be recognized."

General Chaim Abrahms left the room accompanied by the Israeli Army captain.

"Two, M, zero, six," said Erich Leifhelm. "And, if you wish, I will submit to the drugs for verification. I will not be associated with such treacherous pigs."

"I want the combination," pressed Joel, writing. "And I won't hesitate to send you up into space to get it."

"Inversion," said the German. "Reverse the order of the symbols in the second sequence."

"He's yours, Doctor." Converse nodded to the man behind Leifhelm's chair. "We can't take the chance of blowing this one."

General Erich Leifhelm, once the youngest field

marshal of the Third Reich, got up and walked slowly out of the room, followed by the doctor from Bonn.

"You're all unworthy, all blind," said General Jacques-Louis Bertholdier with imperious calm. "I prefer to be shot."

"I'm sure you would, but no such luck," answered Joel. "I don't need you now, and I want to know you're back in Paris, where everyone can see you. Take him to his room."

"The room? I thought I was free to leave, or was that another lie?"

"Not at all. Just a matter of logistics—you know what logistics are, General. We're a little short of transportation and drivers here, so when the doctor's finished, I'm lending the three of you a car. You can draw straws for who drives."

"*What?*"

"Get him out of here," said Converse, addressing a former sergeant major in the French Army once stationed at Algiers.

"*Allez, cochon!*"

The door opened, only coincidentally for Bertholdier. It was Valerie and she looked at Joel. "Stone's on the telephone. He says hurry."

It was 2:05 A.M. when the Mystère jet dropped out of the night sky and landed at the airstrip eight miles from Cuxhaven, West Germany. It taxied to the north end of the runway where the stately, white-maned figure of Johnny Reb waited by a black Mercedes sedan.

The doors of the plane opened and the short steps swung down in place; Converse climbed out, taking Valerie's hand as she descended after him. Next came the former sergeant major from Algiers, followed by a fourth passenger, a slender blond man in his mid-forties who wore tortoiseshell glasses. They walked away from the aircraft as the pilot retracted the steps and closed the automatic doors; the twin engines accelerated and the plane swerved around heading back toward the maintenance hangars. The Rebel came away from the car and met them, extending his hand to Joel. "Ah've seen your picture here and there and it's a pleasure, sir. Frankly, I never thought I'd meet you, leastways not in this world."

"There were a number of times I had my doubts just how long I'd be here. This is my wife, Valerie."

"Ah'm enchanted, ma'am," said the Southerner, bringing Val's hand to his lips as he bowed gallantly. And then to Joel: "Your accomplishments have astonished some of the best minds in my former profession."

"I hope not *too* former," interjected Converse.

"Not at the moment, son."

"This is Monsieur Lefèvre and Dr. Geoffrey Larson. Stone said you've been briefed."

"A pleasure, sir," exclaimed the Rebel, shaking the Frenchman's hand. "My hat's off to you, to all of you for what you did with those three generals. Absolutely *remarkable!*"

"Such men have enemies," said Lefèvre simply. "They are not hard to find and Inspector Prudhomme knew that. We are in many places with many memories. Let us hope they will be put to rest tonight."

"Let's hope," said the Rebel, turning to the fourth passenger. "Dr. Larson, so nice to meet you, sir. I understand you know just about everything there is to know about every computer ever made."

"An exaggeration, I'm sure," said the Englishman shyly. "But I suspect if it ticks I can make it hum. Actually, I was vacationing in Geneva."

The non sequitur momentarily threw Johnny Reb, who could only utter "Sorry about that" as he looked at Joel.

It had been the most difficult decision Peter Stone had made in all his years of agonizing decisions. To make the wrong move—to telegraph the incursion into the complex at Scharhörn —would result in its destruction by the setting off of explosives all over the communications center. There would be nothing left of the old U-boat station but shattered concrete and twisted equipment. Stone had gone by instincts honed over a lifetime in the shadow world. There could be no elite commando units, no official special forces ordered up for an extraordinary assignment, for there was no telling who within the various government forces could be a member, an officer of Aquitaine. Such a man could make a telephone call and the complex at Scharhörn would be blown up. Therefore the incursion had to be made by rogue elements, men hired by outlaws who had no allegiance to anyone or anything but money and their immediate employers. Nothing was a secret any longer without the master list of Aquitaine. The

President of the United States gave Stone twelve hours, after which he said he would convene an emergency session of the Security Council of the United Nations. Peter Stone could hardly believe he had replied to the most powerful man in the free world with the words: "That's meaningless. It would be too late."

The Rebel finished his briefing, his flashlight still shining on the map spread over the hood of the Mercedes. "As I told you, this is the original layout we got from the Zoning Commission in Cuxhaven. Those Nazis sure were particular when it came to specifics—I figure everyone was justifyin' a salary or a rank. We get over the ocean radar and head to the old strip that was used for supplies, then do our number. Now, mind you, there are still a lot of lights out there, still a lot of people, but a hell of a lot less than there were two days ago. There are some walls, but we got grappling hooks and a few boys who know how to use them."

"Who are they?" asked Converse.

"No one you'd ask into your mother's parlor, my friend, but five of the meanest hornets you could find. I tell you they have absolutely no redeeming social qualities. They're perfect."

"What's the aircraft?"

"The best Petey could get, and it's *the* best. A Fairchild Scout. It holds nine people."

"With a glide ratio of eight to one at four thousand feet," said Joel. "I'm flying."

41

Converse inched the half-wheel forward as he cut the engines and entered a left-bank glide over the small airstrip 2,400 feet below. It was erratically visible through the tails of low-flying North Sea clouds, but Joel guessed it could be seen clearly at 500 feet. He would then start his final circle for the short approach, his touchdown heading away from the old U-boat base, minimizing whatever sound the outsized balloon tires made while braking. The maneuver itself was the nearest thing to a carrier landing he could imagine, and he noted with satisfaction that his hands were as steady as his concentration. The fear he was afraid of did not materialize; it was strangely absent. The anxiety and the anger were another matter.

Valerie and Lefèvre—over the Frenchman's strenuous objections—remained behind on a deserted pier in Cuxhaven where Johnny Reb had managed to install a primitive but functional relay station. It was Val's job to stay in radio contact with the team—either the Rebel or Converse operating the powerful handheld equipment on Scharhörn—and the former sergeant from Algiers was to stand guard, letting no one on that pier. The five "recruits" Johnny Reb had hired for apparently large amounts of money were difficult to appraise, for they said very little and wore dark wool-knit caps pulled down above their eyes and black turtleneck sweaters pulled up around their throats. The same clothing was provided for Joel and the British computer expert, Geoffrey Larson; the Rebel had his in the Mercedes. Each man, except Larson, carried a pistol with an attached silencer that was held firmly in an extended holster strapped to his waist. On the left side of the black leather belt was a long-bladed hunting knife, and beside it a coil of thin wire. Situated in back, above the kidneys, and held in place by clips, were two canisters of a Mace-like gas that rendered their victims helpless and silent. The fact that each, including the aging Johnny Reb, wore his equipment with such casual authority made Converse feel out of place, but the degree of concentration they gave to the installation's plans and the curt suggestions they had for gaining entry and subsequent explorations also made him feel that the Rebel had hired well.

Joel circled slowly, delicately into his final approach, silently gliding over the darkened U-boat base, his eyes on both the strip ahead and the instrument-guidance altimeter. He struck the flaps and dropped; the heavy tires absorbed the jarring shock of contact. *Touchdown.*

"We're down," said Johnny Reb into the radio. "And with a little luck we'll stop, won't we, son?"

"We'll stop," said Converse. They did, no more than forty feet from the end of the airstrip. Joel removed the knit hat, breathing deeply; his hairline and forehead were drenched with sweat.

"We're going out." The Rebel snapped off the

radio and pressed it into the front of his chest; it stayed in place. "Oh," he added, seeing that Converse was watching him. "I forgot to mention it. There's heavy-duty Velcro around the case and on your sweater."

"You're full of surprises."

"You had a fair share yourself during the past few weeks. Let's go catfishin', boy." Johnny Reb opened his door; Joel did the same, and they climbed out, followed by Larson and the five men, three of them carrying rubberized grappling hooks attached to coils of rope.

The second man who had said nothing during the strategy session stood before Converse and spoke quietly, startling Joel with his American accent. "I'm a pilot, mister, and that was supposed to be part of my job. I'm glad it wasn't. You're good, man."

"Where did you fly? With whom?"

"Let's say a new kind of Peruvian airline. The scenic Florida run."

"Come *on!*" The Rebel ordered, starting for the overgrown borders of the airstrip.

They approached the high walls of the old U-boat base, all crouching in the tall grass, studying what was before them. Converse was struck by the sheer immensity of the unending thick concrete. It was like a fortress with no fort inside, no treasured structure that warranted the protection of the massive walls. The only break was over on the left, in a section that faced the airstrip. A pair of steel double doors layered with plates of bolted, reinforced iron stood ominously in the erratic moonlight. They were impenetrable.

"This place has quite a history," whispered Johnny Reb beside Joel. "Half the German High Command had no idea it was here and the Allies never got a smell of it. It was Doenitz's private base. Some said he was going to use it as a threat if Hitler didn't turn things over to him."

"It was also going to be used for something else," said Converse, remembering Leifhelm's incredible story of the rising of the Fourth Reich a generation after the war. Operation Sonnenkinder.

One of the men with a grappling hook crawled over and spoke to the Rebel in German. The Southerner replied angrily, looking pained, but finally nodded as the man crawled away. He turned to Joel.

"Son of a no-account hound dog *bitch!*" he exclaimed under his breath. "He stole me blind! He said he'd make the first assault on the east flank—which you know damn well that mother studied—if I guaranteed him an additional five thousand American!"

"And you'll pay, of course."

"Of course. We're honorable men. If he's killed, every penny goes to his wife and children. I know the lad; we took a building once with the Meinhof inside. He scaled eight stories, dropped down through an elevator shaft, kicked a door open and shot the bastards cold with his Uzi on rapid fire."

"I don't *believe* all this," whispered Converse.

"Believe," said the Rebel softly as he looked at Joel. "We do it because no one else will. And somebody has to do it. We may be rogues, son, but there are times we're on the side of the angels—for a price.''

The muted sound of the rubberized grappling hook taking hold on top of the wall split the air; the rope stretched taut. In seconds the black-clothed man could be seen climbing hand over hand, racing up the dark concrete. He reached the ledge, his left hand disappearing over the top, his right leg swinging up as he vaulted into a prone position, his body level with the ledge of concrete. Suddenly he held out his left arm, waving it back and forth twice, a signal. Then bracing himself, he reached for his holstered weapon with his right hand and pulled it out slowly.

A single spit was heard, and once more there was silence as the man's left arm shot out. A second signal.

The two other men with grappling hooks raced out of the grass; flanking the first man, they swung their hooks in circles and heaved them up, each accurately as the ropes were yanked taut, and then began scaling the wall. Joel knew it was his turn; it was part of the plan if he was up to it and he was determined to be. He rose and joined the remaining two men hired by the Rebel; the American pilot who had spoken to him pointed to the center rope. He gripped it and started the painful climb to the top of the wall.

Only in the last extremity were the elderly Johnny Reb and the slender, professorial Geoffrey Larson expected to use the ropes. By his own admission the Southerner might not be capable, and the risk of injury to the computer expert was unacceptable.

Arms and legs aching, Converse was hauled up the final inches by his German companion. "Pull up the rope!" ordered the man in a heavily accented whisper. "Drop it slowly down the other side and reverse the hooks."

Joel did as he was told, and saw for the first time the interior of the strange fortress—and a uniformed man below on the ground, dead, blood trickling down the center of his forehead from the incredibly accurate shot. In the intermittent moonlight he could make out a series of huge watery slips in the distance broken up by concrete piers on which were giant winches, black wheels of immense machinery, long out of use, relics of a violent past. In a semicircle facing the U-boat docks and the sea were five low concrete one-story buildings with small windows, the first two dimly lit inside. The buildings were joined by cement walkways, wide steps where they were necessary, as the central structures were higher off the ground; these no doubt had once been the officers' quarters, commanders of the behemoths that prowled the deep waters of the Atlantic, killers for an abominable cause.

Directly below the wall where the three ropes now dangled were more wide steps that led up both sides of what appeared to be a concrete podium or platform, the area in front some kind of courtyard, perhaps two hundred feet wide, that led to the rear of the buildings facing the U-boat slips. A parade ground, thought Converse, visualizing rows of submarine crews standing at attention, receiving orders and listening to the exhortations of their officers as they prepared once more to enter the deep in search of tonnage and carnage.

"Follow me!" said the German, tapping Joel's shoulder and grabbing the rope as he slid over the wall and lowered himself onto the concrete platform beneath. On both sides the four men were on their way down, one after the other. Converse, less gingerly than the professionals, rolled over the ledge, his hands gripping the rope, and slid to the ground.

The two men on Joel's left raced silently across the platform and down the steps toward the huge steel doors. The two men on his right, as if by instinct, ran down the opposite steps, returning below to crouch in front of the platform, their weapons drawn. Converse, following the German, swiftly joined the pair at the doors. Both men were studying the bolts and the layers of plating and the complicated lock with tiny flashlights.

"Fuse it and blow it," said the American. "There's no alarm."

"Are you sure?" asked Joel. "From what I gathered, this whole place is wired."

"The trips are down there," explained the other pilot, pointing toward the three-foot-high concrete wall on each side of the parade ground.

"Trips?"

"Trip lights. Intersecting beams."

"Which means there are no animals," said the German, nodding. *"Keine Hunde. Sehr gut!"*

The fourth man had finished stuffing wads of a soft, puttylike substance into the lock mechanism, using his knife to finish the job. He then took out a small circular device no larger than a fifty-cent coin from his pocket, layered another mound of the substance directly over the lock and plunged the coin into it. "Move back," he ordered.

Converse watched, mesmerized. There was no explosion, no detonation whatsoever, but there was intense heat and a glowing blue-white flame that literally melted the steel. Then a series of clicks could be heard, and the American quickly slid back the triple bolts. He pushed the right door open and blinked his flashlight outside. Moments later Johnny Reb and Geoffrey Larson walked through the door into the strange compound.

"Trips," repeated the American to the Rebel. "They're all along those two walls," he said, pointing. "See them?"

"I can," replied the Southerner. "And that means there'll be a few shooting straight up on top for tiptoeing feet. All right, boys, let's do a little crawling. Bellies down with knees and asses wiggling." The six at the door joined the two crouched in front of the platform. Johnny whispered in German, then turned to Larson. "My English friend, I want you to stay right here until us old-timers give you the high sign to catch up with us." He looked at Joel. "Sure you want to come?"

"I won't bother to answer that. Let's go."

One by one, with the German who was $5,000 richer in the lead, the seven men snaked their way across the old parade ground. Barely breathing, trousers torn, knees and hands scraped by the rough, cracked concrete. The German headed for the break between buildings 2 and 3, counting from the right. It was a connecting cement path with gradually rising steps on the left. He reached the open space and stood up.

Suddenly he snapped his fingers once—not very loud but loud enough. Everyone froze where he was under the field of intersecting alarm beams. Converse turned his head on the ground to try to see what was happening. The German was crouched in the shadows as a man came into view, a guard with a rifle slung over his shoulder. Aware of another presence, the guard whipped his head around; the German lunged out of the shadows, his long-bladed knife arcing in midair toward the man's head. Joel closed his eyes, the sound of savagely expunged air telling him more than he cared to know.

The movement began again, and again, one by one, each member of the unit reached the path. Converse was soaked with sweat. He looked at the row of U-boat slips ahead and the sea beyond them and wished to God he could fall into the water. The Rebel touched his elbow, indicating that Joel should take out his gun as the Southerner had done. It was now Johnny Reb who took the lead; he crept out to the front of building 2 and turned right, crouching close to the ground, heading toward the lighted windows. His fingers snapped; all movement stopped, bodies now prone. Diagonally to the left, by the edge of a giant slip were the glow of cigarettes and the sound of men talking quietly—three men, guards with rifles.

As if they had been given an order, three of the five men hired by the Rebel—which ones

Converse could not tell—broke away and started crawling in a wide arc toward the opposite side of the old U-boat berth. Approximately a minute and a half later—the longest ninety seconds Joel could remember—a barrage of muted reports punctured the night breezes off the sea. The subsequent sounds were minimal as hands clutched at heads and bodies snapped before falling to the concrete ground. The hired guns returned and Johnny Reb waved them forward, with Converse forced to be the last as men grabbed his shoulders and passed him. They reached the only lighted window in building 2; the Rebel stood up and inched his way to the glass. He turned and shook his head; the unit proceeded.

They came to the open space between buildings 1 and 2. Cautiously each man ran across, crouching the instant he reached the opposite edge and then racing ahead. It was Joel's turn; he got to his knees, then to his feet.

"Horst? Bist das du?" said a man harshly, walking out of a door and up the cement path.

Converse stood motionless. The rest of the unit was well past the edge of building 1 as the sounds of the North Sea crashing on the rocks in the distance blocked out the intruder's voice. Joel tried not to panic. He was alone, and if he panicked, he could blow the operation apart, destroy the complex at Scharhörn, killing everyone, including Connal Fitzpatrick, if, indeed, the young commander was there.

"Ja," he heard himself saying as he turned away into the shadows, his right hand reaching

across his waist for the hunting knife. He could not trust his gun in the darkness.

"Warten Sie einen Augenblick! Sie sind nicht Horst!"

Joel shrugged, and waited. The footsteps approached; a hand grabbed his shoulder. He spun around, gripping the handle of the knife with such force that it nearly blocked out the terrible thing his mind told him he had to do. He grabbed the man's hair and brought the razor-sharp blade across the throat.

Wanting to vomit, he pulled the man into the darker shadows; the head was all but severed from the body. He raced across the open space and caught up with the others. No one had missed him; each man was taking his turn peering into one of the four lighted windows in a row. Johnny Reb was beyond the first, successively pointing in different directions firmly, rapidly, and each man, after a crisp nod, ducked away. An assault was about to be immediately executed. Converse raised himself to the edge of the last window and looked inside. Instantly he understood why the Rebel had to act quickly. There were ten guards in what could only be described as paramilitary uniforms belonging to no recognizable army. Each was either strapping on a weapon, looking at his watch or crushing out a cigarette. Then, more ominously, they checked the ammunition clips in their rifles and automatics. Several laughed, raising their voices as if making demands at the expense of the others. Joel could not understand the words. He moved away from the window and confronted Johnny Reb, who was close to the ground.

"It's a patrol going out, isn't it?" whispered Converse.

"No, son," replied the Southerner. "It's a firing squad. They just got their orders."

"My *God!*"

"We follow them, staying low and out of sight. You may find your old buddy Fitzpatrick, after all."

The next minutes were straight out of Kafka, thought Joel. The ten men lined up and walked out the door leading to building 2. Suddenly floodlights blazed throughout the parade ground, the trip lights obviously turned off as the squad walked out on the concrete. Two men with automatics in their hands ran to building 4; they unlocked and then unbolted the heavy door, and raced inside shouting orders as lights were turned on.

"*Alles aufstehen! 'Raus! Mach schnell! Schnell!*"

Seconds later, gaunt, manacled figures began straggling out in their ragged clothes, blinking at the harsh lights, some barely able to walk and supported by others who were stronger. Ten, twenty, twenty-five, thirty-two, forty . . . forty-three. Forty-three prisoners of Aquitaine about to be executed! They were marched toward the concrete wall fronting the platform at the far end of the parade ground.

It happened with the hysterical force of a crowd gone mad! The condemned men suddenly bolted in all directions, those nearest the two guards with the automatics crashing the chains of their manacled hands into the stunned faces. Shots rang out, three prisoners fell and writhed on the ground. The firing squad raised their rifles.

"Now, you mother-lovin' catfish hunters!" shouted Johnny Reb as the entire Scharhörn unit raced into the melee, pistols firing, muted spits mingling with the ear-shattering explosions of the unsilenced weapons.

It was over in less than twenty seconds. The ten men of Aquitaine lay on the ground. Six were dead, three wounded, one on his knees trembling with fear. Two men of the Scharhörn unit sustained minor wounds—the American pilot and one other.

"Connal!" roared Joel, racing about the scattered prisoners, relieved that most were moving. *"Fitzpatrick!* Where the hell *are* you?"

"Over here, Lieutenant," said a weak voice on Converse's right. Joel threaded his way through the fallen bodies and knelt down beside the frail, bearded Navy lawyer. "You took your sweet time getting here," continued the commander. "But then junior-grade officers usually have deficiencies."

"What *happened* back there?" asked Converse. "You could all have been killed!"

"That was the point, wasn't it? It was made clear to us last night, so we figured what the hell?"

"But why *you?* Why *all* of you?"

"We talked and we couldn't figure it out. Except one thing—we were all senior officers on thirty- to forty-day leaves, most of them summer leaves. What did it mean?"

1044

"It was meant to throw people off if they began to see a pattern. There are ninety-seven men out in hit teams—all on summer leaves. Numerically you were nearly fifty percent of that number, presumably above suspicion. You were a bonus and it saved your life."

Suddenly Connal whipped his head to the left. A man was running out of building 5, racing down the concrete path. "That's the warden!" shouted Fitzpatrick as loud as he could. *"Stop him!* If he gets into the second barracks he'll blow the whole place up!"

Joel got to his feet and, gun in hand, started after the racing figure as fast as his painful legs would carry him. The man had reached the midpoint of building 3; he had less than thirty yards to go to the door of 2. Converse fired; the bullet was way off its mark, ricocheting off a steel window frame. The man reached the door, smashed it open and slammed it shut. Joel raced to it and crashed the full weight of his body into the heavy wood. It gave way, swinging violently back into the wall. The man was running to a metal-encased panel; Converse fired wildly, frantically, again and again. The man spun, wounded in the legs, but he had opened the panel. He reached up for a bank of switches. Joel lunged, gripping the man's hand, smashing his head against the stone floor.

Gasping for breath, Converse crawled away from the man, his hands covered with warm blood, his empty pistol on the floor. One of the Scharhörn team burst through the door. "Are you fine?" he asked in an accent Joel could not place.

1045

"Splendid," said Converse, feeling weak and sick.

The hired gun walked past Joel and glanced at the still figure on the floor on his way to the open panel. He studied it and reached into his pocket for some kind of small, multifaceted tool. In seconds he was taking out screws and pulling off the interior metal plating. Moments later, with another part of the instrument he was cutting wires far back into their receptacles, leaving nothing but stubs of copper.

"You are not to worry," said the man, finished. "I am best of Norwegian demolitions. Now we do not concern ourselves that a stray pig can do damage. Come, there is much work left to do." The team member stopped and stood above Converse. "We owe you our lives. We will pay."

"It's not necessary," said Joel, getting up.

"It is the custom," replied the man, heading for the door.

Out on the parade ground, Aquitaine's prisoners were sitting up against the wall—all but five, whose bodies were covered with sheets. Converse went over to Fitzpatrick.

"We lost them," said the naval officer, with no strength in his voice.

"Look to the things you believe in, Connal," said Joel. "It may sound banal, but it's the only thing I can think of to say."

"It's good enough." Fitzpatrick looked up, a wan smile on his lips. "Thanks for reminding me. Go on. They need you over there."

"*Larson!*" shouted Johnny Reb, standing above the trembling unhurt guard. "Get in here!"

The professorial Englishman walked hesitantly through the steel door at the base of the airstrip into the floodlights. He came over to the Rebel, his eyes wandering about the parade ground, his expression one of consternation and awe. "Good *God!*" he uttered.

"I guess that says it," said the Southerner as two members of the Scharhörn team came running out of building 5. "What'd you *find?*" yelled Johnny Reb.

"Seven others!" shouted one of the men. "They're in a toilet, which is suitable to their conditions!"

"I *say!*" said Geoffrey Larson, raising his voice. "Would any by chance be the computer chap?"

"We did not ask!"

"Go *ask!*" ordered the Rebel. "Time's run out!" He turned to Converse. "I've been in touch with your lady. The word out of Israel and Rome is downright awful—some of the hit teams eluded Stone's men. The demonstrations began an hour ago, and already twelve government people have been killed. In Jerusalem and Tel Aviv they're screaming for Abrahms to take over. In Rome the police can't handle the riots and the panic; the Army's moved in."

Joel felt the sharp, hollow pain in his lower chest and for the first time noticed the early light in the sky beyond the walls. The day had come, and so had the killing. Everywhere. "Oh, *Jesus,*" he said.

"The computer, *boy!*" roared Johnny Reb, his pistol jammed into the temple of the guard beneath him. "You don't have any choices left, *catfish!*"

"*Baracke vier!*"

"*Danke!* It's in building four. Come on, Brit, let's *go! Move!*"

The enormous, glistening machine covering the length of the fifteen-foot wall stood in an air-filtered room. With Joel's note pad in front of him, Larson spent nine agonizing minutes studying it, turning dials, punching the keyboard and flipping switches on the console. Finally he announced, "There's a lock on the inner reels. They can't be released without an access code."

"What in *goddamned catfish hell* are you talkin' about!" screamed the Rebel.

"There's a predesigned set of symbols that when inserted releases the springs that permit the locked reels to be activated. It's why I asked if there was a computer man about."

Johnny Reb's radio hummed, and Converse ripped it off the Southerner's Velcroed chest.

"*Val?*"

"*Darling!* You're all right?"

"Yes. What's happening?"

"Radio-France. Bombs set off in the Elysée Palace. Two deputies were shot riding to the dawn rallies. The government's calling in the armed forces."

"*Christ! Out!*"

A man was brought into the room by two members of the Scharhörn team, who were gripping him by the arms. "He did not care to admit his function," said the hired gun on the left. "But when all were against the wall, the others were not so secretive.''

The Rebel went to the man and grabbed him by the throat, but Joel, with the hunting knife in his hand, rushed forward, pushing the Southerner aside.

"I've been through a lot because of you *bastards,*" he said, raising the bloodstained blade to the man's nose. "And now it's the *end!*" He shoved the point into the man's nostrils; the computer expert screamed as blood erupted and streamed down. Then Converse raised the blade again, the point now in the corner of the man's right eye. "The codes, or it goes in!" he roared.

"*Zwei, eins, null, elf!*" Again the technician screamed.

"Process it!" yelled Joel.

"They're *free!*" said the Englishman.

"Now the *symbols!*" cried Converse, shoving the man back into the hands of the Scharhörn invaders.

They all looked in astonishment at the green letters on the black television screen. Name after name, rank after rank, position after position. Larson had punched the printout button, and the curling, continuous sheet of paper spewed out with hundreds of identities.

"It won't do any good!" shouted Joel. "We can't get them *out!*"

"Don't be so antediluvian, chap," said the Englishman, pointing to a strange-looking telephone recessed in the console. "This is splendid equipment. There are those lovely satellites in the sky, and I can send this to anyone anywhere with compatible software. This is the age of technology, no longer Aquarius."

"Get it *out,*" said Converse, leaning against the wall and sliding down to the floor in exhaustion.

The world watched, stunned by the eruption of widespread assassinations and random homicidal violence. Everywhere people cried out for protection, for leadership, for an end to the savagery that had turned whole cities into battlegrounds, as panicked, polarized groups of citizens hurled rocks and gas at one another and finally turned to bullets because bullets were being fired at them. Since few could tell who their enemies were, anyone who attacked was assumed to be an enemy, and the attackers were everywhere, the orders issued from unseen command posts. The police were helpless; then militias and state troops appeared, but it was soon evident that they and their leaders were also powerless. Stronger measures would have to be implemented to control the chaos. Martial law was proclaimed. Everywhere. And military commanders would assume control. *Everywhere.*

In Palo Alto, California, former general of the Army George Marcus Delavane sat strapped to his wheelchair, watching the hysteria recorded on three television sets. The set on the left went blank, preceded by the screams of a mobile crew as their truck came under sudden attack and the entire unit was blown up by grenades. On the center screen a woman newscaster, with tears streaming down her face, read in a barely controlled, angry voice the reports of wholesale

1050

destruction and wanton murder. The screen on the right showed a Marine colonel being interviewed on a barricaded street in New York's financial district. His .45 Marine issue Colt automatic was in his hand as he tried to answer questions while shouting orders to his subordinates. The screen on the left pulsated with new light as a familiar anchorman came into focus, his eyes glassy. He started to speak, but could not; he turned in his chair and vomited as the camera swung away to an unsuspecting newsroom editor screaming into a phone, "Goddamned shit-*bastards!* What the fuck *happened?*" He, too, was weeping. He pounded the desk with his fist, then collapsed, dropping his head on his arms while his whole body shook in spasms as the screen again went dark.

A slow smile emerged on Delavane's face. Abruptly he reached for two remote controls, switching off the sets on the right and left, as he concentrated on the center screen. A helmeted Army lieutenant general was picked by the camera as he strode into a press room somewhere in Washington. The soldier removed his helmet, went to a lectern and spoke harshly into the microphone. "We have sealed off all roads leading to Washington, and my words are to serve as a warning to unauthorized personnel and civilians everywhere! Any attempts to cross the checkpoints will be met by immediate force. My orders are brief and clear. Shoot to kill. My authority is derived from the emergency powers just granted to me by the Speaker of the House in the absence of the President and the Vice

President, who have been flown out of the capital for security purposes. The military is now in charge, the Army its spokesman, and martial law is in full effect until further notice."

Delavane snapped off the set with a gesture of triumph. "We *did* it, Paul!" he said, turning to his uniformed aide, who stood next to the fragmented map on the wall. "Not even the whining pacifists want that law reversed! And if they *do* . . ." The general of Aquitaine raised his right hand, his index finger extended, thumb upright, and mimed a series of pistol shots.

"Yes, it's done," agreed the aide, reaching down to Delavane's desk and opening a drawer.

"What are you doing?"

"I'm sorry, General. This also must be done." The aide pulled out a .357 magnum revolver.

Before he could raise it, however, Delavane's left hand shot up out of the inside cushion of the wheelchair. In it was a short-barreled automatic. He shouted as he fired four times in rapid succession.

"You think I haven't been *waiting* for this? Scum! Coward! *Traitor!* You think I trust *any* of you? The way you *look at me!* The way you talk in whispers in the hallways! None of you can stand the fact that *without* legs I'm better than *all* of you! Now you know, scum! And soon the others will know because they'll be shot! Executed for treason against the founder of Aquitaine! You think any of you are worth trusting? You've all tried to be what I am and you *can't do it!*"

The uniformed aide had crashed back into the wall, into the fragmented map. Gasping, blood flowing from his neck, he stared wide-eyed at the raving general. From some inner core of strength he raised the powerful magnum and fired once as he collapsed.

George Marcus Delavane was blown across the room, a massive hemorrhage in his chest, as the wheelchair spun and fell on its side, its strapped-in occupant dead.

No one knew when it started to happen, but gradually, miraculously, the gunfire slowly began to diminish. The restoration of order was accompanied by squads of uniformed men, many units having broken away from their commanders, racing through the streets and buildings and confronting other men. It was soldier against soldier, the eyes of the interrogators filled with anger and disgust, staring at faces consumed with arrogance and defiance. The commanders of Aquitaine were adamant. They were right! Could not their inferiors understand? Many refused to surrender, preferring final assaults that cost them their lives. Others bit into cyanide capsules.

In Palo Alto, California, a legless legend named George Marcus Delavane was found shot to death, but apparently not before he had been able to kill his assailant, an obscure Army colonel. No one knew what had happened. In Southern France, the bodies of two other legendary heroes were found in a mountain ravine, each of whom, upon leaving a château in the Alps, had been given a weapon. Generals Bertholdier and Leifhelm had lost. General Chaim Abrahms had disappeared. On military bases throughout the Middle East, all Europe, Great Britain, Canada and the United States, officers of high rank and responsibilities were challenged by subordinates with leveled weapons. *Were they members of an organization called Acquitaine? Their names were on a list! Answer!* In Norfolk, Virginia, an admiral named Scanlon threw himself out of a sixth-story window; and in San Diego, California, another admiral named Hickman was ordered to arrest a four-striper who lived in La Jolla—the charge: murder of a legal officer in the hills above that elegant suburb. Colonel Alan Metcalf personally made the call to the chief operations officer of Nellis Air Force Base; the order was blunt—throw into a maximum-security cell the major who was in charge of all aircraft maintenance. In Washington the venerated Senator Mario Parelli was called out of the cloakroom by a Captain Guardino of Army G-2 and taken away; while at State and the Pentagon, eleven men in armaments controls and procurements were placed under guard.

In Tel Aviv, Israeli Army intelligence rounded up twenty-three aides and fellow officers of General Chaim Abrahms, as well as one of the Mossad's most brilliant analysts. In Paris, thirty-one associates—military and nonmilitary—of General Jacques-Louis Bertholdier, including deputy directors of both the Sûreté and Interpol, were held in isolation, and in Bonn no fewer than fifty-seven colleagues of General Erich Leifhelm, among them former Wehrmacht commanders and current officers of the Federal Republic's Army

1054

and its Luftwaffe, were seized. Also in Bonn, the Marine Corps guard at the American embassy, on orders from the State Department, arrested four attachés, including the military chargé d'affaires, Major Norman Anthony Washburn IV.

And so it went. Everywhere. The fever of madness that was Aquitaine was broken by legions of the very military the generals assumed would carry them to absolute global power. By nightfall the guns were still and people began to come out from behind their barricades—from cellars, subways, boarded-up buildings, railroad yards, wherever sanctuary could be found. They wandered out on the streets, numbed, wondering what had happened, as trucks with loudspeakers roamed the cities everywhere telling the citizens that the crisis was over. In Tel Aviv, Rome, Paris, Bonn, London, and across the Atlantic in Toronto, New York, Washington and points west, the lights were turned on, but certainly the world had not returned to normal. A terrible force had struck in the midst of a universal cry for peace. What was it? What had *happened?*

It would be explained on the following day, blared the sound trucks in a dozen different languages, pleading for patience on the part of citizens everywhere. The hour chosen was 3:00 P.M., Greenwich Mean Time; 10:00 A.M. Washington, 7:00 A.M. Los Angeles. Throughout the night and the morning hours in all the time zones, heads of state conferred over telephones until the texts of all the statements were essentially the same. At 10:03 A.M. the President of the United States went on the air.

"Yesterday an unprecedented wave of violence swept through the free world taking lives, paralyzing governments, creating a climate of terror that very nearly cost free nations everywhere their freedom and might have led them to look for solutions where no solutions should be sought in democratic societies—namely, turning ourselves into police states, handing over controls to men who would subjugate free people to their collective military will. It was an organized conspiracy led by demented and deluded men who sought power for its own sake, willing even to sacrifice their own fellow conspirators to achieve it, and to deceive others who were seduced into believing it was the way of the future, the answer to the serious ills of the world. It is not, nor can it ever be.

"As the days and weeks go by—as this terrible thing is put behind us—the facts will be placed before you. For this has been our warning, the toll taken in blood and in the shaken confidence of our institutions. I remind you, however, that our institutions have prevailed. They will prevail.

"In an hour from now a series of meetings will start taking place involving the White House, the departments of State and Defense, the majority and minority leaders of the House and the Senate, and the National Security Council. Beginning tomorrow, in concert with other governments, reports will be issued on a daily basis until all the facts are before you.

"The nightmare is over. Let the sunlight of truth guide us and clear away the darkness."

On the following morning Deputy Director Peter Stone of the Central Intelligence Agency, accompanied by Captain Howard Packard and Lieutenant William Landis, were brought to the Oval Office for a private ceremony. The specific honors awarded them were never made public, as there was no reason to do so. Each man, with deep respect and gratitude—but with no regrets—declined to accept, each stating that whatever honors were involved belonged to a man not currently residing in the United States.

A week later, in Los Angeles, California, an actor named Caleb Dowling stunned the producers of a television show called *Santa Fe* by giving them his notice—effective before the start of the new season. He refused all inducements, claiming simply that there was not enough time to spend with his wife. They were going to travel. Alone. And if the residuals ever ran out, hell, she could always type and he could always teach. Together. *Ciao, friends.*

EPILOGUE

Geneva. City of bright reflections and inconstancy.

Joel and Valerie Converse sat at the table where it had all begun, by the glistening brass railing in the Chat Botté. The traffic on the lakeside Quai du Mont Blanc was disciplined, unhurried—purpose mixed with civility. As the pedestrians passed by, both were aware of the glances directed at Joel. *There he is,* the eyes were saying. *There is . . . the man.* It was rumored he was living in Geneva, at least for a while.

By agreement, the second report issued across the free world made a direct but—on Converse's insistence—brief reference to his role in the tragedy that was Aquitaine. He was exonerated of all charges. The labels were removed and refuted, the debt to him acknowledged without specifics on the basis of NATO security. He refused all interviews, and was not pleased when the media dredged up his experiences in Southeast Asia and speculated on correlations with the drama of the generals. But he was consoled by the knowledge that just as the interest in him had dwindled years ago, it would do so again—faster in Geneva, city of purpose.

They had leased a house on the lake, an artist's house with a studio built on the slope leading to the water, the skylight catching the sun from early morning to dusk. The beach house in Cape Ann was closed, the lease paid in full and returned to the realtor in Boston. Val's friend and neighbor had packed her clothes and all her paints, brushes and favorite easel, and sent everything air freight to Geneva. Valerie worked for several hours each morning, happier than she had ever been in her life, permitting her husband to evaluate her progress daily. He judged it to be eminently acceptable, wondering out loud whether there was a market for "lakescapes" as opposed to seascapes. It took him two days to remove the last dabs of paint from his hair.

Nor was Joel without employment; he was Talbot, Brooks and Simon's European branch all by himself. The income, itself, however, was not a vital factor, as Converse never remotely considered himself in the mold of those attorneys in films and on television who rarely if ever collected fees. Since his legal talents had been called upon for crucial evidence, he billed the major governments a reasonable $400,000 apiece; the minor ones, $250,000. No one argued. The total came to something over $2.5 million, safely deposited in an interest-bearing Swiss account.

"What are you thinking about?" asked Valerie, reaching for his hand.

"About Chaim Abrahms and Derek Belamy. They haven't been found—they're still out there, and I wonder if they will ever be found. I hope so, because until they are, it really isn't over."

"It's over, Joel, you've got to believe it. But that's not what I meant. I meant you. How do you feel?"

"I'm not sure. I only knew I had to come here and find out." He looked into her eyes, and at the cascading dark hair that fell to her shoulders, framing the face he loved so much. "Empty, I think. Except for you."

"No anger? No resentment?"

"Not against Avery, or Stone or any of the others. That's past. They did what they had to do; there wasn't any other way."

"You're far more generous than I am, my darling."

"I'm more realistic, that's all. The evidence had to be gotten by penetrating the outside—by an outsider wanting to get inside. The core was too tight, too lethal.''

''I think they were bastards. And cowards.''

''I don't. I think they should all be canonized, immortalized, bronzed and with poems written about them for the ages.''

''That's absolute rubbish! How can you possibly say such a thing?''

Joel again looked into his wife's eyes. ''Because you're here. I'm here. And you're painting lakescapes, not seascapes. And I'm not in New York and you're not in Cape Ann. And I don't have to worry about you, hoping that you're worrying about me.''

''If only there'd been another woman or another man. It would have been so much easier, so much more logical, darling.''

''There was always you. Only you.''

''Try to get away from me again, Converse.''

''No way, Converse.''

Their hands gripped, unashamed tears were in their eyes. The nightmare was over.